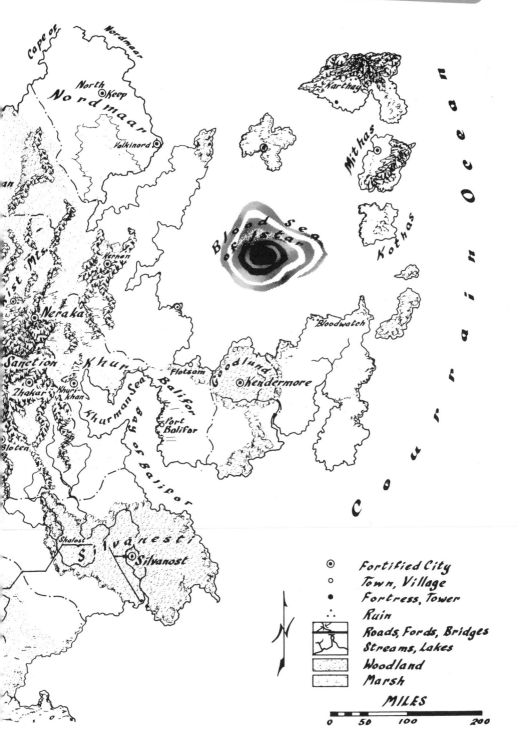

CHRONICLES
VOLUME 4

DRAGONS OF
SUMMER FLAME

by Margaret Weis and Tracy Hickman

CHRONICLES

Dragons of Autumn Twilight

Dragons of Winter Night

Dragons of Spring Dawning

LEGENDS

Time of the Twins

War of the Twins

Test of the Twins

CHRONICLES

VOLUME 4

DRAGONS OF SUMMER FLAME

by Margaret Weis and Tracy Hickman

POETRY BY MICHAEL WILLIAMS
ART BY LARRY ELMORE

DRAGONLANCE® Chronicles
Volume 4

DRAGONS OF SUMMER FLAME

©1995 TSR, Inc.
All Rights Reserved.

First Printing: November 1995
Printed in the United States of America.
Library of Congress Catalog Card Number: 94-68156

Cover and interior art by Larry Elmore

9 8 7 6 5 4 3 2 1

ISBN: 0-7869-0189-6

TSR, Inc.
201 Sheridan Springs Rd.
Lake Geneva WI 53147
U.S.A.

TSR Ltd.
120 Church End, Cherry Hinton
Cambridge CB1 3LB
United Kingdom

TO SOJOURNERS IN KRYNN

May your Sword never break.
May your Armor never rust.
May the Three Moons guide your Magic.
May your Prayers be heard.
May your Beard grow long.
May your Life Quest never blow up in your face.
May your Hoopak sing.
May your Homeland prosper.
May Dragons fly ever in your Dreams.

—Margaret Weis and Tracy Hickman

ICEWALL SERVICE

In southernmost country
*   where the Icewall rises*
in pale and seasonal sun,

where the legends freeze
*   in remembered dew*
and the downed mercury,

they ready the long vats
*   in memory's custom*
pouring gold, pouring amber,

the old distillations
*   of grain, of bardic blood*
and ice and remembrance.

And into the waters the bard descends
*   into gold, into amber*
all the while listening

to the dark amniosis
*   of current and memory*
flowing about him,

until the lung, the dilating heart
*   give way in the waters,*
until he fills with listening

and the world rushes into him
*   deeper than thought, and he drowns*
or addles, or emerges a bard.

In the north it is done otherwise:
*   wisely under the moon*
where the phases labor

out of darkness to the light
*   of coins and mirrors*
in abundant freedoms of air.

I heard you were strangers
*   to the wronged country*
where the bards descend,

to the waters where faith
*   transforms into vision,*
to the night's elixir,

to the last drowning breath
*   given over to memory*
where poetry comes, solitary.

I heard you were strangers
*   in the merciful north,*
that Hylo, Solamnia,

and a dozen unnameable provinces
*   cleansed you past envy, past*
*   loneliness.*
Then the waters told me the truth:

how much you remember your deaths
*   where the halves of a kingdom*
unite in a lost terrain,

how you pass like moons, red and silver,
*   your destination celestial west,*
an alliance of mercy and light.

From the outset the heavens
*   had this in mind, a passage*
through darkness and suspect country,

its vanishing point in sunlight
*   in the air and the earth's horizons—*
not drowning, nor the harp's flood.

O you have never forgotten
*   the bard's immersion, the country of*
*   sleep,*
the time preceding the birth of the worlds

where all of us waited
*   in the mothering dark,*
in the death that the card foretells,

but alone and together you ride
*   into the dying the dying*
the story that means we are starting again . . .

Book 1

1

The landing party. The prophecy.
An unexpected encounter.

t was hot that morning, damnably hot.

Far too hot for late spring on Ansalon. Almost as hot as mid-summer. The two knights, seated in the boat's stern, were sweating and miserable in their heavy steel armor; they looked with envy at the half-naked men plying the boat's oars.

The knights' black armor, adorned with skull and death lily, had been blessed by the high cleric, was supposed to withstand the vagaries of wind and rain, heat and cold. But their Dark Queen's blessing was apparently not responding to this unseasonable heat wave. When the boat drew near the shore, the knights were first out, jumping into the shallow water, laving the water onto their reddening faces and sun-burned necks. But the water was not particularly refreshing.

"Like wading in hot soup," one of the knights grumbled, splashing ashore. Even as he spoke, he scrutinized the shoreline carefully, eyeing bush and tree and dune for signs of life.

"More like blood," said his comrade. "Think of it as wading in the blood of our enemies, the enemies of our queen. Do you see anything?"

"No," the other replied. He waved his hand without looking back, heard the sound of men leaping into the water, their harsh laughter and conversation in their uncouth, guttural language.

One of the knights turned around. "Bring that boat to shore," he said unnecessarily, for the men had already picked up the heavy boat, were running with it through the shallow water. Grinning, they dumped the boat on the sand beach and looked to the knight for further orders.

He mopped his forehead, marveled at their strength and—not for the first time—thanked Queen Takhisis that these barbarians were on their side. The brutes, they were known as. Not the true name of their race. That name—their name for themselves—was unpronounceable, and so the knights who led the barbarians had begun calling them the short-ened version: brutes.

The name suited the barbarians well. They came from the east, from a continent that few people on Ansalon knew existed. Every one of the men stood well over six feet; some were as tall as seven. Their bodies were as bulky and muscular as humans, but their movements were as swift and graceful as elves. Their ears were pointed like those of the elves, but their faces were heavily bearded like humans or dwarves.

They were as strong as dwarves, and loved battle as well as dwarves. They fought fiercely, were loyal to those who commanded them, and—outside of a few grotesque customs, such as cutting off various parts of the body of a dead enemy to keep as trophies—the brutes were ideal foot soldiers.

"Let the captain know we've arrived safely and that we've encountered no resistance," said the knight to his comrade. "We'll leave a couple of men here with the boat, move inland."

The other knight nodded. Taking a red silk pennant from his belt, he unfurled it, held it above his head, and waved it slowly three times. An answering flutter of red could be seen coming from the enormous black dragon-prowed ship anchored some distance away. This was a scouting mission, not an invasion. Orders had been quite clear on that point.

The knights sent out their patrols, dispatching some to range up and down the beach, sending others farther inland, where towering hills of chalk-white rock—barren of vegetation—rose from the trees like cat claws to tear at the sky. Breaks in the rock led to the island's interior. The ship had sailed around the island; now they knew it was not large. Their patrols would be back soon.

This done, the two knights moved thankfully to the meager shadow cast by a squat and misshapen tree. Two of the brutes stood guard. The knights remained wary, watchful, even as they rested. Seating themselves, they drank sparingly of the fresh water they'd brought with them. One of them grimaced.

"The damn stuff's hot."

"You left the waterskin sitting in the sun. Of course it's hot."

"Where the devil was I supposed to put it? There was no shade on that cursed boat. I don't think there's any shade left in the whole blasted world. I don't like this place at all. I get a queer feeling about this island, like it's magicked or something."

"I know what you mean," agreed his comrade somberly. He kept glancing about, back into the trees, up and down the beach. All he could see were the brutes, and they were certainly not bothered by any ominous feelings. But then they were barbarians. "We were warned not to come here, you know."

"What?" The other knight looked astonished. "I didn't know. Who told you that?"

"Brightblade. He had it from Lord Ariakan himself."

"Brightblade should know. He's on Ariakan's staff, though I hear he's asked to be transferred to a fighting talon. Plus Ariakan's his sponsor." The knight appeared nervous, asked softly, "Such information's not secret, is it?"

The other knight appeared amused. "You don't know Steel Brightblade very well if you think he would break any oath, pass along information he was told to keep to himself. He'd sooner let his tongue be ripped out by red-hot tongs. No, Lord Ariakan discussed things openly with all the regimental commanders before deciding to proceed."

The knight shrugged. Picking up a handful of pebbles, he began tossing them idly into the water. "The Gray Knights started it all. Some sort of augury revealed the location of this island and that it was inhabited by large numbers of people."

"So who warned us not to come?"

"The Gray Knights. The same augury which told them of this island warned them not to come near it. They tried to persuade Ariakan to leave well enough alone. Said that this place could mean disaster."

The other knight frowned, glanced around with growing unease. "Then why were we sent?"

"The upcoming invasion of Ansalon. Lord Ariakan felt this move was necessary to protect his flanks. The Gray Knights couldn't say exactly what sort of threat this island posed. Nor could they say specifically that the disaster would be caused by our landing on the island. As Lord Ariakan pointed out, disaster might come even if we did nothing. And so he decided to follow the old dwarven dictum: It is better to go looking for the dragon than have the dragon go looking for you."

"Good thinking," his companion agreed. "If there *is* an army of Solamnic Knights on this island, it's better that we deal with them now. Not that it seems likely."

He gestured at the wide stretches of sand beach, at the dunes covered with grayish green grass, and, farther inland, a forest of the ugly, misshapen trees butting up against the clawlike hills. "I can't imagine why the Solamnics would come here. I can't imagine why anyone would come here. Elves wouldn't live in a place this ugly."

"No caves, so the dwarves wouldn't like it. Minotaur would have attacked us by now. Kender would have walked off with the boat *and* our armor. Gnomes would have met us with some sort of fiend-driven fish-catching machine. Humans like us are the only race foolish enough to live on such a wretched isle," the knight concluded cheerfully. He picked up another handful of rocks.

"Perhaps a rogue band of draconians or hobgoblins. Ogres even. Escaped twenty-some odd years ago, after the War of the Lance. Fled north, across the sea, to avoid capture by the Solamnic Knights."

"Yes, but they'd be on our side," his companion answered. "And our knight wizards wouldn't have their gray robes in a knot over it. Ah, here come our scouts, back to report. Now we'll find out."

The knights rose to their feet. The brutes who had been sent into the island's interior hurried forward to meet their leaders. The barbarians were grinning hugely. Their near-naked bodies glistened with sweat. The blue paint, with which they had covered themselves, and which was supposed to possess some sort of magical properties such as causing arrows to bounce right off, ran down their muscular bodies in rivulets. Long scalp-locks, decorated with colorful feathers, bounced on their backs as they loped easily over the sand dunes.

The two knights exchanged glances, relaxed.

"What did you find?" the knight asked the leader, a gigantic, red-haired fellow who towered over both knights, could have probably picked up each of them and held them above his head, and who regarded both knights with unbounded reverence and respect.

"Men," answered the brute. They were quick to learn and had adapted easily to the Common language spoken by most of the various races of Krynn. Unfortunately, to the brutes, all people not of their race were known as "men."

The brute lowered his hand near the ground to indicate small men, which might mean dwarves but was more probably children. He moved it to waist height, which most likely indicated women. This the brute confirmed by cupping two hands over his breast and wiggling his hips. His comrades laughed and nudged each other.

"Men, women and children," said the knight. "Many men? Lots of men? Big buildings? Walls? Cities?"

The brutes apparently thought this was hilarious, for they all burst into raucous laughter.

"What did you find?" repeated the knight sharply, scowling. "Stop the nonsense."

The brutes sobered rapidly.

"Many men," said the leader, "but no walls. Houses." He made a face, shrugged, shook his head and added something in his own language.

"What does that mean?" asked the knight of his comrade.

"Something to do with dogs," said the other, who had led brutes before and had started picking up some of their language. "I think he means that these men live in houses only dogs would live in."

Several of the brutes now began walking about stoop-shouldered, swinging their arms around their knees and grunting. Then they all straightened up, looked at each other, and laughed again.

"What in the name of our Dark Majesty are they doing now?" the knight demanded.

"Beats me," said his comrade. "I think we should have a look for ourselves." He drew his sword partway out of its black leather scabbard. "Danger?" he asked the brute. "We need steel?"

The brute laughed again. Taking his own short sword (the brutes fought with two, long and short, as well as with bows and arrows), he thrust it into the tree, turned his back on it.

The knight, reassured, returned his own sword to its scabbard. The two followed their guides. Leaving the beach, they walked deeper into the forest of misshapen trees. They walked about half a mile along what appeared to be an animal path, then reached the village.

Despite the antics of the brutes, the knights were completely unprepared for what they found. It seemed that they had come upon a people who had been stranded in the shallows, as the great river Time flowed past them, leaving them untouched.

"By Hiddukel," one said in a low voice to the other. " 'Men' is too strong a term. *Are* these men? Or are they beasts?"

"They're men," said the other, staring around, amazed. "But such men as we're told walked Krynn during the Age of Twilight. Look! Their tools are made of wood. They carry wooden spears. And crude ones at that."

"Wooden-tipped, not stone," said the other. "Mud huts for houses. Clay cooking pots. Not a piece of steel or iron in sight. What a pitiable lot! I can't see how they could be much danger, unless it's from filth. By the smell, they haven't bathed since the Age of Twilight either."

"Ugly bunch. More like apes than men. Don't laugh. Look stern and threatening."

Several of the male humans—if human they were, it was so difficult to tell beneath the animal hides they wore—crept up to the knights. The "man-beasts" walked bent over, their arms swinging at their sides, knuckles almost dragging on the ground. Their heads were covered with long, shaggy hair; unkempt beards almost hid their faces. They bobbed and shuffled and gazed at the knights in openmouthed awe. One of the man-beasts actually drew near enough to reach out a grimy hand to touch the black, shining armor.

A brute moved to interpose his own massive body in front of the knight.

The knight waved the brute off, drew his sword. The steel flashed in the sunlight. He turned to one of the squat trees. With their twisted limbs and gnarled trunks, the trees very much resembled the people who lived underneath them. The knight raised his sword and sliced off a tree limb with one swift stroke.

The man-beast dropped to his knees, groveled in the dirt, making piteous, blubbering sounds.

"I think I'm going to vomit," said the knight to his comrade. "Gully dwarves wouldn't associate with this lot."

"You're right there." The knight continued his inspection. "You and I between us could wipe out the entire tribe."

"We could, but we'd never be able to clean the stench off our swords," said the other.

"What should we do? Kill them?"

"Small honor in it. These wretches obviously aren't any threat to us. Our orders were to find out who or what was inhabiting the island, then return and make our report. For all we know, these people may be the favorites of some god, who might be angered if we harmed them. Perhaps that is what the Gray Knights meant by disaster."

"I doubt if that could be the case," said the other knight. "I can't imagine any god treating his favorites like this."

"Morgion, perhaps," said the other, with a wry grin.

The knight grunted. "Well, we've certainly done no harm just by looking at them. The Gray Knights can't fault us for that. Send out the brutes to scout the rest of the island. Let's go back to the shore. I need some fresh air."

The two knights walked back to the beach. Sitting in the shade of the tree, waiting for the other patrols to return, they passed the time talking of the upcoming invasion of Ansalon, discussing the vast armada of black dragon-prowed ships, manned by minotaur, that was speeding across the Courrain Ocean, bearing thousands and thousands more barbarian warriors. All was nearly ready for the two-pronged invasion of the continent, which would take place on Summer's Eve.

The Knights of Takhisis did not know precisely where they were attacking; such information was kept secret. But they had no doubt of victory. This time the Dark Queen would succeed. This time her armies would be victorious. This time she knew the secret to victory.

The brutes returned within a few hours, made their reports. The isle was not large, perhaps five miles long and as many miles around. The brutes found no other people. The tribe of man-beasts had all slunk off, probably hiding in their mud huts until the strange beings left.

The knights returned to their shore boat. The brutes pushed it off the sand, leaped in, grabbed the oars. The boat skimmed across the surface of the water, heading for the black ship that flew the standard of the Knights of Takhisis: the death lily, the skull, and the thorn.

The knights left behind an empty, deserted beach.

But their leave-taking was noted, as their coming had been.

2

The Magical Isle. An Urgent Meeting. The Decider.

he black dragon-prowed ship vanished over the horizon. When no trace of it could be seen, the watchers climbed down from the trees.

"Will they come back? Is it safe?" asked one of the man-beasts of another, a female.

"You heard them. They've gone to report that we are 'harmless,' that we pose no threat to them. And that means," the female added, after a moment's thought, "that they will be back. Not now. Not soon. But they will return."

"What can we do?"

"I don't know. We came together to live on this isle to keep our secret safe. Perhaps that was a mistake. Perhaps it would have been better to remain scattered throughout the world. Here we are vulnerable to discovery and attack. There we could at least hide among the other races. I don't know," she repeated helplessly. "I can't say. It will be up to the Decider."

"Yes." The male appeared relieved. "That is true. And he will be awaiting our return with impatience. We should go quickly."

"Not like this," warned his companion.

"No, of course not." He gazed unhappily back out to sea, peering through unkempt shaggy hair. "It's all so terrible, so frightening. Even now I don't feel safe. I keep seeing that ship looming on the horizon. I see the dark knights. I hear their voices—the spoken and the unspoken. Talk of conquest, battle, death. Surely . . ." He was hesitant. "Surely we should warn . . . someone on Ansalon. The Solamnic Knights perhaps."

"That is not our responsibility," the woman returned sharply. "We must look out for ourselves, as we have always done. You can be certain," she added, and her tone was bitter, "that in a similar circumstance, they would have no care for us. Come, return to your true form and let us go."

The two muttered words of magic, words that no wizard on the continent of Ansalon could understand, let alone speak: words every wizard on Ansalon would have given his very soul to possess. None ever would or could. Such powerful magic is born, not acquired.

The shambling, filthy husk of the man-beast fell away, as the ugly

shell of the chrysalis falls away to reveal the beautiful duskfaery imprisoned within. Two extraordinarily beautiful beings emerged from the
disguises.

It is difficult to describe such beauty. They were tall, slender, delicate-
boned, with large, luminous eyes. But there are many on this world who
can be described as such, many on this world considered beautiful. And
what may be beautiful to one is not beautiful at all to another. A dwarf
male considers a dwarf female's side-whiskers most alluring; he thinks
the smooth faces of human women are denuded and bland. Yet, even a
dwarf would realize these people were beautiful, no matter that they
did not embody his idea of beauty. They were as beautiful as the sunset
on the mountains, as the moonglade on the sea, as the morning mist rising from the valleys.

A word transformed the crude animal hides they wore into fine-
spun, shimmering silk. Another word altered the very tree in which the
two had been hiding, relaxed the contorted limbs, smoothed the
gnarled trunks. The tree stood straight and tall; deep green leaves rustled in the ocean breeze. Flowers exuded sweet-smelling perfume. At
another word, all the trees underwent this same transformation.

The two left the beach, headed inland, following the direction the
knights had taken to reach the mud-hut village. The two did not speak;
they were comfortable in their silence. The words they'd just exchanged
were probably more than either had spoken to another of their race in
years. The Irda enjoy isolation, solitude. They do not even like to be
around each other for long periods. It had taken a crisis to start a conversation between the two watchers.

Therefore the scene the two found, on their return, was almost as
shocking as the sight of mud huts and clay cooking pots had been to the
knights. The two Irda saw all their people—several hundred or more—
gathered beneath an enormous willow tree, a circumstance almost
unparalleled in the history of the Irda.

The ugly, misshapen trees were gone, replaced by a dense, lush forest of oak and pine. Built around and among the trees were small, carefully conceived and designed dwellings. Each house was different in
aspect and appearance, but few were ever larger than four rooms, com-
prising cooking area, meditative area, work area, sleep area. Those
dwellings that were built with five rooms also housed the young of the
species. A child lived with a parent (generally the mother, unless circumstances dictated otherwise) until the child reached the Year of
Oneness. At that time, the child moved out and established a dwelling
of his or her own.

Each Irda household was self-sufficient. Each Irda grew his own food, obtained his own water, pursued his own studies. Social interchange was not prohibited or frowned upon. It simply didn't exist. Such an idea would never occur to an Irda or—if it did—would be considered a trait peculiar to other, lesser races, such as humans, elves, dwarves, kender and gnomes; or the dark races, such as minotaur, goblins, and draconians; or the one race that was never mentioned among the Irda: ogres.

Irda join with other Irda only once in their lives, for the purpose of mating. This is a traumatic experience for both male and female, for they do not come together out of love. They are constrained to come together by the magical practice known as the *Valin*. Created by the elders of the race in order to perpetuate the race, the *Valin* causes the soul of one Irda to take possession of the soul of another. There is no escape, no defense, no choice or selection. When the *Valin* happens between two Irda, they must couple or the *Valin* will so torture and torment them that it may lead to death. Once the woman has conceived, the *Valin* is lifted, the two go their separate ways, having decided between themselves which would be responsible for the child's welfare. So devastating is this experience in the lives of two Irda, that this rarely happens more than once in a lifetime. Thus few children are born to the Irda, and their numbers remain small.

The Irda had lived on the continent of Ansalon for centuries, ever since their creation. Yet few members of the other, more prolific races knew of the Irda's existence. Such wondrous creatures were the stuff of legend and folk tale. Each child learned at mother's knee the story of the ogres, who had once been the most beautiful creatures ever created, but who—due to the sin of pride—had been cursed by the gods, changed into ugly, fearsome monsters. Such tales were meant as moral lessons.

"Roland, if you pull your sister's hair one more time, you'll turn into an ogre."

"Marigold, if you keep admiring your pretty face, you'll look into the mirror one day and find yourself as ugly as an ogre."

The Irda, so legend had it, were ogres who had managed to escape the gods' wrath, and so remained beautiful, with all their blessings and magical powers intact. Because they were so powerful and so beautiful and so blessed, the Irda did not hobnob with the rest of the world. And so they vanished. Children, walking into a dark and gloomy wood, would always look for an Irda, for—so legend had it—if you caught an Irda, you could force him or her to grant you a wish.

This had about as much truth to it as did most legends, but it did encompass the Irda's primary fear: If any of the other races ever discovered an Irda, they would try to make use of the powerful magic to enhance their own ends. Fear of this, of being used, drove the Irda to live alone, hidden, disguised, avoiding all contact with anyone.

It had been many years since any Irda had walked on Ansalon—in dark and gloomy woods or anywhere else. Following the War of the Lance, the Irda had looked forward to a long reign of peace. They had been disappointed. The various factions and races on Ansalon could not agree on a peace treaty. Worse, the races were now fighting among themselves. And then there came rumors of a vast darkness forming in the north.

Fearful that his people would be caught in yet another devastating war, the Decider made a decision. He sent out word to all of the Irda, telling them to leave the continent of Ansalon and travel to this remote isle, far beyond the knowledge of anyone. And so they had come. They had lived in peace and isolation on this isle for many years. Peace and isolation, which had just been shattered.

The Irda had come together here, beneath the willow tree, to try to end this threat. They had come together to discuss the knights and barbarians, yet they stood apart, each separated from his or her fellows, glancing at the tree, then askance at each other, uneasy, uncomfortable, and unhappy. The tree's severed branch, cut by the knight's cold steel blade, lay on the ground. Sap oozed from the cut in the living tree. The tree's spirit cried out in anguish, and the Irda could not comfort it. A peaceful existence, which had been perfected over the years, had come to an end.

"Our magical shield has been penetrate." The Decider was addressing the group as a whole. "The dark knights know we are here. They will return."

"I disagree, Decider," another Irda argued respectfully. "The knights will *not* come back. Our disguises fooled them. They think we are savages, on the level of animals. Why should they return? What could they possibly want with us?"

"You know the ways of the human race." The Decider countered, his tone heavy with the sorrow of centuries. "The dark knights may want nothing to do with us *now*. But there will come a time when their leaders will need men to fill the ranks of their armies, or they will decide that this island would be a good location for building ships, or they will feel the need to put a garrison here. A human can never bear to leave anything alone. He must do something with every object he finds, put it to some use, take it apart to see how it works, attach some sort of meaning or significance to it. So it will be with us. They will be back."

The Irda, always living alone, in isolation, had no need for any sort of governmental body. Yet they realized that they needed one among them to make decisions for all of them as a whole. Thus, as far back as ancient time, they had always chosen one from among their number who was known as the Decider. Sometimes male, sometimes female, the chosen Decider was neither the eldest nor the youngest, neither the wisest nor the smartest, neither the most powerful mage nor the weakest. The Decider was average and thus, being average, would take no drastic actions, would follow a median course.

The present Decider had proved far stronger, far more aggressive, than any of the Deciders before him. He said it was due to the bad times. His decisions had all been wise ones, or at least so most of the Irda believed. Those who disagreed were reluctant to disturb the placidity of Irda life and had thus far said nothing.

"At any rate, they will not return in the immediate future, Decider," said the female who had been one of the watchers on the shore. "We watched their ship disappear over the horizon. And we noted that it flew the flag of Ariakan, son of the late Ariakus, Dragon Highlord. Ariakan, like his father before him, is a follower of the dark goddess Queen Takhisis."

"If he were not a follower of Takhisis, then he would be a follower of Paladine. If not Paladine, then one of the other gods or goddesses. Nothing changes." The Decider folded his arms across his chest, shook his head. "I repeat, they will be back. For the glory of their queen, if nothing else."

"They spoke of war, Decider, of invading Ansalon." This came from the male watcher. "Surely that will occupy them for many years."

"Ah, there, you see?" The Decider looked triumphantly around at the assembly. "War. Again war. Always war. The reason we left Ansalon. I had hoped that here, at least, we would be safe, immune." He sighed deeply. "Apparently not."

"What should we do?"

The Irda, standing apart, separate from each other, looked questioningly at each other.

"We could leave this island, travel to another, where we would be safe," suggested one.

"We left Ansalon, traveled to this island," said the Decider. "We are not safe here. We will not be safe anywhere."

"If they come back, we'll fight them, drive them away," said one of the Irda—a very young Irda, newly arrived at the Year of Oneness. "I know that we've never, in our entire history, shed the blood of another race. That we've hidden ourselves away in order to avoid killing. But we have the right to defend ourselves. Every person in the world has that right."

The other, more mature, Irda, were regarding the young woman with the looks of elaborate patience adults of every species adopt when the young make statements embarrassing to their elders.

And so they were considerably astonished when the Decider said, "Yes, Avril, you are correct. We do have the right to defend ourselves. We have the right to live the lives we choose to live in peace. And I say we should defend that right."

In their shock, several of the Irda spoke simultaneously. "You are not suggesting that we fight the humans, are you, Decider?"

"No," he returned. "I am not. Of course, I am not. But neither am I suggesting that we pack up our possessions and leave our homes. Is that what you want?"

One spoke, a man known as the Protector, who had occasionally disagreed with the Decider and had occasionally made his disagreement known. He was, consequently, not a great favorite with the Decider, who frowned when the Protector started to speak.

"Of all the places we have lived, this is the most congenial, the most lovely, the best suited to us. Here we are together, yet apart. Here we can help each other when there is need, yet remain in solitude. It will be hard to leave this island. Yet . . . it doesn't seem the same now. I say we should move."

The Protector gestured to the neat, snug houses surrounded by hedgerows and lovingly tended flower gardens. The other Irda knew what he meant. The houses were the same, unchanged by the magic that had supplied the illusion of mud huts. The difference could not be seen, but it could be felt, heard, tasted, and smelled. The birds, normally talkative and filled with song, were silent, afraid. The wild animals, who roamed freely among the Irda, had vanished back into their holes or up into the trees. The smell of steel and of blood was strong on the air.

Innocence and peace had been ravaged. The wounds would heal, the scars disappear, but the memory would remain. And now the Decider was suggesting that they defend this homeland! The very thought was appalling. The idea of moving was catching hold, gaining supporters.

The Decider saw that he had to swing around, take another tack.

"I am not suggesting we go to war," he said, his tone now gentle, soothing. "Violence is not our way. I have long studied the problem. I foresaw disaster coming. I have just returned from a trip to the continent of Ansalon. Let me tell you what I have discovered."

The other Irda stared at their Decider in amazement. So isolated were they—one from the other—that no one realized their leader had even been gone, much less that he had risked walking among outsiders.

The Decider's face grew grave and sorrowful. "Our magic-blessed vessel took me to the human city of Palanthas. I walked its streets, listened to the people talk. I traveled thence to the stronghold of the Solamnic Knights, from there to the seafaring nations of Ergoth. I passed into Qualinesti, the land of the elves. I entered the gates of Thorbardin, realm of the dwarves. Invisible as the wind, I slipped over the borders of the cursed elven land of Silvanesti, walked the Plains of Dust, spent time in Solace, Kendermore, and Flotsam. Finally, I looked upon the Blood Sea of Istar and, from there, passed near Storm's Keep, from whence came these same dark knights.

"Over twenty-five years—in human time—has passed since the War of the Lance. The people of Ansalon hoped for peace, hope that was in vain, as *we* could have told them. As long as the gods war among themselves, their battles will spill over onto the mortal plane. With these dark knights to fight for her, Queen Takhisis is more powerful than ever.

"Their lord, Ariakan, son of Highlord Ariakus, had the nerve and the temerity to point out to the Dark Queen wherein her weakness lay. 'Evil turns in upon itself.' The War of the Lance was lost due to the greed and selfishness of the Dark Queen's commanders. Ariakan, a prisoner of the Knights of Solamnia during and after the war, realized that the Solamnic Knights had achieved victory through their willingness to make sacrifices for the cause—sacrifices that were epitomized in the death of the knight Sturm Brightblade.

"Ariakan put his ideas into practice and has now created an army of men and women committed body and soul to the Dark Queen and, more importantly, to conquering the world in her name. They will give up anything—wealth, power, their own lives—to achieve victory. They are bound in honor and in blood to each other. They are an indomitable foe, particularly since Ansalon is, once again, divided against itself.

"The elves are at war with each other. Qualinesti has a new ruler, a boy, the son of Tanis Half-Elven and the daughter of the late Speaker of the Sun, Laurana. The boy was first tricked and then constrained into accepting the role of king. He is, in reality, little more than a puppet, whose strings are being pulled by some of the old order of elves, isolationists who hate everyone different from themselves. That includes their Silvanesti cousins.

"And because these elves have grown in power, the dwarves of Thorbardin fear attack and are considering sealing shut their mountain once again. The Knights of Solamnia are building their defenses—not in fear of the dark knights, but in fear of the elves. Paladine's Knights have been warned against the dark paladins of evil, but they refuse to believe that the tiger could have altered his stripes, as the saying goes. The

Solamnics still believe that evil will turn upon itself, as it did in the War of the Lance, when Dragon Highlord Kitiara ended up battling her own commander, Highlord Ariakus, while the black-robed wizard Raistlin Majere betrayed them both. That will not happen this time.

"The balance is once again shifting in the Dark Queen's favor. But this time, my friends"——the Decider gazed around at his people, his eyes going to each in turn, gathering them all in "——this time, it is my belief that Queen Takhisis will win."

"But what of Paladine? What of Mishakal? We pray to them now as we have done in the past. They protect us." The Protector spoke, but many others were nodding in agreement.

"Did Paladine protect us from the evil knights?" asked the Decider in stern tones. "No. He permitted them to land on our coast."

"They did us no harm," the Protector pointed out.

"Yet," the Decider said ominously, "the gods of good, on whose protection we have so long relied, can do little for us. This terrible incident has proven that. Our magic, their magic, has failed us. It is time we rely on something more powerful."

"You obviously have some idea. Tell us," the Protector said, his voice grim.

"My idea is this: That we use one of the world's most powerful magical artifacts to shield us—once and for all—from outsiders. You know the name of the artifact to which I am referring—the Graygem of Gargath."

"The Graygem is not ours," the Protector said sternly. "It does not belong to us. It belongs to the peoples of the world."

"Not anymore," the Decider stated. "We were the ones who sought out this artifact. We found it. We acquired it and brought it here for safekeeping."

"We stole it," the Protector said. "From a simpleminded fisherman who found it washed up on the shore, who took it to his house and kept it for its sparkling facets and the delight he took in showing it off to his neighbors. He made no use of it, knew nothing of its magic, cared nothing for its magic. And so, the Graygem could make no use of him. Perhaps he was intended to be its keeper. Perhaps, in taking it from him, we have unwittingly thwarted the plans of the gods. Perhaps that is why they have ceased to protect us."

"*Some* might call what we did theft." The Decider stared very hard at the Protector. "But I say that, in recovering the Graygem, we did the world a favor. This artifact has long been a problem, wreaking havoc wherever it goes. It would have fled the simpleton as it has fled so many others before it. But now it is bound by our magic. By holding it here, under our control, we are benefitting all of mankind."

"You told us, as I recall, Decider, that the Graygem's magic would protect us from incursion from the outside world. That is not, apparently, the case," the Protector said. "How can you say now that its magic will shield us?"

"I have spent long years studying the Graygem and have recently made an important discovery," the Decider answered. "The force that propels the Graygem, causes it to roam the world, is not peculiar to the stone itself, but is, I believe, hidden *inside* the stone. The stone is only a container—a vessel—which holds and constrains the power within. This magical force, once released, will undoubtedly prove to be immensely powerful. I propose to the assembly that we crack open the Graygem, release the force within, and use it to protect our homeland."

The Irda were clearly unhappy. They did not like to take action of any kind, preferring to spend their lives in meditation and study. To take such drastic action was almost unthinkable! Yet, they had only to look around them to see the damage done to their beloved homeland, their last refuge from the world.

The Protector ventured a final protest. "If there is a force trapped inside the Graygem, it must, as you say, be very powerful. Are you certain we can control it?"

"We are able to control the Graygem itself quite easily now. I see no difficulty in our controlling this power and using it to defend ourselves."

"But how can you be sure you're controlling the Graygem? Perhaps the Graygem's controlling you, Decider!"

A voice—harsher than the musical tones of the Irda—came from somewhere behind the Protector. The Irda all turned their heads in the voice's direction, drew back so that the speaker could be seen. It was a young woman, a human woman of indeterminate age, somewhere between eighteen to twenty-five human years. The young woman was, to the eyes of the Irda, an extraordinarily ugly creature. Despite her homely looks—or maybe because of them—the Irda cherished the young woman, doted on her, spoiled her. They had done so for years, ever since she had come—an orphaned infant—to live among them.

Few Irda would have dared make such an impertinent statement to the Decider. The young human should know better. All eyes turned disapprovingly to the Irda who had been placed in charge of the human—the man known, for that very reason, as the Protector.

He appeared considerably embarrassed, was speaking to the young woman, apparently endeavoring to convince her to return to their house.

The Decider assumed an expression of extreme patience. "I'm not certain what you mean, Usha, my child. Perhaps you could explain yourself."

The young woman appeared pleased at being the center of so much attention. She shrugged free of the Protector's gently restraining hand, strode forward until she stood in the center of the circle of Irda.

"How do you know the Graygem isn't controlling you? If it was, it wouldn't be likely to tell you, now, would it?" Usha glanced around, proud of her argument.

The Decider conceded this argument, praised the human's cleverness, and carefully kept from smiling. The idea was, of course, ludicrous, but then the girl was human after all.

"The Graygem has been quite submissive since taken into our presence," he said. "It rests on the altar we constructed for it, barely even glimmers. I doubt if it is controlling us, Child. You need have no worries along that line."

No other race on Krynn was as powerful in magic as the Irda. Even the gods—so some of the Irda, the Decider among them, had been known to whisper—were not as powerful. The god Reorx had lost the gem. It was the Irda who had discovered it, taken it, and now held it. The Irda knew the stories of the Graygem's past, how it had spread chaos and havoc wherever it went throughout the world. The Graygem was, so legend had it, responsible for the creation of the races of kender, gnomes, and dwarves. But that was before the Irda had been in charge of the gem. It had been in the care of humans. What could you expect?

The meeting continued, the Irda trying every way possible to wriggle out of this situation without resorting to any sort of drastic action.

Usha soon grew bored—as humans easily do—and told her Protector she was going back to their house to fix dinner. He looked relieved.

Walking away from the meeting, Usha was inclined, at first, to be angry. Her notion was a good one, had been dismissed all too quickly. But being angry took a lot of energy and concentration. She had other matters on her mind. She walked into the wilderness, but not to gather herbs for the evening meal.

She walked instead to the beach. When she reached the shoreline, she stood staring down, fascinated, at the footprints left in the sand by the two young knights. Kneeling down, she rested her hand in one of the prints. It was much bigger than her small hand. The knights had been taller, bigger than she. Picturing them in her mind, a pleasurable and confusing tingle coursed through her body. It was the first time she'd ever seen another human, a human male.

They were ugly, certainly, compared to the Irda, but not as ugly as all that. . . .

Usha remained on the beach, dreaming, a long, long time.

The Irda reached a decision, decided to leave the matter of the Graygem in the hands of the Decider. He would know how best to handle this situation. Whatever he determined needed to be done would be done. This concluded, they returned to their dwellings, anxious to be alone, to put all this unpleasantness behind them.

The Decider did not return immediately to his dwelling. He summoned three of the eldest of the Irda, drew them apart for a private discussion.

"I did not bring this matter up publicly," the Decider said, speaking softly, "because I knew the pain it would cause our people. But there is one more action we must take in order to ensure our safety. *We* are immune to the temptations generated by the Graygem, but there is one living among us who is not. You all know of whom I speak."

The others—by their dismayed and forlorn expressions—knew.

The Decider continued. "It grieves me to have to make this decision, but we must cast this person out. You all saw and heard Usha today. Because of her human blood, she is in danger from the Graygem."

"We don't know that for certain." One ventured a meek protest.

"We know the stories," the Decider said sharply. "I investigated and discovered them to be true. The Graygem corrupts all humans who come near it, filling them with longings and desires they cannot control. The sons of the war hero Caramon Majere nearly fell victim to it, according to one report. The god Reorx himself had to intervene to save them. The Graygem may have already seized on Usha and is trying to use her to cause dissension among us. Therefore, to ensure her safety as well as ours, Usha must be sent away."

"But we've raised her since she was a baby," another of the elders protested. "This is the only home she has ever known!"

"Usha is old enough now to live on her own, among her own kind." The Decider relaxed his stern tone. "We have commented before on the fact that she is growing restless and bored among us. Our studious, contemplative life is not for her. As do all humans, she requires change in order to grow. We are stifling her. This separation will be as much to her advantage as our own."

"It will be hard, giving her up." One of the elders wiped away a tear, and the Irda do not easily cry. "Especially for the Protector. He dotes on the child."

"I know," said the Decider gently. "It seems cruel, but the swifter we act, the better it will be for all of us, including the Protector. Are we all agreed?"

The Decider's wisdom was honored. He went to tell the Protector. The other Irda hurried back to their separate homes.

3

Farewells.
The Protector's parting gift.

eave?" Usha stared blankly at the man she had always known as Protector. "Leave the island? When?"

"Tomorrow, Child," said the Protector. He was already going about the small house they shared, gathering up Usha's things, placing them on the bed, preparatory to packing them. "A boat is being readied for you. You are an adept sailor. The boat is magically enhanced. It will not overturn, no matter how rough the seas. If the wind quits, the boat will never lie becalmed, but will sail on, sped by the current of our thoughts. It will carry you safely across the ocean to the human city of Palanthas, which lies almost due south of us. A journey of twelve hours, no more."

"Palanthas . . ." Usha repeated, not truly comprehending, not even knowing what she was saying.

The Protector nodded. "Of all the cities on Ansalon, I think you will find Palanthas most suitable. The population is large and varied. The Palanthians have a greater tolerance for cultures other than their own. Oddly enough, this is probably due to the presence of the Tower of High Sorcery and its master, Lord Dalamar. Though a mage of the Order of Black Robes, he is respectful of the—"

Usha didn't hear any more. She knew Prot, knew he was talking out of desperation. A silent, reclusive, mild, and gentle man, those words were the most he'd spoken to her in months, and he was likely speaking these just to comfort both of them. She knew this because, when he picked up a doll with which she'd played as a child, he suddenly ceased talking, drew it to his breast, and held it as he had once held her.

Usha's eyes filled with tears. She turned away swiftly so that he wouldn't see her cry.

"So, I'm being sent to Palanthas, am I? Good. You know I've wanted to leave for a long time now. I have my journey all planned. I was thinking of going to Kalaman, but"—she shrugged her shoulders—"Palanthas will do. One place is as good as another."

She hadn't been thinking of going to Kalaman at all. The city's name was the first that popped into her head. But she made it sound as if she'd planned this trip for years. The truth was, she was frightened. Terribly, horribly frightened.

The Irda know where I was last night! she thought, feeling guilty.

They know I was out on the beach. They know what I was thinking, dreaming!

Her dreams had conjured up the images of the knights: their youthful faces, their sweat-damp hair, their strong and supple hands. In her dreams, they had met her, talked to her, swept her away on their dragon-headed ship. They had sworn they loved her; had forsaken the battle and the sword for her. Silly, she knew. How could any man love someone so ugly? But she could dream she was beautiful, couldn't she? Usha blushed hotly to think of her dreams now. She was ashamed of them, ashamed of the feelings they woke inside her.

"Yes, we both know it's time for you to leave," the Protector said, somewhat awkwardly. "We've talked about it before."

True, Usha *had* talked of leaving for the past three years. She would plan her journey, decide what she would take, even go so far as to set a day. A tentative day, a vague day: "Midsummer's Eve" or "the Time of the Three Moons." The days came and the days left. Usha always remained. The sea was too rough or the weather too cold or the boat inadequate or the omens unfavorable. Her Protector always mildly agreed with her, as he agreed with everything she said and did, and no more was said. Until the next time Usha planned her trip.

"You're right. I was meaning to go anyway," she said, hoping that the quiver in her voice would be taken for excitement. "I'm already half packed."

She swiped a hand over her eyes and turned to face the man who had raised her from infancy. "Whatever are you doing, Prot?" Her childish name for him. "You can't imagine I'm going to Palanthas carrying my doll, do you? Leave it here. It will be company for you while I'm gone. You two can talk to each other until I come back."

"You won't be coming back, Child," said Prot quietly.

He did not look at her, but fondled the well-worn doll. Then, silently, he handed the doll to her.

Usha stared. The quiver formed into a lump, and the lump brought more tears to her eyes. Snatching up the doll, she hurled it across the small room.

"I'm being punished! Punished for speaking my mind! Punished because *I'm* not afraid of that man! The Decider hates me! You all hate me! Because I'm ugly and stupid and . . . and human! Well!" Usha wiped her tears with the backs of her hands, smoothed her hair, drew in a deep, shaking breath. "I wasn't planning on coming back anyway. Who would want to? Who cares about a dull place where no one talks to anyone for months at a time? Not me! I'll leave tonight! Now! The hell with packing! I don't want anything from you ever! Ever! Ever again!"

She was crying now—crying and watching to see the effect of her tears at the same time. The Protector was gazing at her helplessly, just as he always did whenever she wept. He would give in. He always gave in. He would do anything to placate her, soothe her, give her whatever she wanted. He always had.

The Irda are not accustomed to displaying their own emotions, unless such emotions are extraordinarily strong. Consequently, the Irda were baffled by the tempestuous vagaries of human temperament. They could not bear to see anyone in a state of strong emotional throes. It was embarrassing, unseemly, undignified. Usha had learned, early on, that tears and tantrums would win her anything she wanted. Her sobs increased in volume; she choked and gulped and secretly exulted. She would *not* be sent away. Not now.

I will leave! she thought resentfully, but only when *I'm* good and ready!

She'd reached the painful hiccuping stage and was thinking that it was time to quit and give Prot a chance to humbly apologize for upsetting her, when she heard something astonishing.

The door shutting.

Usha gulped, fumbled for a handkerchief to wipe her eyes. When she could see, she stared around in astonishment.

The Protector was gone. He'd walked out on her.

Usha sat alone in the silent, empty little house that had been hers for however many years had passed since they'd brought her here as a tiny baby. She'd once tried to keep track, marking off the years from the day on which Prot said she'd been born. But she'd quit counting at about thirteen. It had been a game up until then, but at that age—for some reason—the game had become hurtful. No one would tell her much about her parents or why they weren't around. They didn't like to talk about such things. It made them sad every time she brought up the subject.

No one could tell her who she was . . . only what she wasn't. She wasn't an Irda. And so—in a fit of pique—she'd ceased to mark the years, and when they had started to be important to her again, she'd lost track. Had four or five years passed? Six? Ten?

Not that it mattered. Nothing mattered.

Usha knew then that this time tears wouldn't help.

* * * * *

The next day, around sun's zenith, the Irda came together again—twice in two days, something practically unprecedented in their history—to bid the human "child" good-bye.

Usha was armored by anger now, anger and resentment. Her farewells were distant and formal, as if she were bidding good-bye to some estranged cousin who'd happened to drop in for a visit.

"I don't care."

Those were the words the Protector heard her say—none too softly—to herself. "I'm *glad* I'm leaving! You don't want me. No one ever did want me. I don't care about any of you. It's not as if you cared about *me!*"

But the Irda did care. The Protector wished he could tell her that, but such words came with difficulty, if at all. The Irda had grown quite fond of the carefree, singing, laughing child, who had jolted them out of their studious contemplation, forced them to open their sealed and locked hearts. If they had spoiled her—and they had spoiled her, the Protector knew—it had been unintentional. It made them happy to see *her* happy and, therefore, they had done everything possible to keep her that way.

He was beginning to think—dimly—that this may have been a mistake. The world into which they were shoving her so roughly did not care anything about Usha. Whether she was happy or sad, dead or alive, were not the world's concerns. It occurred to him now—a bit late—that perhaps Usha should have been disciplined, taught to handle such indifference.

But then, he had never truly thought he'd have to set the wild, singing bird free. Now the time was at hand and, although there were no overt displays of emotion, the Irda showed their feelings in the only way in which they knew how—they gave her gifts.

Usha accepted the gifts with ungracious thanks, taking them and stuffing them into a leather pouch without ever giving them so much as a glance. When the giver attempted to explain what the gift did, Usha brushed the explanation aside. She was hurt, deeply hurt, and she intended to hurt every one of them back. The Protector really couldn't blame her.

The Decider made a touching speech, to which Usha listened in stone-cold silence, and then the time was at hand. The tide was right; the wind was right. The Irda murmured their prayers and good wishes. Usha turned her back on them all and stalked away through the forest, heading toward the beach, clutching their gifts tightly against her chest.

"I don't care! I don't care!" she repeated over and over in what the Protector hoped was a strengthening mantra.

He was the only one who accompanied her to the boat. She refused to speak to him, and he was beginning to wonder if perhaps he'd misjudged her. Perhaps she was one of the unfeeling, uncaring humans. About halfway to the beach, when the two of them were alone together in the woods, Usha stumbled to a halt.

"Prot! Please!" She threw her arms around him, hugged him close, a show of affection she hadn't made since she'd left childhood behind. "Don't send me away! Don't make me go! I'll be good! I won't cause any more trouble! I love you! I love you all!"

"I know, Child, I know." The Protector—his own eyes misting over—patted her awkwardly on the back. He had strong memories of doing this for her when she was a baby, cradling her in his arms, trying his best to give her the love her mother would never be able to give.

When Usha's sobs quieted, he held her at arm's length, looked into her eyes.

"Child, I wasn't supposed to tell you this. But I can't let you go, thinking that we don't love you anymore, that you've disappointed us in some way. You could never do that, Usha. We love you dearly. I want you to believe that. The truth is . . . we are going to work magic—very powerful magic, in an effort to keep the evil knights from returning. I can't explain, but this magic might be harmful to you, Usha, because you are not an Irda. It might endanger you. We are sending you away because we are concerned about your safety."

A lie, perhaps, but a harmless one. In truth, Usha was being sent away because she might endanger the magic. The human, Usha, was the one flaw in the perfect crystalline structure of enchantment the Irda planned to use to contain the power of the Graygem. The Protector knew that this was the true reason the Decider had decreed that Usha be sent away.

Usha sniffed. The Protector wiped her nose and face, as he had done for her when she was a little girl.

"This . . . this magic." Usha swallowed. "It will keep you safe? Safe from the evil?"

"Yes, Child. So the Decider says, and we have no reason to doubt his wisdom."

Another lie. The Protector had now told more lies in this one day than he had in a lifetime that spanned centuries. He was extremely amazed to find he was good at it.

Usha made a feeble attempt at a smile. "Thanks for being honest with me, Prot. I'm . . . I'm sorry I was so beastly to the others. You'll tell them for me. Tell how much I'll miss them and how I'll think of you—all of you—every day. . . ." The tears threatened again. She gulped, shook them out of her eyes.

"I'll tell them, Usha. Now, come. Sun and tide wait for no one, or so the minotaur say."

They walked to the beach. Usha was very quiet. She looked dazed, disbelieving, numb.

They reached the boat—a large, two-masted sailboat of minotaur make and design. The boat had been obtained by the Irda several years ago, for use in the acquisition of the Graygem. That task accomplished, the Irda had no more use for the boat and had given the Protector permission to teach Usha how to sail it. Though he had dreaded it, he'd always feared this day must come.

Usha and the Protector carefully stowed her two packs—a small one holding personal items that could be slung over her back, and a larger pouch, which held the Irda's gifts. Usha wore what the Irda deemed sensible clothes, suitable for traveling in the heat: pants made of light green silk, loose and flowing, gathered around the ankles, held in place by an embroidered band; a matching silk tunic, open at the neck, tied around her waist with a gold sash; and a vest of black velvet, hand-embroidered in vibrant colors. A green silk scarf covered her head.

"All those packs . . . You look just like a kender." The Protector attempted a small joke.

"A kender!" Usha forced a laugh. "You've told me stories about them, Prot. Will I get to meet one, do you think?"

"Easier to meet them than to get rid of them. Oh, yes, Child." The Protector smiled at old memories. "You will meet the lighthearted, light-fingered kender. And the grim and dour dwarves, the cunning and crafty gnomes, bold and handsome knights, silver-voiced elves. You'll meet them all. . . ."

As he spoke, the Protector watched Usha's gaze turn from him. She looked out across the sea. The expression on her face altered, no longer dazed, numb. He saw the hunger now, the eagerness to see and hear and taste and touch life. On the horizon, white clouds massed, building higher and higher. Usha was seeing not clouds, but cities, white and shining in the sun. He had the feeling that if the ocean had been made of slate, she would have run across it then and there.

The Protector sighed. The human side had seized control of the orphan child at last. Excitement glistened in her eyes; her lips parted. She leaned forward in unconscious yearning, ready—as were all humans—to rush headlong into the future.

He knew, far better than she—for he was one of the few Irda to have walked the world—what dangers Usha, in her innocence, faced. He almost warned her; the words were on his lips. He had told her of knights and kender. Now he must speak of cruel draconians, evil goblins, humans with corrupt souls and hearts, dark clerics who committed unspeakable acts in the names of Morgion or Chemosh, black-robed wizards with life-draining rings, rogues, thieves, liars, seducers.

But he didn't tell her. The warnings were never given. He did not have the heart to dim her glow, tarnish her bright radiance. She would learn soon enough. Hopefully the gods would watch over her, as it was said they watched over slumbering children, stray animals, and kender.

The Protector helped Usha into the boat. "Magic will guide the craft to Palanthas. All you need do, Child, is keep the setting sun on your left cheek. Fear no storm. The boat cannot be capsized. Should the wind die, our magic will be your sea breeze, help speed the boat on its way. Let the waves rock you to sleep. When you awake in the morning, you will see the spires of Palanthas shining in the sun."

Together they raised the sail. All during this process, the Protector was distracted, arguing with himself, trying to reach a decision. At length, he made it.

When the craft was ready to launch, the Protector settled Usha in the stern, repositioning her possessions neatly around her. This done, he drew forth a scroll of parchment tied with a black ribbon. The Protector handed the scroll to Usha.

"What is this?" she asked, regarding it curiously. "A map?"

"No, Child. It is not a map. It is a letter."

"Is it for me? Does it"—her face brightened with hope—"does it tell me about my father? Why he left me? You promised one day you would explain, Prot."

The Protector flushed deeply, taken aback. "It . . . um . . . does not, Child. You know the story already. What more could I add?"

"You have said he left me after my mother's death, but you never said why. It's because he didn't love me, isn't it? Because I was the cause of my mother's death. He hated me—"

"Where did you ever get that notion, Child?" The Protector was shocked. "Your father loved you dearly. You know what happened. I've told you."

Usha sighed. "Yes, Prot," she said. All their conversations about her parentage ended like this. He refused to tell her the truth. Very well, it didn't matter. She'd find her own truth.

The Protector tapped the letter, anxious to change the subject of their conversation.

"The missive is not for you, but when you have lost sight of our island, you may open this and read it. The one to whom you are to deliver it may have questions which only you can answer."

Usha regarded the letter with a puzzled expression. "Then who is it for, Prot?"

The Protector was silent a moment, wrestling with himself. Shaking his head to rid himself of doubt, he answered. "There is a powerful wizard

who dwells in Palanthas. His name is Dalamar. After you have read this letter, take it to him. It is right that he should know what we plan. In case . . ."
He stopped himself, but Usha was quick to catch on.

"In case anything goes wrong! Oh, Prot!" She clung to him, now that the moment of parting was at hand. "I'm afraid!"

You will be, Child, all your life. That is the curse of being human. He leaned over, kissed her on the forehead.

"Your mother's blessing—and your father's—will go with you."

He climbed out of the boat. Pushing the boat off the shore, he sent it skimming over the waves.

"Protector!" Usha cried, reaching out her hand as if to seize him.

But the water, or the magic, or both, carried the boat swiftly away. The lapping of the waves on the shore drowned her words.

The Protector stood on the sandy beach as long as the boat was in sight. Even after the tiny white speck had disappeared over the horizon, he stood there still.

Only when the tide had risen, washed away all trace of Usha's footprints on the sand, did the Protector turn around and leave.

4

A letter to Dalamar.

sha, alone on the boat, watched the slender form of the Protector grow smaller and smaller, watched the shore of her homeland dwindle to nothing more than a black line across the horizon. When the Protector and the shoreline were out of sight, Usha gave the tiller a shove, to turn the boat around, sail it back.

The rudder would not respond. The wind blew strong and steadily Irda magic kept the boat sailing toward Palanthas.

Usha cast herself down in the bottom of the boat and indulged in her grief, cried until she nearly made herself sick.

The tears did nothing to ease the pain in her heart. Instead, they gave her the hiccups, caused her eyes to itch and burn, her nose to run. Fumbling for a handkerchief, she found the letter the Protector had given her. She opened it without much enthusiasm—expecting it to be another justification for getting rid of her—and began to read.

My Usha. You lie asleep as I write this. I look on you—resting peacefully, your arm flung over your head, your hair mussed, the stains of tears on your cheeks—and I am reminded of the child who brought joy and warmth to my life. I miss you already, and you are not even gone!

I know you are hurt and angry at being sent away, alone, like this. Please believe me, my darling child, that I would have never done so had I not been convinced that this departure was in your best interests.

The question you raised in the meeting, concerning the Graygem and its control over us, is a question many of us have been asking. We are not certain that breaking the Graygem is the best course of action. We accede to the wisdom of the Decider because, quite frankly, we do not feel that we have any other choice.

The Decider has decreed that no hint of what we are planning should be given to the outside world. In that, I think he is wrong. For too long we have kept ourselves aloof from the world. This has resulted—more than once—in tragedy. My own sister . . .

At this point, whatever had been written had been blotted over. Prot had never mentioned he had a sister. Where was she? What had happened to her? Usha attempted to decipher the handwriting underneath the blot, but failed. Sighing, she read on. The next part was addressed to Lord

---

Dalamar, master of the Tower of High Sorcery, Palanthas.

Usha skimmed through polite introductions and a description of how the Irda had managed to steal the Graygem—a story she'd heard countless times and which she now found boring. She skipped down to the interesting part.

> The Graygem rests upon the altar which we have built specially to hold it. At a single glance, the stone seems unpretentious in appearance. Closer examination makes the Graygem more interesting. Its size appears to vary with the beholder. The Decider insists it is as large as a full-grown cat, while I see the stone as the size of a hen's egg.
>
> It is impossible to determine the number of facets. We have all of us counted them and none of us has reached the same conclusion. The numbers do not vary by ones or twos, but are radically different, as if each of us had been counting the facets on a different stone.
>
> We know the gem is chaotic in nature. We know further that the god Reorx has made many efforts to recapture the Graygem, but that these have always failed. The Graygem is beyond his power to keep. Why, then, are *we* permitted to keep it?
>
> The Decider's answer to this question is that the god Reorx is a weak god, easily distracted and undisciplined. That may be true, but I wonder why the other gods have never made any attempt to control the gem. Could it be because they, too, are weak against it? Yet, if the gods are all-powerful, how can this be possible? *Unless* the Graygem itself possesses a magical power far stronger than that of the gods.
>
> If that is so, the Graygem is immensely more powerful than we are. And this means that the Graygem is not under our control. It is tricking us, using us—to what end or purpose, I do not know. But I fear it.
>
> That is why I have included a copy of the history of the creation of the world and of the Graygem, as we Irda know it. You will find, my lord Dalamar, that it differs considerably from other recorded histories, and that is one reason why I deem it essential that this information reach the Conclave of Wizards. Perhaps some clues in regard to the Graygem may be gleaned from this account.

"Irda history!" Usha sighed and almost rolled the letter back up. "I've heard this enough times! I know it by heart!"

She had learned to read and write the Irda language and also the language known as Common, which the Irda never spoke among themselves, but which was deemed useful for her to know. Though she'd been good at her lessons, Usha had not particularly enjoyed learning. Unlike the studious Irda, she preferred *doing* things to *reading* about doing things.

But she had nothing to do now except whimper and whine and feel sorry for herself. Leaning over the bulwarks, she dipped her handkerchief into the seawater, bathed her hot face and forehead, and felt better. And so, to keep her mind off her sorrow, she continued reading—bored, at first—but gradually becoming enthralled. She could hear Prot's voice in the words and was, once again, seated at the small table, listening to his account of the creation of the world.

According to our ancestors,* the three gods as we now know them, Paladine, Takhisis, and Gilean, dwelt together on the immortal plane. These three were siblings, having been born of Chaos, Father of All and of Nothing. Paladine was the eldest son, conscientious, responsible. Gilean was the middle child, studious and contemplative. Takhisis was the only daughter, the youngest child and, some say, the favorite. She was restless, ambitious, and bored.

She wanted power, wanted to rule over others. She tried but could not gain ascendance over her brothers. Paladine was too strong-willed, Gilean oblivious. And thus we Irda believe that it was at the instigation of Takhisis that the world of Krynn and all life on this plane came into being.

Takhisis can be quite charming and clever when she wants. She went to her two elder brothers with the idea of creating a world and spirits to dwell within it. To Paladine she laid stress on how these spirits would bring order to the otherwise chaotic universe. Paladine had long been troubled by the fact that their lives had no purpose, no meaning. He and his consort, Mishakal, were pleased with the idea of change, and gave their consent.

"Of course, you have spoken to Father about this," Paladine said. "You have obtained his permission."

"Oh, of course, my dear brother," Takhisis replied.

Paladine must have known that his sister lied, but he was so eager to order the universe that he closed his eyes to the truth.

Takhisis then went to Gilean. She spoke to him of the opportunities for study, a chance to see how beings other than themselves would react in various situations.

Gilean found this notion intriguing. Having no consort (we have no record on what happened to her), Gilean consulted with Zivilyn, a god who came from one of the other immortal planes, simply referred to as

---

* It will be noted by Krynnish scholars that the legend of creation related by the Protector differs in some respects from the legends of creation related by other races. This is natural, considering that each race considers itself central in the universe. The dwarves, for example, refuse to admit that they were created by the confusion caused by the Graygem. They maintain that they are Reorx's creation. Many elves believe that they are the one true race and that other races are mere ink blots on Gilean's Great Book. The Irda are, however, the race in possession of the longest unbroken history of Krynn and therefore we consider that their account probably comes closest to the actual events.

Beyond. Zivilyn is said to exist in all planes at all times.

Zivilyn looked ahead and he looked behind. He looked to his left and to his right. He looked up and he looked down and finally pronounced the idea a good one.

Gilean, therefore, agreed.

"You have, of course, mentioned this matter to Father," Gilean asked, as an afterthought, not even bothering to look up from his book.

"Certainly, my dear brother," Takhisis returned.

Gilean knew that Takhisis lied—Zivilyn had warned him she would. But the opportunity for knowledge was too great a temptation, so Gilean closed his eyes to the truth.

Having obtained agreement from her brothers, Takhisis put her plan into action.

There lived, in Beyond, a god known as Reorx. Nothing much is known about his past, although there are rumors that some terrible tragedy occurred, which led him to shun the company of other immortals. He dwelt alone on his plane, at his forge, spending his time creating things beautiful and horrific, wondrous and terrible. His delight was in the creation. He had no use for any of the objects he made and, once they were finished, he simply tossed them away. We see them still. One will occasionally fall to the ground. They are known as shooting stars.

Takhisis went to Reorx and praised his creations.

"But what a pity," she said, "that you should throw them away! I have in mind a plan. You will create something that will not bore you, but will offer you new challenges every day of your immortal life. You will create a world and populate this world with spirits, and you will teach these spirits all the skills that you know."

Reorx was captivated at the thought. At last, his endless creating would have some use, some benefit. He readily agreed.

"You have cleared this with the Father?" he asked Takhisis.

"I would have never come to you otherwise," she responded.

Reorx—simple and guileless—had no idea that Takhisis was lying.

The gods gathered together: Paladine, Mishakal, and their children; Gilean and his only natural daughter, along with his adopted children; and Takhisis, her consort, Sargonnas, and their children. Reorx arrived, set up his forge, and—in the midst of the dark and endless night of Chaos—he placed a chunk of red-hot, molten metal and struck the first blow with his hammer.

At that moment, the two brothers were forced to open their eyes.

Takhisis had *not* consulted Chaos, Father of All and of Nothing. Well aware that he would be opposed to her plan to bring order to the universe, she had deliberately kept her plot secret from him. And there is no doubt that her brothers knew it.

Chaos could have destroyed his children and their plaything then and there, but—as parents will—he decided it would be better to teach them a lesson.

"You will indeed create order," he thundered, "but I will see to it that order will breed discord, both among you and among those who will dwell in your world."

Nothing could be done to alter what had taken place. Sparks from Reorx's hammer had already become the stars. Light from the stars had given birth to living spirits. Reorx himself forged a world wherein these spirits could dwell.

And it was then that Chaos's curse was made manifest.

Takhisis wanted the newly made spirits under her control, intending to order them about and force them to do her bidding. Paladine wanted the spirits under his control, intending to nurture them and lead them in the paths of righteousness. Gilean could see no advantage to either—in an academic sense. He wanted the spirits to remain free, to choose whatever path they would walk. Thus, the world would be much more interesting.

The siblings quarreled. Their children and gods from the other planes were drawn into the battle. The All-Saints War began.

The Father of All and of Nothing laughed, and his laughter was terrible to hear.

At length, Paladine and Gilean realized that the battle might well destroy all of creation. They allied forces against their sister and, though they could not achieve total victory, they at least forced her to come to terms. She reluctantly agreed that all three should rule the new world together, maintaining a balance between them. Thus they hoped to end the curse cast on them by their Father, Chaos.

The three gods decided that each of them would give the spirits gifts that would enable them to live and prosper in the new-formed world.

Paladine gave the spirits the need to control. Thus they would work to gain control over their surroundings and bring order to the world.

Takhisis gave the spirits ambition and desire. Not only would the spirits control the world, but they would seek constantly to make it better—and to better themselves.

Gilean gave the spirits the gift of choice. Each would have the freedom to make his or her own decisions. No one god would possess absolute power.

All these gifts were good, none of them bad—unless each is taken to extremes. The need to control, taken to extremes, leads to fear of change, suppression of new ideas, intolerance of anything different.

Ambition, taken to extremes, leads to the determination to seize power at all costs, enslavement. Desires can become obsessions, leading to greed, lust, avarice, and jealousy.

Freedom—taken to extremes—is anarchy.

The spirits achieved physical form, springing from the imaginations of the gods. From Paladine's mind came the elves—his ideal race. They delight in controlling the physical world, shaping it to their will. They live long, change little.

Takhisis imagined a race of supremely beautiful creatures, all as ambitious and selfish as herself. These were the ogres and, as their hungers increased, their beauty was consumed. But they are immensely strong and very powerful.

We, the Irda, might be said to be creations of Takhisis, for we were the original ogres. We saw what was happening to our people, and some of us turned to Paladine, begged for his help. He enabled us to break away from the Dark Queen, but the cost was dear. We could not live in proximity to other races, lest we should succumb to temptation and fall once again. We would be an isolated, lonely people, delighting in our isolation, perpetuating our own loneliness. Even coming together to produce progeny would be difficult for us, and so our people would never be numerous. All these conditions we accepted in order to escape the fate of our brethren. And therefore the world knows nothing of us—or what they do know is false.

Gilean imagined into being the race of humans. They have the shortest life span, are the quickest to change, and are easily swayed to one side or the other.

The Father, for his own amusement and to increase the likelihood of turmoil, created the animals. He greatly irritated his children by giving many of the animals advantages; chief among these being the dragons, who possess wisdom, intelligence, long life, magic, strength, and formidable weapons.

Since the arrival of dragons upon Krynn, the other mortal species have either fought the dragons or endeavored to ally with them.

Thus there came about the creation of balance in the world. The elves thought of themselves as the embodiment of "good," while the ogres were the epitome of "evil." (It is interesting to note that, in the ogre view of the world, this is entirely opposite. It is the ogres who see themselves as "good," the elves and those like them, who advocate the extermination of the ogre race, as "evil.") Humans, in the middle, could be moved to join either side and did so—constantly.

Thus it is the humans, in whose blood mingle all the gifts of the gods—the need to exert control, ambition, desires, and the freedom of choice to use these in beneficial or detrimental ways—who race forward through time, creating, changing, altering, destroying. This is called progress.

It was also during this time that magic came into the world. Three of the children of the gods had grown up together and been unusually close: Solinari, son of Paladine and Mishakal; Nuitari, son of Takhisis and Sargonnas, and Lunitari, daughter of Gilean. All the gods possess the power of magic, but in these three that power was enhanced by their love for magic and their dedication to this art. This formed a bond between them, who were unlike in almost all other aspects.

When the All-Saints War occurred, these three were under pressure from their various parents to join one side or the other. The three cousins feared that the war would destroy the thing they loved most: magic. They took a vow to be true to the magic, faithful to each other, and they left the pantheon of the gods. Assuming mortal form, they walked the face of Krynn.

Each cousin found a follower among the mortals and to that follower each gave the gift of magic. This gift could be passed on to other mortals, and those mortals could, in times of need, call upon the three gods for assistance. Then the three cousins left Krynn, yet remained near it, circling in the heavens, watching over with unblinking eyes the mortals who use their gifts. Mortals know these "eyes" as Krynn's three moons: the silver Solinari, the red Lunitari, and the unseen (except by his followers) Nuitari.

We Irda possess immensely strong magical powers, but we are not certain from whence the power emanates. We are not aligned with the wizards of Krynn and are, in fact, considered "renegades." You see us as a threat, a danger to your orders. Our magic is one of the many reasons we shun contact with other species. Magic is crucial to our survival. Every Irda is born with it. Magic is in our blood, so to speak, and comes as naturally to us as do the other senses: seeing, smelling, hearing, touching, tasting. Are we asked to explain how we see? I see no reason for the world to demand that we explain how we perform what are, in their eyes, miracles.

To continue with the history of creation.

The new world was young and wild, as were the spirits of the mortals inhabiting it. The elves worked hard and subdued their part of the world. The ogres learned to adapt to theirs. Humans sought to craft their part and improve on it. Reorx—a lonely god—offered to assist them. It is said that the only time Reorx is truly happy is when he is mingling and interfering in the lives of mortals.

Reorx taught a group of humans innumerable skills, which included the technique of forging steel. The elves and ogres both coveted the metal, which neither of them knew how to produce. They came to the humans to buy steel swords, knives, tools. The humans grew immensely proud of their abilities and began to flaunt them. They forgot—in their pride—to honor Reorx, their teacher. They even shunned the god when he came among them, laughing at him because he was far shorter than they, ridiculing his interest in the very craft by which they were gaining so much wealth.

Infuriated, Reorx cursed these humans. He took from them the skills he had taught them, left them only with the desire to invent, build, construct. He decreed that these humans should be short, wizened, and ridiculed by other races. He changed them into gnomes.

During this time, known as the Age of Twilight, the balance of the world—which had been relatively stable—began to shift. No longer content with what they had, humans began to covet what their neighbors had. The ogres, incited by Takhisis, wanted power. The elves wanted to be left alone and were ready to fight to preserve their isolation.

Hiddukel was one of the gods of Beyond brought to this plane by Takhisis to increase her hold on humans. Hiddukel is a deal maker. He loves to deal and barter and is extremely good at it. He saw in the tilting of the scales of balance a way to increase his own power. War would be good for business, bringing about increased production of weapons, armor, food to feed the armies, and so forth. Since he was also a trader in the souls of the dead, Hiddukel could see a handsome profit to be made in that area as well.

Hoping to further the turmoil, Hiddukel went to Chislev, goddess of woodlands and nature, and—in his best persuasive manner—convinced her that doom was at hand.

"It's only a matter of time before war breaks out," he said dolefully. "And what will that do to the environment? Forests chopped down to make siege towers, saplings turned into bows and arrows, fields scavenged or set ablaze. We need to put a stop to this feuding among the races, once and for all. For the sake of nature, of course."

"And what's your stake in all this?" Chislev demanded. "I can't believe you are interested in the welfare of baby bunnies."

"No one gives me credit for having a heart," Hiddukel complained.

"That's because it's difficult to see beneath the oil slick of your words," Chislev retorted.

"If you must know, war would be extremely upsetting to the financial markets. The value of gold would plunge; it would be practically worthless. Farmers can't get their goods to market if the markets are being invaded. And I'm very fond of rabbits."

"In stews, maybe." Chislev sighed. "Yet, you do have a point. I've seen the growing restlessness among the races, and I've been concerned about it myself. I've spoken to Gilean, but you know what that's like! He never looks up from that book. He's always writing, writing, writing."

"Try to get a word in with Takhisis." Hiddukel sniffed. "Either she's off with Sargonnas, watching minotaur bash each other over the head or she's bringing on plagues, famine, floods, what have you. She hasn't time for the likes of us anymore."

"What do you suggest we do? I take it you have a plan."

"Don't I always, my tree-hugging friend? If neutrality were the ruling force in the world, then the balance would remain constant, never shift. Agreed?"

"I suppose," Chislev said cautiously, not trusting Hiddukel, but unable to argue the point. "But I don't see—"

"Ah! Go to Reorx. Ask him to create a gem that will hold within it the very essence of neutrality. This gem will serve as an anchor to the neutral position. Neutrality will become the strongest force in Krynn, overwhelming the two opposite extremes. They'll be bound to the center, will not be able to deviate far from it."

"And what do we do with this gem once it's created. Give it to you for safekeeping?" Chislev was a gentle goddess, but she had a tendency to be sarcastic, especially around Hiddukel.

"Heavens no!" Hiddukel was appalled. "I wouldn't want such a responsibility! Give it to one of your own number to keep. That would be most sensible, wouldn't it?"

Chislev regarded Hiddukel intently, but he met her scrutiny with the utmost innocence, exhibiting sincere anxiety over the fate of the world. It is said that Queen Takhisis herself has lost in many deals with Hiddukel.

The result of this conversation was that Chislev left her forest and wandered the world in mortal form. What she saw disturbed her greatly. Steel forges burned angry red in the night; elves polished their newly attained swords; humans counted their money; ogres practiced lopping off heads. Grieved, Chislev determined that something must be done.

Chislev considered discussing this matter with her consort, Zivilyn, the god who can see all planes, all times, future and past. But Chislev knew from experience that it was difficult getting a straight "yes" or "no" answer from Zivilyn, who was always making up his mind to do one thing, then—seeing it from another angle—changing his mind to do something else—seeing that from another angle—and changing his mind again until he finally ended up doing nothing at all.

This matter need action, and Chislev decided to take it. She went to Reorx herself.

None of the gods ever visited Reorx, one reason he spent so much of his time chumming around with humans. He was amazed and pleased to have a visitor, particularly a visitor of such delicate beauty and sweet temperament as Chislev.

She, in turn, was overwhelmed by the attention Reorx paid to her, as he bustled about his disorderly dwelling, preparing cakes, stumbling over the furniture, losing the teapot, offering her anything in the universe she wanted to eat.

Chislev suffered a twinge of guilt, for she saw the god's loneliness, and reproached herself for having neglected him. Vowing to visit more often in the future, Chislev drank her tea and presented her request.

Reorx was only too happy to comply. She wanted a gem? She should have a gem. A hundred gems! The finest in the universe.

Chislev, blushing, replied that she wanted only one gem, a plain gem, a gem that would hold within it the essence of neutrality.

Reorx stroked his beard, frowned in thought. "And what would that be, exactly?"

Chislev was somewhat perplexed. "Why, the essence of neutrality would be . . . well . . ."

"Chaos?" Reorx suggested.

Chislev considered the matter, glancing about somewhat fearfully lest the Father of All and of Nothing—the embodiment of Chaos—should overhear. "Could we capture a small part, do you suppose? Not much. Just enough to anchor neutrality in this world."

"Consider it done, Madam," Reorx said with magnificent aplomb. "Where shall I deliver this gem?"

Chislev had long pondered this matter. "Give it to Lunitari. She is closest to the world. She is continually involved with the mortals and their doings. She will be the best to hold it."

Reorx agreed. He kissed her hand, fell over an ottoman, upset his teacup, and, face flushed, left immediately for his forge.

Chislev, relieved of her worries, returned thankfully to her forest.

How Reorx managed to capture and encapsulate a bit of Chaos into the gem is not known. But, according to what happened later, he was obviously able to do so. He produced what he called the "Graygem" and, when it was finished, took it to Lunitari for safekeeping. She was attracted to the gem immediately, and set the gem in the center of the red moon. She rarely let it out of her sight, for the stone had the strange effect of causing all who looked upon it to covet it.

This included, unfortunately, the gem's creator, Reorx. Once he'd given the stone to Lunitari, Reorx was disconcerted to discover that he dreamed of the gem nightly. He regretted having parted with it. He went to Lunitari and humbly requested that she give it back.

Lunitari refused. She, too, dreamed of it nightly and liked to wake to see it shining in the red moon.

Reorx fretted and fumed and at last hit upon a way to retrieve the Graygem for himself. Assuming mortal form, Reorx appeared among the race he had created, the gnomes. He chose one gnome, whose inventions had been least destructive to life, limb, and property values, and showed this gnome—in a dream—the Graygem.

Of course, the gnome wanted the gem more than anything else on Krynn, with the possible exception of a multiheaded, steam-driven screwdriver. The latter being unattainable (stuck in committee), the gnome decided to capture the Graygem. How he went about it is told in other stories, but the recovery effort involved a magical ladder, various winches and pulleys, a magical net, and a bit of a boost from Reorx.

Suffice it to say, the gnome captured the Graygem, removing it in a magical net while Lunitari was on the other side of the world.

"Just the thing," the gnome said, eyeing the stone with admiration, "to power my rotating blade combination pickle slicer and beard trimmer." The gnome was about to put the stone into the invention when Reorx appeared, in the guise of a fellow gnome, and demanded it for himself.

The two quarreled and, during the argument, the Graygem slipped out of its net and escaped.

This was the first indication that there was more to the Graygem than Reorx or Lunitari or the gnome or anyone else had imagined.

Reorx watched in astonishment as the gem sailed away through the air. He chased after it (so did the gnome and a host of his relations), but none was able to capture it. The Graygem rampaged around Krynn, leaving havoc in its wake. It altered animals and plants, affected the spell-casting of wizards, and made a considerable nuisance of itself.

All the gods were now aware of the Graygem. Paladine and Takhisis were both furious with Reorx for having forged it without consulting them first. Chislev shamefacedly admitted her part in the scheme, implicating Hiddukel, who shrugged and laughed uproariously.

His plot had worked. Instead of ensuring the balance, the Graygem had further upset it. The elves were planning to go to war with the humans, the humans were preparing to go to war against the elves, and the ogres were eager to fight all comers.

To draw this story swiftly to a close, a human named Gargath managed to capture the Graygem. He imprisoned it inside his castle with various magical devices. (Or so he thought. I am of the opinion that the Graygem permitted itself to be captured, for no human magic that I have encountered would have held it for long.)

The gnomes, who had been chasing after the Graygem for decades, laid siege to Gargath's castle. They succeeded (accidentally) in breaking through the walls. The gnomes rushed into the courtyard and laid eager hands on the Graygem. One party of gnomes demanded that the stone be cut open on the spot, for they were intensely curious to know what was inside. The other party of gnomes wanted to take the gem back to their dwelling place and hoard it for its value.

A brilliant gray light illuminated the courtyard, blinding everyone. When people could see once again, they found the two groups of gnomes fighting each other. But what was most astonishing, the gnomes were gnomes no longer. The power of the Graygem had altered them, changing those who lusted after the stone for wealth into dwarves and those who wanted the stone out of curiosity into kender.

Those gnomes who had remained outside the walls of the castle, working on their latest invention—the revolving, mass-firing crossbow, known as the Gatling Crossbow, for its inventor, Loosenut Gatling—proved immune to the effects of the Graygem's magical light. They assumed it came from the oil-burning candelabra, which was intended to illuminate the battlefield at night and had been sent up in a gas-filled balloon for that purpose—the gas being produced by a new technique too complex to be described here, but which required lemon juice, metal prongs, and water. Those who survived the subsequent explosion remained gnomes.

The Graygem vanished over the horizon. Reorx and others have made various attempts to capture it. The Graygem permits people to catch it. The gem uses them for its own purposes—or perhaps amusement—then, when it tires of the sport, it releases them. The Graygem "escapes."

But now we Irda have the Graygem in our possession. We are the first to subdue it to our will—or so the Decider claims. This night, he will break open the gem and command the magic within to protect us and our homeland from the incursion of humankind forevermore.

That ended the letter to Dalamar, which was penned in Prot's neat, exact handwriting. A note at the bottom, written in the same hand, but less neat, as if the hand had been trembling, was for Usha herself.

My love and prayers go with you, child of my heart, if not of my body.
Pray for us.

Usha thought long on the postscript. She had laughed over parts of the history. The Protector had often entertained her with "gnome stories," as he called them. Some of the few times she'd seen him smile were when he was describing the gnomes' fantastical machinery. She smiled now, remembering it, but her smile slid slowly away.

Could only her human mind see the danger?

No, she realized, Prot saw it, he knew it. That was why he had given her the scroll. The Irda were desperate. The intrusion of the strangers—uncouth, barbaric, smelling of blood and steel—had frightened them badly. They were acting in defense of a way of life they had known for countless generations.

Usha dropped the letter into her lap. Her eyes filled with tears, but now they were no longer tears of self-pity. They were tears of longing and love for the man who had raised her. Such tears spring from a different source—or so the elves believe. Such tears come from the heart, and, though caused by pain, they have the strange effect of soothing pain.

Exhausted, lulled by the rocking motion of the boat and the humming of the wind among the ropes, Usha cried herself to sleep.

5

The altar and the Graygem. The dwarf arrives late. Cracking open the stone.

The Irda did not come together again. When the time came for the breaking of the Graygem—a time when none of the moons was visible in the sky, particularly not Lunitari, who, so legend had it, still coveted the gem—the Decider alone walked to the altar on which the stone rested.

The other Irda remained in their separate dwellings, each working his or her own magic, each lending aid to the Decider. There was strength in aloneness, or so the Irda believed. Concentration became muddled, energies fragmented, when the one became many.

The altar on which the Irda had placed the stone was located in the geographic center of the isle. The altar was some distance from what the Irda termed a village, though to any other race it would have been nothing but a scattered collection of dwellings. The Irda did not pave streets, they did not open markets, they attended no guild meetings. They did not construct temples or palaces, inns or taverns, nothing but houses, flung around the isle at random, each built where its owner felt most comfortable.

The altar was fashioned of polished wood carved with intricate, arcane symbols. It stood in a glade surrounded by seven gigantic pine trees, which had been magically transported from a secret location on Ansalon to this isle.

So old were these trees that they had likely seen the Graygem pass by the first time it escaped Reorx's control. The pines appeared to be intent on not letting the Graygem escape again. The pines' boughs were intertwined, linked together, presenting a solid front of bark and needle and limb and branch through which even a god might have difficulty in passing.

The Decider stopped in front of the grove of seven pine trees, asked a blessing of the seven spirits who dwelt in the trees.

The pines permitted the Decider to enter the glade, closed up their ranks the moment he was inside. Their massive boughs extended over his head. Looking up, he could not see a single star, much less a constellation. He could not see Takhisis or Paladine. And if he could not see them, he was hopeful they could not see him. The needle canopy of the sacred pines would hide the Decider and the Graygem from any who might try to interfere.

The grove would have been impenetrably dark but for the light cast by the Graygem itself, though the light was feeble, sullen, barely a glimmer.

Almost as if it were sulking, thought the Decider.

But the stone gave light enough to see by. The Decider really didn't need such light. He could have called upon his magic to illuminate the grove as bright as day, had he wanted to, but he preferred not to call attention to what he was doing. Some immortal eye might see that magical glow and wonder what was going on. He was thankful, therefore, for the Graygem's assistance.

Centered, calm, the Decider moved to stand beside the altar. He reveled in being alone, in the solitude the Irda so highly prized. Yet he felt within him the minds and spirits of his people. He bowed his head and drew on that energy. Then, reaching out, he picked up the Graygem in both hands and studied it intently.

The stone was not pleasant to hold. It was sharp and smooth, warm and cold, and it seemed to writhe in his grasp. As he held it, the gray light began to pulse stronger and stronger, until it started to hurt his eyes. He increased his mental control over the Graygem, and the light lessened, became subdued. The Decider ran his fingers over the gem, gliding over the smooth facets, tracing along each sharp edge, searching, probing. At last, he found what he sought, what he'd discovered the first time he'd handled the gem, what had given him the idea.

A flaw. More precisely, an occlusion. He had felt it first, before he'd seen it. Just as insects can be found in amber, some type of foreign matter had apparently been trapped within the Graygem during its formation. Most likely this had occurred as the gem cooled, minerals precipitated, were caught in the complex crystallization. At least, that is what the Decider theorized. The foreign substance itself was not important. What was important was that here was an area of weakness. Here, at this point, cracks would form.

The Decider replaced the gem upon the altar. The arcane symbols that had been carved into the wood wove a spell, held the Graygem enthralled.

The Decider, assisting the spell, had the odd impression that the magic was not necessary, that the Graygem was resting on the altar because it wanted to rest there, not because it was being held there.

This impression was not particularly reassuring. The Decider needed to be in control of the gem, not the other way around. He strengthened the magic.

The gem was now surrounded by a sparkling net of Irda synergy. The Decider picked up two tools—a hammer and a spike. Both were made of silver, crafted in the light of the silver moon, Solinari. Magical incantations had been laid over the tools and on them. The Decider placed the spike's tip at the place of the gem's flaw. He positioned the spike carefully, grasped it firmly, raised the small hammer above it.

The thoughts of all the Irda came together, flowed into the Decider, gave him strength and power.

He hit the spike a sharp blow with the hammer.

*　*　*　*　*

On the beach, several leagues from the Irda village and the altar, a boat had landed. This boat had not sailed across the seas in the usual manner of boats. It had sailed down from the heavens, its originating point a red star—the only red star in the skies. A dwarf, with a full, curly black beard and hair, sat in the boat—an astonishing sight, if anyone had been watching, for no dwarf living on Ansalon or anywhere else in Krynn had ever sailed a boat out of the stars. The Irda were not watching, however. Their eyes were closed, their thoughts centered on the Graygem.

The dwarf, grumbling and talking to himself, climbed out of the boat and promptly sank almost ankle-deep in the shifting sands. Cursing, the dwarf slogged on, heading for the woods.

"So these are the thieves," he muttered into his beard. "I might have known it. No one else could have kept my treasure hidden from me for so long. I'll have it back, though. Paladine or no Paladine, they will return it to me or, by my beard, my name isn't Reorx!"

A chiming sound, as of metal striking against metal, rang through the night.

Reorx paused, cocked his head. "Strange. I didn't know the Irda practiced the fine art of metal forging." He stroked his beard. "Perhaps I've underestimated them."

Another ringing sound. Yes, it was most definitely the sound made by the blow of a hammer. But it lacked the deep resonance of an iron hammer and not even the dwarf could convince himself that the Irda had suddenly taken an interest in making horseshoes and nails. Silversmithing, perhaps. Yes, it was the sound made by silver.

Teapots, then, or fine goblets. Jewelry maybe. The dwarf's eyes glistened. Working with sparkling gems, setting them into the metal . . .

Gems.

One gem. A hammer blow . . .

Fear shook Reorx, a fear such as he had not known on this plane of existence. He endeavored to penetrate the shadows. The god's eyesight was keen. He could see, on a fine night, a steel coin that had been care-lessly dropped on the streets of a town in a country on a continent of a distant star. But he could not penetrate the darkness of the grove of pine trees. Something blocked his view.

Trembling, the dwarf stumbled forward, his terror clutching at him with cold, sweaty hands. He had only the vaguest idea what he feared, a fear enhanced by a certain suspicion that had been niggling at his mind for centuries. He'd never admitted to it, never openly explored it, for the possibility was too dreadful to contemplate. He'd certainly never told any of his fellow immortals.

Reorx considered calling on Paladine, Takhisis, and Gilean for aid, but that would mean explaining to them what he was afraid he might have done, and there was always the chance that he could halt the Irda in their madness. No one would ever be the wiser.

And there was always the chance that he was wrong, that he was worrying about nothing.

The dwarf increased his speed. He could see a flicker of gray light now.

"You can't hide from me long," he cried out, and barreled ahead.

Keeping his gaze fixed on the light, Reorx didn't pay much attention to his immediate surroundings. He crashed headlong through bushes, tripped over exposed tree roots, slipped on wet grass. He thumped and thudded and made noise enough for an army. The noise disturbed the Irda in their concentration. They thought it was an army—the return of the black-armored knights—and that increased *their* fear and despera-tion. They urged the Decider to hurry.

The dwarf reached the grove of pine trees. The gray light welled out from the center; he could see it shining sullenly through the intertwined branches. Reorx searched for a place to enter, but the pines stood as close as soldiers drawn up in battle formation, shields held up to pre-sent a solid wall against the enemy. They would not permit even the god to enter. Panting and cursing in frustration, Reorx ran round and round the grove, seeking a way inside.

The silver ringing increased in intensity. The gray light dimmed a bit with each blow, then shone brighter.

Reorx was certain he knew what was happening, and his terror grew with his certainty. He tried shouting out for the Irda to stop, but the ringing hammer blows drowned out his cries. At last, he gave up yelling, quit running.

Panting, sweat dripping from his hair and beard, he pointed at two of the largest pine trees and cried, in a voice that was like a blast of wind, "I swear by the red light of my forge that I will shrivel your roots and wither your limbs and send worms to eat your nuts if you do not let me pass!"

The pines shuddered. Their limbs creaked. Needles fluttered down all around the furious dwarf. An opening appeared, barely large enough for him to squeeze through.

The rotund god sucked in his breath, wedged his body between the trunks, and struggled and heaved and, eventually, with a gasp, burst out the other side. And just at that moment, just as he staggered out into the glade, blinking in the brightening light, the Decider hit the spike a seventh sharp blow.

A crack that was like the rending of the world split the night. The gray light of the gem flared brilliantly. Reorx, accustomed to staring into his forge fire, the light of which shone in the heavens as a red star, could not bear it and was forced to shut his eyes. The Decider screamed and clutched his head. Moaning in agony, he slumped to the ground. The altar, on which the gem had rested, split asunder.

And then, the light blinked out.

The dwarf risked opening his eyes.

The altar where the Graygem rested was now dark. Not a natural, normal darkness, but a terrible, foreboding darkness.

Reorx recognized the darkness; he'd been born of it.

He tried to move forward, with some wild and panicked idea of repairing the damage, but his boots weighed more than the world he had once forged. He tried to cry out a warning to the other gods, but his tongue was made of iron, would not move in his mouth. There was nothing he could do, nothing except tear at his beard in frustration and wait for what was coming.

The darkness began to coalesce, take shape and form. It took the shape of mortal man, not in homage—as do the gods when they take man-shape—but in savage mockery. It was man enlarged, engorged. A giant emerged from the darkness, grew and grew until he stood taller than the pine trees.

He was clad in armor made of molten metal. His hair and beard were crackling flame. His eyes, pits of darkness. And in their depths burned rage.

Reorx sank, shivering, to his knees.

"Himself!" the dwarf whispered in awe.

The giant roared in triumph. He stretched up his arms, broke through the boughs of the pines as if they were made of straw. His fingertips brushed the clouds, tore them into rags. The stars, the constellations, glittered in terror.

"Free! Free from that wretched prison at last! Ah, my beloved children!" The giant spread wide his arms, gazed up at the stars, which quivered before him. "I have come to visit you! Where is your welcome for your father?" He laughed aloud.

Reorx was in such terror as he had never before known, but he was not scared witless. Greatly daring, while the giant's attention was focused upward, the dwarf crawled on hands and knees to the shattered altar.

In the wreckage lay the Graygem, broken, split in two. Nearby was the Irda who had cracked it open. Reorx put his hand on the Irda to find a pulse. The mortal still lived, but he was unconscious.

Reorx could do nothing to save the Irda; the dwarf would be lucky if he was able to save himself. Something had to be done to stave off calamity, though just exactly what and how, Reorx had no idea. Hastily, he caught up the two halves of the Graygem, shoved the fragments beneath the wreckage of altar, covered them with bits of wood. Then he scuttled backward, as far from the altar as he could get.

The giant, sensing movement, glanced down to find the dwarf attempting to burrow into the roots of the pine trees.

"Trying to escape me, Reorx? You puny, wretched imp of a thankless god!"

The giant leaned down near the cowering dwarf. Cinders from the giant's beard drifted among the pine trees. Tendrils of smoke began to rise from the dried pine needles on the ground.

"You thought you were quite clever, imprisoning me, didn't you, Worm?"

Reorx cast a nervous glance upward. "As . . . as it so happens, revered Father of All—"

"Father of All and of *Nothing*," the giant corrected with an ominous emphasis on the latter.

Reorx was shaken, but he stammered on. "It . . . it was a bit of an accident. I was forging the stone, intending to capture just a tiny wee portion of chaos, when—and I'm still not certain how this happened—but it seems I ended up capturing Yourself."

"And why didn't you free me then?"

The heat of the Father's anger beat on the dwarf. He coughed in the thickening smoke.

"I would have!" Reorx gasped with desperate sincerity. "Believe me, Father of All, I would have freed you then and there, had I known what I had done. But I didn't. I swear! I—"

"Fool!" The Father's rage set the grass all around the dwarf ablaze. "You and my thankless children conspired to imprison me. Am I to be captured by one puny god? It took the powers of all of you combined to hold me captive. But, though you had captured me, you couldn't control me. I did damage enough to your precious toys. And all the while I searched for one of your puppets, who could be tricked into freeing me. And finally I found him."

The giant cast a glance at the Decider. Casually he placed his huge, booted foot on the man's body and stomped it, crushed it, ground it into the dirt. Bones cracked. Blood welled out from beneath the giant's boot.

Reorx, sickened, turned away his head. He had the distinct and unhappy impression that he was next.

The giant knew what the dwarf was thinking. The Father gazed down on Reorx, long and grimly, enjoying watching the god squirm.

"Yes, I could squash you as well, but not now. Not yet." The Father looked again at the heavens, and he shook his fist at the stars. "You refused to pay me homage. You refused to be guided by me. You went your own ways to 'create' a world, fill that world with dolls and puppets. Well, my children, as I gave you life, so I can take it away. I am weak now, since I've been forced to assume mortal form, but my power grows by the second. When I am ready, I will destroy your plaything, then cast you and your creation back into the oblivion out of which you were made. Beware, Children. The Father of All and of Nothing has returned."

The Father turned his attention back to the dwarf. "You will be my messenger. In case they didn't hear me, go to them and warn my children of the doom that awaits them. I will enjoy seeing them try to escape *me* for a change! And show them this!"

The Father plucked a strand of flame from his beard and cast it among the pine trees. First one, then another caught fire, exploding into flame. The still-living trees writhed in agony as their limbs were consumed in the roaring inferno.

Reorx knelt among the smoke and the ashes, helpless to stop the blaze that was rapidly spreading from the pines to the other trees in the tinder-dry forest. Flames leapt from tree to tree. Flames sizzled over the ground. The flames burned even the air, left it scorched and empty. The flames created their own wind, that roared and drove the fire onward.

Within seconds, the firestorm reached the Irda village.

Over the rush of wind, the crackle of flames, Reorx heard the screams of the dying. Covering his face with his hands, the god wept . . . for the Irda, for the world.

* * * * *

The Protector sat stunned and immobile in his house. He knew—all the Irda knew—that the Decider was dead. They heard booming thunder that seemed to be words, but the words were too enormous, too monstrous, to be understood. And then the Protector, looking out his window, saw the red glow of the flames. He heard the cries of the dying pine trees.

The glow grew brighter. He could feel the heat. Cinders began raining down on his house and, soon, his roof was burning. He looked out the window, uncertain what—if anything—to do.

Several elder Irda appeared, attempted to stop the fire with their magic. They summoned rain. It evaporated in the heat. They summoned ice. It melted to water and sizzled away. They summoned wind. It blew the wrong direction, only fanned the flames. The Protector watched as, one by one, the Irda were consumed.

A distant neighbor ran out of her burning house. She was screaming something about the ocean. If they could reach the sea, they would be safe.

Flames, running through the grass, caught hold of the hem of the woman's skirt like a playful, deadly child.

The woman's clothing burst into flame. She became a living torch.

The roof of the Protector's house was engulfed now. From somewhere in the back came a crash: a beam falling. The Protector coughed, choked. While he could still see through the smoke, he searched the house until he found the precious object.

He held the doll clasped to his breast and waited—not long—for the end.

*   *   *   *   *

Far out to sea, the sailboat began to pitch and lurch in a hot wind that was blowing from the north. The erratic motion—a change from the gentle rocking that had lulled her to sleep—woke Usha from a sound sleep. At first she was disoriented, couldn't remember where she was. The sight of sails and masts, pointing toward the heavens and the clustering stars, reassured her.

Hearing thunder, she sat up, scanned the dark skies for the storm. She had no fear the boat would capsize; Irda magic would keep it afloat in the strongest gale.

Flickering lightning came from the north, from the direction of her homeland. She watched it, then saw a lurid red glow light the sky. The Decider must be working his magic.

Usha could not go back to sleep. She sat huddled in the stern, watching the red glow grow brighter and brighter. Then she watched it begin to dwindle, fade away.

Usha smiled. The magic must have been very powerful. And it must have worked.

"You will be safe now, Protector," she said softly.

As she spoke, the clear, sweet call of trumpets drifted over the water. Usha turned.

The sun was rising up out of the water, looking like a red and fiery eye glaring in hatred at the world. Bathed in that strange light, the spires of the city of Palanthas glistened blood red.

BOOK 2

I

The honored dead. A single prisoner. A fated meeting.

he bodies of the Knights of Solamnia had been laid out in a long row upon the sands of the shore of Thoradin Bay. There were not many of them, only eighteen. They had been wiped out, to a man. Their squires lay in a row behind them. These, too, had all died. There was no one left to tend to the dead except for their enemies.

A hot wind swirled among the sand and tall grasses, lifted and plucked at the torn and blood-spattered capes that had been draped across the men's lifeless forms.

A knight officer supervised the burial detail.

"They fought bravely." He pronounced the dead knights' epithet. "Outnumbered, taken by surprise, they might have turned and run and none the wiser. Yet they stood their ground, even when they knew they must be defeated. Lord Ariakan has ordered us to bury them with full honor. Lay out each man properly, place his weapons at his side. The ground is too marshy to bury the bodies. I am told a cave has been found, not far from here. We will entomb the bodies within, seal it up and mark it as a resting place for brave men. Have you examined the bodies? Is there any way we can determine their names, Knight Warrior Brightblade?"

"There was one survivor, sir," the knight reported, saluting his superior.

"Indeed? I hadn't known."

"A white-robed mage, sir. He was captured at the last."

"Ah, of course." The subcommander was not surprised. Mages fought at the rear of armies, casting their magical spells from safe places, since they were prohibited by the constraints of their art from wearing armor or carrying more conventional weaponry. "Odd that Knights of Solamnia should have been using a wizard. That would have never happened in the old days. Still, times change. This mage must know the names of the dead. Have him brought here to identify them, that we may do them honor when we lay them to rest. Where is he now?"

"He is being held by the Gray Knights, sir."

"Go and fetch him, Brightblade."

"Yes, sir. At your command, sir."

The knight left on his errand. His task was not an easy one. The battlefield atop the sea wall was now the only quiet place on the southern coast of Thoradin Bay. The vast stretch of black sand was awash with men and equipment. Shore boats lined the beaches, rubbing side against side, and more boats came ashore each moment. The brutes, under command of dark knights, were unloading stacks of equipment and supplies, everything from massive coils of rope to water casks, from quivers of arrows to huge shields, marked with the death lily—insignia of the Knights of Takhisis.

Horses were being ferried ashore; their handlers keeping close to the beasts, soothing their terror and promising that their long voyage would end soon. Blue dragons, ridden by knights, patrolled the skies, though Lord Ariakan did not have much fear that his landing would be further interrupted. Scouts reported that what few people lived in the nearby fishing village east of Kalaman had all fled.

They would certainly report his arrival, but by the time any substantial force could be mustered and sent against him, he would not be here. His beachhead established, he was planning to march swiftly west, to seize the deep-water port city of Kalaman. Once Kalaman fell, he would summon the rest of his troops from Storm's Keep, the knights' impregnable fortress to the north, in the Turbidus Ocean. With a deep-water port for his ships, his forces massed, he would launch the main assault up the Vingaard River and into the heart of the Solamnic Plains.

His objective: to take the one place on Krynn that had never fallen to enemy assault, the place he'd spent many long years as prisoner. Honored prisoner, to be sure, but a captive nonetheless. To take the one place that he saw nightly, in his dreams. And he could take it, he had no doubt. In that place, they had taught him the secrets of their strength. He already knew the secret of their weakness. Lord Ariakan's goal—the High Clerist's Tower. And from there, the world.

Brightblade picked his way through the confusion, almost deafened by the shouts of the officers, the curses and grunts of the brutes bent beneath heavy loads, the frightened whinnying of the horses and, occasionally, from above, the shrill call of a blue dragon to its comrade.

The early morning sun blazed; already the heat was intense, and it was only the beginning of summer. The knight had removed most of his armor once the battle was over, but still wore his breastplate and bracers, the death lily marking him as a Knight of the Lily. A dragon rider, he had not taken part in the battle, which had been fought on the ground. Following the battle, his talon had been chosen to take responsibility for the dead on both sides, and thus, though second in command, he was placed in the position of errand runner.

Brightblade did not resent this, however, just as his commander did not resent being placed in charge of burial detail. It was part of the discipline of the Knights of Takhisis that they served their Dark Queen in all capacities and gave her glory in the doing.

Halfway across the beach, Brightblade was forced to stop and ask where the Gray Knights, the Knights of the Thorn, had set up their headquarters. He was grateful to discover that they had sought shelter in a grove of trees.

"I might have known," he said to himself, with a slight smile. "I never knew a wizard yet who didn't relish what comfort he could find."

Brightblade left the crowded, hot, and noisy beach and entered the relatively cool shade of the trees. The noise receded, as did the heat. He paused a moment to revel in both the coolness and the stillness, then continued on his way, anxious to discharge his duty and leave this place, no matter how cool and inviting. He was now beginning to experience the customary sense of unease and disquiet all those not endowed with the gift of magic feel around those who are.

He found the Knights of the Thorn some distance from the beach, in a grove of tall pine trees. Several large wooden chests, carved with intricate arcane symbols, rested on the ground. Apprentices were sorting through these chests, ticking off items listed on sheets of parchment. The knight gave these chests a wide berth. The smells issuing from them were sickening; he wondered how the apprentices could stand it, but supposed they must grow used to it over time. The Thorn Knights carried their own equipment, always.

He grimaced at a particularly foul odor emanating from one of the chests. A glance within revealed rotting and unsavory objects, best not defined. He turned his gaze away in disgust, searched for his objective instead. Through the shadows of the trees, he saw a patch of white, gleaming in a shaft of sunlight, yet partially obscured by gray. Brightblade was not particularly fanciful, but he was reminded of fleece-white clouds overtaken by the gray of the storm. He marked it as a good omen. Diffidently, he approached the head of the order—a powerful wizardess of high rank known as a Nightlord.

"Madam, Knight Warrior Steel Brightblade." He saluted. "I am sent by Subcommander Knight Trevalin with the request that your prisoner, the white-robed mage, be conveyed to him. Lord Trevalin is in need of the prisoner to make identification of the bodies of the dead, that they may be entombed with honor. Also," he added in a low voice, not be overheard, "to verify the count."

Trevalin would be glad to know if any Solamnic Knight had escaped, one who might lie in ambush, perhaps hope to pick off a leader.

The Nightlord thus addressed did not return the knight's salute, nor did she appear at all pleased by his request. An older woman, perhaps in her late forties, Lillith had once been a Black Robe, but had switched allegiances when the opportunity had presented itself. As a Thorn Knight, she was now considered a renegade by the other wizards of Ansalon, including those who wore the black robes. This might seem confusing to some, since the sorcerers all served the same Dark Queen. But the Black Robes served Nuitari, god of dark magic first, his mother, Queen Takhisis, second. The Knights of the Thorn served the Dark Queen first, last, and only.

The Nightlord eyed Steel Brightblade intently. "Why did Trevalin send *you*?"

"Madam," Brightblade returned, taking care not to reveal his irritation at this unwonted interrogation, "I was the only one available at the time."

The Nightlord frowned, deepening an already dark line between her brows. "Return to Subcommander Trevalin. Tell him to send someone else."

Brightblade shrugged. "I beg your pardon, Madam, but my orders come from Subcommander Trevalin. If you wish to have him countermand them, then you must apply to him directly. I will remain here until you have conferred with my commanding officer."

The Nightlord's frown deepened, but she was caught on the hooks of protocol. To alter Steel's orders, she would be forced to send one of her own apprentices back across the beach to talk to Trevalin. The journey would likely accomplish nothing, for Trevalin was short-handed anyway and would not send another knight to do what this knight could do with ease.

"It must be Her Dark Majesty's will," the Nightlord muttered, regarding Steel with green, penetrating eyes. "So be it, then. I bow to it. The mage you seek is over there."

Steel had no idea what this odd conversation was in regard to, and he had no desire to ask.

"Why does Trevalin want the mage?" the Nightlord inquired.

Steel counseled patience, repeated himself. "He needs him to identify the bodies. The White Robe is the sole survivor."

At this, the prisoner lifted his head. His face blanched and he grew nearly as pale as the corpses laid out on the sand. The White Robe jumped to his feet, to the startlement of those assigned to guard him.

"Not all!" he cried in a ravaged voice. "Surely, not all!"

Steel Brightblade responded with a respectful yet dignified salute, as he had been taught. *Treat all persons of rank, title, and education with respect, even if they are the enemy. Especially if they are the enemy. Always respect your enemy; thus you will never underestimate him.*

"We believe that to be so, Sir Mage, though we have no way of know-ing for certain. We plan to bury the dead with honor, record their names on the tomb. You are the only one who can identify them."

"Take me to them," the young mage demanded.

His face had the flush of fever. Splotches of blood stained his robes, some of it probably his own. One side of his head was badly bruised and cut. His bags and pouches had all been taken from him and lay on the ground to one side. Some unlucky apprentice would sort through those, risking being burned—or worse—by the arcane objects which, due to their propensity for good, only a White Robe could use.

Such objects would not be of any immediate use to a Gray Knight, for despite the Thorn Knights' ability to draw power from all three moons, white, black, and red, each magic knows its own and often reacts vio-lently to the presence of its opposite. A Thorn Knight might possibly be able to use an artifact dedicated to Solinari, but only after long hours of the most disciplined and intense study. The White Robe's spell compo-nents and other captured magical objects would be held in safekeeping, to be studied, then those that could not be safely handled might be exchanged for arcane artifacts of more value—and less danger—to the Thorn Knights.

Brightblade did note, however, that the White Robe kept with him a staff. Made of wood, the staff was topped by a dragon's claw fashioned out of silver, holding in its grip a multifaceted crystal. The knight knew enough about the arcane to realize that this staff was undoubtedly mag-ical and probably highly valuable. He wondered why the White Robe was permitted to retain it.

"I suppose the mage may go," said the Nightlord ungraciously and with reluctance. "But only if I accompany him."

"Certainly, Madam."

Brightblade did his best to conceal his shock. This White Robe could not be of very high level. He was too young. Add to that the fact that no high-level White Robe would have ever permitted himself to be taken prisoner. Yet Lillith—head of the Thorn Knights' order—was treating this young man with the careful caution she would have treated, say, Lord Dalamar, renowned Master of the Tower of High Sorcery in Palanthas.

The White Robe moved weakly, leaned heavily upon the staff. His face was drawn with pain and anguish. He winced as he walked, bit his lip to keep from crying out. He crept forward at a gully dwarf's pace. It would take them the remainder of the day and into the night to reach the bodies, traveling at this rate. Subcommander Trevalin would not be pleased at the delay.

Steel glanced at the Nightlord. The mage was her prisoner. It was her place to offer him assistance. The Nightlord was regarding them both with a look of displeasure mingled with—oddly—curiosity, as if she were waiting to see what Steel would do in this situation. He would act as he had been taught to act—with honor. If the Nightlord didn't like it . . .

"Lean on my arm, Sir Mage," Steel Brightblade offered. He spoke coldly, dispassionately, but with respect. "You will find the going easier."

The White Robe lifted his head and stared in amazement that quickly hardened to wary suspicion.

"What trick is this?"

"No trick, sir. You are in pain and obviously find walking difficult. I am offering you my aid, sir."

The White Robe's face twisted in puzzlement. "But . . . you are one of . . . hers."

"If you mean a servant of our Dark Queen, Takhisis, then you are correct," Steel Brightblade replied gravely. "I am hers, body and soul. Yet, that does not mean that I am not a man of honor, who is pleased to salute bravery and courage when I see it. I beg you, sir, accept my arm. The way is long, and I note that you are wounded."

The young mage glanced askance at the Nightlord, as if thinking she might disapprove. If she did, she said nothing. Her face was devoid of expression.

Hesitantly, obviously still fearing some sort of evil design on the part of his enemy, the White Robe accepted the dark knight's aid. He clearly expected to be hurled to the ground, stomped, and beaten. He looked surprised (and perhaps disappointed) to find that he was not.

The young mage walked easier and faster with Steel's help. The two soon moved out of the cool shadows of the trees and into the hot sun. At the sight of the landing party, the White Robe's face registered awe and dismay.

"So many troops . . ." he said softly to himself.

"It is no disgrace that your small band lost," observed Steel Brightblade. "You were vastly outnumbered."

"Still . . ." The White Robe spoke through teeth clenched against the pain. "If I had been stronger . . ." He closed his eyes, swayed on his feet, seemed on the verge of passing out.

The knight supported the fainting mage. Glancing back over his shoulder, Brightblade asked, "Why haven't the healers, the Knights of the Skull, attended to him, Nightlord?"

"He refused their help," answered the Nightlord offhandedly. She shrugged. "And, being servants of Her Dark Majesty, there may have been nothing our healers could have done for him anyway."

Brightblade had no answer for this. He knew very little of the ways of the dark clerics. But he did know how to dress battlefield wounds, having experienced a few of his own.

"I have a recipe for a poultice I'll give you," he promised, assisting the mage to walk once more. "My mother—" He paused, corrected himself. "The woman who raised me taught me how to make it. The herbs are easily found. Your wound is in your side?"

The young mage nodded, pressed his hand against his rib cage. The white cloth of the mage's robes was soaked in blood, had stuck to the wound. Probably just as well to leave the cloth where it was. It kept the wound sealed.

"A spear," the young mage replied. "A glancing blow. My brother—"

He halted whatever he had been about to say, fell silent.

Ah, so that's it, Steel reasoned. That's why Solamnic Knights had a magic-user with them. One brother who fights with the sword, the other with the staff. And that is why he is so anxious to see the dead. He hopes for the best, but in his heart he must know what he will find. Should I say something to warn him? No, he might inadvertently reveal information that would help us.

Steel was not being callous. It was simply that he could not understand the young mage's obvious anxiety over the fate of this brother. Surely, a Knight of Solamnia expected death in battle, even welcomed it! A relative of the honored dead should be proud, not grief-stricken.

But then this mage is young, Brightblade reflected. Perhaps this was his first battle. That would explain much.

They continued across the crowded beach, the knight and his prisoner receiving some curious stares. No one said anything to them, however. The Nightlord followed behind; her green-eyed gaze never left them. Steel could have sworn he felt the fierce intensity burn through his heavy metal breastplate.

The sun, dripping with red, had fully risen by the time they reached the site of the battle, where the bodies of the dead were located. The sunrise had been spectacular, a fiery display of angry reds and triumphant purples, as if the sun were flaunting its power over a blistered and dried-up world. This day would be a scorcher. Not even night would bring relief. Heat would radiate up from the sand, covering like a smothering blanket those who tried to sleep on it. Rest would come tonight only to those too exhausted to notice.

Steel escorted the White Robe to his superior, Subcommander Sequor

Trevalin.

"Sir, here is the prisoner, as you commanded."

The subcommander glanced at the prisoner, then shifted his gaze to the Nightlord who had accompanied them. Trevalin, too, seemed surprised to note the honored company in which they traveled. He saluted the Nightlord, who outranked him.

"I thank you for your assistance in this matter, Madam."

"I did not see that I had much choice," she replied bitterly. "It is Her Majesty's will."

The comment apparently greatly puzzled Trevalin. Queen Takhisis oversaw all they did—or so the knights believed—but surely Her Dark Majesty had more important matters to occupy her immortal mind than simply identifying prisoners. Wizards were strange folk, however, and the Nightlord was stranger than most. Who knew what she meant now? Trevalin certainly wasn't going to ask. He proceeded swiftly with the task at hand.

"Sir Mage, if you could give us the names and titles of these knights, we will see that these are recorded, that posterity may honor their bravery as they deserve."

The young mage was exhausted by the walk, the heat, and the pain he suffered. He appeared to be dazed, stood looking at the bodies without recognition, as he might have looked at the bodies of strangers. His arm, resting on Steel's, trembled.

"Perhaps, sir," Steel suggested, "if the mage might have some water. Or a cup of wine."

"Certainly." Trevalin supplied not wine, but a cup of potent brandy he kept in a flask on his belt.

The young mage drank it heedlessly, probably not knowing what passed his lips. But the first sip brought some color back to the pale cheeks. That and the brief rest appeared to have helped. He even went so far as to thrust aside Steel's arm and stand on his own.

The White Robe closed his eyes. His lips moved. He appeared to be offering up a prayer, for Steel thought he heard the whispered word "Paladine."

Strength restored, probably more from the prayer than the brandy, the young mage limped over to the first of the dead. The White Robe bent down and drew aside the cape that had been laid over the face. A tremor of relief, as well as sorrow, shook his voice as he pronounced the name and the title, adding the knight's homeland.

"Sir Llewelyn ap Ellsar, Knight of the Rose from Guthar of Sancrist."

He moved down the row of dead with more strength and fortitude than the young knight would have first credited him.

"Sir Horan Devishtor, Knight of the Crown from Palanthas township; Sir Yori Beck, Knight of the Crown from Caergoth; Sir Percival Nelish . . ." He continued on.

A scribe, summoned by Subcommander Trevalin, followed, recording all the details on a horn slate.

And then the young mage came to the last two bodies. He stopped, looked back over the row of dead. Everyone there could see him taking count. He bowed his head, pressed his hand over his eyes, and did not move.

Steel moved to Trevalin's side.

"He mentioned something to me about a brother, sir."

Trevalin nodded in understanding, said nothing. The White Robe had revealed all the officer needed to know. There were no more knights; none had escaped.

The White Robe knelt down. With a trembling hand, he drew aside the cape that covered the still, cold face. He choked on his grief, sat huddled near the body.

"I beg your pardon, sir," said the scribe. "I didn't understand what you said. This man's name?"

"Majere," whispered the White Robe brokenly. "Sturm Majere. And that"—he moved to lift the cape that covered the other knight's face— "is Tanin Majere."

Bending over them, he wiped the blood from the shattered faces, kissed each one on the chill forehead.

"My brothers."

2

Cousins. A debt of honor.
A death sentence. The parole.

ajere." Steel turned to face the young mage. "Majere. I know that name."

Overcome by his grief, the White Robe did not respond. He had probably not even heard. The Nightlord heard, however. She made a soft hissing sound, breath drawn inward. The green eyes shut partway. She gazed at Steel from beneath lowered lids.

He paid no attention to the Nightlord. Steel walked forward, came to stand beside the mage. The young man was tall, well built, though he lacked the bulky musculature of his soldier brothers. His hair was a rich auburn; he wore it long to his shoulders. His hands were the hands of the mage: supple, slender, with tapered fingers. Now that Steel studied the young man, he could see the resemblance, not only to the bodies lying in the sand, but to the man who had once saved Steel Brightblade's life.

"Majere. Caramon Majere. These"—Steel indicated the dead knights—"must be his two eldest sons. And you are the younger. You are the son of Caramon Majere?"

"I am Palin," the young mage answered brokenly. With one hand, he brushed back the damp red curls from his brother's cold forehead. The other hand clung tightly to the staff, as if drawing from it the strength that was keeping him alive. "Palin Majere."

"Son of Caramon Majere, nephew of *Raistlin* Majere!" the Nightlord whispered with sibilant emphasis.

At this, Subcommander Trevalin—who had been paying scant attention, mulling over the logistics of moving the bodies, the detailing of men to the task—lifted his head, looked with greater interest at the young White Robe.

"The nephew of Raistlin Majere?" he repeated.

"A great prize," said the Nightlord. "A valuable prize. His uncle was the most powerful wizard who ever walked Ansalon." But even as she talked about Palin, the Nightlord kept her eyes on Steel.

The knight did not notice. Staring down at the bodies, yet not truly seeing them, he was turning something over in his mind, making some difficult decision, to judge by the dark expression on his face.

And then Palin stirred, lifted eyes that were red-rimmed with tears. "You are Steel. Steel Brightblade. Son of Sturm—" His voice broke again as he spoke the name that was the same as his brother's.

Steel said, almost to himself, "A strange coincidence, our meeting like this . . ."

"No coincidence," stated the Nightlord loudly. The green eyes were jeweled slits. "I tried to prevent it, but Her Dark Majesty prevailed. And what does it mean? What does it portend?"

Steel cast the woman an exasperated glance. The knight had great respect for the Nightlords and their work. Unlike the Knights of Solamnia, who scorned to blend blade with magic, the Knights of Takhisis used mage-craft in their battles. Wizards were given rank and status equal to that of warrior knights; wizards held honored and respected places at all levels of command. But there was still occasional friction between the two groups, though Lord Ariakan tried his best to eliminate it. The practical soldier, who saw straight from point A to point B and nothing else, could not hope to understand the wizard, who saw not only A and B but all the shifting planes of existence between.

And of all the Thorn Knights, this woman was the most impractical—seeing six sides to every four-sided object, as the saying went, constantly searching for meaning in the slightest incident, casting her seeing stones three times a day, peering into the entrails of roosters. Subcommander Trevalin and his staff had discussed, more than once the difficulties encountered in working with her.

A coincidence. Nothing more. And not such a strange one at that. Knights of Solamnia with a mage-brother meeting their cousin, a Knight of Takhisis. The world was at war, though not all the world was aware of it. These three surely would have met at some time. Steel was thankful for one thing: for the fact that he had not been responsible for the deaths of the two Majere boys. He would have been doing his duty, after all, but still, it made things easier. He turned to his commanding officer.

"Subcommander Trevalin. I ask a favor. Grant me permission to take the bodies of these two knights back to their homeland for burial. I will, at the same time, deliver the White Robe to his people and collect his ransom."

Trevalin regarded Steel in amazement; Palin stared at him in stupefaction. The Nightlord muttered, snorted, and shook her head.

"Where is their homeland?" Trevalin asked.

"Solace, in central Abanasinia, just north of Qualinost. Their father is an innkeeper there."

"But that is far in enemy territory. You would be in immense danger. If you had some special mission related to the Vision, then, yes, I would approve. But this . . ." Trevalin waved a hand. "To deliver bodies . . . No, you are too good a soldier to risk losing, Brightblade. I cannot grant your request." The elder knight looked curiously at the younger. "You do not act on whims, Brightblade. What is your reason for making this strange request?"

"The father, Caramon Majere, is my uncle, half-brother to my mother, Kitiara uth Matar. The dead knights and the mage are my cousins. In addition . . ." Steel's face remained impassive, expressionless, his tone matter-of-fact. "Caramon Majere battled at my side during a fight when I was almost captured in the High Clerist's Tower. I owe a debt of honor. According to Lord Ariakan, a debt of honor is to be repaid at the first opportunity. I would take this opportunity to repay mine."

Subcommander Trevalin did not hesitate. "Caramon Majere saved your life? Yes, I recall hearing this story. And these are his sons?" The knight gave the matter serious consideration, comparing it in his mind to the Vision—the Grand Plan of the Dark Queen's. Each knight at his investiture is given the Vision, shown how his single thread is woven into the immense Tapestry. Nothing was allowed to conflict with the Vision, not even a debt of honor.

However, the battle was over. The objective won. The dark knights would spend time establishing their beachhead before moving west. Trevalin could not see that any one knight would be missed, at least not in the near future. And it was always in the knights' interest to gain as much information about the enemy as possible. Steel would undoubtedly see and hear much on his journey into enemy territory that would be useful later.

"I grant you leave to go, Brightblade. The trip will be dangerous, but the greater the danger, the greater the glory. You will return the bodies of these knights to their homeland for burial. As to the White Robe's ransom, the decision as to what to do with him is up to our worthy comrade."

Trevalin looked to the Nightlord, who had been seething with indignation at being left out of the decision-making process. She was not Steel's commander, however, and could have no say in the matter of his going or coming. The White Robe was her prisoner, however, and she did have the right to decide what to do with him.

She pondered the matter, apparently torn between her longing to keep hold of the mage and her longing for whatever ransom his return might bring. Or perhaps something else was disturbing her. Her gaze flitted from Steel to Palin, and her green eyes burned.

"The White Robe has been sentenced to die," she said abruptly.

"What? Why? For what cause?" Trevalin was amazed and, it seemed, impatient. "He surrendered. He is a prisoner of war. He has the right to be ransomed."

"The ransom demand was already made," the Nightlord returned. "He refused. Therefore, his life is forfeit."

"Is this true, young man?" Trevalin regarded Palin sternly. "Did you refuse the ransom?"

"They asked for what I cannot give," Palin said. His hand tightened around the wood of the staff, and all present knew immediately what the ransom demand had been. "The staff is not mine. It has been loaned to me, that is all."

"The staff?" Trevalin turned to the Nightlord. "All you wanted was that staff? If he refused, then take the damn thing!"

"I tried." Lillith exhibited her right hand. The palm was blistered, burned.

"Did you do that, White Robe?" Trevalin asked.

Palin met his gaze, his eyes clear, though red-rimmed with unshed tears. "Does it matter, sir? The Staff of Magius was given to me in sacred trust. I do not 'own' it. I have only limited control over it. The staff belongs to no one, only to itself. Yet, I will not part with it, not to save my life."

Both dark paladins were impressed with the young man's answer. The Nightlord was not. She glowered at them all, rubbed her injured hand.

"An interesting problem," Trevalin remarked. "A man cannot be constrained to pay for his life with that which he does not own. He may go to his friends and family and ask them to raise ransom money for him, but he may not steal from them. The young man is honor-bound to refuse to turn over the staff. You, Madam, may therefore claim his life. But, it seems to me, that this would not conform to the Vision."

The Nightlord cast Trevalin a sharp glance, opened her mouth to protest. The invocation of the Vision took precedence over everything, however. She had to remain silent until he was finished.

"The Vision requires us to advance the cause of Her Dark Majesty in all things, in all ways. Taking this young man's life does nothing to advance the cause. His soul would fly to Paladine, who would be the gainer, not us. However, if we barter this young man's life for something else, some powerful magical object the wizards of Wayreth have in their possession . . ."

The Nightlord's stern expression softened. She regarded Palin speculatively and, oddly enough, her glance went to Steel as well.

"Perhaps," she was heard to mutter to herself, "perhaps this is the reason. Very well," she said aloud. "I bow to your wisdom, Subcommander Trevalin. There is one thing we will accept in ransom for Palin Majere." She paused, dramatically.

"And what is that, Madam?" Trevalin demanded, impatient to get on with his duties.

"We want the wizards to open the Portal to the Abyss," said the Nightlord.

"But . . . that's impossible!" Palin cried.

"The decision is not yours, young man," the Nightlord replied coolly. "You are under the jurisdiction of the Wizards' Conclave. They must decide. Opening the Portal is not like handing over the Staff of Magius. Such a decision belongs to the Conclave."

Palin shook his head. "What you ask for will not—cannot—be granted. It is impossible. You might as well take my life now. I could not," he added softly, his hand resting on the shoulder of his dead brother, "die in better company."

"Judgment has been passed, White Robe. You are our prisoner and must submit yourself to our will." Trevalin was firm. "You will travel, in the company of Knight Brightblade, to the Tower of Wayreth, there to make your ransom known to the Wizards' Conclave. If they refuse, your life is forfeit. You will be brought back to us to die."

Palin shrugged, said nothing, not caring one way or the other.

"You, Steel Brightblade, accept responsibility for the prisoner. If he escapes, you take his parole upon yourself. Your life will be required in payment. You will be sentenced to die in his place."

"I understand, Subcommander," said Steel. "And I accept the penalty."

"You have a fortnight to complete your journey. On the first night that the red and silver moons are both in the sky, you must report to me, your commander, no matter whether you have succeeded or failed. If your prisoner escapes, you must report to me at once, without delay."

Steel saluted, then left to saddle his blue dragon. Trevalin returned—thankfully—to his duties and ordered a squire to prepare the two corpses for transport. The bodies of the other knights were loaded onto a cart, to be conveyed to the tomb. Palin stayed close to his brothers, doing what he could to clean the bodies, wash off the blood, shut the clouded, staring eyes.

Lillith remained near Palin, watched him closely, intently. She was not afraid he would escape. She was searching, rather, for some clue. Why had this young mage—of all the young mages in the world—

been sent here, to fight in this battle? Why had he been the only person to survive? And, most importantly, why had Palin Majere been brought into contact with his cousin, Steel Brightblade?

She conjured up the image of the two of them, walking together, talking together. She saw no immediate family resemblance. In fact, the two could not have been—on first glance—more dissimilar. Steel Brightblade was tall, muscular, well built. Long, dark, curling hair framed a face that was strong and well proportioned, the eyes dark, large, and intense. He was undeniably a handsome man. But though many women looked at Steel Brightblade with admiration once, they tended not to look again. He was comely, certainly, but all attraction ended there. It was obvious to everyone that he belonged, heart and soul, to a stern mistress: War.

War alone could satisfy his lusts, his desires. His cold, proud, haughty mien came alive only during the charge, the fight. The clash of arms was the music he adored, the song of challenge the only love song he would ever sing.

By contrast, his cousin, Palin Majere, was slight of build, with auburn hair and a fair complexion. Fine-boned, with penetrating, intelligent eyes, he reminded the Nightlord immediately of his uncle. She had once seen Raistlin Majere, and she had recognized his nephew the moment she had come in contact with him. It was the hands, she thought. He has his uncle's delicate, deft touch.

Cousins, the same blood running in each. Yes, the resemblance was there, in the soul, if not the body. Steel knew his strength. Palin had yet to discover his. But it was in him as it had been within his uncle. How to turn it to Her Dark Majesty's advantage? For surely there had to be some reason the two had been brought together!

Not coincidence. No, a great Plan was at work here, but as yet the Nightlord could not unravel it. The answer would come. Of that, she had no doubt. She had merely to be patient. And so she watched and she waited.

Palin—either thinking he was alone or not caring—began to talk to his brothers.

"It was my fault, Tanin," he said softly, through a voice husky with tears. "My fault you died. I know you will forgive me. You always forgive me, no matter what I do. But how can I forgive myself? If I had been stronger in my magic, had studied harder, learned more spells . . . If I hadn't frozen in fear, forgot all I knew, I would not have failed you at the end. If I had been more like my uncle . . ."

More like my uncle!

Lillith heard those words. A shiver of awe and excitement raised the flesh on her arms. She saw the Plan. Her Dark Majesty's thoughts were made clear to her, or at least as clear as they can ever be to a mortal mind. It had to be! This had to be the reason. The two men—one in his doubt and insecurity, the other in his haughty pride—would be each other's downfall.

The Nightlord did not trust Steel Brightblade. She had never trusted him, not since she had discovered his parentage. She had argued long against his admittance into the elite ranks of the Knights of Takhisis. The omens were bad; the seeing stones prophesied doom.

A white stone on the left—that was the father, Sturm Brightblade, renowned and revered Solamnic Knight, honored even by his enemies for his courageous sacrifice. A black stone to the right—that was the mother, Kitiara uth Matar, leader of one of the dragonarmies, renowned for her skill and fearlessness in battle. Both were dead, but—the Nightlord could sense—both were reaching out to the son who had been brought into the world by accident, not design.

Though seemingly calm and steadfast in his loyalty and devotion to the Dark Queen, Steel Brightblade must be a raging sea of turmoil within. At least, so the Nightlord speculated. And she had good reason. Steel Brightblade wore the sword of a Knight of Solamnia—his father's sword. And he also wore (though this was a well-guarded secret) a jewel of elven make. Known as a starjewel, it was nothing more than a token exchanged between lovers. It had been given to Sturm Brightblade during the War of the Lance by Alhana Starbreeze, Queen of the Silvanesti elves. And Sturm Brightblade—or rather the corpse of Sturm Brightblade, if you believed Steel's account—had given the jewel to his son.

A white stone to the left, a black stone to the right, and in the center a stone marked with a fortress. Falling on top of the fortress, a stone marked with fire. Thus Lillith read the signs: the young man was torn in two and this inner conflict would result in disaster. What else could a fortress being devoured by flames represent?

The Nightlord had argued long and hard, but no one had listened. Even the Lord of the Skull, a powerful priestess—an old, old woman who was said to be a favorite with Queen Takhisis—had recommended that Steel be admitted into the knighthood.

"Yes, he wears the starjewel," the old crone had mumbled through her toothless mouth. "The jewel is the only crack in his iron facade. We will use it to see into his heart, and from that vantage we will see into the hearts of our enemies!"

Blathering old fool.

But now the Nightlord understood. She threw the idea on the black cloth of her mind, much as she tossed her seeing stones. It fell to the table clean, did not roll or tumble, landed right side up. Pondering, choosing her words with care, she approached the young mage.

"You spoke of your uncle," she said, standing over Palin, staring down at him, her arms folded across her chest. "You never met him, did you? Of course not. You are too young."

Palin said nothing, gripped the Staff of Magius a bit tighter. The young man had done what he could for his brothers. Now all that remained would be the bitter task of taking them home, of breaking the news to his father and his mother. He was weak and vulnerable now. The Nightlord's task was almost too easy.

"Raistlin left this world before you were born."

Palin glanced up and, in that flashing glance, revealed everything, though he continued to say nothing.

"Left the world. Chose to remain in the Abyss, where he is tormented daily by our dread queen."

"No." Palin was stung into speaking. "No, that is not true. For his sacrifice, my uncle was granted peace in sleep. My father was given this knowledge by Paladine."

Lillith knelt down, to come level with the young man. She moved closer to him. She was an attractive woman and, when she chose, could be charming, as fascinating as a snake.

"So your father says. So he *would* say, wouldn't he?"

She felt the young man stir restlessly beside her and she thrilled, deep within. He did not look at her, but she felt his doubt. He'd thought about this before. He believed his father—yet part of him didn't. That doubt was the crack in *his* armor. Through that crack, she slid her poisoned mental blade.

"What if your father is wrong? What if Raistlin Majere lives?" She sidled closer still. "He calls to you, doesn't he?"

It was a guess, but the Nightlord knew immediately she was right. Palin flinched, lowered his eyes.

"If Raistlin was back in this world, he would take you on as his apprentice. You would study with the greatest mage who ever walked this plane of existence. Your uncle has already given you a precious gift. What more would he not do for a loved nephew?"

Palin glanced at her, nothing more than a glance, but she saw the fire kindle deep in his eyes, and she knew it would consume him.

Satisfied, the Nightlord rose, walked away. She could leave the prisoner now. He was safe—safely entangled in the coils of temptation. And he would, inadvertently, draw his cousin in with him. That was the reason the Dark Queen had brought the two together.

Lillith thrust her hand into a black velvet bag, grabbed a handful of stones at random. Muttering the incantation, she tossed the stones on the ground. The Nightlord shuddered.

What she had surmised was correct. Takhisis must have both souls—and quickly.

Doom was very near.

3

Che city of Palanthas.
A weary search, not quite fruitless.

he heat of the midday sun poured like flaming oil on the waters of the Bay of Branchala. The noon hour was the busiest of the day on the docks of Palanthas, when Usha's boat joined the throng of others crowding the harbor. Unaccustomed to such heat, noise, and confusion, Usha sat in her bobbing craft and stared around her in dismay.

Enormous merchant galleys with minotaur crews rubbed up against the large fishing vessels piloted by the seagoing black-skinned humans of Northern Ergoth. Smaller "market" barges bumped and nosed their way among the crowd, bringing down a storm of curses and the occasional bucket of bilge water or fish heads when they piled up against a larger craft. To add to the confusion, a gnome ship had just entered port. The other ships were hauling up anchor, endeavoring to put as much sea as possible between themselves and the gnomes. No one with any sense would risk life and limb by staying anywhere near the steam-burping monstrosity. The harbormaster, in his specially painted boat, sailed hither and thither, mopping his sweating, bald head and shouting up at the captains through a speaking trumpet.

Usha very nearly hoisted her sail, turned her boat around, and went back home. The cruel-sounding curses of the minotaur (she had heard of them, but never seen one) frightened her; the gnome ship—its smoking stacks looming dangerously close—appalled her. She had no idea what to do or where to go.

An elderly man, bobbing placidly in a small fishing skiff on the outskirts of the turmoil, saw her and, appreciating her difficulty, drew in his line and rowed his boat over.

"Bein' a stranger to these parts, er you?" the old man asked, by which Usha understood him (eventually) to be inquiring if *she* was a stranger.

She acknowledged that she was and asked him where she might dock her boat.

"Not here," he said, sucking on a battered pipe. Removing it from his mouth, he gestured at the barges. "Too dang many farmers."

At that moment a minotaur clipper hove up behind Usha's boat and nearly swamped her. The captain, leaning over the side, promised to split her boat—and her—in two if she didn't move out of his way.

Usha, panic-stricken, laid her hands on the oars, but the old man stopped her.

Standing up in his own boat—a marvelous feat, Usha thought, considering that the boat was rocking wildly—the old man answered the captain in what must have been the minotaur's own language, for it sounded like someone crunching bones. Just exactly what the old man said, Usha never knew, but the minotaur captain ended by grunting and ordering his ship to veer off.

"Bullies," muttered the old man, reseating himself. "But damn fine sailors. I should know. I crewed with 'em regular." He eyed her boat curiously. "A fine craft, that. Minotaur-built, if I'm not mistaken. Where did you come by it?"

Usha evaded his question. Before she left, the Protector had warned against her revealing anything about herself to anyone. She pretended not to have heard the old man—an easy thing, amidst the clashing of oars, the swearing, and the harbormaster's trumpeting. Thanking him for his help, she asked, again, where she should dock.

"Over t'east." The old man pointed with the pipe stem. "Thar's a public pier. Usually a docking fee, but"—he was eyeing her now, not the boat—"with that face and them eyes, likely they'll let *you* in fer naught."

Usha flushed in anger and shame, bit back a scathing retort. The old man had been kind and helpful. If he wanted to mock her homely appearance, he'd earned the right. As for the rest of what he'd said—something about a "fee" and letting her in for "naught," she had no idea what he was talking about. Peering through the tangle of masts, she located the pier to which he referred, and it seemed a haven of peace compared to the main docks. Thanking the old man again—rather coolly—Usha sailed her boat that direction.

The public harbor was far less crowded, being restricted to small boats, primarily the pleasure craft of the wealthy. Usha lowered her sails, rowed in, found a pier, and dropped anchor. Gathering up her possessions, she slung one pouch over her shoulders, hung the other around her waist, and climbed out of the boat. She tied the boat to the dock, started to leave it, then paused to take one last look.

That boat was the last tie to her homeland, to the Protector, to everyone she loved. When she walked away from it, she would be walking away from her past life. She recalled the strange red glow in the sky last night and was suddenly loathe to leave. She ran her hand over the rope that linked her to the boat, the boat that linked her to her homeland. Her eyes filled with tears. Half blind, she turned and bumped into something dark and solid that caught hold of her sleeve.

A voice, coming from somewhere around waist-level, demanded, "Where do you think you're going, girlie? There's a small matter of the docking fee."

Usha, embarrassed to be caught crying, hurriedly wiped her eyes. Her accoster was a dwarf, with a gray, scruffy beard and the weathered face and squinting eyes of those who spend their days watching the sun beat on the water.

"Fee? I don't know what you mean, sir," Usha returned, trying not to stare. She'd never seen a dwarf, either, although she knew of them from Prot's stories.

"A fee to leave your boat where you've docked it! You don't think the people of Palanthas run this operation out of the goodness of their hearts, do you, girlie? There's a fee! How long are you leaving the boat? Day, week, month? The fee varies."

"I . . . I don't know," Usha said helplessly.

The Irda have no concept of money. Their needs being simple, each Irda makes what he or she needs, either by hand-crafting it or magicking the object into being. One Irda would never think of exchanging anything with another. Such an act would be tantamount to an incursion into another's soul.

Usha was beginning to recall stories Prot had told her about dwarves. "Do you mean that if I give you something, you will let me leave the boat here in exchange?"

The dwarf glared up at her, eyes squinting until they were nearly shut. "What's the matter, girlie? Boom hit you in the head?" He altered his voice, speaking in a high-pitched tone, as one might to a child. "Yes, little girl, you give the nice dwarf something—preferably cold, hard steel—and the nice dwarf will let you keep your boat where it is. If you don't give the nice dwarf something—preferably cold, hard steel—the nice dwarf will impound your goddamn boat. Got it?"

Usha's face burned. She had no steel, wasn't even certain what he meant by that term. But a crowd of grinning men, some of them rough-looking, was starting to gather around the two of them. Usha wanted only to get away. Fumbling in one of her pouches, her fingers grasped an object. She pulled it out and thrust it in the dwarf's direction.

"I don't have any steel. Will this do?"

The dwarf took hold of it, examined it closely. The squinted eyes opened wider than they'd probably opened in a hundred years. Then, noting the interest of the men around him, the dwarf glowered at them all, closed his hand hastily over the object.

"Platinum, by Reorx's beard. *With* a ruby," he was overheard to mutter. He waved his hand at the men. "Be gone, you gawkers! Go about your business, or I'll have the lord's guardsmen down on you!"

The men laughed, made a few ribald remarks, and drifted off. The dwarf took hold of Usha's sleeve, drew her down to his level.

"Do you know what this is, Mistress?" He was much more polite.

"It's a ring," Usha said, thinking he might not know what a ring was.

"Aye." The dwarf licked his lips. His gaze went hungrily to the pouch. "A ring. Might . . . might there be more where that come from?"

Usha didn't like his look. She pressed her hand over the pouch, drew it close to her body. "Will that be enough to leave the boat in your care?"

"Oh, aye, Mistress! As long as you want. I'll take real good care of her. Scrub the decks, shall I? Scrape off the barnacles? Mend the sail?"

"Whatever you like, sir." Usha started walking away, heading for the shore and the large buildings that could be seen lining it.

"When will you be coming back for it?" the dwarf asked, his short legs pumping to keep up with her.

"I don't know," Usha said, hoping to sound carefree and careless, not confused. "Just so long as the boat's here when I do come back."

"She will be, Mistress. And I'll be right with her," said the dwarf. The fingers of one grimy hand could be seen working busily, as if he were doing sums. "Might be a few extra charges . . ."

Usha shrugged, continued on her way.

"Platinum!" she heard the dwarf say with a covetous sigh. "*With* a ruby!"

Usha evaded the Palanthas port authority simply because she had no idea who they were or that she was supposed to explain to them who she was and why she was in Palanthas. She walked right past the guards and through the rebuilt portion of the city wall with such perfect poise and cool aplomb that not one of the admittedly overworked guardsmen took the time to stop her or question her. She looked as if she had a perfect right to be where she was.

Her poise was, in reality, innocence. Her aplomb was an ice coating over her terror and confusion.

She spent the next several hours wandering the hot, dust-ridden, and overcrowded streets of Palanthas. At every turn, she saw something that amazed, terrified, dazzled, or repulsed her. She had no idea where she was headed, what she was doing, except that somehow she had to find this Lord Dalamar. After that, she supposed she should find someplace to sleep.

The Protector had made some vague references to "lodgings" and a "job," earning "money." The Protector could not be more specific. He'd had only limited contact with humans during his long life, and though he'd heard of such concepts as "working for one's bread," he had only the vaguest idea what that meant.

Usha had no idea whatsoever.

She stared and gawked, overawed. The ornate buildings—so different from the Irda's small, single-story dwellings—towered over her, taller than the pine trees. She was lost in a forest of marble. And the number of people! She saw more people in one minute in Palanthas than she'd seen during a lifetime of living among the Irda. And all the people seemed to be in a tearing hurry, bustling and shoving and pushing and walking very fast, red-faced and out of breath.

At first, Usha wondered fearfully if the city was afflicted by some sort of dire emergency. Perhaps war. But, on asking a young girl who was drawing water from a well, Usha learned that this was only "market day" and that the city was unusually quiet—probably due to the severe heat.

It had been hot near the bay; the sun reflecting off the water burned Usha's fair skin, even in the shade. But at least on the docks she had felt the lingering cool touch of an ocean breeze. Such relief never reached the city proper. Palanthas sweltered. The heat radiated upward from the cobblestone streets, frying those who walked on them as surely as if they'd been set down on a red-hot griddle. Yet the streets were cool compared to the interiors of shops and houses. Shop owners, who could not leave their businesses, fanned themselves and tried to keep from dozing off. The poor people abandoned their stifling homes, lived and slept in the parks or on top of roofs, hoping to catch the barest hint of a breath of air. The wealthy stayed within their marble-walled dwellings, drank warm wine (there was no ice, for the snows on the mountaintops had almost all melted), and complained languidly of the heat.

The stench of too many sweating bodies, crowded too close together, of garbage and refuse baking in the sun, stole Usha's breath, set her gagging. She wondered how anyone could ever live with such a dreadful smell, but the girl had said she didn't smell anything except Palanthas in the summertime.

Usha traveled all over Palanthas, walked and walked. She passed an enormous building, which someone told her was "the Great Library" and recalled hearing the Protector speak of it in respectful tones as the source of all knowledge about everything in the world.

Thinking this might be a good place to inquire about the whereabouts of Lord Dalamar, Usha stopped a brown-robed young man walking about the grounds of the Great Library and made her inquiry. The monk opened his eyes very wide, drew back from Usha about six paces, and pointed down a street.

Following his directions, Usha emerged from an alley into the shadow of a hideous-looking tower surrounded by a grove of dark trees. Although she had been sweating moments before, she now shook with sudden chills. Cold, dank darkness seemed to flow from out of the woods. Shivering, she turned and fled and was actually relieved to find herself once again in the baking sunlight. As for Lord Dalamar, Usha could only imagine that the monk had been mistaken. No one could possibly live in such a dreadful place.

She passed a beautiful building that was, by its inscription, a temple to Paladine. She passed parks and the magnificent yet sterile-looking homes of the wealthy. (Usha took them to be museums). She passed shops filled with wondrous objects, everything from sparkling jewels to swords and armor such as the young knights had worn.

And always, hordes of people.

Lost and confused, not sure why she'd been sent to this bewildering city, Usha continued to wander the streets. She was weakened by the heat and weariness, and only gradually became conscious, as she walked along, that people were staring at her. Some actually came to a halt and gazed at her in gaping wonderment. Others—generally men, who were fashionably dressed—doffed their feathered caps and smiled at her.

Usha naturally assumed they were mocking her appearance, and she thought this very cruel. Bedraggled, miserable, feeling sorry for herself, she wondered how the Protector could have sent her to such a hateful place. Gradually, however, she came to realize that these stares and cap-doffings and bowings were admiring.

Having some vague idea that the journey had altered her appearance, Usha halted to study her reflection in the glass window of a shop. The glass was wavy and distorted her face, but then so did the water of the small pond she was accustomed to using for a mirror back at home. She hadn't changed. Her hair was still flaxen-silver, her eyes still their odd color, her features regular, but lacking the molded, crafted, exquisite beauty of those of the Irda. She was, as she had always been—in her own eyes—homely.

"What very strange people," Usha said to herself, after a young man had been so occupied in staring at her that he'd accidentally walked into a tree.

At length, when she'd nearly worn the soles of her leather boots through, Usha noticed that the hot sun was finally setting, the shadows of the buildings were growing longer and a hint cooler. The number of people on the street diminished. Mothers appeared in doorways, shouting for their children to come home. Looking through the windows of several fine houses, Usha saw families gathering together. She was worn, weary, alone. She had no place to spend the night, and, she realized, she was ravenously hungry.

The Protector had supplied her with food for her journey, but she'd eaten all that before she had sailed into Palanthas. Fortunately, however, she had accidentally wended her way into the merchandising section of the city.

The vendors were just closing up their stalls, prior to calling it a day. Usha had been wondering what people did for food in this bustling city. Now she had her answer. Apparently, people didn't serve food on tables here in Palanthas. They handed it out in the streets. Usha thought that rather odd, but then everything in this city was odd.

She drew close to a booth that had a few odd pieces of fruit left on it. The fruit was withered and dried, having baked in the heat all day, but it looked wonderful to her. Picking up several apples, Usha bit into one, devoured it, and stuffed the rest into one of her pouches.

Leaving the fruit vendors, she came to a baker and added a loaf of bread to her meal. Usha was glancing about, searching for a booth offering wine, when an unholy commotion burst out around her.

"Catch her! Hold her! Thief! Thief!"

4

An assault. Arrested.
Tasslehoff is surprised.

sha stared in amazement at a tall, thin man in a leather apron, who danced and bobbed around her. "Thief!" he cried, pointing at her. "She stole my fruit!"

"She ran off with my bread," panted a flour-smudged woman, who had been running after the man. "That's it, sticking out of her pouch! I'll have that back, you hussy."

The baker made a grab for the bread. Usha slapped the woman's hand away.

The woman began to howl. "Murder! She tried to murder me!"

The idlers and ruffians who generally hung about the market, swilling raw wine and waiting for trouble, were quick to sniff it. A jeering crowd gathered around Usha. A ragged and uncouth-looking man grabbed hold of her.

"I'll volunteer to search her!" he yelled. "Looks to me like she's got those apples stuffed down her blouse!"

The crowd laughed and pressed closer.

Usha had never experienced such rough treatment. Pampered, coddled, brought up among a society of people who didn't raise their voices, much less their fists, she was shocked almost senseless. She had no weapons, and it didn't occur to her, in her initial panic, to use the magical items the Irda had given her. She wouldn't have known how to use them anyway, having paid scant attention to the instructions given her.

The man's filthy hands tore her blouse; his fingers groped to touch her flesh. His fellows cheered him on.

Panic gave way to fury. The ferocity of a cornered animal burned in Usha. She lashed out wildly, with strength borne of terror. She hit and bit and kicked and flailed, not knowing, not caring who she hurt, wanting to hurt them all, wanting to hurt every living being in this hateful city.

It was only when strong hands took hold of her arm, clasping it and giving it a painful twist, and a clear, firm voice said, "Here now, stop this, young woman!" that the blood-tinged mist cleared from her eyes.

Usha blinked, gasped for breath, and peered dizzily around.

A tall, muscular man dressed in a dull, crimson-colored tunic and leggings, with an official air about him, had hold of her. At his arrival, the crowd rapidly dispersed, with varied and colorful comments about guardsmen who spoiled their fun. The man who had accosted her lay on the ground, groaning and clutching his private parts.

"Who started this?" The guardsman glared around.

"She stole bread from my stall, Y'Honor," cried the baker, "and then she tried to murder the lot of us."

"Them's my apples," accused the fruit vendor. "She walked off with 'em, just as cool as cucumbers."

"I never meant to steal anything," Usha protested, snuffling a little. Tears had always worked with Prot when she was in trouble, and she was quick to fall back on old habits. "I thought the fruit and the bread were set out for anyone to take." She wiped her eyes. "I didn't mean to hurt anyone. I'm tired and I'm lost and I'm hungry, and then that man . . . he touched . . ."

The tears came for real at the horrible memory. The guardsman gazed at her helplessly, attempted to comfort her.

"Now, now there. Don't cry. The heat's likely addlepated you. Give these two fair payment, and we'll call it even. Won't we?" the guardsman added, with a glowering glance at the two vendors, who glowered back, but nodded grudging assent.

"I don't have any money," Usha gulped.

"Vagrant!" the man snapped.

"Worse than that." The woman sniffed. "Obviously no better than she should be. Look at those outlandish clothes! I want her set in the stocks and whipped!"

The guardsman appeared displeased, but he didn't have much choice. The contested bread lay on the street, having fallen out of Usha's pouch during the scuffle, and she reeked of overripe, squashed apple.

"We'll let the magistrate settle all this. Come along, young woman. And you two, you'll have to come as well if you want to swear out a warrant."

The guard marched Usha off. The two vendors trailed behind, the woman stiff with righteous indignation, the apple-vendor wondering uneasily if this was going to cost him money.

Numb and exhausted, Usha paid no attention to where she was being taken. She stumbled along beside her captor, her head bowed, not wanting to see any more of this horrible place. She was dimly aware of leaving the streets and entering a large building made entirely of stone, with an enormous, heavy wooden door guarded by more men wearing the same crimson-colored tunic as the man-at-arms. They opened the door. Her guard led her inside.

The stone-walled room into which she was led was refreshingly dark and cool, after the glare and heat of the streets. Usha looked up and around. The guard was arguing with the two vendors. Usha ignored them. Although she was involved, none of this seemed to have anything to do with her. It was all part of this horrible city, which she was going to leave the moment she delivered her letter.

A large man, looking bored by the whole affair, sat at a desk, writing something down in a greasy-paged book. Behind him was an enormous room filled with people, sitting or sleeping on the cold stone floor. Numerous iron bars, bolted into the ceiling and floor, separated the people inside the large room from those on the outside.

"Here's another one, jailer. Petty theft. Lock her up with the rest of the lot until the magistrate can hear her case in the morning," said the guardsman.

The large man glanced up, saw Usha. His eyes widened. "If the Thieves' Guild is taking on recruits who look like her, I'll join myself!" he said in an undertone to the guardsman. "Now then, Mistress, you'll have to leave those pouches with me."

"What? Why? Don't touch these!" Usha clasped her valuables tightly to her.

"You'll likely get them back," the guardsman assured her with a shrug. "Here, now, young woman, don't start any trouble. You're in enough as it is."

Usha held on to the pouches a moment longer. The large man frowned, said something about taking them by force.

"No, don't touch me!" Usha said, and reluctantly removed both of her pouches—the small one with her clothes, the large one with her gifts—and placed them on the desk in front of the jailer.

"I should warn you," she said, in an anger-choked voice, "that some of the objects in that pack are magic, and you better treat them with respect. Also, I am carrying a scroll that I am supposed to deliver to someone known as Lord Dalamar. I don't know who this Dalamar is, but I'm sure he wouldn't be pleased to know you tampered with his things."

Usha had hoped to impress her captors, and she did, though not quite in the way she'd intended. The jailer, who had been rifling eagerly through the pouches, suddenly snatched his hand away from them as if they might be some gnomish invention that was likely to explode at a moment's notice.

The apple vendor cried out, "I drop all charges!" and made a swift departure.

"A witch," pronounced the baker, standing her ground. "I figured as much. Burn her at the stake."

"We don't do that anymore," the jailer growled, but he was pale and shaken. "Did you say Dalamar?"

"Yes, I did." Usha was considerably startled at all this fuss, but—seeing that the name meant something to these people—she took advantage of it. "And you better treat me well, or I'm certain *Lord Dalamar* will be displeased."

The two men conferred in low voices.

"What should we do?" the jailer whispered.

"Send for Mistress Jenna. She'll know," returned the guard.

"Do I put her in the cells?"

"You want her running around loose?"

The conversation ended with Usha being escorted—respectfully—into the large room behind the iron bars. Almost immediately, she was surrounded by what she thought at first were human children. She was wondering what crimes these children could have committed, when she heard the jailer swear at them.

"Get back, you blasted kender! Here now! Where's my keys? Ah, you rascal! Give me them back! Find a seat, Missy," the jailer yelled at her, making snatches and grabs at the kender all the while. "Someone'll be along soon. And what are you doing with my pipe? And you, hand over that ironweed pouch or so help me, Gilean, I'll—"

Muttering and swearing, the jailer left the cell, retreated thankfully to his desk.

So these were kender! Usha was interested in meeting the people whom Prot had dubbed, the "merry thieves of Krynn." Meeting them was not a problem, since the ever curious kender were always interested in meeting any stranger who came into what they considered to be "their" jail.

All talking at once, asking her thirty questions in the space of five seconds, the kender swarmed around her, jabbering and giggling, touching and patting. The noise, the clamor, the heat, her fear and hunger—it was all suddenly too much for her to bear. The room started to heave, then tilt. The air was shot through with sparkling stars.

The next thing Usha knew, she was lying on the floor, looking up into the anxious face of one of the kender. This kender appeared older than the rest; crinkly lines webbed his eyes, laugh-lines tugged at his mouth. Long hair streaked with gray was gathered in a topknot on his head and hung to his shoulder. His face was as pleasant and friendly and curious as that of a child or all the other kender, but he seemed more grown-up than the rest.

When any of the kender came too close, this elder kender shooed them off. Even the rougher elements of the human population, who were also penned up in the holding cell, appeared to respect him, for they, too, kept their distance.

"What happened?" Usha asked, struggling to sit up.

"You fainted," the kender explained. "And I really think you should lie down some more. I've never fainted myself—at least not that I can remember. I keep thinking I should like to try it sometime, but I never seem to manage it. How are you feeling? The guard said you probably passed out because you haven't eaten in a while and that you'd come around. And, sure enough, you did! Are you hungry? In about an hour they'll bring us some bread and soup. The food's good here. Palanthas has a very nice jail, one of the nicest in all Ansalon. What remarkable eyes you have. Kind of a gold color, aren't they? You certainly do look familiar. Have we met before? Were you ever in Solace?"

"I don't think so," Usha answered wearily. The kender's chatter was comforting, but his innumerable questions confused her. "I've never heard of Solace."

She felt rotten. Her head ached and her empty stomach gnawed at her. Prot had warned her to be wary of kender, but this one was the first person she'd met who'd spoken kindly to her. Looking around, she noticed that her head was pillowed on what was probably—to judge by the vivid green, which was the same color as the pants he was wearing—the kender's cloak.

Usha was grateful and tried a smile. "Who are you?"

The kender appeared shocked, then chagrined. "Didn't I introduce myself? I guess not. I was going to, when you keeled over." He held out a small, nut-brown hand. "My name's Tasslehoff Burrfoot. My friends all call me Tas. What's your name?"

"Usha." She accepted the hand and shook it solemnly.

"Just Usha? Most humans I know have two names."

"Just Usha."

"Anyway, that's a pretty name. Pretty enough for two names together." The kender studied her thoughtfully. "You know, Usha, you really *do* remind me of someone. I wonder who it could be?"

Usha didn't know, and she didn't care. Closing her eyes, feeling protected by her new friend, she let herself relax and drift into sleep.

On the ragged edge of consciousness, she heard the kender murmur in awed tones, "I have it! She has gold eyes—just like Raistlin!"

5

The sorceress.
Mistress Jenna is surprised.

The smell of hot soup woke Usha from her nap. She felt better after her brief rest. Propped against the stone wall, she drank chicken broth from a chipped crockery bowl and wondered what was going to happen to her next. At least she'd solved the problem of where she was going to sleep.

It was now nighttime. The cell was dark, lit only by the light of a few sputtering torches on the wall of the prison's entrance.

The kender, Tas, drank his soup, then offered Usha his hunk of brown bread. "Here, you still look hungry."

Usha had finished her bread in about three bites. She hesitated. "Are you sure you don't want it?"

Tas shook his head. "No, that's all right. If I get hungry, I've likely got something in my pouches to eat." He indicated various bulging bags that were draped about his slender frame.

Usha frowned. "Why do you get to keep your things? They took mine."

"Oh, that's the way it always is." Tas shrugged. "I'm not sure why, but they never take anything from us kender. Maybe it's because they don't have room to store them. We tend to collect things in our travels. Or perhaps it's because it would be too difficult to sort out who belongs to what in the morning. Not that it would matter to us, particularly. We"—he gestured at the other members of his race, who were now pelting each other with bread—"share everything."

"So do my people," said Usha, before she thought.

"Your people. Who are your people? Where do you come from? You certainly don't come from around here, that's for sure." Tas nodded so emphatically that his topknot flipped over his head and smacked him in the nose.

"How can you tell?" Usha asked, ignoring the question.

"Well . . ." Tas stared at her, paused to consider. "You're dressed differently, that's one. You talk differently. Same words, but you say them in a peculiar way. And you're about one hundred times prettier than any woman I've ever seen, with the exception of Laurana—that's Tanis's wife, but you probably don't know him, do you? I didn't think so. Oh, and Tika. She married Caramon. Do you know him? He had a twin brother named Raistlin."

Tas looked at Usha oddly as he asked this question. She recalled hearing the name Raistlin before she drifted off to sleep, but she couldn't remember what the kender had said about it. Not that it mattered. She'd never heard of either of them, and she said as much.

"As for my being pretty, I know you mean well, but you don't have to lie to me. I know what I am." Usha sighed.

"I'm not lying!" Tas protested. "Kender *never* lie. And if you don't believe me, ask those men over in that corner there. They were talking about you. Well, maybe you better not speak to them after all. They're a bad lot. They're *thieves!*" he added, in a shocked whisper.

Usha was moderately confused. "You're not a thief?"

"Great Paladine's beard, no!" Tas's eyes were round and wide in indignation.

"Then why are you in prison?"

"A mistake," Tas said cheerfully. "It always happens to us kender—on a daily basis, if you can believe that! Of course, they know it's a mistake." He nodded at the guardsman. "They never charge us, and they always let us go in the morning. Then they spend the day rounding us up and bringing us all back here at night. Gives us all something to do, you see."

Usha didn't understand, tried to think of how to get information without rousing the kender's suspicions.

"Maybe you can explain something to me, Tas. Where I come from, my people live a lot like you do. We share everything. But here, everyone seems so—well—greedy. I took some man's apples. I was hungry. The apples were spoiled. He would have had to throw them out anyway. Why did he get so mad? And that woman. Her bread would have been stale by morning."

"I know what you mean. It all has to do with *things*," Tas explained. "Humans are very keen on *things*. They like to own things, and when they get tired of owning their things they don't give them away, they demand other things in exchange. Remember that, and you'll get on fine. Where do you come from, by the way, Usha?"

It was a casual question. The kender was probably just curious, but Usha remembered Prot's warning not to reveal that she'd been living among the Irda.

"I'm from all over, really," she answered, watching the kender from beneath lowered eyelids, to see his reaction. "I wander here and there, never stay in one place long."

"You know, Usha," said Tas admiringly, "you'd make a great kender. You've never been to Solace, you said?"

"Oh, I might have. One place is a lot like another. Who can remember names?"

"I can! I make maps. But the reason I asked about Solace is that you look just like—"

Keys clanked in the cell door. The jailer entered. This time he carried a staff, which he used to fend off the kender. He peered around the shadowy cell. "Where's that newest prisoner?" He spotted Usha. "You there. Someone wants to talk to you."

"Me?" Usha thought he must be mistaken.

"You. Get moving. Mistress Jenna ain't got all night."

Usha looked at Tas for information.

"Mistress Jenna's a Red Robe mage," he offered. "She runs a mageware shop in town. A truly wonderful place!"

"What's she want with me?"

"The jailer always calls her to come inspect anything he confiscates that he thinks might be magic. Did you have anything with you that might be magic?"

"Maybe," Usha said, biting her lip.

"You! Apple thief!" The jailer was prodding at the giggling kender with his staff. "Get over here *now*!"

"Come on, Usha." Tas stood up, held out his hand. "Don't be afraid. Mistress Jenna's real nice. She and I are old acquaintances. I've been thrown out of her shop on numerous occasions."

Usha stood. She did not accept the kender's hand. Arranging her face to show careless indifference, she walked on her own over to the iron-barred door.

The jailer let her out and grabbed hold of Tasslehoff just as the kender was sidling past, hiding in Usha's shadow. "Here now? Where are you going, Master Burrfoot?"

"To say hello to Mistress Jenna, of course. I wouldn't want to be impolite."

"You wouldn't, would you? Well, now, you just be good and polite and hustle your way back into that cell."

The jailer gave Tas a shove and slammed the door shut in the kender's face. Tas clung to the bars, peering out, trying to see.

"Hullo, Mistress Jenna!" he yelled, waving his small arms. "It's me! Tasslehoff Burrfoot, one of the Heroes of the Lance!"

A woman wearing a red velvet hooded cloak stood beside the jailer's desk. She turned her head in the direction of the kender's shout, smiled a cool smile, and briefly nodded. Then she went back to what she had been doing—sorting through Usha's possessions, which were now lined neatly on the desk.

"Here she is, Mistress Jenna, the one who was asking about the

Master of the Tower."

The woman drew aside the hood of her cloak to get a better view. She was human, her face lovely but cold, as if it were carved from the same stone as the white marble buildings. Dark eyes gazed intently at and through Usha.

Usha's stomach clenched. Her legs trembled. Her mouth went dry. She realized in an instant that this woman knew everything. What would happen to her now? Prot had warned her. Humans consider the Irda no better—maybe worse—than ogres. And humans slew ogres without mercy.

"Come closer, child," the woman said, beckoning with a shapely, delicate hand. "Into the light."

The woman was probably not much older than Usha herself, but the aura of mystery, power, and magic that surrounded the Red Robe wizardess added immeasurably to her years.

Usha walked brashly forward, determined not to let this sorceress see that she was intimidated. She stepped into the light.

Jenna's eyes widened. She took a step forward, sucked in a swift breath. "Lunitari bless us!" she whispered.

With a swift motion, she drew her hood back up over her head and turned to the jailer. "You will release this prisoner into my custody. I'll take her and her belongings."

The woman gathered up the gifts of the Irda, handling each carefully, with respect, and replaced them safely inside Usha's pouch. The jailer regarded them with deep suspicion.

"I was right, then, wasn't I, Mistress Jenna. They are magic."

"You were quite right to summon me. And I'm glad to see, Torg, that you've learned your lesson about handling strange objects. That spell you accidentally cast on yourself was not an easy one to reverse."

"I won't be doing that again, I promise you, Mistress Jenna!" The jailer shuddered. "You can have her and good riddance. But you've got to sign for her. She's your responsibility. She robs another fruit stand and—"

"She won't be robbing any more fruit stands," Jenna said crisply, picking up Usha's pouches. "Come along, child. What is your name, by the way?"

"Usha. And I want my things," she said loudly, far more loudly than she'd intended.

Jenna raised feathery eyebrows.

Usha flushed, chewed on her lip. "They *are* mine," she said sullenly. "I didn't steal them."

"I am aware of that," Jenna replied. "Such valuable, arcane objects do not permit themselves to be stolen. A curse on anyone foolish enough to try." She cast a glance at the jailer, who blushed, ducked his head, and wrote furiously in his book. Jenna handed over the pouches.

Usha took them, followed Jenna to the prison entrance.

"Thank you for getting me out of there, Mistress. If there's ever anything I can do for you, just let me know. Where's your shop? Perhaps I'll stop by it sometime. . . . ."

Jenna was smiling again.

"Yes, indeed you will. Right now. Don't worry, Usha. I plan to take you exactly where you want to go."

"Where's that?" Usha asked in heart-sinking bewilderment.

"To see Dalamar, of course. The Master of the Tower will be quite interested in meeting you, Usha."

"You bet he will!" piped a shrill voice from behind. "Tell Dalamar that Tasslehoff Burrfoot said hullo. And say, Mistress Jenna, don't you think that Usha looks an awful lot like Raistlin?"

The sorceress halted. For as long as it might take someone to count to ten, she stood perfectly still and quiet. Then, slowly, she turned around, retraced her steps.

Usha remained at the entrance, wondering if she should try to run for it. She had the feeling she wouldn't get very far; her legs were the consistency of jelly. And where would she run to anyway? She leaned wearily against the door.

Jenna approached the jailer. "Release the kender into my custody as well."

Torg scowled. "You sure, Mistress? He's a dang nuisance—"

"I'm sure," Jenna said, an edge in her voice as sharp and cold as steel. "Release him now."

Torg drew out his keys, hastened to the cell door, unlocked it.

Tasslehoff—topknot swinging, pouches jouncing—marched out. He offered a polite hand to Jenna.

"How do you do? I don't think we've been formally introduced. I'm Tasslehoff—"

"I know who you are," she said. "I believe Dalamar would like to have a word with you."

"How wonderful! I haven't seen Dalamar in years. Is it true that he's your lover? Well, you needn't look at me like that. Caramon told me. He said you two—"

"Start walking," Jenna said somewhat grimly, steering the kender out of the jail and into the street. "Five paces in front of me, and keep your hands where I can see them. Usha, stay with me."

"I get to lead the way?" Tas was excited.

"If you want to think of it as that," Jenna returned. "No, not that direction. We're going *outside* the city wall, back to my dwelling place."

"But I thought we were visiting the Tower of High Sorcery!" Tas wailed. "I wanted to go through the Shoikan Grove! I saw it once, from a distance. It was truly evil and horrible and deadly. It almost killed Caramon, you know. Please, couldn't we take that route?"

"Don't be ridiculous," Jenna snapped. "No person in his right mind—though I realize that this description precludes kender!—would want to walk the Shoikan Grove, especially at night. *I* do not walk the Shoikan Grove, and I have been a student at the Tower. I will transport us there by a more sedate route, if you don't mind. That is why we are returning to my shop."

Tas was downcast for a moment, then he shrugged. "Oh, well," he said, cheering up. "At least we get to go to the Tower.

"This will be fun!" he added, looking back at Usha as he skipped along ahead of her. For an elder, he certainly had a lot of energy. "The Tower of High Sorcery is a fascinating place! I haven't been there in years, mind you. It's filled with all sorts of magic—most of it evil and all of it very, very powerful. Dalamar's a black-robed wizard, but then I guess you know that, if you want to see him. He's a dark elf and now he's the most powerful wizard in all of Ansalon—"

Usha stopped, stared at the kender.

"A Black Robe? A dark elf? But . . . that can't be right! The Protector wouldn't have sent me to see one of them. Surely . . . maybe there's another Dalamar?"

She heard laughter, like the chiming of silver bells, ring out in the darkness.

"Keep walking," said Jenna, stifling her amusement. "And rest assured, child—there is only one Dalamar."

6

The Tower of High Sorcery. A dinner party. Dalamar is unpleasantly surprised.

n daylight, the Tower of High Sorcery in Palanthas was a place of terror, avoided by all. By night, the tower was ghastly.

Once there had been five Towers of High Sorcery, located throughout the continent of Ansalon. Now there were only two. One of them was in Wayreth Forest and was impossible to reach, unless the mages there wanted you to reach them. At that time, the magical forest surrounding the tower would find you and guide you.

The Tower of High Sorcery in Palanthas was also nearly impossible to reach. It was guarded by the Shoikan Grove, a stand of trees inhabited by undead guardians. The fear the grove generated was so potent that most people could not bear to come within sight of it. Only those loyal to Queen Takhisis or those with a special charm, provided by the tower's master, could enter the accursed grove. And even they did not do so with impunity. Those who had to travel to the tower on business—or, as in Jenna's case, pleasure—generally took a less dangerous route. They walked the paths of magic.

Jenna escorted her charges through the old wall, entered what was known as New City. Designed and built by dwarves sometime during the Age of Might, Palanthas was divided into two sections: Old City and New City. Old City, surrounded by a wall, was carefully laid out like a wheel, with eight roads radiating from a central hub, wherein was located the lord's palace. Palanthas having long ago outgrown the cramped confines of Old City, its people built New City.

Sprawling outside the wall, New City was the center of the merchandising district. All the major guild halls could be found here, as well as dwellings for the merchants.

Jenna's mage-ware shop was located in the best part of New City, rather to the discomfort of other shop owners nearby, who viewed her arcane clientele with deep suspicion. It was known that Jenna was a favorite with Dalamar, Master of the Tower of High Sorcery. And while the Lord of Palanthas was the avowed authority figure in the city, no citizen would have dared do anything to cross the Master of the Tower.

Thus, the merchants grumbled about Jenna, but they did so quietly.

Arriving at her mage-ware shop, which was marked by a sign bearing the images of the three moons—the silver, the red, and the black—Jenna first took the precaution of binding the kender's hands with a silken cord. Only then did she remove the spell guarding the door. She ushered her guests inside.

"Is that necessary?" Usha asked indignantly, pointing at the kender's bindings. "He's not a thief, you know."

Jenna gazed at Usha, lifted her eyebrows.

Usha, wondering what she'd said that was so remarkable, flushed and bit her lip.

"I don't mind, truly," Tas said cheerfully, admiring the silken cord around his wrists. "I'm used to it."

"It's more for his protection and our own, than because I'm worried about losing money," Jenna returned. She spoke a word that sounded to Usha like brittle ice cracking, and a lamp in the room burst into light. Jenna cast a sharp glance at the young woman. "You're not familiar with kender, are you?"

Usha thought frantically of what Prot had told her, wished she paid more attention. She decided to bluff, though she had the heart-sinking feeling that she was wasting her time. "What a strange question. Of course I know all there is to know about kender. Doesn't everyone who lives on Ansalon?"

"Unfortunately, yes. Which is precisely why I asked. This way. Put that down!" Jenna ordered Usha sharply. She had just paused to pick up and study a pretty bottle. "A drop of that on your skin will cause your flesh to fall off in chunks. For mercy's sake, don't touch anything else! You're as bad as a kender. Both of you, come with me."

Usha gingerly replaced the bottle on the shelf. She clasped her hands firmly behind her back and hurried along, trying to see everything at once, with the result that she saw very little. Her chief impression of the shop was the smell, which was enticing and, at the same time, repulsive. Jars of spices and pungent herbs stood beside jars of dead and rotting things. Spellbooks, some of them musty and mildewed, were arranged neatly on bookshelves that covered one entire wall. Jewelry sparkled from inside glass cases.

"In the cellar is my laboratory," Jenna said, opening a door. "You're not to touch anything in here either!"

The door, marked with strange and unreadable symbols, led to a staircase. Jenna personally escorted Tasslehoff, keeping fast hold of his topknot and giving it a painful yank whenever he looked inclined to meddle with anything. She motioned Usha to descend the stairs after them.

The laboratory was underground, beneath the shop. A light came on at their entrance, but it was a dim and eerie blue and illuminated very little. Usha had to watch her footing going down the stairs.

"Now, both of you stand right there and *don't move!*" Jenna commanded when they reached the floor level. She disappeared into the shadows. At length, they heard her talking to someone in low, indistinguishable tones.

Usha caught hold of Tasslehoff by the collar of his green shirt just as he was walking off.

"She said not to move!" Usha scolded.

"I'm sorry," Tas whispered back. He looked truly contrite. "I didn't mean to. It's my feet. My head told them not to move, but sometimes what my head thinks doesn't quite make it down that far. The thoughts seem to stop somewhere around the level of my knees. But don't you think this all terribly exciting? Look over there!" He was breathless with awe. "That's a human skull! I don't suppose she'd mind if I—"

"Yes, I do think she'd mind," Usha said crossly. "Now stay put." She kept fast hold of Tas, not because she was really worried about him disobeying Jenna, but because she desperately needed someone to hold on to.

"I'm glad she brought you along," Usha added impulsively, "though I'm really not sure why. She doesn't seem to like having you around."

"Oh, she didn't have much choice," Tas said, shrugging. "Not after I said what I said about Raistlin."

"What did that mean—my looking like Raistlin? I don't understand. Who is Raistlin?"

"Who is Raistlin?" Tasslehoff repeated, stunned, forgetting to whisper. "You never heard of Raistlin Majere? I didn't think there was anyone in Ansalon who'd never heard of Raistlin!"

Usha, realizing she'd made a mistake, gave a small laugh. "Oh, *that* Raistlin! Well, certainly I've heard of *him.* I just didn't know *which* Raistlin you were talking about. Raistlin's quite a common name where I come from. Several people named Raistlin live in our village. Elvish, isn't it?"

"I don't think so," Tas returned thoughtfully. "Raistlin wasn't an elf, and Caramon certainly isn't an elf! Caramon's big enough to make about three elves, if you chopped him up. And then they were twins, and elves don't tend to have twins a whole lot, as I recall. It's been quite awhile since I've visited Qualinesti. They won't let me across the border, though I know the new Speaker of the Sun. He's Tanis's boy, Gil. You've heard of Tanis Half-Elven, haven't you?"

"Who hasn't!" Usha exclaimed, though she might have included herself.

At least she'd discovered that Raistlin was a "he," something she hadn't been certain about. And that he had something to do with someone named Caramon. Congratulating herself on having covered her tracks nicely, she was thinking up her next question when Jenna returned.

"She knows who Raistlin is. Don't let her fool you, kender. Come along now, both of you. I've spoken to Dalamar and—"

"Dalamar! Is he here? Dalamar!" Tasslehoff waved and hooted. "Yoo hoo! It's me, Tas. Remember me? I—"

"He is *not* here," Jenna interrupted in stern, cold tones. "He is in the tower. We have ways of communicating, he and I. Now, see that circle of salt on the floor?"

Usha didn't; she couldn't even see the floor in the dimness, but at that moment, the light from the lamp suddenly intensified. The circle was clearly visible.

"Step into it carefully," Jenna instructed. "Make certain you don't disturb the salt."

"I know!" Tas cried, highly excited. "I saw Par-Salian do this with Caramon. That was the time I accidentally turned myself into a mouse. You see, Usha, I was in the Tower of Wayreth and I'd found this ring—white with two red stones—and I put it on and—"

"For Gilean's sake, hold your tongue!" Jenna snapped. "Or *I'll* turn you into a mouse! And I'll turn myself into a cat."

"Could you really? What kind of a cat?" Tas chattered on. "Maybe you could turn me into a cat instead? I've never been a cat . . ."

"Take hold of my hands, both of you," Jenna continued, ignoring the kender. "Close your eyes and you won't become dizzy. And no matter what happens, don't let go of my hand."

She spoke words that crawled and twisted inside Usha's head. The floor seemed suddenly to give way. Usha's stomach gave way with it and she had the fearful impression of wind buffeting her. She needed no urging to hang on to Jenna's hand. She clung to the sorceress in terror.

And then Usha was standing on solid ground. The sound and feel of wind ceased. The darkness was gone. She squinted her eyes shut against a bright light.

"You can look now," came Jenna's voice. "We have arrived. You stand safely in the Tower of High Sorcery in Palanthas."

Usha wasn't certain she wanted to open her eyes. From the kender's description, this Tower of High Sorcery must be an evil, horrible place. Tasslehoff was already talking eagerly with someone, who was answering the kender in the polite but distracted tones of one whose thoughts are elsewhere.

"Open your eyes, Usha," Jenna repeated sternly.

Blinking, Usha obeyed and was amazed to find herself, not in some sort of horror-filled dungeon, with bodies chained and manacled, hanging from the walls, but in a beautifully decorated room. Colorful tapestries, portraying fantastical animals, covered the stone walls. Woven rugs, with lovely, intricate patterns, were spread over the floors. Usha had never seen so much furniture in one place at one time.

"Welcome, Usha. Welcome to my tower," said a voice.

Usha turned to see what could only have been—from Prot's description of them—an elf. Tall and slender, with features almost rivaling those of the Irda in beauty, the man was clad in soft black robes, decorated with cabalistic symbols.

"I am Dalamar," said the elf.

His voice was as sweet and clear and seductive as flute music. He advanced toward her, and his movements were graceful, fluid, sinuous. His hair was dark and soft, worn shoulder-length. She was charmed by him, captivated, until she looked into his eyes. They caught her, held her, began to absorb her. Frightened, she tried to shift her gaze. The eyes refused to release her.

"Those pouches look heavy. I'll take them," Dalamar offered.

Usha relinquished the packs without a thought.

"You're trembling, my dear," Dalamar observed, adding in soothing tones, "Don't be afraid. I mean you no harm and might mean you a great deal of good. Please, sit down. May I pour you some wine? Offer you food?"

He gestured to a table, and with that gesture, he released Usha from the enchantment of his gaze. She glanced over at the table. Tempting smells rose from covered pots. Bowls of chilled fruit glistened in the bright light of a candelabra. Tasslehoff had already seated himself, was lifting lids and sniffing in appreciation.

"This really looks good. I'm hungry. Aren't you hungry, Usha? I can't imagine why. I just ate only about an hour ago. But then jail-house soup doesn't stay with you long. Not to say anything bad about the Palanthas jail soup," Tas added, looking anxiously at Dalamar. "You won't tell them I didn't like it, will you? I mean, it's truly quite tasty. I wouldn't want to hurt the cook's feelings."

"I won't say a word," Dalamar promised with a grave smile. "I only hope my poor repast is as good. Roast fowl, bread, fruit, sweetmeats, sugared nuts—all I can offer, this late at night, I'm afraid."

Usha was suddenly extremely hungry.

"It looks wonderful!" she said, and before she quite knew what she was doing, she sank down into one of the comfortable chairs and began ladling food onto her plate.

"I've never been so hungry in my life," she confided to Tas.

"Me neither," he mumbled incoherently, having shoved an entire baked apple into his mouth. With a tremendous effort, he chewed, swallowed, returned to his plate for more. "Must be all the excitement."

"Must be," said Jenna, biting into the crispy brown skin of a baked chicken breast.

The taste was so exquisite, she sighed with pleasure, devoured the chicken breast, and started in on another. It was only then that she realized that she and Tas were alone in the room.

"Where do you suppose Jenna and Dalamar went?" Usha asked, not particularly caring. She took a drink of hot, spiced cider, thought she had never tasted anything so delicious, and drank two more glasses.

"Dunno." Tas was gnawing vigorously on a hunk of bread. "I didn't see them leave. But then that's not unusual. People come and go like that all the time around here. Say, look, your pouches are gone, too."

"So they are." Usha, for some reason, found that funny.

She laughed. Tasslehoff laughed. Their laughter made them thirsty, and they drank more cider. Their thirst made them hungry, and they kept eating . . . and eating.

Pausing at last, Usha wiped her hands on a clean cloth. Then, settling back in her chair, she said to Tas, "Tell me more about this person named Raistlin."

* * * * *

In another room, Jenna spread the contents of Usha's pouch onto a table. Dalamar bent over them, taking care not to touch them, but studying each with a critical eye.

"That's the lot," said Jenna.

"What's in the other pouch?"

"Clothes, all made of silk, like those she's wearing. Nothing else."

"You said she said something about having a message for me."

"That's what she told the jailer. Three possibilities: she's lying, she's carrying it in her head, or she has it on her person."

Dalamar considered this. "I doubt she's lying. With what intent? She obviously has no idea who I am."

Jenna sniffed. "She claims she doesn't recognize the name Raistlin Majere, either."

"That's possible, all things considered." Dalamar continued inspecting the contents of the pouch. Placing his hand over them, he recited certain words. Every object on the table began to glow with a soft light, a few shining brighter than the rest. He lowered his hand, sighed with satisfaction. "You are right. All of them magical, some of them extremely powerful. And, none of them were made by any mage in any of the orders. You agree with me, my love?"

"Most assuredly." Jenna slipped her hand over his shoulder, kissed him lightly on the cheek.

Dalamar smiled, but did not withdraw his attention from the magical paraphernalia. "I wonder what spells are locked inside?" he said longingly.

He extended his hand again, this time moving toward a smallish piece of amber, which had been skillfully carved into the shape of a deer. Hesitantly, grimacing—as if he knew what was going to happen—he touched the amber with the tip of one finger.

A blue flash, a sizzling sound. Dalamar gasped in pain and hastily withdrew his hand.

Jenna, pursing her lips, shook her head.

"I could have told you that would happen. They are intended to be used by one person and one person only."

"Yes, I guessed as much myself. Still, it was worth a try."

The two exchanged glances, arrived at the same conclusion.

"Of Irda make?" Jenna asked.

"No doubt of it," Dalamar replied. "We have a few such artifacts stored in the Tower of Wayreth. I recognize the workmanship and"—he shook away the pain in his injured hand—"the effects."

"We can't use them, but obviously, since the Irda gave them to this girl, she can. Yet, I sense none of the art about her."

"Still, she must have some talent. If she is who we think she is."

Jenna looked amazed. "Do you have any doubts? Didn't you see her eyes? Like liquid gold! Only one man on Krynn had eyes like that. Even the kender recognized her."

"Tasslehoff?" Dalamar glanced up from his study of the artifacts. "Did he? I wondered why you risked bringing him along. What did he say?"

"Too much. And too loudly," Jenna replied grimly. "People were starting to take notice."

"The kender as well." Dalamar walked over to the window, stared out into the night that seemed merely a deepening of the perpetual darkness surrounding the tower. "Can it be that the legend is true?"

"What else? The girl has obviously been raised in some place far from Ansalon. She has with her magical objects of great value crafted by the Irda. The kender recognized her and, beyond all of that, she has the golden eyes. She would be of the right age. And then there is the very fact that she was guided here."

Dalamar frowned, not altogether pleased at the notion. "I remind you again that Raistlin Majere is dead. He has been dead for well over twenty years."

"Yes, my dear one. Don't be upset." Jenna ran her hand through Dalamar's soft hair, gently kissed him on the ear. "But, there *was* that little matter of the Staff of Magius. Locked up inside the tower laboratory. Guarded by the undead with orders to allow no one to pass, not even you. Yet, who has the staff now? Palin Majere, Raistlin's nephew."

"The staff could have been a gift from Magius as well as Raistlin," Dalamar said irritably, withdrawing from her touch. "Magius being the more likely, since he was friends with the knight Huma, and all know that Palin's brothers were planning on entering the knighthood. I explained this all to the Conclave—"

"Yes, my love," Jenna said, lowering her eyes. "Still, you are the one who refuses to believe in coincidence. Was it coincidence that brought that young woman here? Or something else?"

"Perhaps you are right," Dalamar said, after a moment's thought.

He walked over to a large, ornately framed wall mirror. Jenna joined him. For a moment, they saw only their own reflections. Dalamar reached out, brushed his hand across the glass. The reflections vanished, were replaced by Usha and Tasslehoff, eating the charmed food, drinking the enchanted cider, laughing at nothing and at everything.

"How strange," Dalamar murmured, watching them. "I thought it no more than legend. Yet there she sits."

"Raistlin's daughter," Usha said softly. "We have found Raistlin's daughter!"

7

The Inn of the Last Home.
A discussion between old friends.

t was nighttime in Solace. The day's heat remained, rising from the dirt, the trees, the walls of the houses. But at least the night banished the angry, fiery sun, which glared down from the heavens like the baleful eye of some infuriated god. At night, the eye closed and people breathed sighs of relief and began to venture out.

This summer was the hottest and driest anyone in Solace could remember. The dirt streets were baked hard; cracks had formed. A choking dust, rising whenever a cart trundled by, hung in the air, cast a pall over the valley. The beautiful leaves of the gigantic vallenwood trees wilted, drooped limp and seemingly lifeless from dried-out, creaking boughs.

Life had turned upside-down in Solace. Usually the days were bustling, busy times, with people going to market, farmers working in the fields, children playing, women washing clothes in the streams. Now the days were empty, lifeless, drooping, like the leaves on the trees.

The crops in the fields had withered and died in the blaring heat, so the farmers no longer went to market. Most of the stalls in the market closed. It was too hot to play, so the children stayed indoors, fretting and whining and bored. The rushing streams had shrunk to meandering, muddy puddles. The waters of Crystalmir Lake were unnaturally warm. Dead fish washed up on the shoreline. Few people left the relative coolness of their homes during the day. They came out at night.

"Like bats," Caramon Majere said gloomily to his friend, Tanis Half-Elven. "We've all turned into bats, sleeping during the day, flying about by night . . ."

"Flying everywhere except here," Tika remarked. Standing behind Caramon's chair, she fanned herself with a tray. "Not even during the war was business this bad."

The Inn of the Last Home, perched high in the branches of an enormous vallenwood tree, was brightly lit, generally a welcome beacon to late-night travelers. Shining through the stained glass, the warm light conjured up images of cool ale, mulled wine, honey mead, tingling cider and, of course, Otik's famous spiced potatoes. But the inn was empty this night, as it had been for many nights previous. Tika no longer bothered to light the cooking fire. It was just as well, for the kitchen was too hot to work in comfortably anyway.

No customers gathered around the bar to tell tales of the War of the Lance or swap more recent gossip. There were rumors of civil war among the elves. Rumors that the dwarves of Thorbardin had sent out the word to all their people to return home or risk being shut out when the dwarves—fearing elven attack—sealed up their mountain fortress. No peddlers tramped by on their customary routes. No tinkers came to mend pots. No minstrels came to sing. The only people still traveling these days were kender, and they generally spent their nights in local jail cells, not inns.

"People are nervous and upset," Caramon said, feeling called upon to make some excuse for his vanished customers. "All this talk of war. And unless this heat breaks soon, there'll be no harvest. Food will be hard to come by this winter. That's why they're not coming—"

"I know, dear. I know." Tika put the tray on the counter. Wrapping her arms around her husband's brawny shoulders, she hugged him close. "I was just talking. Don't pay any attention to me."

"As if I could ever *not* pay attention to you," Caramon said, running his hand through his wife's hair.

The passing years had not been easy ones for either of them. Tika and Caramon both worked hard to maintain the inn and, though it was work they loved, it was not easy. While most of her guests slumbered, Tika was awake, supervising the cooking of breakfast. All day long there were rooms to be made up, food to be prepared, guests welcomed with a cheery smile, clothes to be washed. When night came and the guests went to bed, Tika swept the floor, scrubbed the tables, and planned out what she would do tomorrow.

Caramon was still as strong as three men, still as big as three men, though much of his girth had shifted location, due to what he claimed was his bound duty to taste all the food. His hair had gone a bit gray at the temples and he had what he called "cogitating lines" marking his forehead. He was genial, affable, and took life as it came. He was proud of his boys, adored his little daughters, dearly loved his wife. His one regret, his one sorrow, was the loss of his twin brother to evil and to ambition. But he never allowed that one small cloud to dim his life.

Though she had been married over twenty-five years, and had borne five children, Tika could still turn heads when she walked through the bar. Her figure had grown plumper over the years, her hands cracked and reddened from being constantly in sudsy water. But her smile was still infectious, and she could proudly boast that there wasn't a strand of gray mingled with her luxuriant red curls.

Tanis could not say the same. His human blood was cooling—rapidly, it seemed to him. The elven blood could do little to warm him. He was strong, still, and could hold his own in battle—though he hoped it wouldn't come to that.

Perhaps it was the sorrow, the worry, the turmoil of these past few months that streaked his hair with silver, his beard with gray.

Tika and Caramon remained for a moment in an affectionate embrace, finding rest and comfort in each other.

"Besides," Tika added, glancing at Tanis, "it's well for you that we're *not* busy. When are they supposed to arrive?"

Tanis looked out the window. "Not until well after dark. At least that was Porthios's plan. It will depend on how Alhana is feeling. . . ."

"Making her tramp about the wilderness! In this heat and in her condition. Men!" Tika sniffed. Straightening, she gave her husband a playful thump on the head.

"What'd you hit *me* for?" Caramon demanded, rubbing his scalp and peering around at his wife. "*I* didn't have anything to do with it."

"You're all alike, that's what," she said, somewhat vaguely. She stared out the window into the gathering darkness, twisting her apron around and around in her hands.

She's middle-aged, Tanis realized suddenly. Odd. I never noticed before. Perhaps it's because, whenever I think of Tika Waylan, I see that saucy red-headed girl who thwacked draconians over the head with her skillet. I used to be able to find that girl again in Tika's green eyes, but not tonight. Tonight I see the lines around her mouth and the sag in her shoulders. And in her eyes—fear.

"Something's wrong with the boys," she said suddenly. "Something's happened. I know it."

"Nothing's happened," said Caramon, with fond exasperation. "You're tired. It's the heat—"

"I'm *not* tired. And it's *not* the heat!" Tika snapped, temper flaring. "I've never felt like this before." She put her hand over her heart. "As if I were smothering. I can't draw a breath, my heart aches so. I . . . I think I'll go see to Alhana's room."

"She's seen to that room every hour on the hour, ever since you got here, Tanis." Caramon sighed. He watched his wife climb the stairs, a worried expression on his face. "She's been acting peculiar all day. It started last night, with some terrible dream she can't remember. But then it's been like that ever since the boys joined the knighthood. She was the proudest person at the ceremony. You remember, Tanis? You were there."

Tanis smiled. Yes, he remembered.

Caramon shook his head. "But she cried herself to sleep that night, when we were alone. She thought nothing of fighting draconians when *she* was young. I reminded her of that. She called me a 'dolt.' Said that was then and this was now and I couldn't possibly understand a mother's heart. Women."

"Where are young Sturm and my namesake?" Tanis asked.

"The last we heard from them, they were riding up north, toward Kalaman. Seems that the Solamnic leadership is finally taking you seriously, Tanis. About the Knights of Takhisis, I mean." Caramon lowered his voice, though the common room was empty, except for the two of them. "Palin wrote that they were going north, to patrol along the coast."

"Palin went with them? A mage?" Tanis was amazed. For the moment, he forgot his own troubles.

"Unofficially. The knights would never sanction having a mage along, but since this was routine patrol duty, Palin was allowed to accompany his brothers. At least that's what High Command said. Palin obviously thought there's more to it than that. Or so he implied."

"What made him think so?"

"Well, Justarius's death, for one."

"What?" Tanis stared. "Justarius . . . dead?"

"You didn't know?"

"How could I?" Tanis demanded. "I've been skulking about in the woods for months, trying my best to keep the elves out of civil war. This night will be the first I've slept in a real bed since I left Silvanesti. What happened to Justarius? And who's head of the Wizards' Conclave now?"

"Can't you guess? Our old friend." Caramon was grim.

"Dalamar. Of course. I should have known. But Justarius—"

"I don't know the details. Palin can't say much. But the wizards of the three moons took your warnings about the dark knights seriously, if no one else on Ansalon did. Justarius ordered a magical assault on the Gray Robes of Storm's Keep. He and several others entered the tower there. They barely escaped with their lives, and Justarius didn't even do that much."

"Fools," Tanis said bitterly. "Ariakan's wizards are immensely powerful. They draw their magic from all three moons, or so Dalamar told me. A small force of magic-users from Wayreth entering the Gray Tower would be marked for disaster. I can't imagine Dalamar going along with a lame-brained scheme like that."

"He came out of it well enough," Caramon said dryly . "You've got to wonder which side he's on in all this. He serves the Dark Queen, too."

"His allegiance is to magic first, though. Just as his *shalafi* taught him."

Tanis smiled at old memories, was pleased to see that Caramon smiled, too. Raistlin, Caramon's twin brother, had been Dalamar's *shalafi*—the elven term for teacher. And though the relationship had ended in disaster—and very nearly the destruction of Krynn—Dalamar had learned a great deal from his *shalafi*. A debt he never hesitated to acknowledge.

"Yes, well, you know the dark elf better than I do," Caramon acknowledged. "At any rate, he took part in the raid, was one of the few to return unscathed. Palin said Dalamar was extremely shaken and upset, refused to talk about what happened. It was the dark elf who brought back Justarius's body, though I guess since Dalamar is keeping company with Justarius's daughter, Jenna, he didn't have much choice. At any rate, the wizards took a drubbing. Justarius wasn't the only one to die, though he was the highest rank. And now Dalamar's head of the Conclave."

"You think he was the one who sent Palin out with the knights?"

"Palin would have had to get permission to leave his studies." Caramon grunted. "The wizards are a lot stricter now than in the old days. Raistlin came and went as he chose."

"Raistlin was a law unto himself," Tanis said, yawning. He wished he hadn't mentioned sleeping in a bed. The thought of clean sheets, soft mattress, fluffy pillow, was suddenly overpowering. "I'll have to have a talk with Dalamar. Obviously, he knows something about these dark knights."

"Will he tell you?" Caramon was dubious.

"If he thinks it's to his benefit," Tanis replied. "Porthios will be staying here for at least a few weeks. Alhana will need time to rest and, though he won't admit it, Porthios himself is on the verge of exhaustion. Hopefully, I can find time to get away, pay Dalamar a visit.

"Which reminds me, I can't thank you enough, Caramon"—Tanis rested his hand over the large hand of the big human—"for letting Porthios and Alhana stay here. Their presence could put you in danger if anyone found out. They have been formally cast out, exiled. They are dark elves, which means they are fair game—"

"Bah!" Caramon waved away the thought, inadvertently driving away a pesky fly at the same time. "The people in Solace don't know anything about elven tiffs, could care less anyway. So Porthios and Alhana have been exiled, branded 'dark elves.' Unless they've both suddenly turned purple, no one here will ever know the difference. An elf's an elf, to us."

"Still, it's rumored that both the Qualinesti and the Silvanesti have assassins out after Porthios and Alhana." Tanis sighed. "Once they were rulers of the mightiest elven nations on Ansalon. By their marriage, they forged an alliance between the two realms that would have made the elves one of the leading political powers on the continent. For the first time in centuries, a child is being born who is heir to both kingdoms! And there are those who have already sworn this child's death!"

Tanis clenched his fists. "What's so damn frustrating is that the majority of elves want peace, not only with their cousins, but with their neighbors. It's the extremists on both sides who are urging that we go back to the days of isolationism, close our borders, shoot any human or dwarf who comes in sight. The rest of the elves follow along because it's easier to do that than to speak out, cause confrontation."

Tanis shook his head. "I don't *think* their assassins would dare attack the inn, but, these days, you never know . . ."

"We survived dragons," Caramon said cheerfully. "We'll survive elves and drought and whatever else comes along."

"I hope so," Tanis said, now in a somber mood. "I hope so, my friend."

"Speaking of Qualinesti, how's Gil doing?"

Tanis was silent for long moments. The pain of Gil's leaving had not diminished, though it had been many months since his son had run away from home, been tricked into becoming leader—or puppet ruler—of the elves of Qualinesti.

Gilthas—named for Laurana's ill-fated brother Gilthanas—was the child both had wanted but had believed they would never have. Laurana's pregnancy had been difficult; Gilthas was a frail baby and was near death several times. Tanis knew he and his wife were overly protective of their son, refusing to allow him to visit the land of his parent's birth, trying to shield him from a racially divided world that found it difficult to accept a child of mixed blood.

When Porthios, Speaker of the Sun of the Qualinesti, left his land to risk his life fighting for the Silvanesti, extremists took the opportunity of his absence to brand him a traitor and choose a new Speaker. They decided on Gilthas, whose mother, Porthios's sister, would be in line for the position, but who had abrogated her right by marrying Tanis Half-Elven.

Believing that Gil, by virtue of his human blood, was a fool and a weakling, who could be manipulated into serving as a puppet king, the extremists persuaded the young man to run away from home and travel to Qualinesti. Once there, Gil proved tougher than the senators had imagined. They had to resort to threats of violence against Alhana

Starbreeze, ruler of the Silvanesti and their prisoner, in order to convince Gil to become Speaker.

Tanis had endeavored—with Dalamar's help—to save his son, but the half-elf had failed.

Or rather, Tanis told himself with sorrowful pride, I succeeded. Gil had chosen to stay, to serve his people, to do what he could to thwart the extremists and bring peace to the elven nations.

But the pain of missing his son did not lessen over time and, to add to it, now an infuriated, vengeful Porthios was massing his forces to declare war on Qualinesti, a tragedy Tanis was trying to prevent. When he felt he could control his voice, he answered.

"Gil's well, or so I hear. I'm not permitted—on threat of death—to see him, you know."

Caramon nodded, his big face soft with sympathy.

"Laurana's still trying to enter Qualinesti. She's been negotiating with them for months now. She says, in her last letter, that she thinks they're beginning to relent. Gil's having something to do with it. He's stronger than they think. But"—Tanis shrugged, shook his head—"I miss him, Caramon. You can't imagine . . ."

Caramon, who missed his own boys, could well imagine, but he knew what Tanis meant. There was a difference. Tanis's boy was a virtual prisoner of his own people. One day soon, Caramon's boys would be coming home.

The two continued to talk of times past and present, when they were interrupted by a soft tap on the door.

Caramon jumped, startled. "Who in the Abyss is that? At this time of night! I didn't hear anyone climb the stairs—"

"You won't," Tanis said, rising to his feet. "That will be Porthios's escort. And these soldier elves are silent even for elves. Moonlight shining on the grass makes more noise than they do."

Reaching the door, Tanis put his hand on the handle. Mindful of what he'd warned Caramon about assassins, Tanis gave a low whistle.

His whistle was answered, in higher pitch. The tapping was repeated.

Tanis opened the door.

An elven warrior glided inside. He cast a quick glance around the room, then nodded to himself in satisfaction. Inspection concluded, he shifted his gaze to Tanis.

"All is secure?"

"All is secure. I introduce your host, Caramon Majere. Caramon, I introduce Samar, of House Protector."

Samar regarded Caramon with cool appraisal. Taking in the big man's spreading paunch and jovial face, the elf didn't seem much impressed.

Those who first met Caramon often mistook his affable grin and slowness of thought as indicative of a simple mind. This wasn't true, as Caramon's friends had come to learn. Caramon never arrived at an answer until he had mentally walked clear around the question, studied it from all sides, examined it from every angle. When finished, he often reached some extremely astute conclusions.

Caramon was not one to be intimidated by an elf, however. The big man gave back as good as he got, standing tall and self-assured. This was, after all, his inn.

Samar's cold face relaxed in a half-smile. "Caramon Majere, a Hero of the Lance. 'A big man, but his heart is bigger than his body.' So my Queen says. I bid you greeting in Her Majesty's name."

Caramon blinked, somewhat confused. He nodded clumsily to the elf. "Sure, Samar. Glad to be of service to Alhana, I mean . . . Her . . . uh . . . Majesty. You just go back and tell her that everything's all ready and she's got nothing to worry about. But where's Porthios? I thought—"

Tanis trod on the big man's foot, whispered, "Don't mention Porthios to Samar. I'll explain later." More loudly he made haste to change the subject. "Porthios will be coming, too, Caramon. Under separate escort. You're early, Samar. I didn't expect—"

"Her Majesty is not well," Samar interrupted. "In fact, I must beg your indulgence, gentlemen, and return to her. Is her room prepared?"

Tika came bustling down from upstairs, her face creased with anxiety. "Caramon! What is it? I heard voices. Oh!" She caught sight of Samar. "How do you do?"

"My wife, Tika," Caramon said proudly. After well over twenty years of marriage, he still regarded his wife as the most beautiful woman in the world, and himself as the luckiest man.

Samar gave a gracious, if hurried, bow. "Madam. And now, if you will excuse, my queen is not well—"

Tika mopped her face with her apron. "Have the labor pains started?"

Samar flushed. Among the elves, such matters are not considered suitable subjects for conversation in mixed company. "I couldn't say, Madam—"

"Has her water broken?" Tika pursued the inquiry.

"Madam!" Samar's face burned. He was obviously scandalized, and even Caramon had gone red.

Tanis cleared his throat. "Tika, I don't think—"

"Men!" Tika snorted. She grabbed her cloak from a hanger on the door. "And just how did you plan to get her up the stairs? Maybe she can fly? Or did you expect her to walk? In her condition? With the baby coming?"

The warrior looked back down at the numerous stairs leading up to the inn. It was obvious he'd not given the matter any thought.

"I . . . couldn't say . . ."

Tika brushed past him, already headed out the door, giving instructions as she left. "Tanis, start the kitchen fire and put the kettle on to boil. Caramon, run and get Dezra. She's our midwife," Tika explained to Samar, catching hold of his sleeve in passing and dragging him along. "I've told her to expect this. Come along, Samovar or whatever your name is. Take me to Alhana."

Samar pulled away. "Madam, you can't! That is impossible. My orders are to—"

Tika fixed her green eyes on him, her jaw set. Caramon and Tanis exchanged glances. Both knew that expression.

"Uh, if you'll excuse me, dear." Caramon squeezed past, was out the door, and headed for the stairs.

Tanis, grinning into his beard, left quickly, retreated to the kitchen. He could hear Tika's voice.

"If you don't take me, I'll go out there and stand in the middle of the market square and yell at the top of my lungs—"

Samar was a gallant warrior. He had fought everything from ogres to draconians. Tika Waylan Majere disarmed him, routed him in a single skirmish.

"No, Madam!" Samar begged. "Please! No one must know we are here. I'll take you to my queen."

"Thank you, sir." Tika was gracious in victory. "Now, get a move on!"

8

Dragon flight.
Dragon counsel. Captor and captive.

he blue dragon and its riders left Valkinord after the sun had set. They flew over Ansalon in darkness, in silence.

The night sky was cloudless and it was cool up here above the wispy clouds, if nowhere else on Ansalon. Steel took off his helm, which was shaped in the image of a skull, and shook out his long black hair, let the wind from the dragon's wings dry the sweat on his head and neck. He had removed most of the heavy plate armor he wore in battle, retaining only the breastplate beneath a dark blue traveling cloak, attaching leather bracers to his arms and above his tall leather boots on his legs. He was heavily armed, for he was venturing into enemy territory. A longbow, a quiver of arrows, and a throwing lance were attached to the dragon's saddle. On his person he bore a sword—his father's sword, the ancient sword of a Knight of Solamnia, the sword that had once belonged to Sturm Brightblade.

Steel's hand rested on the hilt of the sword—a habit he'd grown into. He stared down into the darkness, trying to see something besides darkness. Lights from a village, perhaps, or red moonlight, reflected off a lake. He saw nothing.

"Where are we, Flare?" he demanded abruptly. "I've seen no signs of life since we left the coast."

"I shouldn't suppose you wanted to," the dragon retorted. "Any life we met here would be hostile to us."

Steel shrugged off such considerations, implying they could take care of themselves. Trevalin had spoken of "immense danger," since they were traveling over enemy territory, but the threat, in reality, was small. Their main danger was from other dragons, silver and gold. Those few who had remained on Ansalon when their brethren had returned to the Isle of the Dragons were, according to reports, concentrated in the north, around Solamnia.

Not many people in this part of the country would risk battling a dark knight and a blue dragon. Flare, though small for her race—being only about thirty-eight feet long—was young, fierce, and tenacious in battle. Most blue dragons are excellent magic-users; Flare was the exception. She was too impetuous, lacked the patience needed to cast spells. She preferred to fight with tooth and claw and her devastating lightning breath, which could shatter castle walls and set forests ablaze.

Flare tended to have a low opinion of wizards and had not been pleased at the prospect of transporting one. It had taken Steel a considerable amount of pleading, cajoling, and a deer haunch to at last persuade the dragon to permit Palin to ride upon her back.

"He won't, though, you know." Flare had smirked while devouring the tidbit. "He'll take one look at me and be so scared that he'll soil those nice white robes of his."

Steel had been afraid that this would be the case. The bravest warrior in the world can be unmanned by dragonfear, the terror and awe that dragons inspire in their enemies. Palin had indeed turned deathly pale at the sight of the dragon, with her sparkling blue scales, flaring eyes, and rows of tearing teeth, dripping with the blood of her treat.

At first, Steel had thought he had lost the young man, that they'd have to find another, slower means of travel. But the sight of the bodies of his brothers, strapped onto the back of the saddle, had lent the young mage courage. Palin had pressed his lips together and walked resolutely to the dragon's side, and—with Steel's help—had mounted.

Steel had felt the body of the young mage shiver, but Palin forbore crying out or saying a word. He held himself upright, with dignity—courage for which Steel gave the young man credit.

"I know where I am, in case you think I'm lost," Flare added softly. "Sara and I flew this route . . . that night. The night she came to Caramon Majere. The night she came to betray you."

Steel knew the night to which the dragon referred, and he maintained stern silence. In the seat behind him—the knight had exchanged his one-man saddle for one that accommodated two people—Palin stirred and muttered incoherent words. Not even dragonfear could contend with exhaustion. The mage had fallen into a sleep that was bringing him little comfort apparently, for he flinched, cried out sharply, loudly, and began to flail about.

"Silence him," warned the dragon. "You may see no signs of life on the ground beneath us, but it is there. We are flying over the Khalkist Mountains. The hill dwarves dwell here. Their scouts are alert and cunning. We show up black against the starlit sky. They would easily identify us and pass the word along."

"Much good it would do them or anyone," Steel remarked, but he knew better than to annoy the dragon, and so he twisted around in the saddle and laid a firm, restraining hand on the mage's arm.

Palin quieted at the touch. Sighing heavily, he shifted to a more comfortable position. The two-person saddle had been designed to carry two knights into battle, one wielding steel, the other either magic or clerical spells, useful in counteracting the magical attacks of the enemy.

The saddle was fashioned of lightweight wood covered by leather and was equipped with pouches and harnesses intended to hold not only weapons but spell components and artifacts. The riders were separated by a shelf, covered with padded leather. Inside was a drawer, meant to hold scrolls, supplies or other paraphernalia. Palin rested his head on this shelf, his bloodstained cheek on one arm. His other hand, even in his sleep, kept hold of the Staff of Magius, which—by his instruction—had been lashed to the saddle beside him.

"He relives the battle," observed Steel. Seeing the mage settled, the knight removed his hand and turned back to face the rushing wind.

The dragon indicated what she thought of this remark with a snort and flick of the blue-scaled head. "It was a rout. Don't dignify it by terming it a 'battle.' "

"The Solamnics fought valiantly," Steel returned. "They held their ground. They did not run, nor did they dishonor themselves by surrendering."

Flare shook her mane, but made no comment, and Steel was wise enough not to press the issue. The dragon had fought in the Dragon Wars, twenty-six years ago. In those days, the soldiers of the Dark Queen never missed an opportunity to ridicule or disparage their enemy. Any Dragon Highlord who had dared praise the Solamnic Knights, as Steel had just done, would have been stripped of his rank, possibly his life. Flare, as well as most of the other dragons loyal to Takhisis, was having difficulty adjusting to the new way of thinking. A soldier should respect his enemy—she agreed with Lord Ariakan on that. But praising them went just a bit too far in her mind.

Steel leaned forward to pat the dragon on the neck, indicating that he respected her view and that he would offer no further comment.

Flare, who was quite fond of her master—she doted on him, in fact—showed her appreciation by changing the subject. Though, as might be noted from the topic she chose, blue dragons are not lauded for their tact.

"I don't suppose you've heard anything of Sara?" Flare asked.

"No," Steel answered, his voice hard and cold, keeping his emotions in check. "And you know you are not supposed to mention her name."

"We're alone. Who's going to hear us? Perhaps we'll learn something of her during our visit to Solace."

"I don't *want* to hear anything of her," Steel replied, still in the same harsh tones.

"I suppose you're right. If we did happen to find out where she was hiding, we'd be forced to capture her, return her. Lord Ariakan may praise the enemy all he likes, but he has no use for traitors."

"She is not a traitor!" Steel said, his chill melting in the flash of his temper. "She could have betrayed us any number of times, but she remained loyal—"

"To *you*," said Flare.

"She raised me when my own mother abandoned me. Of course she loved me. It would be unnatural if she did not."

"And you loved her. I mean no disparagement," Flare added, feeling Steel shift uncomfortably in the saddle. "I loved Sara, too, if we dragons can be said to love mortals. She treated us as intelligent beings. She consulted us, asked our opinions, listened to our advice. *Most* of the time. The one time I could have helped her, she didn't come to me." Flare sighed. "A pity she could never understand our cause. She should have been given the Vision. I suggested as much, but, of course, Lord Ariakan paid no attention to me."

"I'm not certain, from what I've heard, that my own true mother would have understood our cause," Steel said caustically.

"Highlord Kitiara?" Flare chuckled, amused at the thought. "Yes, she was one to walk her own path and Takhisis take anyone who stood in her way. What a fighter, though! Fearless, daring, skilled. I was among those who fought with her at the High Clerist's Tower."

"Not a battle that does her much credit," Steel commented dryly.

"True, she was defeated, but she rose from the ashes to strike down Lord Ariakus and gain the Crown of Power for herself."

"Which led to our ultimate downfall. 'Evil turns upon itself.' A credo of jealousy and treachery that meant destruction. Not anymore. We are allied, brothers in the Vision, and we will sacrifice anything in order to bring it about."

"You have never revealed *your* share of the Vision, Steel Brightblade," Flare observed.

"I am not permitted. Since I did not entirely understand it, I related it to Lord Ariakan. He did not understand it either and said it would be best if I kept it to myself, not discussed it with others."

"I am hardly 'others'!" Flare bridled, the blue mane bristling in indignation.

"I know that," Steel said, softening his tone, patting the dragon on the neck again. "But my lord has forbidden that it be discussed with anyone. I see lights. We must drawing near."

"The lights you see belong to the city of Sanction. We have only to cross the Newsea, and we will be in Abanasinia, very near Solace." Flare scanned the skies, tested the wind, which seemed to be dying. "It is nearly dawn. I will set you and the mage down on the outskirts of the village."

"Where will you hide during the day? It would never do for you to be seen."

"I will take refuge in Xak Tsaroth. The city remains abandoned, even after all these years. People believe it is haunted. It is, but only by goblins. I'll breakfast on a few of those before I sleep. Shall I return for you at nightfall or wait until you summon me?"

"Wait for my summons. I am not yet certain what my plans will be."

Both spoke nonchalantly, neither mentioning the fact that they were far behind enemy lines, would be in danger of their lives every second, and could count on no one for support. Certain knights of the Order of Takhisis were living on the continent of Ansalon, spying, infiltrating, recruiting others to the cause. But even if these other knights became known to Steel, he could make no use of them, could do nothing that would disturb the veil they had drawn around themselves. They had their tasks, according to the Vision, and he had his.

Except he wasn't quite certain what that task was.

Flare left land behind, soared over the Newsea. The red moon had not yet set, but dawn's gray light dimmed Lunitari's luster. It sank down into the sea swiftly, almost as if it were thankful to be shutting its red eye to the world.

Palin moaned in his sleep, spoke his dead brother's name, "Sturm . . ."

The name came eerily in the wake of the remembered Vision. Sturm had been the name of the mage's brother, but that brother had been named for Steel's father.

"Sturm . . ." Palin repeated it.

Steel twisted around in the saddle.

"Wake up!" he ordered roughly, irritably. "You're almost home."

* * * * *

Neither Steel nor Palin knew it, but the dragon set them down in almost the very same spot that had once been the meeting place of two friends, many years ago.

The time then had not been much different from the time now. It had been autumn, not summer, but that was about the only difference. It had been a time of peace, as it was now a time of peace. Most said then, as they said now, that peace would last forever.

Palin Majere slumped against the very same boulder on which Flint Fireforge had once rested. Steel Brightblade walked the path once walked by Tanis Half-Elven. Palin looked down into the valley. The tall vallenwood trees normally hid almost all signs of the village that perched in the trees' limbs. But the thick green foliage was now a dusty brown; many of the leaves had died and fallen off. The houses were visible, naked and forlorn and vulnerable.

Though it was early and the people of Solace were wakening and beginning their day, no smoke of fire or forge rose from the valley. It was dangerous to light a fire of any type; only last week, a tinder-dry vallenwood had gone up in a rush of flame, destroying several houses. Thankfully, no lives had been lost; those within had managed to jump to safety. But since then, people had been leery of burning anything.

The Inn of the Last Home was the largest building in Solace and the first building that the two saw. Palin stared down at his home, longing to run to it, longing to run away from it. Steel had removed the bodies of Palin's brothers from the dragon's back. They now lay, wrapped in linen, on a crude, makeshift sled, fashioned by Steel out of tree branches. He was lashing the remaining few branches together now. When he was finished, they would start their journey down the hill.

"Ready," said Steel. He gave the sled a tug. It lurched over a stone and then skidded along the road, raising a cloud of dust as it went.

Palin did not look at it. He heard it scrape through the dirt, thought of the burden it carried, and clenched his fists against the rending pain.

"Are you fit to walk?" Steel asked, and though the knight's voice was grim and rough, it was respectful, did not mock Palin's sorrow.

For this, Palin was grateful, yet he found it humiliating to be asked such a question. Sturm and Tanin would want him to appear strong, not weak, before the enemy.

"I'm fine," Palin lied. "The sleep helped me, as did the poultice you put over the wound. Shall we go now?"

He rose to his feet and, leaning heavily on the Staff of Magius, started to walk down the hill. Steel followed after, dragging the sled behind. Palin, glancing back, saw the bodies jounce, heard the rattle of armor, as the sled lurched over the rough dirt road. He stumbled, losing his balance.

Steel reached out his hand, steadied Palin.

"It is best to look ahead, not behind," the knight remarked. "What's done is done. You cannot change it."

"You talk as if I'd upset a dish of milk!" Palin returned angrily. "These are my brothers! To know that I'll never talk to them again, never hear them laugh or . . . or . . ." He was forced to stop, swallow his tears. "I don't suppose you've ever lost anyone you care about. You people don't care about anything—except slaughter!"

Steel made no comment, but his face darkened at the mention of losing someone. He trudged on, tugging the heavy sled with ease. His eyes, shadowed beneath lowering black brows, were constantly moving, not aimlessly, but taking note of his surroundings. He stared hard into copses and tangled underbrush.

"What's the matter?" Palin glanced around.

"This would be an excellent place for an ambush," Steel remarked.

Palin's pain-drawn face eased slightly. "In fact, it was. Right over there, the hobgoblin known as Fewmaster Toede stopped Tanis Half-Elven, Flint Fireforge, and Tasslehoff Burrfoot and asked about a blue crystal staff. That moment changed their lives."

He fell silent, thinking about the terrible moments that had changed *his* life and had ended the lives of his brothers. Steel's voice did not interrupt his thoughts, but marched along beside them.

"Do you believe in fate, Sir Mage?" Steel asked abruptly, staring at the dirt-baked road. "That moment, the ambush, changed the half-elf's life, or so you say. This implies that his life would have been different if that moment had never occurred. But what if that moment was *meant* to happen, that there was no way to escape it? Perhaps that moment was lying in ambush for him, waiting for him just as surely as the hobgoblins. What if—" Steel's dark-eyed gaze shifted to Palin. "What if your brothers were born to die on that beach?"

The question was like a blow to the stomach. For a moment, Palin couldn't breathe. The world itself seemed to tip; everything he'd been taught slid away from him. Was there some inexorable Fate crouching behind a bush somewhere, waiting for him? Was he a bug, trapped in a web of time, wriggling and twisting in feeble efforts to escape?

"I don't believe that!" He drew in a deep breath and felt better. His mind cleared. "The gods give us choices. My brothers chose to become knights. They didn't have to. In fact, since they weren't Solamnians and didn't have ancestors who had been knights, the way wasn't easy for them . . ."

"They chose to die, then," Steel said, his gaze shifting to the bodies. "They could have run away, but they did not."

"They did not," Palin repeated softly.

Amazed at the dark knight's question, wondering what lay behind it, Palin examined Steel intently. And the young mage saw, for an instant, the iron visage of hard, cold resolution lift, saw the human face beneath. That face was doubting, seeking, suffering.

He's asking for something, but what? Comfort? Understanding? Palin forgot his own troubles, was prepared to reach out, to offer what poor counsel he could. But at that moment, Steel turned, saw Palin staring at him.

The iron visage dropped. "They chose well, then. They died with honor."

Palin's anger and bitterness returned. "They chose wrong. *I* chose wrong. What's so honorable about that!" He gestured at the bodies on the crude sled. "What honor is there in having to tell my mother . . . to tell her . . ."

Turning on his heel, Palin left the place where Tanis had first heard of the blue crystal staff, and continued on down the road.

He heard Steel's voice, musing, thoughtful, behind him. "Still, it is an excellent place for an ambush."

And then the sound of the sled, bumping and skidding through the dust.

9

A WARNING. The elves take up arms.
Tika takes up the skillet.

A shaft of early morning sunlight shot through one of the dia-
mond-paned windows of the inn, struck Tanis full in the eyes.
He woke up, blinded, and realized he had been asleep, had
dozed off in one of the inn's high-backed wooden booths. He sat up,
rubbing his face and eyes, more than a little angry at himself. He had
fully intended to sit up all night, keeping watch. And there he was,
slumbering like a drunken dwarf.

Across the room from him, the exiled elven king, Porthios, was seated at a table covered with maps, a flask of elven wine and a glass at his
elbow. He was writing something; Tanis wasn't certain what. A report,
a letter to an ally, noting down plans, updating his journal. Tanis
recalled that Porthios had been in much the same position when the
half-elf had drifted off to sleep. The wine flask was slightly less full; that
was the only difference.

The two were brothers, though not by blood. Tanis was married to
Porthios's sister Laurana. They had all been raised together, grown up
together. Porthios was the eldest, had been born to the leadership of his
people, and he took his role seriously. He had not approved of his sister
marrying a half-human, as Porthios invariably viewed Tanis.

Porthios lacked the charm of his father, the late Speaker of the Sun.
Porthios was, by nature, stern, serious, plain-spoken to a fault. He
scorned to tell the diplomatic lie. He was a proud man, but his reticence
and diffidence caused pride to seem like arrogance to those who did not
know him. Instead of endeavoring to overcome this flaw, Porthios used
it to isolate himself from those around him, even from those who loved
and admired him. And there was much to admire. He was a skilled general and a courageous warrior. He had gone to the aid of the Silvanesti,
risked his life to fight Lorac's dread dream, which had decimated their
land. It was their betrayal that had soured him. And, for that, Tanis supposed he couldn't blame his brother-in-law for wanting revenge.

The strife had taken its toll. Once tall and handsome, with a regal
bearing, Porthios had grown somewhat stooped, as if the weight of his
rage and sorrow were bowing him down. His hair had grown long and
ragged, was streaked with gray—something one almost never saw,
even among the eldest elves. He was clad in leather armor, stiff and battered; his fine clothes were beginning to show wear, were starting to

fray at the hem, come apart at the seams. His face was a mask, cold and implacable, bitter. Only occasionally did the mask slip to reveal the man beneath, the man who grieved over his people, even as he planned to go to war against them.

Tanis glanced up as Caramon, yawning, lumbered over and settled his great bulk in the booth opposite his friend.

"I fell asleep," Tanis said, scratching his beard.

Caramon grinned. "Yeah, tell me. Your snoring could have sawed down a vallenwood tree."

"You should have wakened me. I was supposed to be on watch!"

"What for?" Caramon yawned again and rumpled his hair. "It's not like we're in a tower surrounded by forty-seven legions of hobgoblins. You'd been riding all day. You needed the rest."

"That's not the point," Tanis returned. "It looks bad."

He cast a glance at his brother-in-law. And though the elf king wasn't looking at Tanis, Tanis knew by the set of Porthios's jaw and the stiffness of his posture that he was thinking to himself, "Weakling! Pitiful half-human!"

Caramon followed Tanis's glance, shrugged. "You and I both know he'd feel the same way if you stayed awake the rest of your life. C'mon. Let's go wash up."

The big man led the way down the stairs to ground level. The morning was already hot. It seemed to Tanis that the very air itself might catch fire. Beneath the inn stood a water barrel. It was supposed to be filled with water. Caramon peered inside and sighed. The barrel was almost half-empty.

"What happened to the well?" Tanis asked.

"Dried up. Most everyone's well went dry around the end of spring. People've been hauling water from Crystalmir Lake. It's a long journey. This barrel was full last night. Some people are setting guards on their water."

Caramon lifted a ladle, bent over the barrel, brought it up. He offered the water to Tanis.

Tanis peered down at the muddy footprints surrounding the barrel. The mud was still damp.

"But not you," Tanis said. Smiling, he drank the brackish water. "You make that trip every day, to Crystalmir Lake and back, hauling water for the inn. And you never see more than half of it because your neighbors are robbing you of it."

Caramon flushed, splashed water onto his face. "Not robbing. I've told them they could take what they needed. But they feel ashamed, some of them. It's too much like begging, and no one's ever had to beg in Solace, Tanis. Not even when times were hard, after the war. No one ever had to steal just to survive either."

Heaving a sigh, Caramon snorted and blew and toweled his face with the sleeve of his shirt. Tanis laved his face, taking care to use the precious water sparingly. Some of the footprints around the barrel were small, child-sized.

Tanis returned the ladle to its hook on the vallenwood tree. "Has Porthios been awake all night?"

He and Caramon walked back to the bottom of the stairs, but did not immediately climb up. A common room filled with grim and dour-faced elves—half of whom were not speaking to the other half—was not the most pleasant place in the world.

"He never even blinked, that I could see," Caramon remarked, looking up at the window beside which the elf king was sitting. "But then, his wife's having a baby. I know I didn't sleep when Tika was . . . in the same condition."

"That I could understand," Tanis returned grimly. "Any husband could. But Porthios looks more like he's preparing for battle than preparing for fatherhood. I don't suppose he's ever even asked about Alhana."

"Not in so many words," Caramon said slowly. "But then Tika's been coming down pretty often, reassuring him. He really doesn't need to ask. I've been watching him, and I think you're wrong about Porthios. I think he truly loves Alhana and that, right now, she and his unborn child are the most important things in the world to him."

"I wish I could believe that. *I* think he'd trade both to have his kingdom back. It's just— What in the name of the Abyss . . . ?"

The rope bridge above their heads—bridges that served as "roads" connecting the tree-built houses of Solace—swayed and rustled. An elven soldier came skimming along, running fast. By the grim expression on his face, the elf was the bearer of bad news. Tanis and Caramon glanced at one another and raced up the stairs. By the time they reached the inn, the elf was already reporting to Porthios.

"What is it? What's going on?" Caramon demanded, arriving late, puffing and red-faced from the unaccustomed exertion. "What are they saying?"

The urgent conversation was being carried on in the Qualinesti Elvish tongue.

Tanis, listening, silenced the big man with a gesture. What he heard obviously disturbed him. Turning to Caramon, Tanis drew the big man behind the bar.

"Their scouts have reported seeing a soldier, human, with long black hair, wearing accoutrements of darkness, walking down the main road, heading for Solace. And Caramon"—Tanis gripped the big man's arm— "he's in company with a white-robed mage. A young mage."

"Palin," said Caramon instantly. "And the other? You're thinking what I'm thinking?"

"The description fits Steel Brightblade."

"But why would Steel come here? Is he alone?"

"Except for Palin, apparently."

"Then what in the name of all the gods are the two of them doing together? Doing *here* together?"

Tanis kept silent about the rest of the report, about the fact that the dark paladin was dragging behind him a sled bearing what appeared to be the bodies of two knights. He had a grim foreboding he knew the answer to those questions, but he might very well be wrong. He hoped and prayed to Paladine he *was* wrong.

Porthios was issuing orders. The entire contingent of elves was on its feet, reaching for bows and arrows, drawing swords.

Caramon looked at the commotion with alarm.

"What are they doing, Tanis? That might be Palin out there!"

"I know. I'll handle it." Tanis crossed the room to Porthios, broke in. "Pardon me, Brother, but the description of the young mage leads me to believe that he is the son of Caramon Majere, your *host*," he added, with emphasis. "The young man is a White Robe. Surely you can't be think-ing of attacking him."

"We are not going to attack them, Brother," Porthios returned, snap-ping the words, impatient at being interrupted. "We are going to ask them for their surrender. Then we will interrogate them both." He fixed Caramon with a baleful glare, speaking in Common. "Your friend's son may be a White Robe mage, but he is in the company of a soldier of evil."

Caramon's face flushed angry red. "What are you implying?"

"Porthios," Tanis intervened, "you know perfectly well that the dark paladin won't surrender. He'll fight, and your people will fight, and—"

"You do any harm to my son," Caramon said coolly, hands clenching to fists, "and you'll regret it."

He took a step forward.

Elven soldiers—those who were Qualinesti—immediately leapt in front of Porthios. Swords rattled; steel flashed.

"What do you *men* think you are doing?"

Her face pale with fury, her voice tight with scorn, Tika shouldered her way past her husband, glared at him and everyone else in the room. Reaching behind the bar, Tika snatched up the old iron skillet that had once walloped so many draconians on the head.

Advancing on the nearest elf, she threatened him with the skillet.

"Have you fools all gone mad?" she asked in a hissing whisper. "You, sir." The skillet pointed in the direction of Porthios. "Your wife is having your baby! And she's not having an easy time of it, let me tell you! Elves and their small hips and all. And you *men*"—she moved the skillet in an arc—"are down here clashing your swords and acting worse than children! I won't have it. Do you hear me? I won't have it."

Bang went the skillet down on one of the tables.

The elves, looking both foolish and grimly determined, held their positions. Caramon wasn't backing off his. Tika tightened her grip on the skillet's handle.

Tanis had slipped over to stand at Porthios's side. He spoke in low tones, in Elvish, so that neither Tika nor Caramon could understand. "Your scout mentioned that the dark paladin was dragging a sled on which were two bodies. It is possible that these bodies are the sons of Caramon and Tika. Would you disturb the rest of the dead?"

This was the one argument that was likely to persuade Porthios to change his mind. Due to their inordinately long life span, elves revere death and honor the dead.

Porthios glanced at Caramon, appeared irresolute.

Tanis continued, pressing his advantage. "I may be wrong, but I think I know this dark paladin. Let me speak to him and the young mage, alone. If what is going on is what I think is going on, then the paladin—servant of the Dark Queen or not—is acting in an honorable and noble manner, at peril of his life. Let me find out the truth, before blood is shed and the dead dishonored."

Porthios considered the matter. "My guards will accompany you."

"That's not necessary, Brother. Look, the worst that could happen is that I get myself killed," Tanis added dryly.

One side of the elf's stern face twitched. Porthios actually smiled. "Believe it or not, Half-Elven, that would grieve me. I have always liked you, though you might not believe it. There have even been times when I actually admired you. I merely consider you an unsuitable match for my sister."

The smile faded, replaced by lines of sorrow, weariness, overwhelming fatigue. Porthios looked up in the direction of the room where Alhana lay, perhaps fighting for her life, for his child's life.

"Go on, Half-Elven," Porthios said softly, wearily. "Go talk to this honorable spawn of evil. You will do things your way. You always have." He looked back up, and his eyes glinted. "But my guards *will* accompany you."

It was a victory of sorts, and Tanis knew better than to try to gain more ground. He'd won this much only because Porthios was too tired and too worried to argue.

Perhaps, Tanis reflected as he strapped his sword around his waist, the stern and unbending elf does love his wife after all. Tanis wondered what Alhana, elf-queen of the Silvanesti, thought of the man she had married for the sake of politics. Had she come to love him as well?

"It's all right," Tanis said to both Caramon and Tika, reverting back to the Common language. "Porthios has agreed to let me deal with the situation. Tika, you better go back to Alhana."

Not understanding, but relieved that the issue had been settled, Tika sniffed, harrumphed, plunked down the skillet, and hastened upstairs.

Tanis was heading for the door when he noted Caramon carefully untying the apron he wore around his large middle. Obviously, he was preparing to accompany his friend. Tanis crossed quickly over to Caramon, rested his hand on the big man's arm.

"Let me handle this one, Caramon. You might be needed here."

Caramon shook his head. "You're right. That boy out there may be Palin. If it is, something's happened to him."

Tanis tried again, a different approach. "You have to stay behind. Keep an eye on these elves. Porthios is desperate, cornered. He could start trouble. We don't want a bloodbath."

Caramon hesitated, glanced over at the outlawed elf-king.

"If it is Palin, I'll take care of him," Tanis continued. "As if he were my own son." His voice trembled slightly, remembering the loved son he hadn't seen or heard from in months.

Caramon shifted his gaze to Tanis, regarded him with steadfast intensity. "You know something you're not telling me."

Tanis flushed. "Caramon, I—"

The big man sighed, then he shrugged. "Go ahead. I know you'll take care of my boy—and Steel, if it's him that's truly there. Who knows, perhaps he's come to our side after all. I'll keep an eye on Grim-and-Dour there." He jerked a thumb at Porthios.

"Thanks, my friend," Tanis said, and left before either Caramon or Porthios had a chance to change their minds.

IO

An excellent place for an ambush.

I n the woods on the outskirts of Solace, Palin and Steel stopped to rest. Or rather, Palin stopped to rest. Steel stopped in order to remain with Palin. The young mage's wound was troubling him; he was in pain, worn out. True, he was close to home, but this homecoming would bring him no comfort, only the terrible task of telling his parents that two of their children were dead. He sat down on the stump of a tree.

"Here, drink this." Steel thrust a waterskin at the mage.

He accepted it, drank sparingly, as he had learned to do on the road with the knights. He handed it back.

"Thank you. I guess I lost mine during the . . . back at the beach."

Steel didn't hear him, didn't see the proffered waterskin. They were in a small glade that—judging from the abandoned toys and refuse scattered about—was used by the local children as a play area. Steel stood gazing upward, into one of the vallenwoods. Palin, following his line of sight, saw a dark, hulking object in the branches. At first he was startled, then memories returned.

"Don't be alarmed. That's only a tree fort," he said. "My brothers used to play war up there when we were little. *Play* war. It was all a game to us back then. They were the fighters, and I was their mage. When they 'died,' I used to use my 'magic' to bring them back to—"

"Children play here, you say," Steel interrupted, talking loudly.

His hand gripped Palin's shoulder hard. The knight wasn't offering sympathy, Palin realized, startled. That grip was a warning.

"Keep talking," Steel said softly. His right hand was on Palin's shoulder, while his left held a dagger. Palin could see the flash of the blade beneath the knight's dark blue cloak.

Palin tensed, his hand instinctively reaching for his bag of spell components. Then he remembered where he was. This was *Solace*, for mercy's sake!

He rose, a bit unsteadily, to his feet. "It's probably just the local kids—"

Steel cast Palin a brief, flashing-eyed glance. "It is not children." His gaze went back to the trees. "Elves. Do as I command, and keep out of my way."

"Elves! You can't be—"

Steel's grip on Palin's arm tightened painfully.

Palin lowered his voice to a whisper. "There aren't any elves within fifty leagues of—"

"Shut up," Steel said coolly. "What magic spells do you have prepared?"

Palin was bewildered. "I . . . I . . . None, really. I never thought . . . Look, this is my home—"

A *pftt* sound, followed by a thunk, interrupted him. A feathered shaft quivered on the tree stump where Palin had been seated. The arrow was of elven make and design.

Five elven warriors dropped out of the trees, landed lightly on the ground. Quicker than the eye could follow, the elves raised their bows, arrows nocked and ready. Four arrows were pointed at Steel. One was aimed at Palin.

He gaped at the elves, astonished and bewildered. The only thought to surface amidst the confusion was that, once again, he'd failed. Even if he had committed to memory his magical spells, what few he possessed were almost worthless—or so he considered them. And the moment he started reciting the words, he'd likely be dead anyway, an arrow through his heart.

Steel released Palin. Shoving the dagger in his belt, the knight drew his sword, faced his enemies.

"You are a creature of evil, though of what manner, we cannot tell," said one of the elves to Steel. "We could have killed you back there, on the road. But your conversation with this White Robe interested us. That and the fact that you have with you the bodies of two Knights of Solamnia. They must be true, then, the rumors we've heard. My lord will be interested in speaking to you."

Steel tossed his cloak back over one shoulder, proudly revealing the insignia he wore upon his breastplate: the skull and the death lily. "See this and see your doom. I am a Knight of Takhisis. I care nothing about what rumors you may have heard and, as for your lord, he can go to the Abyss."

The elves drew back their bowstrings.

"If you're going to do something, Sir Mage, I suggest you do it now," Steel said softly, grimly.

Palin licked dry lips, spoke the first and only magical word that came into his mind. "*Shirak!*"

The crystal ball atop the Staff of Magius burst into radiant light, momentarily blinding the elves. They blinked, turned their heads away.

"Well done!" Steel said and leapt forward, swinging his sword in a lethal arc.

"No! Wait!" Palin caught hold of Steel's arm, attempting to drag him back.

The light of the staff dimmed. The elves could see again, if not perfectly, at least well enough. An arrow tore through the sleeve of Palin's robe. Another struck and bounced off Steel's breastplate. The next two would find their marks.

"*Astanti!*" came the sharp command in what Palin recognized as Qualinesti Elvish.

The elves lowered their bows, searched for the source of the order.

"Put down your weapons, all of you," the voice continued, shifting to the Common language. "You, too, Steel Brightblade."

Startled at hearing his name spoken from behind him, Steel fell back, but only to see what new danger threatened him. He kept his sword raised.

Tanis Half-Elven, accompanied by six elven warriors, strode into the glade. He was alone, bore no weapons, though his sword hung from his belt. His gaze flicked over the two bodies bound to the sled, glanced briefly over Palin and Steel, finally focused on the elven warriors holding the two hostage.

"I have been sent by your lord, Porthios," Tanis said to the elves, continuing to speak Common in order that Palin and—especially—Steel would understand what the half-elf was saying. "Ask your comrades who accompany me, if you don't believe me."

One of the elves who had arrived with Tanis gave a brief nod of his head.

"I know both these men," Tanis continued, moving to stand in front of Palin and Steel, shielding them with his own body. "It is my belief that you have misunderstood their intentions—"

"What intentions do you attribute to this slave of darkness?" one of the elves demanded. "Other than our destruction?"

"That's what I intend to find out," Tanis returned. He placed his hand on Steel's shoulder, cautioning the knight to restrain himself. "Trust me," he said in low tones. "Trust me now as you trusted me in the High Clerist's Tower. I won't betray you. I think I know why you've come."

Steel tried to shake free. His blood was hot; he was eager for a fight.

"You can't win," Tanis repeated softly. "You will die uselessly. Would your queen want that?"

Steel hesitated, wrestling with the battle-lust. The fire faded from his eyes, leaving them dark and chill. With an ill grace, he thrust his sword back in its sheath.

"Your turn." Tanis looked around at the elves.

Slowly, sullenly, they lowered their bows. They might not have done so at Tanis's request, but the elf sent by Porthios added force to the command with a gesture of his own.

"Return to your posts," Tanis ordered. "Leave us alone a moment," he added to Porthios's soldiers.

The elves backed off, retreated into the shadows of the vallenwood trees. But they remained in sight and in arrow range.

Now that they were alone, Tanis turned to Palin. "Tell me, Son. Tell me what happened."

The kind voice, the familiar face, the thought of the tidings he bore were too much. Tears blurred Palin's vision, choked off his voice.

"Courage," said Tanis, adding, "tears are nothing to be ashamed of, Palin, but there is a time for weeping, and this isn't it, believe me! I need to know what you are doing here. Both of you. And I need to know *now*, before we all end up looking like something out of your mother's sewing basket."

Courage, young one, came a whisper. *I am with you.*

Palin started, trembled. He'd heard that voice before, knew it as well as he knew his father's voice. Or, maybe, better. It had not spoken to him in a long, long time.

Surely, he thought, this is a sign!

His tears dried. He related the events of yesterday, events that seemed so very far away.

"We were sent to Kalaman to look over its fortifications and report back how it could best be defended, in case of attack from the north. We were a small contingent, maybe fifty people, altogether. But only about twenty knights. The rest were squires, pages, commoners who drove the baggage carts. We spent several months at Kalaman, supervising the strengthening of fortifications there. Then we rode eastward, intending to go to North Keep. It was on our way there . . ."

He paused, drew a shivering breath, then continued. "We were riding along the coast. We made camp that night. The sea was calm, empty. At dawn, we saw the first ship."

"But surely you had dragons flying with your forces. How did they miss—"

"We had no dragons, Tanis," Palin said, his pale cheeks flushing faint crimson. "High Command didn't think it was necessary, didn't like to impose on them."

"Fools!" said Tanis bitterly. "There should have been dragons. There should have been five hundred knights, not twenty. I told them. I warned them!"

"They didn't really believe anything you said." Palin sighed. "They only sent us in order to 'placate' you. I'm sorry, Tanis. That was what we heard from our commander. None of the knights took what we were doing very seriously. It was more of a . . . a holiday."

Tanis shook his head, glanced over at the shrouded bodies. "Why didn't you return to North Keep to warn the others?"

"There was only one ship at first," Palin explained lamely. "One of the Lord Knights laughed and said something to the effect that we had beaten them twenty-six years ago, we'd beat them now."

"Fools," Tanis repeated, but he muttered it into his beard.

"We drew up along the shoreline, waiting for them. Everyone was joking, singing. And then . . ." Palin's voice trembled. "Then a second ship came into view. And then a third. After that, we lost count."

"And you stayed to fight. Outnumbered, hopeless."

"The enemy could see us from ships," Palin returned defensively. "How would it look if we ran?"

"Sensible?" Tanis demanded.

Palin's flush deepened. He looked down at the bodies, blinked his eyes rapidly.

Tanis sighed, scratched his beard. "They all died?" he asked in low tones.

Palin swallowed, nodded. "I was the only survivor." He spoke so quietly that Tanis had to lean forward to hear him.

"Your brothers, Tanin . . . Sturm . . ."

Palin pointed at the sled.

"Paladine keep them," Tanis said. He put his arm around Palin. The young man was shivering, but holding up well. "You were taken prisoner, I assume." He glanced at Steel.

Palin nodded, unable to respond.

"That much I understand," Tanis continued, "but I'm a bit confused as to why *you* came here, Steel Brightblade." Tanis's voice hardened. "Were you responsible for their deaths?"

Steel was scornful. "What difference would it make if I had killed them? We are soldiers. This is war. I assume they knew the risks, else they would not have been knights."

"It makes a difference, believe me," Tanis said. "You are cousins. Of the same blood. I ask again: did you slay them?"

Palin intervened. "He didn't, Tanis. We were attacked by strange, outlandish men, barbarians who painted their bodies blue. But the barbarians were led by knights."

"I am a knight. I fight on dragonback," Steel said proudly. "The Solamnics fell to the ground forces."

"I see," Tanis said thoughtfully, undoubtedly storing away this vital information to be given to the commander of the Solamnic Knights in the High Clerist's Tower. He shifted his gaze back to Steel. "I still don't understand why you came. If it was for Palin's ransom money, that could have been handled by any messenger. . . ."

"I have come to repay a debt. The bodies of the dead were to be placed in a common tomb. With honor, of course," Steel added, dark eyes flashing. "They fought bravely. They did *not* run, as some might have counseled. But word of their deaths will not reach their families for some time. Perhaps never. When I discovered the name of the young mage here, and found out that his two brothers had been killed in the battle, I took the opportunity of paying back the debt I owe their father, Caramon Majere. I have brought back the bodies of his two sons for proper burial."

"You bring back the dead," Tanis said, regarding the knight with incredulity, "at the risk of your own life?"

Steel shrugged. "What is life without honor?"

"*Est Sularus oth Mithas,*" Tanis murmured. " 'My honor is my life.' You are your father all over again."

Steel's face darkened. His hand clenched over the hilt of his sword. "I am a Knight of Takhisis," he said coldly. "I honor my father's memory, but that is all it is—a memory. I live only to serve my queen."

Tanis's gaze went pointedly to the knight's neck. The sword was not the only gift the dead father had given his son. By some magical means beyond Tanis's understanding, the starjewel Sturm Brightblade had worn around his neck had been transferred to his son. The jewel was an object of good, of elven make, a token of affection. No person whose heart was shadowed by darkness could even touch it, much less wear it. Yet Tanis had seen it shining on Steel Brightblade's breast.

Did he wear it now, concealed beneath the hideous armor with its symbols of death and destruction? Or had he forsworn it, ripped it off, sacrificed it on the Dark Queen's bloodstained altar?

Tanis could not see the jewel. Steel returned the half-elf's gaze coolly, not the least self-conscious. If he wore the jewel, he was disciplined enough to hide any indication of it.

A dangerous man, thought Tanis. If all Takhisis's paladins are like this, we are indeed in trouble.

"Is Kalaman under attack?" Tanis asked, looking at Steel.

"It will be," the knight replied. "And North Keep by now. I am not betraying any secrets. Lord Ariakan *wants* the Solamnics to hear how they were routed."

Tanis regarded Steel in grim silence, then turned back to Palin, who appeared to be on the verge of collapse. "We'll discuss this all later. First, we need to take you home. I will help you break the news of your brothers' deaths to your parents. Remember, Palin, your parents were both soldiers. This will grieve them, certainly, but—"

"There's more, Tanis," Palin said.

Tanis had already guessed as much. "You're being held for ransom."

"Yes. And if the ransom is not paid, my life is forfeit."

"And how much is this ransom? No matter," Tanis added hurriedly. "However much it is, we'll come up with the money. I'll be glad to contribute. So will—"

"It's not money they want, Tanis," Palin interrupted, somewhat impatiently. "I am a magic-user, after all."

"An apprentice," Tanis said, affecting a carelessness he did not feel. He had a terrible foreboding that he knew what was coming, hoped to stave it off. He slapped Palin on the shoulder. "Don't give yourself airs, young man."

Tanis looked at Steel. "As I said, this young mage is an apprentice. He only recently passed the Test. The wizards might exchange a few paltry arcane items for him, but nothing of value. You knights would be far better off settling for money . . ."

"Palin Majere may be only an apprentice mage. But his uncle, Raistlin Majere, was not," Steel returned dryly. "He has given his nephew one valuable gift." The knight gestured to the Staff of Magius. "I have no doubt but that he would provide more if he knew the young man's life was in danger."

"Has the whole world gone mad?" Tanis demanded. "Raistlin Majere is dead! He's been dead for twenty years or more. He didn't give Palin the staff. Dalamar the Dark gave Palin the staff . . ."

Steel gazed at him with those impassive, dark eyes.

"I'm wasting my breath! What is the ransom?" Tanis asked.

"They want the Portal opened," Palin answered quietly. "The Gray Knights want to find the way into the Abyss."

"When the Portal is open," Steel said, "our queen will enter the world. And we will place this world at her feet!"

II

The ransom.
Raistlin's Room. Palin's plan.

Steel stood just inside the door to the Inn of the Last Home. He stood aloof, cold, proud, not moving, showing no emotion as Tanis broke, as gently as he could, the news to Tika and Caramon that their two eldest sons were dead.

"I knew it!" was Tika's first response. She clasped her hands over her heart. "Blessed Paladine, I knew it. I felt it here. Oh, dear gods, why? Why?" She clenched her hands, rocked back and forth in her chair.

Palin put his arms around his mother. "I'm sorry," he said brokenly. "I'm so sorry. . . ."

Caramon sat stunned. "My boys," he whispered. "My boys." And then, with a great sob, he reached out, drew Palin close. "At least you are safe . . ."

Tanis stood apart, waiting for the first transports of grief to subside, waiting to impart even more bad news to the bereft parents. Palin was *not* safe, was in far more danger than they could ever imagine.

At length, Palin wiped away his tears, looked at Tanis.

"You tell them," he said softly.

"Tell us? Tell us what?" Caramon demanded, his head bowed, tense, quivering.

"Palin is a prisoner of the dark knights," Tanis said. "They are demanding ransom."

"Well, of course we'll pay it, whatever it is," Caramon responded. "We'll sell all we own if we have to—"

"It's not money they want, Caramon," Tanis said, searching for some easy way to say this and finding none. "They want the wizards to open the Portal to the Abyss. They want to use Palin to set free the Dark Queen."

Caramon lifted his grief-ravaged face, stared from Tanis to Palin to Steel. "But . . . this is a farce! A mockery! The wizards will never open the Portal! It's a death sentence! You won't take him! You won't!"

Before any in the room could stop him, Caramon sprang from his chair and flung himself at Steel. The big man's weight and momentum sent them both crashing against the wall.

"Caramon, stop!" Tanis and Palin struggled to drag Caramon off the dark knight. Caramon was trying to get his hands around Steel's throat. "This won't help!"

Steel drew no weapon. Reaching up, he seized Caramon's arms, managed to break the big man's hold. He shoved Caramon back into the arms of his son and his friend. Steel stood, breathing hard, wary and watchful.

"I make allowances now for your grief," he said coldly. "I won't another time."

"Caramon! Dearest husband!" Tika clung to him, soothed him. "We'll deal with this. Tanis is here. He'll help us. He won't let them take Palin back. You won't, will you, Tanis?"

Her eyes were frightened, pleading. Tanis wished with all his heart he could tell her what she wanted so desperately to hear. As it was, he could only shake his head.

Tika sank back down in her chair, her hands wrapped up in her apron, clenching the cloth tightly. No tears came to Tika. Not now. Not yet. Her wound was too deep. She couldn't yet feel it, only a chill numbness. And so she sat and stared at the floor and waited for the pain.

"Father," Palin said in low tones. "If I could talk to you . . . "

"Take *me* back, damn you!" Caramon demanded, breaking free of Tika's loving grip. "My life in exchange for my son's. You can hold *me* prisoner until you hear the wizards' answer."

"You speak as a father should, sir," Steel replied, "but you must know such a request is impossible. Our wizards know the worth of the nephew of Raistlin Majere. They deem it likely that the archmage himself might take some interest in the young man's welfare."

"My brother!" Caramon was bewildered. "My brother is dead! What can *he* do?"

"Father!" Palin whispered urgently, tugging on his father's sleeve. "Please! We need to talk!"

Caramon paid no attention.

Steel smiled sardonically, shrugged.

"Let us hope that he can do something, sir." Steel's smile tightened. "Or else you lose a third son."

Tika gasped, moaned, stuffed her clenched fist into her mouth. Tanis was at her side, but Dezra, coming down the stairs, elbowed him away. She put her arms around Tika, whispered soothing words.

"Come. Come with me, dear. Come upstairs and rest."

Tika looked around at her friend as if she didn't know her. Then she closed her eyes, laid her head on Dezra's breast, and began to sob.

Her own eyes shimmering with tears, Dezra looked over at Tanis.

"You might tell that elf lord that his lady's time is almost due. She is in good health and good spirits. I think all will be well with her and with the babe."

"Porthios is waiting outside," Tanis said. Merciful gods, he'd forgotten all about this other crisis. "I'll let him know."

"He should be here, nearby," Dezra said angrily. "What's he doing, running off like that?"

"It was best he left, Dezra. I had trouble enough persuading him to go as it was. We almost had a war break out right here."

Steel, at the mention of the elf, put his hand on his sword's hilt. His lip curled.

"War!" Dezra said bitterly. "A new life coming into a world of sorrow. Maybe it would be better if the baby were born dead!"

"Don't say that, Dezra!" Tika cried suddenly. "Each new child born is hope for a better world. I have to believe that. My boys' lives meant something!"

"Yes, dear. They did. I'm sorry. I wasn't thinking. Come upstairs," Dezra said, weeping. "I . . . I can use your help with Lady Alhana. If you're up to it."

"A new life," Tika murmured. "One leaves. One enters. Yes, I can help. I can help . . ."

"Father," said Palin, when his mother was out of the room. "We need to talk. Now."

Startled by the unaccustomed firmness in his son's tone, Caramon looked around.

Palin's face was deathly pale and drawn. Gray smudges shadowed his eyes.

"I . . . I'm sorry, Son," Caramon mumbled, rumpling his hair. "I . . . don't quite know what I'm doing. You should lie down, though. Go and rest . . ."

"I will, Father," Palin said patiently. He took hold of his father's arm. "Come with me. Come and talk. It's all right if we speak alone?"

Steel, to whom this was addressed, granted permission with a brief nod. "You have given me your word of honor that you will not try to escape, Sir Mage."

"And I will keep it," Palin said with dignity. "Father, please."

"Go with him, Caramon," Tanis urged. "Your other two sons are with Paladine. It is Palin who needs you now."

"I don't understand this, Tanis." Caramon's face twisted in grief and puzzlement. "Raistlin's dead! What more do they want from him? I don't understand."

Tanis had his doubts about that. Was Raistlin truly dead? Or had the gray-robed wizards of Takhisis discovered differently? Tanis guessed that Palin knew more than he was letting on.

"I need to talk to Dalamar," Tanis muttered when Palin and Caramon had left the room. "I need to talk to the Lord Knight. We are in trouble. Real trouble."

But right now, the only person he had to talk to was Porthios.

And that to tell him that his child would soon be born.

One leaves the world. One enters.

Hope?

At the moment, Tanis couldn't see it.

* * * * *

Years ago, Caramon had built for Tika the finest house in Solace. The house was large enough to accommodate a growing family and for many years echoed with the laughter and roughhousing of the Majeres' three boys. Later, two daughters came into the world—for the express purpose of teasing their elder brothers, or so Palin often maintained.

By that time, Caramon and Tika were full owners and proprietors of the Inn of the Last Home. The boys were soon grown to manhood and off on adventures of their own. The house was some distance from the inn. The walk there and back, at all hours of the day and night (Tika often woke up with the firm conviction that the inn had caught fire and was constantly sending Caramon over to check on it) was time-consuming and wearing. Eventually—though both of them loved the house—Tika and Caramon decided that it would be easier to sell their dwelling place and take up residence in the inn itself.

One room in the old house had been denoted Raistlin's Room. In the early days, after his twin brother had turned to the Black Robes and moved into the Tower of High Sorcery in Palanthas, Caramon had maintained the room in the fond but deluded hope that one day Raistlin would see the error of his ways and return.

Following Raistlin's death, Caramon had planned to make the room "just another room," but his hopes and dreams had centered on it so completely that they were like ghosts, refused to be dislodged. Raistlin's Room continued as such until the day the house was sold. When the Majeres moved into the inn, no thought was given to creating another "Raistlin's Room" until one day Caramon was startled to overhear his two little girls referring to one of the rooms—a small storage room in the back—as Raistlin's Room.

Tika put this down to the fact that the girls were attempting to make their new and unfamiliar home as much like the home they'd left as possible. Caramon agreed, but both fell into the habit of terming the room Raistlin's. A traveling mage, staying at the inn, happened to overhear them and begged to be allowed to see the room in which the famous mage had undoubtedly spent much of his time.

Caramon did his best to dissuade the wizard of his mistaken notion—this part of the inn had not even existed during Raistlin's lifetime. But the Red Robe was adamant and, because he was a regular and valued customer (he paid in steel, not in lizard's teeth), Caramon permitted the guest to visit the storage room.

The wizard found the room charming, though a bit cluttered with brooms and the wood box. He asked if he could leave a magical ring—as a "token of his esteem." Caramon couldn't very well refuse. The wizard placed the ring on top of an empty ale barrel and left.

Afraid to touch the arcane object (Caramon had seen enough magic to know that he might end up a lizard himself), he left it where it was. A month later, two white-robed mages arrived, coming specifically to visit the "shrine." Apparently, the first wizard, after leaving the inn, had run into a phenomenal streak of good luck. This being rather unusual for the Red Robe, he immediately attributed it to Raistlin's goodwill. The wizard had spread the tale, and these two were here to add their small "tokens."

The ale barrel acquired a scroll and a potion. The wizards stayed two nights, spending money and talking of Raistlin with Caramon, who was always pleased to reminisce. A month following that, a Black Robe arrived. She came and left without speaking to anyone, except to inquire the location of "the room." She didn't stay the night, but she did order the best wine in the house and paid for it in steel.

Soon, mages from all over Ansalon were visiting the inn. Some left arcane objects as gifts, others left their spell components to be "enhanced," returning to pick them up later. Those who did this swore that the objects increased in magic.

Tika scoffed at the notion that the room had any special "powers." She attributed the notion to the general weirdness of mages. Caramon agreed, until one day—rummaging through some of Otik's old papers—the big man came across a crude diagram of the old inn, prior to its destruction by dragons during the War of the Lance. Looking at it, reliving bittersweet memories, Caramon was amazed (and considerably taken aback) to discover that "Raistlin's Room" was situated directly over the place near the fire where his brother had been accustomed to sitting.

Following this discovery, (which gave even Tika "the shivers" or so she said), Caramon emptied out the storage room, removed the brooms and the wood box (though he left the ale barrel, which now had innumerable mysterious-looking items resting on it).

He began keeping careful record of all the arcane objects. He never sold any of those bequeathed as "gifts," but he often gave them away to mages who had fallen on hard times or to young mages about to take the grueling and sometimes lethal Test in the Tower of High Sorcery at Wayreth. He had the feeling that such gifts would be particularly blessed, for—despite his many faults—Raistlin had always felt a special kinship for the weak and downtrodden and would go out of his way to aid them.

It was to this room, to Raistlin's Room, that Palin now took his father.

The small room had changed considerably over the years. The ale barrel was still there, but specially carved wooden chests had been added to hold the many magical rings, brooches, weapons, and spell pouches. A rack placed against one wall contained all the various scrolls, tied neatly with white, red, or black ribbons. Spellbooks lined one wall; the more gruesome arcane objects were hidden in a shadowed corner. A small window let in sunlight and—what was more important to the mages—the light of the red and silver moons and the unseen light of the black moon. A bowl of freshly cut flowers rested on a table beneath the window. A comfortable chair had been placed inside the room for the convenience of those who came to meditate or study. No kender were ever allowed anywhere near this room.

Caramon entered, without truly knowing where he was or caring, and sat in the room's only chair. Despite his wound and his weariness, Palin was stronger than his father at this moment. For Palin, the terrible debilitating grief was starting to recede. Perhaps it was the calming influence of this room—which he'd always loved. Or perhaps it was the voice inside his head—the voice he knew so well, though he had never heard it in life—that was responsible. Somewhere, somehow, Raistlin lived.

"It is my duty to find him, if I have to enter the Abyss itself."

"What?" Caramon jerked his head up, regarded his son with darkening brow. "What did you say?"

Palin hadn't realized he'd been speaking out loud. He hadn't meant to broach the subject so abruptly, but—since he'd blurted it out and since obviously his father knew what he was thinking—Palin decided it was best to carry on.

"I wanted you to know this, Father. I have formed a plan and intend to act on it. I . . . don't expect you to approve it." Palin paused, swallowed, then went steadily on. "But you should be aware of what I'm doing, in case anything goes wrong. I'm *not* going to the Tower of Wayreth—"

"Good lad!" Caramon exclaimed in relief. "We'll think of something. I'll fight Takhisis herself to keep you safe. I won't let these evil knights take you—"

"Father, please!" Palin said sharply. "I'm not going to the Tower of Wayreth because I am going to the Tower of High Sorcery in Palanthas. I'm going to try to enter the Abyss. I'm going to try to find my uncle."

Caramon's jaw went slack; he stared at his son in bewilderment. "But Raistlin's not in the Abyss, Son. Paladine accepted his sacrifice. Your uncle was granted peace in eternal sleep."

"You don't know that for certain, Father. The last you saw of him, he was inside the Abyss."

"But I saw him, Palin! I saw him asleep, as he used to sleep when we were children."

"It was a dream, Father, you said so yourself. You know what the bards say: that Raistlin is being held prisoner in the Abyss, tormented daily by Takhisis, his body torn and bleeding. That every day he dies in agony, only to be brought back to life and—"

Caramon was no longer bewildered. It generally took the big man time to think through a problem, but there could be only one answer to this question. He rose to his feet.

"I know what the bards say," he said grimly. "I know that the bards have it that Sturm Brightblade traveled to the red moon! All nonsense! Raistlin is dead! He has been dead and at peace all these many long years! I forbid you to go. You will stay here, and we'll negotiate with Lord Ariakan. Tanis will help us . . ."

The Staff of Magius was warm in Palin's hand, warm to the touch. The warmth surged through him like hot, spiced wine, gave him courage.

"You *want* to believe Raistlin is dead, Father. To think otherwise means that you abandoned him."

The blow was struck, the arrow fired, the spear thrown.

The wound inflicted was dreadful.

Caramon went dead white; he might have lain down in the grave with his two sons. His breathing came fast and shallow. He opened and shut his mouth, not saying anything. The big body trembled.

Palin bit his lip, held fast to the staff for support. He was aghast at what he'd done, what he'd said. He hadn't meant to. The words had flown from his mouth before he could stop them. And now that they were sped, Palin could no more take the hurt back than he had been able to halt the life draining from his brothers' bodies.

"You don't mean that," Caramon said in a low, shaking voice.

"No, Father, I don't. I'm sorry. I know you would have risked anything to go back after Raistlin. I know the dream brought you comfort and that you sincerely believe in it. But, Father," Palin continued, "you could be wrong."

You could be wrong . . .

The words echoed in his head, took life and form and shape until he could almost imagine that he saw them burning in front of him, in front of his father.

Caramon gulped, shook his head, seemed to be fumbling for arguments.

He's going to try to talk me out of this. I can't let him, Palin realized. I might be too easily dissuaded. I remember what it was like, once before, in the tower. And that was only illusion, only my Test. But the fear, the terror, was real.

"I've thought this out, Father. Steel Brightblade is sworn to accompany me. He will take me to the tower. Once I am there, I will talk with Dalamar, persuade him to let me try to pass the guardian. If he won't"—Palin's voice hardened—"I will try it myself. The specter let me pass once before—"

"That was an illusion!" Caramon was angry now. "The wizards made it all up! You know that! They told you."

"Did they make up this, Father?" Palin thrust forward the Staff of Magius. "Is this illusion? Or is this my uncle's staff?"

Caramon glanced uneasily at the staff, did not answer.

"The staff was locked inside my uncle's laboratory, along with the Portal to the Abyss. Not even Dalamar himself can enter that room. Yet, somehow, the Staff of Magius left it. And it came to me. I'm going into that room, Father. I'm going to find my uncle. He's going to teach me all he knows. Never again will anyone die because I am too weak to save them!"

"You're going to try to open the Portal yourself? And where is the true cleric who will help you? Have you forgotten? The Portal can be entered only by a mage of great power, in the company of a true cleric. That was why your uncle needed Lady Crysania . . ."

"*I* don't intend to open the Portal, Father," Palin said, his voice low. "It won't be opened from this side at all."

"Raistlin!" Caramon shouted. "You expect Raistlin to open it for you! This is madness!" He shook his head. "The dark knights have set a ransom impossible to fulfill. You owe them nothing! Don't worry," he added grimly, "between us, Tanis and I will deal with Sir Brightblade out there."

"I gave my pledge of honor, Father, that I would not escape," Palin returned with asperity. "Would you have me break it, you who always taught me that my spoken pledge was my bond?"

Caramon gazed steadily at his son; tears glimmered on his lashes. "You think you are clever, don't you, Palin? You've driven me into a corner, used my own words against me. Your uncle used to do that. He was good at it. He was good at getting his own way, no matter who he hurt. Go then. Do what you will. I can't stop you, anymore than I could stop him."

With that, Caramon rose and, with dignity, walked past his son and out of the room.

Chilled, shaken, Palin remained seated. His father was right, of course. Palin had often used his quick wits and his glib words to run circles around his slower-thinking father and brothers, like a dog baiting a chained bear. And they had always given way. It was after one such cajoling that his brothers had permitted him—against their better judgment—to ride with them to Kalaman. He'd pleaded, argued, manipulated. They had given way. And now, because they'd been preoccupied over protecting him instead of concentrating on their fighting, they were both dead.

His wound throbbed. Palin stared at the chair in which his father had been sitting, and remembered.

*　*　*　*　*

Run. It was the sensible thing to do.

Fleeing the oncoming enemy would have been sensible, and the small band of knights and their young mage talked about running, in those few flurried moments in which they had time to talk.

The black-prowed ships stood out to sea. Boats filled with men plied to shore. The wings of innumerable blue dragons cut off the light of the sun. On the beach, where they had ridden for the pleasure of the day, to enjoy the beauty of the seascape, the small band of Solamnic Knights, caught in the open, was vastly outnumbered.

"If we flee, we will get separated, scattered," their commander said to them, shouting his words to be heard over the crashing surf.

"And where can we go that the dragons will not follow us?" Tanin said. "They'll chase after us and pick us off, one by one, and mock forever the cowardice of Solamnic Knights! I say we stand and fight."

"We will stay," Palin said firmly.

"No, Palin, not you." Tanin turned to him. "You travel light. Your horse is swift. This is no place for you. Ride back to Kalaman. Warn them of what is coming."

"What? Me ride off and leave you two, my brothers, to fight alone?" Palin was outraged. "You really think I'd do that?"

Tanin and Sturm had exchanged glances. Sturm shook his head, averted his gaze, stared back out to the sea filled with boats that were full of men. They did not have much time. Tanin rode close to Palin, grasped his arm.

"Sturm and I knew the risks when we took the oath of knighthood. But not you, Palin . . ."

"I won't leave," Palin said grimly. "You're always sending me home, Tanin, whenever there's trouble. Well, not this time."

Tanin, his face flushed in anger, leaned over his saddle. "Damn it, Palin! This isn't some fight against the neighborhood bully! We're going to die! And how do you think Father and Mother are going to feel when they have to bury all three of their sons? Especially you, their youngest?"

For a moment, Palin could say nothing. He had a mental image of turning tail, racing away, forced to tell his parents shamefacedly, "I don't know what happened to my brothers . . ."

Palin lifted his head. "Would *you* leave *me* behind, Tanin?"

"No, but—" Tanin tried to argue.

Palin continued. "Am I less honor-bound because I am a wizard? We take oaths of our own. By the magic and by Solinari, I will stay and I will fight this evil with you, though it cost me my life."

Sturm smiled wryly. "He's got you, there, Tanin. Not much you can say against that."

Tanin hesitated. Palin was his responsibility, or so he considered it. And then, suddenly, he held out his hand. "Very well, my brothers." His gaze included Sturm and Palin. "This day we fight for Paladine and"—he smiled slightly—"and for Solinari."

The three brothers clasped hands, then separated to join the other knights, who were deploying along the sandy beach.

That was all Palin remembered clearly. The battle had been brief, hard-fought, bitter. The blue-painted barbarians, wildly shrieking, jumped from their boats and ran up the shore, their mouths open wide, as if to drink the blood of their enemies, their eyes gleaming with battle-lust. They broke upon the knights like a tidal wave, battling with unnerving ferocity, delighting in the slaughter.

The knights, more disciplined, better warriors, cut down the first row of attackers; one of Palin's fireball spells exploded right in the barbarians' midst, blasting flesh, leaving corpses scorched and smoldering.

But there was a second wave and a third, men trampling the bodies of their comrades in order to reach the knights who had slain them. Palin remembered his brothers closing ranks in front of him, trying to protect him—or at least, he thought he remembered that. About that time, something struck him on the head—a thrown spear, perhaps, partially deflected by one of his brothers.

That was the last he saw of them alive.

When Palin came to his senses, the battle was over. Two dark knights stood guard over him. He had longed to ask of the others, but had forbore, dreading to know the truth.

And then Steel came and Palin knew . . .

* * * * *

Palin sighed, stood up. He went to the door to Raistlin's Room, looked out into the hallway, down the stairs that led into the common room, which was all but deserted. Steel was there alone, sitting rigid, upright in a chair, refusing to let his guard down, refusing to sleep, though the gods knew he must have needed it.

Palin stared into the common room and missed seeing his brothers, missed their laughter, missed their teasing, which had once driven him to distraction. He would have given all the wealth in Ansalon to sit through another of Tanin's "elder-brother" lectures, to hear Sturm's chortling laughter. He missed the little sisters, whose teasing drove him wild. Due to the arrival of the elves and the possibility of trouble, Caramon and Tika had sent the girls to stay with Goldmoon and Riverwind, tribal leaders in Que-shu. Yet he was truly thankful that the little girls, Laura and Dezra, were not here to see their older brothers buried in the ground. Bad enough that they would come home and find the graves. At that moment, their carefree childhood would end.

Tanis Half-Elven came up the stairs, paused at the top.

"You've made up your mind to go, so Caramon tells me."

Palin nodded. "Where is Father?"

"With your mother. Leave him be, Palin," Tanis advised gently. "Let him work this out in his own way, his own time."

"I didn't mean—" Palin began, swallowed, then started over. "I have to do this, Tanis. My father doesn't understand. No one understands. It's his voice. I hear his voice . . ."

Tanis regarded Palin in concern. "You'll stay for the burial rites?"

"Of course," Palin answered. "But after that, we will leave."

"Before you go anywhere, you must rest and eat and drink. You and Steel Brightblade both," Tanis said, "if I can convince him that he's not going to be poisoned or stabbed in his sleep. How like his father he is!" Tanis added, accompanying Palin into the common room. "How many times have I seen Sturm Brightblade, sitting just like that, dead tired, but too proud to admit it."

Steel rose to his feet as the two approached. Whether he stood out of respect for Tanis or out of wariness or both was uncertain. His face was stern and implacable, gave no hint of his thoughts or feelings.

"It is time we were away," he said, looking at Palin.

"Sit down," Palin said. "I'm not leaving until after my brothers are properly buried. There's food and drink. The meat's cold, but so is the ale. I'll fix a room for you. You can sleep here tonight."

Steel's face darkened. "I have no need—"

"Yes, you do," Palin returned. "You'll need your rest, where we're going. Travel to Palanthas will be safer for us after dark anyway."

"Palanthas!" Steel frowned. "Why should we want to go to Palanthas—a stronghold of the Solamnic Knights? Unless this is some sort of trap—"

"No trap," Palin said, sinking wearily into a chair. "We're going to Palanthas because the Portal is there, in the Tower of High Sorcery at Palanthas."

"We want the wizards to agree to open the Portal. This countermands my orders," Steel returned.

"I am going to open the Portal," Palin said. "With my uncle's help," he added, noting that Steel appeared highly dubious.

Steel made no reply. He studied Palin, appeared to consider the question.

"The journey will be dangerous," Palin continued. "I intend not only to open the Portal, but to try to enter it, enter the Abyss. I'm going to find my uncle. You can come along or not, as you choose. I should think," he added offhandedly, "that you might like the chance to speak to your queen in person."

Steel's dark eyes suddenly caught fire, burned. Palin had said something that pricked through the cold armor, touched flesh. His reply was characteristically terse, laconic.

"Very well. We will go to Palanthas."

Palin sighed. He had won two hard-fought battles. Victorious, he could now give himself up to sleep. He was too tired to even go to his room. He laid his head down on the table. Just as he was sliding under sleep's soothing waves, he heard a voice, whispering . . .

Well done, young one. Well done!

I await your coming.

12

Usha's claim. Dalamar is not convinced.
A startling discovery.

hat was truly the most wonderful meal I've ever eaten," said Tasslehoff Burrfoot. "I feel positively stuffed."

He was leaning back in his chair, with his feet on the table, examining the silver spoons. They were quite remarkable silver spoons, each of them marked with intricate designs that Tas guessed were elven.

"Maybe Dalamar's initials," he said to himself drowsily.

He really had eaten too much, but then it had all tasted so good! His fingers stroked the spoon lovingly. He fully intended to return it to the table, but his fingers absentmindedly carried the spoon to his shirt pocket and deposited it there. Tas yawned. Truly a delightful meal!

Usha evidently felt the same. She lay sprawled in a chair, her legs outstretched, her hands folded over her stomach, her head lolling to one side, her eyes half-closed.

She was warm and safe and wonderfully content. "I don't think I've ever tasted anything like that!" she murmured, yawning.

"Me neither," said Tas, blinking his eyes, trying hard to stay awake. With his topknot, he looked very much like a tufted owl.

When Dalamar and Jenna entered the room, both Tas and Usha smiled up at them in a hazy, surfeited torpor.

The wizards exchanged a conspiratorial glance. The dark elf made a cursory examination of the room, swiftly catalogued its contents.

"Only one spoon missing," he remarked. "And the kender's been left alone in this room for over an hour. I believe that must set some sort of record." Reaching down, he plucked the silverware from Tas's pocket.

"I found it on the floor," Tas said and, without really knowing what he was doing, sleepily ran through an entire litany of kender counsel for the defense. "It fell into my pouch by accident. Are you sure it's yours? I thought you didn't want it anymore. You just walked off and left it. I was going to wash it and give it back to you."

"Thank you," said Dalamar, and replaced the spoon on the table.

"You're welcome," said Tas, smiling, and closed his eyes.

Dalamar turned to Usha, who—grinning foolishly—waved her hand at him. "Great meal."

"Thank you. I understand you carry a letter for me," Dalamar said.

"Oh, yeah. Here. Here somewhere." Usha slid her hand into one of the pockets of her silken trousers. Retrieving the scroll, she waved it blithely in the air.

"What did you put in that cider, my love?" Jenna whispered to Dalamar. Retrieving the scroll, she examined it carefully.

"Is this it, child? Are you certain?"

"I'm not your child," Usha said crossly. "You're not my mother and you're not much older than I am, so quit giving yourself airs, lady."

"Whose child are you?" Dalamar asked casually, accepting the letter.

He did not open it at once, but stood regarding Usha thoughtfully, searching for some resemblance between her and his *shalafi*—a man whom the elf had admired and loved, feared and hated.

Usha gazed up at him from lowered eyelids. "Whose child do you think I am?"

"I don't know," Dalamar returned, seating himself in a chair near Usha's. "Tell me about your parents."

"We lived in the Plains of Dust," Usha began.

"You did not." Dalamar's voice was sharp, flicked across Usha like a whip. "Don't lie to me, girl."

She flinched, sat up straighter, regarded him warily. "I'm not lying . . ."

"Yes, you are. These magical items"—Dalamar tossed the pouch into Usha's lap—"are of Irda make. I recognize them." He held up the letter. "Undoubtedly this tells me the truth . . ."

"No, it doesn't," Usha returned. Her head was beginning to throb her tongue was dry and felt thick and fuzzy. She didn't like this place anymore, didn't like the black-robed mage. She'd done her errand. It was time to leave. "It's just a story about a rock. I don't know why Prot thought it was important." Gathering up her pouches, she rose—somewhat unsteadily—to her feet. "And now, since I've delivered the letter, I'll be going. Thanks for the meal—"

She stopped. Jenna's hand rested on her shoulder.

"There's no way out," said Dalamar, tapping himself on the lips with the rolled-up scroll, "unless *I* provide it. Please, sit down, Usha. You are my guest for a time. You and the kender. There, that's better. Now," he continued in a pleasant, dangerous tone, "tell me about your parents."

"I don't know anything," Usha said, alarmed, wary. "Not really. I was an orphan. The Irda took me in, raised me from the time I was a baby."

Jenna seated herself on the arm of Dalamar's chair.

"They must have told you something else."

"They didn't," Usha hedged. "But I managed to find out some on my own. Have you ever heard of the *Valum*?"

"*Valin*," corrected Tasslehoff. Curiosity and sleep were waging a battle for him. Yawning, he pinched himself to stay awake. "The word is *Valin* . . ."

"I know that," Usha snapped, casting the kender a swift, baleful glance. Smiling limpidly, she turned back to Dalamar. "*Valin*, of course. It must be the cider, makes me mispronounce things."

Dalamar said nothing, squeezed Jenna's hand when she would have spoken.

"Anyway," Usha went on, "one night, when I was supposed to be in bed, I heard someone come into our house. Irda almost never have company and so I crept from my bed to see who it was. The visitor was a man the Irda call the Decider. He and Prot were talking and they were talking about me! So, of course, I listened.

"They said lots of things I didn't understand—about the *Valin* and how my mother had been an Irda who'd left her people and gone into the world. How she met a young magic-user in a tavern in an enchanted forest. She was accosted by some thugs in this tavern and the mage and his older brother—"

"Twin brother," Tasslehoff said, but the words were lost in a prodigious yawn.

"—and the mage saw my mother's face and thought she was the most beautiful woman he'd ever seen in his life. And she looked at him and the *Valin* happened between them and—"

"Explain the *Valin*," Dalamar said quietly.

Usha frowned. "You said you knew what it was."

"No," Dalamar protested mildly. "*You* said I knew what it was."

"I know what it is!" cried Tas, sitting bolt upright and waving his hand in the air. "Let me tell!"

"Thank you, Burrfoot," said Dalamar coldly. "But I would prefer to hear the Irda side of the story."

"Well . . . the *Valin* is . . . something that happens . . . between a man and a woman," Usha began, her cheeks flushing crimson. "It . . . er . . . brings them together. I guess that's what it does." She shrugged again. "Prot never told me much about it, except to say that it wouldn't happen to me."

"And why not?" Dalamar asked softly.

"Because I'm part human," Usha answered him.

"Indeed? And who is your father?"

"The young magic-user in the story," Usha said offhandedly. "His name is Raistlin. Raistlin Majere."

"Told you so," said Tasslehoff.

Dalamar pursed his lips, tapped them with the edge of the scroll. He stared at Usha so long, in silence, that she grew nervous, uneasy, tried to shift away from the gaze of the fathomless eyes. At length, the dark elf rose abruptly, walked over to the table. Usha gave a sigh of relief, as if she'd just been released again from her prison cell.

"This is very fine wine," Dalamar said, reaching for the carafe. "You should try some. Mistress Jenna, will you help me serve our guests?"

"What is it?" Jenna asked in a low voice. "What's the matter?"

Dalamar poured the golden wine into crystal glasses. "I don't believe her," he said in a low voice. "She's lying."

"What did you say?" Tasslehoff asked loudly, shoving his head between the two of them. "I didn't hear what you said."

Irritably, Jenna reached into a pouch on her belt, drew forth a handful of sand, and tossed it into the kender's face. "*Drowshi,*" she commanded.

"*Ah-choo!*" Tas sneezed and, almost before the sneeze was completely out, he sighed contently, slumped forward onto the table, and was fast asleep.

"That story of hers. I don't believe it," Dalamar repeated. "She got it from the kender. It was a mistake, leaving the two of them together."

"But the gold eyes—"

"Possibly every single Irda born has gold eyes," Dalamar returned. "How would we know? *I've* never seen one. Have you?"

"Don't be snippy, dear," Jenna said spiritedly. "Of course, I've never seen one. No one on Ansalon has. What does the letter say?"

Dalamar, in a bad humor, slid the black ribbon off the scroll, unrolled it, glanced through it hurriedly. He snorted. "It appears to be the story of the creation of the world. No, my dear, we're not likely to find our answer here."

He flung the letter down on the table where Tasslehoff lay, snoring softly. Grains of sand clung to his graying topknot.

Dalamar brushed sand off the lace tablecloth. "There might be a way yet to find out the truth."

"See if she has the talent," Jenna suggested, guessing his thought. She picked up the letter, began reading it more carefully. "You do that; I'll go through this. There must be something important in it, for the Irda to have sent it to you."

Dalamar returned to Usha, who was now curled up in the chair, her head resting on the arm, more than half asleep.

Dalamar shook her by the shoulder.

"Huh? Waddya want? Leave me alone." Usha squirmed around, attempted to hide her face in the cushions.

Dalamar tightened his grip.

"Ow!" Usha sat up, glared at him. "That hurts."

Slowly, Dalamar released her. "If you are the daughter of Raistlin Majere—"

"I am," Usha said with haughty dignity.

"—then you must have inherited some of his skills in the art."

"What art?" Usha was suspicious.

"The arcane art. Magic. Raistlin was one of the most powerful wizards ever to have walked on Ansalon. Magical talent is generally hereditary. Raistlin's nephew, Palin Majere, has inherited a great deal of his uncle's skill. Raistlin's daughter must surely possess great power . . ."

"Oh, I do," Usha said, lounging among the cushions.

"Then you won't mind demonstrating your talent for Mistress Jenna and myself."

"I would," Usha said, "but I'm not permitted. The Irda warned me, you see. I'm too powerful." She glanced around. "I'd hate to wreck this nice room."

"I'll risk it," Dalamar said dryly.

"Oh, no. I couldn't possibly," Usha returned, wide-eyed, innocent. "Prot warned me never—"

"Great Lunitari!" Jenna drew in her breath sharply. "Blessed goddess of the red moon. If this is true—"

Dalamar turned. "If what is true?"

Jenna held out the letter. "You didn't read far enough, my love. Go to the very bottom."

Dalamar read swiftly, looked up.

"The Irda have the Graygem," Jenna said.

"They claim to . . ." Dalamar mused. "What do you know of this, girl?" he demanded, rounding on Usha.

Fully awake, Usha gazed at him perplexed.

"What do I know about what?"

Dalamar was like a snake dozing in the bright, hot sun. His soft voice, with its hissing elven lisp, was soothing and deceiving. He charmed his prey with elegant manners and his delicate beauty and, when they were completely in his thrall, he would devour them.

"Don't play stupid!" He uncoiled, glided toward her. "What do you know about the Graygem? And this time, Mistress, spare me your lies . . ."

Usha swallowed, licked her lips. "I wasn't lying," she managed in a small voice. "And I don't know anything about the Graygem. I only saw it once—"

"What does it look like?"

"It was a gray . . . gem . . ." she began.

Dalamar's feathery black eyebrows came together in displeasure. The almond eyes glittered.

Usha gulped, went on hurriedly. "It had lots of facets, more than I could count. And it gave off a sickening sort of gray glow. I didn't like to look at it. It made me feel funny inside, as if I wanted to run off and do crazy things that didn't make any sense. Prot said that was the way the stone affected humans . . ."

"And the Irda intend to break open the stone?" Dalamar's voice was taut.

"Yes," Usha said, shrinking away from his terrible intensity, huddling back into the cushions of the chair. "That was why they sent me away. The Decider said, because I was human . . . part human," she corrected herself, "I would interfere with the magic . . ."

"What if they have cracked the Graygem?" Jenna asked. "What would that mean?"

"I don't know. I doubt if anyone does, maybe not even the gods themselves." Dalamar fixed his devouring gaze on Usha. "Do you know what happened? Did you see anything before you left?"

"Nothing," Usha said. "Except . . . a red glow in the sky. Like a fire. I . . . I suppose it was the magic . . ."

Dalamar said nothing more, paid no more attention to Usha. She was careful to keep her mouth shut, burrowed down into the cushions, hoping to escape further notice. The dark elf paced the room several times. Jenna watched him, worried and anxious. Tasslehoff slumbered fitfully, twitching and whiffling. At length, Dalamar made up his mind.

"I will call the Conclave together. This coming day. We must leave for Wayreth at once."

"What are you thinking?"

"That I don't like this," Dalamar said grimly. "The strange weather, the terrible heat, the unusual drought, other odd happenings. This may be the answer."

"What will you do with the girl and the kender? Take them with us?"

"No. She's told us all she knows. If word got out among the Conclave that Raistlin's daughter was loose on Ansalon, it would cause an uproar. We'd get nothing accomplished. Best to keep her here, safe and quiet. The kender, too. He is friends with Caramon Majere, might carry the tale to him."

He and Jenna started for the door.

"Wait!" Usha cried, jumping to her feet. "You can't leave me here! I won't stay! I'll scream! Someone will hear me—"

Jenna turned, tossed a handful of sand over Usha. The young woman blinked, rubbed her eyes, shook her head groggily.

"I won't stay, I tell you—"

"She's resisting the magic," Jenna observed. "Interesting. I wonder if she's doing that herself, or if she's been given a charm—"

"Whatever the case we have no time for that now."

Dalamar snapped his fingers. Usha swayed on her feet, collapsed back among the cushions. Her eyes closed.

A door opened onto a spiral staircase that wound around the interior walls of the Tower of High Sorcery. The narrow stone stairs led upward, to the laboratory, where no one—not even the Tower's master—walked. The stairs led down to rooms where the apprentices lived and studied, down farther still to the Chamber of Seeing. Shutting the door, Dalamar locked it with a silver key.

"That won't stop the kender," Jenna remarked. "And the sleep spell will wear off before we are likely to return."

"True, the lock might not stop him, but this will." Dalamar spoke words in a cold, spidery language.

At Dalamar's command, two white, disembodied eyes materialized in the darkness of the Tower's interior, a darkness that had never known even dreams of light.

The specter moved near Dalamar. "You summoned me, Master. What is your command?"

"Keep watch on this room. Allow no one to go in or out. If the two inside try, don't harm them. Merely prevent them from escaping."

"That makes my task more difficult," said the specter. "But I obey your command, Master."

Dalamar began to speak the words of the spell that would take them along the roads of magic to the distant Tower of High Sorcery at Wayreth. Jenna did not immediately join him. She stood staring at the door, at the specter posting ceaseless watch.

Dalamar interrupted his spell casting.

"Come along," he said, annoyed. "We have no time to waste."

"What if she *is* telling the truth?" Jenna asked softly. "She might be powerful enough to escape even the specter."

"She wasn't powerful enough to avoid getting caught stealing food," Dalamar returned irritably. "Either she's exceptionally cunning or she's a lying little fool."

"Why would she lie? What can she hope to gain by pretending to be a wizardess? Surely she would know that we would know the truth."

"But we don't, do we?" Dalamar said. "The Irda are clever, their magic powerful. Who knows what they have in mind? Perhaps they sent her as a spy, and they knew the only way she would get in was by pretending to be what she is not. I will find out when I have time to speak to her further. It is my opinion that she is lying, that she is no more powerful in magic than the kender. Still, if you don't trust my judgment—"

"I do, my love, I do," Jenna said, hastening to stand at his side. She tilted her head back to be kissed. "It's other parts of you I don't trust."

Dalamar obligingly kissed her, though it was obvious his mind was on other, more urgent, matters. "I am always faithful to you, my dear. In my own way."

"Yes," said Jenna, with a small sigh. "In your own way. I know."

Hands entwined, they spoke the spell together and stepped into the darkness.

*　*　*　*　*

Locked in the Tower room, Usha and Tasslehoff slept under the enchantment. Usha dreamed dreams tinged with fire, dreams that frightened her, but from which she could not awake.

Tasslehoff dreamed kender dreams, which meant that though he was still asleep, his hands were busy. His fingers closed over the handle of the silver spoon and, still dreaming, he slid the spoon into his pouch.

"I guess you must have dropped it," he murmured.

13

The Siege of Kalaman.

t was early morning in Kalaman, a bustling port city on the northern coastline, east of Palanthas. Kalaman was not as large as Palanthas, not as refined, but—as the Kalamites liked to boast—the city had more common sense. This was due undoubtedly to the burgeoning middle class, which had grown in power and wealth since the dark days of the War of the Lance. Palanthas was a city of lords and ladies, knights and mages. Kalaman was a city of tradesmen and craftsmen. The guild ruled in Kalaman, overseen by a governor elected by guild members.

Any man or woman, elf, human, dwarf, or gnome who owned a business belonged to a guild. There were the Silversmiths' Guild, the Swordmakers' Guild, the Innkeepers' Guild, the Ale-brewers' Guild, the Seamstresses' Guild, the Tailors' Guild, the Shoemakers' Guild, the Jewelcutters' Guild, and a hundred more, including the one guild in all of Ansalon run by kender—the Finders' Guild. Anyone who lost anything in Kalaman went immediately to the Finders' Guild.

The city had its own militia, made up of a mixture of hired mercenaries and townspeople, under the leadership of veteran soldiers. The mercenaries were not the usual brawling adventurers, willing to help you fight goblins for the price of a wineskin, just as willing to help the goblins fight you for the same amount. All mercenaries hired to fight for Kalaman were given a house in the city proper as part of their payment. They had their own guild and had voting privileges. Thus the mercenaries who accepted this deal were soon transformed into citizens who had a stake in the city and would be more than willing to fight for it.

The Kalaman militia was loyal, adequately trained, and about as brave as could be expected. Against what was coming, they didn't stand a chance.

The morning sun glared over the eastern wall. Roosters greeted it; most citizens were still in bed. The harbor watchmen, ready to be relieved, yawned and thought longingly of their beds.

"Ship on the horizon," said one. "Anything due in this hour?"

The other consulted the log. "Could be the *Lady Jane* out of Flotsam. She sent word that she was coming in to pick up that load of grain, but, if so, she's early. We weren't expecting her until midday at least."

"Must have had a fair wind," said the other. He turned away to see if his replacement was coming up the boardwalk. When he turned back, he blinked, stared. A second sail suddenly showed on the horizon. "That's odd. There's another ship. And another after that."

Concern altered his tone. "By Hiddukel, it's a fleet! Hand me that spy glass!"

The watchman handed over the spy glass and found one for himself.

"Four, five, and six," said the watchman, awed, counting. "Black ships, with dragon-head prows. I've never seen the like. What flag do they fly?"

"None at the moment." The man was uneasy. "I don't like this. I think we should sound the alarm."

"Wait until we're certain. Seven, eight."

The ships with their tall sails glided over the smooth sea, which was stained red with the fire of the sunrise. The wind favored the ships, that day; they had all sails set and were making good time.

"Look! The lead ship's unfurled their pennant—a skull and a death lily. Sound the alarm. I'll send Hayes to report to the governor."

The clang of the harbor bell rang out over the water, echoed among the buildings on the sea wall, woke those people with homes near the harbor. The alarm was picked up by other bells in the city, bells that hung in the guild halls, bells that hung in the temples devoted to the various gods of Krynn. The governor, roused from his bed, came racing down to the harbor, tucking his shirttail into his trousers as he ran.

By the time he arrived, he could see the dragons.

They flew above the ships—there were now sixteen—in three long, evenly spaced lines, keeping formation, their wings moving in rhythm. They were still far enough away to look black against the sun-lit sky, but every now and then the light would flash off a blue scale. The dragons flying above, the ships sailing below, had a kind of beauty about them, a deadly beauty. Already a few small vessels, having seen what was bearing down on them, were fleeing the harbor, trying to scoot to the safety of the open seas.

"Call out the militia," ordered the governor. He was a half-elf, a silversmith by trade, and had been the governor for three years now.

"Perhaps they're not coming here," ventured the watchman hopefully. "Perhaps they're on their way to Palanthas."

"They're coming here," said the governor grimly, lowering the spy glass. He'd served in the War of the Lance, and he knew the signs. He also knew what the people of Kalaman were about to face. He was not a praying man, generally, but he said a prayer that moment to every god who could conceivably be expected to listen.

The governor acted quickly. He had one slim hope: the harbor defenses. Those had been built up and reinforced, following the War of the Lance. They might be able to hold off the ships and the men aboard them. The two large catapults and four ballistae were manned by experienced crews, all facing the harbor entrance. These weapons were the pride of the militia, and well maintained.

Fire ships, whose wooden decks and masts were soaked with oil, were made ready to set sail into the harbor entrance. Daring crewmen would set the ships ablaze, then stay with the burning ships as long as possible, guiding them in to wreak burning destruction upon the enemy fleet.

The city bells were ringing wildly, frantically now. Men went racing to their posts. Women were drawing water from the wells, filling buckets, horse troughs, anything that would hold liquid, to be used in fighting fires. Children were sent down into cellars, told to be brave.

The governor saw the dragon-prowed ships slow, saw them lower their sails, start to drop anchor. His spirit soared in hope, which was immediately dashed by a messenger, dragging with him a frightened farm girl.

"An army, sir!" The young woman gasped. "An army of blue giants, coming this way! They passed our farm, set fire to the buildings. My father . . . dead . . ." She choked, almost broke down, but managed to fight back the tears. "I rode as fast as I could. They're right behind me, on foot."

"Blue men? Giants?" The governor suspected the girl was crazed with grief. "Calm down, girl, and tell me this story straight. Someone bring her a glass of wine."

She shook her head. "I tell you, sir, these men were as tall as our house. They are stark naked, their bodies smeared with blue paint. They—"

A soldier arrived on horseback, jumped down, ran to the knot of men. "Governor, sir. The general says to tell you that an army has been sighted, coming up the main road. They have siege engines, sir. Siege engines pulled by huge beasts the like of which we've never seen!"

The governor ceased his prayers.

The first wave of dragonfear struck those manning the walls. The shadow of blue dragon wings slid over the town.

* * * * *

It was noon. Lord Ariakan stood aboard his flagship, his officers gathered around, watching the siege of Kalaman through a spy glass. Signal flags slid up and down, carrying Ariakan's commands to the rest of the fleet and to his officers on shore.

Ariakan was sweating in his heavy armor. The sun beat down on the ship, was reflected off the water. He didn't mind the heat. He knew that the people of Kalaman were sweating far more than he was. They were sweating with fear.

His dragon flights circled above the city, not attacking, letting the fear they engendered drive men in panic from the walls. Occasionally, a blue dragon would unleash a blast of lightning, knock down a guild hall tower, set fire to a warehouse. But the dragons had orders not to attack.

The legions of brutes drew up beneath the city walls, surrounded the city six deep, their bodies heaving against the walls like a living, savage ocean. They raised their siege engines with impunity; few were left on the walls to try to knock them down. The brutes clashed their swords against their shields, shouted threats in their uncouth tongue, and fired arrows at anyone brave or foolish enough to show himself. But that was all. They, too, held off the attack.

The fleet remained out to sea, except for two frigates, which had been sent in to deal with the harbor defenses. As they approached the harbor wall, the first battery of ballistae opened fire on the lead frigate, catching it amidships, but above the waterline. Its crew worked to repair the damage, and carried forward with speed. The catapults fired, missed both shots. The frigates dashed into the mouth of the harbor and grappled the fire ships, just starting to blaze up. Two blue dragons circled low over the harbor wall and blasted the emplaced weapons into the sea; their crews jumped into the frothing water.

The lone ballistae battery on the far side opened fire on the dragons as they flew past. Neither dragon was hit, but one of the dragonriders pitched off the side of the beast, plunging into the water.

The frigates secured the fire ships to long tether lines and began to drag them from the mouth of the harbor, to let them burn out at sea. The valiant ballistae crews, fearful of the wrath of the dragons, fled back to the city proper.

By midafternoon, Ariakan had decided that the town had sweated enough. He called for his herald, gave the man his orders, sent him— bearing a flag of truce—into Kalaman.

The envoy rode to the city gates, a white flag fluttering above his head. He was escorted by three of Ariakan's knights, wearing neither mail nor bearing arms, to indicate that they intended no violence. The city refused to open the gates to admit the envoy, but the governor did agree to a parley from atop the wall. He stood plainly visible in bowshot range, an act of courage for which the dark knights accompanying the herald gave the half-elf a salute.

"What do you want?" the governor demanded. "You minions of evil who come without cause to attack a peaceful town."

"We come to demand that the city of Kalaman be surrendered to the might of Ariakan, Lord Knight of Takhisis, soon to be ruler of all Ansalon."

"Other servants of Takhisis have boasted that in the past, and they now serve her in the Abyss, which is where I would consign your master." The governor talked boldly to hearten his men, those who had courage enough to withstand the dragonfear. He didn't feel bold, however. He was crushed, despairing. Kalaman could not hope to fight off such numbers, coming at it from land, sea, and air. "Let us hear your terms," he added grimly.

The herald recited them. "The people of Kalaman will lay down their arms, open the city gates, and permit entry of Lord Ariakan and his troops. The people of Kalaman will swear allegiance to Lord Ariakan as their liege lord. Men of fighting age are to report to the city square, where they will be offered the opportunity to join the ranks of Lord Ariakan's forces. Those who do not want to join will be made prisoner.

"If you accept Lord Ariakan's terms, he will spare your city harm. He will leave your women and children in peace. If you do not accept his terms, but persist in refusing Lord Ariakan entry into your city, he promises that the stones of your buildings will be razed, your houses burned to the ground, your men taken as slaves, your women given to the barbarians for their pleasure, your children slaughtered before their mothers' eyes.

"Lord Ariakan gives you until the sun sets to consider these terms."

"How do we know this Lord Ariakan will keep his word?" the governor asked.

"Lord Ariakan is a Knight of Takhisis," the herald returned proudly. "His word is his bond. He leaves you with this promise. Surrender and know peace. Fight and know destruction."

The herald rode off, the knightly guard of honor falling in behind him. The governor climbed down from the walls, went to consult the guildmasters. The blue dragons circled overhead, reducing what courage remained in Kalaman to ashes.

"If there is a chance that this Ariakan will keep his word," the governor told the guildsmen, "we must take it. Otherwise, we sentence our people to death or worse."

The guild masters reluctantly agreed.

Lord Ariakan had his answer well before sundown.

The city gates opened, and his troops marched inside. The people waited fearfully to be brutalized, mistreated, butchered.

Able-bodied men were rounded up, taken to the city square, and given a speech by one of Ariakan's officers about the glories and honors awaiting those who joined the ranks of Takhisis. Not a man did. They were then chained and manacled and led away, some to serve on the black dragon ships, others to work cutting down trees to build the rafts that would carry Ariakan's forces swiftly downriver.

The rest of the citizens of Kalaman were told to return to their homes.

Ariakan's fleet sailed into the harbor. He himself entered the town with little fanfare, set immediately about business. His knights patrolled the streets.

The next day, the citizens of Kalaman woke to fear, only to find the dragons departed, the army of blue-painted barbarians vanished, the city intact. The market opened, under orders from Lord Ariakan. Shopkeepers were told to unbar the shutters and commence business as usual.

Dazed, disbelieving, the people slowly began to go about their business. The only visible difference between today and yesterday was the knights in black armor patrolling the walls and walking the city streets. Here and there a wife wept for her prisoner husband, a child cried for its missing father, a father mourned his lost son, but that was all.

Kalaman had fallen with hardly a whimper.

Ariakan, seated at his desk in the governor's mansion, unrolled a map and looked to Palanthas.

14

The wheel turns. The wheel stops. The wheel turns again.

hat evening, before sundown, Caramon and Tika buried their two sons.

It was the custom, in Solace, to plant a young vallenwood tree on every new grave. Thus, it was believed, the soul of the dead would enter the tree and therefore never truly die. This is one reason the vallenwood trees are sacred to the people of Solace, one reason that no living tree is ever cut down.

Tanin and Sturm Majere were to be buried in a small family plot within sight of the Inn of the Last Home. Here rested Otik, the inn's founder, lifelong friend to both Tika and Caramon. Here the husband and wife would one day rest themselves, when they left the world and its cares behind them. They had never thought that two of their children might precede them.

Caramon started digging the grave alone, but word soon spread through Solace, and it was not long before a neighbor came to help, then another, and another until every man in the town was there to lend a hand. They worked in the heat, taking turns, pausing to rest in shade that—due to the hot, incessant wind—offered little respite. The men dug the grave in silence, for the most part, having spoken their few broken words of condolence when they arrived. They generally ignored Porthios and his elves, who were standing guard around the inn, where their queen lay. The elves generally ignored them.

The women of Solace came as well, bringing gifts of food and flowers and baby clothes—for word of the birthing had spread, too. Tika packed the baby clothes away, to be given to Alhana in secret before the exiled elven royalty left to continue their attempts to win back their thrones—and to win peace and stability for the elven nations. Tika was well aware that Porthios would never accept the cast-off "leavings" of humans, but, as she told Dezra, "The parents have nothing but the clothes on their backs. What's the poor babe to wear? Leaves?"

Tika worked fiercely all day, refusing to stop to lie down or rest. There was much to be done, what with the baby coming and the guests arriving and the townsfolk to be fed.

"I'll pack my tears away for today," she said to Dezra. "The gods know that they'll still be here tomorrow. As for the aching in my heart . . . it will be here always."

Palin slept the day through. His sleep was so deep that when his father lifted his slumbering form from the table and carried him to his bedroom, the young mage never stirred. Steel slept, too, in a room in the back of the inn, his sword hilt under his hand, his breastplate standing guard duty against the door. The knight had resisted all attempts to persuade him to rest, until Tanis Half-Elven had curtly pointed out that Steel's refusal to trust them impinged on their honor.

"When we escorted you to the High Clerist's Tower to pay homage to your father, both of us pledged our lives to protect you, to protect Sturm Brightblade's son. It is dishonorable of you to refuse to accept that pledge."

Steel went haughtily to his bed and fell asleep almost instantly.

Tanis spent the day with Porthios, not because he particularly enjoyed his brother-in-law's company, but because the proximity of so many humans was making the elven lord edgy.

The day was tense and sorrowful. One of the men digging the grave succumbed to the heat, collapsed, and had to be carried into the inn, where the women sat, sweating and fanning, talking of the bad harvest and wondering how they would get through the winter. Young children, not quite understanding what was going on, but realizing that this was not a day to play and make noise, kept close to their mothers.

The exiled elves stood in the branches of the vallenwood trees, keeping watch and dreaming of their homelands.

And then, at sunset, came the funeral.

Palin and Tika and Caramon stood with a cleric of Mishakal at the head of the grave. Tanis was near them, thinking tender thoughts of his own son, who—though still living—was lost to him.

The bodies of the two brothers, wrapped in their linen shrouds, were lowered reverently to their final resting place, for they were to be buried together. The cleric asked a blessing. The townsfolk filed past the open grave, either dropping some small token of remembrance into the grave or relating a fond tale of some exploit of the brothers, who had been well loved.

When this small ceremony was concluded, the men started to fill in the grave when, to the amazement of everyone, Porthios arrived, accompanied by a contingent of elven warriors. He spoke with awkward kindness to Caramon and Tika, then, standing at the grave site, the elf lord sang a song of lamentation for the dead. Though no one understood the words, the song's sad, yet hopeful, melody brought tears that eased grief's bitter pain, left behind only gentle sorrow. Tika wept then, cradled in her husband's arms.

Porthios finished his song, stepped back. The men picked up shovels and began to fill the grave with dirt. It was customary at this point to drop flowers on the bodies, but the flowers had all withered in the heat long ago. The mound of dirt covering both young knights was tamped down with loving care. The cleric of Mishakal was about to offer a final blessing when the crowd at the graveside suddenly parted. People fell back in alarm.

Steel Brightblade strode into their midst.

Outraged at the intrusion into their grief, the townspeople called for him to leave. Porthios glowered; the elves—hands on their weapons—gathered more closely around their lord.

Steel ignored them, walked up to stand at the head of the grave site.

The cleric of Mishakal said severely, "Sir, your presence here is not welcome. It is an insult to the dead."

Steel made no comment. He stood in silence, stern and aloof, ignoring the cleric, ignoring the insults and threats. He carried in his hands a bundle that had been lashed to the cart bearing the bodies.

Caramon, perplexed, looked at his son. Palin could only shake his head. He had no idea what was going on. In troubled silence, all watched and waited to see what the dark knight would do.

Steel knelt on one knee, unwrapped the bundle, and spread it out upon the withered brown grass.

The last rays of the dying sunlight shone upon Tanin's broken sword. The haft of his brother's shattered spear lay beside it. Removing the weapons, Steel laid each carefully upon the grave site. Then, kneeling, his head bowed, he began to chant words in a strange and unfamiliar language.

The cleric of Mishakal hastened to Tanis, plucked him by the sleeve. "Stop him!" she said urgently. "He is casting some sort of evil spell upon the dead!"

"No, he's not," said Tanis quietly, his eyes filling with tears, his heart with memories. "The language he speaks is Solamnic. He is reciting the knights' Prayer for the Dead."

> Return this man to Huma's breast
> Beyond the wild, impartial skies;
> Grant to him a warrior's rest
> And set the last spark of his eyes
> Free from the smothering clouds of wars,
> Upon the torches of the stars.
> Let the last surge of his breath
> Take refuge in the cradling air
> Above the dreams of ravens, where

Only the hawk remembers death.
Then let his shade to Huma rise,
Beyond the wild, impartial skies.

All remained hushed until he had finished. Standing then, Steel drew his sword, gave the knight's salute. He brought the hilt of his sword to his lips, extended the weapon outward in a sweeping arc. Making a formal bow to the stunned family, the dark paladin turned on his heel and walked slowly and haughtily through the crowd, who parted in awe for him.

As he was leaving, Steel paused to stand in front of Porthios. A mocking smile played upon the dark knight's lips.

"Do not concern yourself with the civil war between the elven nations, sir. Soon, the Qualinesti and the Silvanesti will be united— under the boot heel of Lord Ariakan."

Porthios drew his sword. Tanis, who had foreseen trouble, moved swiftly to halt him.

"Think of where you are, Brother. Think of Alhana," he urged, speaking Elvish. "These are merely words of bravado from young blood. You've heard all this before. Ignore it."

Porthios might well have ignored Tanis, but at that moment a faint cry—a newborn cry—wavered in the air. With a final baleful glance, Porthios shouldered Steel aside and hastened to the inn. His elven escort departed as well, not without exchanging glances that were as good as blows with the dark knight.

Steel met them with that mocking smile, then, half-turning, he glanced over his shoulder. "Palin Majere. You are my prisoner still. Pay your farewells. It is time we were leaving."

"Palin!" Tika cried and stretched out trembling hands to her son.

"It will be all right, Mother," Palin said, with a glance at his father. The two had agreed to say nothing of Palin's intent to his mother. "The mages will pay the ransom. I will be home soon." He leaned forward, kissed her on the cheek.

"Take care of yourself," Tika said softly, brokenly, then startled Palin by adding, "Raistlin wasn't all bad. There was some good in him. I never liked him much, but then I never understood him. Perhaps . . ." She paused, drew a deep breath, then said crisply, "Perhaps what you are doing is right."

Palin stared at her in astonishment. He looked at his father, who shrugged. "I didn't say a word, Son."

Tika smiled sadly, rested her hand on her boy's hand. "I always knew when you were up to mischief. Remember? You and your brothers . . . "

She swallowed. Tears welled from her eyes. "Paladine go with you, my son!"

"Take care, Son," Caramon said. "If there's anything I can do . . ."

"Thank you, Father. Thank you for everything. Good-bye, Mother."

Palin turned away, left quickly, his own tears half-blinding him. But he was master of himself by the time he reached Steel.

"Do you have everything you require?" the knight asked.

Palin flushed. He carried a single pouch of spell components; at his low rank, he needed no more. What clothes he had, he wore—white robes, stained with travel and blood. He had no spellbooks, no scroll cases. But in his hand was the Staff of Magius.

"I'm ready," he said.

Steel nodded, made a graceful, chill salute to Caramon and Tika. Palin did not look back, but began trudging down the road. The two disappeared into the lengthening shadows.

That evening, at the Inn of the Last Home, Caramon and Tika planted two young vallenwoods on the grave of their sons.

Alhana Starbreeze, exhausted from the long birthing, slept. Porthios stood by her side. When she was sleeping and all others had left the room, he leaned over, kissed her tenderly.

Assured that his wife was safe and his newborn son was healthy, Porthios returned to the common room and sat with his warriors. He planned to unite the elven kingdoms, if he had to kill every elf in Ansalon to do it.

Tanis left on a swift journey to the High Clerist's Tower, to tell the knights once more what he had been telling them for five years: that the Dark Queen's forces were again on the move.

Lying in his cradle, wearing human baby clothes much too large for him, the newborn elf child blinked and stared about in astonishment at this strange, new world in which he found himself.

15

Steel vows revenge.
Palin hears the familiar voice.
The journey to Palanthas.

alin and Steel joined up with the blue dragon about five leagues north of Solace. Flare had spent the night in the ruined city of Xak Tsaroth. Said to be haunted, the city remained abandoned, except for gully dwarves and roving bands of goblins and draconians. Flare was still picking bits of goblin from her teeth when they found her. She would not, she told her master with disdain, eat gully dwarf.

Well fed and reunited with Steel, Flare was in a good humor. While the dark knight studied a map of their route north, Flare took delight in attempting to intimidate Palin, already affected by the dragonfear. She unfurled her massive wings, spread them to the sun, flapped them gently to cool herself and her master. When Steel complained that the breeze was fluttering the map, making it difficult for him to read, Flare enjoyed a small fit of temper. She dug her claws in the ground, tore at it, sending up huge clods of dirt and brown grass. She slashed her tail wickedly from side to side, tossed her mane, all the while gazing from beneath lowered lids with her red, reptile eyes to see Palin's reaction.

Palin held himself aloof, purposefully standing near the dragon, though the effort it cost him was plainly visible in his clenched jaw, his white-knuckled hand clinging tightly to the Staff of Magius.

"If you've finished showing off," Steel said to the dragon, "I'd like to go over our route."

The blue dragon snarled, bared her teeth, pretending to be offended. Steel patted her neck, unrolled the map on a boulder, and indicated what he considered to be the best way. Palin mopped sweat from his brow and, keeping tight hold on the staff, moved even closer to the dragon to take part in the discussion.

"This affects me, too," he said, answering Steel's baleful look. "Flying over Solamnia will prove far more dangerous than traveling over Abanasinia."

Since the time of the War of the Lance, the Knights of Solamnia had regained favor with the local populace. It was now considered fashionable for a family of breeding and consequence—not to mention wealth—to have at least one son in the knighthood. Consequently, the ranks of the knights had swelled, and their coffers were full. They had rebuilt many of the crumbling keeps around Solamnia, dispatched troops to man them. Their allies, the silver dragons, kept watch on the skies.

Once reviled, the Knights of Solamnia were now seen as protectors of the weak, defenders of the innocent. Wiser lords had risen in the ranks; the laws set down by Vinas Solamnus thousands of years ago—laws that had been religiously, strictly, and, some said, obtusely followed in the modern era—were being revised and modified, brought up to date.

The Knights of Solamnia, instead of being stoned when they rode into a village—as had been the case in the old days—were treated as honored guests, their help and advice eagerly sought and generously funded.

Dragon and master were well aware of the knights' growing influence. Lord Ariakan had been a prisoner of the knights for several years following the war, and he had not spent his time among them in idleness. He had learned not only their ways—which he admired and copied, making changes where needed—but he had also learned their tactics, strategies, the locations of their strongholds. He had found out their strengths and—most importantly—their weaknesses.

When Tanis had first discovered the existence of the Knights of Takhisis, almost five years previous, he had gone immediately to the Solamnic Knights and warned them of their peril.

"Lord Ariakan knows everything about you—from the color of your smallclothes to your accustomed orders of battle," Tanis warned. "He knows which keeps are fortified and which are empty. His knights are able and intelligent men and women, recruited by him, trained by him, given the Vision by Her Dark Majesty. They will not betray their masters for the sake of gain as we saw during the last war. These people are loyal to the Dark Queen and to each other. They will sacrifice anything for their cause. You must institute changes now, my lords, or it is my belief that Lord Ariakan and his dark knights will make these changes for you."

The lord knights had listened politely to Tanis, had agreed with him politely while he was present among them, and had pooh-poohed him when he was absent.

Everyone knew that those allied with the Queen of Darkness were selfish, greedy, cruel, and completely lacking in honor. History had proven this, time and again. The knights could not imagine that such drastic changes in the ranks of darkness could have occurred in the short span of twenty-six years.

And so the ranks of light made few changes of their own.

Steel was pointing at the map. "We cross the Straits of Schallsea here, skirting Caergoth, for the knights have established a fortress there. We keep to the east, travel over water, with Coastlund on our right. Thus we avoid Thelgaard Keep. North of that, we continue along the coastline, putting the Vingaard Mountains between us and the High Clerist's Tower. We enter Palanthas from the north."

On hearing this, Palin ventured to suggest, "You won't be able to enter the city unless you're disguised. I thought of this," he added with some pride, "and I brought some of my father's clothes—"

"I will *not* walk the streets of Palanthas dressed as an innkeeper," Steel said sternly. "I wear this armor for the glory of my queen. I won't hide who I am."

"Then we might as well march to the High Clerist's Tower and lock ourselves up in a cell," Palin returned. "Because that's where we're going to end up."

"*You* will not, White Robe," Steel observed, with a half-smile.

"Oh, yes, I will. They'll arrest me fast enough when they find out I'm with you. The knights have little love for magic-users."

"Yet you fought in their ranks."

"Because of my brothers," Palin said in a low voice and said no more.

"Do not worry, Majere," Steel said, the smile now in his dark eyes. "We will enter Palanthas safely enough."

"And supposing we do make it through Palanthas," Palin argued. "We still have to walk the Shoikan Grove."

"The accursed wood? I've seen it—from a distance. Didn't your father tell you? I grew up in Palanthas. We lived there until I was twelve, when Lord Ariakan came to enroll me in the knights. As you might imagine, the Shoikan Grove is a temptation to every mischievous child in the city. I forget how many times we dared each other to get close to it. Of course, the moment even the topmost branches of the giant trees came into sight, we turned tail and fled. I remember to this day the feelings, the fear . . ."

He stopped, frowning, then shook the memories off, as a dog shakes off water. He continued, more briskly, "This grove is said to be deadly to every mortal who tries to gain admittance—no matter where his loyalties lie. But surely *you* have safe passage, Sir Mage."

"Don't call me that," Palin said, irritated. "It's not accurate. I'm of low rank in my art. In military terms, I am equivalent to a foot soldier."

He couldn't help the bitterness creeping into his voice.

"All of us start at the bottom, Majere," Steel said gravely. "There is no shame in that. I worked ten years to achieve my rank and I am far from the top."

"You sound just like my brother Tanin. All that metal you knights wear must go to your heads. It's what I used to tell him. And, no, I don't have safe passage through the Shoikan Grove. I could ask for it, I suppose. Dalamar thinks well of me. . . ."

At the mention of that name, Steel's expression changed. His color deepened, the smile in his eyes disappeared, consumed in a sudden, intense fire.

Palin did not notice. He was abstracted, tempted to contact Dalamar and beg a way safely through the grove. "No," he decided at last. "I can't ask Dalamar. That would mean telling him why I wanted inside the tower. And if he knew in advance, he would stop—"

Palin caught a glimpse of Steel's face, looked about hastily, thinking that they might be under attack. Seeing nothing, he asked, "What's wrong?"

"Dalamar the Dark, that is the man of whom you speak?"

"Yes," said Palin, "the master of the tower. The—" Suddenly, Palin remembered his history. Inwardly, he groaned.

"He is the man who killed my mother," Steel said. His hand went to the hilt of his sword. "I look forward to meeting this Dalamar."

The dark elf had killed his former lover only in self-defense; Kitiara had attacked him first. But that argument was likely to be lost on Kitiara's son.

"I suppose it's no use reminding you that Dalamar is the most powerful wizard in Ansalon," Palin said testily. "That he could turn you inside out and upside down with just a wave of his hand."

"What does that matter?" Steel replied, angered. "Do you think I would attack only those weaker than myself? I am honor-bound to avenge my mother's death."

Blessed Paladine, why didn't I think of this before? Palin wondered despairingly. Steel will end up dead. Dalamar will think *I* tried to have him assassinated. He might well destroy me in the bargain. . . .

Trust me, young one, came the voice. *Leave Dalamar to me.*

Palin shivered, thrilled, exulting. He knew now the voice was real, not imagined. It was speaking to him, guiding him, directing him, *wanting* him!

His fears eased. He relaxed.

"We haven't reached the tower yet. We have yet to make it safely inside Palanthas and through the Shoikan Grove. Let us deal with Dalamar and whatever we find in the tower when—if—we make it that far."

"We'll reach it," Steel predicted grimly. "You've given me added incentive."

The two mounted the dragon and, bathed in Lunitari's blood-red light, they flew northward, toward Palanthas.

They traveled all night, encountered no one. But, with the sunrise, the dragon grew uneasy.

"I smell silvers," she reported.

After a brief consultation with Steel, the dragon landed in the foothills of the Vingaard Mountains.

"We do not want to enter Palanthas by daylight anyhow," Steel told Palin. "Better that we rest this day, travel on when it is dark."

Palin chafed at the delay. He was certain that his uncle was alive, needed only to be released from the dread prison of the Abyss. The young mage felt rested and well. Thanks to Steel's poultice, Palin's wound scarcely bothered him. He was eager to journey on, but he couldn't very well argue with a blue dragon or the dragon's master.

"Shouldn't one of us keep watch?" Palin asked, watching Steel unfasten two bedrolls.

"We both need our rest," Steel returned. "The dragon will guard our slumber."

After a short search, they found a shallow recess in a cliff that would offer some shelter, though not much concealment, if anyone happened by. Palin spread his blanket, ate some of the massive quantity of food Tika had found time to prepare for them. Steel ate, lay down, and, with the discipline of a soldier who knows he must take his rest when and where he can find it, was soon fast asleep. Palin stretched himself out on the cool ground, prepared to spend the day in sleepless anticipation of night.

He woke sometime around sunset.

Steel was up, saddling the dragon. Flare was well rested and, by the looks of it, well fed. The carcasses of several deer lay strewn about.

Palin stood up, moving slowly, stiff and sore from lying on the ground. Usually his sleep was troubled by strange, half-remembered dreams. Not this time. He could not remember having slept so soundly or deeply in his life.

"You are turning into an old campaigner." Steel grunted, effortlessly hoisted the heavy saddle onto the dragon's back. "You even snore like one."

Palin muttered some apology. He knew why he had slept well, was somewhat ashamed. It seemed a betrayal of his family, his home, his upbringing. For the first time in his life, ever since he'd felt the hunger, ever since he'd been old enough to throw pretend magical dust in the faces of his playmates, he was at peace with himself.

"Don't apologize, Majere. You did well. We'll need our strength for what we must face this night."

The Shoikan Grove. A terrible place, a deadly place. Caramon had attempted to enter once, had nearly lost his life. And now Palin could scarcely contain his impatience. The grove held no terrors for him. Neither did the grove's master. Raistlin had promised to deal with Dalamar. Palin's thoughts centered on what would come after the grove.

The Portal. His uncle.

The dragon soared into the darkening sky, flying in lazy circles, using the heat thermals to carry her upward.

Within a few short hours, the city lights of Palanthas came into sight. They flew around it, skirting New City on their right. The Old City wall circled the city like the rim of a wagon wheel; torches burned bright at its gates. The famous library was dark, except for a light in one window. Perhaps Astinus, who some claimed was the god Gilean himself, was up late, recording history as it flowed past him.

Perhaps he was, at this very moment, writing about them. Perhaps he might soon be recording their deaths. That thought came unbidden, as Palin looked down at the chill patch of darkness that was the Shoikan Grove. Hastily, he averted his eyes, shifted his gaze to the Tower of High Sorcery. Lights burned within its windows, mostly on the lower level, where the apprentice mages would be awake, committing to memory their spells. Palin knew which room was Dalamar's, searched for light within.

It was dark.

Opposite the tower stood the Temple of Paladine, its white walls shining with a pale radiance, as if they had captured the moonbeams of Solinari and used them to brighten the night. Remembering his errand and the nature of his companion, Palin could not look long on the temple either.

The dragon took them over the palace of the Lord of Palanthas. It was aglitter with lights; His Lordship must be hosting a party.

How could people have fun at a time like this? Palin wondered, irrationally angry. His brothers were dead; other good men had given up their lives. For what? For this—that the Lord of Palanthas and his wealthy friends could drink themselves senseless on smuggled elven wine?

Palin wondered what would happen if he were to leap off the dragon, rush in on the merrymakers in his bloodstained robes and shout, "Open your eyes! Look at me! See what lies ahead for you!"

Probably nothing. The butler would throw him out.

The blue dragon veered to her left, skirted the palace, left behind the glittering lights. She flew above the Old City wall, past New City, and out over the bay. The water was startlingly dark in contrast to the city. Only a few tiny points of light marked the guardhouses of the night watch.

The night watch must have slumbered, for no one saw the dragon dip down from the sky and land on the shoreline.

16

The High Clerist's Tower.
An unwelcome messenger.

Built by Vinas Solamnus in the Age of Might, the Tower of the High Clerist guarded the only pass through the Vingaard Mountains—the major overland route from the rest of Ansalon into the great city of Palanthas. The tower was immense, massive, a mighty fortress. Yet, due to the tower's unusual design, the dwarf, Flint Fireforge, a Hero of the Lance, was once overheard to declare that the builder of the tower was either drunk or insane.

The tower had been built by humans, so the good dwarf's criticism must be taken with, as the gnomes put it, a grain of saltpeter. And it is true that when Flint made the statement, he was not aware of the true nature of the tower's unusual defense system, which the dwarf soon saw put into action.

Not long after Flint made that remark, the dragons of Highlord Kitiara's army attacked the tower. The Solamnic Knight Sturm Brightblade died in that assault, but—due to Sturm's sacrifice—the other knights rallied and, with the help of a kender, an elfmaid, and a dragon orb, the tower was saved.

The High Clerist's Tower was formidable in appearance. Rising some one thousand feet in the air, surrounded on all but the southernmost side by snow-capped mountains, the tower had reputedly never fallen to an enemy while men of faith defended it. An outer curtain of stone formed an octagon as the tower's base. Each point of the octagonal wall was surmounted by a turret. Battlements ran along the top of the curtain wall between the turrets. An inner octagonal wall formed the base of eight smaller towers, built around the larger central tower.

What had so disturbed Flint Fireforge was the fact that no fewer than six gigantic steel gates breached the outer walls, three of which opened onto the Solamnic plain, all of them leading into the heart of the tower Any dwarf worth his weight in stone will tell you that a good, solid fortification has only one entrance, which can be sealed shut, readily manned and defended against enemy attack.

The knights might have answered Flint by terming dwarven tactics unimaginative, lacking in subtlety. The High Clerist's Tower was, in actuality, a masterpiece of cunning design. The six gates opened into restricted courtyards—killing fields where the knights on the high walls above could dispatch their enemy with concentrated fire. Those who won through to the stairs leading to the central tower found themselves bottled up by hidden traps.

Those familiar with the history of the War of the Lance will recall that the three doors opening onto the Solamnic plain were actually dragontraps. A magical dragon orb placed within the center of the converging hallways would call to evil dragons, seduce them into flying inside the tower itself, rather than attacking it from the outside. The dragons were then killed by the Solamnic Knights, attacking the trapped creatures safely from behind stone defenses. Thus the tower's other, forgotten name, Dragondeath. And thus fell many evil dragons during the War of the Lance.

Many long years had passed since Sturm Brightblade stood alone upon the battlements, awaiting certain death. During the War of the Lance, the dragon orbs were reportedly lost to the world, or so most people devoutly hoped. The evil dragons, now knowing the secret of the tower's defenses, could no longer be lured into its deadly trap and, since dragons live incredibly long lives, it was likely that their memories of those halls, wet with dragons' blood, would prevent them from making the same mistake twice.

The tower had been rebuilt after the war, refurbished, modernized. With the loss of the dragon orbs, the tower's central defense against dragons was no longer effective, and the three dragontrap gates had become more of a liability than an asset. The Knights of Solamnia had realized the truth of the dwarf's statement concerning the three steel doors "Might as well invite the enemy inside for tea!" Flint had grumbled. They had taken precautions to seal all three of them with white granite "plugs," ornately carved to resemble the original gates.

Following the war, the Tower of the High Clerist became a bustling hub of activity. Overland traders clogged the roads in and out. Citizens came to seek counsel, advice, justice, or help in defending their towns against marauders. Couriers on important missions rode at a gallop to the gates. Kender were rounded up by day, their pouches searched, and released the following morning with strict orders to "move along," which the kender gleefully obeyed, only to be replaced by a new batch.

During the summer, traders set up stalls along the road leading from the plains below to the tower's main gate. There they sold everything from ribbons and silk scarves (for fair ladies to bestow as favors on their chosen knights), to food, ale, elven wine, and (below the counter) dwarf spirits.

Tourneys, featuring jousting, archery contests, mock battles, drill formations, and exhibitions of proficiency in riding horses and dragons, were held regularly to train the young knights, keep the older ones fighting fit, and delight the public.

Times for the knights had been good . . . until this summer.

As the sun's heat baked the dirt roads, travel across Krynn withered and died like the crops in the field. The man whose only harvest is dust and dirt cannot pay the roving tinker to mend his plow. The tinker cannot pay his bills at the inn. The innkeeper has no money to buy food needed to serve her guests.

Couriers still arrived, more than usual, bearing ominous tidings of famine and fire. A few die-hard travelers wandered in, half-dead from the glaring sun. The traders closed up their stalls and moved back to Palanthas. Tourneys were no longer held. Too many knights, clad in their heavy armor, had collapsed in the heat. Only the kender, afflicted by their national disease known as Wanderlust, continued to frequent the tower on a regular basis, arriving sunburned and dusty and commenting cheerfully on the remarkable change in the weather.

A group of kender were being ushered out the evening Tanis Half-Elven arrived. The knight in charge turned them loose, ordered them away from the gate. After making a quick head count, the guard vanished precipitously, returning with two more kender, who had become separated from the group and were discovered in the dining hall. The knight relieved them of several pieces of cutlery, six pewter plates adorned with the seal of the knights, two linen napkins, and a pepper box.

Ordinarily, the kender would have loitered outside the tower, hoping for a chance to get back in. This morning, however, the kender were distracted by the arrival of Tanis on griffin-back.

As soon as the griffin set down outside the front gate, on the main road leading into the tower, the kender swarmed around, staring with friendly interest at the griffin. That fierce beast—not liking kender—glared back at them with its beady black eyes. When any strayed too close, the griffin ruffled its feathers in irritation and gnashed its beak threateningly at them, much to the kender's delight.

Foreseeing that one or more kender might end up as the griffin's breakfast, Tanis, with many expressions of gratitude, dispatched the beast back to Porthios. The griffin left swiftly and gladly. The kender sent up a wail of disappointment and immediately attached themselves to Tanis.

Keeping fast hold of his sword in one hand and his money pouch in another, the half-elf waded through the kender sea, trying to reach the tower and not making much headway. Fortunately, the sound of hooves, galloping in the distance, caused the kender to abandon Tanis and turn their attention to this new arrival. Tanis hastened quickly toward the entrance.

The knight on duty saluted Tanis, who was a frequent visitor to the tower.

"Welcome, my lord. I will see that you are escorted to the guest hall, to rest after your long—"

"No time," Tanis said abruptly. "I must see Sir Thomas immediately."

Tanis's old friend and former leader of the knights, Lord Gunthar uth Wistan, had retired last year. Thomas of Thalgaard, Lord Knight of the Rose, was now commander of the High Clerist's Tower. A man in his early forties, Sir Thomas had the reputation for being a tough, able commander. His lineage in the knighthood was long. Thomas's grandfather had been a Knight of Solamnia, but had been robbed of his holdings by a sect of false priests during the dark years after the Cataclysm. Thomas's father had swallowed his pride, indentured himself to the priests in order to work as a slave on the land his family had once owned. Young Thomas's first mount, therefore, had been a plow horse; his first battles were fought against grubs and weevils. He had watched his father work himself to death, saw him die a slave, and vowed that he would become a knight.

Thomas had had his chance during the War of the Lance. His small village lay in the path of the dragonarmies. Fearing imminent attack, the false priests fled, taking with them everything of value and leaving the people to the mercy of the draconians. A youth of twenty, Thomas rallied his friends and neighbors, urged them all to seek shelter inside the castle. He defended his holdings with such skill and daring that the castle held out against the might of the dragonarmies until the war's end.

Tanis did not know Sir Thomas well, but, from what he had seen of him, the half-elf judged the knight to be a man of intelligence and common sense.

"I must see Sir Thomas at once," Tanis repeated. "I have urgent news."

"Certainly, my lord," the knight answered, and dispatched a messenger in search of the commander.

Tanis was not kept waiting long. Never one to stand on ceremony, Sir Thomas himself appeared. He greeted Tanis cordially, then, noting the half-elf's impatience, invited him to take a private walk along the battlements.

"You have news," Thomas said, when they were alone together. "And, to judge by your expression, it's not good."

"Then you have not received the report, my lord?"

"Report of what? I've heard nothing this past week."

"Lord Ariakan has launched his assault. North Keep and Valkinord have both fallen. Kalaman might now be under siege. As near as I can judge, the dark knights are launching a two-pronged attack, one army advancing through the Khalkist Mountains, the other planning on coming downriver from Kalaman."

The commander stared at Tanis in astonishment.

"My lord, the knights sent to fortify Kalaman were wiped out, almost to a man," Tanis said quietly. "They fought bravely, but they were vastly outnumbered. I have with me a list of the dead." He withdrew a folded packet, handed it to Lord Thomas. "To give Ariakan credit, my lord, the dead are being accorded all respect."

"Yes, he would," Thomas commented, glancing down the list, his face stern, jaw hard-set. "I knew them, every one," he said at last. Refolding the list, he tucked it into his belt. "I will see to it that their families are notified. You knew two of them, I believe. The Majere boys."

"I knew them. I helped bury them," Tanis returned grimly. "Their younger brother, Palin, was taken prisoner, is being held for ransom. It was his captor, a Knight of Takhisis, who brought us this news. You know this knight, too, my lord. His name is Brightblade, Steel Brightblade."

"Son of Sturm Brightblade. Yes, I recall that incident. You tried to save the young man from evil. He ended up desecrating his father's tomb, stealing his sword."

That wasn't quite what happened, but Tanis—who had been arrested and brought up on charges for his part in the "incident"—knew better than to argue. He'd presented the facts before the Knights' Council and had, at least, cleared his name and that of his friend Caramon. But he had not been able to convince the knights that it was Sturm himself who had bequeathed his sword to his son. Nor, looking back on it now, was Tanis certain of what had truly happened. It seemed to him that he and Sturm had both failed. Steel Brightblade was, as far as Tanis could judge, completely given over to the side of darkness.

"Kalaman under siege . . ." Thomas shook his head, baffled. "I find it hard to believe, Half-Elven. No disparagement, but Ariakan has only a handful of knights."

"My lord, according to Palin, Lord Ariakan's army is far more than a handful. His army is immense. He has recruited barbarians from lands to the east, humans who stand as tall as minotaur and who fight just as fiercely. They are led by knights on dragonback and have, among their ranks, renegade magic-users. Dalamar, head of the Wizards' Conclave on Ansalon, can testify to the power of these sorcerers."

"No doubt he can, since he is on their side."

"No, my lord. You are mistaken. This is not generally known, but recently the wizards of the three moons led an attack against the Gray Knights, as they are known. The wizards of the three moons were utterly vanquished. One of their number, Justarius, was killed. I'm not certain whose side Dalamar is on, but I don't think it is Ariakan's. Dalamar cannot forgive his queen for turning her back on him, in order to grant greater power to her own mages."

Thomas frowned. Like all knights, he distrusted magic-users of any color, wanted as little to do with them as possible. He waved the discussion of magic aside as being unimportant and irrelevant.

"Kalaman can withstand a siege for a long time. Time enough for us to send reinforcements."

"I'm not so certain—" Tanis began.

"My lord!" A young page came dashing, panting, up the stairs. "My lord, a courier has arrived. He—"

"Where are your manners, boy?" Thomas brought the page up short. "Here with me is a lord to whom you owe proper respect, as well as to myself. Discipline must be maintained," the knight added in an undertone to Tanis.

The page, scarlet to his ears, straightened, then hastily bowed, first to Tanis, then to Sir Thomas. But before his bow was half-finished, the boy was talking again.

"The courier, my lord. He's downstairs. We had to help him off his horse. He's ridden that hard . . ." The page halted, out of breath.

"More bad news, I fear," Sir Thomas observed wryly. "No one ever rushes to tell us *good* news."

The two men descended, returned to the front gate.

The courier lay stretched out on the floor, a cloak beneath his head. At the sight of him, Sir Thomas frowned, for the man wore the livery of the city guard of Kalaman. His clothes were stained with dried blood.

"He was so stiff we had to lift him off his horse, my lord," the knight at the gate reported. "He has had nothing to eat, he says, but has ridden day and night to reach us."

"My lord!" The man, seeing Sir Thomas, struggled to rise.

"No, no, Lad. Rest easy. What is your news?" Thomas knelt beside the man.

"Kalaman, my lord!" The soldier gasped. "Kalaman . . . has fallen!"

Thomas looked up at Tanis. "You were right, it appears," he said quietly.

"They came from the sea, my lord," the soldier was explaining in a weak voice. "From the sea and the air. We . . . had no warning. They attacked . . . in the night. Dragons and . . . huge beasts the knights termed mammoths . . . The city . . . surrendered . . ."

The man tried to continue, but fell back. A Knight of the Sword—a follower of the god Kiri-Jolith, who was granted the power to heal— began attending to the injured courier. After a cursory examination, the knight looked up at Sir Thomas.

"He is not severely wounded, my lord, but suffers from loss of blood and exhaustion. He needs to rest."

"Very well. Find him a comfortable bed. Let me know when he's able to talk again. I need details. The rest of you men, keep this to yourselves. No man breathes a word."

They bore the courier away on a litter, took his foundered horse to the stables.

"I know all I need to know anyway," Sir Thomas remarked to Tanis. The two stood alone in the hall; the knight at the entrance had returned to his duties. "Kalaman has fallen. This is dire news. If it reaches Palanthas, we'll have a riot on our hands."

Tanis was doing some quick figuring. "As I said, Ariakan has an immense army, one he can split with impunity."

"I see his plan," Sir Thomas said thoughtfully. "He attacks the east coast with half his strength, marches them west through the mountains. With the other half of his army he attacks the northeast, brings those troops south to meet up with the advancing forces on the other side of the Khalkists. On the way, he'll pick up the ogres and goblins and draconians who've been hiding out in the mountains. He'll have to leave troops to hold Kalaman and protect his supply lines, but, with the additional forces, by the time he arrives here, he'll be back up to full strength."

Sir Thomas smiled ruefully.

"I know him, you see. We used to discuss a plan very much like this, Ariakan and I, back in the old days. We were friends while he was a prisoner here. Ariakan was always a good soldier," Thomas added reflectively, shaking his head. "We made him a better one."

"So what will be his next move?" Tanis asked.

Sir Thomas gazed out the front gate, looked to the east. "He's on his way here. And there's not a damn thing we can do to stop him."

17

Eluding the patrols.
An odd sort of fish-wife.
One-Eye and Yellow Eye.

I don't know whether they had these in your day or not, but now what they call 'smugglers patrols' walk the docks at night," Palin whispered to his companion. "Then there's the port authority. They've rebuilt the Old City wall. Guards patrol there now. They've never forgotten Dragon Highlord Kitiara's raid on the city."

Palin could see Steel and the dragon only dimly. The knight worked in the lambent light cast by the moon and stars, and reflected off the water, to unload the supplies. They had landed on a peninsula that formed the western shore of the Bay of Branchala. Occasionally, Palin caught a flash of moonlit armor, or could see the tall, muscular figure outlined in silhouette against the star-pocked night sky.

Steel removed the bundle carrying the weapons that were never worn on dragonback unless the knight was flying into battle. He buckled on his long sword, thrust a short sword into his belt, slid a dagger into the top of his boot. He left the arrows, bow, and lance with the dragon.

"If my mother and your uncle had worked together, instead of at cross purposes," Steel remarked, "*I* might be the one hosting that party at the lord's house."

Palin did not miss the subtle reminder that Raistlin had been in league with the dark powers, then—as perhaps he was now. The memory of the Test in the Tower of High Sorcery, when Palin had met his uncle—at least he had thought it was his uncle—nagged at the edge of his mind. The image of Raistlin had been pure illusion, conjured up by Dalamar and the other wizards in order to test Palin, to see if he would succumb to the same temptations that had once beset his uncle.

The wizards believed that Caramon would never permit Palin to take the Test, a grueling ordeal that all wizards must pass before they can advance in their arcane art. The Test leaves none unscathed, none unaltered. Caramon would not risk losing his beloved son, as he had once lost a beloved brother. The wizards feared that Caramon's over-protective love would cause Palin to rebel outright, perhaps turn to evil, as had his uncle. The wizards took the matter out of Caramon's hands, had tricked both him and Palin.

In his Test, Palin believed that he had entered the Abyss, had there found his uncle being tortured by the Dark Queen. He had freed his uncle, led him back through the Portal, only to discover that Raistlin planned to leave the Portal open to permit the Dark Queen entrance. In return, she would give Raistlin rulership of the world.

Raistlin offered to make Palin his heir, if only Palin would turn to evil, would assume the black robes. Palin had refused and had been prepared to sacrifice himself in order to prevent his uncle from succeeding. It was then he had discovered that everything—his uncle, the Portal, the Abyss—had been part of his Test. None of it had been real.

Or had it?

Palin could still hear Raistlin's words.

I have trimmed my ambition. No longer will I strive to be a god. I will be content with the world. . . . This will be my gift to the Dark Queen, to prove my loyalty—admittance to the world. And the world will be her gift to me. Here she will rule and I . . . I will serve.

So his uncle had said. But had it really been his uncle? Dalamar claimed that the image of Raistlin had been nothing more than illusion. The Raistlin Palin had met had been a Raistlin of Dalamar's creation.

But the Staff of Magius, held fast in Palin's hand, was certainly not an illusion.

"We'd better hurry," Palin said abruptly. "It is near midnight."

Steel was patting the dragon on the neck, exchanging a few soft words. Palin caught the phrase, "Dargaard Keep," guessed that was where Flare would be hiding out. Lord Soth, the dread death knight, ruled that place still. Soth had once been a Knight of Solamnia. Forbidden love for an elfmaid had driven him to break his knightly vows, led him to commit murder. The gods' curse was on him. He would never die, but lived forever in bitter torment, hating the living, envying them. He was loyal to the Dark Queen and her cause. No mortal dared venture within a hundred leagues of his accursed castle. And, according to legend, the soul of Steel's dead mother was constrained to remain in Dargaard Keep with the knight. The blue dragon would be safe there, amidst such dark company.

Numerous fishing shanties dotted the beach. Either they were uninhabited or their occupants had long since gone to bed. Palin kept uneasy watch on them, fearful that someone would wake.

"Hurry," he repeated, nervously. "I thought I heard something."

"Don't worry, Majere." Steel displayed the skull-handled dagger. "If anyone sees us, I'll shut his eyes permanently."

"No killing, for gods' sake!" Palin protested. "I have a *sleep* spell memorized. I'll use that if we're discovered."

"Sleep spell." Steel snorted in derision. "Will that work on the undead guardians of the Shoikan Grove, do you think?"

"It will probably do about as much good as your dagger," Palin returned crossly, not liking the reminder. The glimpse of the Shoikan Grove, seen from the air, had shaken him.

Steel said nothing more. The knight's eyes glinted with what may have been amusement. He returned the dagger to his boot.

Flare used her powerful hind legs to propel her off the sandy ground. She leapt into the air, spread her wings, caught the meager sea breeze blowing from the ocean, and soared into the sky.

Palin watched the dragon leave with a certain amount of regret. He and Steel were on their own now, and the two of them seemed terribly inadequate.

"Coming, Majere?" Steel asked. "You were the one in such a hurry."

They found a small fishing boat that had been beached on the shore. Steel loaded the supplies into the boat, pushed it out into the water. He held it near shore long enough for Palin—hampered by his robes—to climb in, then Steel towed the boat into the water, splashing into the waves up to his knees, before climbing on board himself.

He took hold of the oars, slid them into the water, and silently, stealthily, rowed the boat toward the harbor.

"There's a lantern in the bottom. Light it," he ordered Palin. "We don't want to look suspicious."

The other, larger ships in the harbor had lanterns hung out, in order to keep other boats from ramming into them. Palin did as he was told, using tinder and flint he found in the prow. As he worked, it struck him as odd that there should be a lantern on board this small fishing boat and, if so, how Steel had known it would be there. In fact, how had Steel known the boat would be there? Perhaps the fishermen used the light for night fishing or smuggling—a far more lucrative trade than fishing these days.

Palin held the lantern aloft as Steel propelled the boat forward; the mage made certain he kept the light from shining on the dark knight's armor.

The night was still and hot. They lost the sea breeze almost the minute they entered the shelter of the harbor. Palin was bathed in sweat. Steel must be in far more discomfort, for he kept his cloak on over his breastplate and other accoutrements underneath. Palin, glancing back as they passed very near a tall, three-masted, minotaur ship, saw the knight's face glistening with perspiration. His black hair was wet, curling about his temples.

He made no complaint, but plied the oars with an effortless strength and skill Palin envied. His own arms ached, just watching.

A gruff voice from the minotaur ship hailed them. Looking up, Palin saw a horned head, outlined against the stars.

"Avast there, you lubbers! Keep clear! Put a hole in my ship and I'll plug it with your miserable bodies!"

"Drunk," Steel observed. "We're nowhere near him."

But Palin noticed that the knight leaned on the oars, sent their boat skimming rapidly across the dark water. Palin waved the lantern in apology, received a parting curse in response.

"Douse the light!" Steel ordered when they were near the docks.

Palin did so, blowing the lantern out with a puff of breath.

Steel stopped his rowing, let the boat glide forward of its own momentum, helped along by the incoming tide. Occasionally, he dipped an oar in the water to correct the direction. Reaching the docks, he caught hold of one of the supporting poles, held on as the boat veered around, nearly sliding under the dock.

"Get out!" he ordered.

Palin searched for the dock's ladder, found it. He was going to have to stand up in a small, rocking boat, grasp the ladder, haul himself up. He looked down into the inky black water that gurgled and lapped against the poles.

"What about my staff?" he demanded, turning to face Steel. "I can't carry it with me."

"I'll hand it to you!" Steel said, gripping the post with both hands, fighting the tide that was attempting to carry the boat into shore.

"No . . ." Palin clung to the staff.

"Then ask it to follow you up there on its own! Hurry up, Majere! I can't hold on much longer!"

Palin hesitated, not out of fear, but out of concern for leaving his valued staff behind.

Steel made a hissing sound, cast the young mage a furious glance. "Now, damn you!"

Palin had no choice. He had to trust, as Steel had intimated, that the staff would take care of itself. Laying the staff gently upon the seat, he rose to his feet, struggled to maintain his balance. Steel managed, by sheer force of strength alone, to swing the boat close to the dock. Palin flung himself at the ladder, caught hold of it, and clung to it in terror as the boat slid out from under him.

His feet scrabbled for purchase, found the last rung. With a gasp of relief, he climbed, tripping over his robes, but making it safely to the top. Immediately, he turned, leaned over to retrieve his staff.

He saw, with horror, that it wasn't there.

"What have you done with my staff?" he cried, forgetting, in his fear and outrage, that they were supposed to be quiet.

"Shut up!" Steel said through clenched teeth. "I haven't done anything with it! One minute it was there and the next it wasn't!"

Palin, panic-stricken, his heart constricting in pain, was on the point of throwing himself into the filthy, murky water when, putting his hand down on the dock, he felt his fingers close over warm, smooth wood.

The Staff of Magius lay at his side.

Palin gasped, almost dizzy with relief.

"Never mind," he whispered shamefacedly to Steel. "I've found it."

"Praise Her Dark Majesty!" Steel muttered.

Standing up in the boat, he caught hold of the ladder and—despite being burdened by his armor and his weapons—swung himself up with graceful ease. The boat drifted away.

Steel stood on the dock, but almost immediately crouched behind a large barrel, pulled Palin down with him.

"What?" Palin whispered.

"Patrol going by," Steel whispered back. "They can see us against the boat lights."

Palin couldn't see them, but—now that the knight had drawn his attention—he could hear the tramp of booted feet. Palin and Steel remained hunched on the dock, hiding behind the barrel, until the sound had faded into the distance.

Rising, Steel strode forward swiftly but silently, padding soft-footed along the dock. Palin marveled that the knight could move so quietly. Any other warrior Palin had ever known would have jangled and clanked, his sword thumping against his thigh, his armor rattling or squeaking. Steel was as silent as the darkness itself.

Palin pictured legions of such knights, marching noiselessly across Ansalon, conquering, enslaving, killing.

And here I am, he realized, suddenly appalled at himself, allied with one of them, my sworn enemy, one of those responsible for killing my brothers. And I'm taking him to the one place where the Dark Queen's knights will probably be able to enhance their power! What am I doing? Have I gone mad? I should cry out to the guards now! Denounce him! Turn him over to them.

No!—came the voice—*We need him, you and I. You will need his sword to win your way through the grove. You will need him inside the tower. Once he's brought you safely that far, then you can be free of him.*

This isn't right, Palin said to himself, but the warnings of his conscience weren't nearly as loud as his uncle's voice, so he was able to ignore them. Besides, Palin reflected wryly, I did give Steel my word. And after I made such an issue of that with my father, I can't very well go back on it now.

Having squared matters with his conscience—or at least rationalized his way out—he gripped the staff tightly and hastened on.

Steel was headed in the direction of the Old City wall. He took long, rapid strides, and Palin, hampered by his wet robes flapping around his ankles, had to walk swiftly to keep up. The guard posts showed clearly, well lit. The patrols' voices carried in the still, night air. Palin had a dozen glib lies prepared in order to get them through the wall and into the city. Unfortunately, none sounded the least bit convincing. He studied the wall anxiously, thinking that they could find some dark, unguarded spot, climb over it.

Iron spikes, spaced about a hand's-breadth apart along the top, ruled out that idea.

Palin was just wondering if there was family resemblance enough between himself and his cousin to convince the gate guard that they were brothers, when he noticed that they were no longer walking in the direction of the main gate. Steel had veered to his right, to a collection of ramshackle buildings huddled beneath the wall.

It was extremely dark in this section; the wall's shadow blocked the moonlight, and a large ship, docked nearby, cut off the ships' light from the harbor. An ideal place for smugglers to hide, Palin thought uneasily, and he jumped, his heart lurching, when he felt Steel's hand touch his arm. The knight drew Palin into the darker shadows of an alley.

Despite the fact that it was so dark Palin couldn't see his nose on his face—an old kender expression—his nose told him precisely where he was.

"Fishmongers!" he said softly. "Why—"

Steel's hand on Palin's arm tightened its grip, warning him to be silent.

A patrol tramped by, marching slowly through this section, peering down the alleys. Steel pressed himself back against the wall of the building. Palin did the same. The guards were making a thorough investigation, evidently sharing Palin's belief that this was an ideal hideout. One actually started to venture into the alley. Palin felt Steel's hand slide away, guessed that the hand was now grasping the hilt of the dagger.

Uncertain whether to stop Steel or help him, Palin waited tensely to be discovered.

A scuffling sound, some distance away, caught the guards' attention. The captain called off his man and the patrol hastened down the docks.

"We've got one!"

"Where?"

"I can see him! There he is!" cried one of the guards.

Boots thumped on the docks; truncheons whacked. A shrill scream echoed over the water. Palin stirred uneasily; that scream didn't sound like a vicious smuggler to him.

Steel grunted at Palin. "Don't move. It's not our concern."

One of the guards yelped. "Damn! He bit me!"

There came the sound of more whacking. The scream dissolved into sniveling.

"No hurt! No hurt! Me not do nothing bad! Hunt rats. Fat rats! Juicy rats!"

"Gully dwarf," pronounced one of the guards in tones of deep disgust.

"He bit me, sir!" repeated the guard, now sounding truly worried. "I feel sick."

"Should we run him in, sir?" asked another.

"Take a look in that sack he's carrying," ordered the captain.

There seemed some reluctance to obey this command, because the captain was forced to repeat it several times. Finally, one man apparently did. They could hear him retching.

"Rats all right, sir," said another. "Dead or dying."

"I give you all rats!" said the sniveling voice. "You take all, General, Your Worshipfulness! Make fine supper. Don't hurt poor Slug. Don't hurt."

"Leave the wretch alone," said the captain. "If we take him in, they'll only have to delouse the jail again. He's no smuggler, that's for sure. Come along, Lieutenant. You're not going to die of a gully dwarf bite."

"You don't know that, sir." The man whimpered. "I heard tell of a man who did. Right awful, it was, sir. He foamed at the mouth and his jaws locked together and—"

"We'll take you to Paladine's temple," the captain said. "Two of you men go with him. Sergeant Grubb, come with me."

The patrol marched off for the main gate. When the guards were safely out of earshot, Steel left the alley, moving so suddenly that Palin had to jump to keep up.

"Where are you going?" he demanded.

Steel made no reply. He walked straight toward the sound of snuffling. Reaching into the darkness, the knight plucked forth a wriggling, disreputable figure that smelled only slightly worse than the alley in which it was hiding.

"Help! Help! Murderers! Robbers! No hit! No hit!" begged the gully dwarf. "You want rats? Me give . . ."

"Shut up," said Steel, shaking the gully dwarf until he couldn't whine for his teeth rattling. "Quit screeching. I'm not going to hurt you.

I need some information. Which shop is One-eyed Kate's?"

The gully dwarf went limp in the knight's grasp. "Me know," he said cunningly. "What it worth?"

"How about your miserable life?" Steel said, shaking the creature again.

Palin intervened. "You won't get anything out of him that way." He rummaged in one of his pouches. "Why are we going to a fishmonger's?" he asked in a low voice. "Unless you've got a sudden craving for halibut . . ."

"I have my reasons, Majere. And you're wasting time," Steel said impatiently.

"Here," said Palin, pulling out a coin and handing it to the gully dwarf. "Take this."

The gully dwarf snatched it, peered at it through the darkness. "Copper?" He sniffed. "Me want steel."

Palin handed over another coin hurriedly. He had heard the knight suck in an exasperated breath. "Now, where is this One-eyed . . . what was the name?"

"Kate," Steel said, grinding the word with his teeth.

"Two shops down," said the gully dwarf. "No more than two."

Palin sighed. "That could mean anything from two to twenty. What does the shop look like?"

"Big fish on sign. Only got one eye."

The gully dwarf practically poked out his own eye, trying to get a good look at his prize. He was apparently satisfied, for he stuffed the coins in a shabby pocket and suddenly ran off, probably fearful Palin might have second thoughts and take the money back.

Steel started walking along the docks. "I need light. I can't see a damn thing. A pity we didn't bring that lantern."

"What about the guards?" Palin asked.

"They won't be able to see us. Their view is blocked by that big ship. Not that it matters—"

"*Shirak*," Palin said.

The crystal, clutched by a dragon's claw atop the Staff of Magius, began to glow with a soft radiance. Steel gave Palin an approving glance.

"Well done, Majere."

"Thanks, but I didn't have anything to do with it," Palin said, with a return of his bitterness. "The staff does it all by itself. I'm not even certain how the spell works." He held the staff up and shone the light on the signs of the shops they were passing.

"Why do you belittle yourself?" Steel asked. "A man should know his own worth."

"I do. I'm worth precisely nothing. But that will soon change."

"When you find your uncle. But he wore the black robes, didn't he? You wear the white. Will *you* change, Majere?"

A good question. Palin had been wondering that himself. "No," he said, at length. "I made my decision during my Test. I am satisfied with *who* I am, though perhaps not *what* I am. If I'm ambitious, if I want to better myself, that's not a bad thing. My uncle will understand."

"And he will teach his black art to a White Robe?" Steel snorted. "That's the day I become a cleric of Paladine!" He glanced sidelong at Palin. "You'll change, Majere. Mark my words."

"You better hope I don't," Palin said coolly. "If I do, I certainly won't feel honor-bound to keep my word and remain your prisoner. You might find my dagger in your back."

Steel smiled, very nearly laughed out loud. "A good answer. I'll keep that in mind."

"There's your sign." Palin pointed, ignoring the sarcasm. "A one-eyed fish."

"Ah! Excellent!" Steel walked up to the door. Glancing around to make certain no one was in sight, he knocked on the door in a peculiar manner.

Palin, mystified, waited in silence.

Apparently whoever lived here was a light sleeper, if the owner was asleep at all. After the briefest delay, a panel set into the door opened a crack. A woman, wearing a black eye-patch, peered out. "We're closed, good sirs."

"Yet the tide is rising," Steel returned conversationally. "All those who would take advantage should have their boats in the water."

The panel slammed shut, but almost immediately the door opened.

"Come in, sirs," said the woman. "Come in."

The two entered the fish shop. It was clean, the floor scrubbed. The tables normally used for displaying the freshly caught fish were bare, would not be filled until the boats came in with the morning's catch. Brown bottles containing fish oil stood in a row on a shelf. The smell of fresh fish was quite strong, but not unpleasant. The woman shut the door behind them, gazed keenly at Palin's staff and its softly beaming light.

"It's magic," Palin explained, "but it won't hurt you."

The woman laughed. "Oh, I am well aware of that, Master Mage I know all about the Staff of Magius."

Palin, not certain he liked that answer, tightened his grip on the staff, studied the woman closely. She was middle-aged, attractive, despite the eye-patch. She was fully dressed, which Palin might have thought odd for this time of night, but then his being here at all was so strange and irrational that a female fishmonger wearing an eye-patch, up and dressed in the middle of the night, seemed just another part of a waking dream.

"I am Steel Brightblade, my lady," said the knight, bowing over the woman's rough and reddened hand as if it were the soft hand of a noble gentlewoman. "Knight of the Lily."

"I had word of your coming, Sir Knight," answered the woman. "And this would be Palin Majere."

She turned to Palin, her one visible eye gleaming in the staff's light. Her clothes were as plain and simple as those of any peasant, but her bearing was regal; her voice cultured, educated. And here she stood in a fish shop!

"Yes! I am Palin . . . Majere, my . . . my lady," he said, astonished. "How did you know?"

"The dragon, of course. I am Katherine, Warrior of the Lily, a member of Her Dark Majesty's knighthood."

"A Knight of . . . of Takhisis?" Palin gaped.

"Of *high* rank," Steel added, with emphasis. "Lady Katherine fought in the War of the Lance."

"Under Lord Ariakus's command," Katherine explained. "That is how I lost my eye, in a fight with an elf."

"I'm . . . I'm sorry, my lady," Palin stammered.

"Don't be. The elf lost more than his eye. I knew your uncle, by the way, Raistlin Majere. He had just assumed the black robes when I met him. I found him . . . charming. Sickly, but charming." Lady Katherine turned back briskly to Steel.

"You want to enter Palanthas unnoticed?"

"Yes, my lady, if that is possible."

"Nothing easier. That is, of course, one of the reasons why I am here. And why I maintain this disguise." She looked directly at Palin as she said this, as if guessing his thoughts.

He felt his face burn, but a chill gripped him. Through this shop the servants of the Dark Queen infiltrate Palanthas! Spies, recruiters for the knights, perhaps murderers, assassins come to the fishmonger's. She helps them enter the city unobserved. Why have they shown this to me? Unless they know for certain that my tongue will be silenced. How not? I'm a prisoner, after all.

Of half a mind to flee, Palin glanced back at the door. He could probably make it before Steel caught him, at least outside. His shouts would bring the guards.

Palin imagined himself screeching for help—very much like the gully dwarf—and his face burned even hotter.

Lady Katherine smiled at him and, again, Palin had the impression she knew everything he had been thinking.

"This way, then, if you are determined to enter. You found the shop without difficulty, Knight Brightblade?" She led the way over to a wooden fish table shoved up against the back wall.

"A gully dwarf told us where you were located, my lady."

"Ah, that would be Alf. Yes, I posted him to keep a lookout for you."

"Not much of a lookout," Palin said. "He told us he'd never heard of the place."

"And he managed to get some money out of you, didn't he, White Robe? Cunning creatures, gully dwarves. People don't give them enough credit. Here we are." Katherine placed her hands on the table. "We must move this to one side."

"Allow me, my lady," Steel offered, and shifted the heavy table with ease.

Katherine walked over to what appeared to be a solid wall of stone. Placing her hand on it, she pushed. A section of the wall turned on a pivot, revealing a hidden passageway.

"Proceed through the tunnel. You will emerge in an alley. It is on the property of the Thieves' Guild, but we pay them well for their silence—and their protection. Yellow Eye will accompany you, to ensure that there is no trouble."

Katherine whistled in a peculiar manner.

Palin assumed Yellow Eye was one of the lady's henchmen, wondered where the man had been keeping himself. The mage was startled out of his notion and nearly out of his wits by a raucous caw and a rush of black wings. Palin instinctively raised his arms to ward off attack, but the bird lighted gently on his shoulder. It was, Palin could see now, a crow.

Cocking its head, Yellow Eye peered at Palin. The bird's eyes gleamed like amber in the lamp light.

"He likes you," said Lady Katherine. "A good omen."

"For my side or yours?" Palin spoke before he thought.

"Do not be disrespectful, Majere," Steel said angrily.

"Don't scold him, Brightblade." Lady Katherine intervened. "The young man says what he thinks—a characteristic he must have inherited from his uncle. If Paladine and Takhisis both stood before you, Palin Majere, to whom would you pray for assistance? Which one, do you suppose, would be most likely to help you achieve your goal?"

Palin realized suddenly, guiltily that he had *not* asked Paladine for his divine help.

"It's getting late." Palin turned to Steel. "We should be going."

Lady Katherine's smile broadened to a grin. The crow let out another ear-splitting caw, which sounded very much like laughter. Edging along Palin's shoulder, the bird playfully nibbled at the mage's ear.

The crow's beak was sharp, its bite painful. Its claws dug into Palin's shoulder.

Steel gave his thanks and bid the lady a gracious and courteous farewell.

Lady Katherine returned the compliment, wished them success in their endeavor.

Accompanied by the crow, riding triumphantly on Palin's shoulder, Palin and Steel entered the narrow tunnel. The staff lit their way. As the tunnel grew darker, the staff's light grew brighter—a phenomenon Palin had noticed before. The tunnel was taking them beneath the Old City wall, he realized, wondering how the knights had managed to dig it without arousing anyone's suspicion.

"Magic, I suppose," he said to himself, recalling the Gray Knight wizards. There were probably some of those very wizards in Palanthas itself, living right under Dalamar's nose.

Wait until I tell him about this, Palin thought, reveling in the idea. Such information alone surely should be worth the price of the wizard's help!

The tunnel was not very long, only as long as the City Wall was wide. Another door led them out into an alley. Steel paused before opening it.

"You better douse that light," he said.

Palin agreed. "*Dulak*," he whispered, and the crystal went dark.

In complete darkness, Palin could see nothing, not even the crow that remained perched on his shoulder. He heard the bird rustle its feathers, heard Steel groping for the door's handle.

The door opened a crack. Silver light poured inside. Lunitari was setting, but Solinari was on the rise, for which Palin was deeply grateful. He could draw on the moon for assistance with his magical spells, enhance their power. He would need all the help he could get, traveling through the deadly Shoikan Grove. He was about to pray to Paladine, and then he remembered Lady Katherine's question.

Palin said no prayers. He decided to trust to himself.

"Keep close to me," Steel warned softly.

Palin recalled that they were near the Thieves' Guild. The young mage's hand slid into his pouch; took hold of a few rose petals. The words to the *sleep* spell were on his lips. Steel had his hand on the hilt of his sword.

They crept out into the alley.

Unexpectedly—they'd neither heard nor seen a thing—a tall, dark figure loomed up right in front of them, blocked their way.

Before Steel could draw his blade or Palin could frame the words for his spell, Yellow Eye emitted a loud and stern-sounding caw.

The figure vanished, as if it had never been.

"Impressive," Palin said, expelling his breath in a relieved sigh.

"Sneaky, like vermin," Steel said disparagingly, but he kept his hand on his sword and started searching the alleyway.

"What do we do with Yellow Eye?" Palin was about to ask, when the crow flapped its wings, emitted another loud caw, and then bit Palin—hard—on the neck.

He cried out in pain, clapped his hand over the wound.

"What the—?" Steel turned so fast he nearly lost his balance.

"That damn bird bit me!" Palin said, furious and hurting.

"Is that all?" Steel demanded angrily. "I thought a legion of thieves had jumped you, at the very least."

"The blasted bird drew blood!" Palin removed his hand and looked at the dark smear left on his fingers.

The crow gave another caw—this one sounding snickering—and winged its way back over the wall.

"You won't die of a crow bite," said Steel. He walked to the end of the alley, peered into the street.

The street was silent, deserted. A few lights shone defiantly, impudently in the warehouse-type building that housed the Thieves' Guild, but none of its members walked the streets. Or, if they did, neither Steel nor Palin saw them.

Steel looked up and down the road cautiously, then raised his gaze above the rooftops. "That's the tower, there."

He pointed at a tall structure, the tallest in Palanthas. Solinari's light did not touch the tower; it stood in a shadow of its own creation. Yet, they could both see it quite clearly. Perhaps the black moon shed its unholy radiance upon the blood-red minarets. Palin nodded, unable to speak. The enormity of his task suddenly daunted him.

"I'm a fool," he said to himself. "I should turn around and go back home right now."

He wouldn't and he knew it. He'd come too far, risked too much . . .

Come too far . . .

Palin stared around, confused.

"Where are we?" he asked.

Steel smiled—a knowing smile. "Inside the walls of the city of Palanthas."

Palin blinked. "How . . . how did we get here?"

"You don't remember?"

"No . . . I . . . I have no idea . . ." Palin put his hand to his head. He felt dizzy, disoriented.

"Dwarf spirits do that to a man," Steel remarked offhandedly. "You'll feel better soon."

"Dwarf spirits? I . . . I don't drink. And you would never stop at a tavern! Not when we're in such danger." Palin was suddenly quite angry. "Tell me what's going on here! You have to tell me!"

"No," said Steel calmly. "I don't."

Palin felt a stab of sharp pain and something warm trickling down his neck. Reaching behind, he found that he'd been wounded, was bleeding.

He couldn't recall how that had happened either.

Steel started walking down the street, heading in the direction of the tower.

Palin, bewildered, followed.

From somewhere above came the eerie, mocking caw of a crow.

18

Cemple of Life.
Grove of Death.

he summer night was dark, hot. The citizens of Palanthas slept fitfully if at all. Lights flickered in many homes. People could be seen hanging out their windows, searching the skies in vain hope of rain, or walking back and forth in their bedrooms, trying to soothe whimpering, fretful children. Steel and Palin kept to the shadows, avoiding notice and questions, particularly those about why a man should walk in this heat wrapped in a cloak.

The two were near their destination. Steel could see the tower above him, yet—frustrated—he couldn't seem to find the street leading to it. Palin was no help. He had been to the tower before, but had traveled there only along the roads of magic. Arriving at an intersection, the two spent a moment debating which way to turn. Palin left it up to Steel, but he took the wrong street, apparently, for they ended up standing on a wide expanse of grassy lawn that stretched, like a carpet of welcome, from the street to a building made of white marble. The smell of flowers hinted at gardens that could be only dimly seen by Solinari's silver light and the white light flowing from the building itself.

Pain constricted Steel's heart, pain long forgotten, its ache stirred up in the cauldron of the past.

"I know where we are," he said.

"The Temple of Paladine! The last place we want to be!" Palin sounded alarmed. "We've come a street too far east. We should have turned right back there, not left." He glanced at Steel. "I'm surprised you should know of the temple "

"When I was a child, Sara prought me here, after the attack on Palanthas. We lost our house to the fires that raged through the city. Sara came here to give thanks that we hadn't lost our lives. It was here I learned of my mother's death—and who was responsible."

Palin made no response. He rubbed the place on his neck where Lady Katherine's familiar—the crow—had bitten him. The pain would not last long; the magic of that bite would last a lifetime, prevent Palin from remembering that he'd ever met a lady knight turned fishmonger. Palin was set to retrace their footsteps. Steel started to follow, but didn't. He paused to linger a moment before the temple, even took a step or two on the close-cropped grass.

Dark bundles dotted the lawn, and for a moment Steel thought that there must have been a battle and these were the bodies left behind. Then he realized that these bodies were living; the only battle they fought was one against the heat. People were slumbering peacefully on the lawn.

Steel knew this place well, far better than he had implied. Perhaps his coming had not been accidental. Perhaps he had been drawn here, as had often happened before.

Steel's youth had been a troubled one. He never lived the easy, carefree days of childhood touted by the poets. The war between light and dark, between conflicting emotions and desires was not a new one. He had fought this battle since his earliest days. The dark, represented by the image of his mother in her blue dragon armor, had impelled Steel even as a child to rule, to control—no matter what the cost to himself or others.

And when he couldn't, when the other children had rebelled against his authority, refused to obey him, the darkness had urged him to lash out, to hurt them. The light, represented in his dreams by the image of an unknown, silver-clad knight, caused Steel to be remorseful afterward. He wrestled with the turbulence in his soul, felt pulled two different ways by powerful forces he did not understand. Sometimes he feared he must be rent in twain if he did not choose one or the other. At times like these, he had fled to this refuge. He had come to Paladine's temple.

Steel had not known why. He was young, as immortal as the gods, he thought, and so had no great need of the gods. He had not gone into the temple itself. Its marble walls were stifling, confining. Not far from where he stood was an aspen tree. Beneath the tree was a marble bench, an old one, a relic of some noble family of ancient days. Cold and hard, the stone bench was not comfortable to sit upon and was generally avoided by most worshippers.

Steel loved it. A frieze had been carved into the back of the bench. Of crude workmanship, probably done by some apprentice learning his trade, the frieze portrayed the funeral of a Solamnic Knight and had been done as a memorial. The frieze pictured the knight, lying on his stone bier, his arms folded across his chest, his shield leaning (improperly, but such is artistic license) at the side of the bier. On either side of the knight's body—all of them identical and all looking very solemn and stern—were twelve knight escorts.

Steel remembered sitting on the grass, his chin on his arms, his arms on the bench. Here, for a brief time, the tumult in his soul ceased, the hot fury in his brain subsided, his clenched fists relaxed. He stared at the frieze, endowed it with boyish, imaginative life. Sometimes, the funeral was his own; he'd died performing heroic deeds, of course. He liked to imagine that he had died saving the lives of the other children—his so-called friends—and that *now*, too late, they had come to appreciate him. Other times he pictured himself attending the funeral of another knight. Steel saw himself not as one of the mourners, but as the knight's slayer. The tourney had been an honorable one. The knight had died heroically, and Steel had come to his funeral to pay him homage.

Almost exactly what had recently happened with the Majere brothers.

The thought made his skin shiver, and Steel was not ordinarily prey to such sensations.

"You're being a fool, Brightblade," he told himself sternly, ashamed of his momentary lapse into superstition.

"Still, it is strange," he told himself, peering through the darkness, trying without success to catch a moonlit glimmer of the bench's cold white marble, "I had forgotten all about that old bench. . . ." He smiled to himself in the darkness, a soft smile, a sad one.

He knew about the gods now. He had dedicated his life to one of them, a dark goddess, the goddess who ruled the darkness of his soul. She would punish him, should he seek out that restful bench. Not only that, but undoubtedly Paladine would vent his anger on any servant of Her Dark Majesty who would dare venture into his holy precinct. Just to step on the grass, as he had done, would be considered sacrilege.

Palin was staring at him, about to speak, when a low, deep-throated growl silenced them both.

The growl was savage, fearless, and it came from behind.

"Don't move!" Palin warned softly. He was facing Steel, could see the knight's back. "It's a tiger. About ten paces behind you. It—"

"Don't be alarmed, Gentlemen," said a calm, cool voice from the darkness. "This is Tandar, my guide. He won't hurt you. It is late to walk the streets. Are you lost? Troubled? Is there any way I can be of help?"

Steel moved, pivoting slowly, carefully, his hand on his sword's hilt. Palin hastened to the knight's side.

The tiger stepped into a glade of silver moonlight. It was a white tiger, extremely rare in Ansalon. Its stripes were black and gray, its eyes green with flecks of gold, dangerously intelligent. The beast was huge, massive in girth, its paws the size of a man's head. A golden collar gleamed on its neck. Dangling from the collar was a medallion bearing a golden dragon—the symbol of Paladine.

It was not the tiger who had spoken, though by its intelligent look, the beast might have. The speaker was a woman. She emerged from the shadows to stand at the tiger's side, her hand resting gently on its head.

"My guide," she had termed the animal. As she stepped into Solinari's light, Steel saw why she walked the night in the company of this great beast.

This woman must always walk the night, for she would never see daylight. The woman was blind.

Steel recognized her then. Revered Daughter Crysania, High Priestess of the Temple of Paladine, the leader of the god's worshippers on Ansalon.

Some twenty years had passed since Crysania, out of an ambition as dark as the mage's own, had accompanied Raistlin Majere into the Abyss. She had very nearly died there. Only when she was lying in that dread place, alone and blind, had she, at last, been able to see. She had returned to the world, blind to its beauty, but no longer blind to its pain. The church had grown strong under her wise leadership, its clerics beloved.

Her skin was as white as Solinari's glow, her hair black, netted in silver. The marks of her trials and struggles were etched on her face, yet serenity and faith graced her. She was beautiful, as the temple itself was beautiful—cool, stalwart, blessed.

Steel looked to Palin to speak, but the mage was apparently tongue-tied. The dark paladin might have suggested that they slip away, make good their escape, but for the tiger, who was watching them narrowly.

"A mage and a knight," Lady Crysania said, approaching them. "I presume you are not lost wanderers, then, but on some sort of mission. Have you come to seek Paladine's blessing?"

The tiger growled again, softly. Obviously, it was time to speak up. Steel elbowed Palin, nudged him in the ribs.

"Not . . . not exactly, Revered Daughter," Palin said faintly. His face was pale and glistened with sweat, not all of it due to the night's heat.

White-robed mages were expected to revere Paladine and follow his precepts. Rescuing a notorious black-robed wizard from the Abyss was probably not high on the god's list of things he would expect his followers to accomplish.

"Palin Majere," said Lady Crysania. "I bid you welcome."

"How . . . how did you know?" Palin gasped.

Crysania laughed, her laughter like the music of silver bells. "How did I know? I can smell the spice and rose petals of your spell components, and so I knew you were a mage. When you spoke, I recognized your voice. You have the tone of your father, but the way you talk . . . you remind me of your uncle." The last she said in a low voice.

Palin's face, formerly pale, was now bright red, as if Lunitari were shining on him. He had no reply to this, nor did the Revered Daughter appear to expect one. Smiling pleasantly, she turned the dark, sightless eyes on Steel.

"I knew the knight by the rattle of his sword. Surely Palin Majere walks in company with one of his warrior brothers. Do I have the pleasure of addressing Tanin Majere or Sturm Majere?"

There were many ways Steel might answer. The easiest: to feign to be one of the Majere brothers. A hoarse and raspy tone would disguise the voice, could be explained away by a cold in the head. A brief exchange of pleasantries and they would be on their way. Whereas, if Steel told the truth . . .

He looked at the tiger. The beast stared at him. There was a wisdom in the eyes not to be found in the eyes of any dumb animal, no matter how intelligent. If the tiger attacked, the beast's weight would carry Steel to the ground. He might be able to stab it but not before its yellow teeth would tear out his throat.

Certain bold words came back to him.

I will not enter Palanthas dressed as an innkeeper . . .

Nor hide behind another man's name.

"You are mistaken, Revered Daughter," Steel said coolly, politely. "My name is Steel Brightblade, Knight of the Lily. I have the honor to serve Her Dark Majesty, Takhisis."

Palin rolled his eyes, shook his head. "Now you've done it!" he whispered.

The tiger muttered softly in its throat. Lady Crysania soothed her guide with her hand. Her brow was furrowed, her expression troubled.

"You proclaim this in the open, in the city of Palanthas?" she asked, not threatening, but in wonder.

"I proclaim it to you, Revered Daughter," Steel returned. "A sighted man could see who I am. There is no honor, only shame, in taking unfair advantage of one whom the gods have chosen to walk in shadow. Still greater shame lies in deceiving a woman as noble and courageous as yourself, my lady."

Crysania's sightless eyes widened.

"What Tanis Half-Elven told us years ago about you knights was right," she murmured. "Paladine help us!" Her sightless gaze turned inward, pondering, then her face shifted once again to Palin. "What are you doing here, young mage? Why do you travel in company with this knight, who—though honorable—is nevertheless dedicated to evil?"

"I am this knight's prisoner, Revered Daughter," Palin replied. "My brothers are both dead. The Knights of Takhisis have landed on the northern coast, near Kalaman. Tanis Half-Elven is on his way to give this news to the knights in the High Clerist's Tower."

"A prisoner. Then they have demanded ransom."

"Yes, Revered Daughter. That is why we are here." Palin fell silent, obviously hoping the cleric would ask him nothing else.

"You are going to the Tower of High Sorcery."

"Yes, Revered Daughter," Palin answered.

The tiger suddenly shook himself, as if he'd just stepped out of the sea and was shaking off the water. The great head moved restlessly beneath Crysania's fingers.

"If you wanted ransoming, young mage, you would go to the Tower of High Sorcery at Wayreth. The Wizards' Conclave decides such issues." Crysania's voice had sharpened.

"Forgive me, Revered Daughter," Palin said with quiet firmness. "But I am not at liberty to discuss this. I have given this knight my word of honor."

"And should we be considered less honorable than our enemies?" Crysania asked with a half-smile. "That is what you imply. My lord Dalamar does not know you are coming, does he?"

"No, my lady," Palin replied softly.

"You are planning to enter through the Shoikan Grove. You will not survive. Your word of honor will not be of much use to you in that dread place. I know," she added, with a shiver. "I have walked it."

She was silent. Again the sightless gaze turned inward.

Steel wanted to leave, yet he was uncertain how to extricate himself. Lady Crysania lifted her head, faced them both, her eyes staring somewhere in between them.

"You are wondering, perhaps, why I do not summon the city guards to deal with you. This meeting does not come about by chance. I do not often walk the temple grounds after midnight. But this night, I couldn't sleep. I supposed it was the heat and went out to seek a breath of cooler air. But now I know it was Paladine's will that I find you, that we find each other. And whatever you are doing, I feel his will guiding you."

Palin stirred, cast a sidelong glance at Steel. The dark paladin shrugged, smiled. Queen Takhisis was known to work in mysterious ways.

"You will never win your way through the Shoikan Grove alive. Here." Lady Crysania reached to her throat, drew forth a medallion. Gold flashed in the silver moonlight. Unfastening the clasp, she removed the medallion, held it out. "Take this, Palin Majere. It will not protect you from the undead guardians of that dread place, but it will lift the fear from your heart, give you courage to walk the darkness."

Palin looked stricken, as guilty as any thief caught with his fingers in the poor box. "I can't accept this, Revered Daughter. It . . . isn't right.

You don't know . . ." He fell silent.

Lady Crysania reached for the mage's hand. She found it, pressed the medallion into his palm.

"Paladine be with you," she said.

"Thank you, my lady." Palin clutched the medallion, not knowing what else to do or say.

"It is time we were going," Steel said, deciding to take command of the situation. He made a formal bow to Lady Crysania. "I would offer to provide you safe escort back to your chambers, my lady, but I see that you are already well protected."

Lady Crysania smiled, though immediately afterward, she sighed. "I believe you would, Sir Knight. It grieves me to see such nobility of heart and spirit dedicated to darkness. And how will *you* enter the Shoikan Grove, Sir Knight? Your queen does not rule there. Her son, Nuitari, is the dread monarch of that evil place."

"I have my sword, my lady," Steel answered simply.

She took a step nearer, the sightless eyes staring at him, and suddenly it seemed to him—startlingly—that she could see him. She reached out her hand to him, rested her hand on his breast, on the armor with the death lily, the skull. The cleric's touch was like a flame, searing his soul, and it was like cool water, bringing him ease. For the first time in his life, Steel was helpless, had no idea what to do.

"You, too, have a guardian, I see," Lady Crysania said to him. "Two guides! One of dark, one of light. The guide who stands on your left, on your heart-side, is a woman. She wears blue armor and carries the helm of a Dragon Highlord in one hand and a lance in the other. The tip of the lance is wet with blood. She is nearest to your heart. The guide on your right is a man, a Knight of Solamnia. He holds no weapon. His sheath is empty. A bloody hole, made by a lance, pierces his body. This man is nearest to your soul. Both want to guide you. Which will you choose to follow?"

She finished speaking, removed her hand. Steel slumped, as if she had been holding him up. He sought proud words, but none came. He could only stare at her in amazement. What she had described had been the Vision—given to him by Queen Takhisis.

The tiger padded up, pressed the white-and-black-striped body protectively against Crysania. She bid Palin and Steel good night.

"My blessing go with you," she said to them softly.

Her hand upon the tiger's head, the cleric of Paladine retraced her steps, was soon lost in the shadows.

Palin was staring, openmouthed, at Steel. The dark knight was in no mood to talk. Half-angry, half-frightened, wholly embarrassed, Steel turned on his heel and walked rapidly back down the street, back the way they'd come. He heard the footsteps of the mage, the flapping of his robes, as Palin hurried to catch up.

Steel walked even more swiftly, as if he could outwalk the fiends plucking at his soul.

"I don't need a guide!" he whispered furiously. "I grew up alone. I don't need either of you—father *or* mother!"

He didn't cease his rapid pace until he emerged from an alleyway and there, before him, stood the trees of the ancient, dreaded Shoikan Grove.

There had once been five Towers of High Sorcery on Ansalon. Strongholds of the mages, the towers were viewed as threats by those who feared the wizards' power. In order to protect themselves from attack, the wizards gave each tower a guardian forest. The forest for the Tower of Daltigoth caused a debilitating lethargy to overcome any who ventured into it; they would fall into a deep and dreamless sleep. The Tower of Istar—shattered during the Cataclysm—caused those who entered to forget completely why they'd come. The Tower of the Ruins raised such heated passions in the breasts of those who encroached upon its grounds that they lost all interest in anything else. The forest surrounding the Tower of Wayreth evades trespassers. No matter how hard they try, they cannot find it. But of all these, the Shoikan Grove is the most terrible. The others were blessed by the followers of Solinari and Lunitari. The followers of Nuitari, the Black Robes, blessed the Shoikan Grove.

Its gigantic oak trees stand unmoving. No wind, not even the violent winds of cyclone and hurricane, can cause so much as a single leaf to shiver. Their massive boughs intertwine, forming a canopy so thick that the sun's light cannot penetrate it. The Shoikan Grove is shrouded in perpetual night. Its shadows are never warmed, are as chill as death.

Nuitari himself cast the enchantment of fear on the grove. All who approach it—even those who come invited by the master within the tower—experience crippling terror that strikes at the heart of every living person. Most cannot even stand to come within sight of the trees. Those of extraordinary bravery who actually make it as far as the grove itself usually do so only by crawling on their knees. Few have ever made it farther. One was Caramon Majere. One was Revered Daughter Crysania. Another was Kitiara. Both of these latter two were given medallions to counteract the fear, to help them through. As for Caramon, he had barely escaped with his sanity intact.

Now Steel Brightblade stood in the shadows of the Shoikan Grove. The enchantment seized him, casting on him the fear—terrible, helpless, debilitating, and unreasoning. It was the fear of death, a surety to those who would set foot within; the fear of the torment and torture that would precede the end; and the even greater fear of the eternal torment and torture promised after.

He could not fight such fear, for it was god-inspired. The fear wrung him, drained him, gripped his bowels, clenched his stomach. Fear dried his mouth, constricted his muscles, dampened his palms. Fear very nearly drove him to his knees.

He heard the voices of the undead, as dry and brittle as bone.

"Your blood, your warmth, your life. Ours! Ours! Come closer. Bring us your sweet blood, your warm flesh. We are cold, cold, cold beyond endurance. Come closer, come closer."

The darkness of the grove, darkness eternal, never brightened by any light, save perhaps the unseen light of the black moon, flowed over Steel. He prayed to Takhisis, though he knew his prayer would not be answered. Her Dark Majesty's rule ended at the border of these woods. Here her son, Nuitari, lord of dark magic, reigned supreme. And all knew that he rarely listened to his parent.

To die in battle—Steel had always assumed that would be his fate. To lie on a marble bier, the weapons of his enemy at his feet, mourned, praised by his comrades—that was Steel's dream of death.

Not this. Torn apart by the rending, tearing nails of the undead; dragged beneath the ground, clawing and grasping, sinking, suffocating. And then, after death came as a mercy, his soul would be held in thrall, forced to serve the god of the undead, Chemosh.

A voice, a new voice, interrupted that of the chill hissings of Chemosh's slaves. A woman, clad in blue armor, strolled out from the shadows of the tall trees. The woman was lovely, her hair cropped short to fit comfortably beneath her helm. Dark curls framed her face. Her dark eyes were alluring. She smiled—a crooked smile—and laughed. She laughed at him.

"Look at you! Sweating and shivering like a child on the Night of the Eye! Did I bear a coward for a son? By my queen, if I did, I'll feed you to Chemosh myself!"

The Blue Lady approached him, her walk swaggering. A sword hung from her hip; a blue cloak stirred restlessly around her, though the night air was breathless and still.

Steel knew her. He had never seen her in life, but he knew her. She had come to him once before—in the Vision.

"Mother . . ." he whispered.

"Don't call me 'Mother'!" Kitiara jeered. "You are no son of mine. My son is not a coward. *I* walked that dread grove. And here you stand, thinking of turning tail and running!"

"I'm not!" Steel retorted, all the more angrily because he *had* considered retreating. "I—"

But the vision vanished, withdrew back into the darkness.

Gritting his teeth, his hand closing over the hilt of his sword, Steel strode forward, heading straight for the Shoikan Grove. He had forgotten about Palin, forgotten that such a being as the mage existed. It was a battle now, between the grove and himself. He did not hear the footsteps hastening after him. He jumped, startled, when a hand touched his arm. Whirling, he drew his sword.

Palin, breathing hard, fell back a step before the knight's fey look. "Steel, it's me . . ."

The light of the Staff of Magius shone brightly on the young mage's face. Steel gave a great sigh of relief, of which he was immediately ashamed.

"Where have you been, Majere?"

"Trying to catch up with you, Brightblade!" Palin answered. "You ran off so fast . . . It's going to take both of us to get through that cursed grove . . . if we make it at all."

They could both hear the voices of the undead now.

"Warm blood, sweet flesh, come to us . . . come . . ."

Palin was white to the lips. The hand holding the staff was white-knuckled, slippery with sweat.

"Blessed Paladine!" Palin grabbed hold of Steel's arm. "Look! Dear gods! It's coming straight for us!"

Steel turned back, sword raised. And then, he lowered it.

"What are you doing?" Palin fumbled frantically for his spell components. "We have to fight . . ."

"My father won't hurt us," Steel said softly.

Two guides, Lady Crysania had said.

A knight clad in armor that shone like silver in the moonlight stepped from the shadows of the grove. The armor was decorated with the rose, the crown, the kingfisher. It was old-fashioned armor, dating back practically to the Cataclysm. The knight wore no sword; he had given his to his son.

The knight came to stand before Steel.

"You have promised, on your honor, to enter this accursed place?" Sturm Brightblade asked.

"I so promised, Father," Steel replied, his voice steady. His hand on his sword was steady now, too.

Sturm's eyes, careworn, sad, loving, proud, seemed to take the measure of the living man. Sturm nodded once, solemnly, and said, "*Est*

Sularus oth Mithas."

Steel drew in a deep breath, let it out slowly. "I understand, Father."

Sturm smiled. Lifting his hand, he pointed at his son's throat. Then, turning on his heel, he walked away. He did not disappear into the shadows; it seemed that the shadows parted for him. He vanished in a glade of silver moonlight.

"Do you know what he means?" Palin asked in a hushed voice.

Steel reached his hand beneath his armor, took hold of a jewel he wore around his neck. He drew it forth. The jewel was of elven make and design—a token elven lovers often exchange. It had been Alhana's gift to Sturm: token of love eternal. It had been Sturm's gift to his son. The jewel's light shone bright and cold—a clean, piercing cold, like a shaft of ice. Or like the sharp blade of a lance.

" 'My honor is my life.' I will not shame my mother. I will not fail my father. We will enter the grove now," Steel Brightblade said.

19

Tas is bored.
Conversation with a specter.
Powerful kender magic.

asslehoff Burrfoot heaved a sigh. Plunking his small body down on a chair, he looked around, sighed again, and made an announcement.

"I'm bored."

Now, at the sound of these dreaded words, anyone who had lived long on Ansalon would have made every attempt to flee for his life. Go up to any seasoned warrior and ask him, "Pardon me, sir, but which would you rather be locked up in a room with—an army of ogres, a regiment of trolls, a brigade of draconians, a red dragon . . . or a bored kender?"

The warrior will pick the ogres, trolls, draconians *and* the red dragon hands down, every time. He will tell you, as will everyone you meet, that nothing on Krynn is more dangerous than a bored kender.

Unfortunately, Usha, never having lived among kender, didn't know this.

The two had spent the first night of their arrival, the next day, and well into the next night slumbering under the enchantment cast on them by Dalamar and Jenna. Tas awoke first and, being a considerate kender, he took pains not to wake Usha, even refraining—with a heroic effort of will—from rummaging through her pouches, one of which she was using as a pillow.

He explored the room, which was filled with interesting objects collected from all over Krynn by Raistlin. Dalamar had added to the collection, and Tas admired the delicate wooden statues of animals carved by the Wilder elves; shells and sponges brought up from the Blood Sea of Istar; porcelain boxes decorated with fanciful paintings of peacocks from Northern Ergoth; huge, ornately carved cedar chests produced by the dwarves of Thorbardin; and various other objects of interest.

Any and all of these (with the exception of the cedar chests) might have ended up in Tas's pouches, and more than one item did actually tumble in by accident, only to tumble out just as rapidly. The room had obviously been kender-proofed.

"My goodness!" said Tas, as a crimson-stained shell of a spiny sea urchin leapt from the kender's pouch back onto its shelf. "Would you look at that!"

"Look at what?" Usha said sleepily.

"Why, every time one of these things jumps into my pouch, it jumps itself back out again. Isn't that marvelous? Come and watch!"

Usha watched, but she didn't appear much impressed.

"Where is Lord Dalamar and that woman—Jenna? Where did they go?"

Tas shrugged. "People are always disappearing around this place. They'll be back." He turned his attention to the locks on the cedar chests.

"I don't want them to come back," Usha said irritably. "I hate this place. I don't like that Dalamar. I want to leave. And I'm going to. Come on. Now's our chance, while they're gone."

Gathering up her packs, she marched over to the door, grasped the handle, and pulled.

The door didn't budge.

Usha rattled the handle, tugged on it, even kicked the door.

It didn't open.

Tas glanced over. "I'd say it was bolted," he offered helpfully.

"But why?" Usha was bewildered. "Are you sure?"

This state of affairs being nothing new or out of the ordinary for the kender, Tas nodded. "People always seem to be locking me up or locking me out or both. You get used to it."

The locks on the cedar chest also proved immune to kender prying. The hole where the key was supposed to fit kept darting from one side to the other, in a most unsportsmanlike manner. While this proved highly diverting for the first ten minutes, Tas soon grew bored with chasing the locks about and again made the pronouncement that would have sent most people running, screaming, for the exit.

"I'm bored."

Usha, pacing like a restive cat, made no reply. Passing the window, she stopped, looked hopefully out. It was a long, long drop to the spiked rails of the tall iron fence below. She drew back hurriedly.

"Well," Tas added, slapping his hands on his knees, "I'd say we've done just about all there is to do around this place. Let's leave."

Fumbling about in one of his pouches, he produced the lock-picking kit that is a kender's birthright. "I'm sure Dalamar didn't mean to bolt us in. The latch probably fell down on its own when he left." He eyed the lock, added severely, "So long as it will *hold still*, I can fix his oversight."

Producing several interesting-looking tools, Tas—no longer bored—walked to the door and set to work.

Usha came over to watch. "Where do we go once we leave this room? Do you know the way out?"

"Yes," Tas said eagerly. "It's through the Shoikan Grove, a really horrible haunted forest filled with undead who want to devour your flesh and hold your soul in torment throughout all eternity. I know. I saw it once, but I never got to go inside. Only Caramon got to go. Some people have all the luck."

He paused a moment, misty-eyed, remembering the good times. Then, whistling a dwarven marching tune, he wiped his nose on his sleeve and cheerfully returned to the task at hand.

The pick rattled inside the lock.

The lock remained locked.

Tas frowned, slid the pick back into his kit, selected another, and tried again.

"Then it doesn't matter whether we get out of here or not. If we can't get through this grove, we're still trapped here!" Usha sounded disheartened.

Tas paused to consider. "I know the grove keeps people out, but I never heard anything about it keeping people *in*. Maybe we won't have any problems at all."

"Do you think so?" Usha regarded him with renewed hope.

"It's worth a try." Tas pried away at the lock energetically. "The worst that can happen is that skeletal hands will reach up out of the ground and try to grab our ankles and drag us under the dirt, where we'll die in terrible agony."

Usha gulped, apparently not seeing the fun in all this. "Maybe . . . maybe we should just stay here after all, wait for Dalamar to return." She returned to her chair and sat down.

"Got it!" Tas cried triumphantly.

The lock made a loud *snick*. Tas threw open the door.

Two cold, disembodied white eyes stared at him from the darkness.

"Oh, hullo there," Tas said to the undead being, somewhat taken aback at its sudden appearance.

"Shut the door!" Usha cried urgently. "Shut it quick! Before that . . . that *thing* comes in here!"

"It's just a specter," Tas said, and he politely held out his hand. "How do you do? My name is Tasslehoff Burrfoot. Oh, I guess you must find it hard to shake hands, seeing as how you don't have any. I'm sorry. I hope that didn't make you feel bad. I know I'd feel really bad if I didn't have any hands. But it's very nice to meet you. What's *your* name?"

The specter didn't respond. The eyes floated nearer. A bone-numbing chill flowed into the room.

Usha jumped out of her chair, ran behind it. "Shut the door, Tas! Please, please! Shut the door!"

"It's all right, Usha," Tas called, though he involuntarily backed up a pace or two. "Come in," he invited the specter politely. "We were just leaving . . ."

The unblinking eyes moved inexorably back and forth.

"We're *not* leaving," Tas guessed, and he was starting to grow a bit miffed. He had really spent as much time in this room as he wanted. Perhaps the specter was lonely, wanted to engage in some pleasant conversation.

"You're one of the undead, aren't you? Would you happen to know Lord Soth? He's a death knight and a great friend of mine."

The specter's eyes glittered in a decidedly hostile manner. Tas suddenly recalled that Lord Soth, having tricked Kitiara into almost murdering Dalamar, probably wasn't highly revered among those who guarded the tower.

"Uh, mmm, not really a friend," the kender admitted, backing up another pace or two. As the eyes floated nearer, the temperature in the room fell to an uncomfortable level. "More like an acquaintance. He never comes to visit or drops by for lunch or anything. Well, it's certainly been nice chatting with you. Now, if you'll just step aside, we'll slip out and not bother you anymore. . . ."

"Tas!" Usha screamed.

The kender tripped on the trailing skirt of the tablecloth and fell down.

The specter hovered over him a moment, then, suddenly, it was gone. The door slammed shut. The chill abated.

Usha, shaking all over, crouched behind the chair. "What *was* that thing?"

"Extremely rude," Tasslehoff remarked, picking himself up and dusting himself off. "I admit that most undead I've met aren't very good conversationalists, with the exception of the spectral minions we ran into in Darken Wood, who very obligingly told us their life stories, all about how they were cursed and everything. Only they talked by using Raistlin's mouth. They had mouths of their own—no lips, only mouths. It was truly wonderful. This specter doesn't have any mouth, which I guess is why it never says anything. Would you like to hear the story about Darken Wood? Since Raistlin is your father and all—"

"I just want to get out of this horrible place!" Usha snapped. She shivered with fear, but she was growing angry, too. "Why are they holding us prisoner? I don't understand!"

"Probably because Raistlin is your father," Tas suggested after considering the matter. "Dalamar was Raistlin's apprentice, but the dark elf was also the Conclave's spy on Raistlin, because he was a renegade wizard, and they didn't trust him. Raistlin knew that Dalamar was a spy, and he punished Dalamar by boring holes in the elf's flesh. The bloody holes are still there, and they still hurt him, but don't ask Dalamar to let you look at them, because that puts him in a *really* bad mood. I know. I did once.

"After that, Dalamar was going to kill Raistlin when Raistlin tried to come back through the Portal of the Abyss after almost defeating the Dark Queen, which was when Caramon tried to go through the grove and Tanis almost fought with Lord Soth, only he couldn't because I stole his magical bracelet . . ."

Tas had to pause here to breathe. Usha stared at him, wide-eyed.

"This Raistlin . . . I mean my father . . . My father did all that! You never told me that part!" She sank back down, limp, in her chair. "No wonder Dalamar doesn't trust me! He'll never let me go! He . . . he might even kill me!"

"I don't think so." Tas pondered the issue. "But they might take you before the Wizards' Conclave. If they do, will you take me with you?"

Usha groaned, put her hands to her head. "I don't *want* to go to any Wizards' Conclave. I just want to go home!"

Tas had difficulty understanding this notion, having been afflicted by Wanderlust at an early age. He knew, from long association, that homesickness was a failing among humans.

"I could probably get us out of here if I truly put my mind to it. But what about all those magic items you have?" Tas pointed at Usha's pouch. "You told Dalamar you were a very powerful wizardess. Being Raistlin's daughter and all, of course, you must be. I *adore* magic spells! I'd really like to see some of yours."

Usha glanced nervously at the pouches, particularly the one that held the magical objects. "I don't think there's anything in here that will help."

"But maybe you don't know that for sure. Let's look! I can help you sort out all your things," Tas offered magnanimously. "I'm really good at sorting and finding. It's amazing what people turn up when they go through my pouches. They find stuff that they didn't even know they'd lost!"

"I'm certain there's nothing in here that will help," Usha said, drawing her pouches closer to her, which proved that she was starting to learn a bit about kender after all. "But why don't you look in yours.

Maybe *you'll* find something."

"That's true. You never know." Tas plopped down on the floor, began fishing around in his pouches. Out came half a moldy piece of cheese, a dead and remarkably stiff bat, a spindle, an inkwell (dried up), a book with the name "Haplo" written on the flyleaf ("Never heard of him"), a hard-boiled egg, and a silver spoon.

"Ah, ha!" Tas let out a shout.

Usha, surreptitiously looking into her own pouch, jumped. "What? What is it?"

"I've found it!" Tas said reverently. "A holy artifact." He held it to the light. "The Kender Spoon of Turning!"

"Are you sure?" Usha leaned forward, examined it closely. "It looks like the spoons we used last night at dinner. It's even got strawberry jam on it."

"Don't be frightened, Usha, but that's blood," said Tas solemnly. "It's the Kender Spoon of Turning. I'd know it anywhere. My Uncle Trapspringer carried one with him all the time. He had a saying: 'Most undead are more afraid of you than you are of them. They just ask to be left alone, to haunt and howl and rattle their chains. But occasionally you'll run into one who wants to suck out your liver. *That's* when you need the Kender Spoon of Turning.' "

"How does it work?" Usha appeared dubious.

Tas scrambled to his feet. "You must present it boldly. Hold it up in front of the specter or the skeletal warrior or whatever sort of ghoul you might chance to encounter. And then you say, in a very firm tone, so that there's no misunderstanding, 'Leave.' Or maybe 'Begone.' I'm not sure. Anyway, when the specter is concentrating on the spoon—"

"I'll sneak past it, out the door," Usha joined in eagerly. "And then when the specter goes to look for me, you sneak past it, out the door. How does that sound?"

Tas found this puzzling. "But we won't *need* to sneak past it, Usha. By the time I get finished with it, the specter will be obeying my every command. Maybe," he added, inspired, "we'll take it with us!"

Usha shuddered. "No, I don't think that would be a good idea."

"But you never know when a specter could come in handy!" Tas said wistfully.

Usha started to argue logically, to point out that the specter would be a very unpleasant, not to mention dangerous, companion. She swallowed logic just in time. She was learning a great deal about kender.

"What would Dalamar think of us if we stole his specter?" Usha said gravely. She draped her packs around her. "He'd be mad, and I wouldn't blame him."

"I wouldn't steal it!" Tas protested, shocked at the accusation. "I only want to 'borrow' it for a while, show it to a few people . . . Oh, well, I guess you're right. I can always come back and pick up one later. "

He scooped all the articles he owned inside his pouches. One or two he didn't own happened to fall in there as well, but they jumped back out again.

Gripping the spoon in his left hand, he held it up in front of him boldly, and walked over to the door.

"You open it," he said to Usha.

"Me?" She gasped. "Why me?"

"Because I have to stand here boldly holding the spoon," Tas replied, somewhat irritated. "I can't be bold and open the door at the same time."

"Oh, all right!"

Usha crept over to the door, flattened herself against the wall. Reaching out with one hand, she gingerly grabbed hold of the door handle and, holding her breath, she gave the handle a yank.

The door creaked open. The two disembodied eyes—now narrowed in anger—started to float inside.

Tas thrust the spoon in what he presumed to be the specter's face. "Leave this place immediately! Be gone! Return to . . . to wherever it is you came from." Tas wasn't exactly clear on that point. He assumed it was the Abyss, but then you never knew, and he didn't want to hurt the specter's feelings.

"Haunt this door no more." That was a rhyme. Tas was rather proud of it, repeated it. "Haunt this door no more. . . ."

The specter wasn't regarding the spoon with the respect it ought, considering that this was the holy Kender Spoon of Turning. The undead eyes were, in fact, glaring at Tas with a most deadly expression. A chill like the chill of the grave made the kender's teeth chatter. But at least the specter was glaring at Tas, not at Usha, who was almost through the door and heading for the hallway.

At that moment, the eyes started to shift.

"Hold!" Tas shouted with about as much boldness as he could manage. "Cease and desist!" He'd heard a constable say that once and was rather fond of the expression.

The specter's gaze was still moving around.

"Run, Usha!" Tas shouted.

Usha couldn't. The cold numbed bone and muscle, froze the blood in the veins. She shook and shivered, unable to move another inch. The specter was almost on her now.

Tas, truly outraged—this was *the* Kender Spoon of Turning, after all—leapt forward, straight at the specter.

"Go away!" the kender shouted.

The eyes shifted to Tas, to the spoon. Suddenly, the eyes widened, blinked, closed, and vanished.

The chill receded. The door remained standing open.

In the distance, a silver bell chimed faintly.

Usha was staring, not at the spoon, but somewhere in the back of the room.

"I turned it!" Tas sounded slightly amazed. "I turned it! Did you see that, Usha?"

"I saw something," she said, a quiver in her voice. "Behind you. A man. He was wearing black robes. A hood covered his face. I couldn't see—"

"Likely another specter," Tas said. Whipping around, he again presented the spoon boldly. "Is he still here? I'll turn him, too."

"No. He's gone. He left when the specter did. When that bell sounded."

"Oh, well." Tas was disappointed. "Maybe another time. Anyhow, the door's open. We can leave."

"None too soon for me!" Usha started for the door, hesitated, peered outside. "Do you think the specter's truly gone?"

"Sure it is." Tas polished the spoon on his shirt front. This done, he thrust the spoon in his topmost pocket, to be available in case of need, and strolled out the door.

Usha followed closely behind him.

They emerged onto a broad landing. Stairs spiraled up and stairs spiraled down. The tower's interior was dark but, at their coming, flickering flames appeared, burning from some invisible source on the walls. In the dim light cast by these eerie flames, Tas and Usha could see that the stairs had no railing, no enclosure. The tower's center was hollow. One misstep on the narrow stairs would be the last.

"It's certainly is a long way down," Tas remarked, leaning precariously over the edge of the stairs to stare into the shadows.

"Don't do that!" Usha grabbed the kender by the strap of one of his pouches, dragged him back against the wall. "Where do we go from here?"

"Down?" suggested Tas. "The way out is down."

"I guess," Usha mumbled. Neither up nor down appeared particularly promising. She cast one last glance behind, at the room they were leaving, half-fearful, half-hoping to see that strange, black-robed figure again.

The room was empty.

Hugging the wall, holding each other by the hand—"In case one of us should slip," Tas said helpfully—they slowly and carefully descended the stairs. No one and nothing disturbed them until they reached the lower levels.

Here, on the ground floor, the apprentice mages, who studied under Dalamar's tutelage, had their living quarters. Tas was just breathing a sigh of relief at reaching the end of the incredibly long descent, when he heard the rustle of robes, the patter of slippered feet, the sound of raised voices. Light shone up the dark stairwell.

"My, I wonder what's going on," Tas said. "Maybe it's a party." He started eagerly down the stairs.

Usha pulled him back.

"It's Dalamar! He's come back!" she whispered fearfully.

"No, that doesn't sound like his voice. It's likely some of Dalamar's students." Tas listened to the voices for a moment. "They sound awfully excited. I'm going to go see what's happening."

"But if his students catch us, they'll put us back in that room!"

"Why, then, we'll have the fun of breaking out again," Tas said cheerfully. "Come on, Usha. We'll think of something. We can't just stand around this boring old staircase all night."

"I guess you're right," Usha said, adding, "Those sound like real, live people. I can deal with real, live people! Besides, if we stay here, someone's bound to find us, and it would look less suspicious if we walked right out in the open."

Tas gazed at her in admiration. "You know, if you weren't part Irda, I'd say you must be part kender. That's a compliment," he added hurriedly. Sometimes, when he said that, people tried to hit him.

But Usha seemed flattered. She smiled, straightened her shoulders, tossed her head, and walked down the stairs and into the light.

Tas had to hurry to catch up. They both nearly bumped into a red-robed mage, who had come dashing around the corner. He brought himself up with a start, stared at them in astonishment.

"What's the problem?" Usha asked calmly. "Can we help?"

"Who in the Abyss are you and what are you doing here?" the Red Robe demanded.

"My name is Usha . . ." Usha paused.

"Majere," Tas inserted.

"Majere!" the young mage repeated in shock. He almost dropped the spellbook he was holding.

Usha glared at the kender. "There, you see! You weren't supposed to tell!"

"I'm sorry." Tas clapped his hand over his mouth.

"Anyway, now you know." Usha heaved an elaborate sigh. "It's so difficult. The notoriety. People just won't leave me alone. You won't tell, will you? Lord Dalamar wouldn't like it."

"I'm Tasslehoff Burrfoot, Hero of the Lance," said Tas, but the Red Robe wasn't impressed, appeared to have forgotten the kender's existence. He was staring at Usha with a worshipful expression, his heart and his soul in his eyes.

"I promise, Mistress Majere," he said softly. "I won't tell a soul."

"Thank you." Usha smiled—a smile that said, *It's you and me, alone, against the world.*

The Red Robe melted. Tas was surprised he didn't see the young man's heart oozing out of his slippers.

"I may be studying here with you," Usha continued, glancing around to see how the place suited her. "I haven't decided yet." She looked back at the mage. "But I think I would like it here."

"I hope you do," he said. "It's quite comfortable."

"Dark, damp, and smells funny," Tas observed. "I've been in better prisons. But I suppose there must be compensations."

The Red Robe blinked, coming suddenly to the realization that there was a kender in the Tower of High Sorcery. He glared at Tas, frowning. "What are *you* doing here? My lord would never permit—"

Usha took hold of the man by the arm, leaned near him. "We were sound asleep—Lord Dalamar gave us his finest guest quarters—when we heard a bell clanging. We thought it might mean . . . "

"A fire!" Tas filled in the blank. "*Is* there a fire? Are we all going to get burned to a crisp? Is that why they're ringing the bell?"

"Ringing bells?" The Red Robe looked as if he'd been hearing bells ever since he laid eyes on Usha. He came to his senses. "Bells! The silver bell! I—I must go." He wrenched himself away.

"There *is* a fire!" Tas grabbed hold of him.

"No, there is not," the young mage said crossly. "Let go of me. And give that back!" He snatched a scroll out of the kender's hands, a scroll that was inches from disappearing into one of Tas's pouches.

"Good thing I found that for you," Tas said gravely. "You might have lost it. There's the bell again! The fire must be spreading."

"It's not a fire. The silver bell means that someone has entered the Shoikan Grove. I've got to go," the Red Robe said again, but he couldn't take his eyes off Usha. "Stay right where you are. You'll be safe here."

"The Shoikan Grove!" Tas said to himself. "And they're going to get dragged down into their graves by skeletons! And I won't be there to see it. Unless—" He had an idea. "Unless I'm there to save them!"

He drew the silver spoon from his pocket and, before Usha or the Red Robe could stop him, made a dash for the tower's entrance.

20

White Robes.
Black Armor.

he hideous voices of the Shoikan Grove were silent. The hands of the undead, which tried to drag their victims down to join them in endless, hungry darkness, stirred restlessly beneath the rotting leaves, but did not attack. The trees kept grim vigil, but appeared prepared to permit the knight and the mage to pass.

Side by side, they entered the dread woods together. Voices of the dead led them on. Voices of the dead lured them on.

The way was not easy. No path existed in the Shoikan Grove, at least not for Steel and Palin. They had to forge a path as they went, battling through thorn-encrusted, tangled undergrowth; the noxious smell of death and decay nearly choked them. In the world outside the Shoikan Grove, the ground was dry and sun-baked, covered with dust. Inside the grove, the ground was wet and soggy, mud oozed beneath their feet, and brackish water filled their footprints as they passed. The air was damp and cold, and moisture—like the sweat of a chill-racked fever patient—beaded on their skin, trickled down their necks.

Each step was terror-filled. The dead of the grove said nothing aloud. They whispered words that were only half heard, but were filled with loathing and horrible desire.

Steel took the lead, his sword drawn, held in both hands, raised to attack. He was watchful, wary, his every move made with extreme caution. Palin came after, walking in the glow of the Staff of Magius, which he used to light their way. It may have been his overwrought imagination, but it seemed to him that the grasping skeletal hands drew back whenever the bones were illuminated in the staff's light.

The journey seemed endless. Fear lengthened seconds to hours, hours to years. The whispering darkness, the breath-snatching stench, the cold that made the bones ache and the fingertips numb, began to work on both warrior and mage.

The ground grew wetter; walking became increasingly difficult. Steel, in his heavy boots, weighted down by his armor, sank up to his ankles in the foul, clinging muck. Each time he moved, it took a great effort to pull his feet free, one after the other. Each step became a battle with the squelching ground, and he was soon breathing hard from the labor. He grew increasingly exhausted. His legs burned from the exertion. He tried to find firmer footing, watched where he put each

step, but it made no difference. With every step, he sank a little deeper; each time it was harder to free himself. Weary, far more weary than
he should have been, almost sobbing for breath, he came to a halt,
looked back at his footprints.

They were filling up with blood.

Palin had no difficulty walking; he trod lightly on the ground, left no
mark of his passing. He could walk, but he couldn't breathe.

The air beneath the trees seemed liquid, flowed into his nose and
mouth like dark, oily water. He choked and swallowed and choked
again. His lungs burned. He inhaled deeply, only to gag and retch as if
he'd drunk swamp water. Tiny pinpricks of light sparked on the fringes
of his vision; he was slowly suffocating, starting to lose consciousness.

Gasping for breath, he was forced to a halt beside Steele.

The dead were waiting for them.

Fleshless hands, nothing but tendon and bone, reached up out of the
black loam and grasped hold of Steele around the shins. Bone-brittle
voices gibbered and laughed. The hands pulled, with inhuman
strength, trying to drag the knight down to join them in unquiet death.

Drawing his sword with a shout, he slashed at the hands with the
shining blade.

More hands clutched the knight's feet, wrapped around his ankles.
His blade severed the hands from the skeletal wrists. One hand would
fall limp, only to be replaced by another and by another after that. He
was losing the battle; was being dragged inexorably under. Already, he
had sunk into the quagmire up to his knees.

Palin plunged forward to help. The words of his magic on his lips, he
struggled to find the breath to say them aloud. But he could not speak;
what air he had, he was forced to use to stave off suffocation. Desperate,
he struck at the hands with the butt-end of the staff.

Bone shattered, tendons snapped.

Elated, he continued the attack, found his breath coming easier. Steel,
too, fought with renewed hope. He could move his legs.

"Take hold!" Palin cried and held out the staff.

Steel reached for it.

Cold bone fingers dug into the back of Palin's neck. Hot, stinging
pain shot through his body. Spasms twisted his limbs. The Staff of
Magius fell to the ground. The bright light of its crystal went out.

Darkness, thick and palpable, rushed in on them, as if it had been
lying in ambush, awaiting its chance. Palin tore frantically at the hands,
panic rising, when suddenly he knew what to do. The memory of his
brothers, training for hand-to-hand combat, came to him with desperate clarity. He saw Tanin grasp Sturm around the throat from behind,

saw Sturm plant his feet solidly and shove backward. He knocked Tanin flat on his back on the ground, breaking his grip.

Palin planted his feet as best he could in the muck, with all his strength, lunged directly backward. He fell through the darkness, no solid body behind him to break his fall. He landed heavily on the ground, driving what breath remained from his body. But the hands had let loose their grip around his throat.

He lay panting for breath, knowing he must move, but too shaken to attempt it yet. Looking up, he thought he saw a star shining through the darkness, and he marveled at how this could possibly be, until he realized that what he saw was the light of the starjewel, shining from around Steel's neck.

"Hurry, Majere!" Steel commanded, offering to help Palin stand. "They've gone . . . for the moment."

Palin ignored the outstretched hand. He lurched to his knees, began scrabbling through the rotted leaves. The darkness whispered around him.

"What's the matter? Are you hurt?" Steel asked.

"My staff! Where is it? I can't find it! I can't see!" Palin ran his hands through the wet leaves.

"Hurry, mage!" Steel urged.

The knight stood protectively over Palin, shielding him with his body and drawn sword.

"I have it!" Palin gasped in relief. His hand closed over the smooth wood and immediately the staff burst into light. Leaning on the staff thankfully, he drew himself to his feet.

And there, before them, was the Tower of High Sorcery.

A tall building, constructed of magic and of black marble, thrust up into the sky, which was dark around it. Not even the stars would come near the Tower of Palanthas. Three moons shone on it. The marble walls glistened in Solinari's light, for though Solinari was a deity revered by the White Robes, he—like his siblings—revered all magic. Lunitari's red beams shone on the blood-red spires atop the tower. Above the spires, above the balcony known as the "Death Walk," floated Nuitari, the black moon, special guardian of this tower, visible only to the Black Robes.

"We've made it," Palin said, a catch in his throat.

The longed-for moment had arrived. He almost broke into a run, but events had taught him caution. He waited for the knight to precede him.

Despite his fatigue, Steel moved forward rapidly. He, too, was relieved to see their journey's end before them. Together, walking now by the light of two moons, they approached the iron gates.

There was no lock that they could see. It seemed the gates would open with a shove. Yet neither put his hand out, neither wanted to touch that iron, which was dripping with the strange, uncanny moisture of the Shoikan Grove.

No one was around. No one was in sight. No lights shone from the windows, but that may have been only illusion. There might—probably were—any number of eyes watching them.

"Well, Majere, why do you wait?" Steel motioned at the gate with his sword. "This is your bailiwick. Go on."

Palin couldn't very well argue the point. He walked forward, reached out to put his hand on the gate.

The gate swung open.

Palin's spirits lifted. He looked back at Steel with a certain amount of weary triumph. Now it was his turn to lead. "Come ahead," he said. "We've been invited to enter."

"Lucky us," Steel muttered, and did not lower his sword. He stepped through the gate and into a garden courtyard. It was a strange sort of garden.

Here grew many herbs and flowers used for spell components. Cultivated and tended by the apprentice mages, most of these plants grew by night, thrived in the unseen light of Nuitari. Nightshade, the death lily, black orchids, black roses, rue, bittersweet, henbane, poppy, mandrake, wormwood, mistletoe—their perfume hung, sweet, cloying, and heavy, in the still air.

"Don't pick or touch any of the plants," Palin warned as they walked the dank gray cobblestone of the courtyard.

"Not a bouquet I would fancy," Steel said, though he did pause to make a slight bow of reverence for the lily that was the symbol of his order.

Palin was just wondering how he would get inside the door—he had some vague memory that there was a bell—when he saw them. Everywhere. All around him.

Eyes. Unblinking eyes. Only eyes.

No skulls. No necks. No arms or torsos or legs.

Eyes and hands.

Dreadful hands. Hands of chill death.

Steel was at Palin's back.

"What are those!" the knight hissed in Palin's ear.

"The guardians of the tower," Palin warned. "Don't . . . don't let them near you."

The eyes glided close. There must have been a hundred, shining pale and cold in Nuitari's light.

"How in the name of the Abyss am I supposed to stop them?" Steel crowded near Palin, guarding the mage's back, as Palin guarded the knight's. "Do something! Say something!"

"I am Palin Majere," Palin called loudly. "Give way!"

Majere . . . Majere . . . Majere . . .

The name echoed off the tower's stone walls, reverberated through the courtyard like the ringing of discordant bells, ended in mocking laughter.

Palin shuddered. Steel's jaw tightened. The knight's face glistened with sweat.

The eyes drew nearer, closing in. White, disembodied hands appeared out of the darkness. Skeletal fingers pointed at the fast-beating hearts of the two living beings. One touch, and their blood would freeze, the heartbeat cease.

"In the name of Chemosh, I command you to stand aside!" Steel yelled suddenly.

The eyes gleamed—but only with anger.

"I wouldn't mention that name again," Palin advised softly. "Only one god is respected here."

"Then *you* do something, Sir Mage!" Steel said harshly.

"I have come to see Dalamar," Palin explained desperately. "I have come to visit your master."

A lie . . . a lie . . . a lie . . .

The words were like the rustle of unseen, ragged robes, the creaking of bony fingers, the flicker in the white, chill eyes.

The spectral guardians moved closer still, formed a circle around the mage and the knight. The two stood back to back, Palin with his staff raised, Steel holding his sword. But the staff's crystal was dimming fast. Steel made a swipe at one of the specters with his blade. The sword whistled, sliced up nothing but the night. The specters moved closer.

"Uncle!" Palin cried. "It is to you I come! Uncle, I need your help!"

The door to the tower opened. Darkness flowed from it. The specters halted their advance; the cold, pale eyes turned that direction.

Palin trembled as fear, elation, awe swept over him. He leaned forward toward the darkness.

"Uncle?" he cried.

A voice answered, "Don't move! Stay right where you are! I'm coming! I'm coming! I'll save you!"

Out of the darkness ran Tasslehoff Burrfoot.

2J

The gate opens. Nuitari's garden.
The way is prepared.

ncle Tas!" Palin gasped in astonishment.

"I take it this was *not* the uncle you had in mind," Steel said grimly.

"No." Palin was baffled. "I never—"

"I've . . . got it right here!" The elder kender was puffing with the exertion of his run. He paused on the stairs leading to the tower door, waving something shiny in the air. "Don't worry . . ."

"Don't come any closer, Tas!" Palin cried fearfully. "Go back! Go back inside!"

"No, no!" Tas called back. "You don't understand. I have it! You'll be safe now!"

And before Palin could say another word, the kender dashed down the stairs and ran straight for the specters.

The dim light of the staff flashed off the object in the kender's hand: a silver spoon.

"Be gone, foul wraiths!" Tas commanded, using a deep, gruff, authoritative voice, such as he imagined a cleric might use. The gruffness proved too much for him to maintain, however; he ended up half-strangling himself. In between the hacks and splutters, he managed to repeat, "Be gone, I say! Be gone! Go away!"

He waved the spoon at the specters.

"We're going to die," Steel said.

"No," said Palin, after a moment's astounded watching. "No, we're not."

Two by two, the chill eyes closed. The deathly white hands drew back into unseen sleeves. The courtyard was empty. The entrance to the tower stood open.

The light of Palin's staff shone bright in Tas's eyes as he came bounding up to greet them. "The Kender Spoon of Turning," Tas said proudly, holding it up for Palin's inspection.

Palin was about to examine the spoon to see if it was in any way magical, but before he could do so, Tas stuffed the spoon into a convenient pouch and moved on to other matters.

He held out his small hand to Steel. "How do you do?" the kender said politely. "I'm Tasslehoff Burrfoot. My friends call me Tas. Except for Palin," he added, as an afterthought. "He calls me 'Uncle Tas.' I'm not really his uncle. Caramon and I are *not* related. I'm a friend of the family. They used to call me 'Granpa' when they were littler than me, but that seemed a bit silly when they all got bigger, so, after some discussion, we changed it to 'Uncle.' I had an Uncle Trapspringer once. He was the one with the spoon. My, that certainly is remarkable armor. So wonderfully evil-looking with those skulls and death lilies. I know! You must be a Knight of Takhisis! I've heard about you, but I've never met one. This is a real privilege. Did I mention that my name is Tasslehoff Burrfoot?"

"I do not discourse with kender," Steel said.

"Even those who save your life?" Palin asked softly.

Steel regarded Tas grimly, finally made a stiff bow. "Steel Brightblade."

"I know you! Tanis told me about you! You're Sturm's son! Sturm and I were great friends!" Tas flung himself forward for a hug.

He was halted by Steel's hand on his head, holding the kender at arm's length.

"It is probable, though not very likely, that I owe you my life, Kender," Steel said coldly. "I am honor-bound to repay the debt, but I am not bound to allow you near my person. I advise you, therefore, to keep clear of me." With that, he shoved Tas backward.

Palin caught hold of Tas, steadied him.

"I forgot," Tas said in a loud whisper, wincing and rubbing his head, "he's Kitiara's son, too!"

Palin was about to advise that it might be beneficial to Tas's health if he steered clear of the knight when a woman's voice called out from inside the tower.

"Tasslehoff! Where are you? Tas? Where did you go?"

Palin raised his gaze, looked toward the door. He breathed a soft sigh. The specters had nearly chilled his heart. Now he felt it catch fire.

A woman like no other he had ever seen in his life stood in the doorway. Masses of silver hair framed a face that was alluring, kept its secrets, yet—by the wide, eager, golden eyes—seemed to require that others give to her all of their own mysteries. Her clothes, made of brightly colored, flowing silk, were outlandish, like no well-bred woman in this part of the country would have worn. Yet, they suited her. She was as exotic, as entrancing, as if she'd fallen from a star.

"Tas!" she called, relief in her voice. She ran down the stairs. "Thank the gods I've found you! Now we can get out of here—"

She halted, stared at Steel and Palin. "Oh." She glanced sideways at Tas, sidled nearer the kender. "Who are these two gentlemen?"

"Friends of mine!" said Tas enthusiastically. "This is Steel

Brightblade. He's Sturm's son. Sturm was a Knight of Solamnia and one of my very best friends. He's Kitiara's son, too, but she wasn't a knight. She was a Dragon Highlord and not exactly a friend, more of an acquaintance. This is Usha."

"My lady," Palin said, staring at the woman, enthralled. But he was disappointed to see her gaze stray to the knight. She tried a tentative smile.

Steel didn't even look at her; his eyes searched the tower windows for signs of danger.

Usha gazed at him longer, studying the armor, which she could now see clearly in the moonlight. Her smile disappeared, her eyes darkened. Her voice trembled in anger. "They were like you—the ones who came. They treated us as if we were dirt beneath their feet. Why did you have to come to ruin our lives?" she cried suddenly. "What did we do to you? We were no threat!"

Now Steel turned his gaze on her, regarded her with interest. "What city are you from, Lady? Kalaman? Has it, in truth, fallen to our might?"

Usha opened her mouth, started to answer, seemed to find the answering difficult. At length, she said, "No, not Kalaman. Near there . . ." Her voice dwindled a moment, then came back strong. "You had no right to invade our homeland!"

"Whatever wrongs you imagine were done to you were done in the name of progress, my lady," Steel returned. "You cannot be expected to understand, so I will not attempt to explain." His gaze shifted immediately back to the tower. He still held his sword in his hand. "We have business here, Majere, if you remember."

"I remember," Palin said, though just barely.

Usha had turned those wonderful eyes on him. "What is your name, sir?" she asked, her cheeks flushing beneath his unabashedly admiring gaze.

"Palin Majere," he said softly. "And yours? I . . . I didn't quite catch it."

"Usha," she replied archly.

"Usha *Majere!*" cried Tas, hopping about in excitement. "Isn't this great? Usha's Raistlin's daughter! I've found Raistlin's daughter."

"No!" Palin cried, stricken.

"What?" Usha, frightened by his intensity, backed away from him a step. "What's wrong?"

"I . . . I am Raistlin's nephew! Caramon Majere is my father and your uncle. We're cousins," Palin said miserably. "*First* cousins!"

"Is that all?" Usha breathed again. "We're first cousins. I don't mind," she said, and she smiled at him.

Her smile glittered around Palin like cascading stardust. He was so dazzled, he could scarcely see.

"Their fathers were twins," Tas said, by way of explanation.

"Now that we have the genealogy straightened out," Steel said acidly, "might I remind you once again, Majere, that time draws short and we have important work to do inside the tower?"

"Inside?" Usha looked back fearfully at the tower, shifted her shadowed gaze to Palin. "You're going inside?"

"We just got outside," Tas informed them, adding, proudly, "Dalamar was holding us both prisoner."

Palin was dubious. "Why would Dalamar hold you prisoner?"

"Does it matter? You came through the grove," Usha said, talking rapidly, not giving Tas a chance to respond. She took hold of Palin's hand, gazed into his eyes. "The Red Robe inside said you must be an immensely powerful wizard to have done such a thing." She leaned close, whispered in his ear. "You and the knight could take us back through the grove, and we could get away from this terrible place!"

Her hand was smooth, soft. Her touch sent the stardust glittering through his blood.

"I can't leave, Mistress," Palin said, still retaining her hand. "I have something here I must do. And you shouldn't try to escape either, not through the Shoikan Grove. It's too dangerous. We barely survived." He turned to Tasslehoff. "I don't understand. Why is Dalamar holding you prisoner?"

"Because she's Raistlin's daughter, of course," Tas answered, his tone matter-of-fact.

Of course. Palin had guessed the answer even before he had asked the question. Dalamar would be very glad to get hold of the daughter of Raistlin Majere. And then it occurred to Palin, with a pang, that perhaps *she* was the reason the voice had led him here. Perhaps his uncle merely needed a guide for the person in whom he was truly interested—his daughter.

Palin withdrew his hand from her grasp. Jealousy gnawed at him, its poisoned teeth biting deep. He was attracted to this woman, jealous of her at the same time, and he understood, finally, the bittersweet relationship that had existed between his father and his father's twin.

Usha felt his sudden coldness, more chill than the specters. She stared at him in puzzled dismay, involuntarily drew away from him.

"You won't help us escape? That's fine. I will go through the grove myself," she said haughtily.

"No, Usha, I'm afraid not," said Palin, his voice raw-edged. "There's a reason you're here—"

"Why? Did Raistlin send for her?" Tas wondered cheerfully. "I thought Raistlin was dead. Do you think he's dead, Palin? You don't, do you! That's why you're here!" The kender was wildly excited.

"Majere—" Steel began impatiently.

"I know. I know! Come on." Palin took hold of Usha's arm, started to lead her inside the tower. "We're going to have a talk with Dalamar—"

"He isn't here!" Usha said, breaking away from Palin's grasp. "He's gone to some wizard's something in somewhere—"

"The Tower of High Sorcery at Wayreth," Tas filled in. "A Conclave. I was at one once. Did I ever tell you about the time Par-Salian turned me into a mouse? Well, I suppose I was the one who turned myself into a mouse, but—"

"Dalamar's gone," Palin murmured.

I will deal with Dalamar. . . .

His uncle had promised. It might all be coincidence, but Palin doubted it. Raistlin was actively working to aid him. But for what purpose? To what end?

"We'd better hurry, then, before Dalamar gets back." Palin started toward the tower door.

A red-robed mage stood inside, blocking entry.

"What are you two doing here? How did you get through the Shoikan Grove and past the guardians? Where *are* the guardians?"

Palin opened his mouth. He wasn't much good at lying, but in this instance, the truth would hardly do. He was about to speak when Tasslehoff interrupted.

"They have been summoned by Dalamar," Tas announced importantly. "As for the guardians, I sent them away with the Kender Spoon of Turning." He exhibited the spoon for inspection.

The mage stared at it, stared at Palin and Steel, stared around the empty courtyard. He looked confused and suspicious.

"Lord Dalamar sent for you," he repeated. "A White Robe and a dark knight?"

"Makes for a nice balance, don't you think?" Tas said, adding, "And how else could they have come through the grove unless Dalamar gave them charms to help them? Now, if you'll excuse us, we have to go upstairs to Dalamar's chambers." Tas looked back around at Palin. "That's where you want to go, isn't it?" he asked in a loud whisper.

The Red Robe frowned. Steel glowered. He had sheathed his sword, but his hand rested on the hilt. "I am Steel Brightblade, Knight of Takhisis. I have come on a mission. Lord Dalamar did *not*—"

"—expect us this early," Tas chimed in loudly and shrilly. "Tell Cousin Steel to keep quiet and let me handle this," he whispered again to Palin, who hoped devoutly that Steel hadn't heard his new appellation.

Tas started moving toward the door. Waving his hand behind his back, he motioned for the others to follow. "We'll just wait for Dalamar in his room. We'd like some tarbean tea, if it wouldn't be too much trouble. Come on, Usha."

Steel followed the kender. Palin was about to, but he noticed that Usha held back. She twisted her hands together nervously, looked up at the tower in dread.

"I just got out of there," she protested. "I don't want to go back!"

The Red Robe was now deeply suspicious.

"You said you were going to study magic with us, Mistress, apprentice yourself to Lord Dalamar. What's going on here?"

"I . . . I haven't made up my mind yet," Usha replied. "I need to go somewhere and think it over. Somewhere *else*! As for studying magic, perhaps I don't need to study, not anymore. I'm quite powerful enough as I am."

"Usha," Palin began.

Steel caught hold of him.

"Let her go," the knight said. "We're wasting time."

Angrily, Palin shook himself loose. "No matter how powerful she is in magic, she'll die if she walks into that grove. Besides," he added in a low voice, "it is possible that we're here because of her."

"What? Why?" Steel glanced at the woman without interest.

"Because if she is Raistlin's daughter, he may be attempting to reach her."

Steel gazed at Palin intently.

"It may be the daughter Raistlin wants, *not* the nephew." Steel shrugged. "He may open the Portal for her? Perhaps you are right. It doesn't matter to me, as long as the Portal opens. Bring her along."

Palin walked slowly back to Usha.

"You can't leave, Mistress," he said. "I ask you to stay with me. Trust me. We'll figure something out."

She looked up at him with her golden eyes. Her gaze was cold, but he saw, now that he was closer, that the frost was a covering for fear. She looked as terrified as a lost child.

"I'll come with *you*," she said softly. "But you must stay with me."

She was warm, her skin soft. Her silver hair, brushing his face, sent tingles of desire through his body. He had never felt this wonderful—or been in such bitter turmoil—in his entire life. Stay with her! He had to enter the Abyss.

The Red Robe, having thought matters over, apparently decided that the kender was right; the best place for this odd group was locked up safely in his lord's chambers.

"I'll accompany you up the stairs to Lord Dalamar's room," the Red Robe announced. "We'll wait for my lord together."

This wouldn't do at all, as Steel reminded Palin with a grim look. They had to find the Portal to the Abyss and had better find it while Dalamar was gone.

"Thank you, but that won't be necessary," Tas said politely. "We know the way. And, besides, Palin's been here before. He's a close personal friend of Dalamar's."

The Red Robe raised his eyebrows in disbelief.

"Don't you recognize him?" Tasslehoff exclaimed. "He's Palin *Majere*! Raistlin Majere's nephew! Usha is Raistlin's daughter. And this"—the kender waved his hand at Steel Brightblade—"is Raistlin Majere's half-nephew. I *think* that's right." The kender's brow furrowed in thought. "Let's see. Kitiara was Raistlin's half-sister. Perhaps that would make Steel only a quarter of a nephew—"

"It's a family reunion," Steel said and, shoving the Red Robe into the wall, the knight strode past him and into the tower.

The Red Robe did *not* follow them to Dalamar's rooms. He did, however, make certain that several of the spectral guardians went along. The pale, unblinking eyes kept watch on them until they were safely inside Dalamar's chambers and had shut the door.

"But they'll be waiting for us," Palin predicted. "Not to mention the one that guards the laboratory. That specter has orders from Dalamar not to admit anyone—not even Dalamar himself. The laboratory has never been opened, not since my uncle . . ."

Palin paused, didn't finish his sentence. What he'd stated wasn't quite true. The laboratory door had been once opened. The Staff of Magius had been inside and now he held the staff in his hand.

"Oh, you don't need to worry about the specter," Tas said confidently. "We have the—"

"Kender Spoon of Turning. I know." Palin sighed. He was in no mood for kender nonsense. "Look, Uncle Tas, I saw the crest on the spoon. It's just an ordinary tablesp—"

Movement caught his eye. He looked up. A black-robed mage stood in the room. Not unusual for the Tower of High Sorcery, except that this mage had white hair, golden skin, hourglass eyes. Palin's tongue cleaved to the roof of his mouth. He started to speak.

"Uncle . . ."

Raistlin made a swift, negating sign with his hand. His golden, hourglass eyes rested briefly on the kender. And then the apparition vanished.

"Yes?" Tas looked up from admiring the spoon. "You were saying something about the spoon being ordinary?"

Palin looked swiftly about. Had anyone else seen the vision?

Apparently not.

Steel was searching the room, testing the walls, looking under tapestries, trying to find another way out. Usha, half-asleep, was curled up disconsolately in a chair. Tasslehoff was fondly patting his spoon.

"This spoon is *not* ordinary!" the kender continued. "It's a holy relic, given to my Uncle Trapspringer by Mishakal herself. Or was it Reorx? I forget. Anyway, it works. You saw it work."

No one else had seen Raistlin. He had come to Palin, no one else. Weariness, pain, disappointment fell from him like a discarded cloak. He would get into the laboratory. The way was prepared. As had once been said of Raistlin Majere:

For him, the door would open. . . .

"Here, let me see it again." Palin took the spoon from Tas, studied it. The spoon matched exactly the other spoons on the table.

"You're right, Tas," Palin said softly. "It *is* a holy artifact. Most holy, indeed."

22

Suspicions. Introspection.
Raistlin's laboratory.

hey left Dalamar's chamber; Tas led the way to the laboratory,
the silver spoon held boldly before him.

Steel was not pleased with the kender as a companion, but
Palin—to Steel's amazement and ire—did not try to dissuade him.

"Only a kender can use the magic Kender Spoon of Turning," Palin
said with a half-smile.

"You and I both know the spoon is not magic," Steel retorted.

"You saw it turn the specter," Palin replied.

"Did I?" Steel demanded. "Or is that what you want me to think I
saw?"

Palin avoided the question. "We'll take the kender along, keep an eye
on him. Or would you rather have him traipsing after us on his own?
'Never turn your back on a kender,' or so the dwarves say."

"Do they?" Steel said coldly. "I heard it was 'Never turn your back on
a mage'!"

The disembodied eyes flickered, flared, then disappeared.

A tablespoon in a kender's hand could not turn such wraiths. Steel
knew it, and he knew Palin knew it. Palin seemed suddenly eager to
reach their destination. His doubts, his fears, had been laid to rest. He
was relaxed, confident. Something had happened; he'd seen something,
had received some sign. But Steel had no idea what. Was the young
mage far more powerful than he'd led Steel to believe? Was this strange
woman with the golden eyes part of a plot? Were they leading the
knight into a trap? Never one to trust magic-users, Steel determined to
watch Palin and the woman closely.

They climbed the shadowy stairs, round and round in a leg-aching
spiral, hugging the wall to keep from tumbling over the edge into the
darkness below. No one approached them. No one interfered with
them. No one stopped them. The tower might have been deserted
except for them.

The infamous laboratory of the Tower of High Sorcery was near the
top of the tower. The only remaining Portal to the Abyss was inside that
laboratory.

Perhaps.

"Tell me about this Portal, Majere," Steel said as they were wending
their way upward.

Palin appeared extremely reluctant to talk. "I know very little," he began.

"I know a lot!" The kender spoke up eagerly.

Steel ignored him.

"You're a mage, aren't you, Majere? I suppose they must teach you these things in mage-school or wherever you study."

"I know the history," he answered evasively.

"I do, too!" Tasslehoff chimed in. "I was there for a lot of it. I was with Caramon and Raistlin when Raistlin wasn't Raistlin, he was Fistandantilus and he entered the Portal and tried to fight the Dark Queen, except he failed. Would you like to hear that story?"

"No," said Steel. "I want to hear about the Portal, since we're *both* going to be entering it," he added pointedly, watching Palin intently.

The Staff of Magius shone bright on the young mage. Palin's face was deeply flushed, his eyes shining, exultant.

Catching Steel's gaze on him, Palin took care to move the staff away, withdraw into the shadows.

He *is* plotting something, Steel said to himself, and he redoubled his watch.

"Are we going back into the Abyss?" Tas asked, and the kender did not sound as excited as most kender would have at the prospect. "I hope you know that the Abyss is not a very nice place. Horrible, in fact. I'm not really sure I want to go with you."

"Good," Steel said. "Because you're not. Continue your tale, Majere."

"Just keep talking," Usha said. "It's not as frightening when someone's talking.

Palin said nothing, however. They continued to climb until they came to a broad landing. Out of breath, muscles aching, they halted, of one accord. The door to the laboratory was still far above them, outlined in torchlight. They sat down on the landing, stretched out their legs, glad for the rest.

"The Portal?" Steel gave the mage a nudge.

"There's not really much to tell," Palin said with a careless shrug. "Long ago, five Portals existed, located in each of the five Towers of High Sorcery. Created by magic, the Portals had been devised in order to provide the wizards with the ability to travel between towers, without the need for expending their energies on teleportation spells.

"Thinking to open doors only to each other, the wizards did not realize that they had accidentally created a route from this world to another plane of existence. Queen Takhisis knew this, however. Trapped in the Abyss, she and her evil dragons had long sought entry into Krynn, but were blocked by Paladine and his good dragons. Paladine had little control over magic-users, however, who were known to go their own ways.

"Takhisis found a black-robed wizard who might be open to temptation. Assuming the form of a beautiful woman, Takhisis appeared to the wizard every night in his dreams, whispered seductive promises. He became obsessed with the lovely woman, vowed to find her and make her his own.

" 'I am a prisoner on another plane, in another time,' Takhisis told the wizard. 'Only you, with your power, can free me. To do so, you must enter the Portal. Keep my vision in your mind, and I will guide you.' "

Palin halted abruptly at this point. His face, illuminated by the staff's light, had gone extremely pale.

I will guide you. The words hung in the air.

"What happened to the wizard?" Usha asked.

"I know! I know!" Tas raised his hand.

Palin, after clearing a huskiness from his throat, continued. "The lust-filled wizard entered the Portal, the vision of Takhisis burning in his blood. What happened to him there, no one knows, for he never returned. Once the Portal was opened, Queen Takhisis and her legions of dragons swarmed into Krynn and that, so legend has it, was the cause of the First Dragon War.

"The gallant Knight of Solamnia, Huma, drove the Dark Queen back into the Abyss. The wizards, deeply ashamed, tried to seal shut the Portals. Unfortunately, the wizards who had created them had been lost in the Dragon War, and so had their knowledge and the power. The surviving wizards could not shut the Portals. They could make it impossible to enter—or so they thought. And so they made it a condition that the only two people who could enter a Portal would be a black-robed mage in company with a white-robed cleric. Such an unholy alliance would, they believed, be impossible to achieve, and so the Portals were safe.

"In time, with the rise of Istar, when magic-users were persecuted by the church, three of the Towers of High Sorcery were either lost or destroyed. Their Portals were destroyed with them. The wizards who lived in the Tower of Palanthas agreed to abandon it, in return for the promise from the Kingpriest that they could continue to practice their magic in Wayreth. Before they left the tower, however, the wizards moved the Portal to the fortress at Skullcap for safekeeping, fondly imagining that no one would find it there."

"I found it!" Tas cried. "Well, I sort of found it. I was with Caramon and Raistlin, back in time, only I wasn't supposed to be. And Crysania, who was a white-robed cleric, and Raistlin entered the Portal, and that's how Raistlin got into the Abyss. And Crysania went with him, and the Dark Queen almost killed Crysania, only she stayed alive, except that she was blind, and Caramon went in and brought her out, and Raistlin realized that he'd made a terrible mistake and that the Dark Queen was going to get into the world, and so he—Raistlin, I mean—sacrificed his life by staying in the Abyss and keeping the Portal sealed shut. Caramon believes that his brother was granted peace in eternal sleep for his sacrifice, which would mean that Raistlin isn't in the Abyss after all—

"Oh!" Tas jumped up in excitement. "Is *that* why we're going into the Portal, Palin? To look for Raistlin? In that case, I'll go with you," the kender offered magnanimously. "Raistlin and I were great friends. Until he killed Gnimsh the gnome." Tas grew more solemn. "I've never really forgiven him for that."

"You're going in there to search for Raistlin Majere?" Usha asked. She did not look at Palin as she spoke, but played nervously with the hem of her tunic.

"We have yet to enter the laboratory," Palin pointed out. "We're a long way from walking into the Abyss in search of anyone!"

"And none of us is a black-robed wizard or a white-robed cleric," Steel said. "Which means, according to your story, Majere, that we have no chance of entering, that we never *have* had a chance of entering." He leapt to his feet, his hand on the hilt of his sword. "You have known this all along. What sort of trick did you have in mind? Or is there something you have omitted telling us?"

"No trick," Palin said softly. "I've told you the truth—as far as I know it." He looked up at Steel. "I have no idea how I'm going to get inside—"

"Yes, you do. Or you would not have come this far. What is it? What do you know, Majere?"

Palin grasped the Staff of Magius, rose to his feet. "I know that I gave you my word of honor, and I will not break it."

"The word of a wizard is slippery as an eel," Steel said, sneering.

"The word of a Majere is not," Palin answered with dignity. "Shall we go on?"

*　*　*　*　*

They continued the climb, up and up the winding stairs. They were being watched, they knew, though they could not see the watchers.

Every step brought memories to Palin, memories of his Test, which had taken place in this tower. All illusion, according to Dalamar. Had it been? It had seemed so real. But then, the Test always seemed real to the mages who took it, who risked their lives in order to possess the magic.

Perhaps the Test had been reality, the rest of Palin's life illusion.

Closing his eyes, Palin leaned back against the chill wall of the tower and, for the first time in his life, gave himself up to the magic. He felt it burn in his blood, caress his skin. The words it whispered were no longer of doom, but of welcome, of invitation. His body trembled with the ecstasy of the magic. . . .

Palin recalled that moment of his Test with a pang. He had not experienced the ecstasy in a long, long time. He had never admitted it to anyone, not even himself, until now. Magic had become drudgery. Spells studied alone in the depths of the night, words recited over and over, taking care to achieve the proper inflection, the correct pronunciation. Magical words tumbled about his head when he tried to sleep; spell components tainted his dreams. The tingle in the blood when the spell was cast, the feeling of satisfaction when the magic did what it was supposed to do—he experienced that. But it never outweighed the feeling of inadequacy, the helpless emptiness and terror that came when the spell did *not* work.

And more and more often, the magic was not working. The words got all mixed up in his head, jumbled together. He couldn't remember whether he pronounced the first word with the accent on the last syllable or the last word with the accent on the first. He couldn't find the proper spell component, which had been in his pouch only moments before. . . .

When had the fear started to grow within him? Not on his first adventure, traveling with his brothers, meeting the dwarf Dougan Redhammer and setting out to recapture the Graygem of Gargath. Then the magic had been intoxicating, the danger exhilarating.

He'd returned to his studies eagerly, though he had no master to teach him. No mage on Krynn wanted the nephew of Raistlin Majere for a pupil. Palin understood. He hadn't felt the need for a master at that point in his life. He would work alone, as his uncle had worked alone.

At first, Palin had done well, only to have nothing to show for it. Months passed. He made little or no progress. Sometimes it seemed he regressed. He traveled to the Tower of Wayreth, to the Conclave, seeking counseling.

"Patience," Dalamar had intoned. "Patience and discipline. Those who take the white robes achieve greater power, ultimately, than those who wear the red or the black, but you pay a price. *You* must walk before you can run."

My uncle didn't walk! Palin felt the frustration burn inside him. He chafed at the repeated rote learning, at the interminable scroll making, at the hours wasted grubbing in the dirt in his herb garden. And running beneath it all, like refuse water, contaminating his life and his work, was the growing fear that he wasn't good enough, that he would never be anything more than a low-ranking mage, fit to practice his magic for children's name-day parties.

To prove his own worth to himself was one reason he'd abandoned his studies and ridden with the knights. He had failed most miserably . . . and it was his brothers who had paid the price.

Palin climbed the stairs, one after the other, forcing his pain-filled legs to take another step, and yet another; his mind was so entangled in the past that he was oblivious to the present. He was no longer cognizant of his whereabouts, didn't realize that they had reached their destination until the kender tugged on the mage's white robes.

Dazedly, Palin stared at Tas, at first without recognition. Then he blinked, came abruptly back.

"Yes? What is it?"

"I think we're here," Tas said in a loud whisper, pointing. "Is that it?"

Palin raised his staff. Light from the crystal banished the darkness.

They stood on a large landing, directly below a wooden door with wrought-iron hinges. A short flight of stairs led up to the door.

"I know this place." Palin answered as best he could. His throat and mouth were so dry that talking was difficult. "I took my Test here. Yes"—he paused, licked dry lips with a dry tongue—"this is the laboratory."

No one spoke, not even Tas. They drew close, within the staff's circle of light. Outside the circle, the darkness gibbered and whispered. Half-seen shadows flitted past, groped for them with wispy hands. If the staff's light should fail, they would be plunged into blinding darkness.

"Go on, Majere!" Steel Brightblade's voice was rough-edged, jagged. "Advance. Open the door."

A vision of the past came to Palin.

Two cold white eyes stared at him out of the darkness—eyes without a body, unless the darkness itself was their flesh and blood and bone. . . .

"Stand aside," said Dalamar. "And let us pass."

"That cannot be, Master of the Tower. Your command was to 'Take this key and keep it for all eternity. Give it to no one, not even myself. And from this moment on, your place is to guard this door. No one is to enter. Let death be swift for those who try . . .'"

"We have to get by the guardian," Palin said.

"What guardian?" Steel demanded impatiently. "There is no guardian!"

Palin stared. Darkness reigned. The only light that shone was the light of the Staff of Magius. And before that light, the darkness gave way.

The specter was nowhere to be seen. The whispers in the darkness were not threatening, Palin realized suddenly. They were exulting. Could they be anticipating the return of the true Master of the Tower?

"This is all wrong!" Palin whispered.

No, nephew. This is eminently right!

Tears stung Palin's eyes. He trembled; the light of the staff wavered in his shaking grasp. What I am doing here? He's using me . . .

"Well, of course the guardian's gone!" said Tasslehoff Burrfoot in satisfaction. "It heard about my spoon. Come on, Palin! I'll lead the way!"

Tucking the spoon inside his pocket, the kender dashed up the stairs.

"Tas! Stop! Don't go in there!"

Such words, unfortunately, are not in the kender vocabulary.

Palin watched fearfully, more than half-expecting to see the guardian appear, the kender drop dead on the staircase.

Nothing happened.

Tasslehoff reached the laboratory door safely. He rattled the handle, peered at the lock, gave the door a shove.

The door swung silently open.

Chill air flowed out, heavy with must and mildew and other, more unpleasant, odors. Usha gagged and covered her mouth and nose with her scarf. Steel grimaced and drew his sword.

"It smells of death," he said.

Tasslehoff hovered on the stoop, staring inside.

"Wow!" they heard him say. And then the kender, with a hop, leapt over the stoop and vanished into the darkness.

Palin envisioned the jars of spell components, the magical artifacts, the spellbooks, the scrolls—all in easy reach of a kender's deft fingers. Here was danger far greater than any spectral guardian ever given unholy life.

"Tas!" Palin shoved past Steel. Gathering up his robes, the mage raced up the stairs. "Tas! Come out of there! Don't touch *anything*!"

He stood in the doorway, suddenly fearful, reluctant to enter. This was wrong, all wrong. Palin shone the staff's light inside.

Tasslehoff had advanced to the middle of the room, was standing in front of an enormous table, staring at the objects on it in wide-eyed wonder.

"Tas!" Palin scolded, cross with relief. "Come out of there!"

He could hear, behind him, Steel mounting the staircase.

The staff's light went out. Darkness engulfed them, roiled around them, crashed over them, drowned them.

Steel cursed. Usha gave a frightened cry.

"Don't anyone move!" Palin warned, having terrible visions of them all falling off the spiral stairs, plummeting to the stone floor far, far below. "*Shirak!*"

The command failed. Either that, or the staff refused to obey. The darkness grew deeper, stronger.

"What is going on, Majere?" Steel demanded. "Light the damn staff!"

"I'm trying!" Palin said, frustrated and angry with himself. Again, the magic had failed him.

Armor scraped against stone. Booted feet came down heavily on the stairs. Steel was trying to find him.

"Palin!" Usha called out fearfully. "I'm coming up to you! Don't move."

"Usha, be careful!" Palin half-turned, to try to go back, to try to reach her.

"Palin!" Tas's voice echoed shrilly. "I've got hold of something. Maybe this will help!"

"Tas! No!" Palin cried, turning back.

A crash came, the ominous sound of breaking glass.

Groping forward, tapping with the staff like a blind beggar in the market, Palin edged his way into the pitch-dark laboratory. Steel was right behind him. The knight stood poised on the threshold, then he stopped. He did not enter.

The door slammed shut.

23

Dalamar returns. A message. Usha's magic.

ajere!" Steel Brightblade threw himself at the closed door in an attempt to break it down. "Damn you, Majere! Open the door!"

"Palin!" Usha was beside him, pounding on the door with her fists.

The knight heard faint cries and thumping from the other side of the door. It might have been Palin attempting to open the door . . . or it might have been the mage sealing it shut.

Steel assumed it was the latter. "Go back to the landing," he ordered the woman.

"What are you going to do?"

"Try to break down the door. I thought I felt it give a moment before. Go on. You're in my way."

"But . . . it's so dark!" Usha protested, her voice shaking. "I can't see! What if . . . what if I fall?"

Steel didn't give a damn whether she fell or not, but he curbed his impatience. "Feel your way down. Stay close to the wall. You'll know when you reach the landing. Once you get there, don't move."

He heard her cautious footsteps, moving slowly down the stairs, then he forgot about her, focused on the door. He would have to run up the stairs to reach it, which did not provide him with the correct leverage . . .

The woman screamed. "Knight! Behind you!"

Steel turned, sword raised.

Two pale eyes shone in the darkness.

"Leave, Sir Knight. The way is forbidden."

"You let the mage inside! *And* the kender," Steel retorted.

"*I* did not let them in."

"Then who did?"

"The Master of the Tower."

"Lord Dalamar is returned? Then tell *him* to let me inside!" Steel demanded.

The eyes drifted closer. The deadly chill of the netherworld struck through to the marrow of the knight's bones. He gritted his teeth to keep them from clicking together, gripped his sword more tightly.

"I do not refer to Dalamar," said the specter. "Leave this place now, Sir Knight, or you will never leave it at all."

"Help!" Usha cried. "Someone, please help us!"

Her voice echoed eerily through the darkness, circling round and round the tower's inner walls, falling like a stone dropped in a well. The sound was so strange and terrifying that she didn't repeat her call.

Help could come or not, as it chose. Steel's prisoner was on the other side of the door. Steel's duty lay on the other side of that door. He had failed once. He had hesitated on the threshold instead of entering. This realm of wizards was unsettling, unnerving. The very air was clogged and fouled with sorcery, the darkness alive with unquiet spirits. He longed for an enemy he could see, feel. He longed to breathe fresh air, hear the clean clash of sword against sword. He longed to leave this mage's keep, but he could not abandon his duty, not even in death.

He struck at the specter. His sword whistled in the air, clanged against the stone wall with a shower of sparks.

The pale, gleaming eyes grew enormous, swelled and bulged. Hands reached out, their cruel touch lethal.

Steel slashed at it again. "Takhisis," he shouted, "be with me!"

"Your prayers are in vain, Sir Knight," said a voice. "Our queen has no jurisdiction here."

A globe of warm yellow light, held in the hands of a red-robed wizardess, drove the darkness back. Beside her, standing on the landing, was a sorcerer—an elf wearing black robes. At first amazed, Steel then realized that the man must be a dark elf, one who had turned against the light, gone against the precepts of his people. This must be Dalamar the Dark, Master of the Tower of High Sorcery.

Or was he merely subletting it?

Dalamar looked upward, to the knight standing at bay on the stairs. "I heard intruders had broken in, that a knight and a white-robed mage had passed safely through the Shoikan Grove. I could not believe it at first. Now I understand. A Knight of Takhisis. But where is the White Robe who accompanied you? Where is Palin Majere?"

"In there!" Usha answered, pointing at the laboratory. "He went into that . . . that room. The kender went with him. And then the door slammed shut and we haven't been able . . ."

Her voice sank. Dalamar's face was livid. The infuriated sorcerer turned to the guardian, who continued to hover near.

"You failed in your duty! I gave you orders to allow no one to enter!"

"Your orders were countermanded, my lord Dalamar," the hollow voice returned, "by the true Master of the Tower."

Dalamar did not reply. His face was set and cold, colder than if the chill hands of the undead had touched him.

Steel felt the power of the dark elf, felt the heat of his rage. The knight would not have been surprised to see the tower walls start to melt from it. Usha shrank away, hugging the stone wall. Even the elf's companion, the wizardess, took an involuntary step backward. Steel held his ground only because he could not in honor do anything else.

And then, Dalamar relaxed. The flame in the burning eyes died, their gaze abstracted. He had turned inward, was communing with himself. "Perhaps this is for the best after all. *He* may know something . . ."

Dalamar's mouth twisted in an ironic smile. "This is out of our hands, apparently, Jenna. For the moment, at least."

"So it would seem," the wizardess agreed, her gaze going to the sealed door, to the knight standing before it, and the woman crouched against the wall. "What will you do with these two?"

Dalamar's gaze returned to the knight, and the dark elf seemed to see him for the first time. "Are you, by chance, Steel Brightblade?"

Steel concealed his astonishment, reminded himself that he was in the presence of a powerful sorcerer. "I am," he said proudly.

"Kitiara's son!" Dalamar exclaimed. "I should have seen the resemblance. I knew your mother," he added wryly.

"You *murdered* my mother," Steel returned in dire tones.

"Which, of course, you consider a debt of honor, one that must be repaid with my blood." Dalamar shrugged. "Very well. You challenge me. I accept. You attack me. I kill you. A waste of a good soldier. Takhisis would not be pleased with either of us. I slew your mother in battle, Steel Brightblade. It was self-defense. She struck first. I can show you *that* scar. Unfortunately, I cannot show you the other scars she left on me."

The last words were spoken low. Steel could not be certain he heard them, and chose to ignore them anyway. He was consulting the Vision, as did all the Knights of Takhisis when faced with a dilemma. Was it Her will that he fight this dark elf and very probably lose his life in the attempt? Was it Her will that he make a futile stand at this laboratory door? Or did She have other plans for him?

He looked into the Vision. An image of his mother entered his mind. She bore her sword, carried it unsheathed, in her hand, as if she would use it herself. But behind his mother he saw another figure—a five-headed dragon. His mother stood in the dragon's shadow. It was still confusing . . .

"Sir Knight!" Dalamar was calling to him, had been calling to him for some time now, apparently, trying to regain Steel's attention.

"What did you say, my lord?" Steel asked, frowning, still attempting to read his Dark Queen's will.

"I said that someone has been attempting to contact you," Dalamar repeated patiently. "Your commander, I believe."

"How is that possible, my lord?" Steel was suspicious. "No one knows I am here. What does he say?"

"I have no idea," Dalamar said, with a touch of irritation. "I am not a messenger boy. As for how he knew you were here, I presume someone told him. Possibly the same someone who guided you safely through the Shoikan Grove. If you will abandon your post, Brightblade, I will take you to where you may commune with your officer. I assure you," Dalamar added, "your quest here is futile. Not even I could enter that laboratory. The uncle has sent for his nephew. We must leave it to the two of them."

"Palin Majere was my prisoner," Steel said, still hesitating. "I accepted his parole."

"Ah," said Dalamar, instantly understanding. "Then you do indeed have a difficult decision to make."

Steel took only a moment to make it. His commander knew he was here. It must be Takhisis's will that her knight turn his footsteps in a different direction. It must also be her will that he remain alive. Steel sheathed his sword, descended the stairs.

Immediately, the two pale eyes resumed their place, guarding the door.

"I will take you to the Pool of Seeing," Dalamar said as the knight joined him on the landing. "There you may communicate with your commander. We will travel the corridors of magic. Much faster and far less strenuous than these stairs." The dark elf laid his hand on Steel's arm. "You may experience a dizzy sensation—"

"What about me?" Usha, who might have been a solid stone statue, came suddenly to life. "What will you do with me? And what has happened to Palin? I want to go with him!"

"Jenna, attend to her," Dalamar ordered.

The wizardess nodded, smiled.

Dalamar spoke words of magic.

The darkness opened in front of Steel. He remembered wanting to flee, but the sorcerer propelled him forward.

Then his feet touched solid ground. He stood at the edge of a pool, saw himself reflected in the still, dark water.

* * * * *

Usha had gone along with the others mainly because she didn't want to be left alone in the room. And also, she admitted to herself now, because she found the young mage very attractive. He was the first male she'd met who hadn't been stupid and boorish, like the thugs who'd attacked her, or cunning and frightening, like the wizard, or cold and cruel, like the dark knight.

Palin was different. He reminded her in many ways of her Protector. He was gentle, vulnerable; she sensed the fear in him, akin to her own. The shadow of some great grief, some secret sorrow hung over him. And yet he was strong, both in will and in courage. She called his face to mind and experienced a wrenching, twisting sensation in her heart that was uncomfortable, painful, exquisitely delightful.

"I want to go with Palin," Usha said.

"Go ahead." Jenna gestured at the laboratory door, at the disembodied eyes of the guardians.

Usha had second thoughts.

"I want to leave," she stated. "Everyone else has gone. You can't keep me here against my will."

"No, I can't," Jenna replied coolly. "Such a powerful sorceress as you could go wherever she wanted."

Usha wanted, more than anything else she had ever wanted in her life, to be far from this evil tower. She wanted to have nothing more to do with it or the people inside it . . . with the possible exception of Palin Majere.

She glanced up at the door through which he'd vanished. The eyes of the specter stared down at her.

"I will leave, then," Usha said, and she opened her pouch.

She stared in perplexity at the various objects inside. She knew that they were magic, but that was all she knew about them. She bitterly regretted that she had not paid more attention to the instructions. There were several rings; an amulet made of milk quartz, one of garnet, and another of obsidian; two scrolls tied up with purple ribbons; a small bag containing some sort of sweet-smelling herbs; a short length of rope, useless, as far as she could tell; several tiny, carved animal figures; and a small glass vial.

She shut her eyes, concentrated, tried to bring back the image and words of her people.

The images came, comforting, warm, and forever lost.

Tears burned her eyes. She'd been so cold, so selfish. She longed to take back that moment, replace it with another in which she told them how grateful she was to them, how much she loved them, how much—how very much—she would miss them.

"If you're ever in danger and you want to escape, use this . . ."

She could see the Protector clearly, hear his counsel, feel him press an object into her hand.

What object? Which?

"If you don't want to be trapped alone on the stairs in the dark, I suggest you come with me," Jenna advised, adding dryly, "unless you are leaving us."

"I am leaving," Usha answered.

It was either the obsidian amulet or the glass vial, one or the other. One had something to do with shadows, which wouldn't likely be of much help to her. This foul place already had more shadows than it knew what to do with. The other would take her out of danger. How? Usha couldn't recall, but anything was better than this.

Obsidian was black and so were shadows. Logic rejected the amulet, told her to try the vial.

Usha had lived around magic all her life, but only magic that was used for good and practical purposes. She had never seen evil or harmful magic—until she had come to this dread tower. And so she wasn't particularly frightened about trying an unknown magic. Her Protector had given it to her; she trusted him.

Usha plucked the vial from her pouch, cracked open the wax seal that covered it.

Jenna sprang at her, but it was too late.

A thin sliver of whitish yellow smoke rose from the vial. It smelled sweet, like newly mown grass, and banished the stench of death and decay that seemed to linger in the air.

Usha held the vial to her nose. She inhaled the smoke . . .

She became smoke.

24

The Chamber of Seeing.

Where are we now?" Steel asked.

"We stand in the Chamber of Seeing," said Dalamar. "It was created by my *shalafi*, Raistlin Majere."

They stood in a circular room in the center of which, taking up almost the entire area, with the exception of a small walkway, was a pool of dark water. A blue flame spurted from the pool's center. The flame gave off no smoke, and what it used for fuel—unless it burned the water— could not be told. And though the flame was bright, it provided little light. The chamber remained dark.

"And what does this Chamber of Seeing do," Steel inquired, glancing around in disgust, "besides give off a foul smell?"

His gaze caught movement around the edge of the pool; his hand went to his sword's hilt.

"Relax, Sir Knight," Dalamar said quietly. "They cannot hurt you."

Steel, not exactly trusting the Black Robe, did not let loose his sword. He stared hard in the direction of the movement, sucked in a hissing breath.

"What in the Queen's name is that?"

"At one point in his notorious career, my *shalafi* attempted to create life. These were the result. They are known as the Live Ones."

Bleeding, larvalike masses, the Live Ones crawled, writhed, or pulled themselves along the side of the pool. They made noises, but whether they were speaking or merely bleating in pain-filled distress, Steel could not tell. The knight had seen many horrible sights, seen his comrades hacked to death in battle, seen dying dragons plummet from the skies. For the first time in his life, he was forced to avert his gaze, forced to sternly calm the quaking of his stomach.

"Sacrilege," he said, wishing the creatures would cease their pitiable wailings.

"True," Dalamar agreed. "My *shalafi* had no great respect for the gods—any gods. But do not waste your sympathy on these. The Live Ones are better off, and they know it."

"Better off than what?" Steel demanded harshly.

"Those known as the Dead Ones. But, come, Sir Knight. Your commander desires to speak with you, and we are wasting his valuable time. He seemed quite impatient."

"How do I talk to him? Where is he?" Steel peered into the shadows as if he expected Subcommander Trevalin to step out of the stone walls.

"I have no idea where he is. He did not tell me. Look into the pool."

The Live Ones yammered in excitement. Several dragged their bodies near the edge, pointed to the water with their misshapen appendages. Steel regarded them, the dark elf, and the pool with suspicion.

"Go to the edge," Dalamar instructed impatiently, "and look into the water. Nothing dreadful will happen to you. Get on with this, Sir Knight. Your commander's time is not the only time wasted. Critical events are happening in this world, as I believe you are about to discover."

Steel, still dubious, but accustomed to obeying orders, walked to the edge of the pool, careful not to step on any of the Live Ones in the process. He stared down into the dark water and, at first, saw nothing except the reflection of the blue flame. Then the flame and water blended, rippled. He had a terrifying feeling that he was falling into the pool, put out his hands to stop himself, and very nearly touched Subcommander Trevalin.

The subcommander stood in a burned-out shell of a castle. Scorch marks charred the walls; the ceiling beams had fallen in; the roof was now the sky.

The subcommander was holding a staff meeting, apparently, for many knights under his command were assembled in the large room. At the far end of the room sat another knight, this one clad in the armor of the Knights of Solamnia. Steel might have taken this knight for a prisoner, but the armor was charred and blackened like the fire-scourged castle walls. Eyes as red as flame burned through the slits of the metal helm. Steel knew then the name of this dread knight, knew where his commander was.

Dargaard Keep, home of the death knight, Lord Soth.

"Subcommander Trevalin." Steel saluted.

The subcommander turned around. "Ah, Brightblade. You are still a guest of my lord Dalamar, I see." The knight saluted. "I thank you, my lord, for conveying my message."

Dalamar bowed, his mouth twisted in a half-smile, a half-sneer. He was in a very awkward position. He had no love for Takhisis's gray-robed wizards, yet he was bound—at least outwardly—to do all he could to forward his Dark Queen's cause.

"How goes your mission, Brightblade?" Trevalin continued. "The Gray Knights are most anxious to hear." A quirk of his eyebrow expressed exactly what he thought of the Gray Knights and their anxiety.

Steel faced his superior steadfastly, unblinking. "My mission has failed, Subcommander. The White Robe, Palin Majere, has escaped."

Trevalin was grave. "This is most unfortunate, Brightblade. Is there any possibility you can recapture the prisoner?"

Steel glanced sideways at Dalamar.

The dark elf shook his head. "Not where he has gone," he said softly.

"No, Subcommander," Steel replied.

"A pity." Trevalin was suddenly cool. "Majere was sentenced to death. You gave your parole for his return. Since you have allowed him to escape, it is you who must take your prisoner's place."

"I am aware of that, Subcommander."

"You will, of course, have the right to state your case before the adjudicator. In this instance, that would be Lord Ariakan himself, since he is your sponsor." Trevalin appeared relieved. "Fortunately for you, Brightblade, and for me, Lord Ariakan is extremely busy at the moment. Your trial will, of necessity, be postponed. You are a skilled and valiant soldier. I would regret losing you on the eve of battle. Which brings me to my point. You are ordered to return to your talon."

"Yes, Subcommander. When?"

"Now. Immediately. There is no time to waste. I have already dispatched Flare to pick you up."

"Thank you, Subcommander. Do I join the talon at Dargaard Keep?"

"No, Brightblade. We will have moved by then. You will meet us in the Vingaard Mountains. At dawn tomorrow, we attack the High Clerist's Tower. You should not have any trouble finding us," Trevalin added, his witticism drawing laughter from the assembled knights. "The gods themselves will look down on this vast army and be amazed. But I will give you directions."

* * * * *

Dalamar watched and listened to this conversation in silence. Toward the beginning, Jenna had entered the chamber, beckoned to him that she needed to speak to him. He gave her a sign to wait. Hearing what he needed to hear, Dalamar moved to the front of the chamber, came to stand beside Jenna.

"What is it? Keep your voice low."

Jenna leaned toward him. "The girl is gone!"

Dalamar raised an eyebrow. "Gone? How?"

Jenna shrugged. "By magic. How else? She took out a vial, broke open the wax seal. Smoke rose from the vial. Before I could stop her, she had inhaled it and *she* changed into smoke. There was no way I could reverse the magic, not knowing what spell the Irda had used."

"You probably couldn't have halted it anyway," Dalamar remarked. "And so she left?"

"The smoke cloud vanished. She vanished with it."

"Interesting. I wonder, if she had this capability, why she didn't leave sooner?"

"Perhaps, as you said, the Irda sent her to spy on us. Does this settle in your mind that she is at least part Irda?"

"No, it does not. A gully dwarf could have used those enchanted objects if someone had shown the creature how. This answers none of our questions about the girl. Well, she's gone, and that's that. We have more immediate worries. The Knights of Takhisis plan to attack the High Clerist's Tower at dawn."

Jenna's eyes opened wide in astonishment. "Blessed Gilean!"

"They will win," Dalamar said, frowning, glancing over at Steel.

Jenna gazed steadily at Dalamar. "Can it be that such news displeases you? Aren't you on the side of your queen?"

"If Takhisis were on *my* side, I would be on hers," Dalamar replied bitterly. "But she isn't. My queen has seen fit to employ her own wizards to do her work. If the High Clerist's Tower falls to her knights, the city of Palanthas will most assuredly surrender. We will be at the beck and call of the Gray Robes."

Jenna was shocked. "Surely you don't imagine they would dare try to take the Tower of High Sorcery from you?"

"In an instant, my dear! The Conclave will fight them, of course, but we saw how well that worked when we raided Storm's Keep."

Jenna nodded, pale and silent. Her father, Justarius, had died in that disaster.

"Nuitari must be finding it difficult to stand up to his mother," Dalamar continued dryly, referring to the god of dark magic, the son of Takhisis. "I notice his power has been waning of late."

"He is not alone," Jenna said. "Lunitari has been strangely powerless and, according to a White Robe I spoke to in Wayreth yesterday, Solinari has been distant from his people as well."

Dalamar nodded. "I believe I will take a little trip, my dear."

"To the High Clerist's Tower." Jenna understood. "What do I do with the knight?"

"His blue dragon is coming to fetch him. Take him up to the Death Walk. I will part the magical shell that protects the tower itself long enough for the dragon to descend and pick up her master."

"Should we let him go? We could make him prisoner."

Dalamar considered the matter. "No. We will return him to his army.

One knight more or less isn't going to make any difference to the outcome of the battle."

"We might use him as hostage—"

"The Knights of Takhisis would do nothing to save him. In fact, he's marked for death if he returns. He lost his prisoner, you see."

"Then he won't go back. Why should he?"

"*Est Sularus oth Mithas.* My honor is my life. The Knights of Solamnia said it first, but the Knights of Takhisis subscribe to the same silly code. Try to make him break it. I'm sure you'll find his response quite amusing.

"Besides," Dalamar added thoughtfully, "I'm not certain but that we may be doing Her Dark Majesty a disservice by returning this particular knight to her. He is not wholly under her command."

Jenna shook her head. "You talk in riddles, my love. He looks pretty well bound to Takhisis to me. What should I do after I get rid of him?"

Dalamar stared into the dark pool. The light of the blue flame flared in his eyes. "If I were you, Jenna, my dear, I would begin packing."

* * * * *

Steel concluded his conversation with his commanding officer. The spell ended; the enchantment lifted. Once more the knight stood beside the pool of dark water. Several of the Live Ones had gathered around him, poking and prodding at his armor with interest. Suppressing a shudder, he backed up swiftly, almost bumped into Jenna.

"You are leaving us, I hear, Sir Knight."

"Yes, Mistress," Steel replied. "My dragon is coming here." He glanced around. "Where is Lord Dalamar?"

"My lord has gone to part the magical shield that surrounds this place. I will take you to the Death Walk. You can meet your dragon there. Unless you would rather walk through the Shoikan Grove again?" she added archly.

Steel, sensing he was being made sport of, maintained cold silence.

"Please follow me, Sir Knight." Jenna motioned to the door. "We will step out into the hallway. I do not want to climb the thousand stairs, and I prefer not to cast a magical spell in this room. The enchantments do not blend well."

Steel accompanied Jenna from the Chamber of Seeing, not sorry at leaving. Once in the hall outside, he drew in a deep breath. The tower's air was dank and smelled of herbs and spice, mildew and decay, but at least it cleared his nostrils of the foul stench of the chamber.

Jenna regarded him curiously. "I must first ask, Sir Knight, if you are *quite* certain you want to leave us."

"Why wouldn't I?" Steel asked, regarding her warily. "Is there a chance to find Majere?"

"Not in *this* life," Jenna replied, smiling. "That wasn't what I meant. Dalamar tells me that if you return to your army, you will be executed."

Steel was calm. "I failed in my duty. The penalty is death."

Jenna regarded him with wonder. "Then why return? Escape while you can!" She moved near him, said softly, "I will send you anywhere you want to go. Bury this armor, and you will be a new man. No one would ever know."

"I would know, Mistress," Steel replied.

Jenna shrugged. "Very well, then. It's your funeral. Shut your eyes. It will help dispel the dizziness."

Steel shut his eyes, heard the wizardess start to laugh.

"Dalamar was right. *Most* amusing!"

25

The well-dressed dwarf.
Double or nothing.

sha stood next to a cart full of fruit with no very clear idea of how she got here or where here was. Her body tingled all over, from head to toe; her head seemed filled with wispy, smoky fog, and her nose tickled.

She vaguely remembered pulling out the vial, sniffing it, inhaling a most pleasant fragrance, and that was all she knew until now, when she found herself standing in what appeared to be an open-air market crowded with people. Usha expected everyone to be staring at her—having just appeared out of nowhere—but no one was paying the least bit of attention.

The people had too many troubles of their own. No one was selling anything in the market, except rumors. People huddled in knots, talking in low, urgent tones. Occasionally someone from one group would leave, go over to another group, ask for news. Usha heard several times the words: "Kalaman has fallen!" spoken in tones of fear and alarm. Usha could make nothing of this. She did overhear enough to convince her that she was, once again, in Palanthas.

Usha sighed. She was not particularly pleased to find herself still in Palanthas, still close to the dread tower. Yet she would have been sad to have left Palanthas, to have left all hope of ever seeing Palin again. Even though she told herself such hope was remote, she nurtured it. She no longer felt friendless and alone. Someone cared for her. And she had someone to care for.

She couldn't see the tower from where she stood, but then she couldn't see over the rooftops of the tall buildings surrounding her. She hoped to slip away while no one was bothering about her, lose herself in the crowd. She must do something to earn these steel pieces which the Palanthians considered so valuable. She was thinking about this, wondering what she could do, when the smoke, lingering in her nose, caused an irritating tickle. She fought it, but could stand it no longer. Usha sneezed loudly.

A flashily dressed dwarf near her jumped in alarm, his boots clattering on the pavement.

"By Reorx's beard, Lass, you gave me a fright!" The dwarf gasped, wheezed for breath; his hand pressed over his heart.

"I'm sorry, sir," Usha began, but was interrupted by another sneeze.

"Have a cold, do you, Lass? I'm susceptible to colds." The dwarf, eyeing her nervously, backed up a step.

Usha shook her head, unable to explain due to the onset of a third sneeze. The dwarf backed up still further, held his hat over his face.

"Bless you," the dwarf said, somewhat belatedly.

Usha nodded her thanks, sniffed, and began to sort through her pouches for a handkerchief.

The dwarf offered his. It was white, lacy, and marked with the initials DR in fanciful stitchery on the corner. The handkerchief looked too fine and elegant to use. Usha, embarrassed, dabbed at her nose with a corner and, blushing, handed it back.

The dwarf stuffed the hankie in a pocket and regarded Usha with bright, cunning eyes.

"What is your name, Lass?"

"Usha, my lord," Usha replied with a curtsey, judging—by his clothes—that this dwarf must be someone important, if not the lord of Palanthas himself.

"Not 'my lord,' Lassie," the dwarf said, though he stroked his full, glossy beard proudly. "Dougan Redhammer, at your service."

Usha knew that the dwarves were skilled artisans, handy with metal and stone, but she had never heard that they were leaders in fashion. The legendary beauty of the halls of the great cavern city of Thorbardin was nothing when compared to the dwarf's red velvet waistcoat with golden buttons; the magnificence of the immense gates of Pax Tharkas dwindled to insignificance when held up against Dougan's frilly silk shirt with lace cuffs.

Red velvet breeches, black stockings, black shoes with red heels, and a wide-brimmed hat with a jaunty red plume rounded out the dwarf's finery. His beard was long and silky black and extended well past his stout middle; long black hair curled over his shoulders.

The fragrant smells of fresh fruit, which had been sitting in the hot noontime sun, distracted Usha's attention from the dwarf. She had not expected to be hungry again, following the feast in the Tower of High Sorcery, but that had been some time ago, her stomach informed her. Usha took a quick, surreptitious glance at the vendor, was relieved to see it was *not* the one who'd had her arrested.

Still, she'd learned her lesson. She tore her gaze away with a sigh, ordered her insides to think about something else. They refused with a growl.

The dwarf saw the look, however, heard the sigh and the growl.

"Help yourself, Lass," he said, waving his hand. "The plums are not as fresh as they were this morning, but the grapes are fine if you don't mind them a bit shriveled from the heat."

"Thank you," Usha said, refusing to look in the direction of the fruit, "but I'm not hungry."

"Then you've swallowed a small dog," Dougan said bluntly. "I can hear the beast barking from here. Eat up. I've had my lunch, so you'll not be offending me."

"It's not that." Usha's cheeks were pink. "I . . . I don't have any of what they term 'coins' . . ."

"Ah, that is a problem." Dougan stroked his beard, regarded Usha thoughtfully. "New to the city, eh?"

Usha nodded.

"Where are you living?"

"Nowhere in particular," Usha said evasively. The strange dwarf was taking far too great an interest in her personal affairs. "If you'll excuse me—"

"What do you do for a living?"

"Oh, this and that. Look, sir, it's been very nice talking with you, but—"

"I understand. You're newly arrived in the city and looking for work. Find it all a bit overwhelming, don't you?"

"Well, yes, sir, it's just—"

"I think I might be able to help you." Dougan eyed her critically, his head cocked to one side. "You sneaked up on me pretty good. I never heard you coming, and that's a fact." Reaching out, he took hold of her hand, studied it. "Slender fingers. Deft, I'll reckon. Quick? Skilled?"

"I . . . I suppose so." Usha regarded the dwarf with confusion.

Dougan dropped her hand as if it had been a piece of sun-baked fruit, stared at her feet a good, long time, then lifted his gaze to her face, muttering to himself. "Eyes that would charm Hiddukel from his money-counting. Features that would raise Chemosh out of his own grave. She'll do. Yes, indeed, Lassie," he said, raising his voice. "I know some people who are looking for talent just like yours."

"What talent?" Usha asked. "I don't—"

But Dougan wasn't listening. Plucking up a bunch of grapes, he thrust them in Usha's hands. He added several plums, a large squash, and would have added turnips, but Usha couldn't hold anything more. This done, the dwarf started to leave.

"Hey! You! Haven't you forgotten something?" The vendor—a large human—had been talking over the rumored fall of Kalaman with several friends. The sight of someone attempting to make off with his wares drove all thoughts of impending war right out of his head. He loomed over the dwarf. "I said, 'Haven't you forgotten something?' "

Dougan paused, twirled his mustache. "I believe I have. The turnips." Catching up several, he again started to leave.

"A small matter of my money," the vendor said, blocking their way.

Usha stuffed a handful of grapes in her mouth, gulped and swallowed them hurriedly, determined to eat as much as she could in case she had to give the fruit back.

"Put it on my tab," Dougan said airily.

"This ain't no alehouse, Shorty," snarled the man, crossing his arms over his chest. "Pay up."

"I'll tell you what, my good man," Dougan said affably, though he appeared a bit displeased at the term "shorty," "I'll flip you for them." He produced a gold coin. The vendor's eyes lit up. "The lord's head up two times out of three, and the fruit is mine. Agreed? Agreed."

Dougan flipped the coin. The vendor, scowling, watched it spin in the air. The coin landed on the cart rail, the lord's head up.

The man stared closely at it. "Hey, that ain't no Palanthas coin. And that ain't no lord. That head looks like yours . . . "

Dougan snatched up the coin hastily. "Must've grabbed the wrong one." He tossed the coin before the man could protest. The head—lord or dwarf—landed up again.

"Ah, too bad," Dougan said complacently, reaching out to pocket the coin.

The vendor was quicker, however. "Thank you," he said, snatching it up. "That should just about cover your purchases."

Dougan's face flushed red. "You lost!" he roared.

The vendor, closely examining the coin, started to turn it over.

"Well, never mind," Dougan added. Walking hurriedly away, he tugged at Usha to accompany him. "It's not whether you win or lose, but how you play the game, I always say."

"Hey! Dwarf!" the vendor shouted. "You tried to cheat me! This coin has two heads! And both of them look like—"

"Come along, Lass," Dougan urged, quickening his pace. "We don't have all day."

"Hey!" The vendor was screaming at the top of his lungs. "The gold's rubbing off! Stop that dwarf—"

Dougan was running now, his thick boots clomping on the cobblestone streets.

Usha, clutching her food, hastened to keep up. "They're chasing us!"

"Turn right. Down this alley!" Dougan huffed and panted.

The two dashed into a dark alleyway. Usha, looking behind, noticed that those chasing them skidded to a halt at the alley's entrance.

The vendor pointed, cajoling, pleading.

Shaking their heads, the men walked away.

The vendor—after shouting a few threats at Dougan—stalked off in a rage.

"They're not coming after us," Usha said in wonder.

"Thought better of it," Dougan said. Slowing down, he began to fan himself with his hat. "Probably noticed I was wearing a sword."

"You're not," Usha pointed out.

"Their lucky day," the dwarf said with a sly wink.

Usha glanced around nervously. The alley was cleaner than any other she'd seen in Palanthas. It was also darker and emptier, quieter. A crow walked up, cool and confident, began pecking at a plum she'd dropped.

Usha shivered. She didn't like this place. "Do you know where we are?"

The crow ceased its pecking, cocked its head, stared at her with beady yellow eyes.

"Yes, Lass, I do," Dougan Redhammer said, smiling. "There's folks live around here I want you to meet. They're needing someone like you to do a few small jobs for them. I think you'll suit them just fine, Lass. Just fine."

The crow opened its beak, gave a raucous, laughing caw.

26

The laboratory.
Tasslehoff takes the initiative
(among other things).

O h, my!" Tasslehoff whispered, too thrilled and awestruck to speak aloud.

"Don't touch anything!" were Palin's first words, uttered in stern and urgent tones.

But since these are generally the first words spoken by anyone in the presence of a kender, the warning went right in one side of Tas's head and out the other, ending up nicely rationalized in between.

Don't touch anything!

"Sound advice, I suppose," Tas said to himself, "since it's given in the laboratory of one of the greatest, most powerful Black Robes who ever lived. Touch something in here and I might end up living inside one of those jars like that poor, dead thing inside that one jar, which there couldn't be any harm in my just taking the lid off to get a closer look . . ."

"Tas!" Palin removed the jar from the kender's hand.

"I was moving it back so it wouldn't fall," Tas explained.

Palin glared at him. "Don't touch!" he reiterated.

"Gee, he's in a really bad mood." Tas continued talking to himself, wandering to another (darker) part of the laboratory. "I'll just leave him alone for a while. He doesn't really mean 'don't touch anything,' because I'm already touching something. My feet are touching the floor, and it's a good thing, too, or I'd be floating around like all this dust in the air. That would be quite entertaining. I wonder if I could manage it. Maybe that bottle with the blue-green gunk in it is some type of levitation potion. I'll . . ."

Palin—his face grim—snatched the bottle from Tas's hand and prevented him from pulling out the stopper. After removing several objects: a stub of a dust-covered candle, a small stone carved in the shape of a beetle, and a spool of black thread, from the kender's pouches, Palin marched Tas over to a dimly lit, empty corner and told him, in the most angry tone Tas had ever heard almost anyone use, to "STAY PUT AND DON'T MOVE!

"Or I will send you out of here," Palin finished.

Tas was well aware that this threat was empty, because, while he'd been poking around the laboratory, he'd been vaguely aware of the fact that Palin was beating on the door with his fists, attempting to pull it open, and had once even struck at it with his staff, to no avail. The door wouldn't budge.

The knight had also banged on the door for a while, but on the other side. Now the outraged thunderings of Steel Brightblade could no longer be heard.

"He must have left," Tas said. "Either that or the specter got him."

This would have been an interesting sight and one Tas was disappointed to have missed. Still, a kender can't be everywhere at once, and Tasslehoff wouldn't have lost this opportunity for all the specters in the world, with maybe a banshee or two thrown in.

"Palin doesn't mean to be a grouch. He's just frightened," Tas remarked, sympathy in his voice. The kender was not personally familiar with that particularly uncomfortable emotion himself, but he had known it to afflict many of his friends, and so he decided—out of compassion for his young companion—to do as Palin asked him to do.

Tas stood in the corner, feeling virtuous and wondering how long such a feeling would last. Probably not long, virtuousness bordering on boredom. Still, it would do for a while. Tas couldn't touch anything, but he could look, and so he looked with all his might and main.

Palin walked slowly around the laboratory. The Staff of Magius shed a bright light over everything in the room, as if it were pleased to be back home.

The room was enormous, certainly far bigger than anyone could have reasonably expected it to be, considering its location and the size of all the other rooms in the tower. Tas had the eerie and exciting impression that the room had grown when he stepped inside and, even more exciting, that the room was *still growing*! It was an impression received from the fact that no matter where in the room he looked, whenever he took his eyes away and then looked back, he saw something that he was positive hadn't been there before.

The biggest object in the laboratory was a gigantic table. Carved of stone, it took up almost the whole middle of the room. Tasslehoff could have lain end to end about three times and have had room left for his topknot. Not that he would have wanted to lie in all that dust, which was extremely thick and covered everything. The only tracks Tas could see across the dusty floor were his own and Palin's, not even little mice skitterings. There were no cobwebs either.

"We are the first living beings to set foot inside this chamber in years," Palin said softly, unknowingly echoing the kender's thoughts.

The young mage passed a worktable, shone the staff's light on innumerable shelves filled with books and scrolls. Some of the books, bound in night-blue bindings, Tasslehoff recognized as the spellbooks belonging to the infamous mage Fistandantilus. Other books, in black bindings with silver engraving or red bindings with gold lettering, might have been Raistlin's own, or were perhaps left here by the tower's previous inhabitants.

Palin stopped in front of these spellbooks, gazed at them with eager, hungry eyes. He reached out a hand to one, then abruptly pulled it back.

"Who am I kidding?" he said bitterly. "If I were to even look at the flyleaf, I'd probably go mad."

Having been a traveling companion of Raistlin's, Tas knew enough about magic-users to know that a mage of low rank attempting to read a spell that wasn't meant for him would go instantly insane.

"That's a safety feature," Tasslehoff pointed out, in case Palin didn't know. "Raistlin explained it to me once, the time he took the spellbook away from me. He was quite nice about it, saying he didn't want to have an insane kender on his hands. I said it was awfully kind of him to be so considerate, but that I wouldn't mind being insane, and he said yes, but *he* would, and I think he added something to the effect that he'd rather have twenty ogres with twenty sticks beating him about the head and shoulders, but I could be mistaken on that point."

"Uncle Tas," said Palin in a nervous, half-suffocated, smothered kind of voice, "I don't mean to be rude, especially to someone your age, but would you please shut up!"

He continued walking around the room, shining the light of the staff more closely on this item or that, not handling, not touching anything. He covered the entire laboratory twice, with the exception of one little part.

He didn't go into the back of the chamber, located almost directly across from where Tasslehoff was standing. That part was very dark and, Tas began to suspect, Palin was deliberately keeping the light away from it.

Tas knew what was in that part of the laboratory, though. Both Caramon and Tanis had told him the story.

Palin kept glancing that direction, then looking back at Tas, as if confused about what he was supposed to do.

Well, Tas knew exactly what they were supposed to do.

"But he's still frightened," Tas commented with a shake of his topknot. "That has to be it. I can't imagine why else he's wandering around here, when we should be getting on with things. I could tell him what to do.

"No, that wouldn't be a good idea. As I recall from when I was a mere kender lad, advice from an older person, such as myself, to a younger person, such as Palin, is generally *not* well received. Perhaps I could give him a hint, nudge him along, so to speak. After all, we haven't got all day. It's getting along about supper time and, as I recall, the meals in the Abyss, while perhaps being nutritious, were distinctly lacking in flavor. So. Now—wait until he's not looking."

Palin was inspecting the scrolls in a desultory manner, interested in them, but obviously having something more important on his mind. He glanced at them, sighed, and put them back with obvious reluctance.

"Come on—find one that you can use!" Tasslehoff muttered.

And suddenly Palin apparently did so. He examined the wax seal that had been stamped on the ribbon binding the scroll, brightened considerably, and, breaking the seal open, began to scan the contents.

Tasslehoff Burrfoot, moving as silently as kender can, which meant that the dust drifting to the floor made as much noise as he did, left his place in the corner, stole stealthily across the room, and boldly mounted the stone dais on which stood the Portal to the Abyss.

"This is interesting, Tas," Palin said, turning to look at where the kender had been. A note of concern crept into his voice when he noticed the kender wasn't there anymore. "Tas!"

"Look what I found, Palin," Tas said proudly.

Grasping hold of a golden silk rope hanging at the side of purple velvet curtains, he gave the rope a pull.

"No, Tas!" Palin cried, dropping the scroll and leaping forward. "Don't! You could get us—"

Too late.

The curtain lifted, dust shaking down off its folds in a cloud that nearly choked the kender.

And then Palin heard that ominous word—generally the last word those who have the misfortune to travel with a kender ever hear in this life.

"Oops!"

27

The Thieves' Guild.
The New Apprentice.

The Thieves' Guild in Palanthas could boast—and usually did, with some pride—that it was the oldest guild in the city. Although no official date marked the guild's founding, its members were probably not far wrong in their reckoning. Certainly there were thieves in Palanthas long before there were silversmiths or tailors or perfumers or any of the number of other guilds that now flourished.

The Thieves' Guild traced its roots back to ancient times, to a gentleman known as Cat Pete, who had led a band of brigands in the wilds of Solamnia. His band preyed on highway travelers. Cat Pete (his name was not given him because he was silent and catlike in his grace, but because he had once been soundly whipped with a cat-o'-nine-tails) was very selective of his victims. He avoided lords who traveled with armed escorts, all mages, mercenaries, and anyone wearing a sword. Cat Pete maintained that he was extremely loathe to shed blood. So he was—especially his own.

He chose to rob the lone and unarmed traveler—the itinerant tinker, the wandering minstrel, the hardworking peddler, the impoverished student, the poor cleric. Needless to say, Cat Pete and his band found it rather difficult to make ends meet. Pete was always hopeful that someday he would accost a tinker who happened to be hiding a load of jewels on his person, but this never happened.

During one particularly hard winter, when the band was reduced to such extremes that members were eating their own shoes and starting to look hungrily at each other, Cat Pete decided to better himself. He sneaked out of camp, determined to seek his fortune—or at least a crust of bread—in the newfound city of Palanthas. He was crawling over the walls in the dead of night when he stumbled across a city guard. Those who view Cat Pete in a romantic light say that he and the guard engaged in a vicious battle, that Pete hurled the guard from the top of the wall to the ground below, that the highwayman then entered the city triumphant.

Those who have bothered to read the true history of Cat Pete will find the true version of the tale. Upon being accosted on the wall by the guard and threatened with imminent demise, the bold Cat Pete fell to his knees, clasped the guard about the legs, and begged for mercy. The

guard at this moment slipped on a patch of ice. Due to the fact that
Pete's arms were locked firmly around his knees, the guard could not
catch his balance. Arms flailing, he tumbled off the wall.

Cat Pete, who'd had sense enough to let go at the last moment, continued to retain his cool presence of mind. He descended to the ground
by more conventional means, robbed the body of the dead man, and
sneaked into the city, where he took up residence in a cow shed.

One could say the guild rose from the cow droppings.

Pete always claimed he started the Thieves' Guild, but it was really
his lover—a dwarven woman by the name of Quick-hand Bet—who is
credited with being the founder. "Thieves fall out" is an old saying and,
as the city grew larger and wealthier, the thieves in Palanthas were
falling out on a regular basis. They would often find themselves ran-
sacking a house that had been ransacked the night previous or, as happened on one noteworthy occasion, three separate groups of burglars
showed up to burgle the same lord's mansion at the same time. This
resulted in a brawl among the thieves, which roused the household. The
lord and his servants captured the lot, shut them in the wine cellar, and
hanged them the next morning. Cat Pete was, unfortunately, among
their number and is said to have fought like a fiend before his end,
though records indicate he collapsed in a blubbering heap at the foot of
the scaffold and had to be hauled up the stairs by the scruff of his neck.

Following this disaster, Quick-hand Bet called together as many cut-
purses, cut-throats, and pickpockets as she could persuade to come out
of hiding and gave them a rousing speech. It would be far better, she
said, for them to pool their talents, stake out territory, divide the spoils,
and not tread on each other's toes. They had all seen the bodies of their
comrades swinging on the gibbets. The thieves agreed, and they were
never sorry.

The Thieves' Guild proved such a success that more and better talent
made its way to Palanthas. Through intelligent leadership, the guild
prospered. Its members established bylaws and codes of conduct, to
which all who joined the guild ascribed. The guild received a share of
every thief's spoils and, in return, offered training, alibis that would
occasionally stand up in court, and hiding places when the lord's men
were on the prowl.

The guild's current headquarters was an abandoned warehouse
inside the city wall, near the docks. Here the thieves had thrived for
years with impunity. The Lord of Palanthas would make, on a regular
basis, a promise to the citizenry that he would shut down the Thieves'
Guild. On periodic occasions throughout the year, the city guards
would raid the warehouse. The guild's spies always knew when the

guard would be coming. The guard always found an empty warehouse on its arrival. The lord would tell the citizens that the Thieves' Guild was out of business. The citizens, accustomed to this, continued to bolt and lock their doors at night and stoically count their losses the next morning.

Truth be told, the citizens of Palanthas—though they detested the thieves—were rather proud of their Thieves' Guild. The ordinary money-grubbing burgher, whose inflated prices robbed people on a much smaller scale, could complain about it loudly. Young girls dreamed of the handsome, daring highwayman they would rescue, with their love, from a life of crime. The Palanthas citizenry looked down upon lesser towns that had no Thieves' Guild. They spoke with disdain of such cities as Flotsam, whose thieves were unorganized and—it was felt—of generally a much lower class than the Palanthas thieves. The Palanthians were fond of recounting stories of the noble burglar who, upon entering the house of the poor widow to rob her, was so struck by her woeful plight that he actually left money behind. Poor widows of Palanthas would have had occasion to dispute this tale, but no one asked them.

It was to this warehouse—or the guild hall as it was grandiosely termed—that Usha and Dougan turned their steps. The alley was dark and deserted. Usha entered it without hesitation. The memory of the tower haunted her. As long as she was anywhere away from that dread place, she was content. She liked the bluff and gruff manner of the dwarf, admired his elegant style of clothing and, in short, trusted him.

She knew nothing of the eyes watching them as they traversed the alley. She was blissfully ignorant of the fact that, had she been in this place alone, she would have had her throat slit.

The eyes knew and approved Dougan, however. The bird whistles and cat howls that Usha thought, innocently, belonged to birds and cats, guided the dwarf and his companion safely through the gauntlet of spies and guards.

The warehouse was a gigantic building that butted up against the city wall. Because it was made of the same stone as the wall, it looked rather like a growth or tumor that erupted from the wall's surface, spread into the streets. It was gray, mottled, sagging, crumbling. What windows it had were either filthy or broken; blankets had been stuffed into the holes (to be removed should the building ever come under attack. They were ideal for archers.) The door was thick, massive, made of wood banded with iron, and bore a peculiar mark on it.

Dougan knocked on the door in a strange and involved manner.

A panel slid open near the bottom. An eye peered out. The eye studied

Dougan, shifted to Usha, shifted back to Dougan, narrowed, then vanished as the panel slid shut.

"You don't mean to say people live here?" Usha said, looking around in disgust and astonishment.

"Shh! Hush! Keep your voice down, Lass," Dougan cautioned. "They're quite proud of this, you know. Quite proud."

Usha couldn't see why, but she kept silent, thinking that was only polite. She glanced back over her shoulder. The Tower of High Sorcery, though far away, was visible. She could even see—or so she imagined—the window of Dalamar's study. She pictured the mage standing at the window, staring out into the streets below, searching for her. Shuddering, she edged closer to Dougan and wished whoever lived in this building would answer the door.

She looked back to find the door already open. Usha stared, startled. She hadn't heard a sound. At first she didn't see anyone in the doorway. All was dark beyond, and a dreadful smell—of garbage and worse—caused her to wrinkle her nose. She thought at first it was coming from inside the building, when a voice spoke from the odoriferous shadows.

"What you want?"

"Why, it's a dwarf!" said Usha, relieved.

"Bite your tongue!" Dougan growled. "It's a gully dwarf. No relation," he added stiffly.

"But it—I mean he . . ." She thought it was a he, but it was hard to tell through the rags. " . . . looks just like—"

She was about to say "you," but a ferocious glint in Dougan's eye warned her to amend. "A . . . a dwarf," she finished lamely.

Dougan, clearly indignant, made no answer. He spoke to the gully dwarf. "I want to see Lynch. Tell Lynch that Dougan Redhammer is here and that I won't be kept waiting. Tell Lynch that I have something for him that will be to his advantage."

The gully dwarf started, on three separate occasions—each time Dougan finished a sentence—to leave on his errand, only to turn around whenever Dougan spoke.

"Stop!" the gully dwarf shouted suddenly. "Me dizzy." He did look queasy.

Usha was beginning to feel queasy herself, but that was from the smell.

"Me not feel good," the gully dwarf said thickly. "Feel like gotta barf."

"No, no!" Dougan cried, stepping hastily out of range. "Just rest yourself. There's a good chap."

"Barfing not bad," the gully dwarf argued, brightening. "If meal was good going down, it be just as good coming back up."

"Fetch Lynch, you little maggot," Dougan ordered, mopping his face with a handkerchief. The heat, in the breathless alley, was stifling.

"Who's Lynch?" Usha asked as the gully dwarf obediently trotted off.

"His full name is Lynched Geoffrey," said Dougan in an undertone. "He's the guildmaster."

"What an odd name," Usha whispered. "Why is he called that?"

"Because he was."

"Was what?"

"Lynched. Don't mention the rope burn on his neck. He's very sensitive about it."

Usha was curious to know how a man who'd been lynched was still walking around. She was about to ask when Lynched Geoffrey appeared in the doorway. He was tall and lithe and slender, with over-large hands and thin, long fingers that were in constant motion—snapping, twitching, wiggling, or waving. A skilled pickpocket, who had reportedly once stolen a silk shirt off a nobleman's back, leaving his jacket untouched, Lynch maintained that these exercises kept his fingers supple. A thick scar of fiery red encircled his throat. His face was nondescript. The scar was his most interesting feature.

"What are you staring at, girl?" Lynch demanded angrily.

"N-nothing, sir," Usha stammered, forcing her gaze up from the scar, to meet the man's small, weasel-like eyes.

Lynch snarled, unconvinced, turned to Dougan. "Where've you been hiding out, old friend? We was talking about you the other day. Could have used you for a little tunneling job we had. You dwarves are good at that sort of thing."

"Yes, well, I've been involved in other matters," Dougan muttered, appearing displeased at the sneering way in which the man said "you dwarves," but swallowing his ire. "Now, down to business. My young friend, here"—he indicated Usha—"is new in town. She needs a place to sleep."

"This ain't a boarding house," Lynch said, putting his hand on the door, which started to shut.

Dougan inserted his large, heavy-booted foot, propped the door ajar. "If you'd let me finish, Lynch, old friend, I was about to say that the lass here needs a way to earn a living. She needs a bit of training in the art. I'm willing to pay the cost of her teaching," the dwarf added surlily.

Lynch again opened the door. He took a close look at Usha, who didn't at all like the way he stared at her, as if he were peeling back not only the layers of her clothes but the skin beneath. She flushed hotly. She didn't like this place or this odious man with his insect-wriggling hands. She wasn't at all certain that whatever he had to teach, she wanted to learn. She was about to bid them all good-bye when, glancing back at the end of the alleyway, she saw a black-robed mage standing there.

There were many black-robed mages in Palanthas, and more than a few had dealings with the folk in the warehouse. But Usha instantly assumed that this mage was Dalamar.

The mage was at the alley's opening. His head, covered with his hood, was turning this way and that, as if searching for someone. The alley, at the end of which she and the dwarf were standing, was long. The shadows were deep. It was probable he had not yet seen her.

Usha sprang forward, grasped Lynched Geoffrey by his splay-fingered hand, shook it until she nearly shook it off. "I'm so pleased to make your acquaintance," she said breathlessly. "I'll work hard. I'm a hard worker." Skipping past him, she ducked into the darkness of the warehouse, gulped in the foul-smelling air with relish.

Dwarf and thief appeared somewhat taken aback by her enthusiasm.

"She moves quick enough, I'll say that for her," Lynch remarked. He wrung his hand. "Got a good, strong grip, too."

Dougan drew a money purse from his broad black belt, hefted it in his hand.

"Done," said Lynch and politely invited Dougan to step inside. "Now, what's your name, girl?"

"My name is Usha," she said, looking around her curiously.

The interior of the warehouse was cavernous. Part of the floor was filled with tables and chairs, resembled the common room of an inn. Torches blazed on the walls. Thick candles burned on the tables. People sat around the tables, drinking, eating, gaming, talking, or sleeping. Every age, every race living on Ansalon was represented. The Thieves' Guild may have had its faults, but prejudice wasn't one of them. Two humans sat drinking companionably with three elves. A dwarf played at dice with an ogre. A hobgoblin and a kender were engaged in a drinking contest. A red-robed wizardess was involved in a heated discussion about Sargonnas with a minotaur. Children ran among the tables, playing rough-and-tumble games. The rest of the warehouse was lost in shadow, so Usha couldn't see what it contained.

No one looked at her. No one paid her the slightest attention. Thinking that it wouldn't hurt to impress her future employer, she added, "My full name is Usha Majere. I'm Raistlin's daughter."

"Yeah," said Lynched Geoffrey. "And I'm his mother." He spit on the floor.

Usha stared, taken aback. "I beg your pardon?"

"Raistlin's daughter!" Lynch laughed unpleasantly. "That's what they all say. I had three come here last year, claiming that very thing." His voice hardened. The weasel eyes were cold, flat. "Who are you really? Not a spy?" With a suddenness the eye couldn't follow, a knife glinted in Lynch's hand. "We deal short and swift with spies, don't we, Brothers?"

The other guild members were on their feet. Knives slid out of boots and swords rattled in their sheaths. Spell words and prayer chants crackled in the air, accompanied by the eerie sound of a whirling hoopak.

Usha stumbled backward until she bumped into the closed, barred door. Dougan put his rotund body between her and the guildmaster. The dwarf held up the purse.

"You know me, Lynched Geoffrey! What would I be doing, bringing a spy in here? So the lass claims her father's Raistlin Majere." Dougan appeared somewhat flustered at this, glanced at Usha out of the corner of his eye, but continued gamely on. "Who's to say it isn't so? How many of you"—he now cast a beetle-browed, scathing gaze around the assembled company—"can swear an oath as to who *your* fathers were?"

By the mutters and head-noddings that went around, most seemed to think the dwarf's contention sound. The fat purse, clinking comfortably with the ring of steel, added weight to his argument.

"Sorry if I was a bit hasty, girl," Lynch said, the knife in his hands vanishing as swiftly and mysteriously as it had appeared. "I'm of a highly sensitive nature, and I'm subject to nerves." He turned to Dougan. "We'll take her on as apprentice, standard terms. What do you want her trained for?"

"A special job," Dougan said evasively.

Lynch frowned. "What kind of job, dwarf?"

"That's for me to know and you not to," Dougan snapped. "I'm paying you to train her. That's all."

Lynch might have been less willing to yield had the size of the purse been smaller. As it was, he said, scowling, "The guild comes in for its cut. Don't forget that."

Dougan looked around at the people standing, watching. He looked especially at the children. His severe expression softened. He took off his hat with its elegant plume, held it over his chest, as he might if he were taking a vow. "If we succeed, you will all share. That I promise. If we fail, no blame to any of you." He sighed, appeared downcast for a moment.

Lynch deftly snatched the purse. "It's a deal. What do we teach her to do? Picking? Dipping? Shilling? Luring? Baiting?"

He and Dougan went off into a corner and were soon engaged in deep conversation.

Usha found a chair at an empty table and sat down. A ragged child brought her a plate of stew and a mug of ale. She ate hungrily. Thoughts of Palin and concern over his fate cast the only shadow over her contentment. The heart of youth is ever optimistic, particularly when that heart has felt love's first painfully sweet constrictions.

"The gods would not have brought us together if they had meant to then separate us so cruelly." This was Usha's conviction, which said a great deal for her faith, if not much for her knowledge of the harshness of reality.

Finished with her meal, Usha was relaxed and happy in her new situation. As crudely as these people talked, as strange and sinister as they appeared, Usha was no longer afraid of them.

Luring. Baiting.

These people were fishermen, of course.

BOOK 3

I

The warning. Three come together. Tanis must choose.

anis stood on the topmost battlements of the High Clerist's Tower, gazing over them at the empty road that led to the city of Palanthas. He walked that road in his mind, came to the city, imagined the unrest.

Rumor of the oncoming enemy had reached the city at daybreak. It was now noon. People would have closed up shops and stalls, taken to the streets, listening avidly to any and all rumors, the more outlandish, the better believed.

Of course, by this evening, the Lord of Palanthas would have his speech prepared. He would stand on his balcony, read from his notes, reassure the populace that the High Clerist's Tower stood between them and the enemy. Then, on this comforting note, he would go inside to dinner.

Tanis snorted. "I wish someone would come comfort me!"

And someone did come, but he was bringing neither comfort nor reassurance. Neither did he travel the road, but arrived in a far more unconventional manner.

Tanis walked east along the battlements, turned, was about to retrace his steps, when he nearly knocked over a black-robed wizard who stood blocking his path.

"What the—" Tanis gripped the top of the wall to steady himself. "Dalamar! Where did—?"

"Palanthas. I traveled the roads of magic and do not have time to listen to you spluttering. Are you in charge here?"

"Me? Good heavens, no! I'm only—"

"Then take me to someone who is," Dalamar said impatiently. "And tell these fools to sheathe their swords before I turn them into pools of molten metal."

Several knights, keeping watch on the battlements, had drawn their swords and now surrounded the dark elf.

"Put away your weapons," Tanis told them. "This is Lord Dalamar of the Tower of High Sorcery. He is quite capable of carrying out his threat, and we're going to need all the swords we can get. One of you, go find Sir Thomas and tell him that we request a meeting with him at once."

"Indeed you speak truly about needing swords, Half-Elven," Dalamar observed as they proceeded along the battlements, heading for the inner chambers. "Though I think it more likely that what you truly need is a miracle."

"Paladine has provided those for us in the past," Tanis said.

Dalamar glanced around the tower. "Yes, but I see no befuddled old wizard mumbling over his fireball spells and wondering where he's put his hat."

The dark elf came to a halt, turned to face Tanis. "Dark times are coming. You should not be here, my friend. You should leave, return to your home, to your wife. I can assist you if you like. Say the word and I will send you there at once."

Tanis eyed the dark elf. "Your news is as bad as that?"

"As bad as that, Half-Elven," Dalamar answered quietly.

Tanis scratched his beard. "I'll wait to hear it, then decide."

"Suit yourself." Dalamar shrugged, started walking again, moving in haste. His black robes swirled around his ankles. The few knights they passed regarded the wizard with baleful glances and drew hastily away.

Tanis entered the council chambers. An armed escort of knights bore down on them.

"I'm looking for Sir Thomas," Tanis called.

"And he is looking for you, my lord," answered the escort's commander. "I have been sent to tell you that a Knights' Council has been convened to deal with this crisis. Sir Thomas has heard that Lord Dalamar arrives with news."

"Of the most urgent nature," Dalamar said.

The knight gave a stiff, cold bow.

"My lord Dalamar, Sir Thomas extends his thanks for your coming. If you will impart this news to me—or to my lord Tanis Half-Elven, if you prefer—we will not detain you longer."

"You do not detain me," Dalamar returned. "There exist no means by which you could detain me. I came of my own free will and I will leave that way, *after* I have spoken to Thomas of Thalgaard."

"My lord." The knight hesitated, struggling between politeness and policy. "You place us in a most difficult situation. If I may speak bluntly?"

"Do so if that will hurry this along," Dalamar returned with mounting impatience.

"You must know, my lord, that you are the enemy, and as such—"

Dalamar shook his head. "You don't have very far to look to find your enemies, Sir Knight, but I am not among them."

"Perhaps." The knight was not convinced. "But I have my orders. This may be a trap laid by your sovereign queen in order to ensorcel our commanders."

Dalamar's face paled in anger. "If I wanted to 'ensorcel' your commanders, Sir Knight, I could do so from the comfort and safety of my home. At this very instant, I could—"

"But he wouldn't," Tanis intervened hastily. "Lord Dalamar comes in good faith. I swear it. I will answer for him with my life if need be."

"And I will also," came a calm, clear voice from another hallway.

Lady Crysania, led by the white tiger and escorted by a party of knights, walked into the council chambers. The tiger gazed intently at each man present, not with the quick, suspicious gaze of an animal, but with the intent, thoughtful, and intelligent gaze of a man. And it might have been Tanis's imagination, but he could have sworn that Dalamar and the tiger exchanged an oblique signal of recognition.

The commander and his men fell to their knees, bowed their heads.

The Revered Daughter of Paladine bid them rise, then turned her sightless eyes toward Dalamar. The dark elf had inclined his head in a respectful gesture, but he did not bow. At her softly spoken command, the tiger led her to Dalamar, though the beast interposed its massive body between the two of them. Crysania extended her hand.

Dalamar brushed the woman's hand with the tips of his fingers. "I thank you for your support, Revered Daughter," he said, though with a touch of sarcasm.

Crysania turned toward the knights. "Will you now be so good as to escort us, all three, into the presence of Sir Thomas of Thalgaard?"

Although the knights were obviously reluctant to escort Dalamar anywhere except to the dungeons, they had no choice but to acquiesce. The Knights of Solamnia served the god Paladine. Revered Daughter Crysania was the highest official in the church dedicated to the worship of their god.

"This way, my lords, Revered Daughter," the commander said, and ordered his men to fall into ranks behind them.

"How did you know I would be here, Revered Daughter?" Dalamar asked her in an undertone, seemingly not altogether pleased. "Are my movements being watched by the church?"

"Paladine watches all his children, my lord, as a shepherd watches all his sheep, not excluding the black ones," she added with a smile. "But, no, Sir Wizard, I did *not* know you were here. Strange rumors are circulating around Palanthas. No one could give me any information, so I came to find out for myself."

A slight emphasis on the words "no one" and the soft sigh that accompanied them caused Dalamar to regard her more closely. He took a step nearer. The tiger paced along with immense dignity, guiding its mistress's steps and keeping careful watch.

"I take it, then, Revered Daughter, that your god has spoken nothing to you of what is transpiring in the world?"

Crysania did not answer in words, but her troubled, pale face expressed her thoughts.

"I do not ask out of some vindictive sense of triumph, Revered Daughter," Dalamar pursued. "My own god, Nuitari, has been strangely silent of late, as have all the gods of magic. As for my queen." Dalamar shrugged, shook his head. "Nuitari's power wanes and, as a consequence, my own has been affected. The same is true of Lunitari and Solinari. All mages report it. It's almost as if the gods were preoccupied . . ."

Crysania turned toward him. "You are right, my lord. When I heard these rumors, I took them to the god in prayer. You see this amulet I wear around my neck?" She indicated a medallion made of silver, adorned with an image of a dragon done in beaten gold. "Whenever I have prayed to Paladine in the past, I feel his love surround me. This medallion"—she touched it reverently—"begins to glow with a soft light. My soul is quieted, my troubles and fears ease."

She was silent a moment, then she added softly, "Of late, the medallion has remained dark. I know Paladine hears my prayers; I feel that he wants to comfort me. But I fear that he has no comfort to offer. I thought perhaps this threat posed by Lord Ariakan is responsible."

"Perhaps," Dalamar said, but he obviously remained unconvinced. "We may find out more soon. Palin Majere has entered the Portal."

"Is this true?" Crysania was dismayed.

"I am afraid it is."

"How did he get in? You locked up the laboratory! You posted guards—"

"He was invited, my lady," Dalamar said dryly. "I think you can guess by whom."

Crysania went white, the color fleeing her cheeks. Her steps faltered. The tiger pressed comfortingly against her, offering support.

Tanis was quick to come to her aid, took hold of her arm. Feeling her tremble, he cast an angry glance at Dalamar.

"You let Palin go? You should have stopped him."

"I did not have much choice in the matter, Half-Elven," Dalamar returned, dark eyes flashing. "All of us here know firsthand of Raistlin's power."

"Raistlin Majere is dead," Crysania said firmly, her momentary weakness swiftly passing. Standing straight, she withdrew her arm from Tanis's. "He was granted peace for his sacrifice. If Palin Majere has been lured into the Abyss"—her voice softened in sorrow—"then it is by some other force."

Dalamar opened his mouth, caught Tanis's warning frown. The dark elf remained silent, though his lip curled derisively.

The three said no more during the remainder of their walk, each occupied with his or her own thoughts, none of them very pleasant, to judge by the shadowed expressions. The commander led them into a long hallway decorated with flags. Each flag bore the family crest of one of those currently listed on the rolls.

The flags hung unmoving in the hot, breathless air. Tanis, looking down the long row, found the crest of the Majere family, newly designed for the admittance of the two brothers into the knighthood.

The flag bore a rosebud—symbol of Majere, the god for whom the family had been named—submerged in a flagon of foaming ale. Tanis had always thought the crest looked more like a sign for an inn than a knightly standard, but Caramon had designed it and was immensely proud of it. Tanis loved his friend too well to breathe a word against it. As he watched, two young pages, mounted on ladders, were draping the flag with black cloth.

"My lords, Revered Daughter, please enter."

The commander flung open the doors to a large room, invited the three to speak before the Knights' Council.

The Knights' Council is convened only on certain occasions, these governed by the Measure. They include the determination of strategies for war, the assignment of orders, the selection of a warrior lord prior to battle, to hear charges of unknightly conduct, to honor those who have performed valiantly, and to settle questions concerning the Measure.

The council is made up of three knights, one from each of the orders: Rose, Sword, and Crown. These three sit at a large table carved with the symbols of the orders, placed opposite the entrance to the council chamber. Those knights whose duties permit may be present during a council meeting. Those who wish to speak before the council stand in a cleared area directly in front of the table.

After the Code of the Knights, "*Est Sularus oth Mithas,*" is recited by all knights present in the hall, the Knights' Hymn is sometimes sung, if the reason for the council's convening is a joyous one.

At this meeting, the three knights present recited the code and then took their seats. The hymn was not sung.

"I must say, this is a historic occasion," Sir Thomas commented, after introductions had been performed and chairs brought for the visitors. "And, if you'll forgive me for saying it, not one I particularly like. To put it bluntly, this meeting of you three here, at this time . . ." He shook his head. "It smacks of doom."

"Say rather that we have been brought here to avoid doom, my lord." Lady Crysania spoke gently.

"I pray to Paladine you are right, Revered Daughter," Sir Thomas replied. "I see you restless with impatience, Sir Wizard. What news do you bring us that is so urgent as to warrant a Black Robe's appearance before a Knights' Council—a thing that has never happened in all the history of the knighthood."

"My lord," said Dalamar briskly, determined to waste no more time, "I have it on good authority that the Knights of Takhisis will attack this fortification at dawn tomorrow morning."

Lady Crysania drew in a sharp breath. "Tomorrow?" The tiger at her side growled softly. She calmed him with a whispered word, a caressing touch on the head. "So soon? How can this be?"

Tanis sighed inwardly. So this is what Dalamar meant when he warned me not to remain here. If I do, I will be embroiled in the battle. He is right. I should leave, return home.

Sir Thomas of Thalgaard shifted his troubled gaze from Dalamar to Tanis to Lady Crysania and back to Dalamar. The other two members of the council, a Knight of the Sword and a Knight of the Crown, remained seated rigidly upright, their stern countenances betraying nothing of their thoughts. It was left to the highest-ranking knight to speak first.

Sir Thomas tugged on the long mustaches that were a hallmark of the knighthood.

"I trust you will not take it amiss, my lord Dalamar, if I question your reasons for bringing this news to us?"

"I see no need to explain to you my reasons for doing anything, my lord," Dalamar replied coolly. "Suffice it to say, I have come here to warn you to make what preparations you can to meet this assault. Tanis Half-Elven, though he cannot answer for my motives, can answer for my veracity."

"I believe I can answer for his motives," Lady Crysania added in a low voice.

"If you want to know *how* I know, I can easily satisfy you on that score," Dalamar continued, unmoved by the interruption. "I have recently been in the company of a Knight of Takhisis, a man named Steel Brightblade."

"Son of Sturm Brightblade," Tanis reminded them.

The faces of the three knights darkened; their frowns deepened. "The despoiler of his father's tomb," said one.

"Say, rather, the receiver of his father's blessing," Tanis corrected, adding irritably, "Damn it, I've explained the circumstances before this very council!"

The three knights exchanged sidelong glances, but said nothing. Tanis Half-Elven was a legendary figure in Solamnia. A renowned hero, he exerted a powerful force in this part of the world. Following the aforementioned incident with Steel Brightblade in the sacred tomb of the knights, Tanis had been requested to appear before the Knights' Council to explain why he had personally escorted a young man known to be loyal to the Dark Queen into the Tower of the High Clerist and had then proceeded to take him to the tomb, where the young man had committed the dire sacrilege of disturbing the rest of his hero father. Steel Brightblade had destroyed the body, stolen his father's magical sword, and injured several knights while battling his way out. Not only that, but Tanis Half-Elven and his friend Caramon Majere had actually aided and abetted the evil knight in his escape.

Tanis had given his own view of the incident. According to him, Steel had come to pay his respects to his father. He had been given the sword as a gift by his father, perhaps in an effort to turn the young man from the dark path on which he was bound to walk. As to Tanis and Caramon aiding him, they had both made pledges to the young man to guard him with their lives.

The Knights' Council had heard other testimony, notably from Revered Daughter Crysania, who had spoken up for both men, adding her firm belief that Paladine himself had guided their way into the tower, for, though he wore his own armor, adorned with the death lily, evidence indicated that Steel Brightblade had been mistaken by every Solamnic Knight he met for one of their own—until the end.

The knights could not very well rule against such eloquent and moving testimony. They had judged that Tanis Half-Elven had acted out of honor, though it was, perhaps, misguided. The incident had been closed, but—as Tanis now saw—not forgotten.

Nor, apparently, forgiven.

Sir Thomas sighed, pulled his mustaches again. He looked at the other two, who nodded silent agreement to his silent question.

"I thank you for your warning, Lord Dalamar," Thomas said. "I may tell you that your information corresponds to that which we've obtained from other sources. We did not know that the attack was expected so soon, but we have been expecting it. We are prepared."

"I did not see much in the way of preparation," Dalamar said wryly. He sat forward in his chair, indicated a map that was spread out on the table. "My lord, this is not a small force of knights you are facing. It is an army, a great army, numbering in the thousands. They have recruited barbarians from a distant land to fight for them. They have their own sorcerers, powerful wizards—as I have cause to know—who obey no laws of magic except their own."

"We are aware of this—" Sir Thomas began.

"What you may not be aware of, my lord, is that they passed through Neraka. Dark clerics entered the haunted ruins and summoned the shades of the dead to join the fight. They stopped in Dargaard Keep, and I have no doubt that you will find Lord Soth and his warriors among the attacking forces. Lord Ariakan is their leader. You trained him yourselves! You know, better than I do, his worth."

This was apparent, to judge by the grim expressions on the knights' faces.

Sir Thomas stirred restlessly in his chair. "All this you say is very true, Lord Dalamar. Our own scouts confirm it. Yet, I say this to you, the Tower of the High Clerist has never fallen while men of faith defended it."

"Perhaps that's because men of faith have never attacked it," Lady Crysania said suddenly and unexpectedly.

"The Knights of Takhisis have been raised together since boyhood," said Dalamar. "They are unswervingly loyal to their queen, their commanders, each other. They will sacrifice anything, including their lives, to advance the cause. They live by a code of honor as strict as your own. Indeed, Lord Ariakan patterned it after your own. It is my opinion, my lords, that you have never been in greater danger."

Dalamar gestured to the window. "You say you are prepared, yet what have you done? I look out and I see the main road, which should be clogged with knights on horseback and their attendants, lines of foot soldiers, wagons, and carts, bringing in weapons and supplies. Yet that road is empty!"

"Yes, it is empty," replied Sir Thomas. "Do you want to know the reason why?" He folded his hands, rested them on the map. His gaze encompassed all three of them. "Because the enemy holds it."

Tanis heaved a sigh, rubbed his bearded chin. "We sent out couriers, Dalamar. They traveled on dragonback to call the knights to arms. They have been gone three days. You see the response."

"Those knights with land and castles on the eastern borders sent back word that they were already under siege. And some did not answer at all," Sir Thomas said quietly. "In many cases, the couriers sent to fetch the knights did not themselves return."

"I see," Dalamar murmured, his brow furrowed in thought. "Forgive me. I was not aware."

"Ariakan's armies are moving with the speed of a brush fire. He is ferrying his troops and baggage and siege engines down the Vingaard River on a vast armada of barges. The river is ordinarily raging this time of year, but now, due to the drought, it is as smooth and placid as a glass of warm ale. Their barges have traveled swiftly, manned by the barbarians from the east.

"No obstacle can stop his army. He has in his force huge beasts known as mammoths, who are reputed to be able to knock down living trees with their heads, lift the trunks with their long noses, and toss them aside as if they were twigs. Evil dragons fly overhead, guarding the army, poisoning with dragonfear the hearts and minds of any who dare face them. I did not know about the undead of Neraka or Lord Soth, but I can't say that I'm surprised."

Sir Thomas straightened, his expression grave, but stern and dignified. His voice was steady, his gaze steadfast, unwavering.

"We are prepared, my lords, my lady. The fewer the numbers, the greater the glory, or so it is said." The knight smiled slightly. "And Paladine and Kiri-Jolith are with us."

"Their blessings on you," Revered Daughter Crysania said softly, so softly that she was almost inaudible. Thoughtful, musing, she stroked the head of the tiger.

Sir Thomas regarded her with concern. "Revered Daughter, the day is waning. You should return to Palanthas before darkness falls. I will order you an escort—"

Lady Crysania lifted her head. "Indeed, you will do no such foolish thing, Sir Thomas. You need every man you have. A golden dragon, who serves me in Paladine's name, brought us here. Firegold will carry us safely back." She stroked the tiger, who had risen to its feet. "My guide, Tandar, will see that no harm comes to me."

The tiger Tandar gazed at all of them, and Tanis had no doubt that Crysania was as safe with that fierce, savage, and loyal companion as she would be with a regiment of knights.

She rose to take her leave. The knights, Tanis, and Dalamar all stood in respect.

"Several clerics are already on their way to aid you. They are driving a wagon filled with supplies and will arrive here sometime tonight. They volunteered, my lord," she said, forestalling Sir Thomas's objections. "You will need them, I think."

"They will be most welcome," the knight replied. "Thank you, Revered Daughter."

"It is the least I can do," she said, sighing. "Farewell. The gods be with you. I will remember you with my prayers."

She turned away. Her steps guided by the tiger, she left the chamber. In leaving, she passed Tanis. He heard her add, in a soft murmur, "If anyone is listening. . . ."

"I, too, will take my leave," Dalamar said. "I would offer you the aid of magic, but I know it would not be accepted. Though I remind you that Lord Ariakan has made wizards a part of his army equal in rank and status to warriors."

Sir Thomas was properly apologetic. "I am aware of that, Sir Wizard, and I thank you for the offer. Our knights have never practiced the art of combining steel and sorcery. I fear that more harm than good might be done in such circumstances."

"You are probably right, my lord," Dalamar responded with a sardonic smile. "Well, I bid you all good fortune. You won't mind my saying that you will need it. Farewell."

"Thank you, Lord Dalamar," Sir Thomas said. "Your warning may well have saved the day."

Dalamar shrugged, as if the matter no longer interested him. He looked at Tanis. "Are you coming with me?"

Sir Thomas looked at Tanis. Everyone in the room was looking at Tanis.

Would he be leaving or staying?

Tanis scratched his beard, aware that he had to make his decision. The only way to leave safely now was to take Dalamar's path, travel the roads of magic.

Sir Thomas, drawing near Tanis, requested a word in private.

"I will wait for you, Half-Elven," Dalamar said, adding pointedly, "but not for long."

Tanis and Sir Thomas strode outside, onto a small balcony off the Knights' Council room. It was not yet sundown, but the shadows of the mountains brought a premature night to the tower. In a courtyard below stood an immense and magnificent golden dragon, Firegold, the dragon who served Revered Daughter Crysania. Other dragons, mostly silvers, circled the tower, keeping watch.

Sir Thomas leaned on the balustrade, gazed out into the gathering darkness.

"I will be blunt with you, Tanis," the knight said quietly. "I can use your help. Not just your sword-arm. I need you in command. The knights left to defend the tower are mostly young men, new to the knighthood. Their fathers and elder brothers—those whom I would normally put in command—are home defending their own manors and towns."

"Which is where I should be," Tanis said.

"I grant you that," Sir Thomas agreed readily. "And if you leave, I will be the first to bid you godspeed." The knight turned, looked at Tanis directly. "You know the situation as well as I do. We face overwhelming odds. The High Clerist's Tower must stand, or all of Solamnia will fall. Ariakan will control the north of Ansalon. He will establish this as his base of operations. From here he can attack the south at his leisure. It will be long months before we would be able to regroup and take the tower back—if then."

Tanis knew this, knew it perfectly well. He knew, too, that if the people of Ansalon had only listened to him and Laurana and Lady Crysania and, yes, even Dalamar, five years ago, this would have never happened. If the elves and dwarves and humans had only put aside their petty quarrels and concerns and come together to form the alliance they had proposed, then the tower would have defenders, more than it needed.

Tanis could see it in his mind: elven archers lining the battlements, doughty dwarven warriors manning the gates, all fighting shoulder-to-shoulder with their human comrades.

It was a fine picture, but one that would never be painted.

If I return home, he thought, it will be to an empty house.

Laurana would not be there. She and Tanis had said their farewells. Both had known at the time that this parting might be their last. He remembered.

*　*　*　*　*

Stopping by his house on his way from Solace to the High Clerist's Tower, Tanis had expected his usual warm welcome.

He didn't get it.

No one came running from the stables to tend to the needs of the griffin on which he'd flown. No servant greeted him at the door; those bustling past on errands gave him hurried curtseys and disappeared into other parts of the large mansion. His wife, Laurana, was nowhere to be found. A large traveling chest sat squarely in the center of the entryway; he had to squeeze his way past it. He could hear voices and footsteps, all of them in the upper levels. He climbed the stairs in search of an answer to all this upset and confusion.

He found Laurana in their bedroom. Clothes were spread out on the bed and over all other available surfaces, draped over chairs, flung over the hand-painted standing screens. Another traveling chest, this one smaller than one downstairs, was in the center of the room. Laurana and three maidservants were sorting, folding, packing. They never noticed Tanis standing in the doorway.

Tanis remained silent, taking this brief moment to watch his wife unobserved, to watch the sunlight shine through her golden hair, to admire the grace of her movements, to hear the music of her voice. He captured an image of her, to hold in his mind, as he kept her painted portrait in miniature near his heart.

She was elven, and the elves do not age as rapidly as do humans. Laurana, at first glimpse, would seem to any human onlooker to be in the early years of womanhood. If she had remained in her elven homeland, she might have maintained that appearance of eternal youthfulness. But she had not. She had chosen to marry a half-breed; she had cut herself off from her family and friends, had taken up her residence in human lands. And she had spent these intervening years working ceaselessly and tirelessly for an end to the conflict that divided the two races.

The work, the burden, the flashes of hope, followed by the destruction of dreams, had dimmed the bright elven serenity and purity. No lines or wrinkles marred her skin, but sorrow cast its shadow over her eyes. No gray was tangled with the gold of her hair, but the luster was dimmed. Any elf, looking at Laurana, would say that she had prematurely aged.

Tanis, looking at her, loved her more now than he had ever loved her in his life. And he knew, at this moment, that this might very well be the last time they ever met in this life.

"Ahem!" He cleared his throat loudly.

The maidservants started, gasped. One dropped the dress she had been folding.

Laurana, looking up from bending over the trunk, straightened and smiled to see him.

"What's all this?" Tanis demanded.

"Finish packing," Laurana instructed the servants, "and put the rest of these clothes in storage." She wended her way among the cloaks and hats, finally reached her husband.

She kissed him affectionately. He held her in his embrace. They took a moment to let their hearts speak to each other in companionable silence. Then Laurana led Tanis to their study, shut the door. She turned to him, her eyes alight.

"Guess what?" she said and answered before he could begin to guess, "I've had a message from Gilthas! He has invited me to come to Qualinesti!"

"What?" Tanis was astonished.

Laurana had been working unceasingly to force the Qualinesti elves to admit her into their land, to be near their son. Time and again, her request had been refused. She was told that if she or her husband ventured anywhere near the border of the elven homeland, they would be in dire peril of their lives.

"Why the sudden change?" Tanis was grim.

Laurana did not answer. She unrolled the scroll, which had been sealed with the mark of the sun, the mark of the Speaker of the Sun, now Gil's title.

Tanis studied the broken seal, unrolled the scroll, read it through.

"Gil's handwriting," he said, "but not our son's words. Someone dictated, and he wrote down what they told him to write."

"True enough," Laurana said, unperturbed. "But it is an invitation nonetheless."

"An invitation to disaster," Tanis said bluntly. "They held Alhana Starbreeze prisoner. They threatened her life, and it is my belief they would have killed her if Gil had refused to go along with the senators' schemes. This is some sort of trap."

"Well, of course, it is, silly," she said to him, amusement glinting her eyes. She gave him a swift kiss on his cheek, ruffled her hand through his beard, a beard in which he had lost count of the strands of gray. "But as dear Flint used to say, 'A trap is only a trap if you step in it before you see it.' I can see this one a mile off. Why"—she laughed, teased him— "even you spotted it without benefit of your spectacles."

"I only wear those for reading," Tanis said, pretending to be irritated. His aging was the subject of a long-standing joke between them. He held out his arms to her; she nestled in his embrace. "I don't suppose I received a similar invitation?"

"No, dear one," she said gently. "I'm sorry." She pulled back from him, looked into his eyes. "I will try, when I get there . . ."

He shook his head. "You won't succeed. But I am glad that you, at least, will be there. Porthios and Alhana—"

"Alhana! The baby! I never asked! How—"

"Fine. Fine. Mother and son. And I must say this. If you had seen Porthios holding that baby, you wouldn't have recognized him."

"I would have," Laurana said. "He is my elder brother, after all. He was always kind and loving to me. Yes, he was," she added, seeing Tanis's look of doubt. "Even when he was being his most pigheaded and prejudiced, I knew he was only trying to spare me pain and sorrow."

"He didn't succeed," Tanis said remorsefully. "You married me anyway, and look where I led you."

"You led me home, dearest husband," Laurana said quietly. "You led me home."

They sat and talked a long, long while, spoke of the past, of friends distant, of friends gone from this world. They talked of Gil, shared their memories, their love, their hopes, their fears. They spoke of the world, of its troubles, old and new. They sat and talked and held each other by the hand, knowing, without saying, that this moment was precious, that it must soon end.

They said their good-byes. He was to fly north that night, to reach the High Clerist's Tower by the next day. She was to start her journey to Qualinesti that morning.

She accompanied him to the door at midnight. The servants had gone to bed. The house was silent; soon it would be empty. Laurana and Tanis had agreed to dismiss the servants. They knew they would both be gone a long, long time. Already the house had an empty feel to it. Their footfalls echoed in the stillness.

Maybe they would always echo like that when they were both gone. Maybe their spirits would walk this house, blessed spirits of love and laughter.

They held each other tightly, whispered broken words of love and farewell, and they parted.

Tanis, looking back, saw Laurana standing in the open doorway in the moonlight. No tears. She smiled at him and waved.

He smiled, waved back.

You led me home, the words echoed. *You led me home.*

* * * * *

Memory receded. Tanis considered his decision. He could return to their dwelling, but he would be alone in the empty—so very empty—echoing house. He saw himself pacing the floor, wondering what was happening at the tower, wondering if Laurana was safe, wondering if Gil was well, wondering if Palanthas was under attack, fuming with impatience at not knowing anything, running to the door every time hoofbeats were heard, blaming himself . . .

Ask the gods for guidance.

In the courtyard below, Revered Daughter Crysania was seated on Firegold's back. The tiger with the human eyes crouched protectively at her side. Tanis, gazing down at her, heard her words.

If any are listening . . .

The tiger lifted its head, looked up, directly at Tanis. And then, as if her guide had imparted some information to her, Crysania turned the unseeing eyes, which seemed to see so much, on the half-elf. She raised her hand in blessing . . . or was it farewell?

The pain of choosing eased. Tanis knew then that he'd already made his decision. He'd made it long ago, the very moment in the Inn of the

Last Home when the blue crystal staff, Goldmoon, and Riverwind had entered his life. Tanis recalled that moment and his memorable words on that occasion, words that had changed his life forever.

"I beg your pardon! Did you say something?" Sir Thomas eyed the half-elf in perplexity and some worry.

He's probably thinking the strain is too much for the old man. Tanis grinned, shook his head.

"Never mind, my lord. Just reliving old memories."

His gaze shifted from Lady Crysania to a place on the battlements, a place marked by a splotch of crimson, a place held in reverence by the knights, who never walked over it, but avoided treading on the blood-stained stones, circled them in respectful silence. Tanis could almost see Sturm standing there, and the half-elf knew he'd chosen rightly.

Tanis repeated the words now, as he had said them then. No wonder Sir Thomas looked puzzled. The words were not inspiring, not words that would echo through the vaults of history. Yet, they said something about that strange, disparate, unlikely group of friends, who had gone forth to change the world.

"We'll go out through the kitchen."

Turning, laughing, Tanis walked back inside the tower.

2

The Return. The trial.
Sentence is passed.

I t was nighttime in the Plains of Solamnia, though few of those inside the encampment of the Knights of Takhisis could have told it. The armies of darkness had banished the darkness. Campfires were prohibited; Lord Ariakan had no desire to start a fire, the grass of the plains was tinder-dry from the drought. But the Knights of the Thorn, the gray-robed wizards, had provided enormous globes made of crystal, which gleamed with an incandescent gray light. Suspended from tree branches, the globes turned night to eerie day.

Steel saw the light while still some distance away. Lord Ariakan scorned to hide his numbers in shadows. Let the enemy see the full might of his army and lose heart. Circling the encampment on the back of his blue dragon, Steel himself was impressed. Flare landed on a plowed field, its crops withered by the heat. Dragon handlers ran to assist the knight from his saddle, point him in the direction of the main camp, and take care of the dragon's needs.

Flare's only desire was to rejoin her comrades. She had heard them calling her before she could see them and, having ascertained that Steel had no need of her until morning, she flew to where the blues were gathered.

The blue dragons were the favored mounts of the Knights of Takhisis. Dragons are extremely independent and, generally, have a low opinion of humanity. Most dragons find it difficult to obey orders given them by those whom they consider inferior beings, and for certain species of dragon this proves impossible.

Black dragons are devious and selfish and cannot be trusted, not even by those whom they purportedly serve. Black dragons see no need to "sacrifice" themselves for any cause other than their own, and, though they can be enticed to fight, they might well leave the battle in the midpoint to pursue their own aims.

During the War of the Lance, red dragons had been the favored mounts of many commanders, including the infamous Dragon Highlord Verminaard. Enormous, fire-breathing, and vicious, the red dragons had no patience for the subtleties of Ariakan's type of warfare. The red's idea of attacking a city was to burn it, loot it, destroy it, kill everything inside it. The notion that the intact city, its inhabitants alive and well, is of more practical use to the Dark Queen than a pile of rubble and rotting corpses, was anathema to the reds. Let the smoke of burning, the stench of death, proclaim Her Majesty's glory, not forgetting the glitter of gold stashed in the red dragons' lairs.

Green dragons proved useless in battle during the last Dragon War. Greens will fight when cornered, but not until then. They prefer to use their powerful magical spells to ensnare an opponent. Thus greens have little respect for military commanders, though they would obey the Knights of the Thorn—the gray-robed wizards—if the greens thought they might gain something for themselves.

White dragons, accustomed to living in cold climes, had all but disappeared in the summer's unusual and devastating heat, which had turned ice floes to rivers, melted their ice caverns.

Lord Ariakan chose blue dragons on which to mount his knights, and he had been well rewarded. The blue dragons actually liked mortals and were incredibly loyal to their riders and to each other. They obeyed orders, fought well as a cohesive unit, and—most important—could clearly understand the Vision and their part in it.

Steel left Flare to the companionship of her fellows, who greeted her with glad cries in their own language. A few blue dragons circled in the air, keeping watch, but most were on the ground, resting for the great battle. Ariakan had no fear of assault. His back was secure. His huge army had swept across northern Ansalon like a raging fire, consuming everything in its path.

Steel entered the encampment on foot, searching for the standard that would mark the location of his talon. This soon proved almost impossible, given the size of the force assembled on the plain. Seeing that he might search for his unit all night and never find it, he stopped to ask an officer, who directed him to the proper location.

Trevalin was in a meeting with his officers. On Steel's arrival, Trevalin broke off, motioned the knight to join them.

"Knight Warrior Brightblade, reporting for duty, sir," said Steel, saluting.

"Brightblade." Trevalin smiled. "I am glad to see you. Truly glad. Some seemed to think you might not return."

Steel frowned. This was an affront to his honor. He had the right to confront his vilifier. "Who might that be, Subcommander?"

"The Nightlord who was responsible for sending you on that fool mission in the first place." Trevalin grimaced, as if he had a bad taste in his mouth. "She said nothing outright, mind you. She knows better than to publicly insult the honor of one my knights. But she's been skulking about all day, making insinuating remarks. Relax, man. Forget about it. You have more urgent worries."

Trevalin's smile had hardened into a straight, grim line. Steel guessed what was about to come next.

"Lord Ariakan was here, in person, looking for you. He left orders. You are to report to him immediately." Trevalin's expression softened as he placed a supportive hand on Steel's arm. "I think he means to bring you to trial tonight, Brightblade. He's done so with others. 'Discipline must be swift to be maintained,' he says." Trevalin gestured. "That's his tent over there, in the center. I'm to take you there myself. We'd best go now. Lord Ariakan said to report at once."

Steel's jaw set. He was to be tried tonight, most certainly convicted. His execution would follow. Tears burned beneath his eyelids, not tears of fear, but of bitter disappointment. Tomorrow, the knights would attack the High Clerist's Tower in what was bound to be the decisive battle of this campaign, and he would miss it.

Slowly, half-blinded, all things blurring in his vision, he drew his father's sword from its sheath, held it out to Trevalin. "I surrender myself to you, Subcommander."

The sword of the Brightblades was reputed to have belonged to one of the ancient heroes of the knighthood, Bertel Brightblade. It had been passed down through the centuries from father to son, and would, according to legend, break only if the man wielding it broke first. The sword had been lain to rest with the dead, only to pass, once more, into the hands of another Brightblade when he came of age. Its antique steel blade, which Steel kept lovingly polished, gleamed, though not with the cold gray light of Takhisis's wizards. The sword shone with its own bright silver light.

Trevalin eyed the hilt, with its decoration of the kingfisher and the rose—symbols of the Knights of Solamnia—and the subcommander shook his head.

"I'll not touch it. I'm going to need my hands tomorrow. I don't want them burned off in Paladine's wrath. It amazes me that you can handle such an artifact with impunity. It amazes the Nightlord, too. That was one of the remarks she mentioned against you."

"The sword was my father's," Steel said, wrapping the belt around the sheath with prideful care. "Lord Ariakan gave me permission to carry it."

"I know, and so does the Nightlord. I wonder what you did, Brightblade, to cause her to hate you so? Ah, well. Who can tell with wizards? Wait here while I inform the others where we're going."

The walk was not a long one. Neither was the trial.

Ariakan had ordered a watch kept for them, apparently, for the moment they arrived, a knight on the lord's staff recognized them, drew them forth from the large but orderly crowd of officers, couriers, and aides, all waiting to gain Lord Ariakan's attention.

The knight led them into the large tent, over which flew Ariakan's flag: black, adorned with a death lily, entwined around a sword. The lord himself sat at a small blackwood table, which had been a gift to him from his men on the anniversary of the founding of the knighthood. The table traveled with Ariakan, was always carried among the baggage. This night, most of the shining black wood was covered with rolls of maps, which had been tied neatly and shoved aside. In the center of the tent, in front of Ariakan, was an enormous box filled with sand and rocks, arranged to represent the battleground.

The Battle Box was Ariakan's concept, one of which he was extremely proud. The sand and rocks could be smoothed over, reshaped to form any type of terrain. Large rocks stood in for the Vingaard mountains. Palanthas—its buildings made of gold, surrounded by a wall made of pebbles—was located in the western corner of the box next to a patch of crushed lapis that represented the Bay of Branchala. In the pass between the mountains was a miniature High Clerist's Tower, carved of white jade. Small knights cast of silver stood near the High Clerist's Tower, along with silver and a few gold dragons.

The Knights of Takhisis, done in shining obsidian, had the tower surrounded. Dragons of blue sapphire perched on the rocks, their heads all pointed in one direction: the tower. The disposition of battle had been thus determined. Each talon now had its orders. Steel saw his own talon's flag, carried by a tiny knight astride a tiny blue dragon.

"Knight Warrior Brightblade," came a stern, deep voice. "Advance."

The voice was Ariakan's. Subcommander Trevalin and Steel walked forward, both men conscious of the stares of those crowded around the outside of the tent.

Ariakan sat alone at his table, writing in a large, leather-bound book, a history of his battles, on which he worked whenever he had a moment to spare. Steel was close enough to see neat marks on the page, marks that approximated the disposition of the troops represented in the Battle Box.

"Subcommander Trevalin, reporting with the prisoner as ordered, my lord."

Ariakan added a final flourish, paused a moment to review his work, then—beckoning to an aide—he shoved the open book to one side. The aide sprinkled sand on the page to dry the ink, and removed the volume.

The Lord of the Night, commander and founder of the Knights of Takhisis, turned his attention to Steel.

Ariakan was barely fifty, in the prime of his manhood. A tall man, strong, well conditioned, he was still an able warrior, held his own in joust and tourney. He had been a handsome youth. Now, in his middle years, with his sharp, beaked nose and bright, far-seeing black eyes, he reminded one of the sea hawk. It was an appropriate image, since his mother was purported to be Zeboim, goddess of the sea, daughter to Takhisis.

His hair, though graying at the temples, was thick and black. He wore it long, swept back into a clubbed tail, held at the base of his neck with a braided silver-and-black leather thong. He was clean-shaven, his skin tanned and weathered. He was intelligent, could be charming when he wanted to be, and was well respected by those who served him. He was reputed to be fair and just, as dark and cold as the water in the depths of the ocean. He was devoted, body, mind, and soul, to Queen Takhisis, and he expected no lesser devotion from those who were loyal to him.

He gazed now at Steel, whom he had first taken into the knighthood when the boy was twelve, and—though there was sadness in the eyes—there was no mercy, no compassion. Steel would have been surprised, and probably disappointed in his commander, to have discovered otherwise.

"The accused, Knight Warrior Brightblade, stands before us. Where is his accuser?"

The gray-robed sorceress, who had concurred in sending Steel on the ill-fated mission, stepped out of the crowd.

"I am the accuser, my lord," the Nightlord said. She did not look at Steel.

He, in his turn, kept his gaze proudly on Ariakan.

"Subcommander Trevalin," the lord continued, "I thank you for your services. You have delivered the prisoner as ordered. You may now return to your talon."

Trevalin saluted, but did not immediately leave. "My lord, before I go, I request permission to say a word on the prisoner's behalf. The Vision prompts me."

Ariakan raised his eyebrows, nodded. The Vision took precedence over all else, was not invoked lightly. "Proceed, Subcommander."

"Thank you, my lord. May my words go on record. Steel Brightblade is one of the finest soldiers it has been my privilege to command. His bravery and skill are above reproach. His loyalty to the Vision is unswerving. These attributes have been proven time and again in battle and should *not* now be questioned." As he said this, Trevalin cast a baleful glance at the Nightlord. "The loss of Knight Warrior Brightblade would be a grievous loss to us all, my lord. It would be a loss to the Vision."

"Thank you, Subcommander Trevalin," Ariakan said, his voice cool and dispassionate. "We will take what you have said into account. You are dismissed."

Trevalin saluted, bowed, and, before he left, whispered a few words of encouragement to Steel.

The knight, holding fast to his father's sword in both his hands, nodded his thanks, but said nothing. Trevalin left the tent, shaking his head.

Ariakan motioned. "Bring forth your sword, Knight Warrior."

Steel did so, advancing to the table.

"Take the blade from its sheath," Ariakan continued, "and place it before me."

Steel obeyed. Removing the sword from its battered and well-worn sheath, he placed the blade—turned lengthwise—in front of his lord. The sword no longer gleamed, but appeared gray and lusterless, as if overshadowed by Ariakan's dark presence.

Steel walked five paces backward, stood erect, motionless, his hands at his sides, his eyes straight ahead.

Ariakan turned to the Gray Robe. "State your charges against this knight, Nightlord."

In strident tones, Lillith related how Steel had volunteered to take the bodies of the two dead Knights of Solamnia back to their father—a debt of honor, she conceded. Ariakan, glancing at Steel, indicated his approval with a slight inclination of the head. The lord was familiar with Steel's history, knew that the knight owed his liberty and very possibly his life to Caramon Majere. That debt was now expunged.

The Nightlord went on to say how Steel had further taken charge of the young mage, Palin Majere, how he had accepted the mage's parole, how Steel had offered to take upon himself the prisoner's death sentence should the prisoner escape.

"The Knight Warrior is back in our midst, my lord," the Nightlord concluded her summation. "And his prisoner is not. Brightblade's mission has failed. He has permitted his prisoner to escape. Indeed, my lord," she added, gliding forward to his desk, bending over it, moving close to him as if she were about to uncover some dread conspiracy. She lowered her voice, which was throaty, hissing. "Considering Brightblade's lineage, it is my belief that he assisted his prisoner to escape."

"Make yourself clear, Nightlord," Ariakan said, with a hint of impatience. Although he recognized and appreciated the value of magic-users, like most men of the sword he tended to grow weary of their penchant for obfuscation. "I dislike vague innuendoes. If you have a complaint against this knight, state it in words we simple soldiers can understand."

"I thought I had, my lord," the Nightlord said. Drawing back, standing straight, she regarded Steel with enmity. "This knight wears an elf bauble at his throat. He carries the sword of our enemies. I say to you, my lord, that this knight is *not* completely loyal to our glorious queen or to the Vision. He is a traitor to our cause, as witnessed by the fact that his prisoner escaped. I submit, my lord, that Brightblade should be made to pay the penalty he himself agreed to accept. Steel Brightblade should be put to death."

Ariakan shifted his gaze back to Steel. "I have known this man since he was a boy. Never has he given me cause to question his loyalty. As for the sword and the jewel, these were given to him by his father, a man who, though our enemy, is honored among us for his courage and bravery. I knew of these gifts at the time," Ariakan continued, slightly frowning, "and approved them, as did the High Priestess of Takhisis. Do you question *our* loyalty, Nightlord?"

Lillith was shocked that Ariakan could imagine such a thing, devastated that she should be so misunderstood. "Certainly not, my lord. Your decision was undoubtedly a wise one—*at the time it was made.*" She lingered over the phrase, gave it emphasis. "But I remind my lord that times change, as do the hearts of men. There remains the question of the prisoner. Where"—she spread her hands—"is Palin Majere? If he may be brought forward, either alive or dead, then I will withdraw all my accusations and beg this knight's forgiveness."

She smiled, folded her arms across her chest, and gazed at Steel in venomous triumph.

"What is your response, Knight Warrior?" Ariakan asked Steel. "What have you to say in your own defense?"

"Nothing, my lord," Steel answered.

A low murmur rose from the knights gathered to witness this trial—and there were many more now than when it had started, word having spread rapidly through the camp.

"Nothing, Knight Warrior?" Ariakan appeared astonished and troubled. He cast a sidelong glance at the Nightlord and very slightly shook his head. The gesture told Steel plainer than words that Ariakan was on Steel's side. "Let us hear your story."

Steel could have told them his story, could have won admiration by relating how he had made his way safely through the infamous Shoikan Grove—a heroic feat few people on Krynn would dare attempt, much less live to tell about. He could have further excused himself by saying that Palin Majere had undoubtedly received help in his escape from his uncle Raistlin Majere, of infamous memory. Once the facts were known,

Steel had no doubt that Ariakan would judge in his favor.

But Steel said simply, "I offer no excuses, my lord. I accepted this mission, and I failed in it. I gave my word of honor. I lost the prisoner I was bound to keep safe. I accept your judgment, my lord."

"My judgment will be death," said Ariakan, his frown deepening.

"I am aware of that, my lord," Steel answered calmly.

"Very well, then. You leave me no choice, Knight Warrior."

Ariakan rested his hand upon the sword's hilt. An expression of pain contorted his face—the sword was an artifact dedicated to Paladine and thus did Paladine punish those who followed the paths of darkness. Ariakan did not release the sword. Slowly, gritting his teeth, he turned the blade's point toward Steel. Only then did Ariakan let go.

"Steel Brightblade, you are hereby sentenced to die by this very sword which you have disgraced and dishonored. The sentence of death will be carried out . . ."

It will be carried out now, thought Steel, who had seen similar trials before. Discipline must be swift, to be maintained. He tried to prepare himself to meet his queen. What would he say to her, who could see into his heart? Who knew the truth?

His body stood firm, his soul trembled, and he did not, at first, hear Ariakan's words. The low murmur of approval from the assembled knights, mingled with a few scattered cheers, brought Steel back to the world of the living.

He stammered, not believing. "What . . . what did you say, my lord?"

"The sentence will be carried out in one month's time," Lord Ariakan repeated.

"My lord!" The Nightlord was swift to protest. "Is this wise? This man has admitted to his treachery! What harm might he do among us?"

"This knight has admitted to losing his prisoner," Ariakan returned. "He has submitted willingly to just punishment. I remind you, Nightlord, that his commander, invoking the Vision, asked that this knight be spared to fight in the upcoming battle. I, too, have consulted the Vision, and thus my judgment stands."

Ariakan's voice was cold and soft, but all present could sense his anger. The Nightlord bowed her head, withdrew, but not before she had cast Steel Brightblade a look that, were looks capable of killing, would have carried out his execution then and there.

Dazed, still not quite believing he was to live, Steel stood unmoving. Ariakan was forced to motion twice before the knight walked forward to retrieve his weapon.

Lord Ariakan gestured to the sword, careful not to touch it. The palm of his right hand was blistered and inflamed, as if he had grasped red-hot metal. "Take back your weapon, Knight Warrior. You have the chance to restore your honor in this battle, so that your soul may face our queen proudly, not crawl before her."

"I thank you, my lord," Steel said, his voice thick with emotion. He lifted the sword reverently, slid it back into its sheath.

"I must order you to remove your spurs, however," Ariakan said. "You are stripped of rank and title. I am placing you in command of a company of foot soldiers. You will have the honor of leading the charge upon the front gate."

Steel lifted his head, smiled. Leading the charge, fighting on foot, the first to enter the tower, the first to face the brunt of the enemy's defense, he would be among the first to die. Ariakan was doing him a great favor.

"I understand, my lord. Thank you. I will not let you down."

"Return to your talon for the time being, Brightblade. You will be reassigned in the morning. You are dismissed, unless you have anything further to say to me."

Ariakan was, once again, giving Steel a chance.

In that moment, Steel longed to unburden himself. But he knew if he did so, the pride and affection in his liege lord's manner would freeze, change to anger and bitter disappointment.

"No, my lord. I have nothing more to say except to once more offer my thanks."

Ariakan shrugged. Rising to his feet, he walked over to the Battle Box. His officers surged around him, bending over it, moving units here and there, once more discussing strategy and tactics. A dark cleric came bustling up to cast a spell of healing on the lord's injured hand.

Steel was forgotten. He slipped out the back of the tent to avoid the crowd. Leaving the light and the noise behind, he made his way beyond the camp's outer perimeter to someplace where he could be alone.

He would die on the morrow, die with honor, spare his lord, his com rades from ever knowing the tumult in his soul, from ever knowing the truth—that he had hesitated on the laboratory threshold, hesitated because he'd been afraid.

3

Ariakan's battle plan.
Steel's own battle.

I t was hours before dawn, but the army of Lord Ariakan was already on the move, winding its way from the plains into the Virkhus Hills, heading for Westgate Pass and their target, the Tower of the High Clerist.

The road was clear; the Knights of Solamnia could not afford to waste their forces in defending it. Ariakan's armies moved rapidly, their way lighted by fire of torch and fire of magic. Steel, walking in the vanguard, turned to look and marvel. The line of men, equipment, and machines stretched from the hills back down to the plains. Massed on the road, moving with well-trained precision, the army appeared as a flaming snake in the darkness—a gigantic snake that would soon wind around and crush the life out of its victim. The army's numbers were incalculable. In the history of the world, no mightier force had ever been assembled on Ansalon.

The defenders of the High Clerist's Tower would be able to see the army clearly now. They would be watching that dread serpent make its inexorable approach. Steel could imagine their awe, their dismay. Any hope the Knights of Solamnia might have entertained of holding their tower must surely be gone by now.

As he buckled on his sword, Steel recalled stories he had heard of his father's brave stance, alone on the battlements of the very tower his son was about to attack. Sturm Brightblade had foreseen his death as well. He had also seen beyond, seen the bright victory that awaited him.

Steel felt closer to his father now than his warrior mother. Sturm understood the decision his son had made, the decision to choose death over dishonor. His mother, Kitiara, did not.

Throughout the night, Steel had felt the heat of their battle, a war he had known all his life. He could hear his father's voice speaking of honor, self-sacrifice, his mother's voice urging him to lie, connive, or charm his way out of trouble. The fight had been a long one and exhausting; it had continued even in his sleep, apparently, for he dreamed of silver armor and blue, the clash of weapons.

Dreams ended with the trumpet call to arms. Steel woke feeling well rested, exhilarated, empty of fear. He and his men—a force of barbarian swordsmen and archers, all of whom were as excited as their commander—marched rapidly, so rapidly that they had to occasionally slow their pace, to avoid tripping on the heels of the talon in front of them.

Steel would die this day, he knew it for a certainty. But he would die gloriously, and this night his soul would stand before his queen, his loyalty proven beyond question, the tumult within him ended forever.

* * * * *

Lord Ariakan assembled his army on the Wings of Habbakuk, an apronlike stretch of flatland located just below the High Clerist's Tower. The strongest bastion of defense on Ansalon, the fortress held no mysteries for Ariakan. He knew every hallway, every secret entrance, every cellar, knew its weaknesses, knew its strengths. He had been awaiting this moment since the day he'd left, long years ago.

Ariakan could recall sitting on his horse on this very hillock, looking up at the tower and planning how he would take it. The memory gave him an eerie sense of having done this all before, though that time the men standing around him had been Knights of Solamnia, some of whom might well be waiting to meet their old comrade in battle this day.

His servants set up his command tent in the dark. His officers assembled as the first streaks of orangish pink stained the skies. Five officers were present, the three leading strike army commanders, the commander of the draconian force, and the commander of a force that had come to be known among the troops as the Minions of Dark—an army composed of goblins, hobgoblins, ogres, and human mercenaries, many of whom had been skulking about the Khalkist Mountains since the end of the War of the Lance, awaiting their chance for revenge. Also among these was a large force of minotaur, under the leadership of their own kind, since the minotaur scorn to take orders from mere humans.

Ariakan went over his battle plan again. The first, second, and third strike armies were to attack, breach, and penetrate the tower's curtain wall by way of the main entrances. Each would be given siege engines to accomplish the task. The first army to breach the defenses was to clear the curtain wall to allow the other forces to enter.

The Minions of Dark were to attack the main entrance to the Knights' Spur. If successful, they were to work their way into the main tower and assist the strike armies in the destruction of the enemy.

The fifth army, the draconian force, was joining with the Knights of Takhisis, who would attack from the air. The draconians, mounted on the backs of blue dragons, would drop from the skies onto the battlements and clear the way for the strike armies. The knights would remain on dragonback, fighting the silver dragons, who would certainly rush to the aid of the Solamnic Knights.

After the meeting, Ariakan dismissed his officers and ordered his servants to bring him breakfast.

* * * * *

The waiting was hard. Steel paced restlessly, unable to sit still. The excitement coursing through his veins needed an outlet. He walked over to watch the engineers assemble the siege engine that would assault the main gate. Steel would have joined in the work, just for something to do, but he guessed he would be more of a hindrance than a help.

The huge battering ram was made of the trunk of a once-mighty oak. Its head, fortified with iron, was fashioned in the shape of a snapping turtle (to honor Ariakan's sea-goddess mother), and was mounted on a wheeled platform that would be rolled over the road, right up to the main gate. The ram hung suspended from the top of the siege engine in a cradle of leather, connected to a complex series of pulleys. Men tugging on strong ropes would pull the ram back. When the ropes were released, the ram would fly forward, striking the gates with enormous impact. An iron roof over the ram offered protection from flaming arrows, boulders, and other weapons the defenders would use in an effort to destroy it before it could do significant damage.

Knights of the Thorn endowed the infernal engine with various kinds of magic. Knights of the Skull, led by the High Priestess of Takhisis, advanced and gave their dark blessing to the siege engine, calling on the goddess to assist their cause. The tower's huge ironwood gates, banded by steel, were further strengthened by magic, and, it was feared, would not fall without the Dark Queen's personal intervention.

But was Takhisis here? Had she come to witness her army's greatest triumph? It seemed to Steel that the high priestess faltered in her prayer, as if uncertain whether or not anyone was listening. The Knights of the Skull, flanking the priestess to her right and left, appeared uneasy and stole sidelong glances at each other. The engineer, who had been forced to cease work during the prayers, was impatient with the whole business.

"Lot of nonsense, if you ask me," he grumbled to Steel when the prayers had ended. "Not but what I'm a man of faith," he added hastily, glancing around to make certain the clerics hadn't heard him. "But I've spent six months of my life, day and night, on the design for that engine and another six months building it. A bit of stinking wizard-dust and a few mumbled prayers aren't going to win this battle. Our Dark Lady will have a lot more important work to do today than hang about, knocking on the Solamnics' front door." He gazed at his machine with moist-eyed pride. "My engine will do that little job for her."

Steel politely agreed, and the two moved on to discuss the coordination of their two forces. This done, Steel left to return to his barbarian troops.

He found the brutes playing at some game popular among their kind. One of them, one of the few who spoke the Common tongue, tried to explain the game to Steel. He listened patiently, attempted to look interested. He soon found himself lost in the complexity of the rules of the game, which was played with sticks, rocks, pine cones and involved the seemingly careless tossing about of large and deadly-looking bone-handled knives.

The brute explained that the occasional bloodletting excited the men, prepared them for battle. Steel, who had been wondering how the barbarians had acquired all those strange-looking scars on their legs and feet, soon left the brutes to their dangerous pleasures and returned to his pacing.

His gaze went to the battlements of the High Clerist's Tower, where he could see small figures milling about, peering over the crenellation. It was long past dawn, long past the hour when armies usually attacked. If the waiting was hard on Steel, he could guess that it must be far harder on those inside the tower. They would be wondering why the delay, wondering what Ariakan was plotting, second-guessing their own strategies. And all the while, fear would gnaw at their hearts, their courage diminish by the hour.

The sun rose higher in the sky; the shadows cast by the tower grew shorter. Steel sweated beneath his heavy armor and looked with envy on the brutes, who went into battle stark naked, their bodies covered with some sort of foul-smelling blue paint, which, they claimed, had magical properties and was all they needed to protect them against any weapon.

Steel braved the heat to walk over to where the knights, his own talon, were preparing their dragons for battle. Subcommander Trevalin spotted him, waved, but was too busy adjusting his lance—a copy of the famed dragonlances—to talk. Steel saw Flare, who had a new rider. Steel didn't envy the knight. Flare had been furious when she had found out about Steel's demotion, had even spoken of refusing to fly into battle. Steel had talked her out of deserting, but it was obvious she was still sulking. She was loyal to the Vision and would fight valiantly, but she would also manage to make life as difficult as possible for her new rider.

Smothering the feelings of regret and envy, Steel returned to his own command, sorry that he had left. He was feeling the heat, his enthusiasm was starting to wane, when a swirl of movement in the army's center caught his eye. Lord Ariakan had emerged from his tent. A hush fell on those around him.

Accompanied by his bodyguards, standard bearer, wizards, and dark clerics, Ariakan mounted his horse—a coal-black charger known as Nightflight, and rode forward, taking up a position just behind the rear squadron of the second strike army. He ordered the battle standard raised.

The standards of all the other armies were hoisted; the flags hung limp in the still air. Ariakan lifted a baton made of black obsidian, decorated with silver death lilies, topped by a grinning skull. Taking a final glance around, noting that all was in readiness, Ariakan lowered the baton.

The single clear note of a trumpet sounded on the heat-shimmering air. Steel recognized the call, "Advance to Contact," and the blood pulsed in his veins until he thought his heart would burst from the thrill.

Trumpets of all the armies of Takhisis sounded the response, joined by the higher-pitched horns of the various squadrons, blending together in a blaring, ear-splitting cacophony of war. With a roar of voices that must have shaken the foundation stones of the tower, the army of Takhisis launched the attack.

4

A discussion between old friends. Sturm Brightblade asks a favor.

n the early dawn, Tanis Half-Elven climbed the stairs leading to the battlements near the central tower, not far from where Sturm Brightblade's blood stained the walls. Here he would soon take up his position, but he did not call his troops to follow him. Not yet. Tanis had chosen this particular place deliberately. He sensed the presence of his friend. And he needed his friend at that moment.

Tanis was tired; he had been awake all night, meeting with Sir Thomas and the other commanders, trying to find a way to do the impossible, a way to win against overwhelming odds. They made their plans, good plans, too. Then they had stepped out on the battlements, watched the armies of darkness, bright with light, flow up the hill—a rising tide of death.

So much for good plans.

Tanis sank down on the wall's stone floor, leaned back his head, closed his eyes. Sturm Brightblade stood before him.

Tanis could see Sturm clearly, the knight in his old-fashioned armor, his father's sword in his hands, standing on the very battlements on which Tanis now rested. Oddly, Tanis wasn't surprised to see his old friend. It seemed right and proper that Sturm should be here, walking the battlements of the tower he'd given his life to defend.

"I could use some of your courage right now, old friend," Tanis said quietly. "We can't win. It's hopeless. I know it. Sir Thomas knows it. The soldiers know it. And how can we carry on without hope?"

"Sometimes winning turns out to be losing," said Sturm Brightblade. "And victory is best achieved in defeat."

"You talk in conundrums, my friend. Speak plainly." Tanis settled himself more comfortably. "I'm too tired to try to figure out riddles."

Sturm did not immediately answer. The knight walked the battlements, peered over the wall, stared at the vast army amassing below.

"Steel is down there, Tanis. My son."

"He's there, is he? I'm not surprised. We failed, it seems. He's given his soul to the Dark Queen."

Sturm turned away, turned to face his friend. "Watch over him, Tanis."

Tanis snorted. "I think your son is extremely capable of watching over himself, my friend."

Sturm shook his head. "He fights against a foe beyond his strength. His soul is not completely lost to us, but—should he lose this inner struggle—he will be. Watch over him, my friend. Promise me."

Tanis was perplexed, troubled. Sturm Brightblade rarely asked for favors. "I'll do my best, Sturm, but I don't understand. Steel is a servant of the Dark Queen. He's turned away from all that you tried to do for him."

"My lord . . ."

"If you'd only explain to me—"

"My lord!" The voice was accompanied by a hand, shaking his shoulder.

Tanis opened his eyes, sat bolt upright. "What? What's going on?" He reached for his sword. "Is it time?"

"No, my lord. I'm sorry to wake you, my lord, but I need to know your orders. . . ."

"Yes, of course." Tanis rose stiffly to his feet. He looked swiftly around the battlements. No one else was there, just himself and this young knight. "Sorry, I must have dozed off."

"Yes, my lord," the knight agreed politely. "You were talking to someone, my lord."

"Was I?" Tanis shook his head, trying to rid himself of the sleep-fog that clouded his brain. "I had the strangest dream."

"Yes, my lord." The young knight stood patiently waiting.

Tanis rubbed his burning eyes. "Now, what was your question?"

He listened and answered and carried on with his duties, but whenever silence fell, he could hear softly spoken words.

Promise me . . .

* * * * *

Dawn came, but the sun's light brought only deeper despair. The tower's defenders looked down on a sea of darkness that had risen in the night, was about to break over them in a tidal wave of blood. News spread of the enormous force arrayed against the knights. Commanders could be heard sharply ordering their men to remain silent, maintain their positions. Soon the only sounds that could be heard were the calls of the silver dragons, circling in the air, shouting defiance to their blue cousins.

The knights braced for the attack, but it didn't come.

An hour passed and then another. They ate breakfast at their posts, bread in one hand, sword in another. The armies gathered below made no move, except to increase their numbers.

The sun rose higher and higher; the heat grew unbearable. Water was rationed. The mountain stream that had once flowed through the tower's aqueduct had dried to barely a trickle. Men standing on the stone walls, their armor heated by the blazing sun, keeled over, passed out.

"I think we could boil the oil without benefit of the fire," Sir Thomas observed to Tanis on one of the Lord Knight's many tours of inspection.

He pointed to a huge cauldron, filled with bubbling oil, ready to be poured on the enemy. The heat from the fire forced all to keep their distance, except for those given the onerous task of stoking the blaze. They had shed armor, clothes, were stripped to the waist and sweating profusely.

Tanis mopped his face. "What's Ariakan up to, do you think? What's he waiting for?"

"For us to lose our nerve," Sir Thomas replied.

"It's working," Tanis said bitterly. "Paladine have mercy, I never saw an army that large! Not even during the war, in the last days before the fall of Neraka. How many troops do you think he has?"

"Gilean only knows," Sir Thomas said. "It's hopeless to try to figure. 'Every man counted in fear is a man counted twice,' as the old saying goes. Not that it matters much."

"You're right, my lord," Tanis agreed. "It doesn't matter at all." He considered asking how long the knight thought the tower could hold out, realized that this didn't matter much either.

A trumpet call split the air.

"Here they come," said Sir Thomas, and left hastily to take up his command position on one of the balconies off the gardens on level six.

Tanis sighed in relief, saw that same relief reflected on the faces of the men under his command. Action was far better than the terrible strain of waiting. Men forgot the terrible heat, forgot their fear, forgot their thirst, and leapt to take their posts. They could at last relax and let go; their fate was in Paladine's hands.

A blare of trumpets and a roar of challenge split the air. The army of darkness charged. The sun glittered off the scales of blue dragons; the shadows of their wings slid over the tower walls, the shadow of their coming slid over the hearts of the tower's defenders. Dragonfear began to claim its first victims.

The silver dragons and their knight riders, armed with the famed dragonlances, flew to do battle. A phalanx of blues clashed with the silver. Lightning flared; the blue dragons attacked with their breath weapons. The silvers retaliated by spewing clouds of smoking frost, which coated their enemies' wings, sent them tumbling from the skies.

Tanis wondered at the small number of blue dragons, was already suspecting that this initial attack was a diversion, when a cry rang out. Men were pointing to the west.

What appeared to be a swarm of blue dragons was flying in from that direction, far outnumbering the silver. Each of these blues did not bear a single rider, but numerous riders. The young knights stared in puzzlement, but the veterans, those who had fought in the War of the Lance, knew what was coming. The moment the first blue dragons appeared over the tower, dark, winged shadows began to descend through the skies.

"Draconians!" Tanis shouted, drawing his sword and readying himself for the attack. "Remember: The instant you kill one, toss its body over the wall."

Dead draconians were as dangerous as living draconians. Depending on their species, the bodies either turned to stone, trapping any weapons left inside; or the bodies blew up, destroying their destroyers; or dissolved into pools of acid deadly to the touch.

A Bozak draconian, its stubby wings spread to cushion its fall, thudded on the top of the wall directly in front of Tanis. Not suited to flying, the Bozak landed heavily, was momentarily stunned by the impact. It would recover quickly, however, and Bozaks were magic-users as well as expert fighters. Tanis jumped to attack the dazed creature before it could gather its wits. He swung his sword; the draconian's head parted from its neck and blood spurted. Sheathing his sword, Tanis grabbed the body before it could topple, dragged it up over the wall, and shoved it over the edge.

The dead Bozak fell among a group of barbarians attempting to scale the wall. The body blew up almost immediately, doing considerable damage. The barbarians retreated in confusion.

Tanis had little time for elation. Mammoths pulled an enormous siege engine toward the tower's front gate. Ladders were being thrown up against the walls. Tanis ordered his archers to the fore, instructed the knights manning the cauldron of oil to make ready to upend it on the heads of those below. With luck, they might even set the siege engine on fire. The men in his command were quick to do his bidding. He was well respected, known to be a knight in spirit, if not in truth.

A courier came dashing up, slipped in the draconian's blood, and nearly fell. He recovered himself, reported to Tanis.

"Message from Sir Thomas, my lord. If the front gate falls, you are to take your men and reinforce the troops guarding the entrance."

If the front gate falls, there won't be much left to guard, Tanis thought gloomily, but he refrained from saying the obvious, merely nodded and changed the subject. "What was that yelling I heard a moment ago?"

The messenger managed a tired grin. "A force of minotaur tried to sneak inside through the aqueduct. Sir Thomas guessed that the enemy might think of that, what with the drought and all. Our knights were waiting for them. They won't try *that* again soon."

"Good news." Tanis grunted, shoved the messenger to one side, and attacked a draconian who had very nearly landed on top of the young man.

That small break-wall of hope soon gave. The tide of darkness poured through, continued to rise throughout the afternoon. The knights were driven from one position after another. Retreating, they regrouped, tried to hold on, only to be pushed back again. Tanis fought until he was gasping for breath. His muscles burned, his sword hand was cramped and aching.

And still the enemy came.

Tanis was conscious only of clashing steel, the screams of the dying, and the splatter of what he thought at first was rain.

It turned out to be blood—dragon's blood, falling from the skies.

Over and above the din came the underlying, nerve-shattering *boom*, *kaboom* of the great ram, beating like a dark heart, pulsing with strong, terrible life.

There came a momentary lull in the fighting. The enemy was waiting for something. Tanis took advantage of the respite, leaned against the wall, tried to catch his breath.

From below came a splintering crash and a triumphant shout. The massive gates of the Tower of the High Clerist gave way.

A force of enemy troops, which had been held in reserve behind the siege engine, rushed the entrance. They were led by a knight in armor fighting on foot, and they had gray-robed wizards among them.

Rallying his men—those who were still able to stand—Tanis ran to defend the front gate.

5

Promise made.
Promise kept.

Steel deployed his troops behind and on each side of the huge siege engine. The brutes were skilled archers; their bows stood taller than most humans, and they fired strange arrows that made an eerie whistling noise during flight. Steel used his archers to keep the battlements clear of defenders, permit the siege engine to do its work uninterrupted.

This strategy worked, for the most part, with the exception of a small group of Solamnic Knights who hung on to their post with grim determination, beating off draconian attacks from above and fending off the brutes' arrows from below. They proved to be a nuisance to the siege engine, dumping boiling oil on it, nearly setting it ablaze; hurling large rocks, one of which smashed a mammoth's head to a bloody pulp; and using archers of their own with deadly effect.

Long after other defenders had given way or been killed, these knights remained. Even as he chafed at the delay, Steel saluted them and their unseen commander for their courage and bravery. But for them, the ram would have battered down the gates by midafternoon.

Eventually, inevitably, the ram did its work, bursting open the heavy wooden gates. Steel brought his troops forward, prepared to enter, when the head engineer—after taking a quick look inside—ran back to report.

"There's a damn portcullis blocking the way." The engineer looked personally affronted by this unexpected obstacle. "It wasn't on Lord Ariakan's map."

"A portcullis?" Steel frowned, tried to remember. He'd entered the tower this way himself five years ago, couldn't remember seeing a portcullis then either. But he did recall some construction work going on at the time. "They've added it apparently. Can you break it down?"

"No, sir. The engine won't fit under the wall. This'd best be wizard work, sir."

Steel agreed, dispatched a courier to carry the news to Lord Ariakan. Nothing to do now but wait.

He recalled the time he'd entered this gate, the time he'd gone down to the Chamber of Paladine to pay his respects to the memory of his father. The body had lain in state on the bier, preserved, some said, by the magic of the elven jewel Sturm had worn around his neck. The sword of the Brightblades had been held fast in the still, cold hands. Admiration for the dead man's courage and bravery, regret to have never known him, a hope to be like him—all these emotions had moved Steel's soul to reverence and love. His father had returned that love, given his son the only gifts Sturm Brightblade had to give—the jewel and the sword—fey gifts, both blessed and cursed. Though the midafternoon sun was grueling, Steel shivered slightly beneath his armor.

Beware, young man. A curse will fall on you if you find out the true identity of your father. Leave it be!

It was Lord Ariakan's warning, given to Steel when he was still very young. The warning had come true. The curse had fallen like an axe, cleaving Steel's soul in two. Yet, it had been a blessing as well. He had his father's sword and a legacy of honor and courage.

Up there, on those battlements that had been defended with such bravery and tenacity, his father's blood stained the stone. His son's blood would stain the rocks below. One defender, one conqueror. Yet, eminently fitting.

The courier returned, bringing with him three Knights of the Thorn. None of them, Steel noted in grim relief, was the Gray Robe who had been his accuser.

Steel recognized their commander, a Lord of the Thorn. The man was in his middle years, had fought in the War of the Lance, and was Ariakan's personal wizard. He was accustomed to working with soldiers, accustomed to blending blade with magic.

He gestured casually to the tower entrance, shouted to be heard above the noise of battle. "My lord has ordered us to take out the defenses within. I'll need your troops to guard us while we work."

Steel drew his forces into position. The master wizard and his assistants took their places in the rear. A cloud, coming from behind, indicated that the second strike army was forming, ready to enter when the way was clear.

The Lord of the Thorn motioned with his hand.

Steel raised his sword, saluted his queen. With a ringing battle cry, he led his troop, followed by the gray-robed wizards, inside the shattered gates of the High Clerist's Tower.

The iron portcullis stood between the knights and the central courtyard. Defenders on the other side fired a deadly barrage of arrows through the bars of the gate.

An old hand at dealing with such defenses, the Lord of the Thorn and two other, lower-ranking Gray Knights, handled their work swiftly and cleanly. Steel, always somewhat distrustful of magic, watched them in astonished admiration, while his own archers fired arrows back through the iron grillwork, forcing the defenders to keep their distance.

A few arrows, fired by Solamnic archers, fell among the magic-users. The two Gray Knights took care of these. Using various shield and disintegrating spells, they caused the arrows to either bounce off an invisible barrier or crumble to dust before they struck.

The Lord of the Thorn, working as coolly and calmly as if he'd been safe in his own laboratory, removed a large vial containing what appeared to be water from his pouch. Holding the vial in his hand, he dropped in a pinch of dirt, replaced the stopper, and began to chant words in the spider-crawling language of magic. He opened the vial again and, still chanting, tossed its contents onto the stone wall into which the portcullis was mounted.

The water ran down the stone in rivulets. The wizard tucked the empty vial carefully back into his pouch, clapped his hands, and instantly, the wall began to dissolve, the stone changing magically into mud.

His work done, the Lord of the Thorn folded his hands in the sleeves of his robes and stepped back.

"Push on it," he said to Steel.

The knight ordered three of the largest brutes forward. They set their shoulders against the iron and, with two or three heaves, ripped the portcullis from its moorings and flung it to the floor.

The Lord of the Thorn, looking bored, rounded up his assistants.

"Unless you need me for something significant, we'll be returning to my lord."

Steel nodded. He was grateful for the wizards' help, but he wasn't sorry to see them go.

"Alert me when the tower falls," the mage added. "I'm supposed to break into the treasury."

He left, his assistants hastening after him. Steel ordered his men to rid themselves of bows and arrows, draw their swords and knives. From here on, the combat would be hand-to-hand. Behind him, he heard shouted orders. The second strike army was preparing to advance.

Steel led his men over the shattered gate, beneath the dripping mud, and down the hallway leading to the central courtyard of the High Clerist's Tower. He stopped his forces at the hall's end.

The courtyard was empty.

Steel was uneasy. He'd expected resistance.

All was quiet inside the tower's heavy walls, too quiet.

This was a trap.

Unused to attacking fortifications, the brutes would have dashed heedlessly into the open. Steel rasped out a command, was forced to repeat it twice before he could make the brutes understand that they were to await his signal to advance.

Steel studied the situation carefully.

The courtyard was formed in the shape of a cross. To Steel's right were two iron doors, marked with the symbol of Paladine, which led deeper into the tower's interior. At the far end of the cross stood another portcullis, but Steel had no intention of fooling with that. The corridor led to the dragontraps—ancient history, as far as the Knights of Takhisis were concerned.

On each side of the portcullis were two staircases, which wound down from the battlements. Steel stared hard at those staircases. Ordering the brutes to keep silent, he listened carefully, thought he heard a scraping sound, as of armor against stone. So that's where they were hiding. He would draw them out, and he knew just how to do it.

Pointing to the iron doors to his right, those marked with the kingfisher and the rose, Steel gave his orders in a loud voice.

"Break down those doors. Downstairs is a tomb containing the bodies of accursed Solamnic Knights. Our orders are to loot it."

Several of the brutes went to work on the door, hurling their massive bodies at it, hacking at the lock with their swords. Steel entered the courtyard swaggering, undisputed master of the tower. Removing his helm, he called for a waterskin, took a long drink. The brutes clambered after him, laughing and jabbering. Grabbing torches off the walls, they jeered impatiently at the slow work of their comrades, who were not having much luck breaking down the door.

Steel had not expected they would. He had been given no orders to loot the tomb; he had no intention of permitting the barbarians access to that hallowed hall. But his ruse had worked. Sauntering near the staircase, he now heard clearly the clink of metal against metal and even a low murmur of anger, swiftly hushed.

Keeping up the act, pretending he had heard nothing, he stalked over to berate the brutes.

"You weaklings!" Steel fumed. "Must I call in the wizards every time we come to a door? I would do better with an army of gully dwarves! Put your backs into it—"

A clatter, the clash of swords, and sudden outcry to his left informed Steel that the defenders had left their hiding place, were attacking.

A contingent of Solamnic Knights burst into the midst of Steel's force. The suddenness and swiftness of their attack caught even Steel off guard. Several of the brutes were cut down before they had a chance to raise their swords.

The knights had, apparently, an able and intelligent commander They did not attack in a mob, but with precision, driving a wedge through the main body of Steel's force, splitting up his troops while maintaining unity among their own. With the second strike army entering from the front, Steel's force had nowhere to go, was trapped in the courtyard.

He had foreseen this, of course. He did not expect to win this battle, but at least the second strike army would find the way clear.

Steel left the brunt of the attack to his men. His responsibility was to find the able and intelligent commander, perhaps the same man who had fought so determinedly on the battlements, and eliminate him.

"Chop off the head, and the body will fall," was one of Ariakan's dictums.

Replacing his helm, closing the visor, Steel pushed and shoved his way through his own men. He knocked aside swords, stopped to fight when he was forced. But his attention remained centered on locating the officer in charge. That proved difficult. All the knights were wearing armor—most of it dented and bloody. He was hard-pressed to distinguish one from another.

Battling his way into the center of the melee, Steel heard, above the tumult, a commanding voice raised, issuing new orders. This time, Steel saw the commander.

He wore no helm, perhaps so that his orders could be heard clearly. He was not in full armor, but wore only a breastplate over tooled leather. Steel couldn't see the commander's face—his back was toward the dark knight. Long, graying brown hair indicated he was older, undoubtedly a veteran of many battles.

Part of the man's breastplate swung loose; one of the leather ties had been cut, leaving his back partially exposed. But Steel would have died himself before he attacked any man from behind.

Shoving between one of his own men and a battling Solamnic Knight, Steel reached the commander, laid his hand on the man's shoulder to draw his attention.

The commander whipped around, faced his opponent. The man's bearded face was covered with blood. His matted hair, wet with sweat, hung over his eyes. A tiny, tingling jolt shot through Steel. Something inside him said, "You know this man."

Steel gasped. "Half-Elven!"

The man arrested his attack, fell back, peered suspiciously at Steel.

The knight was furious at this trick fate had played on him, but he could no longer fight, in honor, this man who had once saved his life.

With an angry gesture, Steel raised his visor. "You know me, Tanis Half-Elven. I will not fight you, but I can and do demand your surrender."

"Steel?" Tanis lowered his sword. He was surprised at this meeting, yet, in a way, wasn't surprised at all. "Steel Brightblade . . ."

A young Solamnic Knight, standing near Tanis, surged past the half-elf, a spear aimed at Steel's unprotected face.

Steel raised his arm to counter the blow, slipped in a pool of blood, fell to the ground. His sword—his father's sword—flew from his grasp. The young Solamnic Knight was on him.

Steel tried desperately to stand, but the heavy armor prevented swift movement. The Solamnic Knight raised his spear, prepared to drive the point through Steel's throat. Suddenly spear and knight vanished from Steel's view.

Tanis stood over him, offered him a hand to help him rise.

Pride urged Steel to refuse aid from the enemy, but common sense and the Vision prompted him to grudgingly accept Tanis's assistance.

"Once again, I owe you my life, Half-Elven," Steel said bitterly when he was on his feet.

"Don't thank me," Tanis returned grimly. "I made a promise to—"

The half-elf's eyes opened wide, his face contorted with pain. He lurched forward with a pain-filled cry.

One of the brutes, standing behind the half-elf, jerked free a blood-covered sword.

Tanis staggered; his knees gave way.

Steel caught the half-elf, lowered him gently to the floor. Cradling Tanis in his arms, Steel could feel warm blood wash over his hands.

"Half-Elven," Steel said urgently. "I wasn't the one who struck you! I swear it!"

Tanis looked up, grimaced. "I . . . know," he whispered, with a wry smile. "You are a . . . Brightblade."

He stiffened, gasped, drew in a ragged breath. Blood trickled from his mouth. His gaze slid past Steel, attempted to focus on something behind the dark knight.

Tanis smiled. "Sturm, I kept my promise."

Sighing softly, as if grateful for the chance to rest, Tanis closed his eyes and died.

"Half-Elven!" Steel cried, though he knew he would hear no answer. "Tanis . . "

Steel was aware, suddenly, of a Solamnic Knight standing over him. The knight stared down at the body at his feet with an expression of intense grief, anguish, and sorrow.

The Solamnic Knight wore no helm, carried no weapon. His armor was antique in design. He said nothing, made no threatening move. He shifted his gaze, regarded Steel with an intense expression that was both sorrowful and filled with pride.

Steel knew then who stood over him. No dream. No vision. Or, if so, his imagination gave the dream form and body.

"Father!" Steel whispered.

Sturm Brightblade said no word. Bending down, he picked up the body of Tanis Half-Elven, lifted it in his arms, and turning, walked slowly, with measured tread, from the courtyard.

The sound of defiant shouts and clashing arms roused Steel. The iron doors, marked by the symbol of Paladine, burst open. A new force of Solamnic Knights rushed into the courtyard, coming to the aid of their comrades. A knight shouted that Tanis Half-Elven was dead; another knight vowed to Paladine to avenge his death. They pointed at Steel.

Steel, retrieving his sword, advanced to meet them.

6

The dragons silent. The door open. Someone waiting on the other side.

"Oops," said Tasslehoff Burrfoot, stunned and awed. Then he added, with a wail, "I broke it! I didn't mean to, Palin! I'm always breaking things. It's a curse. First a dragon orb, then the time-traveling device! Now I've really done it! I've broken the Portal to the Abyss!"

"Nonsense," snapped Palin, but his voice lacked conviction. The thought occurred to him—alarmingly—that if anyone on Krynn could "break" the Portal to the Abyss, it would be Tasslehoff.

More logical thought prevailed. The Portal had been constructed by powerful mages using powerful magic that not even a kender could unravel. But, if that was true, then what was wrong?

Palin, cautiously approaching the Portal for a closer look, regarded it in perplexity.

"I saw it once before, you know, Palin." Tas gazed at the Portal and sadly shook his head. "It was truly wonderful in a horrible sort of way. The five dragon heads were all different colors and they were all shrieking and Raistlin was chanting and inside were swirly lights that made you dizzy to watch and I heard terrible laughter from inside and . . . and . . . " Tas sighed and slumped gloomily to the floor. "Look at it now."

Palin was looking. He had never seen the Portal, not really, only in the illusion Dalamar had created. But Palin had studied the Portal—as do all mages. A huge oval door mounted on a raised dais, the Portal was ornamented and guarded by the heads of five dragons, their sinuous necks snaking up from the floor. The five heads looked inward: two on one side, three on the other. Their five mouths were open, singing endless, silent paeans to the Dark Queen.

Inside the Portal was a darkness that only the eyes of magic could penetrate.

Whenever the curtain concealing the Portal was lifted, the five heads would come to life, glowing with light: blue, green, red, white, black. They would kill and devour any mage foolish enough to attempt to enter on his own, as it had been during his Test. . . .

The light blinded Palin. He blinked painfully and rubbed his burning eyes. The dragon heads shone only more brilliantly, and now he could hear them each begin to chant.

The first: From darkness to darkness, my voice echoes in the emptiness.

The second: From this world to the next, my voice cries with life.

The third: From darkness to darkness, I shout. Beneath my feet, all is made firm.

The fourth: Time that flows, hold in your course.

And finally, the last head: Because by fate even the gods are cast down, weep ye all with me.

. . . His vision blurred, and tears streamed down his cheeks as he attempted to see through the dazzling light into the portal. The multicolored lights began to whirl madly, spinning around the outside of the great, gaping, twisting void within the center. . . .

"Why, would you look at that!" Tas said suddenly. Jumping to his feet, he ran over to tug on Palin's sleeve. "I can see inside! Palin, I can see inside! Can you?"

Palin gasped. He *could* see inside the Portal. A flat, empty gray landscape spread out beneath a flat, empty gray sky.

The five dragon heads were silent, gray. The eyes of the dragons, which should have been gleaming in fierce warning at this attempt to break through their guardianship, were dull, lackluster, empty.

"That's the Abyss," said Tas solemnly. "I recognize it. That is, I sort of recognize it. But it's the wrong color. I don't know if I've told you or not—"

"You have," Palin murmured, knowing it would make no difference.

Tas continued. "But I was in the Abyss once, and I was considerably disappointed. I'd heard such a lot about it: fiends and imps and revenants and ghosts and souls in torment, and I was really looking forward to a visit. But the Abyss isn't like that. It's empty and horrible and boring. I was very nearly bored to death."

One man's heaven is another man's hell, as the saying went, and that was certainly true of kender.

"Almost as boring as it is around here," Tas added—an ominous statement for a kender, as Palin should have noted.

He was lost in thought, however, trying to explain the inexplicable. What was the matter with the Portal?

Tas rambled on. "But I clearly remember that the Abyss was not this gray color. It was sort of pinkish, like a fire burning in the distance. That's how Caramon described it. Maybe the Dark Queen decided to redecorate." The kender brightened at the thought. "She could have chosen a better color scheme—all that gray just doesn't quite do it for me. Still, *any* change would be an improvement."

Tas gave his tunic a tug, checked to make sure he had all his pouches, and started forward. "Let's go take a look."

Palin was only half paying attention; his mind was occupied in recalling everything he'd ever heard or read about the Portal and the Abyss. The part of him that was constantly on the alert when around kender—a survival trait many humans developed—rang a warning, interrupted his thoughts.

Jumping forward, tripping over the dais in his haste, Palin managed to grab hold of Tas seconds before the kender would have walked straight into the Portal.

"What?" Tas asked, wide-eyed. "What's wrong?"

Palin was having difficulty breathing. "The spell . . . might have activated. . . . Not permitted inside . . . Could have . . . been killed . . ."

"I suppose I could have," Tas said on reflection. "Then, on the other hand, I suppose I couldn't. That's the way the fireball bounces, as Fizban used to say. Besides, Raistlin seems to be getting impatient. I don't think it would be polite to keep him waiting any longer."

Palin stopped breathing altogether. His flesh went cold; his heart shriveled. "My . . . uncle . . ."

"He's standing right there." Tas pointed into the Portal, into the empty gray landscape. "Can't you see him?"

Palin gripped the Staff of Magius, leaned on it for support. He looked inside the Portal again, fearing what he would see. . . .

Raistlin's body hung limply from the wall by his wrists, the black robes in tatters, the long white hair falling across his face as his head lolled forward. . . . From chest to groin, Raistlin's flesh had been ripped apart, torn asunder by sharp talons, exposing living organs. The dripping sound Palin heard was the sound of the mage's lifeblood, falling drop by drop into a great stone pool at his feet.

Raistlin stood, wearing the black robes, his arms folded across his chest. His head was bowed, brooding, but he would occasionally glance in the direction of the Portal, as if waiting for someone. Then he would return to his thoughts; unpleasant ones, to judge by the grim expression on the thin, pale face.

"Uncle!"

It was only a whisper; Palin barely heard himself speak the word.

But Raistlin heard him. The archmage lifted his head, turned the gaze of the golden, hourglass eyes on Palin.

"Why do you hesitate, Nephew?" a dry, rasping voice demanded irritably. "Hurry! You've already wasted enough time! The kender has been here before. He will guide you."

"That's me," cried Tas in excitement. "He means me! I'm going to be a guide! I've never been a guide before. Except to Tarsis, which wasn't by the sea when it should have been, but that wasn't my fault." He grabbed hold of Palin's hand. "Come on, follow me. I know exactly what to do. . . ."

"But I can't!" Palin wrenched his hand out of Tas's pinching grip. "Uncle!" he called. "What about the Portal? According to the laws of magic, we can't—"

"Laws," Raistlin said softly, musingly. He looked away, looked at the distant horizon, the pale gray of the endless sky. "All laws are suspended, Nephew, all rules broken. You may enter the Portal safely. No one will stop you. No one."

Laws suspended. Rules broken. What a strange thing to say. Yet, Palin had evidence of that—or something like that—right before his eyes. He could enter the Portal without hindrance. The Dark Queen would not try to stop him. He was in no danger.

"Wrong, Nephew," said Raistlin, answering Palin's thoughts. "You are in very great danger, you and every other mortal on Krynn. Come to me, and all will be explained." The hourglass eyes narrowed. "Unless you are afraid . . ."

Palin was afraid. He had good reason to be afraid, but he said quietly, "I've come this far, Uncle. I won't go back."

"Well said, Nephew. I'm glad to see I haven't wasted my time on you. When you are here, come find me."

Palin drew in a deep breath, held fast to the staff in one hand and took hold of Tasslehoff with the other.

Together the two walked up to stand before the five dragons' heads.

"We *will* enter," Palin told them, and he took a step forward.

The dragons did not move, did not speak, did not see, did not hear.

"The Portal isn't broken," Palin said to himself softly. "It's . . . dead!"

Tas and Palin entered the Portal to the Abyss with the same ease as they would have walked through Tika's kitchen door.

7

The Abyss. The search.
An immortal council.

They stood in the midst of gray: gray ground, gray sky. There was no sign of life, not even cursed life.

Raistlin was nowhere in sight.

"Uncle!" Palin started to call.

"Shh! Hush! Don't!" Tas cried, clutching at Palin and nearly knocking him over. "Don't say a *word*. Don't even *think* it!"

"What? Why not?" Palin asked.

"Things happen in a very strange way around this place," Tas whispered, glancing furtively about. "When I was here, I thought about how nice it would be to see a tree. And one appeared—right like that. Only it wasn't a green, leafy tree. It was a dead tree. And then I thought about Flint, 'cause, according to Fizban, I'm supposed to meet Flint under a tree in the Afterlife. And a dwarf appeared, only it wasn't Flint. It was an evil dwarf named Arack and he came at me with a knife and—"

"I understand," Palin said softly. "What we wish for, we receive, only not quite the way we want it. Do you suppose, then, that Raistlin . . . that he was just an illusion? Because I wanted to see him?"

"He seemed awfully real, didn't he?" Tas said after a moment's reflection. "That mysterious bit about laws suspended and rules broken—that's Raistlin all over. And the way he told us to meet him here and then left before we came. That's like him, too."

"But he told us to hurry. . . ." Palin considered the matter. " 'Laws suspended . . . rules broken . . . When you are here, come to find me . . .' Tas," he said, with a sudden idea. "How do you travel through this place? You don't walk, do you?"

"Well, you can, but the scenery's nothing special, not to mention that we don't know where we're going. . . Do we know where we're going?"

Palin shook his head.

"Then I wouldn't advise it," Tas said. "The last time I was here, I remember this really gruesome character with a beard that sprouted out of his skull and a smell like a gully dwarf picnic only worse. He was the one who found me and took me to see the Dark Queen. She was *not* nice," Tas added severely. "She said to me—"

"How did you get to see the queen?" Palin interrupted, keeping tight hold of the reins of conversation, well knowing that, if allowed to run loose, the kender would veer off into any of a half-dozen conversational side roads.

Tas's brows wrinkled in thought. "Well, it wasn't by carriage. I would have remembered that. I believe . . . Yes. The gruesome character put his hand—it was more of a claw than a hand, as I recall—put it around a medallion he wore on his neck and one minute we were someplace and the next minute we were someplace else."

"You're sure he wore a medallion?" Palin asked, disappointed.

"Yes, positive. I remember because it was such an interesting-looking medallion—it had a five-headed dragon on it—and I would have liked to borrow it for a while, just to get a closer look, and—"

"The staff," said Palin.

"No. Medallion. I'm certain. I—"

"I mean, we might be able to use the staff to find my uncle. Here, take hold of my hand." Palin grasped the staff more tightly.

"Magic?" Tas asked eagerly. "I do love magic. I remember once when Raistlin magicked me into a duck pond. It was . . ."

Palin paid no attention. Closing his eyes, he grasped the staff in his hand, felt the smooth wood warm beneath his touch. He thought about his uncle, remembered him as he had seen him, heard his voice, heard it clearly.

Hurry! Come to me. . . .

"Oh!" Tas gasped. "Palin! Look! It worked! We're moving."

Palin opened his eyes.

The gray, unchanging landscape slid beneath his feet; the gray sky revolved around him, swirled around them, faster and faster, until Palin was sick and dizzy at the sight.

The swirling gray surrounded him, spun around him. The ground fell away, but the gray held him, would not release him.

Round . . . and round . . . and round . . .

Round . . . and round . . . and round . . .

Spinning his senses away, drawing consciousness from him like a thread drawn from the spindle, spinning, spinning on a great wheel, round and round . . . and round . . . spun thinner and thinner and—

Snap.

Palin couldn't breathe. A hand was pressed over his mouth. He struggled, tried to lift his own hands to break the smothering grip . . .

"Hush!" said a whispering voice. "Speak no word! Make no sound. We are not supposed to be here."

Palin opened his eyes, stared into golden, hourglass eyes. The hand covering his mouth was thin and bony, the fingers long and delicate. The skin was gold-tinged. It was his uncle's hand, his uncle who held him.

Palin nodded to indicate he understood. Raistlin released his grip, and Palin drew a deep breath.

Something wriggled at his side. Tasslehoff.

The kender was saying something, but Palin couldn't hear him. He knew Tas was talking, because the kender's mouth was moving, but no words were coming out.

Tasslehoff, looking extremely puzzled, felt his throat, spoke again. Nothing.

Cupping his hand over his ear, Tas tried again. No sound came out.

In desperation, the kender stuck out his tongue, nearly went cross-eyed trying to see what was wrong with it.

Raistlin, moving close to Palin, spoke softly. "The spell is not permanent. Don't let go of him."

Again Palin nodded, though he couldn't help wondering why Raistlin had brought the kender along at all. He was about to ask, but Raistlin—glaring at him—sternly enjoined silence.

Palin and Raistlin and Tas were hidden in deep shadows behind an enormous marble column, gleaming white, with black and red striations. Next to Palin was another column—black marble, with red and white striations. And beyond that, a third column of red marble, with white and black markings swirled through it. There was no floor or ground beneath their feet; only darkness.

Palin gasped slightly. A strong hand closed over his; thin fingers dug painfully into his arm.

Raistlin said no word. None was necessary. Palin shut his mouth, resolved to make no further sound. He grabbed hold of Tas, who was starting to creep away. Together, they looked down.

A group of people stood in a circle. Beneath their feet was a marble floor. In the center of the floor was a black circle of nothingness. Radiating out from that circle were bands of alternating color: white, black, red. The people—men and women—stood on the edge of the circle, each one on his or her own color. The people were talking, arguing.

Palin glanced at Raistlin in puzzlement.

The archmage inclined his hooded head in the direction of the people, touched his ear.

Palin listened closely, and, when he realized the import of their conversation, the enormity of what they were saying stole his voice away. He could not have made a sound if he had wanted to. He listened and watched with rapt attention while his soul trembled. Even Tas was, at last, truly quiet, overawed.

The people on whom they were spying were the gods of Krynn.

"It is all Hiddukel's fault!" Chislev, a goddess, clad in spun green cloth, her brown hair wreathed in leaves and flowers, pointed an accusing finger at a stout god standing on a black band. "He tricked me and the dwarf. Isn't that true, Reorx?"

The dwarf, whose fine clothes were considerably the worse for wear, held his plumed hat in his hands. He was subdued, but anger smoldered in his eyes.

"Chislev speaks truly. I was the one who forged the blasted rock—at her insistence, I might add. Still, it was Hiddukel who thought up this whole scheme."

The god—a large, gross god with a slick manner—smiled aloofly, feigned indifference. His gaze, from out of slit eyes, slid nervously sideways to a beautiful, cold-faced, cold-eyed woman wearing shining black armor, who stood at the head of the circle.

"Well, Hiddukel?" Takhisis's voice seemed to embody darkness. "What have you to say for yourself?"

"What I did was perfectly legitimate, my queen," Hiddukel replied, oiled and smooth. "We all know the history of the Graygem. There's no need to repeat it. A harmless little plot, intended merely to further expand the glory of Your Majesty."

"And turn a profit for yourself?"

"I look out for myself," Hiddukel whined, shrinking back from Takhisis's anger. "What's the harm in that? If some people"—his greasy face turned to Chislev—"are so naive as to fall for it, then that's their problem, isn't it? And if some"—Hiddukel glanced disparagingly at the dwarf—"are so stupid as to try to capture Chaos—"

"That was an accident!" Reorx roared. "I intended to snatch only a part of Chaos—a wee morsel. You must believe me, sir."

The dwarf turned humbly to a tall, grim-faced god wearing silver armor, who occupied a white band next to Takhisis. "I had no intention of capturing Himself," Reorx added in subdued tones.

"I am well aware of that," said Paladine. "We are all to blame here."

"Some more than others. Powerful magic was needed to hold Chaos," growled Sargonnas, a tall, horned god who stood near Takhisis. "It seems to me that the blame lies with our rebellious children."

The three gods of magic drew together.

"It wasn't our fault," Lunitari said.

"We knew nothing about it," Nuitari replied.

"No one consulted us," Solinari protested.

Reorx grumbled. "It was Lunitari who lost the Graygem!"

"Your grubby little gnome stole it!" Lunitari flashed back.

"If only someone had asked me," Zivilyn complained, "I could have looked into the future and warned you—"

"When?" Morgion asked sarcastically. "In another six or seven millennia? It would take you that long to make up your mind about which future was which."

The lesser gods began to argue loudly, each blaming the other. In each voice, on each face, strain and fear were evident. The bickering and accusations dragged on interminably. Gilean read long passages from his book, attempting to either fix blame or shift it, as the various gods requested. Reorx gave an impassioned speech in his own defense. Hiddukel held forth at great length, talking very long and saying very little. Sargonnas blamed everything on the weak, puny, and sniveling races of humans and elves and ogres, claiming that if they'd only had sense enough to become servants of the minotaur, this calamity would never have happened. Zivilyn responded by showing innumerable versions of the future and past, which completely confused and confounded the issue, resolved nothing.

The argument went on so long and was so wearing and unproductive that Palin several times drifted off to sleep. He would wake again with a start when some particularly loud voice was raised, only to drift off yet again. He had the distinct and somewhat uneasy feeling of the passing of time, but that time was somewhere else, not here.

He would have questioned Raistlin, but when he tried to speak, Raistlin shook his head, the golden eyes narrowed. He appeared highly displeased. Tasslehoff was sound asleep, snoring softly.

At length, just when Hiddukel stated that he was prepared to cite several important legal precedents, all of which had a direct bearing on his case, Paladine and Takhisis, who had remained silent during the argument and who continued to remain silent, exchanged glances.

There was a sudden flash of brilliant light, and only the three elder gods were left standing in the circle. The lesser gods had been banished.

"It was useless to bring them here," Takhisis said bitterly.

"We had to try." It was the hitherto silent Gilean who spoke. He held a large book, in which he was constantly writing. "We might have learned something that would aid us."

"It is obvious to me that none of them knows how this happened," Paladine returned. "Somehow, Chaos apparently became trapped inside the Graygem, and—rightly or wrongly—he blames us."

"*If* he's telling the truth," Takhisis said. "This could be a ruse."

"I believe he *was* trapped inside," Gilean said thoughtfully. "I've given the matter careful study, and it would explain a great deal: the havoc that the Graygem has wreaked all over Krynn, the fact that none of us could control it—"

"Your Irda managed to control it, Brother," Takhisis interrupted, with an accusatory glance at Paladine.

"It controlled them, you mean," the god answered sternly. "Chaos at last discovered people he could manipulate, people strong enough in magic to free him, yet not strong enough to stop him. They have paid for their folly."

"And he is determined to make *us* pay. The question is, can he do it, my brothers? Is he strong enough? We have grown in strength ourselves over the centuries."

"Not nearly as strong as we need to be," Gilean said with a sigh. "As you yourself reported, Sister, Chaos has caused a great rift to form in the Abyss. He has grown in power, far beyond anything we could ever dream. He is summoning forth his armies: fiends and dread shadow warriors, fire dragons. When he is ready, he will attack Krynn. His object: to destroy everything we created. When that is accomplished, the rift will be vast and deep, so vast and deep that it will swallow the world. All that is now will be nothing."

"And what of us?" Takhisis demanded. "What will he do to us?"

"He gave us life," Paladine said heavily. "He could take it away."

"The question is, what do we do now?" Gilean asked, looking from one sibling to another.

"He's toying with us," said Paladine. "He could destroy us all with a flick of an eyelash. He wants to see us suffer, to see our creation suffer."

"I say we leave, Brothers, slip away before he knows we are gone." Takhisis shrugged. "We can always create another world."

"I will *not* abandon those who trust in me." Paladine was stern. "I will sacrifice myself for them if need be."

"We might be doing them a favor by leaving," Gilean pointed out. "If we leave, Chaos might follow us."

"*After* he destroyed the world," Paladine insisted, glowering, "our 'plaything,' as he calls it. He will show no mercy. I will stay and fight him—alone if need be."

The other two gods were silent, thoughtful.

"Perhaps you are right, Brother," Takhisis said, with sudden, disarming sweetness. "We *should* stay and fight. But we will need the help of the mortals, don't you agree?"

"They will need to help themselves, that much is true," Paladine said, eyeing his sister distrustfully.

"We could never destroy Chaos," Gilean said, "but there might be ways to force him to leave. In this, the mortals could aid us."

"*If* they were united," Takhisis said. "It wouldn't do to have armies of humans and elves turn on each other when they were supposed to fight the legions of Chaos."

"They would unite," Paladine said grimly. "They would have no choice."

"Perhaps. Perhaps not. Do we dare risk it, my brothers? For their sakes, as much as ours?"

"State your meaning plainly, Sister," Paladine demanded. "You have some plan in mind, I see."

"One that will undoubtedly be to her advantage," Gilean added in a whispered aside to his brother.

Takhisis heard him, looked hurt at the thought that they could so misunderstand her. "What benefits one benefits us all, if we manage to rid the world of Chaos. Is that not true, dear brothers?"

"What is your plan?" Paladine repeated.

"Only this. Give control of Ansalon to my knights. Permit them to hold sway. Under their rule, law and order will prevail. This endless bickering and fighting among the mortals will cease. Peace will come to Ansalon. The mortals will be unified and therefore prepared for Chaos's attack."

"Unity? The unity of slaves! The peace of the prison house! I cannot believe this, not even of you, Sister," Paladine returned angrily. "Never have we faced such peril, and even now, while your very existence hangs by a thread, you scheme and plot to have your own way. I will *not* agree."

"Now, wait a moment, Brother," Gilean said in mollifying tones. "Certainly our beloved sister is double-dealing, trying to play both ends against the middle. What else did you expect? But the plan she has proposed does have some merit. A unified and peaceful Ansalon, even if it is unified under darkness, would be better prepared to face the armies of Chaos than an Ansalon that is fragmented, divided, in turmoil."

Paladine was thoughtful, troubled. His gaze went to Takhisis, back to Gilean. "Do you stand with her on this?"

"Yes, Brother, I'm afraid I must," Gilean said gently. "Otherwise, I see no hope."

"Come, Brother, don't be selfish," Takhisis advised, her tone mocking. "You speak very glibly of sacrificing yourself for your precious mortals. But when it comes to the point where you must do so, you balk. Are you all talk? Or do you really mean what you say?"

Paladine was silent a long, long time. His brow furrowed in thought, he turned his sorrowful gaze out toward the world. At length, he shook his head. "I cannot see the future. Flame and smoke block my vision. I am not certain you two are right, yet, if you both are against me, I have little choice but to acquiesce. I agree, Sister," he said, with a bitter sigh. "Ansalon will be yours."

"You have chosen wisely, Brother," Takhisis said, cool and dark, magnanimous in triumph.

"But you rule only until the forces of Chaos are destroyed," Paladine insisted.

"Or we are," Gilean added gloomily. He exhibited the book, in which he continued to write. "It could be, dear brother, dear sister, that I am penning the last chapter."

"Then," said Takhisis, "we had better make it a good one. Farewell, my brothers. I have a battle to win."

She disappeared. Paladine left immediately after. Gilean alone remained. He sat down, continued writing in the great book.

8

Disappointment. Victory is ours.
The surrender.

teel Brightblade was alive.

He didn't want to be. He wasn't supposed to be. He should have died in the assault on the High Clerist's Tower, died nobly, bravely in battle, his life sacrificed for his queen, his honor restored.

And he had been meant to die—his armor pierced by a spear wielded by a noble enemy. Tanis Half-Elven had thwarted fate by saving Steel from that spear. Tanis Half-Elven had died Steel's death.

Steel stood in the central courtyard of the High Clerist's Tower, his bloodied sword in a hand that was sticky and gummed with blood—some of it his own, most of it belonging to others. He couldn't quite comprehend what was happening; the battle-lust burned hot in him still. His most vivid memory was of his father, bearing away Tanis's body. And he wondered now if he might not have imagined all that, but for the fact that Tanis's blood stained the stones at his feet.

After that, he knew nothing but the strange silence of battle—the silence that encompasses the clash of arms, the grunts of the dying, the shouts of orders, the trampling of feet. Yet all these sounds are blotted out by the silence within, the silence of the warrior, who must concentrate his being on his objective, who must let nothing distract him, nothing interfere.

For Steel, the silence was broken when he looked around for another opponent to fight—and realized there were none.

"Victory! Victory is ours!" Subcommander Trevalin—his armor blood-spattered and dented, his face covered with sweat and grime—strode into the central courtyard, shouting the news.

"Tell this to my Lord Ariakan!" Trevalin commanded, catching hold of a squire and shoving him toward the entrance. "Tell him—if he hasn't heard already—that the Solamnics want to discuss terms of surrender."

Trevalin glanced around, saw Steel, standing, dazed and bewildered, in the center of the courtyard. Trevalin strode over, clapped his arms around his friend.

"Brightblade! Sheathe your sword! We've won!"

"Won . . ." Steel repeated. The battle had ended and he was alive.

Trevalin, exhilarated, continued on. "A glorious campaign! It will live forever. The High Clerist's Tower falls for the first time in recorded history! A stunning victory! Palanthas is ours next. Once they hear that their protectors have been defeated, the good dragons fled, the citizens will drop like rotten fruit into our hands. And you, my friend! I've heard tales of your valor already! They say you are the slayer of Tanis Half-Elven."

"No," Steel mumbled. The fire of battle that had raced through his veins was slowly being stamped out, leaving nothing but ashes and smoke. He was alive. "No, I didn't kill the half-elf. He saved—"

But Trevalin wasn't listening. A courier from Lord Ariakan had ridden into the courtyard. His horse—trained for swiftness, not battle—shied at the sight of the bodies, the stench of blood. The courier fought to hold the animal steady, searched for someone in authority.

"His Lordship has seen a white flag displayed from the top of the tower. Messengers report that the tower's defenders wish to discuss terms of surrender. My lord has also heard that the silver dragons and the golden dragons have abandoned the field, left the battle. Is any of this true, Subcommander?"

"It's true, all of it. I myself saw the so-called 'good' dragons flee." Trevalin laughed. "Perhaps Paladine sent them a message, ordered them to retreat."

The courier didn't seem to find this funny. His horse stamped and snorted, cantered about nervously, its hooves slipping on the blood-covered stones. The courier hung on gamely, guiding the restive animal this way and that, while talking to Trevalin.

"His lordship suspects a trick."

Trevalin nodded, more soberly. "I wouldn't be surprised if the dragons have fled only to regroup somewhere, increase their numbers. All the more reason to accept the surrender of the knights and take command of this fortress quickly."

"Are these their officers?" the courier asked in a low voice, leaning over his horse's neck. "These men coming toward us?"

Three Knights of Solamnia advanced into the courtyard. One, the commander, a Lord Knight of the Rose, walked in front; the other two walked solemnly to either side. They had removed their helms—either that or they had lost them in battle. The three knights bore marks from the fray; their armor was battered, covered with dust and blood. The commander limped badly, grimaced in pain with every slow and halting step. Another's face was covered with blood from a gash on his head; he carried one arm stiffly. The third had a crude bandage wrapped about one eye; blood seeped beneath it, trickled down his cheek.

They carried, between them, a length of white cloth.

"Those are the officers," Trevalin confirmed.

The courier rode to meet them. Halting his steed, he saluted.

The defeated Solamnic commander lifted his haggard gaze. He was middle-aged, but he appeared far, far older. "Are you from Lord Ariakan? Will you carry a message to him?"

"I will, Sir Knight," the courier replied politely. "What message am I to carry to His Lordship?"

The Solamnic Knight rubbed his hand across his face, perhaps wiping away blood, perhaps tears. He sighed. "Tell His Lordship we ask permission to remove our dead from the field."

"This means, my lord, that you surrender this tower?"

The knight nodded his head slowly. "On condition that there be no more bloodshed. Too many have died this day."

"It may be that His Lordship requires unconditional surrender," the courier returned.

The knight's expression hardened. "If such is the case, we will continue fighting until not one of us is left alive. A grievous waste."

At this point, one of the knights accompanying the commander spoke in urgent tones, appeared to renew an argument.

The commander silenced him with a motion of his hand. "We have discussed this once. I will not send any more young men to their deaths in what would be a wasted effort. I know Ariakan. He will act honorably. If not—" He shook his head, returned his grim gaze to the courier. "Those are our terms. Tell your lord he can take them or leave them."

"I will do so, Sir Knight."

The courier galloped off. The three defeated knights stood off to themselves, held themselves aloof. They said nothing to each other, kept their eyes straight forward, refusing to acknowledge the presence of the enemy.

"He'll accept them," Trevalin predicted. "The battle's done. All else is useless slaughter. As I said, my guess is he'll want to take control of the tower swiftly, before the gold dragons return. And now I must go back to my command. You will be pleased to know, Brightblade, that Flare survived the battle without injury. She fought well, though she seemed to me to be lacking spirit. Missed her true master, I guess. I—Brightblade, what is this?"

"My sword," said Steel darkly, bitterly. "I surrender myself up to you, Subcommander. I am your prisoner."

Trevalin was at first confused. Then he remembered. "Damn! I had forgotten all about that." He shoved the proffered sword aside, moved closer, spoke softly. "Listen to me, Steel. Don't say a word to anyone. His Lordship will have forgotten all about this, too. As to that Nightlord—well, Ariakan will hear of your valor this day. What is the loss of one measly mage compared to the duel between you and Tanis Half-Elven? A duel you won!"

Steel was cold, calm. "I am your prisoner, Subcommander."

"Brightblade, damn it," Trevalin began, exasperated.

Steel unbuckled his swordbelt, held his sword in his hands.

"Very well, Brightblade," Trevalin said in a low voice. "I place you under arrest. But the first opportunity I have, I will personally speak to Lord Ariakan on your behalf, ask him to take into account your bravery—"

"Please do not, Subcommander," Steel said in the same chill tone. "Thank you, but I ask you to say nothing. My lord will think that I am begging for my life. Take me to wherever it is they are holding the prisoners."

"Very well," Trevalin said, after a moment's pause, waiting—hoping—Steel would change his mind, "if that is what you want."

Trevalin gestured for Steel to precede him, indicated a door at the far end of the courtyard.

Outside the tower walls came the blare of trumpets and the shouts of men, celebrating victory. Steel heard the clatter of hooves. Lord Ariakan was approaching, riding in triumph, riding as conqueror to the fortress he had once entered as the conquered.

Steel did not wait to watch. He did not want to spoil the moment, did not want his lord—in his glory—to see Steel in his shame. Lifting his head, his jaw set firm, Steel walked across the crimson-stained stones toward the prison cells of the High Clerist's Tower.

9

Che Portal. Old friends return. Casslehoff's confession.

ell," muttered Tasslehoff Burrfoot, "as Bupu would have said, this is a fine kettle of rat stew!" He blinked, gasped. "I heard myself! My voice has come back! Did you hear that, Raistlin? I—"

"Uncle," said Palin, troubled, "what does this—"

"Not now, kender," Raistlin interrupted. "Nor you, either, Nephew. Questions later. We must leave swiftly, before we are discovered."

Relieved that he could talk again, excited to realize that he was going to be magicked yet again (twice in one day), Tas hoped they were going someplace as interesting. Another duck pond, perhaps.

Raistlin said nothing, did nothing. But suddenly the column behind which they had hidden began to dissolve, dwindle, disappear.

The magic whirled around Tas, or perhaps he whirled around the magic. He couldn't tell, due to the extremely gratifying sensation of having his stomach flattened up against his spine and his topknot wrapped around his eyes.

When the whirling stopped, his stomach fell back into its proper place. He dragged the hair out of his eyes, looked around, and sighed.

No duck pond, nothing but gray sky above, gray ground beneath. They were back where they had started.

There was the Portal. Beyond the Portal was the laboratory, exactly as they had left it—filled with jars and bottles containing the most interesting, if disgusting, things; books and scrolls; perhaps a magical ring or two. Tas had always had lots of luck with magical rings.

The laboratory had seemed pretty boring to the kender before they had entered the Abyss. It looked as good as market day in Flotsam now.

Tas was all set to dash back through the Portal when he remembered his manners. He turned, held out his small hand to Raistlin.

"Well, good-bye, Raistlin. It was nice seeing you again, even if you did murder poor Gnimsh. I've forgiven you for that, though, because Caramon said you tried to make it all up by sacrificing yourself and closing the Portal when you knew the Dark Queen was waiting to rip you open and tear your guts out."

At this point, a thought occurred to the kender. "I say, Raistlin. Is the Dark Queen going to come back and chain you to the wall and rip you open and tear your guts out? Not that I want her to, of course. You must find that extremely unpleasant. But if she absolutely insisted on it, I'd sort of like to watch."

Raistlin's eyes narrowed. "If you think you'd enjoy it, Master Burrfoot, perhaps I'll ask Her Dark Majesty to rip *your* guts out."

Tas considered this a truly generous offer, but he finally shook his head. "It's nice of you to think of me, Raistlin. I've never had my guts ripped out before and, while it would certainly be entertaining, I don't suppose it would be conducive to a long life. Tanis is always telling me to think before I do anything, whether or not it would be conducive to a long life, and not to do it if it wasn't. I'd say that comes under that last category."

Palin looked truly alarmed. "The Dark Queen's *not* coming, is she, Uncle? To . . . to torture you . . . ?"

"She would like to. Takhisis has a long memory. She does not forget or forgive. She would take her vengeance on me if she could, but I am protected from her wrath." Raistlin spoke dryly. "As the kender said— a reward for my sacrifice."

"Then you're not going to be tortured?" Tas asked.

"No, I am not," Raistlin said. "Sorry to disappoint you."

"That's all right," Tas reassured him. "This trip has been really great, just the same. Getting to see all the gods up close like that. Of course, I did sort of miss Fizban, but I could see where he wouldn't have been of much help in a desperate situation like this. And now I've seen what Paladine looks like when he isn't setting his beard on fire and losing his hat. And Gilean seemed awfully familiar, but I can't recall where I've seen him before. Chemosh was frightfully ugly, wasn't he? Is that skull really his face? And Morgion, all his flesh falling off like that. I probably should have said 'hello' to Paladine. It would have been polite, since he and I are such close personal friends, but I was having trouble with my voice. Maybe the cat got my tongue. But if that were so, what happened to the cat? And why would a cat want an extra tongue in the first place?"

"You must go," Raistlin said firmly. "You are wasting time."

"I'm ready," Tas announced, and he started walking back into the Portal. "Good-bye, Raistlin!" he called over his shoulder. "I'll tell Caramon you said, 'hi,' even though you didn't."

The kender realized suddenly he was alone. "Palin, aren't you coming?"

Palin stood still, his hand running nervously up and down the staff. He looked at Raistlin. "You're not coming with us, are you?"

"No, Nephew. I am not."

"But you could if you wanted to. You're not dead. You gave the staff to me. You were the one who brought us here."

"Yes, I could return," Raistlin said quietly. "You are right. I am not dead. Yet neither am I truly alive. But why should I go back? The world held little pleasure for me when I was in it. I've done my part—bringing you here, showing you the danger. You have done what no other mortal being has ever done. You have been witness to a meeting of the gods. Now you must return, warn people, warn the knights of both Takhisis and Paladine, warn the wizards of the three moons and those of the Gray Robes. Warn your father and tell him to spread the warning. Tell them all what you have seen and heard."

"I will tell them," Palin said. "But I am not certain that I fully understand what I've seen and heard. I can warn them that Chaos is intent on destroying the world. I can tell them that Paladine has given us into the hands of darkness. I wonder if anyone will believe me. But you, Uncle. They would believe you. Come with me!"

Raistlin gazed intently at Palin. "That is not your only reason for wanting me to return, is it, Nephew?"

Palin flushed, replied quietly, "No, Uncle. It is not. I came here to find you . . . because I wanted you to teach me."

"There are numerous teachers of mage-craft in the world. You are gifted in the art, Nephew. Surely there must be many who would want such a brilliant pupil."

"Perhaps, but they don't want me," said Palin, his flush deepening.

"And why not you?" Raistlin asked softly.

"Because . . . because of . . ." Palin hesitated.

"Because of me?" Raistlin said with an unpleasant smile. "They still fear me that much, do they?"

"I don't mean to hurt your feelings, Raistlin," Tas offered helpfully, "but there were times when you weren't a very nice person."

Raistlin fixed the golden, hourglass eyes on the kender. "I thought I heard someone calling you."

"You did?" Tas listened, but he didn't hear anything. "Where?"

"Over there!" Raistlin pointed.

And then Tas did hear something—a gruff, grumbling voice.

"And what do you think *you're* doing here, Tasslehoff Burrfoot? Up to nothing good, I reckon. Likely getting yourself and those poor fools with bad luck enough to be stuck with you into no end of trouble . . ."

Tasslehoff whirled around so fast that the flaps of his pouches flew open, scattering his prized possessions all over the Abyss. But for once in his life, Tas didn't care.

"Flint!"

Long gray beard and disapproving scowl and gruff voice and all. Tas was preparing to hug Flint, whether the dwarf liked being hugged or not (which he generally didn't, but then this was a special occasion), when Tas noticed two people standing behind Flint.

"Sturm!" Tas gasped with pleasure. "And Tanis! What are you doing here? Wait! I know! We're going on another adventure! Where are we going? Wherever it is, I'm sure to have a map. My maps are up to date now. Tarsis by the Sea isn't anymore—by the sea, I mean. Tarsis is still where it always was. I say, Flint. Hold still so I can hug you."

Flint snorted. "As if I'd let a kender within a foot of me, much less hug me! Keep your distance, and I'll keep my money pouch."

Tas knew Flint didn't truly mean it, tried again to hug his friend. But the kender's arms wrapped around nothing but gray air.

Tas stepped back. "Flint, quit joking about. How can I go adventuring with you if you won't hold still?"

"I'm afraid you're not going with us, Tas," Tanis said gently. "It's not that we don't want you—"

"It's not as if we did, either," Flint grumbled.

Tanis smiled, rested his hand on the dwarf's shoulder. "We came because your old friend wanted to have a word with you."

The dwarf shifted uncomfortably from one foot to the other, smoothed his beard, and got very red in the face.

"Yes, Flint, what is it?" Tas asked, considerably subdued and even feeling the beginnings of a snuffle coming on. He had a strange sort of ache in his heart, as if his insides knew something was not quite right but hadn't gotten around to telling his outsides about it. It didn't seem right for Tanis to be here.

"What did you want to say to me, Flint?"

"Well, Lad," Flint said after a few wheezes and throat-clearings, "I was saying to Tanis, when I first saw him—"

The ache in Tas's heart grew until it was almost too much to bear. He put his hand over it, hoping to make the ache go away, at least until Flint was done.

"I said to Tanis, when I first saw him, that I am . . . well . . . getting a bit lonely, you might say."

"Under your tree, you mean?" Tas asked.

"Don't get me wrong," Flint growled. "I'm very well situated. That tree of mine—it's a wondrous sort of tree. Every bit as pretty as the vallenwoods back home. Tanis himself said so, when he saw it. And it's warm there, next to Reorx's forge, and interesting, too. Creation never stops, you see, or else one part or another needs a touch of mending. Reorx works there, hammering away. And he tells stories, wonderful tales about other worlds that he's seen . . . ."

"Stories!" Tas cheered up. "I love to hear stories! And I'll bet he'd like to hear a few of mine, like the time I found the woolly mammoth—"

"I'm not finished!" Flint roared.

"Sorry, Flint," Tas said meekly. "Go ahead."

"Now I forgot where I was," Flint said irritably.

"About being lonely . . ." Tas hinted.

"I remember!" Flint folded his arms over his chest, drew in a deep breath, let it and the words out in a rush. "I wanted to tell you, Lad, that if you ever are of a mind to come see me, you'll be welcome. I don't know why it is." The dwarf did appear extremely confused. "And I know I'm going to regret saying this, but I . . . I've come to miss you, Lad."

"Well, of course, you have," Tas said, amazed that the dwarf hadn't figured this out earlier. "I can't help thinking—and I hope your tree isn't offended—but sitting in one place all day watching a god hammer on the world doesn't sound very exciting to me. Which reminds me. Speaking of gods, we just saw Reorx. And all the rest of the gods, too! And the most wonderful—I mean terrible—things are happening in the world. Here, I'll get Palin to come tell you about them. Palin!" The kender turned, yelled, and waved. "And there's Raistlin. This is quite the reunion, isn't it? You've never met Palin. That's odd, why doesn't he come over and say hello?"

Palin glanced over, waved his hand, the sort of wave which says, *You're having fun, good. Keep on having fun. Now leave me alone.*

Flint, who had been trying to say something for the past several minutes and never getting the words out, due to Tas interrupting him, finally stated, "He can't see us, you ninny!"

"Of course, he can see," Tas said, a bit irritably. "It's only Tanis who needs spectacles—"

"Not anymore, Tas," Tanis said. "Palin can't see us because he is alive. We exist in a different realm now."

"Not you, too, Tanis?" Tas said in a small voice.

"I'm afraid—"

"You must have done something that was not conducive to living a long life," Tas continued hastily, blinking and giving his eyes a swipe with his hand. He grew stern. "Which I must say wasn't very smart of you, Tanis. I mean, you're always telling me not to do things that are not conducive to leading a long . . . long . . ." His voice began to quiver.

"I guess I just wasn't thinking," Tanis said, smiling. "I lived well, Tas. I had many blessings in my life. It was hard to leave those I loved," he added, "but I have friends here."

"As well as enemies," Flint said grimly.

Tanis's face grew shadowed. "Yes, we will be fighting our own battles in this realm."

Tas pulled out a handkerchief (one of Palin's), mopped his eyes, and blew his nose. He sidled closer to Flint.

"I'll tell you a secret, Flint," Tas said in a loud whisper, which could probably be heard in most parts of the Abyss, "I'm not the adventurer I used to be. No." The kender heaved a great sigh. "I sometimes think—and I know you're not going to believe this—but I sometimes think of retiring, settling down. I can't understand what's come over me. It's just not fun anymore, if you know what I mean.

"Ah, you doorknob," Flint said gruffly. "Can't you figure it out? You're getting old."

"Old? Me!" Tas was thunderstruck. "I don't feel old, inside, I mean. If it wasn't for the occasional annoying pain in my back and my hands and the strong urge to take naps by the fire instead of shouting taunts at minotaur—they get *really* angry, did you know that? Especially when you go 'mooo' at them. It's amazing how fast an angry minotaur can run when he's chasing you. Anyway, where was I?"

"Where you should be," Tanis said. "Good-bye, Tas. May the minotaur never catch you."

" 'Moo' at a minotaur!" Flint humpfed. "Of all the doorknobs! Take care of yourself, Lad." He turned quickly, walked away very fast, shaking his head. The last thing Tas heard, the dwarf was still muttering, " 'Moo!' " to himself.

"Paladine walk with you, Tas," Sturm said, and he turned and followed after Flint.

"Just so long as he *walks* with me and doesn't try any fireball spells," Tas said, somewhat dubious.

He watched until he couldn't see them anymore, which was almost instantaneously, because one moment they were there and the next they weren't.

"Tanis? Flint?" Tas called their names a couple of times. "Sturm? I'm sorry I took your bracers once by accident."

But there was no answer.

After a couple more blubbers and a few hurting sobs seized the kender unexpectedly, Tas drew in a deep, hiccuping breath, wiped his nose on his sleeve—the handkerchief was wet past using—and sighed, somewhat irritably.

"People need me, Tanis says. Well, they're always needing me, it seems. Banish a ghoul here, fight a goblin there. Never a moment's peace. Still, that's what comes of being a hero. I guess I'll just have to make the best of it."

Gathering up his pouches, Tas, shuffling his feet through the gray sand, walked slowly back to the Portal. Palin was still talking to

Raistlin.

"I wish you would reconsider. Come back, Uncle. Father would be so pleased to see you."

"Would he?" Raistlin asked softly.

"Why, yes . . ." Palin stopped, uncertain.

Raistlin smiled, shrugged. "You see? Things are best as they are. Look!" A faint light was beginning to beam from the Portal. "The queen is once more bending her thoughts this way. She is now aware that the Portal is open. You must go back through and shut it again. Use the staff. Swiftly."

The sky grew dark, the gray deepening to black. Palin looked at it uneasily, but still he hesitated.

"Uncle . . ."

"Go back, Palin," Raistlin said, his voice cold. "You do not know what you ask of me."

Palin sighed, then he looked at the staff in his hand, looked back at Raistlin. "Thank you, Uncle. Thank you for having faith in me. I will not fail you. Come on, Tas. Hurry! The guardians are returning."

"I'm coming."

But Tas dragged his feet. The thought of five multicolored, screaming dragon heads, all of them maybe trying to devour him, didn't excite him in the least. Well, not much.

"Good-bye, Raistlin. I'll tell Caramon you said . . . Why, hullo, Kitiara! Gosh! People certainly do pop up from out of nowhere around here, don't they? Remember me, Kitiara? I'm Tasslehoff Burrfoot."

The dark-haired woman, wearing blue dragon armor, a sword at her side, shoved the kender brutally aside. She came to stand in front of Palin, blocked his way back to the Portal.

"I'm very glad to meet you at last, Nephew," Kitiara said, smiling the crooked smile. She extended her hand, took a step closer. "Why don't you stay a little longer? There's someone coming who would very much like to meet you. . . ."

Tas shouted a warning. "Palin, look out!"

Kitiara drew her sword; the blade shone with a dull, sullen gray light. She advanced on Palin. "You have heard what you were not meant to hear. My queen does not take kindly to spies!"

Kitiara swung her blade. Palin lifted his staff, countered the blow, tried to shove Kit backward. The two stood locked in the struggle. And then Kit fell back suddenly. Palin, overbalanced, stumbled forward. Kit leapt to the attack.

Tasslehoff searched about frantically for something to hurl at Kitiara. He had nothing but the objects in his pouches and himself. Figuring that his most prized possessions, while undeniably valuable, wouldn't do much to stop an enraged Kitiara, Tas hurled himself, launching his small body in her general direction, hoping to knock her down and avoid impaling himself on her sword at the same time.

He forgot he was in the Abyss. The kender flew at Kitiara, flew through Kitiara, and flew out the other side of Kitiara without ever touching her. But he did accomplish something; he managed to bump her sword, which—strangely—had substance to it. Kit's lunge, aiming for Palin's heart, went awry.

Tas landed on all fours, shaken and confused.

Palin staggered backward. A splotch of red blossomed on his white robes. He clutched his shoulder, swayed, and sank to one knee. Kitiara, cursing, lifted her sword and advanced again.

Scrambling to his feet, Tas was about to have another go at the sword, when he heard Raistlin chanting strange words. Black robes swirled in front of Tas. The dragons of the Portal began shrieking, and just when everything was at its most interesting, something struck Tasslehoff right between the eyes.

He saw the most fascinating collection of stars on the backside of his eyelids, felt himself toppling, and was overtaken by an inadvertent nap.

10

A prisoner. The lashing.

he key rattled in the lock. The cell door swung open.

"Visitor, Brightblade," said the jailer.

Steel sat up on his straw pallet, rubbed the sleep from his eyes. He wondered if it was day or night; he had no way of knowing. The dungeons, located on the first level of the tower, had no windows. Steel blinked in the torchlight, tried to see who was entering.

He heard the whisper of robes, saw a glimmer of gray.

Steel rose slowly, chains clanking, to his feet. He must show this woman respect, for she was his superior, but he wouldn't hurry about it.

"Nightlord," he said, watching her warily.

She drew close, her gaze darting all over him, taking in every aspect of his degradation, from his filthy clothes to his matted hair and manacled wrists.

"Leave us." The Nightlord, Lillith, turned to the jailer. "Shut the door."

"Don't keep him long, Nightlord," the jailer growled, placing the burning torch in an iron sconce on the wall. "He's got work to do."

"I will be only a few moments." Lillith waited until the jailer had left, then turned back to Steel. Her eyes shone eerily. She regarded him with an intensity that seemed to give them a baleful, inner light.

"Why have you come, Nightlord," Steel asked finally, growing weary of this silent scrutiny. "To revel in my downfall?"

"I take no pleasure in this, Brightblade," Lillith answered abruptly. "What I do, I do for the glory of our queen. I came to tell you why it is necessary that you must die."

Steel shrugged. "Then you have wasted your time, Nightlord. I know why I must die. You said it yourself. I lost the prisoner entrusted to my care."

"You were meant to lose him," the Nightlord said calmly. "I sent you on a fool's errand, knowing full well that you would lose him. I did not, however, expect you to return. I had hoped," she continued, speaking in a detached manner, "that you would both die in the Shoikan Grove. Barring that, I trusted the Dark Queen would kill you and the mage in the Abyss. That plan also failed. But, hopefully, by now, the mage is dead. And shortly you will be, too." She nodded several times, repeated, "You will be, too."

Steel was confounded, could find nothing to say. That this woman should hate so completely, so malevolently, without cause was beyond his understanding. At length, seeing that she expected him to speak, he said, "I fail to understand why you have come, Nightlord. If it is to taunt me—"

"No, not that. I take no satisfaction in this. I came because I wanted you to understand. I would not want you to stand before our queen and accuse me of having had you executed falsely or unjustly. Her Majesty can be . . . most vindictive."

The Nightlord was silent, brooding.

Steel was not inclined to be sympathetic. "What you did was tantamount to murder, Nightlord, treacherous and deceitful, unworthy of one of Ariakan's knights."

Lillith paid this scant consideration. "I looked into the future, Steel Brightblade. I saw you and the mage, the White Robe, together on a field of battle. I saw lightning strike the tower. I saw death, destruction, the fall of the knighthood." The strangely lit eyes turned to him. "You and the White Robe must die. Only then will doom be averted. Do you understand? Surely you accept this as necessary!"

"I accept my lord's judgment," Steel said, choosing his words carefully. "If my death benefits the knighthood, then so be it."

The Nightlord seemed less than satisfied with this answer. She gnawed her lower lip, rattled the seeing stones in their pouch.

The jailer opened the cell door. "You have another visitor, Brightblade."

Subcommander Trevalin entered. He appeared displeased to find the Nightlord. She was not overjoyed to see him. She said no further word to Steel. Pivoting on her heel, she swept out of the cell, her gray robes swirling around her. Trevalin stepped back, took care to keep out of the way of their touch.

"What was *she* doing here?" he asked.

"Wizard talk," Steel said, deeply troubled. "Omens, that sort of thing. She said"—he paused, hesitated—"she says my death is necessary or else the knighthood will fall. She has foreseen it, she says."

"Rot!" Trevalin snorted. He lowered his voice. "I know our lord sets great stock in these magic-users, but you and I are soldiers. We know that the future is what we make it, with this." He rested his hand on his sword's hilt. "You are a valiant warrior, Brightblade. You served our queen well. You should be rewarded . . . I don't suppose I can persuade you, one last time, to speak to Lord Ariakan?"

Steel hesitated. The thought of leaving this foul jail cell, of being returned to his command, of once again riding into battle, was almost too much for him, almost overcame his resolve. This was a glorious hour for Lord Ariakan, for their queen. The armies of the Knights of Takhisis were thundering across Ansalon. No one was able to stop them. Palanthas had already fallen. The knights were preparing to go to war against the elves. And Steel would miss it. Manacled, chained hand and foot, he was working at slave labor. In another fortnight, he would be walking out that cell door the last time, to his own execution.

He had only to speak to Lord Ariakan, but to tell him what? The truth?

"I am sorry, Subcommander," Steel said with a faint smile at Trevalin's obvious disappointment. "I have nothing to say."

Trevalin gazed at him in silence, hoping he would change his mind.

Steel stood silently, unbending.

Trevalin shook his head. "I am sorry, too, Brightblade. Well, I have done all I could." He rested his hand briefly on Steel's arm. "Our talon leaves this day. We are being sent to aid the fighting in Northern Ergoth. I could have used you. I shall not see you again, I suspect. Her Dark Majesty be with you."

"And with you, Subcommander. Thank you."

Trevalin turned on his heel, left, just as the jailer entered.

"Time for work detail, Brightblade."

Steel moved slowly, stalled for time. He did not want Trevalin to see him being led ignominiously out of his cell in chains, to be lined up with the other prisoners, marched off to the quarries. When he was certain he could no longer hear Trevalin's footsteps, Steel walked out of the cell.

He joined a group of other prisoners, Knights of Solamnia who had either been captured during the battle or who had surrendered. Most were young—younger than Steel.

The Solamnic Knights knew he was the enemy. They believed he was responsible for Tanis Half-Elven's death. They had first thought him a spy in their midst. But then they had learned the truth from their guards, how Steel had lost a prisoner, had voluntarily returned to face his punishment, which was death. An act of such courage and honor earned him the young knights' grudging respect. They said little to him, but they no longer shunned him, spoke freely among themselves when he was among them. Occasionally—during the brief rest periods—they even attempted desultory conversation. Their attempts were coldly rebuffed.

Steel walked in a bleak despair that would admit no comfort.

Lord Ariakan was not harsh to his prisoners, but he was not kind to them either. He saw to it that they were adequately fed and watered—

a weak, sick man is not fit for hard labor—but he worked them mercilessly and did not spare the lash when he needed them to work harder. Ariakan had won a great victory, but he hadn't yet won the war.

He knew dragons, knew that they couldn't be trusted. He guessed that the silver and gold monsters had flown away to regroup, summon others of their kind, were preparing to return to attack in force. He kept his troops on alert, worked his prisoners day and night, rebuilding, repairing, refortifying the High Clerist's Tower.

The prisoner knights had expected Steel to use his rank and his allegiance to garner favors from the guards. Steel could have done so, in fact. His enemies were not the only ones to admire him. His voluntary return to face his punishment, his bravery in battle, his subsequent stoic acceptance of his own imprisonment and execution were praised nightly around the watch fires.

But Steel scorned to accept any favors. He did not deserve them.

Therefore, he threw back the extra food the guards gave him, thrust away the extra dipper of water. He worked side by side with the captured Solamnic Knights: stone-cutting in the mountain quarries, hauling the huge blocks back to the tower, struggling to fit them into place. All the work was done in the glaring light of the merciless sun. But he was never struck, never lashed like the other prisoners. So bound up was he in his misery that he had never noticed this difference.

The prisoners were marched off to the quarry as usual. Their task was to load giant blocks of granite onto large wooden sleds, which were then dragged by the huge mammoths to the tower. The blocks were pulled by ropes up a ramp, onto the sled. Prisoners, positioned behind the blocks, shoved them along the incline.

Steel's thoughts were centered on Trevalin, on his talon. He imagined his comrades flying into what was bound to be a challenging fight with the Ergothians, humans of enormous courage and prowess, who had held their lands all during the War of the Lance and who were determined to hold them now.

Steel pictured the engagement, fought the battle in his imagination. The guide rope he was supposed to be holding went slack. Warning cries and shouts jolted him from his reverie. The huge block of granite, half on the sled and half off, had tilted, tipped, and overturned the sled.

"Clumsy bastard! Pay attention to what you're doing!" The overseer snarled and struck out with his lash. He did not strike Steel. He struck the young knight standing next to Steel.

The whip laid open the flesh of the young knight's bare back; the blow knocked him to the ground. The overseer stood over him, whip raised, ready to strike again.

Steel caught hold of the overseer's arm.

"The fault was mine," Steel said. "He did nothing. I let go of the rope."

The overseer stared at Steel in astonishment. So did the other prisoners, who had all ceased work, were watching in disbelief.

The overseer recovered himself. "I saw it all. The Solamnic—"

"—did nothing to merit punishment." Steel shoved the overseer aside. "And don't call me knight. I am a knight no longer. And don't do me favors, ever again."

He walked over, helped the young Solamnic to his feet. "I am sorry this happened, sir. It won't happen again. Will you accept my apology?"

"Yes," murmured the knight. "Yes, of course."

Satisfied, Steel went back to the overseer. "Strike me."

The overseer grunted. "You're wasting time. Get back to work."

Steel repeated, "Strike me. As you struck him. Or else I will report you to my lord for dereliction of duty."

The overseer was, by now, angry enough at Steel for making a fool of him that he welcomed inflicting the blow. He brought the lash across Steel's bare shoulders, flaying the skin almost to the bone.

Steel bore the pain without flinching. No grimace crossed his face. No cry escaped his lips. The overseer struck once more, then, with a snarl, turned away.

Seeing his punishment was finished, Steel went back to work. His back was raw, bleeding. Flies began to buzz around the open wounds.

The overseer began to harangue the other prisoners, urging them to shift the block onto the sled. The young knight took advantage of this opportunity to draw near Steel, awkwardly offering his thanks.

Steel turned away. He wanted no thanks; he had not done this out of any misguided sense of compassion. The sting of the lash had returned him to reality. He had no right to even imagine himself as one of Takhisis's chosen. The Dark Queen knew his guilt.

He could have entered the mage's laboratory—that was the knowledge that tormented him. The door held open a moment for him. He could have gone in after Palin, but he had hesitated, only a moment, unwilling to walk into that gibbering, whispering, death-dealing darkness. And then the door had slammed shut.

Takhisis had seen into his heart. She knew him for a coward. She had refused to grant him an honorable death, and now, apparently, she wanted him further punished. He would not stand by and see another punished in his place.

Steel lifted the guide rope, returned to his work. The salt sweat running into his wound stung like fire. He was, now, like all the other prisoners.

Except that in a fortnight, in the dawn of the day celebrated as Midsummer's Eve, if Palin Majere did not return or was captured, Steel Brightblade would die. And if, as the Nightlord had said, his death would save the knighthood, as his father's death had saved the Solamnic Knighthood, then, perhaps, he could feel more at peace.

But he would serve Chemosh for all eternity before he asked Takhisis to forgive the Nightlord.

II

Queen's Vengeance.
Raistlin's Choice.

asslehoff woke with a pain in his head and the feeling that he'd been trodden on by a woolly mammoth, such as the one he'd once helped rescue from an evil wizard.

Sitting up, rubbing his head, Tas demanded, "Who hit me?"

"You were in the way," Raistlin returned shortly.

Tas rubbed and blinked and saw more stars and wondered aloud. "Where am I?"

And then he remembered where he was. They were in the Abyss. The dragons' heads were glowing very brightly now, and they had to get back through the Portal.

"Come over here, kender," Raistlin ordered. "I need your help."

"They always need my help," Tasslehoff muttered. "*After* they knock me down because I'm in the way. And my name's Tasslehoff," he added, "in case you forgot."

He blinked some more, and finally the stars quit bursting long enough for him to see.

Raistlin was crouched over Palin, who lay, unconscious, on the gray ground. Tas picked himself up, hurried over.

"What's the matter with him, Raistlin? Is he going to be all right? He doesn't look at all well. Where did Kitiara go?"

The archmage glared at him. "Shut up."

"Sure, Raistlin," Tas said meekly. And he truly meant to. The next words just sort of popped out by mistake. "But I *would* like to know what happened."

"My beloved sister stabbed him, that's what happened. She would have finished the job, but I stopped her. She is no match for me, and she knows it. She has gone off to seek reinforcements."

Tas hunkered down beside Palin, inspected the wound. "It doesn't seem too bad," he said, relieved. "It's in his right shoulder, and there's not a lot of important parts in your right shoulder. He's passed out. Why—"

"Didn't I tell you to shut up?" Raistlin said.

"Probably." Tas sighed. He was feeling sad and low-spirited. "You usually do." He would have added more, but Palin groaned and began to twitch and writhe.

"What's wrong with him, Raistlin?" Tas asked, suddenly afraid for his young friend. "He looks like . . . like he's dying."

Raistlin shook his head. "He *is* dying. Palin has to return to his plane of existence quickly."

"But the wound isn't serious—"

"The blade that stabbed him was of *this* realm, kender, not your own. You managed to block her killing stroke, but the blade entered his flesh. The curse is already working on him. If he dies here, his soul will remain here—a captive of Chemosh."

Raistlin rose to his feet, stared at the Portal. The eyes of the dragons stared back. The sky was gray, streaked with black strands, like tentacles, snaking out toward them.

Tas looked from Palin to the Portal to the sky and back to Palin. "I suppose I could drag him that far, but what would I do for him once I got him back inside the laboratory?" He thought a moment, then brightened. "I know! Maybe there's a magic spell you could teach me that I could use on him. Will you, Raistlin? Will you teach me some magic?"

"I have sinned enough against the world," Raistlin said dryly. "Teaching magic to a kender would ensure my damnation." He frowned, pondering.

"You have to go back with him, then, Raistlin," Tas said. "I suppose you *can* go back?"

"I can go back," Raistlin said. "My physical body did not die in the world. I may return to it. The question is, why would I want to? The only pleasure I ever found in that world was in my magic. And if I returned, do you suppose the gods would let me keep my powers?"

"But what about Palin?" Tas argued. "If he stays here, he'll die!"

"Yes." Raistlin sighed. "What about Palin?" The archmage smiled bitterly, gazed with enmity up into the dark sky. "So I am to go back. Is that what you want? Weak and defenseless as I am! Thus do you, my queen, have your revenge!"

All this made little sense to Tasslehoff. He reached out to give Palin a soothing pat. But when he touched Palin's skin, it was cold. The young man's lips were blue; the flesh starting to turn a sickly white.

"Raistlin!" Tas cried, gulping. "You better do something quick!"

Raistlin knelt swiftly at Palin's side, rested his hand on the young man's neck. "Yes, he's very far gone."

With sudden decision, he reached down, caught hold of Palin's shoulders. "Kender, you and I between us will carry him."

"My name's Tasslehoff. You seem to keep forgetting." Tas jumped to help, noticed something lying on the ground. He pointed. "What do we do with the staff?"

Raistlin stared at the Staff of Magius. The archmage's thin, nervous fingers twitched. He reached out to it suddenly, eagerly. "On second thought, there could be a way . . ."

And then his hand stopped, withdrew.

"You bring his staff, Kender," Raistlin said in a low voice. "I will take care of Palin. Hurry!"

"Me?" Tas could barely speak for the thrill. "Me? I get to carry the . . . the staff?"

"Quit dithering and do as you're told," Raistlin ordered.

Tas clasped his hand around the famed Staff of Magius, lifted it up. He'd longed to touch the staff from the very first moment he'd seen Raistlin holding it, back in the Inn of the Last Home.

"I'm ready!" Tas said, gazing up at the staff with pride.

Raistlin was not strong enough to lift Palin. The archmage placed his hands under the young man's shoulders, dragged him over the gray ground, and managed, by a great effort, to carry Palin to the Portal.

The dragons' heads gleamed with a strange, hideous beauty.

Raistlin halted, breathing heavily, and now, for the first time since he'd met him, Tas heard Raistlin begin to cough.

"Kender," he ordered in a choked voice, "raise the staff! Raise it high, so the queen can see."

Tas, thrilled to the very soles of his green shoes, did as he was told. He lifted the staff in the air as high as he could.

The dragons' heads shouted defiance, but the Portal remained open.

Tas walked into the Portal, holding the staff. It was the kender's proudest moment.

Raistlin, dragging Palin, followed. The dragons shrieked in deafening tones, but did not try to halt them.

The cool, dusty darkness of the laboratory closed over them. Raistlin laid Palin gently on the floor. The archmage straightened, took a step toward the Portal.

"I'm coming back into the Abyss," he cried. "Let me return! Do what you want to me, Takhisis. Don't leave me here, bereft of my power!"

Light flared, blinding light, painful to witness. Tas's eyes burned and watered; the lids wanted to shut, but Tas knew that if they did, he might miss something, and so he held them open with his fingers.

Raistlin, coughing, took another step toward the Portal. The light grew brighter still. Tas's eyelids outvoted him two to one and shut. The last he saw, Raistlin had lifted his arms as if to ward off a blow . . .

Raistlin cursed. Tas heard a swooshing sound, and the light went out.

Tas risked opening his eyes.

The velvet curtain hung, once again, over the Portal. A faint, mocking light shone from underneath. The rest of the laboratory was shrouded in black.

Raistlin stood in front of the curtain, staring at it. Then, abruptly, he turned away, disappeared into the darkness. Tas heard him walking away.

The darkness wasn't an ordinary darkness, the kind of darkness one liked to have in one's bedroom, the kind of darkness that was soft and woolly and lulled you into sleep and pleasant dreams. This was altogether a different sort of darkness, a chill, decaying, whispering darkness, a darkness that made you want to stay very much awake.

"Raistlin? Where are you?" Tas asked.

He wasn't afraid, not exactly, but he was starting to think that a little light would be a pleasant sort of thing to have about now. He was about to try to cause the staff to light. He knew the magic word—he was pretty sure he knew the magic word—and was just about to speak it when Raistlin's voice came from the darkness. His voice was like the darkness, chill, whispering.

"I am in the front part of the laboratory. Keep near Palin," Raistlin said. "Let me know if he moves or speaks. And put down that staff!"

Tas crept over to sit beside Palin. The kender heard Raistlin rustling about, then a light flared—a soft, comforting sort of light. Raistlin appeared, carrying a candle in a wrought-iron holder fashioned in the shape of a bird. He set the candle down beside Palin.

"I think he's somewhat better," Tas said, reaching out to touch Palin's forehead. "He's warmer, at least. But he's not awake yet."

"The curse still chills his blood, but he can be healed now." Raistlin eyed the kender. "Didn't I tell you to put down that staff!"

"I did!" Tas protested. Investigation proved—to his immense astonishment—that the staff was still in his hand. "My! Isn't that remarkable. I think it likes me. Perhaps I could make it light up—just once. What's that word you say to make the light go on? Shelac? Shirley? Shirleylac?"

With a grim expression, Raistlin took hold of the staff and, with some difficulty, pried the kender's fingers loose.

"Just once let me light it, Raistlin! Please! I'm sorry I took your magical eyeglasses that time. If I ever find them, I'll give them back to you. That's odd, isn't it, the way my fingers seem to have stiffened up like that . . ."

Raistlin wrenched the staff free. Removing the staff to a distant part of the laboratory, he stood it up against the wall. The archmage seemed as reluctant to part with it as the kender. Raistlin's hand caressed the wood. His lips moved in what might have been the language of magic.

But nothing happened.

Raistlin removed his hand and turned away. Going over to the gigantic stone table, he lit another candle, held it high, stared down at Palin.

"Tas?" Palin murmured in a weak voice.

"I'm here, Palin!" Tas forgot the staff, turned back to his patient. "How do you feel?"

"My arm burns . . . but all the rest of me is so cold," Palin answered through chattering teeth. "What . . . what happened?"

"I'm not really sure," Tas answered. "I said hullo and was going to shake hands, when the next thing I knew Kitiara had her sword and was about to stab you, and Raistlin bumped into me and I took a nap."

"What?" Palin was momentarily confused, then memory returned. He struggled weakly to sit up. "The Portal! The Dark Queen! We must . . . get back . . ."

"We are back," Tas said, gently pushing Palin down again. "We're in the laboratory. Raistlin's here, too."

"Uncle?" Palin stared up into the light that reflected off the golden-skinned face, framed by long white hair. "You came after all!"

"He came through the Portal to save you, Palin," Tas explained.

Palin's wan face flushed with pleasure. "Thank you, Uncle. I'm very grateful." He lay back, closed his eyes. "What did happen to me? I feel so cold . . ."

"You were struck by a cursed weapon from the Abyss," Raistlin explained. "Fortunately, the sword only harmed your flesh. If it had stabbed through to the heart, you would be serving Chemosh now. As it is, I believe I have something here that will give you ease."

Raistlin returned to the inner portion of the laboratory to examine a row of jars lined up on a dust-covered shelf.

"Who was that woman?" Palin asked, with a shudder. "Some minion of the Dark Queen's?"

"In a manner of speaking, yes, though I've no doubt she was not acting on orders, but furthering her own pursuits. That was my sister," Raistlin replied, "your late aunt Kitiara."

"We certainly have been running into a lot of old friends lately," Tas said. "Well, I guess you couldn't call Kitiara a friend now, but she was once, long ago. Why, I remember the time she saved me from a bugbear in a cave. How was I supposed to know that bugbears sleep all winter and wake up hungry? But she's gone." Tas heaved a sigh. "And now Tanis is gone, too. So many . . . gone. At least," he added, cheering up a bit, "we have you back, Raistlin."

"So it seems," Raistlin replied, and almost immediately he went into a fit of coughing. The fit doubled him over. He clutched his chest, gasped for breath. At length, the spasm eased. Wiping his lips with the sleeve of his robe, he drew a ragged breath. "My return was unintended, I assure you."

"He tried to go back," Tas added, "and when he tried to go back, the heads screamed at us. It was really quite exciting. But then Raistlin shut the curtain. I don't suppose I could just take a peek? See if the heads are—"

"Don't go near it!" Raistlin snapped. "Or else you will find yourself taking another nap. And this one will not be brief!"

Finding the jar he wanted, the archmage took it down from the shelf, removed the stopper. He sniffed at it, nodded, and walked over to Palin.

Raistlin spread a bluish unguent over the wound.

"This may sting."

Palin grit his teeth, drew in a sharp breath. "I take it we weren't supposed to have been eavesdropping on the gods." He half sat up, peered at his shoulder, trying to see his wound. The lines of pain were smoothed from his face. He breathed easier and had stopped shivering. "That does feel better. Is it magic?"

"It is," Raistlin replied, "but not of my making. It was a gift, from a cleric of Paladine."

"Lady Crysania, I expect," Tasslehoff said, nodding wisely. "She thought quite a lot of you, Raistlin."

Raistlin's face was impassive, grim. Turning, he stood and walked back over to resume his examination of the shelves' contents.

"Tas!" Palin whispered, shocked. "Hush!"

"Why?" Tas whispered back crossly. He was feeling out of sorts. "It's the truth."

Palin cast an uneasy glance at his uncle, but—if Raistlin heard—he was ignoring them both.

Tas's head hurt. He was dreadfully unhappy to think that Tanis was gone and he'd never able to hear his laughter, see him smile, borrow his handkerchiefs. And now, to add to his misery, he was bored.

Tas knew very well that if he even so much as looked at a dead bat in this laboratory, Raistlin and Palin would both yell at him. And if they yelled at him, the ache in his chest would cause him to yell back at them and probably say some things that would hurt their feelings. Which would mean that one or the other might end up by turning him—Tasslehoff Burrfoot—into a bat, and while that sounded like fun . . .

Tasslehoff wandered over to the laboratory door. He tried to open it, but it wouldn't budge. "Drat! We're stuck in here!"

"No, we are not," Raistlin said coldly. "We will leave when I am ready to leave, not before."

Tas regarded the door thoughtfully. "It sure is quiet out there. Steel was hammering on this door like thunder when we left. I suppose he and Usha and Dalamar got tired and went to dinner."

"Usha!" Palin stood up, then almost immediately sagged back weakly in a chair. "I hope she's all right. You must meet her, Uncle."

"He's already met her," Tas pointed out. "Well, sort of. Since she's his daughter—"

"Daughter!" Raistlin snorted. He was shaking fragrant leaves from a large bag into a small leather pouch. "If she claims that, she's a liar. I have no daughter."

"She's not a liar. The circumstances were . . . um . . . singular, Uncle," Palin said defensively. He made his way from the chair to the corner where his staff stood, took hold of it. Almost immediately, he appeared to feel stronger. "You *could* have had a daughter and not known about it. Because of the Irda magic."

Raistlin coughed, started to shake his head, then looked up. "Irda? What have the Irda to do with this?"

"I . . . Well, it's a story that people tell about you, Uncle. Father never paid much attention to it. Whenever anyone would bring it up, he'd say it was all nonsense."

"I would be interested to hear this tale," Raistlin said with a hint of a smile on the thin lips.

"There are several versions, but—according to most—you and father were returning from your Test in the Tower of Wayreth. You were ill. The weather was turning bad. You both stopped at an inn to rest. A woman entered, asked to spend the night. She was muffled and cloaked. Some ruffians attacked her. You and father saved her. She tried to keep her face hidden, but her scarf fell off. She was beautiful," Palin said softly. "I know how you must have felt, Uncle, when you looked at her! I have felt the same way." He was silent, smiling, entering his own fable.

"And then what happened?" Raistlin asked, jolting the young man from his daydream.

"Well, um," Palin stammered. "To make a long story short, you and she . . . well, you, uh . . ."

"Made love," Tas said, seeing that Palin appeared rather confused on this point. "You two made love, only you didn't know it, because of the Irda magic, and she had a baby that had golden eyes, and the Irda came and took the baby away."

"I made love to a beautiful woman and I didn't know it. Just my luck," Raistlin said.

"That wasn't quite the way it happened. She'll have to tell you. You will like her, Uncle," Palin continued with enthusiasm. "She is charming. And kind, and very, very beautiful."

"All of which proves she is no child of mine," Raistlin returned caustically. He pulled the thong shut on the leather pouch, hung it carefully from his belt. "We had best leave now. We have a great deal to do and little time in which to accomplish it. Too many days have passed, I fear."

"Days? No, Uncle. It was midmorning when we left. It must be about twilight now." Palin paused, looked about the laboratory. "Don't you want to take any of your spellbooks? I'm feeling better. I could help you carry them—"

"No, I do not," Raistlin returned calmly, coldly. He did not glance in their direction.

Palin hesitated, then said, "Would you mind if I took them, then? I was hoping you might teach me some of the spells."

"Spells of the great Fistandantilus?" Raistlin asked, and he appeared highly amused. "Your robes would have to turn a lot darker than they are now before you could read those spells, Nephew."

Palin was calm. "Perhaps not, Uncle. I know that a Black Robe has never in the history of the Three Moons apprenticed a White Robe. But that doesn't mean it's not possible. Father told me how you once changed a life-draining spell into a life-giving spell, the time when Uncle Tas was poisoned in the Temple of Neraka. I know the work will be arduous and difficult, but I will do anything—sacrifice anything," he added emphatically, "to gain more power."

"Would you?" Raistlin gazed at Palin intently. "Would you really?" He lifted an eyebrow. "We will see, my nephew. We will see. And now"—he strode toward the door—"we must leave. As I said, time grows short. It is twilight, but not of the day you left. A month has passed on Ansalon."

Palin gasped. "But that's not possible! It . . . it's only been hours . . ."

"To you, perhaps, but time as we know it on this plane of existence means nothing in the realm of the gods. A month ago this day, Lord Ariakan rode in triumph through the gates of the High Clerist's Tower. Once that fell, nothing could stop him. The city of Palanthas is now ruled by the Knights of Takhisis."

Tas was at the door, his eye to the keyhole, trying to see out. "What if the specter's still there?"

"The guardian is gone. Dalamar is here, but he will not be staying long. Soon, as in the days after the Cataclysm, the tower will be deserted."

"Dalamar, gone! I . . . can't believe it." Palin seemed dazed. "Uncle, if the dark knights are in control, where will *we* go? No place will be safe."

Raistlin did not reply.

There was an eerie quality to his silence.

"I have dreamed of it . . . for so long," Raistlin said softly. "We will go home, Nephew. I want to go home."

BOOK 4

I

A CHANGING WORLD. THE INN.
AN UNEXPECTED VISITOR.

With the fall of Palanthas came the fall of northern Ansalon. The great and ancient city secured, its wealth in hand, its port open to the black dragon ships, Ariakan lost no time in seizing all the land that he could take easily, while building up his forces for the battles that would be difficult and long-fought.

Rumor turned out to be his best weapon. It spread faster than even his knights on their blue dragons could fly. Tales of armies led by Lord Soth, armies formed of skeletal warriors, who butchered any living being and drank their blood, were whispered everywhere, believed everywhere. Dragonfear added to the terror, as did tales of the cruel barbarians, who were said to spit children on their spears and roast them alive over their fires. By the time his troops reached most major cities, the citizens were in such a panic that they flung wide the gates and invited the dark knights to enter without a fight.

A month had passed, and Ariakan controlled Nordmaar, eastward through the Khalkist Mountains, south as far as the Plains of Dust, west into Solamnia and Abanasinia. Northern Ergoth still held out, its darkskinned seafaring race battling fiercely, refusing to give in. The hill dwarves were said to be mounting stiff resistance in the Khalkists, where renegade draconians had entered the fray. Ariakan had not yet attempted to take the elven lands of Silvanesti and Qualinesti. He knew that such a battle would be costly; he hoped instead that the fruit would fall into his hand, rotted from the inside.

The Plains of Dust he ignored, for the time being, as being worth very little. When the remainder of the continent was in his control, then he would pick off the scattered tribes of Plainspeople, led by the cleric Goldmoon and her husband, Riverwind.

As for the gnomes of Mount Nevermind, they, unfortunately, fell to themselves. Having heard rumors of the dark knights' planned invasion, the gnomes feverishly launched into operation all their most powerful war machines. No one was exactly certain what went wrong, but a powerful explosion rocked Northern and Southern Ergoth. An enormous cloud of black, acrid smoke appeared in the sky, hung over the mountain for a week. When the smoke cleared, most of the top of the mountain was said to be missing. Casualties were reported to be high, but the sounds of clanking and banging could once more be heard echoing from the mountain. In gnomish philosophy, there is no such thing as a disaster—merely opportunity.

Kendermore did not fall without a fight, due mainly to the efforts of the kender's cunning war leader, Paxina, the daughter of Kronin Thistleknot, a hero of the Dragon Wars. Paxina "Stinging" Thistleknot had heard that Lord Ariakan had deemed the kender "worthless nuisances" and planned to have all kender rounded up and put to death. Paxina announced this to her people, hoping to rally them to battle. She received shrugs, yawns, and "So what else is new?" in return.

Something else was needed to stir kender blood. Paxina thought the matter over, then started a rumor that the dark knights were coming to loot Kendermore, steal all the kender's most prized possessions.

This did the trick.

Appalled, the kender put up such a stiff resistance that, even though he crushed them, they managed to win Ariakan's admiration. He determined that the kender might prove useful after all, if they could be convinced to serve the Dark Queen. Thus Kendermore survived, much to the disgruntlement of those knights forced to serve there.

Within a matter of weeks, Lord Ariakan was ruler and master over more territory than the Dragon Highlords had been able to gain during the War of the Lance. This with fewer casualties, on both sides.

Life changed for the conquered, but only in subtle ways not readily apparent. Those who feared wholesale butchery and slaughter, such as they had witnessed during the last war, were surprised to find that the knights treated those they conquered fairly, if harshly. Strict laws were laid down and coldly, dispassionately, sometimes brutally enforced. Schools, except for those teaching the lessons of the Dark Queen, were closed. Any wizard caught outside the bounds of the Tower of Wayreth was in peril. Those who broke the laws were put to death. No arguments, no appeals. The rollicking town of Flotsam, known for its rough and rowdy citizenry, was, by the end of the month, subdued, quiet, peaceful.

There were some who maintained that this peace was good. It was about time the land was quiet, made safe for honest men. There were others who thought that this peace, bought in exchange for their freedom, was obtained at too high a price.

*　*　*　*　*

Tika Waylan Majere shut the door on the last customer, dropped down the heavy wooden bar, and heaved a sigh. She did not immediately return to her work—and there was plenty of it: mugs to be washed and dried, plates scraped and carried to the kitchen, tables to be cleaned. Tika stood at the inn's door, her head bowed, twisting her apron in her hands. She stood so long, so silently, that Caramon left off wiping down the bar and came over to his wife.

He put his arms around her. She leaned back against him, clasped her hands over his wrists.

"What's wrong?" he asked softly.

Tika shook her head. "Nothing." She sighed again. "Everything." Her hand wiped across her eyes. "Oh, Caramon! I never used to be glad when I shut the inn up at night. I used to be sorry to see the last customer go. But now I'm sorry when I open it up in the morning. Everything's changed! It's all changed!"

Turning around, she buried her face in her husband's chest and began to sob. Caramon stroked her red hair soothingly.

"You're just tired, dear. The heat's getting to you. Come, sit down. We'll let this all go until morning. Dirty dishes won't go anywhere, and that's a fact. Here, you rest, and I'll fetch you a glass of cool water."

Tika sat down. She didn't really want a glass of water, which would be tepid at best. Nothing stayed cool in this heat, not even the ale. Their customers were learning to like warm beer. But waiting on her made Caramon happy, and so she sat and let him fuss over her, bringing in water and her favorite cookies and shooing away Raf, the gully dwarf, who had come in from the kitchen, eager to "clean" the plates, which he did by devouring all the leftover food.

No one ever needed a garbage pail with a gully dwarf around.

Tika could hear the disappointed Raf wailing in the kitchen. Caramon, his face grim, flung in a stale loaf of bread and slammed the door shut again. The wail subsided.

Tika nibbled on a cookie. She wasn't hungry, but if she didn't eat, Caramon would continue to fuss and worry over her until she did. As it was, he smiled broadly, sat down beside her, and patted her hand.

"I knew those cookies would tempt your appetite."

"They're delicious, dear," Tika said, lying. The cookies tasted like dust. Everything tasted like dust to her these days. But Caramon, seeing her eat, brightened with pleasure, and somehow his pleasure flavored the cookies. She found herself eating another one.

"Oh, Caramon." Tika sighed. "What are we going to do?"

"About what?"

"About . . . well, about . . . this." She waved a hand vaguely.

"About the dark knights? Not much we can do about them, my dear," Caramon said solemnly. "They've improved business, I'll give them that." He was silent a moment, then said quietly, "Some people are saying this occupation isn't such a bad thing."

"Caramon Majere!" Tika flared. "How *could* you?"

"I didn't say it," Caramon pointed out. "I said some people were saying it. And they have a point. The roads are safe. When this heat lets up—and it's sure to do so any day now—people will be traveling again. The knights are gentlemen. Not like the draconians who held the town during the last war. Ariakan didn't send his dragons in to burn the place down. His soldiers don't steal. What they buy they pay for. They don't get drunk; they're not rowdy. They're—"

"Not human," Tika finished bitterly. "They're like some weird gnome machine that's taken it into its head to be human, but inside it's still a machine. These knights have no heart, no feelings about anything. Yes, they're polite to me, but I know perfectly well that if they were ordered to slit my throat for their Dark Queen's glory, they'd do it in a moment."

"Well, there is that . . ." Caramon admitted.

"And what about—" Tika's storm was building, gaining in fury. She ate four more cookies. "What about the people who've just disappeared? People like Todd Wainwright."

Caramon's face darkened. "Todd's been begging for trouble for a year. He's a brawling ruffian. I've either thrown him out or carried him out feetfirst more than once. You yourself told him not to come back here."

"That may be true," said Tika crisply, "but the Dark Queen's soldiers didn't take Todd away because he was a mean drunk. They took him away because he didn't fit into their grand plan, because he was a troublemaker and a rebel."

"Still, things *are* more peaceful without him around," Caramon argued. "They have to maintain law and order—"

"Peace!" Tika sniffed. "Law and order. We've got that, all right. We have laws enough to choke a gully dwarf. *And* order. Some people fear change, fear anything different. They walk the safe, well-traveled path because they're afraid to leave it. This Ariakan has carved a nice little rut in the road, and he expects everybody to walk in it. Anyone who doesn't, who wants to take a side path or leave the road altogether, is spirited away in the middle of the night. You'd be safe and sound in the bottom of a dark, dry well, Caramon Majere, but I don't suppose you'd accomplish much."

Caramon nodded. He'd said nothing during Tika's tirade, but had very quietly set about slicing a loaf of bread, adding some cheese to it, and put it in front of his wife. Having finished the cookies, Tika began on the bread and cheese.

"They've stopped the elven wars," Caramon mentioned.

Tika tore into a hunk of bread voraciously, chewed it as though she were chomping down on the detested knights. "By turning Tanis's own son into one of their mindless machines," she mumbled between bites.

"*If* you believe Porthios," Caramon said calmly. "He claims Gilthas is considering selling out to the knights to save his own skin. I've met young Gil, and I think better of him than that. He is Tanis's son, remember, and Laurana's, too. The dark paladins killed his father. I'm not certain what game the young man is playing, but I'll bet it isn't one the knights think he's playing. Qualinesti hasn't fallen yet."

Tika shook her head, but didn't argue. Talking about Tanis still upset her; the night Laurana came to tell them the sad news of his death was etched vividly in her mind: the three of them sitting together in the darkness because they were afraid of lighting a lamp, speaking, through their tears, of old times.

"Besides," Caramon continued, unobtrusively slicing up more cheese and shoving it toward his wife, "bad times have a way of bringing people together—like we saw during the War of the Lance."

"Few examples and far between," Tika muttered. "Most were too happy to run up the white flag, and Takhisis take their neighbors."

"Now, my dear, I have a better opinion of people than that," Caramon said. "And how about a bit of dortberry pie to finish off?"

Tika looked down, saw bread crumbs and cheese crumbs and cookie crumbs, and she began to laugh. Her laughter changed swiftly to tears, but they were tears of love, not sorrow. She patted her husband's big hand.

"I see your plan now, and, no, I don't want any pie, not after all those cookies. I've eaten quite enough, thank you."

"About time, too. You've eaten more in ten minutes than you've eaten in ten days," Caramon said severely. "You've got to keep up your strength, Beloved." He gathered his wife in his arms. "I don't want to lose you, too," he added, in a husky voice.

Tika leaned against her husband, feeling, as she always did, that he was her best solace, her greatest comfort. "You won't lose me, dearest. I'll start taking better care of myself, I promise. It's just . . . I keep thinking about Palin." She sighed, looked out the window, into the darkness. "If his grave were out there, with the other two boys, at least I'd know . . ."

"His grave's not there because he's not dead," Caramon said.

"Caramon," Tika argued gently, "you know what Dalamar told us. . . . Palin and Tas went into that laboratory and never came out. It's been over a month and no sight or sound of them. . . ."

"He's *not* dead," Caramon said. He broke free of Tika's embrace. "I'll fix us each a cup of tarbean tea," he said, and headed for the kitchen.

Tika knew better than to go after him. Caramon had to work things out on his own. She heaved another sigh, then—looking at all the mess—sighed again and stood up. Wars and dark knights and evil dragons would come and they would go. Dirty dishes would be around forever.

She was stacking plates when she heard the sound. Uncertain whether she'd heard rightly, what with the crockery clattering, Tika ceased her work, held her breath, listening.

Nothing.

She tried to identify the noise.

Footsteps on the stairs. Footsteps that were soft, stealthy.

She did not hear the sound again, though she kept quiet for a long time. Shrugging, deciding that it must have been the cat, she began stacking dishes again. She had gathered them all on a tray, had picked the tray up, was holding it in her hands, on the way to the kitchen, when she heard metal scraping against wood.

Turning, she watched the bar across the door rise, completely of its own accord. It lifted. The door began to swing open.

Tika dropped the tray—with a crash—and reached for a skillet. Swiftly, she darted behind the door. Any dark knights who tried to take her or her husband or her little girls would get a cracked head for their pains. . . .

"What the—?" Caramon came barging out of the kitchen.

"Shh!" Tika put her finger to her lips, raised the skillet.

Someone opened the door a crack, stepped inside. Tika couldn't get a good look; he was wearing a gray cloak, despite the heat. She could see only her target, the back of his head. She aimed . . .

Caramon gave a great roar and surged forward, knocking aside tables and smashing chairs.

"Palin!" Tika whispered. Too stunned to move, she collapsed back against the wall and watched, with tear-filled eyes, her husband fold their son in his embrace.

"Where's Mother?" Palin asked, searching around.

"Hiding behind the door," Caramon said through his own tears. "Getting ready to whomp you one!"

Tika, flushing, flourished the skillet, then dropped it with a clang and ran to her son.

"Palin, dear Palin!" She wept and laughed. "All these days I've prayed for you to come back to us safely and, when you do, I nearly bean you! I thought you were . . . one of them."

"It's all right, Mother," Palin said, hugging her close. "I understand. I know what's happening around here. We've spoken to Dalamar."

"We?" Tika glanced past him.

Palin stepped back to face his parents. "Mother, Father. Someone else is with me, someone you haven't seen in a long, long time. He wanted me to tell you first. He . . . wasn't certain he'd be welcome. . . ."

With a wild, pain-filled cry, Caramon rushed for the door, flung it wide.

A figure clad in black robes, dark against the darkness, stood on the stoop. At the sight of Caramon, the figure drew back the cowl covering his head. Light streaming out of the inn glistened on golden skin, shone in hourglass eyes.

"Raist!" Caramon cried, and swayed on his feet.

Raistlin looked long at his brother, did not move from his place outside the door.

"Caramon," he said at last, softly, and the name seemed wet with his heart's blood. "Caramon, can you . . . can you . . ." He began to cough, but he struggled to continue to talk. "Forgive . . ."

Caramon reached out, drew his brother inside. "Your room is ready for you, Raist. It always has been."

2

Regrets. Instructions.
Choices.

he rising sun, fierce and fiery, even this early in the day, glittered in the stained-glass windows of the inn. The twin brothers sat watching it. Tika had long ago gone to bed, as had Palin—still somewhat weak from his wound. Caramon and Raistlin had stayed up. They were awake all night, talking first of the distant past, of past times, of past mistakes and past regrets.

"If you'd known how it would turn out, would you have chosen differently, Raist?" Caramon asked.

"No," Raistlin returned with a hint of his old irritability. "For then it would not have been me doing the choosing."

Caramon didn't quite understand, but he was accustomed to not understanding his brother and he didn't let it worry him. He understood enough. He began to tell his brother about the family.

Raistlin sat hunched in a corner of the booth, nursing in his hands a cup of the tea that soothed his cough. The archmage listened to Caramon's stories, saw Palin and his brothers clearly in his mind, knew things about them that Caramon did not. All those years spent on that distant plane, peaceful in his deathlike slumber—such visions had been Raistlin's dreams.

It was not until the very darkest hour before the dawn that the two spoke of the present . . . and of the future.

Now Caramon gazed, troubled and disturbed, out the window, watching the sun rise through the brittle brown leaves of the vallenwood.

"The end of all things, you say," Caramon murmured. "Of *all things*," he repeated, turning to face his brother. "I know I'm going to die. Everything, even the elves, has to die. But . . . I always knew that this"— he made a gesture that encompassed window, tree, grass, dirt, and cloudless sky—"would still be here when I'm gone. You're saying nothing . . . *nothing* would remain?"

"When Chaos comes to destroy this 'plaything of the gods,' the ground will open, fire will spew up from the cracks. A wind with the fury of a thousand storms will roar down from the heavens, fan the flames. Fire dragons, ridden by fiendish warriors, will ride over the land, and soon the fire will consume everything. Lakes will evaporate, oceans boil. The air itself will be scorched; people will die just breathing it. No one, nothing will survive."

Raistlin spoke in a calm, detached voice that was utterly convincing, utterly frightening. His words sent a thrill of horror through Caramon.

"You sound like you've seen it," he said in a low voice.

"I have," Raistlin returned. His gaze shifted. He had been staring into the steam rising from the tea. Now he turned his gaze toward his brother. "You have forgotten what I see with these cursed eyes of mine. I see time as it moves forward and, thus, I have seen time stop."

"But it doesn't *have* to be like that," Caramon argued. "I've learned that much. The future is what we make it."

"True," Raistlin agreed. "There are alternatives."

"And?" Caramon persisted, eternally hopeful.

Raistlin stared back into the cooling tea. "I have told you the worst that can happen, my brother." He was thoughtful, silent, then added, "Or perhaps that was the best."

"What?" Caramon was shocked. "The best? People being burned alive! Oceans boiling! That's the best?"

"It depends on how you look at it, my brother." Raistlin shoved the tea away. "I can't drink that. It's grown cold." Coughing, he drew his robes closer around him, though it was already stifling inside the inn.

"We can't just sit here and do nothing!" Caramon protested, rising and heading for the kitchen. He returned with a kettle of hot water. "We'll fight, fight alongside the gods, if need be."

"Oh, yes," Raistlin said. "We will fight. And many of us will die. We might even win. And that could be the greatest loss of all."

"I don't understand, Raist—" Caramon began.

" 'I don't understand, Raist . . .' " Raistlin mimicked.

Caramon flushed uncomfortably, looked down at his feet.

Raistlin sighed. "This time, Caramon, I don't understand either. No, don't fix me any more tea. We haven't time. We have a long journey ahead of us."

"We? You . . . you want me to come?" Caramon asked hesitantly.

"Of course," Raistlin replied brusquely. "I need the support of your strong arm. And you are the only one who ever knew how to brew this properly." He waved his thin hand at the teacup.

"Sure, Raist. I'll go anywhere with you. Where are we going?"

"To the Tower of Wayreth. Dalamar will meet us there. He is calling a Wizards' Conclave."

"Then we'll be taking Palin with us . . ."

"No, Palin is going on another errand. He must journey to Palanthas."

"Alone?" Caramon frowned. "But he would be in danger on the

road—"

"He is not going by the road," Raistlin interrupted irritably.

"Ah, then you're going to magic him there," Caramon said.

"No, I am not," Raistlin said shortly. "Speaking of Palin, I must have a word with him. Come, come, my brother," Raistlin continued, noting Caramon still standing there, the teakettle in his hand. "Make haste! Every minute that passes is another minute closer to disaster. We need to be ready to leave in an hour."

"Sure, Raist," Caramon said, and he started to return to the kitchen.

In the doorway, he paused, watched his brother. Raistlin rose slowly to his feet, leaning on the table to help himself up. Once, long ago, he would have leaned on his staff. Pausing, he picked up the bag containing the tea mixture and hung it from the belt around his thin waist. No other bags dangled from his belt, no smell of rose petals clung to him. He carried no scroll case, no book . . .

And then, for once, Caramon understood.

"They've taken away your magic, haven't they, Raist?" he said softly.

Raistlin was silent for long moments, then said—oddly, "I notice you drink nothing stronger than water, my dear brother."

"Yes," Caramon said steadily. "But what—?"

Raistlin carried on, as if he hadn't heard. "Why? Why nothing but water?"

"You know why, Raist. The dwarf spirits take hold of me. Once I start, I can't quit. . . ." Caramon paused, his face twisted in a puzzled frown. "Do you mean it's the same? You . . . ?"

"I might not have been able to resist the temptation," Raistlin said quietly.

"But . . . what's coming. Won't we need you?"

"We have Palin," Raistlin said.

Caramon's flush vanished. He was pale, unhappy. "You can't mean that, Raist. He's young yet and he's not high ranking—"

"Neither was I, my brother," Raistlin said softly. "Neither was I."

Caramon swallowed. "Yes, but you . . . Well, you . . ."

"Had help?" Raistlin sneered. "Yes, I had help. Fistandantilus was with me. And so will Palin have help. So will Palin . . ." He coughed, sank back down in his chair. "But don't worry, my dear brother. Palin will have the choice, as did I."

Caramon did not find that knowledge at all comforting. He left his twin sitting at the table, watching the day dawn as hot as summer flame.

*　*　*　*　*

Palin came down to breakfast to find the house in turmoil. His mother stood at the bar, cutting hunks of the warm, fruit-laced bread she always baked whenever anyone in her family was traveling. "Walking bread," the boys called it, because they ate it while walking, though—as older brother Sturm once said jokingly—the bread was hard enough that it also could be walked on while eating.

The smell conjured memories both vivid and painful. Palin was forced to stop on the staircase and hold fast to the staff until the blurring cleared from his eyes and the choke from his throat. He descended just as Caramon emerged, carrying a large knapsack, which he deposited at the door.

"Father," said Palin, in astonishment, "are you coming with us to Wayreth?"

"He is coming with me, Palin," Raistlin said, turning. "I'm glad you are up. I was just going to wake you."

"But, I'm going with you, too," Palin protested. "I feel perfectly well. My shoulder is a little stiff, but I used more of that ointment this morning and the wound is healing—"

"What wound?" Tika said sharply, looking up from her work.

"A slight injury he suffered on his travels. Nothing serious," Raistlin returned.

"We'll see about that. Caramon, finish cutting this bread and then put some in those sacks. As for you, young man, sit down there where I can take a look at you. I wondered why you kept your cloak on last night."

"Mother!" Palin felt his cheeks burn. He cast his uncle an embarrassed glance. "It's all right, Mother, really. There's no need to fuss over me—"

"Tika," Caramon broke in, "there isn't time—"

She turned, hands on her hips. "Are dragons going to attack us in the next five minutes, Caramon Majere?"

"Well, no," Caramon began. "But—"

"Then there's time." Tika motioned to a chair. "Sit down, young man, and let me take a look at that shoulder. What did you do with the bloodstained robes? Hide them under your bed, like you used to when you were little?"

Palin sent out a silent plea for reinforcements, but his father had already been routed and was leaving the field. His uncle, a ghost of a smile on his face, came over to take a seat across from Palin.

"I need to give you instructions, Nephew," Raistlin said. "Besides, sometimes it is pleasant to be 'fussed over.' "

Caramon halted in his bread-cutting, stared at his brother in amazement. Then, smiling a little sadly, shaking his head, the big man began stuffing the bread into sacks.

Palin squirmed out of the sleeve of his robe, submitted to his mother's touch.

Tika poked and prodded and peered and sniffed, then, nodding, said, "It's healing well enough, but it should be washed out. There's little bits of fiber stuck to it. I'll be back."

She went to the kitchen for hot water and a cloth.

"And now, Nephew," said Raistlin, "here are your instructions. Your father and I are going to Wayreth. I want you to return to Palanthas . . ."

Palin opened his mouth to protest.

"That young woman you mentioned," Raistlin continued. "The one who claims to be my daughter. I want you to find her."

Palin shut his mouth on his protest. "Yes, Uncle," he said instead, so quickly and with such eagerness that his father, lifting his head, gave his son a long, hard look. "Do you believe her story, then?"

"No," Raistlin returned coldly, "but her connection with the Irda intrigues me."

"I'll be glad to find her for you, Uncle," Palin said, ignoring his father's grin, his teasing whistle, "but are you certain she's still in Palanthas?"

"According to Dalamar, she is. That sorceress companion of his keeps in contact with her. She'll know where the young woman can be found."

"You and Dalamar discussed this, then. Why didn't you include me?"

"You were resting," Raistlin said. "We did not want to disturb you. Here." He reached into a pocket of his black robes, withdrew an ordinary-looking ring, and handed it to Palin. "Take this. Dalamar has arranged for your transportation back to Palanthas."

"*He* arranged," Palin repeated with a sigh. Taking the ring, barely glancing at it, he thrust it into a pouch, "Because I could not do so myself. But, you, Uncle. *You* could cast the *Span Land and Time* spell. I would like to hear it, even though I can't yet cast it— What is it, Father? What do you want?"

Palin had gradually become aware of his father, frowning at him and shaking his head.

"Your uncle's not feeling well this morning, Son," Caramon said sternly. "Do what he tells you and don't badger him."

Palin noted that Raistlin did look extremely pale. "I didn't mean— Of course, if you're not well . . ."

"I am well," Raistlin retorted, "at least as well as I ever am. You deserve to know the truth. I have no magic anymore, Nephew. It was taken from me. That was the condition I was forced to make in order to return to this plane of existence."

"And you didn't want to return. You came because of me. Uncle, I—"

"Do not pity me," Raistlin snarled. The golden eyes glared fiercely, hotter than the sun.

Palin, startled, fell silent.

"I take it as a compliment," Raistlin said, his anger cooling. "It is a sign that she fears me still. But enough talk. Caramon, we should be on our way. Go say your good-byes to Tika and give her my thanks for the hospitality. I want to have a few words in private with Palin."

"Sure, Raist," Caramon said, but he didn't move. He glanced uncertainly at his son.

"Go along, Caramon," Raistlin repeated. He was about to add something further, but his words were cut short by a spell of coughing. "Go!" he gasped. "Don't you see how you upset me?"

Caramon hesitated, looked from his son to his twin brother. Then he left, reluctantly, heading for the kitchen.

When they were alone, Raistlin beckoned Palin to come nearer. He spoke in a whisper, his throat raw from coughing. "When you have located this young woman, I forget her name—"

"Usha," Palin said softly.

"Don't interrupt me! I barely have breath enough to speak as it is. I repeat, when you have found her, take her with you to the Great Library. I will meet you there the day after tomorrow, on midnight of Midsummer's Eve."

"I understand, Uncle," Palin replied, subdued. "Midnight of Midsummer's Eve. I will be there."

Raistlin relaxed, breathed easier.

"And now, Nephew, you had best go say your own good-byes and be on your way. The ring is simple to use. Put it on your finger, form an image of Palanthas in your mind, and the spell will carry you there."

"Yes, Uncle," Palin said, adding bitterly, "Of course it's simple. I couldn't handle anything complicated."

Raistlin regarded him silently a moment, then, reaching out, he rested his wasted hand on Palin's bare shoulder. The archmage's touch was unnaturally hot, almost burning. Palin flinched beneath it, forced himself to hold still as the thin fingers bit into his flesh.

Raistlin bent near and his whispering words brushed against Palin's cheek. "You will be made the offer, as I was. You will be given the choice."

"When?" Palin grasped his uncle's hand. "Soon? How will I know?"

"I can say no more." Raistlin straightened, drew back. "I have said more than I was supposed to. Choose wisely, Nephew."

"I will," Palin said, standing. "I've thought about this a long time. I know what choice I will make."

"Good for you, Nephew," Raistlin said, smiling, and there was a chill in the smile.

Shivering, feeling again the touch of the cursed blade, Palin drew his robe up around his injured shoulder.

"And now, go fetch your father, young one," Raistlin ordered. "Time moves, and we are standing still."

3

Brothers. Together again.

ong ago, during the reign of the Kingpriest of Istar, the world was ruled by the forces of good—at least, that is what they termed themselves. Some people questioned whether prejudice, intolerance, hatred, and persecution were truly virtues of Paladine, but the Kingpriest had covered these sins in fine, expensive white robes until not even he saw the corruption beneath.

The Kingpriest and his followers feared all who were different from themselves. This was a long list and grew daily, but magic-users were at the top. Mobs attacked wizards of any allegiance, stormed their towers, torched their schools, stoned them or burned them at the stake. The wizards, with their power, could have fought back, but they knew that to do so would bring more bloodshed and mayhem. They chose to retreat, and they left the world to hide in the one place that was safe: the Tower of High Sorcery at Wayreth.

And that was where the wizards went now, except—ironically—they were not fleeing the forces of light. They were fleeing the forces of darkness.

It is said that you never find the Tower of Wayreth if you go hunting for it. The tower finds you, and whether or not that is good or bad depends on your motive in coming. You may fall asleep in a field of grass one night, only to wake up and find a wilderness surrounding you the next morning. What that wilderness decides to do with you is up to the mages in the tower.

All creatures are wary of the tower. Not even dragons—of any color or allegiance—will fly near it. The black dragon, sent by Dalamar to bear Raistlin and Caramon swiftly and safely over the Kharolis Mountains to the general vicinity of the tower, would go no closer than the road.

The black dragon set them down, stood restless and uneasy, flapping its wings and craning its neck, sniffing the air and apparently finding whatever it smelled little to its liking. It clawed the ground and eyed Raistlin askance, anxious to leave, but careful to show the archmage no disrespect. Caramon helped his brother dismount, removed the two knapsacks. The dragon lifted its head, looked eagerly to the sky.

"You have leave to go," Raistlin told the creature, "but do not go far. Keep watch along this road. If we do not find what we seek, we will need your services again."

The dragon inclined its head; red eyes flashed. It spread black wings and, powering itself off the ground with its hind legs, leapt into the air and soared back northward.

"Ugh," complained Caramon, grimacing and tossing the two knapsacks onto the ground in disgust. "The smell! Like death warmed over. Takes me back to that time in Xak Tsaroth, when the black dragon captured you and would have finished all of us if it hadn't been for Goldmoon and the blue crystal staff."

"Did it? I don't remember," Raistlin remarked offhandedly. Bending over, he searched through his own knapsack. He picked out two or three pouches, which he himself had packed before they had left, and hung them on his belt.

Caramon was staring at him in astonishment. "You don't remember? Bupu and the Highbulp and Riverwind dying and coming back to life and—"

Raistlin stood on the dusty road, gazing out across a field of dry, parched wheat. He looked long and hard, searching for something, apparently not finding it. He frowned, his lips compressed, and he shook his head.

"Time," he muttered. "Time is slipping away! What can those fools be doing?"

"You don't remember Xak Tsaroth? Any of that?" Caramon persisted.

Raistlin turned his head to his brother. "What were you saying? Oh. The war." He shrugged. "I remember some, now that you mention it. But it all seems to have happened to another person, not to me."

Caramon regarded his brother sadly, uneasily.

Raistlin shrugged again, turned away. "We have more pressing problems, my dear brother. The forest is not here."

"Seems to me it's never here when you want it," Caramon grumbled. "Act as if we *don't* want it. Mark my words, you'll find it standing right on top of us. I wonder if there's a creek around anywhere, one that hasn't dried up. I've got to wash this dragon slime off my hands before I vomit."

He gazed around. "Maybe that grove of trees over there. See, Raist? Near that giant willow? Willows grow where it's wet. Shall we head that way?"

"One way is as good as another, it seems," muttered Raistlin, in an ill humor.

The two left the road, struck out across the field. The way was difficult. Stalks of the dry, dead wheat thrust up out of the baked ground, jabbed through the leather soles of Caramon's boots, tore at the dragging hem of Raistlin's robes. The heat of late afternoon was stifling; the sun beat down mercilessly. Dust raised by their passing flew up into their faces, set Caramon sneezing and caused Raistlin to cough so that he was forced to lean on his brother's arm in order to remain standing.

"You wait here, Raist," Caramon said at last, when they were little more than halfway to the grove. "I'll go on."

Raistlin coughed, shook his head, clutched his brother's arm.

"What is it?" Caramon asked anxiously.

Raistlin gasped for breath, managed to whisper, "Hush! I heard . . . something."

Caramon glanced around swiftly. "What? Where?"

"Voices. In the grove." Raistlin drew a breath, choked.

"You're swallowing too much dust," Caramon said in concern. "What do we do? Go back?"

"No, my brother. That would look suspicious. We've made noise enough for an army of dwarves. We've been seen and heard. Now it is our turn. I want to get a look at whoever it is who is looking at us."

"Probably the farmer who owns this field," Caramon said. His hand crept to his side. Unobtrusively, he loosened his sword in its sheath.

"Come to do what? Harvest dead plants?" Raistlin asked caustically. "No. There's some reason the Forest of Wayreth is staying away from us when it knows I have great need to enter. I think this may be it."

"I wish you had your magic," Caramon growled, clomping through the dried-up field. "I'm not the swordsman I used to be."

"It doesn't matter. Your sword would avail you little against these. Besides, I am not defenseless. I had anticipated we might run into trouble." As he spoke, Raistlin reached into one of the pouches. "Ah, I was right. Look, in the shadows of those trees."

Caramon turned, squinted. "My eyes aren't what they used to be either. What is it?"

"Knights of the Thorn, the gray-robed wizards of Takhisis, six of them."

"Damn!" Caramon swore softly. "What do we do?" He looked back at his brother.

Raistlin had drawn his black hood well down over his face. "We use our brains instead of brawn, which means that you keep your mouth shut. Let me do the talking."

"Sure, Raist," Caramon said, smiling. "Just like old times."

"More than you know, my brother," Raistlin said softly. "More than you know."

The two walked on together; Raistlin leaned on Caramon's arm—but not his sword arm. They entered the grove.

The Gray Knights were waiting for them. Rising from the grass where they had been sitting, the knights formed a semicircle that almost immediately closed around them.

Raistlin lifted his head in feigned astonishment. "Why, greetings, Brethren. Where did you spring from?"

Removing his hand from his brother's arm, Raistlin slid both hands into the sleeves of his black robes. The mages tensed. But since Raistlin kept his hands in his sleeves, and addressed the knights as "brethren," they relaxed somewhat.

"Greetings, Black Robe," said one of the knights, a woman. "I am Nightlord Lillith. What business have you here?"

"The same as you, I imagine," Raistlin returned pleasantly. "I'm seeking to enter the Forest of Wayreth."

The Gray Knights exchanged frowning glances.

The Nightlord, obviously their leader, said, "We hear that Dalamar the Dark has called a Wizards' Conclave. We were hoping to attend."

"And so you should," Raistlin returned. "You would hear much that would astonish you, receive timely warnings—if you would listen. However, I doubt that's the true reason you want to attend the Conclave. How many of your brethren lie hidden around here?" He glanced about with interest. "Twenty? A hundred? Is that enough, do you think, to take the tower?"

"You mistake us," the Nightlord said imperturbably. "We pose no threat to you—our brethren, Brother."

Lillith bowed. Raistlin bowed in return. Straightening, the Nightlord pursued the conversation, all the while staring at Raistlin intently, trying to see the face that was hidden in the shadow of the cowl.

"What do you mean, timely warnings? Warnings against what?"

"Imminent peril. Ultimate destruction. Certain death," Raistlin said coolly.

The Nightlord stared, startled, then she laughed. "You dare to threaten us? The rulers of all Ansalon? How amusing. Tell Dalamar so, when you see him."

"That is not a threat," Raistlin said. "It is a certainty. And Dalamar did not send me. Caramon, why do you stand there gawking? You came here for water. Go and fetch it."

"Caramon!" the Nightlord repeated, turning to look at him. "Caramon Majere?"

"That's me," Caramon confirmed grimly, after an uncertain glance at his brother.

He was obviously reluctant to leave, but he did as he was told, though he made certain not to turn his back on the Gray Knights.

Walking sideways, he descended the hill, heading for the creek that was little more than a trickle of brackish water. He pulled out the waterskin, bent to fill it.

Raistlin, bereft of his brother's support, stepped closer to the gigantic willow, rested his back against it.

"Caramon Majere, so-called Hero of the Lance," the Nightlord said, her gaze going back to Raistlin. "Traveling in the company of a black-robed wizard. How strange."

Raistlin withdrew his hands from his sleeves, pulled back his cowl. "Not so strange—for brothers to travel together."

Caramon, looking at his twin, dropped the waterskin.

Raistlin's face was no longer gold-skinned. It was bone-white, as was the skin of his hands. His lips were bluish. The hourglass eyes stared out from dark, greenish hollows.

The Nightlord gasped, fell back a step. "Raistlin Majere! By Chemosh!" she cried. "You are dead!"

"So I am," said Raistlin softly. "Yet I stand before you. Here, touch me!" He stretched out his thin, ashen-skinned hand toward the Gray Robe.

"Keep away!" she commanded, drawing forth a silver skull pendant, which she wore on a silver chain around her neck. The other Gray Nights were all fumbling with spell components and scrolls.

"Put away your magic," Raistlin commanded scornfully. "I mean you no harm. As I said, I come bearing a warning. Our queen herself has sent me."

"Takhisis sent you?" the Nightlord asked dubiously.

"Who else?" Raistlin demanded. "Who else has the power to clothe my restless spirit in flesh and bone? If you are wise, you will leave this place at once, bear my warning to your lord—Ariakan."

"And what are we to say to Lord Ariakan?" The Nightlord, after the initial shock, was starting to regain her composure. She was eyeing Raistlin closely.

Caramon, retrieving the waterskin, was filling it with one hand, keeping the other near the hilt of his sword.

"Tell Ariakan this," Raistlin said. "His victory was hollow. He is now, in his moment of triumph, in greater danger than ever. Caution him not to relax his vigilance, but to increase it tenfold. Look to the north, for from that direction, doom will come."

"From where? The Knights of Solamnia?" Lillith scoffed. "Those who survived have surrendered to us and are now locked up in their own dungeons! I don't think they—"

"Do you dare mock the words of your queen?" Raistlin hissed. He stretched out both his hands. Fists closed, suddenly opened. "Beware her power!"

A blinding flash of light, accompanied by an explosion, burst amidst the Gray Knights, who flung up their arms to protect their eyes. Their leader, the Nightlord, lost her balance and slid halfway down the hill. A cloud of foul-smelling, greenish black smoke hovered on the hot, still air. When the smoke cleared, Raistlin was nowhere to be seen. All that remained was a charred spot on the grass.

Caramon dropped the waterskin again.

Lillith picked herself up. She appeared shaken, though she made an attempt to conceal her nervousness. The others gathered around her, taking care to avoid coming anywhere near the charred spot.

"What do we do, Nightlord?" asked one of the wizards.

"That was a message from our queen! We should take it immediately to Lord Ariakan," said another.

"I am aware of that," the Nightlord snapped. "Let me think." She glanced suspiciously at the charred spot, then looked at Caramon, who was standing in the creek, turning this way and that, staring around in perplexity. The smell of sulfur lingered on the air.

The Nightlord frowned. "Where is your brother?" she demanded.

Caramon scratched his head. "Beats the hell out of me, Lady," he answered.

Lillith regarded him long and searchingly. Her eyes narrowed. "I have the feeling this is some sort of trick. But"—she raised her hand, stopping the shocked outburst of her subordinates—"trick or not, Lord Ariakan needs to be warned that Raistlin Majere now walks this mortal plane. Perhaps he *was* sent by our queen. Perhaps he is here for his own purposes, as he came once before. Either way, he could be a nuisance."

The Nightlord glanced out across the barren field, in what was reputedly the direction of the Tower of Wayreth.

"And if Raistlin Majere walks free of the Abyss, you can be certain that his nephew, Palin Majere, came back with him. We've wasted time enough here. Let us be gone," she said. Gracefully waving her arm three times around her head, she vanished.

The other Knights of the Thorn were swift to follow. Casting a final, baleful glance at the charred patch, they muttered their incantations and, one by one, disappeared.

Caramon splashed out of the creek. Holding out his hands tentatively in front of him, he groped through the air. "Raist?" he whispered, baffled and awed. "Raist? Where are you? You . . . you won't leave me here . . . will you? Raist?"

"I am here, my brother," came a voice, tinged with smothered laughter. "But you must help me."

Caramon lifted his head, shocked to the core of his being. It was the willow tree that spoke.

He gulped, swallowed. "Uh, Raist . . ."

"*Inside* the tree, you thick-headed boob! Come around this direction!"

"Inside . . ." Caramon hastened around to the side of the tree near the charred spot on the ground. Hesitantly, fearfully, he parted the willow's long, dangling branches.

A hand—a white, wasted hand—beckoned imperiously to him from the willow's massive trunk.

Caramon breathed a sigh of relief.

"Raist! You're alive! But"—he sounded puzzled—"how did you get inside the tree?"

Raistlin snorted, but, when he spoke, he sounded well pleased with himself. "In the name of Hiddukel the Trickster, don't tell me you fell for that old ruse? Here, help me. I can't move. I'm caught on something."

Caramon took hold of Raistlin's hand, was vastly relieved to find that the flesh was warm. He followed the arm up, discovered his brother, gazing out at him from inside the trunk of the willow.

Understanding at last, Caramon began to chuckle, though his laughter had a shaky quality to it.

"I don't mind saying you gave me quite a scare, Raist. And you should have seen those Gray Knights! Their robes aren't gray any longer, most of 'em. Here, don't move. I see the problem. Your hood's snagged. Lean forward just a bit. I can't reach my hand in . . . Just a bit more . . . There! That's got it."

Raistlin emerged from the tree's interior. He began brushing off the dirt and cobwebs, shaking bits of bark out of his white hair.

Caramon regarded his brother with pride. "That was really something! The white paint and everything! When did you do that?"

"While we were on the back of the dragon," Raistlin said complacently. "Here, help me down to the creek. I need to wash this stuff off. It's beginning to itch."

The two descended to the creek bed. Caramon retrieved the waterskin. Raistlin laved his face and hands. The chill white of undead flesh bubbled away downstream.

"It was sure realistic. I thought you had your powers back," Caramon said.

"You mean you thought I'd lied to you about losing them," Raistlin countered tersely.

"No, Raist!" Caramon protested, a little too volubly. "I didn't. Truly. It's just . . . well . . . you might have given me a hint . . ."

Raistlin smiled, shook his head. "You have no power of dissembling, my dear brother. One look at your honest face and the Nightlord would have known all. As it was, she was suspicious, I think."

"Why didn't she stick around to investigate, then?"

"Because I had given her a perfect excuse to leave with her dignity still intact. You see, my brother, these Gray Robes were here with the purpose of attacking the Tower of Wayreth. They thought they could enter the forest unawares."

Raistlin lifted his head, gazed around intently. "Yes, I can sense the magic. They used various spells in an attempt to find the way in. They had no luck. I doubt the Nightlord wanted to return to Ariakan with news of her failure. Now they have news of a different sort to take him."

"You knew all this!" Caramon was admiring. "Before we even came?"

"Of course not," Raistlin returned, coughing a bit. "Here, just don't stand there. Help me up this hill. I knew we might meet trouble on the road and so I came prepared, that is all. Having heard from Palin some of the more interesting legends that are being told about me, I decided that it would be easy to take advantage of the situation. Some white paint on my face and hands, a bit of charcoal dust and some of Tika's pistachio nut paste under the eyes, a handful of flash powder, and— behold! The Dead Wizard from the Abyss."

"I might have figured the rest out, but the disappearing act. That was what boggled my mind." Caramon helped his brother up the small rise.

"Ah, that was an unexpected touch." Raistlin returned to the willow, pointed to the tree's interior. "I hadn't intended to do that. But when I leaned against the trunk, I felt a large crack. Glancing inside, I discovered a portion of the tree is hollow. Evidence within indicates that the local children have used it for a tree house. It was a simple matter for me to pop inside under cover of the explosion and the smoke. Less simple to get out, unfortunately."

"Well, all I can say is that you— What in the name of— Where in the Abyss did that come from?"

Caramon had been bending over to see inside the willow. Turning, he almost walked into a gigantic oak tree, which had not been there only moments before. He looked to his left and found another oak. On his right, still another. The dead field, the dried-up wheat, even the creek, were gone. He stood in a vast, dark forest.

"Relax, my brother. Have so many years passed that you have forgotten?" Raistlin again folded his hands in the sleeves of his robes. "The Forest of Wayreth has found us."

The trees parted. A path appeared, leading them deeper within.

Caramon eyed the forest grimly. He'd walked that path before, several times before. The memories it brought back were not happy ones. "Raist, one thing I don't understand. The Gray Knights laughed at your warning. Lord Ariakan will, too. They won't fight on our side . . ."

"They will, my brother," Raistlin said, sighing. "You see, there are no longer 'sides.' We all fight together. Or we all die."

Both stood a moment in silence. The rustle of the leaves of the trees sounded troubled, uneasy. The calls of the birds were hushed.

"Well," said Caramon, gripping his sword tightly, glaring balefully ahead into the enchanted wood, "I suppose we'd better get on with this."

Raistlin rested his hand on his brother's arm. "I will enter alone, Caramon. You go back home."

"And leave you?" Caramon was adamant. "No, I won't—"

"My brother," Raistlin chided gently, "you are falling into old habits again. I thank you for escorting me this far. I have no need of you any longer. Your place"—his grip tightened on his brother's arm—"is with your family and the people of Solace. You must return, prepare them to face what is coming."

"They won't believe me," Caramon said bluntly. "I'm not sure I believe it all myself."

"You will think of something, my brother," Raistlin said. Coughing slightly, he wiped his lips with a white cloth. "I have faith in you."

"You do?" Caramon flushed with pleasure. "You know, maybe I could put it out that I was forming a secret resistance movement. Then I—"

"Yes, yes," Raistlin interrupted. "Just don't get yourself hanged in the process. Now, I must be going. I've wasted time enough. Return to the road. The dragon will be watching for you, will carry you safely back."

Caramon looked extremely dubious, but he knew better than to argue. "Will you be coming too, Raist?" he asked anxiously.

Raistlin paused, considered. "I cannot promise," he said, shaking his head.

Caramon opened his mouth to cajole, caught his brother's glinting glance, shut it. He nodded, cleared his throat, hoisted his knapsack to his shoulder. "You will take care of Palin, won't you?" he asked gruffly.

Raistlin smiled, grim, thin-lipped. "Yes, my brother. *That* I promise!"

4

FatheR anÒ ÒaughteR.

he Thieves' Guild in Palanthas had fallen on hard times.
At first, some in its membership had been pleased to see the
Dark Queen achieve victory. They had worked hard for this
time, when night should finally rule the land. The thieves prepared to
be richly rewarded.

They were in for a nasty shock.

The Knights of Takhisis marched triumphantly into Palanthas. The
hooves of their steeds clattered with the ring of iron on the city streets.
The pennants of the skull and lily escorted them, the flags hanging limp
in the hot and breathless air. The citizens were commanded to turn out
to do honor to Lord Ariakan. Flowers were thrust into the hands of
small children, who were ordered to throw them at His Lordship's feet.
The children proved terrified of the rictus grins of the knights' skull-
helms, and of the blue-skinned brutes, who made ferocious faces and
lifted their voices in blood-chilling war chants. The children dropped
their flowers, screamed, and wailed in their mothers' skirts. Parents
grabbed them and hustled them away, lest they bring down the wrath
of the dark knighthood.

And so Lord Ariakan's arrival was greeted with tears, wilted flowers,
and fear. He did not mind. He had not expected more. If, here and there,
he heard a cheer from the throng, he turned his eyes toward that person
and pointed him or her out to his aide. One of those persons thus indicated was Lynched Geoffrey, who, drunk as a skunk in honor of the day,
was yelling his lungs out.

When he had sobered up, Lynched Geoffrey went to pay his respects
to His Lordship the very next day. He was refused admittance.
Undaunted, Geoffrey came back daily and finally, several weeks later,
the guildmaster was admitted.

Ariakan had commandeered a house in the center of town, near that
of the Lord of Palanthas, who was under house arrest. Ariakan could
have taken the lord's palace, but the commander of the Knights of
Takhisis did not propose to remain long in Palanthas. His place was
back at the High Clerist's Tower, from which he would lead his armies
to conquer all of Ansalon. He was in Palanthas only long enough to set
up a provisional government, firmly establish his grip on the city.

He spent his days seated at his favorite desk, which had been placed in the center of the dining hall, papers spread out before him, drafting edicts, writing laws. Aides and servants stood nearby, ready to run instantly on whatever errand he commanded. Suitors and well-wishers awaited His Lordship's pleasure in a small antechamber that had been cordoned off by the knights.

Lynched Geoffrey was made to wait among this number several hours before being invited in to see His Lordship. Geoffrey didn't mind the wait; he spent his time profitably, lifting the purse of the head cleric of the Order of Chemosh.

Lynch was finally admitted into Ariakan's presence. The thief greeted Ariakan with a swagger, a leer, and a cheeky, "Well, it's about time!"

No chair being placed for him in front of His Lordship, Geoffrey remedied the oversight by dragging one up for himself. He plunked the chair down at one end of Ariakan's desk, threw himself into the chair, slouched back, and, lifting his skinny legs, rested his boots comfortably on the table.

Ariakan said nothing. He did not look at the thief. His Lordship was busy with the proper wording of one of his laws. He did not even raise his eyelids.

The blade of a poleaxe crashed down, splintering the table, and slicing off the heels of Lynch's boots. He was fortunate the blade did not slice off the boots themselves and his feet along with them. Geoffrey snatched his feet off the table. He stared at his ruined boots, cursed loudly.

Ariakan made a slight gesture with the crook of his index finger.

His Lordship's aide grasped Lynch by the scruff of his scarred neck, jerked him to his feet, withdrew the chair, and ordered him, in a cold voice, to speak his piece in language suitable to His Lordship's rank and station and then be gone about his business.

Lynched Geoffrey gathered the shreds and tatters of his dignity about him. Fingers twitching, he sullenly reminded Lord Ariakan that they were both on the same side, that he—Geoffrey—was a leader to his people just as Ariakan was to his knights, that the Thieves' Guild expected the knights' cooperation in certain projects they had in mind and that, in return, the knights could expect to receive a little something for their pains.

At which point Lynch shoved over a money bag to Lord Ariakan, who, much to Lynch's discomfiture, had neither ceased to write nor had looked up once during the thief's entire recitation.

Lynch might have escaped with being merely tossed out on his head, but for the fact that the cleric of Chemosh came rushing in, panting and sweating, to cry that his money bag had been stolen.

Ariakan lifted his head, looked at the money bag, saw there the horned skull that was the symbol of Chemosh.

Lynch, with a smirk and a gibe, shrugged his skinny shoulders.

"It's all going to the same cause, ain't it, Masters?" Lynch remarked with a sly laugh and a wink. "This is just *my* way of serving Her Dark Majesty."

Ariakan lifted his head, looked at Lynched Geoffrey for the first— and last—time.

"And this is mine," said His Lordship. "Hang him."

The sentence was carried out immediately, atop the city wall. The hanging went off quite well; some said because Lynch had already had practice.

News of their leader's sudden demise hit the Thieves' Guild a stunning blow. The guild hall echoed with their outrage and vows to make the knights pay for what the thieves saw as an act of treachery against their own kind. Most switched allegiances on the spot. Paladine gained more supporters in a space of ten minutes than a cartload of clerics could have converted with a lifetime of prayer. Expecting to be attacked by the knights at any moment, the thieves made ready. They sent messengers to alert and round up all the membership, ordered everyone to report to the guild hall. When all were gathered, their leaders passed out weapons, removed the blankets from the windows, posted archers and spies, and waited for the assault.

Few shed tears for Lynched Geoffrey. Usha was certainly not one of them. He had found her lodging in a room above a tavern, had fixed her up with a job waiting tables in the tavern, and had then thrown himself on her bed and told her exactly what he expected in return for his magnanimity. She had refused his advances with anger and indignation.

Not being one to take "no" for an answer, Lynch might have forced his desires on her, but, having a bit of larceny planned for later in the evening, he had decided that he couldn't afford the time it would take to make the girl come to appreciate him. He had left her then, but he continued from that day on to press his odious attentions on her.

It didn't take Usha long to learn, to her horror, that these people were not fishers of fish, but of other people's property. She had also learned— at the point of a knife—that once admitted into the guild's secrets, no one left with the knowledge—alive.

"Unless you can magic yourself out, Raistlin's Daughter!"

The last had been spoken in a sneering tone by Lynched Geoffrey, smarting from Usha's continual rebuffs. The name drew a laugh, and she was baptized "Raistlin's Daughter" by a cleric of Hiddukel, who solemnized the ceremony by dumping a mug of ale over her head. From then on Usha was termed Raistlin's Daughter, the appellation always accompanied by either a laugh or a sneer.

Usha had no recourse, no one to help her. Dougan Redhammer had vanished. She hoped he would come back to see her. She wanted to demand of him why he had given her over to these terrible people. But he never appeared, never returned. Not that even he would have been able to do anything for her. The thieves never let her out of their sight. Someone, somewhere, was always watching her.

There were even eyes in her room. A crow often came to visit her. The bird flew uninvited in through the open window of her wretched lodgings. Once Usha left her window shut, preferring the room's heat to putting up with her black-feathered visitor. Undeterred, the crow pecked on the outside of the glass until Usha was forced to let the bird in or risk the landlord's ire. Once in her room, the crow would hop about, pecking at and picking up any object it happened to find. Fortunately, she had hidden inside the straw mattress the magical objects given to her by the Irda. The bird never discovered those, but neither did Usha, fearful of those beady yellow eyes, dare bring the artifacts out into the open.

She took the thieves' "training," which she was afraid to refuse. The first skill she learned was the fine art of pocket picking. This was taught by a truly horrible old woman who hung small bells on her clothes and then ordered Usha to attempt to remove some object—a purse, a silken handkerchief, a necklace or brooch—without causing any of the bells to ring. If Usha failed, if a single bell chimed a single note, the old woman whacked Usha a stinging blow with a cane on whatever part of her body happened to be within striking range.

Usha was next taught how to move through a darkened room filled with objects and not bump into anything or make a single sound. She was taught how to focus on her objective, to complete it, no matter what distractions were going on around her. She learned to scale walls, climb ropes, slide through windows. She was not a very apt pupil, until the realization came to her one night that she could use all this knowledge to escape the very people who were teaching it to her.

The thieves had been pleased with her progress ever since.

That had been almost a month ago. This day, the day Lynched Geoffrey was hanged, was the day she decided she would make good her escape.

The guild hall was awash in defiance, bravado, and liquor. The thieves were prepared to fight, either to the last drop of blood or the last drop of dwarf spirits, whichever ran out first.

The time passed slowly. The day was long, hot and sweltering, and boring. Heads began to ache from the consumption of too much courage.

Night's shadows fell, bringing renewed spirit and energy. The thieves always took heart in darkness. Their spies had nothing to report. The streets around the guild hall were quiet. The knights were said to be going about their business. They were not assembling, not being called to arms. Most thought that this was merely an attempt to lull the thieves into complaisance. They hunkered down and waited.

Usha was among their number in the guild hall. She'd been given a weapon, a small dagger, but she didn't plan on using it. She had discovered, during one of Lynched Geoffrey's drunken ramblings, the existence of a secret passage, which led from the guild, underneath the wall, to the harbor. She had cleaned out her lodgings, brought along her few possessions, some clothes and the Irda magical artifacts. These she wrapped in a bundle and kept under her table, at her feet. When the knights attacked, she planned to escape during the confusion.

Once away from this heinous place, she would find her boat and flee this doomed city. Her one regret was in leaving Palin, but she had heard nothing from him in weeks and was beginning to conclude, with an aching heart, that her faith in the gods had been misplaced. She would never see him again.

It was nearly midnight in Palanthas, and no army massed in the streets. It began to occur to the thieves that the knights weren't going to attack after all.

"They're afraid of us!" someone cried.

That boast, the ale, and the dwarf spirits were passed around freely.

The thieves, in truth, had nothing to fear, at least for the moment. Lord Ariakan was not afraid of the Thieves' Guild. He fully intended to clean out the "maggots' nest" as he said to an aide. The intention was on his list—at the bottom of his list. The thieves were an annoyance, an irritant, nothing more. At this critical time, engaged in battle for the control of all of Ansalon, he would not, he said, "waste the manpower needed to clean out a dung heap."

The thieves knew nothing of this, however. They were convinced that they had scared off the vaunted Knights of Takhisis. They spent the night drumming on each other's backs, congratulating themselves. So loud and boisterous was the celebrating that they did not, at first, hear the knock on the door.

Murf, the gully dwarf, who, for some reason known only to the gods, could drink a great deal and never get drunk, was the only one to hear soft scratching on the door. He thought it was rats, scrabbling in the alleyway. Feeling a bit hungry, after all the spilled ale he'd been lapping off the floor, the gully dwarf hurried to secure his dinner. He slid open the peephole, peered outside. He saw nothing but thick, velvety blackness.

Thinking this was just the night, the gully dwarf flung open the door.

A hooded figure, robed in black velvet, stood in the doorway. The figure stood so still that Murf, eager to find his dinner, did not see the robed person. The gully dwarf fell to his hands and knees and began to search for supper.

The robed and hooded person appeared to be accustomed to gully dwarves and their ways. He waited patiently until Murf, thinking he'd seen a rat run underneath, reached out to lift the black robes and take a look.

A booted foot trod upon the gully dwarf's hand, pinned it to the ground.

Murf did what any gully dwarf would do under similar circumstances. He let out a shriek that sounded like some gnomish invention letting off a full head of steam.

At the sound of the scream, which might have been heard in Solace, the thieves dropped their mugs and grabbed their weapons. Their current leader, a rogue known as Widower Mike, due to the fact that all his wives kept unaccountably dying on him, ran to the door. Six brutish followers clattered on his heels.

Everyone in the guild hall had fallen silent, was staring at the door in suspicion and alarm. Their spies, who should have warned them of the approach of this visitor before he even stepped foot in their alley, had been strangely silent. Widower flung the door wide. Light from torch and candle illuminated the alley. Usha, looking out, saw what could only be a black-robed wizard.

Panic seized her. Dalamar had found her! She wanted to run, but she couldn't move. Her feet were too cold and numb to support her; her whole body shook. She could do nothing but stare.

The man lifted his hand, which was thin and wasted, and drew a letter in the air.

Widower grunted. He glanced back at his followers. "He knows the sign," he said, and they lowered their weapons, though they did not sheathe them. Several of the guild's mages had their hands in their pouches or were unrolling scrolls, prepared to defend the membership should this intruder abuse their hospitality.

Murf continued to howl, though the mage had removed his foot.

"Shut your gob!" ordered Widower, and he kicked the gully dwarf. "Some lookout you are!" he muttered unjustly, since Murf was the only one who had been cognizant of the stranger's presence.

"What do you want, wizard?" Widower asked. "And the answer better be good, or there'll be hell to pay."

"I'm looking for someone," came the voice from the depths of the hood. "I intend you no harm and may mean you some good."

The voice didn't sound like Dalamar's, but then it was so soft and whispering, it was hard for Usha to tell. She was taking no chances. She had recovered her senses and her courage. She began to stealthily creep away, to seek the safety of the back exit and secret passageway.

She had not gone far, however, when a hand closed over her arm. One of the thieves swiveled around, peered up at Usha with bloodshot eyes.

"Pour me more ale!"

Fearing that if she refused, she'd draw attention to herself, Usha did as she was commanded. Keeping her head down, she grasped the ale pitcher in her hand and was starting to pour when the robed figure spoke again.

"I am searching for my daughter."

Usha began to tremble. She dropped the pitcher with a crash.

"Hey! He's lost his daughter!" Widower said, laughing. "Should I let him in, Sally Dale?"

He cast a questioning glance backward. A tall woman, wearing a red tunic and numerous pouches slung from her belt, nodded her head.

The man entered. Widower slammed shut the door behind him, threw the bolt.

"Take yer hood off. I like to look a man in the eyes," Widower demanded jocularly.

Slowly the man lifted both hands. Slowly he removed the hood that covered his head. He opened his eyes wide and turned their gaze on Widower, who appeared to be extremely sorry that he'd made the suggestion.

The mage's face was gaunt, the skin stretched taut over high cheekbones. He was not yet middle-aged, but his hair was white. His face had a golden tint to it, glistened with a metallic sheen in the firelight. The eyes were his most forbidding feature, for their pupils were formed in the shape of an hourglass.

Widower blanched, grimaced, and said thickly, "By Hiddukel, wizard, you've got a face out of a nightmare! I pity that daughter of yours if she looks like you."

"You would do well to pity any child of mine," the mage said softly. His golden eyes slid without interest over every person in the room until they came to Usha.

"What is your name?" he asked.

Usha couldn't answer. She had lost the power of speech. She could not even draw a breath. Pinpoints of flame flickered before her eyes.

"Her?" Widower shrugged. "Why we call her Raistlin's . . . Raist . . ." The word ended in a startled hiss.

The hiss was echoed in a gasp from Sally Dale.

She ran forward, caught Widower by the arm. Nearly squeezing his limb off, she spoke a name urgently in his ear.

Widower went livid. He backed away. The name was whispered sibilantly from one thief to another, making it sound as if the guild hall were alive with snakes.

Sally Dale prodded Widower, who gulped and gabbled, pointed at Usha. "There's your daughter, Master! Take her! We ain't laid a finger on her. I swear it. No matter what she says. We didn't know, Master. Who would have thought? I didn't mean . . . Don't take offense . . ."

"Be gone," Raistlin commanded. "Get out. The lot of you."

His voice was soft, yet it reached into dark corners, stole up among the rafters, settled like choking smoke over the room.

Widower gave a weak laugh, ventured to protest. "Get out? Us? I say, Master, that's hardly fair. Why don't you leave? It's *our* guild hall. . . ."

Raistlin frowned. The golden eyes narrowed, glinted. His hand slid toward a pouch he wore on his belt.

Sally Dale shook Widower, shook him until his bones rattled. "You fool! This is Raistlin! Raistlin Majere! The wizard who fought the Dark Queen herself! He could blast this hall to Lunitari if he chose, and us along with it!"

Widower still hesitated. He eyed Raistlin.

The archmage, for his part, remained calm. He drew a pouch from his belt, began to slowly open it. . . .

The hall emptied. The thieves ran for the doors, the windows, for every conceivable nook and cranny.

Within minutes, Raistlin and Usha were alone.

Usha stood terrified. Her gaze was fixed, fearfully, upon the man whom she had claimed as father.

Raistlin drew from the pouch a handful of herbs. Going to a table, near Usha, he selected the cleanest cup he could fine, sifted the herbs into the cup.

"Bring hot water," he told Usha.

She blinked, startled by the command, but hastened to do as she was bidden. Hurrying to the fireplace, she lifted the black kettle and brought it back to the table. Carefully, trying to control her shaking hand, she poured the water into the cup.

Steam, perfumed with smells of catnip, mint, and other, less pleasant, odors, spiraled up from the cup.

Raistlin sipped the tea quietly. Usha replaced the kettle, took a moment to gather her courage, then came back and sat down across from the mage.

He raised his head. The black robes rustled; she smelled spice, roses, death.

She shrank away, lowered her gaze. She couldn't bear to look into that cold, metallic face.

A chill hand touched the top her head, and she shuddered. The touch was gentle, but the fingers were cold. Not corpselike, the fingers were alive. But it was reluctant life. Long ago, or so she had heard, the fire that had burned within this man had been so hot as to consume him and all who came around him. Now the flame was quenched, the ashes scattered. It could no longer be rekindled.

His hand lingered on the top of her head, smoothed the silvery hair. Then the fingers slid down her face, touched her chin. Raistlin's hand lifted her chin, forced her to look into the strange, misshapen pupils of his golden eyes.

"You are no child of mine," he said.

The words were frozen hard. But as fish live beneath the surface of an ice-bound lake, as life is maintained in the depths of chill darkness, Usha heard beneath the awful pronouncement a wistful sadness.

"I could be," she said, aching.

"You could be the child of any man," Raistlin remarked dryly. He paused, regarded her intently. His fingers on her chin sent a chill over her. "You have no idea *who* your real father is, do you?" He appeared puzzled. "Why did you choose me?"

Usha swallowed. She longed to pull away from his touch, which was starting to burn as ice burns the skin. "The kender . . . told me about the legend. I thought . . . Everyone seemed to respect you . . . I was alone and . . . " She shook her head. "I'm sorry. I never meant any harm."

Raistlin sighed. "The harm would not have come to me. You nearly brought it upon yourself. I wondered . . ." He didn't finish his sentence, let the matter drop. He sipped his tea.

"They would never tell me," Usha said, feeling the need to explain further. "They said it didn't matter."

"By 'they' you mean the Irda."

She nodded. He started to say something more, but suddenly he broke into a fit of hoarse coughing that shook the frail body and flecked his lips with blood.

"Are you all right? Let me get you something." Usha rose to her feet.

Raistlin's hand grasped her wrist, held her fast. He continued to hold on to her as he coughed and gasped for air. Each spasm caused his hand to constrict around hers painfully, but she did not flinch or try to pull away. At length, the coughing fit passed. He drew in a shattered breath, blotted the blood from his lips on the sleeve of his black robe.

"Sit down," he commanded in a voice that was nearly inaudible.

She sank down into her chair. His grip on her arm relaxed. He let go of her, but his hand rested upon her arm and she did not pull away. Instead, she edged closer. She felt a warmth in that hand that had not been there before, and she understood that he had drawn it from her, from her youth, her vitality.

"What is your name?" he asked.

"I am called Usha," she replied.

"Usha . . ." he repeated softly. "Do you know what it means?"

"Why, no," she said, blinking. "I never thought about it. I never supposed it meant anything. It's . . . just a name."

"A name that comes from another world, another time. Usha means 'the dawn.' I wonder . . ." Raistlin mused, gazing at her. "Did the one who named you know the meaning? Did he or she have foreknowledge of what was to come? It would be interesting to find out."

"I *could* be your daughter." Usha wasn't interested in her name. She wanted to be this man's daughter, wanted it as much for him as for herself now. He wore his loneliness and isolation as he wore the black robes, proudly, defiantly. Yet still his wasted hand lingered near hers. "I have golden eyes, eyes the same color as yours."

"So did your mother," he replied.

Usha stared at him. A hunger rose in her, a desperate need for the sustenance for which she'd been starving all her life. The Irda had attempted to feed that hunger with sugar buns and candied fruit and all manner of sweets and confections. They had not understood. They had not realized she needed simple fare on which to grow and thrive.

"You know who my parents are," she cried, and her hand closed over his. "You know who I am! Tell me, please. How did you find out? Did you go to see Prot. Is he well? Does he miss me?"

"I did *not* visit the Irda," Raistlin replied. "I had no need. I was once known as the Master of the Present and the Past. Time holds no constraints for me. The river's waters carry me wherever I want to go."

He drank his tea, moistened his throat. His voice grew stronger, and he continued.

"When I first heard of you, heard of your claim, I disregarded it. My brother, Caramon, told me the legend, of how a mysterious woman seduced me, bore away my seed within her, and cast on me a magic spell of forgetfulness. I did not believe it. What magic exists that could be powerful enough to banish the knowledge from my heart that I had once been loved. Not even death can do so much," he added softly, almost to himself.

Usha kept silent, hoping, dreading.

"And so I paid little attention to your claims," Raistlin went on. "Caramon assured me there had been others before you and, I assume, there will be others to come after. I thought little more of the matter until I attended the Wizards' Conclave in Wayreth Tower. Again your name was spoken in connection with mine, only this time it was spoken seriously. Dalamar the Dark made the claim."

Raistlin's voice hardened. "Yes, Usha, you do well to shiver at that name. He intended to use you, if the claim proved true, use you to gain a hold over me. I had no choice. I must know for certain. I waded Time's dark river; I ventured into the still waters of the Irda's stagnant pond. I found the truth."

He coughed again, but only briefly.

"I do not know where your parents were from originally. I did not venture back so far. When I first saw them, they had been captured and made slaves by minotaur, were sent to serve aboard a minotaur ship. The minotaur do not treat their slaves kindly. One night, believing that death could hold no terrors for them equal to what they already knew, your mother and father gave their lives into the hands of Zeboim. They cried to her for mercy and jumped overboard into a raging sea.

"Zeboim is a capricious goddess. She will turn with savage fury on those who serve her faithfully. She rewards those who might seem least deserving. She was flattered that these two had sought her protection and provided them with the wreckage of a raft. Her breath guided them to a safe landfall and, in this, I think the goddess intended mischief. She led them to the secret isle of the Irda.

"The Irda took pity on the two, who were discovered cast ashore, more dead than alive. The Irda gave your parents shelter and food. They took care of your mother when it was apparent that you were on the way. Yet, though not brutal or cruel as were the minotaur, the Irda inflicted their own form of torture. They did not intend it," Raistlin added, shrugging. "They simply could not understand the needs of two humans. When your parents were well, they wanted to leave, to return to their homeland. The Irda refused. They feared that your parents would betray them to the rest of the world. They made them virtual prisoners. Your father rebelled, defied them openly."

Raistlin gaze steadily at her. "The Irda killed him."

"No!" Usha faltered, shocked. "That can't be true. I don't believe it! They could never have done such a thing! Why, Prot wouldn't even crush a spider!"

"The Irda didn't mean to. You know them, Usha. Can't you picture how it was? They were repulsed and angered by the man's anger, his violence. They intended only to teach him a lesson. But their magic was too powerful, they went too far. None of their healing arts, none of their prayers, would revive him.

"Not long after that, you were born. Your mother, in her grief, wrapped you well one night, laid you down in your cradle. Then she walked into the sea and drowned. The Irda found her footsteps on the shore, but they never found her body. Perhaps, after all, Zeboim demanded a price for her previous kindness."

Usha sat with her head lowered, tears clinging to her lashes.

"Remorseful, the Irda raised you," Raistlin continued with the story. "They lavished on you all kindness, denied you nothing except the knowledge of who you are. They could not tell you the truth without telling you all. And that they would never do."

"I understand," Usha said, choking. "The Irda did not want to make me unhappy."

"They did not want to admit that they had acted wrongly," Raistlin said, his voice sharp. "The pride and arrogance of the Irda, which in ancient days brought ruin on their own race, is now likely to bring ruin to us all. Still," he added grimly, "I must not be uncharitable. They have paid for their folly. . . ."

Usha was not listening. She had been lost in her own thoughts, seeking back through her childhood, hoping to find some fragment of memory, a scrap of a lullaby, the last loving look of her mother's eyes. Only half hearing, she looked up. "What did you say? I'm afraid I wasn't paying attention."

"Never mind. It wasn't important." Raistlin rose from the table. "I must go. But, first, I give you this advice, Usha, whose name means 'the dawn.' You are thinking of fleeing Palanthas in an effort to escape your 'teachers.' "

Usha stared. "How did you—"

"There is no need," he said, cutting short her question. "Your training is complete. You are free to leave the guild this night and never return."

"They won't let me," Usha began.

"I think that, once they know who you are, they'll let you go."

"What do you mean?" Usha lifted her eyes. "You're . . . not going to tell them . . ."

"I see no reason to do so. This remains between you and me and, perhaps, Dalamar, if he oversteps his bounds. Besides, I have a reason for wanting you to stay. Someone is on his way to Palanthas now. He comes seeking you, and you, I think, will want to be where you can be found. This is someone," Raistlin added dryly, a slight smile touching his thin lips, "who will be very glad to know that you and he are *not* related."

"Palin?" Usha whispered. "He's safe? He's coming here, for me?"

"I gave him that task," Raistlin said. "It was one he accepted with alacrity."

Usha's face grew hot, as if she'd been drinking sparkling wine. She sat wrapped in warmth, reveling in the sweet, bubbling taste of youthful, joyous love, thrilling in the knowledge that she was loved in turn. But the bubbles soon burst upon her tongue, the taste of the wine turned sour. It occurred to her that she would have to admit to Palin that she had told a lie, a monstrous lie.

The realization was like a bitter draft poured into her sweet drink. She started to ask Raistlin for help, only to find that Raistlin was gone.

Startled, uneasy, Usha looked around. She had not seen him leave, yet the door stood open to the night. She went to the door, stared out into the alley. But if the archmage were there, he had melted into the night, become one with the shadows.

"Raistlin?" she risked calling, once.

Overhead, a crow circled, answered with a single, mocking "Caw!"

Shivering, despite the heat, Usha went into the hall, grabbed her possessions, and made her way back to her lodgings.

5

Return to Palanthas.
The Mage Ware Shop.
A Gray Knight's Suspicions.

hen the mists of the ring's magic cleared, Palin stood on a street inside a city that, after a moment's brief disorientation, he recognized as Palanthas. The blood-tipped minarets of the Tower of High Sorcery gleamed sullenly in the bright sunlight. Nearby, the Temple of Paladine was in shadow, its white marble dimmed, as if obscured by clouds. But there were no clouds in the eye-aching, brilliant blue sky.

Palin glanced around the street in which he'd materialized. Fortunately, it was a side street, probably in the merchandising part of the city. Shops, not residences, lined the paved road. Several passersby, startled by his sudden appearance, had paused to stare, but—noting the white robes of a mage—they merely gave him a wide berth and continued on about their business. Palin quickly drew the ring off his finger, slid it into a pouch, and tried to appear nonchalant.

He was amazed at the sight of the large number of people in the street, most of them walking along calmly, moving about as if this were just another ordinary business day. He wasn't certain what he'd expected in a city occupied by the dark knights—people locked up inside their houses, perhaps, troops patrolling the streets, gangs of slaves being marched along with their legs in irons. But here were housewives off to market, their children tugging at their skirts; guildsmen trotted along, looking—as always—as if they were in a hurry to be somewhere important. There were even the usual loafers and loungers and ne'er-do-wells hanging about outside the ale houses, beggars on the corners.

The city was so much like the Palanthas he'd known from years past that Palin wondered if his uncle hadn't been mistaken. Perhaps Palanthas had not fallen to the Knights of Takhisis. It was all very perplexing. And perhaps the most perplexing question of all: Why was he standing on a strange street corner?

He had expected the ring to take him to the tower. Why had it brought him here? Dalamar must have had a reason.

Palin looked closely at the signs hanging above the doors, hoping to find out what part of town he was in. Almost immediately he had what he thought was the answer to his question. Directly across the street was a mage-ware shop, as denoted by the sign with three moons—the silver, the red, and the black—hanging over the door.

Thinking that even if Dalamar didn't mean him to come here, this would be a good place to start—and perhaps trade for a few useful magical items while he was here—Palin crossed the street.

The door to the mage-ware shop was open wide in welcome, not unusual, since it was midafternoon of a busy market day. But Palin was surprised to see that no hulking guard stood outside, ready to turn away tourists, gawkers, and kender, who are drawn to mage-ware shops like bees to sugar water.

Palin entered the shop and stood for a moment just inside the door, waiting for his eyes to accustom themselves to the deep shadows after the glaring sunlight. The familiar scents made him feel at home, relieved his uneasiness: the sweet fragrance of dried flowers, not quite able to mask the underlying reek of decay and death, mingled with the musty smell of mildew and the scent of old leather.

The shop was a large one and, apparently, quite prosperous. No fewer than six wooden display cases with glass covers were filled with rings and brooches, pendants and crystals, bracelets and bracers—some of them beautiful, some hideous, some relatively ordinary in appearance. Glass jars containing everything from newt eyeballs suspended in some sort of viscous liquid to what appeared to be licorice whips in another were arranged on shelves. (No spell that Palin had ever heard of involved candy, and he could only assume the licorice was for mages with a sweet tooth.) Rows of spellbooks lined the walls, categorized by the color of their bindings and the occasional rune engraved on their spines. Scrolls, rolled and tied neatly with variously colored ribbons, were ensconced in dusty little nooks. Scroll cases and pouches made of leather, velvet, or plain cloth (for poorer mages) were displayed upon a table, along with a fine selection of small knives.

Everything was in the shop except the shop's owner.

A red curtain sealed off the back end of the shop. Assuming the owner was there, Palin was about to call out when a voice spoke right behind him.

"If you're hunting for Mistress Jenna, she's just stepped out a moment. Perhaps I could help?"

A man, clad in the gray robes of a mage, but wearing a sword at his side, stood next to Palin.

A Knight of the Thorn, Palin realized. The knight must have been hiding in the shadows behind the door.

Palin recognized the name of the owner: Mistress Jenna, a powerful red-robed sorceress and Dalamar's lover, by all accounts.

"Thank you, no," Palin said politely. "I'll wait for Mistress Jenna's return. I need to ask her a question about a spell component."

"Perhaps I can answer your question for you," said the Gray Knight.

"I doubt it," Palin returned. "The spells I cast and those you cast have nothing whatsoever in common. If you don't mind, I'll wait for Mistress Jenna. Don't let me keep you from leaving. You must have been on your way out the door when I came in."

"I wasn't leaving," the Gray Knight said. His tone was pleasant; he even seemed amused. "I am posted here. By the way, I don't believe you have signed the book. If you'd step over here . . ."

The Gray Knight led the way to a small desk that stood to the left of the door. On the desk was a large, leather-bound book with neatly spaced lines drawn across it. Palin, looking down, saw a list of names, followed by what appeared to be a record of purchases or trades. There were not many names, he noted, and the date of the last one was two days prior to this.

"Sign here." The Gray Knight indicated a line. "And then I'm going to have to ask you to show me all your arcane paraphernalia. Don't worry. I'll return the items to you—those which are not on the list of contraband deemed to be a hazard to the state. If they are, they'll be confiscated. But you will be compensated."

Palin couldn't believe he'd heard right. "Hazard . . . Confiscated! You . . . you can't be serious!"

"I assure you, White Robe, I am extremely serious. That is the law, as you undoubtedly knew when you walked in here. Come, come. If the guards let you in at the front gates, you must not be carrying anything too powerful."

I didn't enter at the front gates, Palin started to say, caught himself just in time. He could fight, but with what? His little knife against this wizard's sword? And how came these wizards to be wearing swords anyway? No wizard on Krynn had, up until now, been permitted to combine sword and sorcery! The Dark Queen was certainly granting her minions favors!

Palin knew without doubt that this knight-wizard was more powerful than he was. He could only go along with the man, pretend to be cooperative and pray to Solinari that the Gray Knight didn't get too curious about the Staff of Magius.

Letting the staff fall against a counter, as if it were nothing of value or important, Palin feigned great reluctance in taking off and handing over his pouches and the few scroll cases he carried. He spread them out in front of the Gray Knight, who did not touch any of them. Muttering a few words, he cast an enchantment on them.

Each pouch and scroll case began to glow with an eerie light—some with a red cast to it.

Satisfied that they were all magic, the Gray Knight ordered Palin to empty the contents of pouch and scroll case onto the table.

Palin put up a brief protest, but did as he was told. Rings, including the one given him by Dalamar, rolled out onto the tabletop. He removed the scrolls, untied the ribbons, permitted the Gray Knight to glance over the spells. All the while, his anger at this treatment mounted, as did his concern.

What would happen when the Gray Knight turned his attention to the Staff of Magius?

Palin glanced surreptitiously around the shop in hopes of finding something to use as a weapon. The brooches and other enchanted objects were locked in cases, which were undoubtedly further guarded by magical spells. He had no idea what any of them did, might well grab a ring that would be more harmful to himself than the Gray Knight. The same held true with the scrolls and the spellbooks; he didn't have time to go leafing through them.

If nothing else, I can always hit him over the head with a jar, Palin determined grimly, and chose the one he would grab.

The knight had his head bent, scanning the contents of one of Palin's small spellbooks.

Palin began edging his way over to the shelves, was just reaching out his hand to take hold of the jar, when the Gray Knight raised his head.

"Oh, there you are! What are you doing over there?"

"Just looking to see if this marjoram in here is fresh," Palin replied, lifting the jar down from the shelf. He removed the stopper, sniffed. "Quite nice. Care to smell for yourself?"

The Gray Knight's eyes narrowed in suspicion. "Put the jar down and come back over here. These I'm keeping." He gestured to a large pile of scrolls, rings—including Dalamar's—and other objects. "These"—he pointed to the spellbook, a pouch containing sand, and one containing bat guano—"you can have back."

Palin flushed in anger, started to protest, but the Gray Knight turned away. He reached for the staff. "Now, let's take a look at this."

"It's an ordinary walking staff," Palin said, barely able to speak past the tightness in his throat. "You can see for yourself that I am of low rank. What would I be doing with a magical staff?"

"What indeed? But that's quite an unusual adornment for a walking staff—a dragon's claw clutching a crystal. You won't mind if I inspect it more closely?"

The Gray Knight spoke his words, cast the spell that would reveal the magical properties of the staff, just as it had revealed the magical properties of everything else Palin carried.

Palin tensed, waited for the telltale glow to spread over the staff. The moment the knight went to touch it, Palin was ready to hurl himself bodily at the man, wrestle him to the floor.

The staff did nothing.

Palin gaped in astonishment. The Staff of Magius, one of the most powerful arcane artifacts in all of Krynn, stood propped against a counter, looking as plain and innocent as any kender hoopak.

The Gray Knight frowned. He was certain that the staff was magical, but could not very well admit that he doubted his own spell-casting. He glared at Palin suspiciously, thinking that perhaps the young mage had managed to slip one past him.

Palin stood with his hands folded in the sleeves of his robes. He smiled deprecatingly. "I told you."

"You did indeed," the Gray Knight returned. He stared at the staff, was obviously tempted to cast the spell again, perhaps realized this would make him look foolish. He contented himself with a rebuke. "A fancy-looking staff like that could get you into trouble, young man. If you insist on playacting a wizard, wait until the Night of the Eye. At least you'll get a cookie out of it."

Palin's face burned at the insult. He dared say nothing, however; certainly he could not argue. Swallowing his pride, he comforted himself by imagining the expression on the knight's face if he ever learned that he'd had in his grasp the famed Staff of Magius and let it go.

"Sign your name." The Gray Knight shoved the book at Palin.

Lifting the quill pen, Palin was about to comply, when footsteps, the rustle of robes, and the heady fragrance of some expensive perfume caused him to turn his head.

A woman—one of the most lovely and exotic women Palin had ever seen—entered the shop. She was dressed in red robes, expensive red robes, made of velvet and silk, trimmed with golden stitchery. She wore the perfume to mask the occasionally unpleasant smells of the spell components she carried in silken bags that hung from a braided leather-and-silver chain belt. She was alluring, powerful, mysterious, and, at her arrival, even the Gray Knight straightened, bowed.

She paused, regarded Palin curiously. "How do you do, Master Mage? I am Jenna, owner of this shop. I apologize for not being here when you arrived. I was called to the lord's house. One of the servants broke a valuable vase and they asked me to mend it. A menial task, and one I would ordinarily refuse, but there are so few magic-users left in town these days. What can I do for you?"

"Mistress Jenna," Palin said, with marked admiration, "my name is

Pal—"

"Palas! Palas Margoyle!" Jenna swept forward, took him by the hand. "My dear boy, I should have recognized you sooner. But then it's been so long and you've changed. When did we last meet? Almost five years ago. During your Test. And you are here for your scroll-writing session. You're early, but, never mind. I don't seem to do much business these days," she added, with a cool glance at the Gray Knight.

Jenna clasped Palin's arm, started to lead him away, to the part of the shop that was curtained off from the rest.

"He hasn't signed the book, yet, Mistress," the Gray Knight said.

Jenna halted, cast Palin a look of warning that chilled his blood.

"Oh, yes, we must sign the book," Jenna said archly, turning around. "How else would the Knights of Takhisis keep track of who comes to visit me and what they buy? Not that many come to buy anything anymore. Soon I shall be destitute and then no one will have to sign the book ever again. Ah! Look! Someone has spilled the marjoram. Palas, help me clean this up."

Palin did as he was instructed, cleaning up the minute amount of dried leaves he had scattered.

Jenna leaned down to help him, whispered as she drew near, "They are searching for you! There is a warrant for your arrest!"

Palin's hand jerked, nearly spilling the leaves again. He managed to deposit them back into their jar. Jenna replaced the stopper, returned the jar to the shelf.

"Go, sign the book, then, Palas. Hurry up. I'll be in the laboratory. Through these curtains and down the stairs."

She walked through the curtains. Palin heard her descend the stairs. Light-headed, from either nervousness or her nearness or perhaps both, he wrote the false name, awkwardly, left an ink blot at the finish. This done, under the distrustful, suspicious gaze of the Gray Knight, Palin walked through the curtains and nearly tumbled headfirst down the stairs, which gaped unexpectedly at his feet.

He started to shut the curtains behind him.

"Leave them open," the Gray Knight instructed him, and moved to take his place at the head of the stairs, where he could see down into the laboratory and still keep an eye on the front door.

Palin sat next to Jenna, who brought out a tablet made of wax.

"The advantages of writing down a magical spell on a scroll are obvious," she began, speaking in a loud, didactic tone. "You don't have to commit the spell to memory beforehand, and thus are able to use it at will. Writing down certain spells, particularly complex spells, permits you to keep your mind free to memorize others. The main disadvantage is the difficulty of penning the spell, far harder than pronouncing it. For in writing, not only must you pronounce the words as you write, but you must also form the letters perfectly. Any sloppiness, and the spell will not work.

"Of course, we are not going to truly write spells today. You are not advanced enough in your studies for that. Today we will practice forming the letters. We will be writing them on wax, so you may rub out any mistakes. Thusly."

Lifting a stylus, Jenna pressed it into the wax, began tracing letters. Palin, who had learned all this years before and was, in fact, quite adept at preparing scrolls, paid little attention. He was angry at himself. Of course the knights would be searching for him. He had been a fool not to consider this possibility.

Jenna nudged him with her elbow. She was regarding him sternly, pointing at the tablet.

"There, copy down what I have written."

Palin took the stylus, looked at the letters, looked at them again, and finally understood what was going on. Jenna was not writing magic. He read: *Dalamar told me of your coming. I have been trying to find Usha. I believe she is still in Palanthas, but I'm not certain where. There is little I can do. I am constantly watched.*

Seeing that Palin had read her message, she rubbed it out.

Palin wrote: *How will I find her?*

Usha returned: *It is too dangerous for you to walk around town. The knights have us locked in a grip of iron. Patrols, checkpoints. All citizens must have the requisite papers. But don't despair. My agent is hunting for her. He reported that he was close and that he would certainly have word today.*

"It's awfully quiet down there," the Gray Knight said, peering at them from the top of the stairs.

"What do you expect? We are studying," Jenna returned crisply.

A tiny bell, hanging from the ceiling by a silken thread, rang three times.

Jenna did not bother to turn around. "Is that a customer in the shop? Tell them I will be with them momentarily."

"I am not your servant, Madam," said the Gray Knight caustically.

"Feel free to leave anytime, then," she replied, rubbing out the writing on the wax. "That may be my agent now," she said to Palin in an undertone.

The heavy boots of the knight could be heard, crossing the shop floor. Then, alarmingly, there was a yell and sounds of a scuffle.

"That's him," Jenna said, and, rising to her feet, she hastily ascended the stairs.

Palin was right behind her, bumped into her when she stopped at the top.

She whispered, "Pretend you don't know him. Say nothing. Leave the talking to me."

Palin, mystified, nodded. Jenna stepped into the shop.

"What is this?" she demanded.

"A kender," said the Gray Knight grimly.

"I can see that for myself," Jenna returned.

Palin stared, remembered—just in time—that he wasn't supposed to know this person.

Squirming in the hands of the knight was Tasslehoff Burrfoot.

6

Jenna's agent. The Goose and Gander.
Awfully fine ginger beer.

I—Ouch, that hurts! How would you like it if someone nearly squeezed your arm off? I tell you that Mistress Jenna wants to see me. I'm her agent. Oops! Oh, my. I'm awfully sorry. I didn't mean to bite you. Your hand just sort of got in the way of my teeth. Does it hurt too badly? I— Ooh! Ooh! Stop it! You're pulling out my hair! Help! Help!"

"For Gilean's sake, let him go," Jenna said.

The knight had hold of Tas by his topknot.

"You do not want a kender in your shop, Madam," the knight intoned.

"It is *my* shop—at least for the moment," Jenna snapped. "Until you drive me out of business and you knights take over. For now, this is my business, and I will run it as I choose. Let the kender go!"

The knight did so with obvious displeasure. "Very well, Madam, but you must be responsible for the consequences."

"If I were you, I would go upstairs to my apartment and wash out that wound," Jenna advised. "Or perhaps you should have one of your clerics treat it. You never know, the kender might be rabid."

"I wouldn't be surprised," the knight returned coldly. "Remember this, Madam—your shop remains open by the sufferance of the Knights of Takhisis. We could shut you down this minute if we chose, and there's not a single person who would stop us. Indeed, quite a few of your neighbors would probably thank us. So don't try my patience."

Jenna tossed her head scornfully, but did not reply. The Gray Knight trudged upstairs, wringing his injured hand. Tasslehoff winced, rubbed his head.

"Are my eyes slanted now, like Dalamar's? It feels like they are. He pulled so hard, he took my eyelids up with my scalp. He is *not* a nice man," Tasslehoff pronounced and then, leaning close to Jenna, the kender lowered his voice. "I told a lie. I *did* really mean to bite him."

"He deserved it," Jenna said with a smile. "But be more careful next time. My protection stretches only so far. I don't want to have to bail you out of jail again. Did you find the necklace I am seeking?" she asked loudly, loud enough to be heard upstairs.

Tas shifted his gaze to Palin, winked at him several times, and said, equally loudly, "Yes, Mistress Jenna. I found it! I know right where it is!"

"You didn't touch it, did you?" Jenna sounded anxious. "Or let the owner know that it is in any way valuable?"

"The owner never saw me. The necklace didn't either," Tas added confidentially.

Jenna frowned at this statement, shook her head. She turned to Palin. "Master Mage, we seem to be getting nowhere with our lesson today. It is time for afternoon meditation. Would you do me a favor and see if you could acquire this necklace for me? It is magic, but the owner doesn't know this, has no idea of its true worth."

Palin had, by this time, figured out that the necklace must be Usha. At the thought of seeing her again, his heart beat rapidly and a pleasant, tingling sensation warmed his blood. All notions of danger disappeared, or at least got shoved well to the background.

"I would be honored, Mistress Jenna, to obtain this necklace for you," he said, struggling to sound indifferent, though he was near shouting in excitement. "Where is it?"

"The kender will show you. Leave now, before I close up shop."

She rolled her eyes upstairs. Palin took the hint.

He bowed silently.

Jenna held out her hand. "Good luck," she said softly.

Palin, taking her hand, brought it respectfully to his lips. "Thank you, Mistress," he whispered. He hesitated, then said quietly, "I saw the way that knight looked at you. You're in danger here yourself. . . ."

Jenna shrugged, smiled. "I am the only mage left in the city. The Conclave deems my work here important. But don't worry, Palin Majere, I can take care of myself. Walk in Lunitari's light."

"Solinari shed his grace on you, Mistress," Palin replied.

"Thank you, Tas," Jenna said. She removed several valuable objects that had happened to fall off the shelves and into Tas's pouch, and escorted him and Palin out the door.

"I didn't really find a necklace," Tas said the moment they reached the street.

"I know," Palin said hurriedly. "But don't say any more about it until we're far away from here." He proceeded down the street rapidly, looking behind every so often to make certain they were not being followed.

"Mum's the word." Tas trotted along at Palin's side. "How's Caramon and Tika? Did the dragons burn down the inn like they did in the last war? Where's Raistlin?"

"Hush," Palin said, glancing about in alarm. "Don't mention—"

"I had a whole lot of questions to ask Raistlin, all about being dead and everything," Tas continued, not listening, "but Dalamar magicked me out of the tower so fast I never got to ask one. Raistlin was always very good at answering questions. Well, most always. Sometimes he wasn't, but then he'd usually just discovered he'd lost the thing I was asking questions about, but since I most always found it for him, he didn't need to be rude. Where did you say Raistlin went?"

"I didn't!" Palin said grimly. Two dark knights, walking down the street, were looking at them strangely. "Don't mention that name! Where are we going?"

"Oh, nowhere in particular," Tas said evasively. "Just a little inn I found. The ginger beer is excellent."

"What?" Palin pulled Tas up short. "We don't have time to stop and drink ginger beer!"

The two knights had slowed their pace, were taking a great deal of interest in their conversation.

"That's mine, you little thief!" Palin grabbed hold of the first pouch he saw hanging partway out of Tas's pocket. He discovered, to his amazement that the pouch really was his. It was one the Gray Knight had confiscated.

"You must have dropped—" Tas began.

The two knights laughed, shook their heads, and kept walking.

Palin dragged the kender off into an alley. "We don't have time to go to an inn! I'm supposed to find Usha and take her to meet Raistlin at the Great Library tonight!"

"We will," Tas replied. "Only we shouldn't go until after dark. The Thieves' Guild's very particular about such things. I know a nice inn, not too far—"

"Thieves' Guild!" Palin gasped. "Are you telling me that Usha's a . . . a thief?"

"Sad, isn't it," Tasslehoff said, commiserating. "I was shocked to hear that myself. Stealing from people is a very wicked crime, so my mother always used to tell me, and you'd never catch me—"

"Are you sure?" Palin asked nervously. "Maybe you've made a mistake."

"I'll tell you how I found out, shall I? We could go to this very nice inn—"

Two more knights walked past the alley, paused to peer down it.

Realizing that he looked more suspicious standing in an alley talking to a kender than he would out in the open, Palin reluctantly agreed to go to the inn. The two continued through the streets of Palanthas.

"Let's see." Tas thought back. "The first night I came to Palanthas, that would be the night that Raist . . . I mean You Know Who . . . let us out of the laboratory and Dalamar was so incredibly astonished and not very pleased to see us until he and You Know Who had that little confidential talk. You remember?"

"Yes, I remember." Palin attempted to curb his impatience. "Tell me about Usha."

"That's right. Turn here, down this side street. Well, the first night I spent in jail, due to a misunderstanding with a tinker over a very fine little teapot that whistled, and I was just looking to see what they put inside to make it whistle like that, when—"

Palin frowned.

"—and I spent the night in jail," Tas finished with a rush. He sighed. "The Palanthas jail isn't what it used to be. The Knights of Takhisis are in charge now, which I thought at first might be interesting, especially if they tortured people by hanging them upside down by their heels and poking at them with red-hot rods. But they're not. Torturing anyone, I mean. The knights are very stern and strict and were always making us line up and keep quiet and sit down and keep quiet and not move and keep quiet. And, there weren't hardly any kender. But I'll tell you about that later. Here's the inn. It's sort of shabby-looking on the outside, and it doesn't get much better on the inside, but the ginger beer is quite good."

The Goose and Gander Tavern stood on a corner where two side streets met to form one point of a triangle. The tavern had been built on the triangle's tip, and was, consequently, shaped like a slice of pie. Being located near a blacksmith's shop, the tavern had acquired a layer of soot from the smithy's fire. The brick walls, covered with withered ivy, were black with grime. An attempt had been made to wash the mullioned windows, which resulted in nothing more than smearing the dirt. The goose and gander painted on the tavern's sign (with their necks intertwined) had once had white feathers, but now looked as if they had just emerged from a coal bin.

"Tas, really, I'm not thirsty," Palin said.

Two rough-looking customers had just emerged from the tavern, wiping their bearded faces with the backs of their hands, and eyed both mage and kender with dark scowls and grim expressions.

"Oh, yes, you are," Tas said and, before Palin could stop him, he had dashed in through the tavern's door.

With an exasperated sigh, Palin went in after him.

"No kender!" The innkeeper—an exceptionally thin man with a pale, sallow face—was glaring at Tas.

"We're just leaving," Palin said, reaching out his hand to grab Tas.

Instead, Tas caught hold of the sleeve of Palin's robe. "The ginger beer here is awfully nice! I know!"

The few people in the tavern were turning to stare.

Seeing that Tas wouldn't be budged, thinking it would be best to humor him, Palin pulled out a money pouch. "Give us a table. I'll be responsible for the kender."

The innkeeper's gaze went from the full money pouch to Palin's white robes, which were made of fine-spun lamb's wool. The innkeeper glowered, shrugged.

"Pay up front and sit in the back," the innkeeper growled. "An extra steel piece for the nuisance."

"This table," Tas said, trotting through the tavern and selecting a table near the kitchen.

It was the worst table in the place, but it was fine with Palin, who wanted to be able to talk without anyone overhearing. The clatter of plates, the shouts of the cook, the clanging of pans, and the whoosh of the bellows pumping the fire effectively covered all conversation, to the point where Palin found it difficult to hear himself.

"The food's bad, and the wine is worse," Tas said cheerfully. "Which is why no Knights of Takhisis come around here." He winked.

The innkeeper brought over a mug of ginger beer and a glass of wine. Tas took a swig of beer. "We'd like some food," he told the innkeeper.

"I'm not hungr—" Palin began. Tas kicked him under the table.

"Bring us two plates of cornbread and beans, and put lots of peppers in them," Tas ordered.

"I'll send the girl," the man muttered, and left.

"Tell me about Usha!" Palin said, leaning across the table to be heard.

Tas took a good long look around the tavern, then, nodding to himself, he launched into his tale.

"Where was I? Oh, yes. In prison. Well, I met this dwarf in the common cells, and he was most entertaining, being a thief and everything. He said my set of lock-picks, which the knights took away from me, was one of the finest he'd ever seen and that if I wanted to sell it he'd be interested when he got out, which he didn't expect to be for some time due to the fact that the knights take a very dim view of thievery and were doing their best to clean up the town. Which is why there weren't any kender in jail."

Here Tas sighed and paused to take another drink of ginger beer and to look around the inn once more. Palin fidgeted nervously, anxious to hear how this story ended—if it ever did.

Wiping foam from his mouth, Tas continued.

"Well, I remembered that Dalamar had told me to watch out for Usha and no one gets around town like a thief, so I asked the dwarf if he'd seen anyone who looked like Usha, and I gave him her description. He said, yes, that sounded just like a woman who'd joined the Thieves'

Guild. She was proving to be an apt pupil, or would have been if the knights hadn't moved in and ruined everything."

"I don't suppose he made a mistake?" Palin asked hopefully. "Maybe there's another woman who looks like Usha—"

Tas cocked an eye at him over the rim of the mug of ginger beer.

"I guess not," Palin said, with a sigh. "It *must* be her. I know where the Thieves' Guild is. Steel and I went there. But how will we get near the place? It must be well guarded. And we have to go tonight. Like I said, I promised . . . someone . . . I'd meet him at the Great Library."

"Well, visiting the Thieves' Guild's going to be dangerous," Tas said quietly. "People say the knights are going to burn it down."

"But you said . . . Usha! Is she . . ."

"She's all right," Tas reassured him. "You can ask the dwarf. He's sitting over at the table near the window."

Palin twisted around in his chair.

The dwarf, who had been watching them, raised his mug in salute. "Good to see you again, Laddie."

Palin hung on to the table. "That's . . . that's . . ."

"Dougan Redhammer," Tasslehoff said, waving.

The flashily dressed dwarf heaved himself to his feet, clomped over to their table. "Mind if I join you, Laddie?" He winked. "Palin Majere, if I remember correctly."

Palin swallowed. "I . . . I . . . know you . . . You're . . ."

"Easy, Lad," Dougan said softly. "Eyes watching, ears listening. If I were you, I'd order a bite to eat. You look a little peaked."

"Here's the waitress," Tas said, grinning at Dougan, who grinned back, stroked his luxuriant beard.

The woman, carrying a tray of heavy mugs in her hands, stopped on her way to the kitchen. Her hair, wet with sweat and steam, straggled down over her face. She was dressed in what appeared to be castoff clothing—a man's full-sleeved shirt tied at the waist, a long, cotton skirt with the front tied up in knots, to keep from tripping over it. She cast them a quick, bored glance, then shifted her gaze back to the kitchen door.

"Yeah? What d'you want? Make it quick. I've got dishes to wash."

"Usha!" Palin barely found the strength to stand up. He pushed himself away from the table. "Usha, it's me!"

At the sound of his voice, speaking her name, Usha nearly dropped the mugs.

Palin caught them for her. Their hands met and touched, beneath the heavy tray.

"Palin!" she said breathlessly. "I thought you were dead! I never expected to see you again! Where did you go? What are you doing here?"

"Tas brought me It's a long story. I'm not dead. I came looking for you."

The two stood gazing at each other, holding the tray of mugs, oblivious to everything and everyone else.

"You found me," Usha said softly.

"And I won't ever leave you again," Palin promised.

Dougan Redhammer tugged on his mustache. He eyed Palin speculatively.

"Wanna bet?" the dwarf asked, with a quirk of his eyebrow.

7

The brawl. Escape.
Thieves' Way.

No messing about with the customers on *my* time, girl," the innkeeper said, descending on them. "Get to work!"

"Sorry." Palin took the tray from Usha and handed it to the startled innkeeper. "She's quitting."

"What? Palin, I can't quit! I— Well, I—" Usha bit her lip, flushed, finished lamely. "I need this job."

"She needs the job!" The innkeeper mimicked her. Sneering, he slammed the tray full of mugs down on the table. "Yes, she needs it. So she can see who's carrying a fat purse and then mark them for her thief friends! Like the dwarf there."

"Say now!" Dougan roared, clenching his fists. "Mind who you're calling a thief! By Reorx's beard, I'll not stand for that!"

Grabbing a chair, the dwarf brought it crashing down on the head and shoulders of the blacksmith, who was seated behind him.

The drunken smith, growling in anger, staggered to his feet, began flailing away with his fists. He missed the dwarf, connected with the innkeeper.

The innkeeper staggered backward, rubbing his jaw. Tasslehoff caught hold of his apron strings.

"Skinny-butt, skinny-butt!" Tasslehoff sang out, skipping around the dazed innkeeper like a topknotted fiend. "Afraid to eat his own cooking! Ptomaine Bill they call him!"

The blacksmith was now taking on all comers, which included at least half the customers. The other half had gathered around, shouting encouragement and placing bets. The innkeeper hefted the poker and took off after Tas.

Dougan yelled over at Palin and Usha. "Be off with you, Lad! You, too, Lassie. I'll take care of this wee matter!"

Palin looked intently at the dwarf. "It's good to see you again, sir. I wish our second meeting was under happier circumstances."

"I do too, Laddie. By Reorx, I do." Dougan heaved a profound sigh. "It's in the hands of the gods. . . ."

A crockery jug smashed down on top of the dwarf's head. Ale cascaded over his hat, drenching the jaunty plume and soaking the dwarf.

"That does it!" he yelled, spluttering. Leaping up on a chair, he shoved up his sleeves and knocked his opponent flat. "Best hurry, Lad!"

"This way," Usha said, and she led Palin out the inn by the back door.

Outside they heard a whistle, blowing wildly. The call was answered by running footsteps, the sound of shouted orders. The two huddled in the shadows.

"The knights!" Palin reported, peering around a corner of the wall. "A patrol's coming down the street."

"What about Dougan?" Usha asked anxiously. "We can't leave him! And Tas!"

"Here I am!" came a bright voice.

Tasslehoff emerged from behind the compost heap. He was slightly rumpled, his face was filthy, his pouches hung askew, and his topknot had slipped to one side of his head.

"I'm fine," he pronounced.

"Four knights are going in the front," Palin said. "We should leave now, before more come."

Usha held back. "Dougan!" she said again urgently. "He's been really good to me—"

"Oh, he'll be all right," Tas assured her. "He's a god, after all."

Usha stared. "What?"

"We better go now!" Palin urged, tugging Usha along.

"He's a god," Tas said offhandedly, hastening along beside them. "Reorx. I know, you see, because I hang around gods a lot. Paladine and I are great personal friends. The Dark Queen was so fond of me that she wanted me to stay with her in the Abyss. And now Reorx, who is really Dougan. We had a nice little chat, before someone clonked him on the head bone with a stew pot."

"Do you know what he's talking about?" Usha asked Palin in an undertone.

"I'll explain later," he whispered.

"Now where are we going?" Tas asked excitedly.

"To the Great Library."

"Ah! Astinus." Tas was triumphant. "You see? When I was in the Abyss—the second time, not the first—I finally figured out where I knew him from. He knows me, too."

From inside the inn came shouts and shrieks and the clash of steel against iron.

They reached the end of the alley. Palin started to venture out into the street.

Usha caught hold of him.

"What are you doing? You can't just walk out there like that!"

"My dear," Palin said, gently but firmly, "we have to hurry. Don't worry. If the knights see us, they won't connect us with the brawl.

They'll figure we're ordinary citizens, out for an evening stroll."

"That's just it," Usha countered. "Ordinary citizens don't go out for evening strolls anymore. Look around. Do you see anyone in the streets?"

Palin was startled to realize that Usha was right. The streets were empty—except for the knights.

"Read your identification papers," Usha said softly. "Sometimes certain people are given permission to be out at night. If so, it should be stamped on your papers."

Palin stared. "What identification papers? What are you talking about?"

"I don't need an identity," Tas asserted. "I know who I am. I told them so in the jail last night."

"Everyone in Palanthas has to have papers." Usha looked from one to another in consternation. "Even visitors. The knights give them to you at the gate. Are you sure you didn't get any papers? How did you get into town without them?"

"Well," Tas began, "Dalamar said something that sounded like *oogle, bogle, bogle* and—"

"Never mind," Palin interrupted quickly. "Let's say that we both came into town by rather unconventional means. And, no, neither of us has papers. I don't understand. When did this start?"

The door to the inn opened. The knights marched out several men—including the blacksmith and the innkeeper, who was pleading with them not to shut down his business. Four more knights came out, carrying the unconscious dwarf by the arms and heels. The remainder of the patrons melted away into the darkness.

Tas, Palin, and Usha held perfectly still until the knights had left. The lights in the inn still burned. The cook came fearfully to the door, peered out, then—pulling off her apron—she ran for home.

"You see," said Usha. "Everyone's terrified. When the knights took over, they made every person in Palanthas come to the lord's house—which is now the knights' headquarters—and register. You had to say where you lived, who your parents were, how long you'd been living in the city. If people said the wrong thing, they were taken away—no one knows where. All the families of the Solamnic Knights have vanished. Their houses have been taken over— Hush!"

The three ducked deeper into the alley. A patrol of three knights clanked by, their measured footsteps ringing on the cobblestones.

"The knights established a curfew," Usha continued softly, after the knights had passed. "All citizens are required to be in their homes by midnight. To help enforce the curfew and to 'protect the good citizens from marauding raiders' the knights said that we could no longer light the street lamps."

"The lamps," Palin murmured. "I wondered what was different! Even at night, Palanthas used to be as bright as day."

"No one comes out now. The tavern's been losing money. Only the locals stop by for a drink, and now they probably won't even do that anymore. No one wants to run into the patrols."

Usha gestured down the street the knights had taken. "Even if you're on some perfectly innocent errand, you're marched off to one of the knights' headquarters and questioned endlessly. They ask to see your papers. They want to know where you're going and why. Then, *if* your answers satisfy them and *if* your papers are 'in order,' *then* they escort you to your destination. If they catch you in a lie, may the gods help you. And if they caught you, Palin, without papers, in the company of a kender . . ."

Usha shrugged, shook her head.

"Kender aren't allowed in the city at all," Tas added. "They threw me out this morning, along with a few others. I came right back in, of course, but that wasn't as easy as it used to be. A lot of the old cracks and holes in the wall have been repaired. Still, there are a few they missed."

"We can't just stay here, skulking in the alley," Palin whispered. "I must be at the library by midnight. We'll have to chance the streets. We're running out of time."

"What about your magic ring?" Tas asked eagerly. "You could whisk us there in no time. I love being magicked."

"The ring would take *me* there," Palin said, "but not you or Usha. Come on. We should leave now, while it's quiet, before the knights come back."

Usha was silent long moments, then said, "There's another way, a safer way, but you won't like it."

"Why?" Palin asked, chilled. "What is it?"

Usha tossed her silver hair. "The Thieves' Way, it's called. There—I told you, you wouldn't like it."

Even by Solinari's dim white light, Palin could see Usha's face darken. She wouldn't look at him, and she pulled her hand out of his.

"Usha," Palin began awkwardly.

"I was hungry," she added defiantly. "I had nowhere to go, no place to sleep. The dwarf, Dougan Redhammer, found me and was kind to me. He took me to the Thieves' Guild. *They* didn't ask any questions." Usha cast Palin a reproachful glance. "*They* accepted me right off, made me feel at home. They gave me a place to sleep, found me a job, which is a lot more than *some* people did for me."

Palin was confused. Suddenly, *he* was the guilty party, and he wasn't at all sure how that had happened.

"I'm sorry," he said lamely, "but I—"

"I never stole anything!" Usha continued, growing heated, blinking back tears. "Not a single thing! The thieves were only teaching me. Dougan said I was good at it. I have a real knack."

"Usha, I understand. Hush, don't say anything more." He took hold of her hands, held her tightly.

She looked up at him, into his eyes, and for a moment he lost any notion of where he was, what he was doing. His lips were on hers, she was in his arms. They clung to each other, in the darkness, feeling safe in each other's arms, if nowhere else on Krynn.

Palin slowly, reluctantly, pushed Usha away. "I can't let this happen between us," he said firmly. "You're my uncle's daughter . . . my own cousin!"

"Palin . . ." Usha sounded uncomfortable. "What if I told you that I wasn't, well, wasn't really—" She stopped, tried again. "That I hadn't told the truth . . ." She stopped again.

"The truth about what?" He smiled at her, tried to seem cheerful. "About being a thief? But you did tell me. And I understand."

"No, that wasn't it," she said, sighing. "But, never mind. It wasn't important."

Palin felt a tugging on the sleeve of his robe.

"Excuse me," said Tas politely, "but this alley is getting awfully boring, and what time did you say we had to be at the library?"

"Tas is right. We should go now. We'll take your way."

"Follow me, then." Usha turned away from the street, led them farther into the dark alley, until they reached a dead end.

Tall buildings blocked the moonlight. Light from the deserted inn did not illuminate this part of the alley. Usha stumbled over something in the dark. Tas stepped on a cat, which screeched and fled. Palin banged his shin against a crate.

"We need light," Usha muttered.

"Is it safe?"

She glanced back nervously down the alleyway. "We won't be here long."

Palin said, "*Shirak*," softly, and the Staff of Magius began to glow with a pale, cold light. He held the staff high, saw nothing but walls on all three sides.

"Usha, how—?"

"Hush," she whispered, and dropped to her knees. "Help me move this grate!"

"The sewer!" Tas was down on all fours instantly. He began tugging at the grate in excitement. "We're going down into the sewer! I've heard of the Palanthas sewers before. They're supposed to be very interesting, but I never got around to actually going down into one. Isn't this wonderful, Palin?"

Palin thought of several words to describe going down into the sewers of this large, populous city. *Wonderful* was not foremost among them. He crouched beside Usha, just as she and Tas managed to slide the heavy grate to one side.

"This may be a good hiding place, but how is it going to get us to the library? . . . Ugh!"

A terrible smell flowed up out of the darkness, a smell so foul that it seemed to have a shape and life of its own. Palin gagged and covered his nose with his hand. Tasslehoff, who had been staring, open-mouthed, into the hole, tumbled back as if he'd been struck in the face.

"Pew! Yick! Uck!" The kender wrinkled his nose in disgust. "That certainly is . . . . is . . . "

"Indescribable," Palin said grimly.

"Here, put this over your nose and mouth." Usha handed Palin a bar rag, which had been hanging from her belt. "You'll soon get used to it."

The rag smelled only slightly better than the sewer. Palin took it, but hesitated.

"Usha . . ."

She began kilting up her skirt, lifting the hem and tucking it into her belt. "The sewer system can take you anywhere in Palanthas, maybe even to the Tower of High Sorcery. I don't know. The route's not going to be very pleasant, but—"

"It's a lot better than being caught by the dark knights," Tas observed, tying a handkerchief (one of Palin's) around his nose and mouth. "And I think there's three knights coming this way."

Palin turned in alarm. Several figures—moonlight gleaming off black armor—were visible at the end of the alley. He hastily doused the light of the staff. Usha, another bar rag tied over her mouth, had already entered the sewer opening, was climbing down an iron-runged ladder. Tas followed. Palin adjusted the rag around his nose and mouth. Taking a deep breath, trying to hold it, he crouched at the edge of the opening.

His fingers wrapped around the Staff of Magius. He whispered words of magic, and the next moment he was floating through the darkness. His feet touched the bottom of the sewer at about the same time Usha dropped off the end of the ladder.

Palin caught her, steadied her to keep her from falling into the muck.

She looked at him in astonishment. "How did—"

"Magic," he said.

Tas clattered and rattled down the iron stairs.

"I don't think the knights will come into the alley, but if they do, they'll find the grate off the sewer. They'll know someone's down here," Tas reported.

"We have to get away from here," said Usha. "This way."

Holding Palin's hand, she drew him onward into the darkness. Tas, hitting bottom, adjusted his pouches and hurried after them.

"*Shirak,*" said Palin and stared around in amazement.

No one quite knew how the labyrinthine sewer system of Palanthas had come into existence. Some said that the sewers had been designed by the original builders of Old City and were constructed along with the city itself. But other stories persisted, claiming that the sewer system had been here longer than Palanthas, that it had been constructed as a city itself, built by a nation of dwarves long since forgotten. Some versions of the tale had it that the dwarves were routed from their underground tunnels by humans, who—recognizing the enormous potential of the location—planned to develop the city on top of them.

Certainly, as Palin noted to his astonishment, the sewer system resembled a small city far below ground. The walls were made of stone and were shored up with stone archways. The floor was smooth-paved, ran straight and level. There were even old iron sconces on the wall, which—by the charring on the stone around them—had once held torches.

The ceilings were low; only Tas could walk upright. Palin and Usha were forced to bend almost double. The footing was uncertain, the pavement beneath their feet wet and slimy and occasionally littered with piles of rotting garbage. Rats skittered away at their approach. The three walked carefully; none of them wanted to slip and fall. The light of the staff guided them; the crystal seeming to gleam more brightly the darker its surroundings.

The tunnel into which they'd descended ran directly underneath the alley. They might be walking beneath the very feet of the knights. As long as Palin kept moving in a straight line, he had some idea where he was in relation to the city above. But then the tunnel made a series of serpentine turns and opened into an intersection of three other tunnels, all branching off into different directions. He had no idea which to take.

"This is hopeless!" Palin said. His back hurt from walking bent over, and the smell and the knowledge of what was causing it was making him nauseous. He had never considered the air of Palanthas all that fresh, but now he would have given anything for a breath of it. "How can we tell where we are?"

"Did you hear something?" Tas asked, peering behind them. "I thought I heard something."

"Gully dwarves," Usha said, her voice muffled by the bar rag. "Shine the light over there," she instructed Palin, pointing at the upper wall of one of the bisecting tunnels.

Markings—two different types—decorated the wall. One set of marks was obviously incredibly old. The letters had been made out of multicolored tiles, forming a mosaic. Many of the tiles were now missing, leaving gaping holes in the pattern; others were covered with mold and mildew. The characters looked to be of dwarven make.

Beneath the ancient mosaics were more recent markings. These were nothing more than pictures, crudely scrawled on the walls with some sharp instrument, perhaps a knife blade. They looked like a child's drawings of blocks and circles, with arrows underneath.

Usha studied these intently.

"I still say I heard something," Tas insisted. "Footsteps . . . and maybe voices."

"Mice. This way," Usha said, and turned to the central tunnel that branched off slightly to the left.

"How can you tell?" Palin asked, hesitating. He, too, thought he had heard something. He peered over his shoulder, into the noisome darkness.

"That mark." Usha put her finger on one of the drawings on the wall. "That's the Great Library."

Palin turned back, stared. All he saw was a triangle with a series of lines drawn beneath it. He shook his head.

"That's the roof," Usha said, indicating the triangle, "and these lines are the columns. What's the matter? Don't you trust me?"

She snatched her hand from his. Palin attempted to recapture the hand, but Usha was now keeping it to herself.

"Of course I trust you. It's just . . . so strange," he admitted. "Who or what made these pictures?"

Usha refused to answer.

"Thieves, I'll bet!" said Tas excitedly, studying the scrawls. "They put these drawings here so they can find their way around. Look, that's the lord's house—with its five gables. And that big, tall rectangle with the little triangle on top—I'll bet that's the Tower of High Sorcery. And the round dome with the five pointy things—the Temple of Paladine. This is fun! And the arrows show which way to go. Are there more, Usha?"

"You'll find them at every intersection. Are you coming?" she added, with a haughty glance at Palin. "You were the one in such a hurry."

"I'll lead!" Tas announced. "Maybe I'll find some more pictures."

He forged ahead. Usha, after readjusting the rag over her mouth, started to follow him.

Palin caught hold of her, refused to let go.

Usha stirred against him, then tilted her head back, looked up at him earnestly, as if again about to tell him something, yet unwilling, uncertain.

"Usha," Palin said, "what is it?"

Her eyes, above the bar rag, glimmered. She pulled down the handkerchief. "Palin, I—"

"Where *are* you two?" Tasslehoff sang out, his voice echoing eerily in the tunnel. "I—" The echo suddenly changed, became a screech. "Run, Palin! Run— Ulp!"

And then the echo was silent.

8

A frightening encounter. The rescue. Usha's friends.

as?" Palin called out.

He heard what sounded like a scuffle, a man's deep voice cursing. Palin started forward.

Something darker than the darkness sprang out at him, grabbed him around the throat.

"Stop his mouth! He's a mage," came a gruff voice, and a callused hand clapped over Palin's mouth.

He managed to keep firm hold on the staff in his struggle, and its light went out. But the men who had accosted him apparently carried some type of light. A shaft of yellow stabbed forth into the darkness, only to be immediately doused, by command of the gruff voice.

"Quit this! All of you!" called out Usha. "Jack Nine-fingers, don't you know me?"

A sound of scraping iron and the light of a stubby candle glowed. The yellow light flared once again, struck Usha full in the face. Her arms were pinioned to her sides; a shadowy figure had hold of her.

"By Hiddukel, it's Dougan's girl," the gruff voice growled. "Let her go. What have you got there, Allen Scar?"

"A kender," replied the man grimly. "He knifed me," he added, aggrieved, showing off a hand that was cut and bleeding.

The light illuminated a large man, his face disfigured by a long scar. He carried a wriggling, kicking Tasslehoff under one huge arm. The man had stuffed a handkerchief in Tas's mouth, but the gag wasn't stopping the kender from commenting freely, if somewhat incoherently, on his captor's features, parentage, and body odor.

Chuckles came from out of the darkness, echoing up and down the tunnels.

"Kender! Pah! What next?" Jack Nine-fingers spit into the muck. "I can't stand the little thieves."

"He's a friend of mine," Usha protested. "So is the mage. You let me loose, Sally Dale!"

Usha twisted deftly out of the hands of her captor—a middle-aged woman clad in a short red tunic worn over leather pants. The woman looked to Jack Nine-fingers for orders.

He nodded and waved, and the woman backed off.

"Let my friends go, too," Usha urged.

Jack eyed Palin warily. "Release the scroll-speaker. But take his staff and his pouches. And, you, Mage, keep your hands in plain sight and your mouth shut. Sally Dale, listen to him. If he so much as squeals a word of magic, web him."

The woman nodded silently and kept her eyes on Palin. A white-bearded dwarf held the lantern—a kind known as a "dark" lantern, for it had an iron panel that, when closed, permitted no light to escape. He flashed the light straight into Palin's eyes, half-blinding him.

"What are you doing down here, Girl?" Jack Nine-fingers demanded, frowning. He was a short man of slender build, nimble and lithe, clad all in black leather. The absence of his ring finger on his left hand gave him his name. He had long black hair, a black beard. His skin was dark, swarthy. "You've no thieving business on tonight, at least none that you've cleared with the guild." He said the last in an ominous tone. "You're not thinking of going independent, are you, Girl?"

"I'm not on 'business,' Jack Nine-fingers," Usha answered him with a blushing sidelong glance at Palin. "My friend the mage must reach the Great Library by midnight. As you can see, he's a White Robe. He carries no papers."

"Don't say any more, Usha," Palin cautioned. "They'll probably turn us over to the dark knights, especially if they get paid for their trouble!"

"No, they won't, Sir Mage," came a voice from the darkness.

The speaker stepped into the light. She was young, her face partially hidden by a shawl she had draped over her head. She wore the black dress of a widow and carried a baby in her arms.

"They will not give you up to the knights," she said softly. "They have rescued us from them, my child and me. My husband was a Knight of Solamnia. He died in the High Clerist's tower."

The child in her arms slept fitfully. She hugged the baby close. "The dark knights came to my door yesterday and told me to be ready to leave this day, that they would accompany me to a 'place of relocation.' I was frightened. I've heard rumors of such places. I had nowhere to go, no one to turn to. And then he came in the night"—she nodded her head toward Nine-fingers—"and offered to take me someplace where we would be safe. I care nothing for myself anymore," the young woman added, her tears dripping onto the baby's gown. "My life ended with my husband's death. But my child . . ."

She hid her face in the baby's blanket. Sally Dale put her arms around the young woman, comforted the mother as the mother comforted her child. Tasslehoff had ceased his incoherent imprecations, was now sniffing, as was the large man holding on to the kender.

Palin turned to Nine-fingers. "Is that true? Are you taking her somewhere where she will be safe?"

"It's no concern of yours what we're doing," Jack growled. His face split into a grin. "Let's say this—it will be a fine joke when those black-armored devils show up at the lady's door this day and find the bird flown."

"Perhaps I've misjudged you," Palin said stiffly. "If so, I'm sorry."

Nine-fingers laughed, leaned near him. "Don't think too well of us, now, Mage. If I was to meet you in an alley in the dark, you with a fat purse hanging from your belt, I'd just as soon slit your throat for your money, as not. What we do we do for love of no man. We do it to thwart those black-plated bastards who have ruined our livelihood, what with their patrols and their curfews. We plan to do everything we can to make their lives miserable, so long as they are in our city. Those who survive."

Nine-fingers winked, leered, and drew his finger across his throat. Then, eyeing the three, he scowled. "As it is, I'm wondering whether or not it would be well to make certain you spread no word of our ways. It was wrong of the girl to bring you down here, show you our secrets."

"Whatever you do, you best be doing it, Jack," said Sally Dale crisply. "The boat that's to carry my lady here will be wanting to sail with the tide. If you're going to silence this lot, do it quick and we'll be gone."

"Let us go our way in peace, Jack," Usha begged. "I can answer for my friends. They won't say a word."

"My brothers were Solamnic Knights," Palin added. "I swear on their graves that I would do nothing to endanger this lady."

Jack continued to eye Palin. "A White Robe. Well, he'll keep his word. They've a weakness in that area. Be gone with you then. Mind you follow the symbols, Girl. Those who get lost down here end up as rat fodder."

He waved his hand. The large man with the scar dropped Tasslehoff face first into the muck. The dwarf with the lantern led the way. Sally Dale drew the woman and the child into the darkness. The others trooped after her and, within several heartbeats, the thieves were gone as swiftly and silently as they had appeared.

Palin remained standing in the darkness, to calm his fast-beating heart, regain his composure. He was very confused; his view of a neat, well-balanced world had been turned inside out. He recalled his father saying that some people applauded the dark knights for bringing law and order to a troubled land. And he remembered—as if in a dream—the god Paladine saying bitterly, "the peace of the prison house."

"It's safe to have light again," Usha said softly.

"*Shirak*," he said, and the staff's light gleamed. He looked at Usha, troubled. "You seem to know these people well. And they know you."

Usha's face was pale, her lips set tightly. "Yes, I do know them. They were helpful to me. I've already explained this to you. Am I on trial?"

Palin sighed. Once more, it seemed, he was the one at fault. He decided to change the subject. "You started to tell me something earlier. What was it?"

Usha refused to look at him. "It wasn't important." Turning away from him, she bent down to help pick up Tas.

"Are you all right?" she asked solicitously.

The kender, coughing and spitting, stood up, wiped muck from his face.

"Did you hear what that man called me, Usha? 'Little thief'!" Tas was spluttering with indignation. "How *dare* he? *And* he took my knife. Only it wasn't my knife, it was your knife, I noticed, Palin. And now that thief is missing *his* knife, too. I've got it right here. Funny, he must have dropped it . . ."

9

The Great Library. Bertrem is shocked. Astinus of Palanthas.

 e're here," Usha reported in a soft voice. She stood beside a ladder leading upward. The light of the staff illuminated a grate above their heads.

"Where does this come out?" Palin asked.

"Right in the middle of the street, unfortunately, directly across from the library," Usha said. "Needless to say, this exit isn't used a lot." Her voice cool, she spoke to Palin as she might have talked to a stranger.

"I'll go look," Tasslehoff offered. He climbed nimbly up the ladder, shoved on the grate, and lifted it a crack. Peering out, he dropped the grate with a clunk loud enough to be heard in Northern Ergoth.

"Patrol!" he warned, tumbling down the ladder.

"*Dulak!*" Palin stifled the staff's light.

The sound of booted feet rang above them, one knight stepping right on the grate. At that dread sound, Usha moved near Palin. Her hand found his, and their fingers twined tightly together.

The knights marched past, and everyone let out a deep breath.

"I'm sorry," he whispered. "I'm sorry," she began. Both stopped talking, smiled.

"I'll go back up." Tas was prepared to climb when Palin stopped him.

Standing beneath the ladder, he stared up at the metal grate that covered the sewer entrance. This grate was not hidden like the one in the alley. This grate was in a well-traveled street in the center of town. The grate would have to be replaced, or the knights might get suspicious and start searching the sewers. They wouldn't find Palin, but they might find Jack Nine-fingers and the woman he was helping to safety.

"We have to hurry!" Usha reminded him. She was standing very near him, pressing against him in the darkness. "The patrols make their rounds every quarter of the hour."

"I'm trying," Palin said, finding it difficult to think rationally with her so near, the touch of her hand on his. The words to the spell he needed flitted in and right back out of his mind. "This isn't working. Stand over here."

Taking Usha by the shoulders, he positioned her directly beneath the ladder. "Tas, you stay near Usha. When I call, you start climbing."

"What are you going to do?" Tas asked excitedly. "You're going to work magic! Can I come with you and watch?"

"You stay here," Palin repeated, having enough distractions.

Fumbling with the staff, he climbed awkwardly up the ladder. He lifted the grate a fraction, peeped out.

Solinari was high in the sky; its silver light made all objects stand out in sharp relief against a black background. The street was empty.

Removing a leather bracelet he wore around his right wrist, he brought the words of the spell to mind. He needed to enunciate each word properly while performing the correct hand motion, using the spell component in the prescribed manner. He could hear Usha and Tas whispering below him, tried to block their voices out.

He shut his eyes, concentrated. He was no longer in the sewers of Palanthas. He was no longer in danger from the knights. He was no longer in a hurry. He was no longer near the woman he would give his life to possess. He was with the magic.

Palin lifted the loop of leather, began to move it in slow circles directly underneath the grate. At the same time, he spoke the words of magic, placing proper emphasis on each syllable. And as he spoke, he waited, tensely, nervously, eagerly for the rush of warmth, centered at his heart, which would spread throughout his body. The warmth meant that the magic had taken hold of him, was working through him. The warmth was addicting, intoxicating, came only to a chosen few.

He felt the warmth begin and he knew the exquisite joy, the exhilaration of the power tingling in his blood. The magic sparkled and danced within him, like bubbles in wine, rising to the surface of his being. It was a simple spell he cast; any mage of low rank could perform it. Yet even the simplest spell brought this reward, cost this price. For after the words were spoken, the bubbles burst. The warmth receded, leaving behind weariness, depression, and an all-consuming desire to experience the sensation again.

For now, Palin reveled in his art. He moved the loop beneath the grate, spoke the words. The grate began to rise slowly in the air. Palin controlled its levitation by the motions of his hand; every time he drew a complete circle, the grate rose a fraction more. When the grate was high enough to permit a person to climb out, Palin ceased the hand-motion. The grate held still, hovering in the night air.

"Tas! Usha!" he called softly. "Now! Quickly!"

Tas clattered up the ladder, his pouches jouncing around him. Usha came up behind. Palin crawled through the opening; not an easy task, considering that he was forced to keep the loop of leather underneath the grate the entire time. He crouched on the street, his hand beneath the grate, as Tas hauled himself out of the sewer.

"Keep watch!" Palin ordered the kender, who scooted across the street and ducked behind a bush.

Usha came next, scrambling up and out with ease.

Tas motioned to her, and Usha ran to join him.

Palin began to lower the loop of leather, moving it downward in a slow spiral. And then he heard footsteps, marching in rhythm.

He didn't dare hurry. Withdrawing the loop now would cause the grate to fall to the street with an ear-splitting clang. The footsteps were some distance yet, but drawing nearer. Palin moved as swiftly as he could, which seemed torturously slow. The booted feet drew nearer, nearer.

"Palin!" Tas ventured a loud whisper. "Do you hear—?"

"Hush!" Palin hissed. The grate was almost in place. It was touching his hand now.

This was the difficult part. Once the loop was removed, the grate was free of the spell, would start to fall. He had to "catch" the grate, hold it, renew the spell, all in the space of a very few seconds. Carefully, he drew his hand out from underneath it and, with a swift motion, reversed the loop, held it downward, and shifted his hand above the grate.

The footsteps were closer, probably only half a block away now. The buildings were still blocking the knights' view, but when they emerged into the street in front of the library, they would be able to see him, a dark shadow in the bright moonlight.

He heard a rustle in the bushes, heard Tas whisper sharply, "No! Wait here, Usha! It's too dangerous."

Palin lowered the grate into place. The warmth faded from his blood, leaving him suddenly weak, chilled, and empty. For a brief moment, flight seemed useless, a waste of energy. Far easier just to stay here, let the knights capture him.

Palin was accustomed to these feelings of despair and lethargy that came after the magic. He knew better than to give way to them. The knights were very close now. He dove for the shadow of the bush just as the knights emerged into view.

Moonlight glinted off their dark armor. They tramped past, silent, efficient. The three hiding in the bushes kept still, afraid to breathe, fearful that the rapid beating of their hearts might be too loud, give them away.

The knights were gone. Once again the street was empty.

The white marble facade of the Great Library of Palanthas, with its columned portico and narrow, dark windows, was one of the oldest structures on Krynn, held in reverence and respect by all who came near it. People who walked its grounds spoke in hushed tones, not because silence was imposed on them, but because the very air rustling the trees seemed to whisper the secrets of the ages kept locked inside the library. Palin had the impression that, if he took the time to listen, he might hear one of them.

But he didn't have time to listen. Not only was it nearing the hour of his meeting with his uncle, the knights would be coming back this way in a very short time. The enormous double front doors were new, replacing the old doors that had been damaged years before during the Battle of Palanthas. Made of bronze and bearing a book—the symbol of Gilean—the doors were shut, looked extremely imposing. Palin pushed on them. They were, as he had expected, locked.

"Probably barred from the inside," he muttered. "There must be a way—"

"What about this, Palin? Maybe this does something."

Tasslehoff was holding on to a length of rope dangling down from the dark recesses of the portico.

"Tas, don't—"

Whatever Palin had been going to say was boomed out of his head by the clang of a large bronze bell. Its resonating notes thundered through the still night air, reverberated up and down the street.

"Oops!" Tas said, and let go of the rope.

The bell began to swing back and forth, clanging madly, the sound nearly deafening them. Lights flared in the library windows. Lights flared in the windows of buildings up and down the street. A smaller door, set within the great doors, opened tentatively.

"What is it? Fire?" demanded a cracked voice. A tonsured head peered fearfully into the darkness. "Where is the fire?"

Palin had caught hold of the bell cord, stilled the ringing of the bell. "There is no fire, Brother. I'm—"

A strange expression contorted the elderly monk's face. He stared at the mage's white robes, stained and filthy; at Usha, her dress hiked up around her waist, her shoes covered with muck; and at Tasslehoff, dripping slime from his topknot. The monk put his hand over his nose.

"The library's closed," he said in a loud voice and started to shut the door.

"Wait!" Tasslehoff interposed his small body in the doorway. "Hullo, Bertrem! Remember me? I'm Tasslehoff Burrfoot. I was here before—"

"Yes," said Bertrem in frozen tones, "I remember. The library is most definitely closed. Come back in the morning. *After* you have bathed." Retreating, he started to shut the door, paused, added hastily, "All but the kender," and, pushing Tas out, Bertrem pulled on the door.

"Please! You must let us inside!" Palin thrust his staff into the door, stopping it a crack. "I'm sorry we smell like this, but we've been down in the sewers—"

"Thieves!" Bertrem shrieked, trying unsuccessfully to drag the door closed. He raised his voice. "Help! Help! Thieves!"

"Someone's coming!" Usha warned.

"We're not thieves!" Palin was growing desperate. "I'm supposed to meet my uncle here. He told me to wait for him in the office of Astinus. Let me see Astinus!"

Bertrem was so shocked he nearly let loose of the door. "Assassins!" he howled. "Assassins here to murder the master!"

"Knights!" Usha hissed. "Heading this way!"

"Bertrem!" A voice called from within the library.

Bertrem jumped, paled, glanced back over his shoulder.

"Yes, Master?"

"Let them in. I've been expecting them."

"But, Master . . ."

"Do you force me to repeat myself, Bertrem?"

"Yes, Master. I m-mean, no, Master."

Bertrem swung the door open. Backing up, he held the sleeve of his robe over his nose, motioned the three to come inside.

The interior of the library was shadowy, lit only by an oil lamp Bertrem had set on a table so he could answer the door. The speaker whom the monk addressed as "Master" could not be seen.

"Shut the door, Bertrem," ordered the voice. "When the knights come to inquire about the commotion, tell them that you were sleepwalking, that one of the things you do when you sleepwalk is ring the bell. Is that understood, Bertrem?"

"Yes, Master." Bertrem sounded subdued.

"This way," continued the voice from the shadows. "Quickly. History passes unrecorded while I stand idle in this drafty hall. Light your staff, young mage. Your uncle is waiting for you."

Palin spoke the word, and the staff lit the vast hall. The light shone on rows of bound leather volumes and stacks of scrolls placed neatly and carefully on long shelves that extended as far as the eye could see, were swallowed up by the darkness, much as the history they contained was swallowed up by the past.

The light also fell on the author of the books, the writer of the scrolls.

His face was neither old nor young nor yet middle-aged. It was smooth, unlined, as blank as the paper on which he wrote constantly, endlessly, recording the passage of time on Krynn. No emotion marked the face; no emotion touched the man. He had seen too much to be moved by any sight. He had described the birth of the world. He had written of the rise of the House of Silvanos, the crafting of the Graygem, the construction of Thorbardin, the heroics of Huma in the Second Dragon War, the Kinslayer War, the formation of the Knights of Solamnia, the founding of Istar. He had continued to write during the terrible destruction of the Cataclysm, when the walls of the library shuddered around him.

He had written of the fall of the Knights of Solamnia, the rise of the false priests, the return of dragons, the War of the Lance.

Some said that he had, long, long ago, been a monk in the service of Gilean. During his service, he had begun to write his now famous history. Gilean had, so it was told, been so impressed with the work that he had rewarded the mortal man with immortality—as long as he continued writing.

Others said that he was the god Gilean himself.

Those who came into his presence could rarely recall his features, but they never forgot his eyes: dark, roving, all-seeing, without pity, without compassion.

"I am Astinus, Child of the Irda," he replied, though Usha had not asked the question—aloud.

Usha stared, shook her head. "I'm not . . . "

The eyes gazed at her relentlessly. She gave up her denial. "How did you know?" Held by the eyes, fascinated, she crept forward. "*What* do you know?"

"Everything."

"Do you know the truth about me?" Usha faltered, with a sidelong glance at Palin.

"Ask yourself that question, Child of the Irda," Astinus replied offhandedly. "Do not ask me. This is not the place to talk," he added, with a glance at the door. "The knights will be here any moment. Come along."

He turned to his right, proceeded down a hallway. They left Bertrem standing guard—not very happily—at the closed door. The bell rang loudly. The three hastened their steps.

"Hullo, Astinus," Tasslehoff said, trotting along at the chronicler's side, not at all daunted by the imposing presence. "Do you remember me? I remember you. I just saw the god Gilean in the Abyss. Are you really Gilean? You don't look much like Gilean, but then Fizban didn't look like Fizban either. Well, rather, he did look like Fizban, he just didn't look like Paladine. Dougan Redhammer looked a lot like Reorx, but then I've noticed that dwarves haven't much imagination. Have you noticed that? Now if *I* were a god—"

Astinus came to a sudden halt. A flicker of emotion passed over his face. "If kender were gods, the world would certainly be an interesting place. Though none of us would ever be able to *find* anything in it."

"Where is my uncle?" Palin inquired, eager and not eager for him to meet Usha.

"He waits for you in my private quarters. But"—Astinus flicked a glance over at Palin—"surely you do not intend to meet him in that condition."

Palin shrugged. "I am certain that my uncle would understand. We had no choice—"

Astinus came to a halt in front of a closed door. He pointed. "In there you will find water for washing yourself and a change of clothes."

"I thank you, sir, for your thoughtfulness," Palin began, "but my uncle told me to hurry—"

He was talking to Astinus's back. The chronicler had turned away from him. "I have clothes for you as well," he said to Usha and Tas. "Castoffs that we donate to the poor, but they are clean and serviceable. You two, come with me."

Astinus said, over his shoulder as he walked away, "I will return in a few moments, Palin Majere. When you are dressed, I will take you to your uncle. Come, Child of the Irda. You, as well, Master Burrfoot."

"Did you hear what he called me?" Tas was saying proudly to Usha as they followed Astinus. "*Master* Burrfoot."

Palin supposed Astinus was right. Raistlin would not want to meet a nephew who smelled as if he'd been feasting with gully dwarves.

Palin opened the door, walked into the room—a small cell, similar to those in which lived the Aesthetics, the monks who devoted their lives to the service of the library and its master. Sparsely furnished, the room contained a bed and a washstand on which stood a pitcher of water, a washbowl, and a lighted candle. The end of the bed was lost in the shadows, but a lump was probably his change of clothing.

Palin barely glanced at the clean clothes. He approached the washbowl, now suddenly eager to strip off these filthy robes and wash away the muck and the stench that was starting to make him sick to his stomach.

After his ablutions, feeling much better, he bundled the dirty robes in a corner, turned to put on the clean clothes.

Palin halted, stared, sucked in a breath. He grabbed hold of the robes, held them close to the light, thinking that his eyes were playing tricks on him.

No mistake. No trick, at least not one his eyes played.

The robes Astinus had given Palin were black.

10

The Choice.

alin's first thought was that Astinus was playing some sort of joke. Recalling the passionless eyes, Palin discarded that notion. The black cloth was soft to the touch and felt oddly warm in his hand. Palin's words, spoken to Raistlin in the Tower of High Sorcery, returned forcibly to him.

I know the work will be arduous and difficult, but I will do anything—sacrifice anything to gain more power.

And was this the answer? Was this the sacrifice his uncle intended?

A knock sounded. Before Palin could respond, the door swung open. Astinus stood in the doorway. He held a large book in his arms, a quill pen in his hand.

"Well," he commanded, "why are you wasting time? Put them on."

"I don't understand, sir," Palin said. "What does this mean?"

"Mean? What do you think it means? You have already made your decision. Put them on."

"Decision? What decision? I never intended this. I don't want to take the Black Robes. I don't want to use my magic for gain or to harm others or force others to work my will—"

"Don't you?" Astinus was calm. "I should think that allowing a man to die in your place was a decision worthy of the black robes."

Palin protested. "Die? In my place? You must have made some sort of mistake. I never—" He stopped. "My god! You mean Steel! But, no! Surely the knights wouldn't put him to death. He *must* have explained the circumstances to them. There was nothing he could have done. Didn't they believe him?"

Astinus entered the room. Walking up to Palin, the chronicler opened the great book he held, indicated a line written at the bottom of the page.

This day, First Watch rising, Steel Brightblade was executed. He died in place of Palin Majere, who gave his word of honor to return, and broke it.

"First Watch rising," Palin murmured. He lifted his gaze from the book to Astinus. "It's not First Watch yet! It can't be. How—"

"It is several hours until sunrise," Astinus said, shrugging. "Sometimes I anticipate events. It makes the work easier, especially if there is no chance for change."

"Where?" Palin demanded. He held fast to the black robes. "Where is he to die?"

"In the High Clerist's Tower. He dies without honor, stripped of his rank. He will lay his head upon a block of blood-crusted stone. Lord Ariakan himself wields the sword that will sever Steel Brightblade's head from his body."

Palin stood silent, unmoving.

Astinus continued, relentless. "Brightblade's corpse will not be entombed, but will be thrown from the walls, for the carrion birds to feast on. He will be used as an example to other knights. This is what happens to those who fail to obey orders."

Images came to Palin: Steel kneeling at his brothers' grave site, Steel fighting at his side in the Shoikan Grove, Steel saving his life . . .

"But, what does it matter?" Astinus droned on sonorously. "The man is evil. He has given his soul to the Dark Queen. He has killed his share of good men, Knights of Solamnia. He deserves to die."

"Not in shame and dishonor." Palin stared at the book in Astinus's hands, at the writing on the page. "First Watch. It's too late. I would stop the execution if I could, but it's not possible. It takes days to reach the High Clerist's Tower from Palanthas. I could never arrive in time to prevent the execution." He was ashamed of himself, but he felt a vast sense of relief.

A voice whispered in Palin's mind. *Robe yourself in black. When that is done, I will open the spellbook of Fistandantilus to you. You will have earned it.*

A bitter taste, worse than the smell of the sewers, was in Palin's mouth. He ran his hand over the black cloth. It was soft to the touch, soft and warm, would envelop him, protect him. "I've done nothing, Uncle! It's not my fault. I never thought Steel would come to harm because of me. And even if I wanted to go, I could never get there in time."

You have made your decision. Proclaim it proudly! Don't lie to yourself, Nephew! the voice whispered. *You can go. You have the ring, Dalamar's ring. The kender gave it back to you. You can be standing in the High Clerist's Tower before the next beat of your heart.*

Palin trembled. The wood of the Staff of Magius was suddenly warm, warmer than the black cloth in his hand. The ring would take him. He had only to wish it.

But what a terrible wish! He looked up at Astinus. "You've heard?"

"Yes. I hear all words, even those of the soul."

"Is . . . what he says true? Could I stop the execution?"

"If you reached the High Clerist's Tower in time, yes, the knights would halt the execution." Astinus regarded Palin with mild curiosity.

"They would halt *Steel's* execution. Are you prepared for me to cross out his name and insert your own?"

Palin's throat closed; he could barely breathe. No. No, I am not ready to die. I'm afraid of death, afraid of the pain, the unending darkness, the unbroken silence. I want to see the sun rise, listen to music, drink a cup of cold water. I have found someone to love. I want to feel again the tingle of the magic. And my parents. Their grief would be bitter. I don't want to leave this life!

Then don't, Nephew, came the whispering voice in his mind. *Steel Brightblade has dedicated his soul to the Dark Queen. Many would account it a good deed to let him die.*

I gave my word. I promised to go back.

Broken word? A broken promise? What is that? Once Steel Brightblade is dead, who will know or care?

I will, Palin answered.

And what did you expect, Nephew? What did you think the word "sacrifice" meant? I will tell you. It means exchanging everything—everything!—love, honor, family, your soul itself—for the magic. Isn't that what you wanted? Or did you expect to gain it all without giving something in return?

"You're asking me to give my life," said Palin.

Of course.

"Either way," Palin realized, "I give my life."

Either way, said Raistlin.

II

The execution.

teel Brightblade lay upon a pallet of straw, spread on the stone floor of his cell. He had not slept, but had spent the night before his execution in silent, bitter vigil. He did not fear death. He had made peace with death, looked forward to it.

And death had not come, not taken him as he had wanted to die—in honor, in battle. His death would be inglorious, shameful, without honor. He would die in shackles, die the death of the thief, the coward, the traitor.

He could not see the dawn from his windowless cell, but he could hear them call the watch. He'd listened to it all night long. He heard the Last Watch shouted throughout the tower, imagined what it would be like for those standing guard duty.

They would smile, stretch, and yawn. The end of their watch was near. In another hour, they could leave their posts, return to the barracks, slip into the welcome darkness of sleep. Out of that darkness they would return, wake to curse the bedbugs, the heat, the snoring of the man next to them.

Steel Brightblade, in an hour, would slip into the darkness from which there was no return, not unless Chemosh got hold of him, sent him walking the world as one of the restless undead. Steel feared nothing in this life, but the thought of that dread fate shriveled his soul. He had once met the death knight Lord Soth. Awed at the undead's power, Steel had still gazed at the death knight's faceless visage with revulsion and pity and the whispered prayer, "Takhisis, Ruler of the Dark, let any fate be mine except this."

That had been his agony throughout the night. Would Takhisis forgive him? Or would she hand him over to skull-masked Chemosh, to spend eternity as Death's slave.

The thought left him chilled, quaking with terror, his body bathed in a cold sweat. Shuddering, he crouched on the straw pallet and was praying for Her Dark Majesty's mercy, when the key rattled in the cell door.

"Visitor," called out the jailer. His voice was subdued, reverent, and the unusual tone warned Steel that this visitor was not ordinary.

He straightened, rose to his feet. He was clad in the garment he would wear for the execution, a plain, crude black shift, similar to the garment used to clothe the bodies of paupers before they were thrown into unmarked graves. He waited tensely, nervously, thinking, fearing, wildly hoping that perhaps it was Lord Ariakan, come to rescind the sentence of death. The cell door creaked open.

A figure draped in black robes entered. The figure was stooped, bent with age. Steel could not tell, in the shadows of his cell, if the figure was male or female. It seemed little more than a shambling bundle of darkness. The figure was not alone. Another, also robed in black, walked at its side, supportive of the feeble steps.

Yet the voice which spoke was neither weak nor faltering. "Shut the door and lock it."

Memory stirred in Steel. He had seen this, encountered this before. He fell to the damp, dank stone, lying prone upon it, his arms extended out above his head.

"Holiness!" he whispered.

"Light," the high priestess ordered the acolyte who served her.

The younger woman spoke a word, and light gleamed from an unseen source. The light did not banish the darkness. Rather, it seemed to deepen it, make it stronger, give it life.

The high priestess of Takhisis hobbled forward until she came to stand above him.

"Rise," she hissed. "Look at me."

Overcome with awe, Steel raised himself to his knees.

The high priestess had seemed ancient to him when she had blessed his investiture, years ago. She was now old past understanding, past comprehension. Gray hair hung in wisps around her face. Her skin was stretched over bone, seemingly without flesh beneath. Her lips were blue, bloodless, as were the veins on her bone-ivory hands.

Stretching one of those hands forth—the other clutched the acolyte's arm—the priestess took hold of Steel's chin. Her fingers were like talons; long nails, yellowed and sharp, dug into his flesh.

"Your queen has heard your prayers. She is pleased with you, Steel uth Matar Brightblade. You have served Her Majesty well, better than you know. She stands to gain two souls this day. A place has been prepared for you in Her Dark Majesty's dread guard, a place of honor . . ."

Steel shut his eyes. Tears of relief and thankfulness seeped from beneath the lids. "I honor and thank Her Majesty with all my heart—"

"One requirement." The priestess interrupted him.

Steel's eyes flared open.

The priestess's nails stabbed his flesh, drawing blood. She loosed his chin. Her hand lowered, a skeletal finger extended, pointing. "Remove the talisman."

Steel's hand went to his neck, to the chain of fine silver he wore around his neck. From that chain dangled an ornament Steel had always kept hidden. Only four people knew he possessed it, and one of those persons, Tanis Half-Elven, was now dead. Lord Ariakan knew, for Steel had told his lord himself; the priestess knew; and Caramon Majere, who had been a witness, knew. Steel's hand closed over the talisman, the starjewel.

Steel often wondered why he wore it. The jewel was an irritant; its sharp edges scratched and annoyed him. He had, more than once, decided to rid himself of it, had grasped the jewel in his hand, prepared to break its chain, fling it to the dust.

Yet, every time he touched it, a cooling, calming feeling of serenity spread through him, like cold water assuaging a burning thirst. The sensation eased his almost constant inner turmoil, cleared his thoughts, left them crystalline, clean-cut and sharp-edged, like the jewel. Nagging doubts vanished, while confidence in himself, his abilities, was restored.

His fingers touched the silver chain. Knowing how the jewel affected him, Steel was reluctant to touch it. His thoughts were calm now, his inner doubt settled. His queen had forgiven him his sin, had prepared a place of honor for him at her side. The jewel would now only confuse and disturb him.

Yes, the priestess was right. He should remove it, remove it now, so that his soul stood before Takhisis free of restraint.

"I will," he said, and, grasping the chain, he gave it a sharp tug.

The chain did not break.

"Remove it!" ordered the priestess, displeased. Her red-rimmed eyes narrowed. "Or risk Her Majesty's wrath!"

A vision rose before Steel's eyes, a vision of a fleshless hand, scrabbling up from the smothering ground of the Shoikan Grove, seeking the warmth of living blood to banish the chill that could never be banished, and he knew—with stark terror—that the hand was his.

Frantic, desperate, he pulled and tore at the chain until it bit deep into his neck. "Let me go, Father!" he cried, not realizing what he was saying, not even knowing he was saying it. "Let me go! I have made my choice—"

His hand slid along the chain. He grasped the jewel, thinking to use it as leverage.

Light, warm and bright, welled out from between his fingers. His fears, which were like the nightmares of a child, alone in darkness, eased, as if the father's strong arm were there to support him, comfort him, protect him from harm.

He was filled with peace, calm. He was no longer bitter. He knew, suddenly, that though his death might seem dishonorable to some, he would be honored by others. His soul was his own. Takhisis could not claim it, not unless he gave himself willingly. He had yet to make that choice.

He must have faith, if that faith was only in himself.

Steel's hand opened wide, released the jewel, let it fall back against his breast.

The high priestess hissed in displeasure, snarled. "You are doomed! You have betrayed your queen. May your torment be endless!"

Steel shivered at the terrible curse, yet he did not flinch or crouch or grovel. He felt nothing now, was drained of all emotion, even fear.

"Take me away from here!" the priestess ordered.

The acolyte raised her bowed head, flashed Steel a look of hatred, enmity, then did as the priestess commanded, guided the faltering footsteps over the rough stone.

Steel should say something, he knew, but he was suddenly tired, very tired. He was tired of this life. He was impatient to end it, end the suffering and doubt, the feeling of being two separate beings trapped in one body, end the struggle between them for the possession of his soul.

The battle would be over soon. He found himself looking forward to it.

A single trumpet, its note pure silver, sounded First Watch.

Booted footsteps marched with solemn tread outside the cell door. Steel rose to his feet. They would find him standing straight and proud when they came inside to take him.

The door swung open. Two knights, high-ranking knights, members of Lord Ariakan's own personal staff, entered. Steel recognized the honor being accorded him; he was humbly grateful.

"Steel uth Matar Brightblade," said one, speaking in low, solemn tones, "you are hereby summoned to face our lord's judgment. Do you have anything to say in your defense in this, your final hour?"

"No, my lord," Steel answered steadily, "I accept my lord's judgment as just. I accept my punishment as right."

"So be it," said the knight, his tone grim.

Steel was astonished then to realize that the man had been hoping for a different response.

The decision made, the knight's expression hardened. He and his companion approached Steel. They bound his hands with strips of black leather behind his back. They gathered up and tied his long, thick hair with another cord of leather, in order to lay bare his neck to meet the sword. This done, they started to grasp hold of his arms.

He shrugged loose from their grip.

"I will walk on my own," he said.

He walked out the cell door.

The jailer stood to one side, muttered, in a gruff voice, "May the Dark Queen judge you fairly, Sir Knight."

From the darkness of the cells around his came a multitude of voices, "May Paladine defend you, Brightblade!"

Somewhere, in the darkness, someone began to sing, "*Sularus Humah durvey. Karamnes Humah durvey . . .*"

It was the Song of Huma, hero of the Knights of Solamnia. One by one, the other prisoners joined in, their voices rising strong and poignant in the dawning.

"Make them stop that row," said one of the dark knights, but he said it softly, and the jailer walked away, pretending he hadn't heard.

Steel wanted to respond, could find no words, no voice to speak them if they had existed. He nodded his silent thanks. His eyes dim with tears, he walked on.

It was not a long distance from the cell block to the central courtyard, where Steel had fought courageously, where Tanis Half-Elven had died in his arms. Not a long walk to where Steel himself was to die by his own sword, his father's sword.

He was astonished to find that the route was lined with knights. At first, he thought they had gathered to revile him. But, as he walked past, barefoot, clad in his robes of shame, each man or woman present saluted him gravely, solemnly.

All the knights blended together in a blur of shining armor that coalesced into the image of his father, striding before him, silver armor shining in the first rays of the dawn.

Steel emerged into the courtyard, which was filled with knights, all standing in a circle. In the center was a block of black marble, stained and crusted with dried blood. An area had been hollowed out, where Steel would place his head.

With firm, unfaltering step, accompanied by his two knightly guards, Steel Brightblade walked up to the block, stood before it.

Lord Ariakan, as Steel's sponsor and judge, would also be his executioner. Ariakan held in his gloved hands the sword of the Brightblades. His Lordship's face was as cold and unrelenting as the stone.

He looked, not at Steel, but at the two knights. "Has the prisoner any argument to make why this sentence should not be passed on him?"

"No, my lord," answered one of the knights, "he does not."

"He deems the sentence just, my lord," said the other. "The punishment right."

"Then so the sentence will be performed on him." Lord Ariakan's gaze shifted to Steel.

"Her Dark Majesty will be your next judge, Steel uth Matar Brightblade. You will assure her, as you have told us, that you were judged fairly, that you were given every chance to speak in your own defense, and that you refused this opportunity."

"I will do so, my lord," Steel answered, his voice strong and carrying through the air, which was already, even in the early morning, breathlessly hot. "I hold you blameless in my death, my lord. I take it completely upon myself."

Lord Ariakan nodded, satisfied. It was not unknown for Queen Takhisis to take exception at the judgment of mortal men, to send back the soul of the victim to seek revenge on those who had falsely executed him.

"Let the sentence be carried out."

One of the knights escorting Steel offered him a blindfold. Steel, with a shake of his head, proudly refused. The two knights took hold of Steel by the arms, assisted him to kneel before the block. One of them brushed back the black hair, leaving the neck bare.

"Strike him there!" came a hissing voice, the voice of the high priestess. "Strike him along the red mark on his flesh."

The mark left by the silver chain.

Steel turned his head, rested his face on the block of marble, which, despite the heat of the day, was as cold as death itself.

"Pray to your queen, Brightblade," said Lord Ariakan.

"My prayers are made," Steel replied steadily. "I am ready."

He could see the sword rising above him; Ariakan lifted it high, ready to bring it down with a blow that would sever Steel's head from his body. He watched it arc upward. When the blade reached its zenith, it caught the sun's light, flared with a white brilliance like a star.

Steel closed his eyes. The memory of that beautiful flash would be his last. He waited, tensely, for the blow.

What he felt, instead, was a heavy weight, as of another body, crashing into his, knocking him off balance. His hands tied, he had no way to catch himself; he lurched over sideways.

Astonished, almost angry at the interruption, he opened his eyes to see what was going on.

A young man in white robes stood protectively over Steel. In his hands he held a staff topped with a crystal ball, clutched in a dragon's claw.

"What is the meaning of this?" Lord Ariakan thundered. "Who, in the name of the Dark Queen, are you?"

"I am the one you want," said the young man in a halting voice that strengthened as he continued, "I am Palin Majere."

12

OlÒ fRiENÒs.
A pROposeÒ MEEtiNG.

Raistlin Majere stood in the study of Astinus of Palanthas. The archmage was restless, he roamed about the room, his gaze roving coldly and without interest over the volumes of recent history stacked neatly on the shelves. Astinus worked at his desk, writing in the book. At intervals, one of the Aesthetics would appear and, very silently, not disturbing the master, gather up the completed volumes and bear them away to the library, where they were then arranged in chronological order.

The two men had not spoken since Astinus's return to his study. The bells in the town rang out First Watch. Raistlin paused in his restless pacing, looked out the open door and down the hall, as if he were expecting someone.

No one came.

He stood long moments, then, walking back, circled around Astinus's chair, looked to read what the historian had just written. Satisfied, Raistlin nodded to himself.

"Thank you, my friend," he said quietly.

Astinus did not lift his pen from the paper; the flow of ink ceased only when he stopped to dip that pen in the inkwell, and that he did so swiftly that the eye scarcely noticed it.

"I did very little," Astinus replied, continuing to write.

"You showed Palin the book," Raistlin said. "I grant this is not unusual, but you showed him the book in order to force him to make a decision. And you dislike meddling in mankind's affairs."

"Mankind's affairs are my affairs," said Astinus. "How not? I have written them, lived them—every one of them—for centuries."

His writing slowed, finally ceased. He had, just that morning, begun a new volume. It was thick, leather-bound, its vellum pages blank, ready to receive laughter, tears, curses, blows, the cries of the newborn, the sighs of the dying. His fingers seemed permanently bent in a crook to hold his pen. His index finger stained bluish purple from the ink, Astinus thumbed through the blank pages until he came to the end.

"Whatever happens," he said quietly, "this book will be the last."

He picked up the pen, put it to paper. The pen made a harsh scratching sound, ink spluttered, blotting the page. Astinus frowned, tossed the split quill aside, selected a fresh one from a holder on his desk, and began writing again.

"You knew, I think, the decision your nephew would make."

"I knew," Raistlin said quietly. "That was why I sent Caramon back home. He would have interfered. Palin had to make his own choice."

"The right one—for him," Astinus observed.

"Yes. He is young, has never been truly tested. Life for him has been easy. He's been loved, admired, respected. Whatever he wanted was given to him. He's never known hardship. When he wanted to sleep, a bed was prepared for him, a bed with clean sheets in a warm and cozy room. Oh, true, he traveled with his brothers, but that—until the last— was more a holiday than anything else. Not like Caramon and me, when we were mercenaries before the war."

Raistlin mused. "Only once was he truly tested, during the battle when his brothers died. He failed—"

"He did not fail," Astinus remarked.

"He thinks he did," Raistlin said, with a shrug, "which amounts to the same thing. In reality, he fought well with what magic he had, kept his head in the midst of fearful chaos, remembered his spells during a time when one wonders how a man remembers his own name. But he lost. He was doomed to lose. Only when he held the black robes in his hand, only when he had to condemn a man to death unjustly, only then did he come to the sacrifice he must be prepared to make."

"He may well die in gaining such understanding." Astinus, all this time, had not ceased to write.

"That is the risk we all take. So the Conclave judged . . ." Raistlin frowned down at the books, as if he could read their contents and was not finding much of it to his liking.

"As they judged once in your case, old friend."

"They tempted me . . . and I fell, for which I was reviled, for which I paid a heavy price. Yet, had I not fallen, it is very likely that the War of the Lance would have been lost." Raistlin's lip curled in a sneer. "How does that thread weave into the grand design?"

"As do all threads," Astinus said. "Look at the rug beneath your feet. Were you to turn the rug over, you would see what appears to be a confused tangle of many-colored strands of thread. But look at the rug from the top—the strands are neatly, tightly woven, merged together to form a strong fabric. Oh, it is frayed a bit at the corners, but—overall—it has worn well."

"It will need to be strong," Raistlin said quietly, "to withstand what is coming. There is one more thing I would like you to do for me, my friend."

"And that is . . . ?" Astinus did not look up, but his pen flowed across the paper.

"I would like to see Lady Crysania," Raistlin said.

Now Astinus lifted his gaze; now the pen stopped. The historian was rarely astonished by anything, since he had seen, heard, felt everything. This request, however, took him by surprise.

"See Lady Crysania? Why?" Astinus demanded. "What would you say to her? That you are sorry for what you did to her? For the way you used her? That would be a lie. Did you not tell your brother that you would do what you did all over again?"

Raistlin turned. A hint of color stained the pale, wan cheeks. "I used her. What of the way she used me? We were two of a kind, just clad in different color clothes."

"She loved you . . ."

"She loved her ambition more."

"True," Astinus agreed. "And she finally saw that, but only when she could see nothing else. What would you say to her? I am curious, particularly since this meeting you propose will never come about."

"Why not?" Raistlin demanded sharply. "All I have to do is walk over to the temple grounds. They cannot—dare not—keep me out."

"You may walk over there any time you want, but it will avail you little. Have you forgotten what dire calamity faces the world? Lady Crysania has been called to fight her own battle against Chaos, as have many others. Your story, Palin's story, Steel Brightblade's story, are just one of many that I am currently writing."

"The great tangle," Raistlin murmured, scraping his foot across the rug. "Does Lady Crysania go alone?"

"No. Another is with her, a man devoted to her. He travels with her, though she is not aware of his true nature. That, too, is another story. Again, assuage my curiosity. Would you ask her for forgiveness?"

"I would not," Raistlin returned coldly. "Why should I? She got what she wanted. I got what was due me. We are even."

"So, you would not apologize to her. You would not ask for forgiveness. What, then, did you want to say to her?"

Raistlin was silent long moments. He had turned back to the bookshelves, was staring now at the shadows that surrounded the books, staring at a time that would never happen.

"I wanted to tell her that sometimes, in my long sleep, I dreamt of her," he said softly.

13

The Note. Usha's plan.
A disturbance in the library.

Usha had bathed—a cat's bath, as Prot would have called it, meaning that she had given herself a lick and a promise. But at least she had been able to wash away the stench of the sewer and the smell of the tavern's grease and stale ale, which had been almost as bad. She had changed her clothes, too, though she had been almost as startled and very nearly as fearful at the change of clothing she found on her bed as Palin had been of the change he had found on his.

Her old clothes, the clothes the Irda had made for her, clothes that she had thought were packed away in a small wooden box in the small, shabby room over the tavern—her old clothes were here. And here, too, was the pouch containing her only possessions—the magical artifacts of the Irda. The sight of her clothes and especially the pouch frightened her. Someone had not only gone to fetch them, apparently, but someone had gone to fetch them before they could have possibly known she was going to be here!

Usha didn't like that. She didn't like this place. She didn't like the people. The only person she did like was Palin, and she liked him so much that the feeling was more frightening than anything else.

"Why do I keep lying to him?" she asked herself miserably. "One lie on top of another. All tiny and harmless to begin with, they seem to be growing in size."

A tiny pile of sand had changed to a mountain of boulders. She had to labor to keep them in place, for if one shifted, they would all fall, tumble down and crush her. Yet the mountain of lies was now a barrier, was keeping her separated from Palin.

She loved him, wanted him for her own. This past month, she had dreamt of him, reliving their brief time together in the dreadful tower.

Other men, like Lynched Geoffrey, had tried to win her love. Usha had at last begun to realize that people found her pretty. And Usha could at last let herself believe. She looked into a mirror and no longer saw herself as ugly, perhaps because the images of the incredibly beautiful Irda had begun to fade in her mind, like summer roses pressed between the pages of a book.

As other men fell in her estimation, Palin rose. And though she told herself constantly that she would never see him again, the sight of a mage in white robes always quickened her heartbeat.

"How strange," she muttered, "that when he did come in, I was too busy and harassed to take note."

She paused a moment to relive the memory, the wonderful, thrilling warmth that had surged through her when she had heard him speak her name, speak it with such love and longing.

"And I repaid him with more lies," she said, berating herself. The words came so glibly to her tongue, they were out before she knew it. "But I can't bear the thought of losing him again!" She sighed. "And now here is this uncle of his. . . ."

Usha put on her old clothes reluctantly, wary of their mysterious appearance. But it was either wear these or dress again in the muck-stained skirt, the food-spattered blouse. While she dressed, she formed a resolve.

"I'll find Palin. I'll take him away from this place before he has a chance to talk to his uncle, before he can find out that I'm not . . . the person he thinks I am. I'll be doing this for his own good," Usha convinced herself.

A soft tap on her door interrupted her castle-building.

"Usha? It's me, Tas. Open up! Quick!" The voice had a squeezed quality to it, as though it were coming through the keyhole, which, upon investigation, Usha discovered it was.

She opened the door so fast that Tas lost his balance, tumbled inside.

"Hullo, Usha. Do you mind if we shut the door? Bertrem seems to be awfully fond of me, because he told me under no circumstances was I to leave my room and wander about the library without him. But I don't like to bother him. He's so busy. He went to tell Astinus we were ready."

Usha hesitated in shutting the door. "Where's Palin? Can you take me to his room?"

"Sure," said Tas cheerfully. "It's two down from yours and one up from mine." He padded, soft-footed, over to the door and peered out. "We don't want to disturb Bertrem," he said in a loud whisper.

Usha wholeheartedly agreed with this sentiment. Seeing no one in the hall, the two slipped out and ran to Palin's room.

The door was shut. Usha tapped on it timidly. "Palin!" she said in a soft voice. "Palin, it's Usha and Tas. Are you . . . are you dressed?"

No answer.

"I think I hear someone coming!" Tasslehoff said, tugging on Usha's sleeve.

Usha started to tap again, but the door moved beneath her hand, began to swing open.

"Palin?" Usha called.

Tas marched inside. "Palin, I— Oh. You can come in, Usha. Palin's not here."

"Not here!" Usha darted inside, looked around the room. Her search didn't take long, for the room was very small. Robes of soft black fabric lay on the floor, as if they had been picked up, then dropped. The room smelled of the sewer muck, which his boots had tracked across the floor. And there was even the round print of mud left by the bottom of the staff.

"Look, here's a note." Tas pointed to a ripped piece of paper, such as mages use for copying spells, which was lying on top of the black robes. "It's for you," the kender reported, picking it up. "I'll read it . . ."

Usha snatched the note, began to read it feverishly.

The note appeared to have been written in a great hurry; the writing was almost illegible. The paper was stained with ink blots and other marks that might have been tears. Usha read the few, very few, words scribbled on it, and a chill, as of a biting winter wind, made her shiver all over.

"Usha!" Tas was alarmed. She had turned so very pale. "Usha, what is it? What's the matter?"

Silently, with hands that seemed to have gone numb from the cold, Usha handed the kender the note.

" 'Usha, I love you with all my heart. Always remember . . .' I can't read that part, it's all smudged. Something, something . . . 'gone to the High Clerist's Tower' . . . something . . . 'Steel . . . love . . .' " Tas paused, aghast. "He's gone to the High Clerist's Tower!"

"That's the dark knight's stronghold, isn't it?" Usha asked hopelessly, knowing the answer.

"It is *now*," Tas said, subdued. "It didn't use to be. I wonder why Palin went there? And without taking us?"

"He went to throw his life away!" Usha said, frightened and angry at the same time. "That's what the note says. He gave his word to that . . . that horrible knight, Brightsword or whatever his name was. We have to go after him, stop him!" She started for the open door. "The knights will kill him. Are you coming with me?"

"You bet," said Tas promptly, "but he probably wouldn't have walked, Usha. It's something I've noticed about mages. They don't take to exercise. And if Palin has magicked himself into the middle of the stronghold of the Knights of Takhisis, he's going to be in a lot of danger. I think we'd better go tell Raistlin—"

Usha slammed shut the door, turned, stood with her back against it. "No. We won't tell anyone."

Tas halted, amazed. "Why not, Usha? If Palin's truly gone to the High

Clerist's Tower, he's going to need rescuing, and while I'm pretty good at rescuing people myself, I've found that it almost always helps to have a wizard with you. . . . Oh, I forgot! You're a wizard, aren't you, Usha?"

Usha didn't appear to be listening. "Tas, have you ever been to the High Clerist's Tower?"

"Oh, yes," said Tas matter-of-factly. "I've been inside it many times. The first time was when Flint and I were there and Kitiara attacked it and then the dragons flew in and were all trapped and I broke the dragon orb, completely by accident. And Sturm died and Laurana took the dragonlance."

He paused, gave a little sigh, then added, "Anyway, I know my way around the High Clerist's Tower quite well. I'm especially familiar with the location of the jail."

"Good," said Usha, "because that's where we're going. I have an idea."

Walking over, she picked up the black robes, shook them out, slid them over her head. Flushed and breathless, she smoothed her hair, adjusted the robes around her slender body. The robes were a good fit; she and Palin were nearly the same height. She tied them around her waist with a black, silken cord.

"How do I look?" she asked. "Like a black-robed wizard?"

"Well," said Tas, hating to throw cold water on this expedition, but bound to bring up objections, "the knights don't have black-robed mages, only gray."

"That's true." Usha was downcast.

"But!" Tas lit up with excitement. "They do have black-robed clerics! I've seen them walking around town!"

"You're right! I'll be a cleric of Takhisis." Usha paused, regarded the kender in perplexity. "What about your disguise?"

"I could wear black robes, too!" Tas said eagerly.

"Hush," Usha said, frowning, "I'm thinking."

The meaning of the word "hush" being generally unknown in the kender language, Tas prattled on. "Once a cleric of Morgion—that's the god of pestilence and disease—came to Kendermore, looking for converts. Eiderdown Pakslinger had always wanted to be a cleric, so he volunteered. The cleric said Eiderdown wasn't really the type Morgion had in mind, but he'd give him a try. Well, the very week that Eiderdown put on the black robes, almost every kender in Kendermore came down with a severe cold in the head. You never heard such sneezing and coughing and nose-blowing!

"The sickest of all was the cleric of Morgion. He was laid up for a week, wheezing his lungs out. Eiderdown took credit for the whole epidemic. And even though the head cold was something of a nuisance and we all ran out of handkerchiefs, we were really proud of him—poor Eiderdown had never been much of a success at anything before this. Eiderdown said he thought he'd try his hand at bunions next, and maybe ringworm after that. But the cleric of Morgion, once he quit sneezing, took Eiderdown's black robes away from him and left the village rather suddenly. We never did know why—"

"I can't think of anything," Usha said, giving up. "If anyone stops us—which, hopefully they won't—we can just say you're my prisoner."

"It's a role I've had a lot of practice at," Tas said solemnly. "How are we going to get to the High Clerist's Tower? It's an awfully long walk from here."

"We're not walking. I have my magic items all here with me. And I know how to use them," Usha added with a touch of wonder and pride. "Sally Dale showed me. You go look to see if anyone's out there."

Tas opened the door, looked up and down the hall. He thought he saw the flutter of brown robes, vanishing around a corner, and he waited for someone to come, but no one did. Eventually, Tas reported the way clear. The two left Palin's room, hurried back to Usha's.

Once inside, she began rummaging through her pouch.

Always being willing to help, Tas began rummaging through the pouch, too. Usha found what she wanted. Lifting the object out carefully, she closed the pouch.

She reopened the pouch to remove Tas's hand, which had inadvertently stayed behind, then she exhibited what she held. It was a small figurine of a horse, made out of clay, covered with a shining white glaze that seemed to glow in the candlelight. Tas caught his breath. It was truly the most lovely, wonderful thing he'd ever seen.

"What does it do?"

"When I breathe on it, it will take us to the High Clerist's Tower with the speed of the wind. Or at least that's what Sally said she thought it would do."

Usha held the small horse to her lips, breathed into the tiny nostrils.

The nostrils flared, the horse took a deep breath, and suddenly a real, enormous horse materialized in the room.

The beast was shining white, as if it were still covered with glaze, and it whinnied and trumpeted and stamped its hooves in impatience.

Usha gasped. Sally Dale had said nothing about summoning a full-blown animal! Usha didn't have time to marvel—not with the noise the horse was making. Tasslehoff was already clambering onto the animal's back. He helped Usha, who had never ridden any sort of beast in her life and was appalled at the size of the horse. She felt unsafe and unsteady on the horse's bare back.

Tasslehoff, digging in with his heels, grabbed hold of the mane. "Now what?" He had to shout to be heard above the clamor the horse was making.

"Go the High Clerist's Tower," Usha instructed.

"How?" Tas cried.

"Wish it!" Usha closed her eyes and wished.

*   *   *   *   *

Raistlin sat in a chair in Astinus's study, engrossed in a book the chronicler had just completed, dealing with the fall of Qualinesti into the hands of the dark knights, a fall that had been accomplished without a fight.

The knights and their blue dragons had encircled Qualinesti, ringed it round with sword and spear, and yet had not attacked. Ariakan, in what had become almost standard procedure, sent in an envoy, demanding the elves surrender. In secret, he met with representatives of the elven senate.

Within the elven kingdom, the people were divided, torn asunder by fear of the knights and the blue dragons that circled with impunity overhead. The elves sent messages to the golden and silver dragons to come to their rescue, but they received no answer.

At this point, a faction of younger elves demanded that the nation go to war. Porthios and his troops were out in the wilderness, keeping an eye on Ariakan and his troops. Porthios could not hope to attack such a large force with his small band of guerilla fighters, but if the elves would attack from within Qualinesti, Porthios and his forces would attack from their side and catch the dark knights in a closing vice.

The elves were prepared to follow this plan when a senator rose to announce that Qualinesti had sued for peace. The senate had voted for surrender, provided that their king—Gilthas, son of Tanis Half-Elven and his wife Laurana—be allowed to remain the ruler.

The meeting had ended in a near riot; many of the younger elves were arrested, led away in chains by their own people. Gilthas stood silently by, watching, saying nothing. His widowed mother, Laurana, was at his side. All knew then that Gilthas was nothing but a puppet, who danced when the knights pulled his strings.

At least, that's what they thought they knew. Raistlin, reading, smiled now and then.

The water clock on the mantle ticked the passage of time; Astinus's pen recorded it. Second Watch had come and gone. From within the library came an odd sound.

Raistlin lifted his head. "A horse?" he said in wonderment.

"That's what it is," Astinus said calmly, continuing to write.

Raistlin raised an eyebrow. "Inside the Great Library?"

"That's where it is." Astinus wrote on. "Or was."

The sound of the horse was replaced by the sound of sandals, flapping in haste on the floor.

"Enter, Bertrem," said Astinus, before the monk had knocked.

The door opened; Bertrem's head appeared. Receiving no rebuke for disturbing his master, Bertrem's head was soon followed by the rest of him.

"Well," Raistlin demanded, "have they left?"

Bertrem looked to his master.

Astinus, irritated, ceased his work, glanced up. "Well, answer the archmage's question! Have the woman and the kender left?"

"Yes, Master," Bertrem answered with a sigh of thankfulness.

Bertrem had once fought off an attack by draconians, when they had tried to burn the library during the war. He never had nightmares about draconians, however. Bertrem had nightmares about kender—kender loose in the Great Library, kender whose pockets were bulging with books.

"They are gone. They brought in a horse!" he added in shocked disapproval. "A horse in the Great Library!"

"A noteworthy event," Astinus said, and made a note of it. He glanced at Raistlin. "They have gone to rescue your nephew. I am surprised you are not with them."

"I am with them, in my own way," Raistlin said, and returned to his reading.

14

The Nightlord accuses. Palin responds.
A dark omen.

T he two knights who had escorted Steel to his execution now assisted him to stand up from the block. They were forced to lift him to his feet, then prop him up. Steel had been so intent on the next world, had given himself so completely to death, that he was weak and shaking in life. He tottered on unsteady legs and gazed around in bewilderment, wondering what this new life now held for him.

Lord Ariakan had lowered the sword, though he still held it. He commanded discipline in the ranks, silenced the clamor.

Palin stood on the spot where he had materialized. He had not moved, had not spoken since his initial, startling pronouncement. Lord Ariakan had, of course, halted the execution, but it was obvious—from the way he was shifting his gaze from Steel to Palin and back again—that His Lordship had questions.

Ariakan turned to the assembled knights. "Is there someone here who can tell me what is going on? Who is this White Robe? Is this truly the prisoner we seek? Can anyone here identify him?"

Two knights stepped forward, both pushing eagerly out of the crowd, though each had differing motives for their haste. One was Subcommander Trevalin, newly arrived from the triumph in Qualinesti. His face was alight with pleasure, and he cast Steel a congratulatory glance as he came to stand before his lord. The other was the Nightlord, who had eyes only for Palin.

Trevalin would have spoken out immediately, but the Nightlord outranked him. He was forced to contain his eagerness. Lillith had first say.

"My lord Ariakan." The Nightlord bowed. She seemed disturbed, troubled. "This is indeed the prisoner, Palin Majere, for whom Steel Brightblade gave his parole. *I* was the one who captured this young mage in battle. I know him. I so swear before our queen. Yet, I would say, my lord, that this mage's recovery should not, in any way, affect your lord's judgment passed on Steel Brightblade. He lost his prisoner. It was not Brightblade who recovered him. My lord said he was to die. I urge Your Lordship to carry out the sentence!"

Lord Ariakan regarded the woman with a troubled expression, then turned away from her, cutting short her attempt to say more. Ariakan looked to Trevalin.

"Subcommander, do you recognize this White Robe? Will you swear to his identity?"

"I do indeed know this mage, my lord," Trevalin said. "He is the prisoner, Palin Majere, I so swear by my queen and all her hosts! This frees Steel Brightblade of the sentence of death!" He cast a defiant look at the Nightlord.

Ariakan smiled slightly. "That will do, Subcommander." He looked next to Steel. "Brightblade, is this your prisoner?"

"Yes, my lord." Steel spoke in a daze. "This is Palin Majere."

"Nephew of Raistlin Majere, who once again walks this realm!" The Nightlord was avid. "My lord Ariakan, I urge you! Hand this mage and his cousin over to the Thorn Knights at once. Let us deal with both of them. I warn you, Lord, they are plotting together! Why else would this young man arrive and voluntarily give himself up to death? He thinks that he will escape! Kill them both now, my lord, immediately! Otherwise, I warn you, these two will bring about the downfall of the knights!"

The gathered knights glanced at each other, spoke in low, troubled voices. Vehement, impassioned, Lillith was alarmingly convincing.

Ariakan raised his hand for silence, gazed intently at the young mage who stood alone, near the bloodstained marble block.

"I will take the matter of Steel Brightblade under advisement. As to the mage, the Thorn Knights may interrogate the prisoner at their leisure. Only pray let him speak for himself now, before the morning grows any hotter and we are broiled alive."

Though the sun had just risen, its heat was already intense. The sun had a strange look to it as well. It was larger, seemed to have drawn closer to the world, if such a thing was possible. The heat beat relentlessly on the black armor of the knights, causing more than one to cast longing glances at the shadows.

Ariakan wiped the sweat from his forehead with his arm, continued his questioning. "Palin Majere, have you come to ransom yourself?"

"He has come to destroy us!" the Nightlord said loudly.

Ariakan sternly glanced at her, and she fell into a seething silence.

Palin shook his head. "No, I have not," he answered.

"Are you, in fact, allied in treachery with your cousin, Steel Brightblade? Answer me the truth, young mage," Ariakan cautioned. "I have ways of catching you in a lie, ways you would not find pleasant."

"I wear the White Robes," Palin said proudly. "Do you think it likely, my lord, that I would be allied with a knight of evil?"

Ariakan nodded, appeared to accept the response. Lillith ground her teeth in frustration, muttered beneath her breath.

Ariakan, ignoring the Nightlord, continued with the young mage. "You were sentenced to death on your capture if you did not provide ransom. I order that sentence to be carried out forthwith. Have you anything to say before you die?"

"My lord, I do," Palin replied. "I gave my word to return. Before I am put to death, I want to apologize to this knight and explain to him why I broke my word."

"Do not let him speak!" The Nightlord was insistent. "This is a trick of our enemies! Do not trust this mage. He is the nephew of one of the most powerful wizards who ever lived. As I told you, my lord, I met Raistlin Majere near the Forest of Wayreth. He has escaped from the Abyss—"

"My uncle was never in the Abyss!" Palin refuted.

The Nightlord did not care to dispute the point. "Raistlin has returned," she maintained. "*He* was the one who sent you here, isn't that true?"

"It is not true," Palin said, a faint flush staining his pale cheeks. "I came here of my own accord. If anything, my uncle would have stopped me."

Ariakan intervened. "If I might have a word, Nightlord? Thank you. I am familiar with the exploits of members of the Majere family. Courage, it seems, runs in the blood. I want to speak to this young man. If you are so afraid of him, Lillith," Ariakan added dryly, "then bind him with what enchantments you will."

The Nightlord, scowling, stalked over to stand beside Palin. She scorned to touch the bags and pouches containing his spell components. Whatever magic he cast with those she could easily counter. Her eyes fixed covetously, jealously, and suspiciously on his staff.

"He holds the Staff of Magius, Lord Ariakan—one of the most powerful magical artifacts in all of Ansalon."

"Take it, then," Ariakan said impatiently.

"I want him to give it to me, my lord. That will prove to me that this is no trick of his uncle's."

Palin did not look at the Nightlord. He kept his gaze on Ariakan. "You may take up the staff when it falls from my dead hand, my lord, not before. This is no trick, I assure you. I am not involved in some plot with my cousin. May I speak freely, my lord?"

"You cannot trust him!" the Nightlord cried. "You see, he refuses to surrender the staff. It could do us all great harm."

"If he wanted to do us harm, Lillith, I am certain he would have done so before now. I have granted him the right to speak his apology to Brightblade, whom he has wronged. I, for one, would like to hear it."

Palin, nodding his thanks, walked over to stand in front of Steel.

"Cousin, you acted honorably and nobly in bringing the bodies of my two brothers back to be buried in the soil of our homeland. You escorted me safely to the Tower of High Sorcery, that I might try to fulfill the geas laid on me by these gray sorcerers. I think we both knew, in our hearts, that the quest was a false one, given to us for some obscure purpose."

The Nightlord fumed, but she could do nothing at this point to stop Palin from having his say. Ariakan had given his command, and she dared not disobey.

Palin continued. "Each of us continued on to the Tower of High Sorcery in pursuit of our objective. Steel Brightblade was always loyal to his queen in his pursuits. I was perhaps not so honorable in mine. Be that as it may, I entered the laboratory of my uncle, fully expecting that Steel Brightblade should accompany me. The door slammed shut, however, and I could not open it again. Since I could do nothing else, I searched for and found the Portal. I entered it—"

"He lies!" the Nightlord interrupted shrilly. "No mage of his low rank could enter the great Portal to the Abyss! It is written that only a black-robed wizard accompanied by a cleric of Paladine—" The Nightlord suddenly sucked in her breath, aware of what she had said.

Ariakan's eyebrow quirked. "But I thought you sent this young man to open the Portal. Perhaps he found the key. Continue, Palin Majere. You almost make me forget the heat."

"I entered the Portal," Palin repeated. "I needed no key. No constraints were laid on me. The Portal stood open. The Queen of Darkness had abandoned it."

"Lies!" muttered Lillith, but she did not say the word loudly, only loud enough for those standing near to hear.

Ariakan frowned at hearing this part of the tale. The knights in the courtyard exchanged questioning glances.

Palin swallowed, started to continue, coughed, and said faintly, "My lord, may I beg a drink of water?"

Ariakan waved his hand. A squire brought over a dipper full of water. Palin drank thankfully. Steel Brightblade stood unmoving. He had waved off assistance. His dark eyes never left Palin's face.

"Thank you, my lord," Palin said. "Inside the Abyss, I found my uncle. He was *not* being tortured, as the stories have it. He took me and my companion, the kender, Tasslehoff Burrfoot, to witness a most extraordinary event—a gathering of the gods."

The knights' murmurings grew loud. There was much shaking of heads and exclamations of disbelief, even derisive laughter.

Commanders ordered silence among their men.

Ariakan now regarded Palin with suspicion, murmured to an aide, "Are we permitted to put to death the insane?"

Palin overheard, proudly lifted his chin. "I swear to you, my lord, by Solinari and by Paladine, by Mishakal and all the gods of the white pantheon, that what I speak is the truth. I know it sounds unbelievable," he continued, with rising passion, "but what I heard in the Abyss is more unbelievable still.

"The world—our world—is in terrible danger. The Irda recently captured the Graygem and, in an attempt to use its magic to stop you, my lord, from invading their land, they inadvertently broke it open. The Father of the Gods, Chaos, had been imprisoned in the Graygem. When the Irda broke it, they freed Chaos.

"The father has denounced his children and has sworn to destroy their creation. The gods are in league to fight him, and they hope and expect that we mortals will join them. If not, our world is doomed. All of us, every living being on this world, and eventually the world itself, will perish."

Heat rose in waves from the stones in the courtyard. Flies buzzed incessantly around the dried blood on the marble block. The Nightlord rolled her eyes and shook her head, smiled mockingly, making certain all knew what she thought of Palin's tale.

Ariakan's brow furrowed.

"I don't suppose you have any proof to back up your claims, Palin Majere? You must admit, this is a monstrous story you bring us."

"I have no hard proof, my lord," Palin said calmly. He had never expected to be believed—except perhaps by one person, and that was the only person who counted. His gaze went to Steel. "But I heard Paladine make a bargain with your queen. The dark knights were given control over Ansalon, in order that they might unify all the warring people, bring them together to take a stand against the armies of Chaos. The tower fell to your forces, the first time the tower has ever fallen to the armies of darkness."

"I would like to think our overwhelming superiority of arms and men had something to do with our victory," Ariakan said wryly.

Steel turned to face Ariakan. "My lord, may I speak?"

"Certainly, Brightblade. I'm surprised you haven't spoken before now."

"My lord, I believe Palin Majere. I'm not sure why"—Steel shrugged—"except that I journeyed with him and I know him to be a man of honor. This act—his coming here in order to spare my life, at peril of his own—proves it. I ask my lord to recall one strange occurrence during the Battle of the High Clerist's Tower: the withdrawal of the silver and gold dragons. We thought they retreated, expected them to regroup. But they have not reappeared. What other explanation, except that Paladine ordered them to leave?"

Ariakan gave this due consideration. He was a man of faith. He had himself brushed up against the gods. His mother, so many believed, was Zeboim, goddess of the sea. And long ago Ariakan himself had been honored by an audience with Queen Takhisis, had obtained her personal blessing to form the knighthood that was dedicated to her.

"Send for the high priestess," he commanded. "We will soon have the truth of this."

A courier departed. The knights stood, sweating and uncomfortable, in the courtyard, beneath the infernal sun.

A high, piercing shriek split the stillness. A cry of horror and anguish, it raised the hair on the back of the neck, raised the flesh on the arm.

"Now what?" Ariakan demanded.

A commotion broke out among a group of knights standing near the entryway. They all parted, hastening to clear the way.

The courier reappeared, his face chalk white. "My lord! The high priestess is dead!"

Stunned silence descended on the knights. After what they had heard of Palin's story, this sudden death of their highest-ranking cleric seemed the worst possible omen.

"How did it happen?" Ariakan asked, shaken.

"I have with me the woman who was with her at the time, my lord." The courier motioned, and a cleric of Takhisis came forward. The young woman was livid, her hair torn, her robes rent in the transports of her grief.

"Her Holiness was deeply troubled, my lord. Ever since she went to the prison cells to visit the condemned this morning, she seemed abstracted, preoccupied. Her Holiness approached the altar to offer prayer. She was making the ritual sacrifices when her arm brushed up against a vial of holy oil, knocked it onto the altar. The oil spilled, spread over the altar. A bit of flaring wick fell from one of the candles and caught the oil on fire. The fire spread swiftly, consuming the sacrifices before they had been properly anointed. The high priestess stared into the flame with such a look of horror on her face that I shall never forget it, as long as I live. Then, my lord, she dropped down before the burning altar. The flames went out, but when we tried to raise Her Holiness, we discovered that she was dead."

The knights heard the story in a silence that seemed to encompass all the world. Into the silence fell the Nightlord's voice, as disturbing as a pebble dropped into still water.

"I told you, my lord! It is this White Robe's doing! And his as well." She stabbed a finger suddenly at Steel. "They are in league! Both traitors! It is they who are responsible for Her Holiness's death."

"Commanders, dismiss your men," Ariakan ordered. "Return them to their duties. Nightlord, take Palin Majere to a cell. He is to be held for further questioning. The sentence of death will be postponed until this matter is settled. I will be in the temple, investigating this further." Ariakan turned to depart.

Trevalin, greatly daring, spoke up. "My lord!"

Ariakan, irritated, looked back over his shoulder. "Yes, Subcommander, what do you want?"

"My lord, since Steel Brightblade has been vindicated and no *substantial* charges have been leveled against him, I ask that you return him to his rightful rank and place among my command."

"Free him at your own peril, Lord Ariakan!" Lillith said, her voice soft and lethal. "Free him, and the knighthood falls!"

Ariakan gazed at the Nightlord with disfavor. He glanced at Steel, then shrugged. "Very well, Subcommander. Brightblade, I give you permission to return to your talon, but you are not to leave the fortress."

Lord Ariakan left for the makeshift Temple of Takhisis, which had been established outside the walls of the High Clerist's Tower. Though the dark knights officially ruled the tower, they had discovered that no holy object dedicated to Her Dark Majesty could be brought within the tower walls.

The Nightlord, shaking her head over her lord's folly, motioned to several of her knights, gave Palin into their custody. The sorcerers bound Palin by the arms, stripped him of his spell components, and gagged his mouth. He still retained the Staff of Magius, however.

The Nightlord approached. Compressing her lips tightly, determined that she would betray no weakness, she stretched out her hand, suddenly seized hold of the staff, wincing in anticipation of the pain.

Her face cleared, smoothed. She regarded the staff first in amazement, then with triumph. Exulting, she wrenched it free of Palin's grip.

He waited for the staff to react, to punish the Nightlord for her audacity. Nothing happened. The staff might have been an ordinary staff.

"The Staff of Magius appears to have chosen a new owner," Lillith said to him. "This is a mark of Her Dark Majesty's approbation. My lord must be made aware of the truth." Smiling, secret, subtle, she added, "And he will be. He will see for himself."

Caressing the staff, running her fingers over the smooth wood, the Nightlord motioned for the guards to take the young mage.

As the Gray Robes dragged Palin away, he cast a last look at Steel. *You must believe me!* he said silently. *You must convince him!*

Steel remained impassive, but he continued to follow Palin thoughtfully with his eyes until the young man had been removed from the courtyard. Even after Palin was gone, Steel remained standing, staring.

Trevalin clapped Steel on the back, recalled his attention. "Congratulations, Brightblade! Drawn from the brink of death. How do you feel? Elated? Relieved?"

"Confused," answered Steel.

15

Unease. Paths cross.
Dry lightning.

Steel returned to his quarters with the other knights in his talon. His armor and—most importantly—his sword were given back to him, with Lord Ariakan's personal commendation. Steel breakfasted with Subcommander Trevalin and his comrades, who wanted to hear about the knight's adventures with the White Robe.

Steel was not inclined to discuss Palin. The knight sat in brooding silence, made only short answers to his friends' questions. Finding him unwilling to talk, the knights shifted their discussions to their recent travels in Qualinesti, to the battle that never was.

"Elves!" Trevalin sneered. "I've seen toads with more honor. They came crawling to us in the dead of night. Some of their own senators served Qualinesti up—spitted—on a platter. One of them . . . What was his name?"

"Rashas," offered a knight.

"Yes, Rashas. Gave this long speech all about the integrity and nobility of the elves—as opposed to our lack of those qualities—and then calmly sat down and signed the papers that put his people firmly under the heel of my lord's boot. All very civilized." Trevalin laughed. "Their ruler is a mere boy. This Rashas leads the kid around by the ears. He's the son of Tanis Half-Elven, by the way, Brightblade."

Steel, who had been thinking of other things, looked up. "Who is?"

"The ruler of the elves. Gilthas, I think that's his name. Slimy elf words—they slide right out of my head. The boy doesn't have his father's spirit, that's for certain. Or his mother's, either, if all the stories they tell about the Golden General are true."

"I'm not so sure, Trevalin," one of the knights argued. "He may sit on his throne as meek and quiet as a mouse, but he gets a look about him sometimes . . . Well, if I were that fat senator, I'd keep an eye on that boy."

"Bah!" Trevalin snorted. "The only elf worth anything is that fellow Porthios. Now there's a fighter. True to form, the elves sent their only good leader into exile. He lives like a bandit, so they say."

"Word has it that he and his warriors raided Red Talon's camp," another knight offered. "Killed three of their dragons and escaped before anyone knew they were there."

"I wouldn't doubt it." Trevalin nodded. "He's smart and capable and has, for an elf, some shreds of honor, or so I hear. I could meet him in battle and not feel like I wanted to go take a bath afterward. Every time that Rashas elf got near me, I wanted to wash the filth from my hands."

There was more talk about the war, but Steel quit paying attention. He kept hearing Palin's words. They ran over and over in Steel's mind, mingled with the strains of the song the prisoner knights had sung in his honor. Steel dimly recalled having heard the song before, though he couldn't remember where. Probably as a child, growing up in Palanthas during the war. He had not thought about it, certainly, in twenty years. Yet, the melody sang in his memory, solemn, reverent, a hymn of victory, honoring self-sacrifice, yet touched with the sorrow of irretrievable loss. He didn't know the words to it; they were in ancient Solamnic, but that didn't matter, for it was Palin's words he heard, floating on top of the song, like oil on water.

"Brightblade!"

Steel jerked his head up.

Trevalin laid a hand on Steel's shoulder. "Go to bed, my friend. I doubt you've had much sleep these past few nights."

Steel obeyed, more to escape company than because he felt he needed the rest. It was difficult to sleep anyway. The heat was stifling, seemed to suck the air out of the rooms. He lay in bed, bathed in sweat, wondering what the Gray Robes were doing to Palin. Whatever it was, it wouldn't be pleasant.

Steel was not squeamish; he'd seen men die before, seen them tortured. But this was different. The Nightlord wasn't attempting to illicit information from Palin. She was trying to force him to give up the staff, which was his by right. That, to Steel's mind, was stealing, and therefore dishonorable. He was well aware that the Gray Robes viewed acquisition of the enemy's staff the way Steel would view acquisition of an enemy fortress, but he couldn't help his disgust and revulsion. As Trevalin had said about the elf Rashas, whenever Steel was near the Nightlord, he wanted to go away and wash the filth off his hands.

The young mage had behaved most honorably, and he would be treated most shamefully.

"At the very least," Steel determined drowsily, "I could see to it that Palin obtains a quick and painless death. He deserves that much."

Steel was wondering how he might accomplish this when, the next thing he knew, torchlight had replaced the sunlight. He had slept the day through.

* * * * *

Nighttime brought no relief from the heat. The temperature had climbed so high during the day that those standing guard duty in the sweltering sun soon keeled over, had to be constantly replaced by fresh troops. Several of the young page boys had been reprimanded for attempting to cook an egg on the paving stones, but the officer who had caught them carried the fried egg about with him the rest of the day, showed it to everyone he met.

Lord Ariakan completed his investigation into the death of the high priestess, ordered the funeral to be held immediately, the body burned. It would never do to leave a corpse lying about in this heat. He had found no mark on her, no wound, magically caused or otherwise. The woman had been old, over a hundred, some claimed. He judged her death to be of natural causes and spent the remainder of the day trying to quell the rumors that were running rife among the superstitious brutes.

Steel woke to find his comrades just going to their beds. Fully rested and restive, he would never be able to sleep. He sought out Trevalin, asked if the subcommander knew what had happened to the White Robe.

Not particularly interested in the matter, Trevalin said he presumed the Nightlord had taken the young man down to what used to be the abandoned dragontraps, which the Thorn Knights had made their headquarters. Trevalin advised Steel, rather curtly, to have nothing more to do with either the White Robe or the Gray.

On reflection, Steel decided that this was good advice. He could do nothing to save Palin and might actually make matters worse for the young man. He was a mage; he'd chosen his lot in life; he'd chosen his own fate. Determined to put Palin out of his mind, Steel decided to pay a visit to Flare.

The blue dragon had been extremely difficult to work with during the trip to Qualinesti, Trevalin had told Steel. She had complained about every rider, never found one that suited her. She had battled with her mate, inflicted a bite on his snout that had put the blue male out of commission for a week. The dragonmaster could do nothing with Flare, had reported her unfit for duty. The other dragons were keeping their distance.

Steel hoped she would return to normal once he was back, though he knew she would likely sulk for a week before she decided to forgive him. In order to hasten the process, he intended to stop by the kitchen, see if he couldn't persuade the night cook to give him a suckling pig. Flare was fond of pork, and Steel trusted she would accept the morsel as a peace offering.

He was walking the empty and silent corridors, on his way to the tower's fourth level, where the kitchens were located, when a flash of color caught his eye. Any color at all was out of place amid the somber, severe shades of black and gray worn by the knights. It did not belong here. And this was a collision of colors, wildly clashing, appearing extremely bright in the torchlight and completely, suspiciously, out of place.

Adding to his suspicions concerning the glimpse of color was the fact that it moved, vanished, the moment Steel turned to look for it. He thought he heard a sound, as if a voice had been about to speak, but had been immediately and suddenly muffled.

Loosening his sword in its sheath, Steel went to investigate. The sound had come from behind a stone staircase, hidden in a recessed area away from the light. Steel walked soft-footed, hoping to be able to sneak up on the spy—for he had concluded that's what the intruder must surely be. The knight was not wearing his armor in the heat; he made hardly any noise. Rounding the staircase, he saw two forms, dark against the shadows. One was robed and hooded in black. That was not unusual, with all the clerics of Takhisis about, but the other was most unusual. Steel saw—to his astonishment—a kender.

"That's him!" the kender was saying in a muted voice to his robed companion. "I'd know him anywhere! He looks just like Sturm, you see. I think we should ask him—"

Steel advanced, moving swiftly, creeping up on them from behind. The two were so engrossed in their conversation, that he was able to sneak quite close before they heard him. Reaching out, Steel grabbed the kender's topknot, gave it a twist, wrapped it around his hand.

"Ask me what?" he demanded.

"Ouch! Ah! Don't! That hurts!" The kender squealed. Reaching up, he tried unsuccessfully to break Steel's grip.

"Let him go!" ordered the robed figure with a female voice.

Steel ignored the cleric, dragged the protesting kender into the light. He recognized that voice, but he wanted to be certain.

He was.

"What are *you* doing here?" he demanded, giving the kender a shake.

"Ow! Oiy! You're pulling out my hair!" the kender wailed.

The black-robed cleric took hold of Steel's hand, attempted to pry it loose. "I told you to let him go!"

Steel flung the kender back against the wall, turned to the cleric. Her hood had slipped in the struggle. Shining hair glistened silver in the torchlight.

Seeing recognition in Steel's eyes, the woman caught hold of her hood, pulled it over her face.

Too late.

"You!" he said in astonishment.

She said nothing, but cast him a scathing glance. Turning her back on him, she tended to the kender, who was rubbing his head and wiping his eyes and demanding to know—somewhat breathlessly—if he had any hair left.

Steel glanced swiftly around, wondering if anyone else was nearby. The stairs were located in a recessed area off a hallway. The dinner hour was long past; the only people likely to be in this part of the tower were the cook and his helpers. Steel's first thought was to sound the alarm, rouse the guard, have these two arrested. It was his first thought and what he knew he should do—fully intended to do, except that he found himself not doing it.

He took hold of the woman's shoulder, drew her and the kender back again into the shadows.

I'll interrogate them first, he said to himself, then turn them over to the guards. "What in Takhisis's name are you doing here?" Steel demanded aloud. He couldn't recall either the woman's or the kender's name.

The kender started to answer, but shut his mouth when the woman pinched him.

"Not that it's any of your business," the woman said to Steel loftily. "But, if you must know, I'm a cleric of Takhisis now. I'm transporting this prisoner—"

"That's me," the kender said helpfully.

"—to prison," the woman concluded with a frown for the kender.

"He must be an important prisoner," Steel remarked, "for you to miss the funeral ceremonies."

The woman's golden eyes flickered. "Funeral?" she said faintly, plucking at the black velvet cloth with her hand. "I . . . I hadn't heard. Who died?"

"Your own high priestess," Steel said relentlessly. "Every other cleric in this place is in deep mourning. As for that lame story about a prisoner kender, no one would believe that. Any cleric of Takhisis who found a kender wandering around in here would have dispatched him to Chemosh in an instant. You'd better try again."

He had to give the woman credit. She accepted defeat with courage. Though she was white to the lips, and though it took tremendous effort, she managed to regain her composure. Her jaw clenched, her lips tightened, she drew herself tall, and faced him with dignity.

"What will you do to us? Summon the guard?"

"I'm asking the questions. What are you doing here? The truth, this time."

The woman bit her lip, finally admitted, "We're here to rescue Palin.

But we can't discover where they're holding him."

"Not in the jail," the kender added, "I checked there already. See, Usha, I was right! This is Steel, and he likely knows where Palin is."

"Do you?" She leaned near him, put her hand on his arm. "Will you tell us? You don't have to take us there. Just tell us, and then let us go. What harm will that do? Palin came here to save your life. You can't let him die!"

Steel silently cursed the woman, cursed the kender, cursed the luck that had led him into their paths, right when he himself was thinking that Palin did not deserve to die, that there was something ignoble in Steel himself for allowing the young mage to be put to death.

And that made Steel pause to consider. Was it merely bad luck that had led him to these two? Or was it something more? Was it the hand of his queen? Surely, it was Takhisis who had brought him here. He sensed her presence, sensed it in the darkness that shrouded him. Yet . . . what did Her Majesty want him to do? Apprehend these two? Give them over to certain death? Or did she want him to help them free Palin?

When in doubt, every knight was taught to consult the Dark Queen's Vision. Steel had always been confused by the enigmatic, puzzling nature of his own view of the Vision and in this instance, it was of little help. He felt pulled in two directions, one urging him to betray Usha and Tas, the other urging him to assist them.

The one thing of which Steel was certain was the story Palin had told Lord Ariakan. Steel himself had been feeling restless and uneasy. The air crackled of danger, as it crackled with dry lightning. Something somewhere was going terribly wrong.

"Come with me," he said abruptly to Usha and Tas. "Keep your hood pulled low over your face."

"Thank you!" Usha said fervently.

"Don't thank me yet," Steel returned in cold disdain. "I'm not going down there to free Palin. I need to talk to him, find out more about this business about the Graygem. I'm taking you and the kender with me just to keep an eye on you. I may decide to turn you both in. And don't say a word, either of you. If anyone stops us, let me do the talking."

The two nodded; the kender starting to say something, Usha hushing him. Steel wondered how they planned on spiriting Palin out of this fortress, almost asked, but decided that the less he knew, the better. They must have a way; the woman was a mage, after all.

They left the upper levels, heading down into the depths of the tower, into the long unused dragontraps.

16

The Dragontrap.

he High Clerist's Tower had neither place nor provision for magic-users. Not surprising, considering that the Knights of Solamnia had never, in their long history, had any use for wizards. It was said that Huma had gone into battle with a mage at his side, the two of them using both steel and sorcery to defeat their enemies. The wizard's name was Magius, a Red Robe who had been Huma's friend since childhood. The very staff Palin carried had belonged to this same Magius, whose tragic fate was also responsible for the fact that wizards on Ansalon were now permitted to carry daggers. But Magius was almost never mentioned by the knights when *they* told Huma's story. Or, if they brought him into the tale, the mention was grudging and he played only a very minor role. The knights would always emphasize that Huma never relied on Magius, but—more than once— the noble and valiant knight risked all to protect his weaker friend.

The wizards of Krynn tell a different story, of course. In theirs, Magius is the true hero, giving his life for his friend, dying a terrible death at the hands of the enemy. Huma is the minor character when the tale is told in the Tower of High Sorcery—a nice chap, all brawn and heart, relying on Magius to shape the course of the battle.

The truth rests in the lost and forgotten grave where Magius's body lies, in Huma's empty tomb. What is certain is that there are no mage-ware stores, no wizard's laboratories, no bookshelves filled with spell-books in the High Clerist's Tower.

And so, the gray-robed wizards of the Knights of Takhisis had to make their own.

They chose the long-abandoned dragontraps for several reasons, the main one being, of course, privacy. Though the sorcerers were part and parcel of the Knights of Takhisis, living, training, and fighting with their fellow knights, the Gray Knights were still wizards, and wizards require secret places, quiet places, safe places, in which to work.

The dragontraps were all these. No one ever went there without reason. During the War of the Lance, the chamber in which the dragon orb had once stood had collapsed in upon itself. The Solamnic Knights had cleared away the rubble, but "stone remembers death," or so the dwarves claim, for the blood that soaks into stone can never be completely washed away. The stone floors of the dragontraps were discolored with blood: the blood of dragons, the blood of the knights who fought the great beasts down here. It was a place alive with death, a dreadful place, a sad and sorrowful place.

Palin heard the gruesome yells, the tortured cries, the dying screams. More than once he turned his head fearfully, thinking frantic wings beat the air behind him. But the sounds were all his imagination, unless the ghosts of the dragons slaughtered here and the ghosts of the knights slain in the desperate fray continued the battle on some other plane. On this plane of existence, the dragontraps were dark, as cool as any place could be in the sweltering heat, and filled with the small sounds associated with wizards: the scratch of a pen recording a spell, the whispered chant of someone committing a spell to memory, the slow speech of someone puzzling out the magical words, the swish of robes across the dusty floor.

Palin had time to listen to the sounds—both of the living and of the dead. He was not being tortured, as he had expected, at the hands of the Nightlord. Neither had he been killed, as he had also expected. It seemed he had been forgotten. He had been left sitting here in the fortress's inner core, away from the glaring sun, so long that he had lost all track of time. It might have been hours or days since he arrived in the fortress. No one came near him; no one spoke to him.

The gag over his mouth fit tightly, pried his jaws open, gave him a choking sensation. He was thirsty, his throat parched and dry. The bindings on his wrists were cutting off his circulation. He was chained by the ankle to the leg of a large gray marble table, marked all over with cabalistic symbols.

He once attempted to communicate, by incoherent croaks and grunts, his desperate need for water, but the mage walking past at the time ignored Palin, kept on walking.

The Nightlord had taken the Staff of Magius from him, and its loss, perhaps even more than the gag, the thirst, his uncertainty and fear, was a bitter torment. Vanished with the staff was his uncle's voice. Palin felt truly alone—a feeling he had not experienced since receiving the staff.

He wondered what the Gray Knights meant to do to him, and when they meant to do it, and why they had done nothing to him as yet. The more time that passed without anything happening, the more fearful he grew. He hadn't been afraid at all in the courtyard, talking to Lord Ariakan, surrounded by the enemy. Even when he'd looked at the block, seen the dried, caked blood crusted in the dreadful hollow. He could have died in those moments with dignity, without regret, except for the sorrow his death would bring to those he loved.

Fear grew on him steadily as he sat here, alone, in the noisome darkness. His thoughts roamed, sometimes to horrible places. He looked around at the dragontraps, saw how they worked, saw the holes through which knights attacked with the dragonlances. The dragons the knights had killed had been evil, wicked dragons, creatures of the Dark Queen, red dragons and blue, who had butchered countless innocents, tortured and tormented their victims.

The dragon orb, placed on a pedestal in the heart of the tower, had lured the dragons into the trap, calling them with the enchanted words they could not resist. Once they flew inside the gaping gates, the trap was sprung. Portcullises thundered down. The dragons could not escape. The knights attacked with sword and lance and arrow. Picturing the way the dragons had died—trapped, frantic, furious, roaring in rage and agony—Palin found it in his heart to pity the magnificent, doomed creatures.

At length, worn out, exhausted, he dozed, only to wake with a start from terrifying dreams, filled with blood and stabbing pain and, above all, the terror of being caught in a trap, with no way out except death.

Resolutely he thrust such nightmarish images out of his mind, only to find them returning with nagging insistence. He couldn't understand them, but they troubled him, and his fear grew. His horror of being left alone in this dreadful place began to consume him until the thought of torture was almost pleasant, if pain brought with it a living face, a living voice.

And so, when the Nightlord returned, carrying the Staff of Magius in her hand, Palin was irrationally glad to see her.

The feeling did not last long.

The Nightlord held the staff up before him. Palin's dazed mind thought nothing of this at first. Then he recalled how the staff had burned the Nightlord the first time she had tried to touch it. His heart constricted in fear. Had she gained power over the staff? Had the staff abandoned him?

"*Shirak!*" Lillith spoke triumphantly. The crystal atop the staff glimmered with a dull light, flickered sullenly, as if reluctant to obey.

Palin lowered his head, as if the light bothered him. In reality, he hoped the woman would not see his tears.

The Nightlord laughed and leaned the staff against the table; a tiny, tempting fraction out of Palin's reach.

"I knew the staff would come to me sooner or later. I saw it in the seeing stones. What did you say?"

Palin had grunted something. The Nightlord removed the gag with a deft twitch of her hand, ripped it from his mouth.

He tried to moisten his dry mouth enough to speak.

"Water."

"Yes, I thought you might be thirsty." The Nightlord uncorked a water pouch, tilted the liquid into Palin's mouth.

He gulped, choked, looked up at the woman with blurred eyes. "Why haven't you killed me before now? What are you waiting for?"

The Nightlord smiled unpleasantly. "Can't you guess? The hunter does not kill the rabbit before the wolf sticks his head in the snare."

It took Palin a moment to comprehend what the woman had said. When he finally figured it out, he stared at her. "You're setting a trap? For whom? My uncle?" He almost laughed. "I would like to be permitted to live long enough to see *that* encounter."

The Nightlord smiled in her turn. "I would, too," she said softly. Then she shrugged. "Some later date. The trap is not for your uncle, but another a member of your family."

Thinking she must mean his father or mother, Palin shook his head in bafflement. And then a thought came to Palin.

"Steel . . . ?"

The Nightlord's eyes flashed; she raised one eyebrow.

This time, Palin did laugh, though it came out more a croak. "You won't catch *that* wolf with this rabbit. What do you suppose? That he cares enough for me to try to free me?" Palin laughed again, amused at the thought.

The Nightlord bent near, seemed to suck the laughter from him, draw his light into her darkness. "Her Majesty brought you two together for a reason. I have thrown the stones many times, and the answer is always the same. Look, I'll throw again."

Lillith removed a handful of polished agates from a black bag she wore on her left wrist. Taking the stones, she muttered the spell words, tossed the stones onto the gray marble surface. The staff's light gleamed more brightly, shone on the multicolored agates.

"There! Look!" She pointed a fine-boned finger. "The black stone, that is Steel. The white, you. In between, a fortress . . ."

Palin saw a green agate marked with a rune representing a tower.

" . . . and, on top of the fortress, flames."

He stared at a red agate marked with a tiny flicker of fire.

"You on one side, him on the other, doom in between."

Reaching down, she snatched up the stones with a snap of her hand.

"There! Both of you gone!" she whispered. "The two of you dead and—"

"And doom remains," Palin said calmly, gazing at the tower stone and the flame stone. Both still lay upon the table.

The Nightlord blinked, startled. She had intended to pick up all the stones. Somehow, her hand had missed these two. For a moment she hesitated, wondering, undoubtedly, what this new omen portended.

Palin didn't care. He was too tired.

"You heard what I told your lord about the gods," he said wearily. "I saw—"

"—what your uncle wanted you to see!" The Nightlord scoffed. "And so I have told my lord. A trick of Raistlin Majere's. Ah, he is full of tricks, that one. But one day he will play a trick too many." Lillith picked up the two stones she had missed, swept them into her bag. "As for Steel Brightblade, he is a traitor to our queen's cause. And I will prove it to my lord. Then you will both die together, as befits such close cousins!"

The seeing stones rattling in the bag, the Nightlord departed, taking the glowing Staff of Magius with her.

Palin leaned against the table. The darkness closed over him. With the darkness came despair. He was going to die here. They would find him, chained to this pedestal . . .

Voices roused him.

Palin lifted his head groggily, his eyes squinting in the bright light of a single torch. He could dimly make out figures, the glint of armor, perhaps the faint glimmer of a jewel, but nothing more.

The people, whoever they were, held a brief, whispered conversation. A stern, cold, male voice cut it off, ordered, "Stay here. And keep quiet."

Palin recognized that voice, and his heart was in his throat. He tried to speak, but was too amazed, too baffled. The man with the torch and the glimmering starjewel was Steel Brightblade.

He left his two companions behind, and they were immediately swallowed by the darkness that flowed in to replace the light of the torch. Steel advanced toward Palin.

"Majere?" Steel did not lower his voice, his booted footsteps rang throughout the chamber. He walked with confidence, certain of his right to be here. This was *not* a man intent on stealthily freeing a prisoner. He drew closer. "Majere, I must talk to you—"

Bright light flared. In the attack alcoves where, years ago, the Knights of Solamnia had hidden to fight the dragons, now stood Knights of Takhisis.

"You see, my lord!" Lillith's voice was shrill with triumph. The Staff of Magius burned bright in her hand. "You see!"

Lord Ariakan's voice came from the darkness, heavy with sadness, burning with anger. "Steel Brightblade has indeed proven himself a traitor. Seize him!"

17

The trap is sprung.

Knights strode forward, grasped Steel by each arm. He did not struggle. His eyes flicked once to Palin, flicked away.

"You must believe me!" Palin said in a low voice. "I had nothing to do with this!"

"Steel Brightblade, why have you come here?" Lord Ariakan demanded. "Your talon is not on duty. You have no business here."

"The reason is obvious, my lord!" the Nightlord stated. "He has sneaked down here to free the prisoner."

"I am not a sneak," Steel returned coldly, goaded into speaking. "You saw me, heard me. I came openly."

"For what reason?" Ariakan persisted.

Steel would say nothing.

Lord Ariakan shook his head. "It was a mistake accepting you into the knighthood, Brightblade. Some warned me against it"—his glance slid to the Nightlord, who had the grace (or perhaps the presence of mind) not to appear smug—"but others urged me on, the high priestess, who now lies dead, being one of them. You are a good soldier, honorable, courageous, loyal. Yes, I say loyal," he added, with a scathing glance at the Nightlord.

"I truly believe, Brightblade, that you mean to serve our queen with all your heart and soul. But in that heart beats the dark ambition of your mother and in that soul rests the nobility of your father. Both are at war within you. And so you act at cross purposes. You are, therefore, a danger to the cause, a threat to the Vision. I sentence you to death, Steel Brightblade. Let the sentence be carried out immediately."

A knight drew his sword, walked over to face Steel.

Steel did not struggle, or make any protest. Every word his lord had spoken rang true, like a true blade.

The knight raised his sword, prepared to plunge it into Steel's breast.

"My lord!" a knight called out. "He had accomplices." There came the sounds of a cry and a scuffle.

"Is this man never to die?" Ariakan demanded impatiently. "Or," he added to himself as an afterthought, "is Queen Takhisis so determined that he should live? Await my order!" he commanded aloud. "What have you found?"

"Two more, my lord." A knight came forward, dragging Tasslehoff and a slender person clad in black robes, the face and head hidden by the hood. "Brightblade was not alone, it seems."

Palin stood, hope surging through him. "Raistlin!" he whispered. "My uncle has come!"

The Nightlord had the same thought, apparently. She surged forward, the Staff of Magius clasped tightly, protectively in her hand.

"Who are you, Wizard?" the Nightlord demanded. "Remove your hood."

The robed figure lifted its head. The staff's light gleamed in golden eyes.

The Nightlord drew back, at first alarmed. Then, recovering herself, she gave a sneering laugh. "You are no mage. You have no magic in you!" She yanked the hood from the figure's head.

Palin's glad cry changed to one of dismay.

Pale and frightened, Usha stood there, blinking in the light.

"What is going on here?" Ariakan now seemed more puzzled than angry. "A kender and a Black Robe wizardess?"

"Not a wizardess!" the Nightlord said scornfully. "She has no more magic in her than this wall. She is a spy!"

"I don't know what she's talking about!" Tasslehoff spoke up. "We're not with this knight. We're not with anyone—except each other."

"Silence that little worm," the Nightlord said.

"No, let him speak," Ariakan countermanded, frustrated. "Something strange is going on here, and I mean to get to the bottom of it. Put him down. Kender, come over here."

Tas readjusted all his pouches, stepped forward, extended his small hand.

"How do you do, sir? My name is Eiderdown Pakslinger. This is my friend Usha, a *very* powerful evil sorceress, so I wouldn't mess with her if I were you. She is Raistlin Majere's daughter!" He stopped dramatically to give everyone time to be properly impressed.

Ariakan, ignoring the kender's proffered hand, frowned.

The Nightlord snorted. "Spies! You came in here with Brightblade. Tell His Lordship the real reason you are here, kender."

"I'm trying to," Tas told her, dignity offended. He turned back to Ariakan. "You may not know this, but I'm an evil kender. Yes, that's why I'm here, to offer my services to the Dark Queen. Takhisis changed my life. I'm extremely wicked now. I'll do something wicked, if you want me to. Watch this!"

Tas dashed off. Several knights made a grab for him, but the kender was too nimble. He sped across the floor, darting and skipping out of the way of the knights.

"I'll kill this White Robe for you!" Tas shouted.

Tas drew a small knife, feinted a stab into Palin's stomach. Shifting the blade, the kender cut through the bindings on Palin's wrists, cried "Catch!" and tossed Palin the dagger.

Startled, unprepared, his hands and fingers numb from being bound, Palin fumbled with the knife, managed to hold on to it.

Swords rang out. The knight who had been holding Steel prisoner turned to apprehend Palin.

Tasslehoff clambered up onto the table, leapt onto the knight's back. Grasping hold of the man's helm with both hands, Tas pulled it down over the knight's eyes. The sword thrust that would have killed Palin went wild. The knight lost his balance. He and the kender tumbled onto the floor.

Other knights sprang at them.

"Hard as ice!" Usha's voice rang out. She held up a shining, clear crystal.

Sword arms froze, feet could not move, and mouths gaped open. The chill of the Irda magic flowed around the dark knights, encased them in icy magic.

All except Steel. Perhaps the starjewel protected him, perhaps the sword, perhaps the dark influence of his mother. He alone, of all the knights in the chamber, could move.

Palin, the knife in his hand, put his back to the table, looked uncertainly at Steel.

"We are cousins," Palin said. "You saved my life. I don't want to fight you."

Usha ran to his side. She held the crystal in one hand, the tiny figurine of a white horse in the other. "Why don't you join us? Come with us! They mean to kill you, too!"

Steel frowned, troubled. His sword was half in, half out of his scabbard. "My lord is just."

"Like hell he is!" Palin swore. He slashed out with the knife, forced Steel to step back. "You *want* to die, you coward! You're afraid to live!"

Glowering, Steel thrust his sword back into its sheath.

Palin was wary. He lowered his dagger. "You'll come . . ."

Steel lunged forward. Catching hold of the wrist of Palin's knife-hand, Steel flung the mage backward, struck the hand holding the dagger against the stone table.

His hand was cut and bleeding, but Palin clung desperately to his only weapon. Steel slammed his hand into the table again. Palin gasped in pain, let go of the dagger. It fell, clattering to the floor.

An explosion—deafening, heart-stopping—shook the High Clerist's Tower to the very foundations. The floor vibrated; the walls shuddered and cracked. The crystal fell from Usha's hand, landed on the marble table, shattered. The spell was broken.

"What the—?" Ariakan began.

Another horrific boom rocked the tower, knocking many of the knights to their hands and knees. Steel staggered backward, fell into Palin, who instinctively held on to him to steady them both.

"Someone find out what is going on!" Ariakan roared. "Are we under attack?"

Men hastened to do Ariakan's bidding, began running for the exits. Others remained with the prisoners.

"My lord! Where is my lord Ariakan?" A young squire, round-eyed with fear, was pushing and shoving his way through the confusion.

"I am here!" Ariakan cried out, his voice carrying above the turmoil.

"My lord!" The squire could scarcely breathe. "The tower . . . it's been struck by lightning! Twice, my lord! Terrible lightning! I've never seen the like before! It streaked down from the skies like a thrown spear. Twice it hit us," he repeated himself in his awe. "In exactly the same place! And . . . and . . ."

He gulped for air. "Dragons, my lord! Hundreds of them . . . gold, silver . . ."

"We *are* under attack," Ariakan said grimly, and he drew his sword.

"No, my lord!" The squire was reduced to a hoarse whisper, and all around him hushed to hear his words. "Red dragons fly with the gold. Blue fly side by side with silver. A terrible light shines in the northern sky, a hideous red glow that is brightening and spreading, as if every tree in the great forests to the north have caught fire. You can smell the smoke . . ."

Tendrils and wisps of gray were seeping through the open gate. Another boom came, and another shook the High Clerist's Tower. A sconce broke loose from a wall, fell to the floor with a clatter, dousing its torch. The iron portcullis rattled, chains swung back and forth. Choking clouds of dust began to filter down from the ceilings. The knights glanced at each other in alarm. They were brave men; no one doubted their courage, but they did not relish the idea of being buried alive.

Palin and Usha stood close, arms clasped around one another. Tasslehoff, held fast by a knight, was squirming in his captor's grasp. "I want to see!" the kender begged. "Please, please, please! You can kill me later! I promise. Word of honor. Just let me go and see!"

Steel was staring at the Nightlord. "The tower, struck by lightning . . ." he murmured.

Lord Ariakan issued swift commands, sent his troops racing back through the attack alcoves, up the nearest staircases.

"Call a meeting of my commanders," he ordered. He was walking as he talked, his aides and lieutenants gathered around him. "I want reports from all on what they've seen, what they've heard. I'll speak to the dragons myself. Send for the Lord of the Skull."

"What do we do with the prisoners, my lord?" someone demanded.

Ariakan waved his hand impatiently. "I don't—"

"Slay them, my lord!" the Nightlord cried, and she had the temerity to clutch at Ariakan's arm. "Kill them now! They! . . . They are the cause! I have read it in the seeing stones."

Ariakan impatiently shook the woman loose. "May our queen take you and your seeing stones, Lillith! Get out of my way!" He flung the woman backward.

The Nightlord tried to catch her balance, but the Staff of Magius tangled between her feet, tripping her. She sprawled backward onto the floor, beneath one of the iron portcullises used to trap the dragons.

Another ear-splitting peal of thunder reverberated through the tower. The portcullis, loosened by the shock waves of the previous explosions, broke loose from its moorings, plummeted down.

The Nightlord saw death descending, tried to crawl out of the way. She was not fast enough. The iron bars, as sharp as spears, meant to cleave their way through the tough scaly hide of dragons, slid with ease through the Nightlord's soft flesh. The portcullis thudded to the stone floor, pinning Lillith beneath it.

She gave a hideous shriek, clutched at the bars that had impaled her, as if she might wrench them loose. Blood spurted from the terrible wounds. Her hands lost their grip, slid weakly to the floor. Her fingers rested on the Staff of Magius, touched it, twitched feebly. The bag of seeing stones gaped open, spewed the agates into the widening pool of blood. Her eyes fixed in her head. The hand on the staff stiffened, went limp.

Lord Ariakan gazed down at the corpse in horror. He was pale beneath his black beard. Sweat glistened on his skin. "I have seen death in many forms, but few as terrible as that. It is a sign! May our queen have mercy on her soul."

He glanced about, searching. Catching sight of Palin, he motioned. "You, Majere. Come over here. Don't be afraid. What you told me, up in the courtyard, about Chaos seeking to destroy us. Is this the beginning?"

Palin hesitated, then said quietly, "I believe so, my lord, but I don't know for certain."

Ariakan drew in a deep breath, let it out slowly. He wiped sweat from his face. "I want to speak with you further, White Robe. Brightblade, bring him along. Both of you, come with me."

Palin gestured toward Usha and Tasslehoff.

"I want to bring my friends with me," Palin said. "I want to be assured of their safety."

"Very well!" Ariakan was impatient. "Let's get out of here before the damn tower tumbles down around our ears!"

"And," Palin continued, not moving, "I want my staff."

"Take it!" Ariakan was grim. "I doubt if anyone else wants the accursed thing. Brightblade, bring these three to my quarters."

"Yes, my lord," said Steel.

Lord Ariakan hurried away, leaving the four alone in the dragontraps.

Palin walked over to where the Nightlord lay sprawled in her own gore beneath the iron bars. As he bent to retrieve the staff, he caught sight of the Nightlord's staring eyes, pain-twisted face. He could smell the still-warm blood.

Had the staff killed her? Had it acted a role, lured her into its own trap, deliberately tripped her? Or had it all been a freakish accident? Palin's hand, reaching for the staff, halted, trembled.

Usha hastened to his side, wrapped her hands around his arm. He held on to her thankfully.

Tas wiped blood out of his eyes with the end of his topknot. "Hurry up, Palin! I want to see what's going on!"

"I'll fetch the staff if you're too squeamish, Majere," Steel said in disgust.

Palin shoved the knight back. Keeping his eyes fixed on the staff, he drew in a deep breath, reached down, and slid the staff out from underneath the dead hand.

Retrieving it, he started to straighten.

A figure draped and hooded in black stood directly in front of him.

Steel, alarmed, drew his sword. Palin sprang to halt him. "Don't! It's my uncle!"

Raistlin gazed at Steel without, so it seemed, much interest. He soon shifted the gaze to Palin. "Well done, Nephew."

"Uncle, how—" Palin began.

A low rumble of thunder that seemed to rise from the ground, not the heavens, caused the floor to quake beneath their feet. A crash sounded somewhere close.

"No time for questions," Raistlin said. He grasped hold of Palin, motioned for Usha and Tasslehoff to come to his side. "Dalamar arranged my journey. He waits for us at the Tower of High Sorcery."

"You're not going anywhere, Palin," Steel said grimly, "except to see Lord Ariakan. You and your uncle."

Palin hesitated. "I promised I would talk to Ariakan. Perhaps we should—"

"The time for talk is past. The battle has begun. Even now Lord Ariakan walks into the midst of it."

Raistlin's gaze went to Steel. "Your sword is needed elsewhere, son of Brightblade. Permit us to leave in peace."

Steel could hear the truth of that statement for himself. The sounds of battle had penetrated to the depths of the tower.

Raistlin strode forward, black robes whispering across the stone floor. Steel eyed him warily, drew his sword.

"I recognize that blade," Raistlin said calmly. "Your father's, isn't it? I never liked your father much. All that business about knightly honor, nobility. He made such a show of it, flaunted it, threw it in my face."

Steel said nothing, but his hand gripped the sword's hilt more tightly, until the knuckles were white.

Raistlin drew closer still.

"And then I discovered something very interesting about your father. He lied to us. Sturm Brightblade was no more a knight than I was. He was made a knight only shortly before his death. All that time, he wore the armor, carried the sword . . . and it was all a lie."

Raistlin shrugged. "And do you know what? I liked him better after I discovered that."

"Because you supposed he had sunk to your level," Steel said hoarsely.

Raistlin's smile was twisted, bitter. "You *would* think that, wouldn't you, Brightblade? But, no, that's not the reason."

Raistlin moved closer, so close that Steel could feel the chill of the mage's frail body, could hear the breath rattle in the lungs, could feel the soft touch of black velvet.

"Your father lied to every person except one—himself. In his heart Sturm *was* a knight. He had better claim to that false title than many who held it for truth. Sturm Brightblade obeyed laws that no one enforced. He lived by a noble code in which no one else believed. He swore an oath that no one heard. Only himself . . . and his god. No one would have held him to that oath, to the Measure. He did that himself. He knew himself.

"Who are you, Steel Brightblade?" Raistlin's golden, hourglass eyes flickered. "Do you know?"

Steel's face drained of color. He opened his mouth, but no words passed his lips. A tear slid down his cheek. He lowered his head so swiftly that the long black hair tumbled down in front of his face.

With an angry motion, he thrust his sword into its sheath. Turning, not looking at any of them, he ran toward the stairs and the sounds of battle.

All must join as one.

aistlin stood at one of the windows in the upper chambers of the Tower of High Sorcery in Palanthas. The archmage was back in his old study, a room that—he was surprised and somewhat amused to note—Dalamar had left much as it had been when his *shalafi* had left. The study had not been shut off from the world, as had the laboratory, with its dangerously powerful artifacts, its dark and disturbing secrets.

Certain objects, mostly magical in nature, had been removed from the study, taken to Dalamar's rooms, perhaps, or maybe to the classrooms, where young apprentices studied them, worked to unlock the arcane mysteries. But the intricately carved wooden desk was still here. The volumes of books on the shelves were old friends, their bindings familiar—more familiar—than the faces of the people in Raistlin's past. The carpet on the floor was the same, though considerably more worn.

Usha sat in the very chair in which Lady Crysania had once sat. Raistlin looked through the ethers, tried to see Crysania's face. She was veiled in shadow. He shook his head, turned again to the window.

"What is that strange light shining in the north?" he asked.

"The Turbidus Ocean is on fire," Dalamar replied.

"What?" Palin cried, startled, springing out of his chair. "How is that possible?"

"I want to see!" Tas crowded nearer the window.

The night sky was dark everywhere, except to the north. There it glowed a hideous orangish red.

"The sea, burning!" Palin said, awed.

Tas sighed. "I wish I could see it."

"You may yet have the chance." Dalamar was searching among the volumes lining the bookshelves. He paused, turned to face them. "Members of the Conclave were sent to investigate. They report that a vast rift has opened up in the ocean, between Ansalon and the Dragon Isles. Fire springs from it, causes the ocean water to evaporate. What you see are clouds of steam, reflecting the dreadful light.

"Out of that rift spring fire dragons, ridden by fiends and some sort of shadow creatures. Their numbers are incalculable. Every tongue of flame that licks the broken side of the rift erupts into the fearsome dragons, made of fire and magic. The creatures who ride them are created out of the swirling darkness of Chaos. His forces now assault the High Clerist's Tower. Soon they will attack all other strategic points on Ansalon. We have had reports that the dwarves of Thorbardin already battle these fiends in their underground caverns."

"What of the book?" Raistlin asked, unperturbed.

"I can't find it!" Dalamar muttered something beneath his breath and turned back to his search.

"My people." Usha spoke through trembling lips. "What of my people? They . . . they live near there."

"Your people were responsible for bringing this doom upon us," Raistlin observed caustically.

Usha shrank back, shriveling in the mage's view. She looked to Palin for comfort, but he had been avoiding her ever since their return from the tower. All the while, his uncle watched both of them closely. Obviously, Usha had not yet told Palin the truth. Just as well, considering what trials they both faced. Just as well . . .

"What is the Conclave doing?" Palin was asking Dalamar.

"Attempting to determine the construction and nature of these magical creatures, so that we may fight them. Unfortunately, this can only be done by confronting them directly. As head of the Conclave, I have volunteered to undertake the task."

"A dangerous one," Raistlin remarked, glancing back at the dark elf who had once been his apprentice. "And one from which you are not likely to return."

"It won't much matter, will it?" Dalamar said, shrugging. "You were in the meeting of the Conclave when we discussed this. If our theories hold, it won't matter at all."

"I'll go with you, sir," Palin offered. "I'm not of very high rank, but I might be of some help."

"The gods need the help of us all. Especially our Dark Queen. Yet, she still tries to play both ends against the middle," Raistlin mused. "She hopes to emerge from this the victor."

"She'd better hope she emerges from it at all," Dalamar said dryly.

"Then you'll take me?" Palin asked, his hand tightening around the staff.

"No, young mage. Don't look downcast. You will have a chance to die. You are being sent on another task. The head of the White Robes, Dunbar Mastersmate, goes with me, as does Jenna, to represent the Red Robes. Hopefully, even if we fall, our findings will be delivered to the Conclave in time to be of use."

"It won't come in time to help those in the High Clerist's Tower," Raistlin observed, pointing. The fiery glow in the sky glistened on the mountain peaks, burned brighter and brighter, turning night into an eerie and terrifying day. "The knights are already under attack."

"It's too bad Tanis isn't here," Tas said wistfully. "He was always good at this sort of thing."

"Tanis Half-Elven fights his own battle on his own plane," Raistlin said. "So do the elves, the dwarves, the kender."

"Are they attacking Kendermore?" Tas asked, a catch in his throat.

"All places on Krynn, Master Burrfoot," Dalamar answered. "All beings, of all loyalties, will be forced to drop other quarrels, join to fight for their very survival."

"Perhaps they will," Raistlin said. "Perhaps not. Hatred runs deep on Ansalon. Alliance is our only hope . . . and the one with the least chance of occurring."

"Would you send me home, Dalamar?" Tas asked. He drew himself up to his full stance. "Laurana taught me a lot about being a general. I know important things, like you're not supposed to sound 'retreat' at the *start* of the battle, because that gets the soldiers pretty well confused, even if it is a lovely bit of music to play on the trumpet and I was only seeing if I could. So, if you would magick me back to Kendermore, I'd like to do what I could to help."

"Kendermore must do without their general, I'm afraid," Raistlin said. "I believe I remember where that volume was kept." He walked over to help in the search. "Your skills are needed elsewhere."

Tasslehoff gasped. He struggled to speak, managed a croak. "Would you . . . would you say that again, Raistlin?"

"Say what again?" the mage demanded irritably.

"Say that . . . that I'm needed," Tas said, swallowing a lump in his throat. "Fizban used to think so, but then he tended to be a bit fuddled in his mind—a few sandwiches short of a picnic, if you know what I mean. No offense," he added, glancing upward. "He and I decided that since I was a small person, I could help on the small things, like rescuing gully dwarves about to become breakfast for a dragon. The really big stuff I should leave to big people."

"It is the big people who will be looking for your help now," Dalamar said. "We're sending you with Palin."

"Did you hear that, Palin? I'm going with you!" Tas said excitedly.

"I heard." Palin sounded less than enthusiastic.

"Here it is." Raistlin pulled a book from the shelf, set it down upon the desk.

He and Dalamar bent eagerly over the volume, flipped impatiently through pages.

Tasslehoff began to roam about, examining various curious objects that stood around on small tables and adorned the mantelpiece. He picked up what appeared to be nothing more than a solid piece of wood, but, upon closer examination, he found innumerable little drawers cut into it, all cunningly disguised not to look like drawers.

The box was rapidly descending into one of Tas's pouches when the kender stopped. He held the box in his hand, gazed at it longingly, ran his fingers over the wood. Sighing, he reached up, carefully put the box back on the mantelpiece.

"I'm going on an important mission," he said gravely. "And I don't want to be weighted down."

"Now I know we are nearing the end of the world," Dalamar muttered.

"Here is the entry," Raistlin said. "Yes, you see. I remembered it correctly."

Dalamar bent over the book. The two of them read, occasionally whispering strange-sounding words aloud.

Palin did his best to overhear; the words sounded Elvish, but they must have been ancient Elvish, for he could only understand about one word in twenty. Seeing his uncle absorbed, Palin moved over to stand beside Usha.

She sat huddled in the chair, staring fearfully at the red glow in the sky.

Palin put his hand comfortingly on her shoulder. She reached up swiftly, caught hold of his hand, held it tightly.

"I'm afraid for them," she said, her throat constricting. "That glow . . . it's the same one I saw the night I left. Only . . . now it's so much brighter. I'm worried, Palin. What your uncle said is right. They—we—have brought doom on everyone!"

"Don't worry," Palin said gently, stroking her shining hair. "The Irda are strong in magic. When I come back—"

Usha looked up at him. "What do mean, when you come back. Where are you going? I'm going with you!" She was on her feet, her hands clasping Palin's.

"That clinches it, then," Dalamar said, straightening.

"Yes, I believe it does," Raistlin murmured. He began to cough, but recovered himself quickly, wiped his lips with his handkerchief.

A knock sounded on the door. It opened silently. Jenna stood within.

"Dalamar," she said quietly, "it is time. I have the spell components and the scrolls you requested."

"I must go," Dalamar said. "We have no time to lose. You will give Palin and the kender their instructions, *Shalafi*?"

Raistlin shook his head. "You need not call me that. I am no longer your teacher."

Dalamar smiled a dark and twisted smile. His hand went to his breast, unclasped a pin fashioned in the image of a black swan, drew aside the folds of black velvet. Five wounds, the same shape and size as the tips of five fingers, were visible, fresh, bleeding, on the elf's smooth skin.

"You will always be my teacher," Dalamar said. "As you can see, I study the lesson you taught me daily."

"And you have profited by it, it seems," Raistlin remarked coolly. The fingers of his right hand began to tap softly on the desktop.

"I admired you," Dalamar said softly. "I still do." With a quick, jerking motion of his hand, he drew the folds of cloth together, hiding the wounds. "And I will hate you forever."

He turned to Palin. "Farewell, Majere. May all the gods of magic shed their blessings on you."

"On us all," Jenna said quietly. "Farewell, Palin Majere. And farewell to you"—she smiled archly—"Usha Majere."

Jenna extended her hand to Dalamar. He took it, spoke quick words of magic, and the two vanished.

Palin did not return their good-byes. His gaze was fixed on Raistlin.

"Where am I going, Uncle? Where are you sending me?"

"And me!" Tas said eagerly.

"And me," Usha spoke resolutely.

"No—" Palin began.

"Yes," Raistlin cut in smoothly. "The girl goes with you. She must. She is the only one who knows the way."

"Home!" Usha understood him at once. She caught her breath. "You're sending me back home!"

"I am sending you back to fetch this." Raistlin rested a thin finger on a picture in the book he and Dalamar had been reading. Palin leaned over to look.

"The Graygem! But . . . it's broken. The gods said so."

"It is broken," Raistlin agreed. "It will be up to you to mend it. First, though, you must steal it from those who guard it." He glanced meaningfully at Usha.

"Are you coming with us, Uncle?"

"In spirit," Raistlin replied. "I will give what help I can. I am not of this world, Palin," he added, seeing his nephew's disappointment. "My power is gone. I can work only through you."

Palin was puzzled. "I am proud to think you have such confidence in me, but—why am I being sent, Uncle? There are other mages far more powerful—"

"All the mages on Krynn are fighting this war, Nephew. Gray Robes and Red, White Robes and Black, master wizard and lowest apprentice. The Conclave judged you most suitable for this particular task. Why? They had their reasons, some of which I approved, some I did not. Suffice it to say, your bond with the Irda girl was one factor, your bond with me another. You have the Staff of Magius and, perhaps the most important, you once were able to control the Graygem."

"I didn't control it so much as trick it," Palin said ruefully. "And I had help. Dougan Redhammer was there."

"You will have help with you this time as well. You do not go alone." Raistlin glanced at Tasslehoff, who was now seated on the floor, taking inventory of the objects in his pouches.

Palin followed his uncle's gaze, drew near Raistlin.

"Uncle," Palin murmured, "I will go wherever you say and do exactly as you bid me. Usha will go with me, to find out what happened to her people. But are you sure about sending Tasslehoff? Granted, he is the very best kender who ever lived, but . . . well . . . he *is* a kender—"

Raistlin placed his hand on Palin's shoulder.

"That's why he is being sent. Kender have one quality that you will need, Nephew. Kender are immune to fear." Raistlin's grip tightened; thin fingers dug into Palin's flesh. "And where you are going, that quality will be inestimable."

19

Rumors. Thunder and flame. Setting sail.

he docks at the Bay of Branchala were crowded with people that hot, gray, smoke-filled morning. A terrible storm raged in the mountains; people in Palanthas could hear the thunder rumble. Fearful rumors ran through the town, leaping from house to house, feeding off their own fuel, burning faster and more furious the farther they traveled.

An ominous red glow lit the northern sky, turning night into unnatural day. At first, the word went out that there was a great conflagration in the city. Some said the Great Library was burning. Others swore they had heard the Tower of High Sorcery was ablaze. More than a few knew someone who had seen fire pouring out the windows of the Temple of Paladine.

No one could sleep. Everyone was in a state of nervous excitement. People rushed to the temple, to the library, volunteering to fight the blaze, only to find—once they arrived—that there was no fire. The Palanthians wandered up and down the streets, watching the red glow that was growing ever brighter. They joined in tight, tense, small groups, heard the latest rumor, broke free of one group and raced to another. Bells all through the city rang hysterically, breaking out sporadically here and there as one rumor took predominance over another and someone decided that he should announce it.

At first, the Knights of Takhisis attempted to impose order on the city. They turned out in force, marched up and down the streets, dispersed the crowds, urged the people to return to their beds. The knights closed the taverns, tried to silence the bells. But toward morning, the bells were replaced by the beating of drums. The knights who had been marching in the streets were next seen marching out of the gates, heading up the road that led from Palanthas to the High Clerist's Tower.

It soon occurred to the citizens of Palanthas that the city was free.

There was great rejoicing. Rumors flew thick and fast now. The elven nation had risen and launched an assault against the dark knights. The dwarven nation had risen and launched an assault. The dwarves *and* the elves . . . and so on until someone swore that he'd heard an army of kender was sapping through the walls of the High Clerist's Tower. The bells rang out yet again, this time for victory. Their peals were soon muffled.

By midmorning, ships were sailing in haste into the harbor. Their crews reported that they had seen the sea on fire; the red glow in the sky came from a terrible, magical blaze that used water as fuel. Once this spread about, people ran to the docks to hear the sailors' stories and stare at the flickering red glow—sunset at the wrong time of day, in the wrong sky.

And then word came that the forests of the Vingaard Mountains were aflame, that the High Clerist's Tower was being attacked by a force hideous and powerful and unknown, the same force that could burn water as easily as tinder-dry wood. A pall of smoke drifted over the city, rising from the flaming hills. As yet, the forest fires were far away, posed no threat, but if the winds shifted . . .

"Where'd you leave your boat?" Palin asked Usha as the three emerged from the gates of the Old Wall, started to walk to the waterfront.

"In the public harbor. I paid a dwarf to watch it. Oh, Palin," Usha cried, stopping in dismay. "Look at that mob! How will we ever get through it?"

Half the population of the city was down at the docks, waiting for each new ship to arrive, muttering to their neighbors, or standing grimly silent, watching the strange sky. A wall of people stood between them and the public harbor. It was a living wall that shifted with every eddy and current of rumor, but remained densely packed, all the same.

"That? Pooh! That won't be any problem," said Tas cheerfully. "Just follow me."

He walked up to the nearest group of people, several guildsmen, who fanned themselves, mopped sweating foreheads, spoke together in low, excited tones, pausing to ask everyone who passed, "What news?"

"Excuse me," Tasslehoff said loudly. He plucked one of the guildsmen by his long, flowing sleeve. "My friends and I are trying to—"

"Kender!" the man yelled. Grabbing his money pouch with one hand, a jeweled pendant he wore around his neck with the other, he jumped about three steps backward.

This man bumped heavily into the backside of another man, who was talking with another group. That man, turning and seeing Tas, clutched his own money pouch and took three hasty steps back. Soon people were shoving and jostling and elbowing each other out of the way.

"Thank you," said Tasslehoff politely and moved forward—Palin and Usha hastening fast behind—until he hit the next section of human wall, where his shrill "Excuse me!" started the entire process all over again.

Thus the three made their way through the mob far more easily and much faster than they had expected. The fact that their passing was accompanied with sharp orders to "Keep clear!" and repeated cries of "Hey! Give that back!" and the occasional scuffle were minor nuisances, not to be considered.

Most of the people were huddled near the city wall or gathered around the commercial docks, near where the shore boats were ferrying ashore the crew and passengers from the big ships floating at anchor at the harbor's entrance. Once they reached the water's edge, the crowd thinned out.

Warning flags had been hoisted, hung limp above the harbormaster's office. The sailors had no need of them, however. They could see for themselves that no sane person would put out to sea this troubled morning.

Usha was not a sailor. She knew nothing of warning flags, would have paid them little heed if she had. She was going home. She would find out the truth—whatever it was, however terrible it was.

Her fear seemed to enhance her senses, sharpen her sight, for she found her sailboat readily, though it was jammed in among many, many others.

"There!" She pointed.

Palin eyed it dubiously. "It seems awfully small."

"It will hold the three of us."

"I mean . . . small . . . to venture into the sea."

He gazed out across the water. Not even a breath of wind blew down at the harbor. Waves caused by the movement of ships lapped sluggishly beneath the docks. No sea birds skimmed the water's surface or fought over the fish heads and tails. No clouds massed in the sky, though the flash of forked lightning, the rumble and boom of thunder from the east, was constant. The strange and ominous red glow spanned the horizon, was reflected in the water.

Palin shook his head. "There's no wind. We can't row all that distance back to your homeland. We'll have to find some other way."

"No, we won't," Usha replied, tugging him along. "The boat is magical, remember? It will take me home, Palin. It will take me home," she repeated softly.

"Usha," Palin said, pulling on her hand, slowing her eager progress, "Usha . . . "

She saw on his face, heard in the tone of his voice what he was about to say. It was like looking in a mirror, her own fear reflecting back to her.

"I'll be all right," she said. "I have you with me."

Holding fast to his hand, she walked out onto the dock, heading for her boat.

Usha climbed down into the vessel, began to inspect it, to make certain it was still in seaworthy condition. Palin and Tas remained topside, baking in the sun, ready to cast off the ropes when it was time to leave. Several people glanced at them curiously, but no one said anything to them, probably figuring they were making the craft snug to weather the storm, never guessing they were planning to set sail.

Palin wondered if people would try to stop them, what he would do, how he would handle that situation should it arise.

They had to take this route, much as he disliked sailing into that fire-red sky. What Usha had said was right. The magical boat would return to its homeland. There was no other way, since no one else knew where the Irda homeland was, not even the members of the Conclave. Dragons might, but they were fighting their own battles.

"I'm quite a sailor myself," Tas announced, sitting on the dock, swinging his legs and peering down into the sea, trying to catch sight of some fish. "Flint wasn't. Flint hated water. He never could really understand why it was around. 'Reorx gave us ale,' Flint used to say. 'You'd think he would've stopped there, when he'd got it right.' I tried to point out that you couldn't very well sail a boat on ale. Well, you probably could, but the foam would be inconvenient. Flint maintained that boats were accursed inventions anyway. 'Course, this may have been because he almost drowned in one. Did you ever hear the story about how Flint almost drowned? It was one day when your father—"

"Let's not talk about drowning," Palin said. "Or my father."

Danger would be coming to the Inn of the Last Home. Caramon had gone back to warn the townspeople of Solace, to make them ready, to do what he could to protect them against whatever horrors they might face.

"Does my father know what I will be doing?" Palin had questioned his uncle, almost the last words the two had spoken together. "Where I'm going?"

"He knows," Raistlin had replied.

"What did he say?" Palin had asked uneasily.

Raistlin had almost smiled. "That, when this was over, he and your mother would expect you home to dinner."

Palin thought this over, was pleased. His father knew the danger his son would be facing and, instead of trying to deter him (as Caramon would have done in the old days), he was letting his son know that his parents had faith in him, that they believed in him and knew he would do his best.

A small hand was tugging at his sleeve. Palin looked down. Tas was standing right beside him.

"Palin," Tas said in a whisper. "I'm afraid Usha's going to be unhappy once she gets to her home, after what we heard the gods say about it."

"Yes, Tas," Palin said quietly. "She will be very unhappy."

"Shouldn't we tell her now? Sort of . . . prepare her?"

Palin looked down at Usha, who was working busily, stowing away gear, making room for the extra two people who would be going with her.

"She knows, Tas," he said. "She already knows."

* * * * *

As it turned out, no one tried to stop them from leaving the harbor. No one even noticed they were setting sail or, if people did, they had problems enough of their own to consider. The wind that people had prayed for all summer, the breezes from the mountains, bringing cooling air to the stifling city, had suddenly now, perversely it seemed, decided to blow. But the wind did not bring relief from the heat. It brought terror. The forest fires were racing down the mountains, the wind blowing them straight toward Palanthas.

The bells rang out again. People ran to do what they could to try to save their homes and businesses, should the unthinkable happen. The smoke in the air stung the eyes and made breathing difficult. Ashes were starting to drift down on the city. Palin stood in the boat, looked back at the great city of Palanthas, and tried to imagine what it would be like if the fires came. He thought of his uncle, alone in the tower. The apprentices had already gone, traveling to Wayreth to lend their aid in preparing magic. He remembered his last glimpse of his uncle, standing by the Pool of Seeing.

"Here, I will watch," Raistlin had said. "From here, I will do what I can to guide you."

Palin thought of Astinus, writing, writing. He could imagine Bertrem, panicked, and the other monks, working frantically to save the books, the history of the world.

Save them for what? There might be no one left around to read them. We are sailing to an island of death, perhaps sailing toward our own deaths . . .

"Well, we're off!" Tasslehoff announced cheerily. He was perched in the bow, peering ahead, as Usha steered the boat out of the harbor, out into the open sea. "You know," he said with a delighted sigh, "there's nothing quite as exciting as going someplace you've never been before."

20

Cinder and ash.

hey sailed out of the Bay of Branchala, into the Turbidus Ocean, the wind pushing them along as if eager to help. Then, suddenly, the wind that had carried them this far—the same wind that was sending a firestorm onto Palanthas—died. They floated, becalmed, on the water's flat surface.

Usha rested her hand on the rudder, turned the boat's prow to the north. "Home," she commanded.

The boat began to skim across the water, water that seemed to have been painted over with red. The sail fluttered limply, for no breeze stirred it, but the boat sped on, traveling faster and faster until it bounded perilously over the surface, sent the salt spray flying into their faces.

Tas was in the prow, hanging on with both hands, facing into the wind and spray, openmouthed with the thrill of the wild ride. Usha held fast to the rudder. Palin clung to the sides, trying to blink the stinging saltwater from his eyes.

The boat's speed increased. Tas was blown off his perch, landed on a pile of rope coiled at the bottom. Eventually, all three of them were forced to huddle down in the bottom of the boat, the sky reeling above them, the waves crashing over them. Water sloshed around their feet; they were soaked to the skin. Palin worried about the boat taking on too much water, but Usha told him even if it did, the magic would keep them afloat. They hung on to each other now. They could see nothing except the red, glowing sky.

* * * * *

"We're slowing down," said an excited voice. "I think we're here."

Usha woke up, startled to realize that she had dozed off. Palin lifted his head, rubbed his eyes. They all must have fallen asleep. Usha vaguely recalled having dreams about being wet and hungry.

Palin looked toward the sun, whose fiery, glaring eye stared at them above the rim of the horizon.

"We've slept the day away apparently," he said. "The sun's setting."

"It's taking a long time about it," Tas observed.

"What do you mean?" Palin stood up in the boat cautiously.

"I've been watching it for about three hours now, all the time you were asleep. The sun hasn't budged. It just sits there."

Palin smiled indulgently. "You must be mistaken, Tas. It probably hasn't been three hours. It just seemed that long."

Tasslehoff was back on his station at the prow. "Look! There ahead!"

A thin line of darkness was silhouetted against the red sky.

Usha stood up rapidly, forgetting she was in a boat, and setting it to rocking with such violence that she was forced to grab hold of the mast to keep from tumbling overboard. She made her way forward, joining Palin and Tas at the prow, and stared eagerly, her lips parted in joy.

"I think this must be your homeland, Usha," Palin said. "We appear to be heading right for it."

The boat took them nearer.

"Funny-looking trees," Tas commented. "Do you come from a place that has funny-looking trees, Usha?"

"Our trees look the same as all other trees," Usha said. "But you're right, those do look strange . . ."

The waves and its own magic carried the boat still nearer.

"Blessed Paladine," Palin whispered, aghast.

"Oh, my," said Tas in a small voice. "Those trees aren't trees anymore. They're all burned up."

"No," Usha said softly. "This isn't right. The magic isn't working. This boat has taken us to the wrong place. That"—her throat closed on her words, choking her—"that isn't my home."

But the wretched boat kept taking her closer and closer.

"I'm sorry, Usha," Palin said, and reached out his hand to her.

She ignored his words, ignored his hand. Stumbling over coils of rope and waterskins, she ran back to the stern. She grabbed hold of the rudder, shoved on it, tried to change course, to turn the boat around.

The rudder wouldn't budge.

Usha hurled herself on the rudder bodily. When Palin took hold of her, pulled her away, she struck at him with her fists, crying out, and struggling to break free. The boat rocked violently.

"You're going to capsize us!" Palin told her.

"I don't care!" she sobbed. "I don't care if we all die!"

"Yes, you do, Usha," he said gently, over and over. "Yes, you do." He soothed her and brushed back her wet hair and held her tightly.

Her sobs quieted, she rested in his arms. The boat, under its geas, took them in to shore.

By the time they reached the beach, Usha had settled into a silent, frozen calm almost as frightening as her hysteria. She stepped out of the boat and into the water, waded through it ankle-deep until they reached the broad stretch of sand where the Knights of Takhisis had made their own landfall not so long ago.

She stared around at a scene of utter devastation.

Except for where the waves lapped against the shore, the sand—once white—was now black.

Palin, pulling in the boat and beaching it on the shore, thought the black sand a natural phenomenon. But then he saw the debris floating in the water, saw the fine silt that had settled on the top of the waves. He looked at the charred and burned trunks of what had once been living trees, and suddenly he knew why the sand was black. It was covered with cinders and ash.

Palin, sighing, helped Tas climb out of the boat. When he turned back to Usha, she was running wildly, frantically, into what had once been a forest. Palin and Tas scrambled after her, slipping in the shifting sands. She left them both behind. The elder kender, with his short legs and shorter breath, was soon outdistanced. Palin, not accustomed to physical exertion and encumbered by his wet robes, could not keep up.

Her trail was easy to follow, however, pitifully easy, as Tas observed. It was a trail of footprints through ankle-deep ashes, and it led them deeper into a wilderness of desolation. The slightly sweet, sharp, sickening smell of charred wood was overpowering, sapped the breath. Ashes and cinders, stirred by the breeze, stung the eyes and set them both to coughing. Blackened branches hung over them, creaking and swaying, ready to fall.

They came to a stone wall, formed in the shape of a square. A blackened chimney made of stone rose up from one end—all that was left of what must have once been a small, snug house.

"Palin!" Tas called in a strangled voice.

Palin turned. The kender was pointing at something. Palin had no need to draw closer to see what it was. He knew.

The corpse—what remained of it—lay near the house, as if the person might have been running out of the burning building, only to be overtaken by the inferno.

"I saw Que-shu," Tasslehoff said, subdued by the awful sight, "after the dragons had been there. It was like this. The saddest thing I ever saw until now. Do you . . . do you think they're *all* dead, Palin?"

Palin looked at the charred and blasted stumps of the trees, at the thick coating of ash covering the ground.

"We have to find Usha," he said, and, taking hold of Tas by the hand, the two followed her trail through the ashes.

She stood in front of another wall of stone. Nothing recognizable was left of the house or its contents. It had collapsed in upon itself, was a heap of blackened rubble.

She didn't cry or call out. She made no move to touch what little was left.

Palin went to her, put his arms around her. It was as if he were embracing stone. Her flesh was cold, her body stiff, her eyes wide, set, staring.

"Usha!" Palin called, truly frightened at her appearance. "Usha, don't do this to yourself. It won't help. Usha, don't . . ."

She didn't look at him, but stared fixedly at the charred remnants of the house. Her face was chalky white beneath a mask of black soot. A single tear tracked through the smudges on her cheek, as her footsteps had tracked through the ashes on the ground.

"I'm so sorry, Usha," Palin said gently. "But, the Irda are not wholly destroyed. *You* will carry on . . ."

"No," she said with a terrible, remote calm. "No, they are gone, completely, utterly gone. Prot knew this would happen. That's why he sent me away. Oh, I'm sorry, Prot!" She gave a shuddering sob. "So very sorry."

"Don't, Dearest. There was nothing you could have done. Perhaps," he added hopefully, "some of them managed to escape. Their magic . . ."

Usha shook her head. "Even if some could have saved themselves, they never would have left the others behind. No, they are gone. Nothing is left. Nothing."

The eerie red glow of the sun shone through the skeletal trees. A bar of sunlight glanced across her, bathed her in red, making her golden eyes gleam like burnished bronze.

The sun . . .

"Tas was right!" Palin gasped. "The sun hasn't moved! Tas, you were— Tas?"

He looked around.

The kender was gone.

21

Dougan Redhammer. The Graygem.
Minions of Chaos.

hat's more like it," said Tasslehoff, watching Palin and Usha. "They have each other now, and so, of course, everything will be all right. At least everything deserves to be all right for them. I've often found, though," he added with a sigh, "that deserving and happening don't necessarily go together."

He stood watching the two, long enough to see them find solace and comfort in each other's arms. True love—if you're not in it, just happen to be standing there watching it—does tend to be a bit boring. Tas yawned, sneezed violently when some ash flew up his nose, and looked around for something to do.

There, stretching before him among the stumps of burned trees, was a path.

"All paths lead somewhere," is an old kender adage. Combine this with "Every path is the right path except when it's the left fork," and that pretty well sums up kender philosophy.

"And perhaps this path will lead me to the Graygem," he said, on consideration.

Tas was going to tell Palin and Usha he was leaving, then he thought that perhaps they wouldn't want to be disturbed, so he slipped very softly away, following the path he had discovered.

As he walked, moving along very quietly, so as not to bother anyone, he considered what he knew about the Graygem.

"I suppose it's a jewel like any other, except that it's broken, of course, which is a very good thing," Tas said thoughtfully, "because now I don't have to go to the trouble of breaking it."

He recalled Raistlin saying something about the Graygem being guarded, but Tas hadn't paid too much attention to that part. Gems were always guarded, in his experience, and since the guards always tended to be people with a most unreasoning prejudice against kender, Tas really couldn't see why this should be any different. He continued down the path, climbing over burned-out stumps and thinking that the mounds of black ashes were a lot like drifted snow, except for being black and being ashes and smelling kind of putrid, when he suddenly came upon a dwarf, crouched behind a tree.

"My goodness," Tas said, stopping short. "How very strange."

The dwarf was exceedingly well dressed, especially to be hiding behind a flame-ravaged tree in a charred and devastated forest. The dwarf's fine clothes were covered with soot, as was his beard and long hair. The plume of his hat was bedraggled and dirty. He was watching something very intently; his back was half-turned to the path, which meant his back was half-turned to the kender on the path.

"I do believe . . yes, I'm positive," Tas muttered. "It's Dougan Redhammer."

Tas followed the dwarf's line of sight, tried to see what Dougan was watching so closely, but he couldn't, due to another large pine tree—or what was left of it—that was in the way.

The dwarf seemed very intent on his watch. Tas didn't want to disturb Dougan, so he crept forward silently, gliding across the scorched ground as still as a mouse, of which he had firsthand knowledge, having accidentally turned himself into a mouse once. Stealing up on the dwarf, Tas reached out and tapped Dougan on the shoulder.

It was amazing, considering his stoutness, how high the dwarf could jump. And to jump that high, without losing his broad-brimmed hat, was also quite remarkable.

Dougan's jumping up in that sudden manner startled Tas so that he fell back, tumbled over a burned-out log, and landed on the ground. The rotund dwarf, breathing heavily and turning the same red as the sky, pounced on the kender and clapped his hand over Tas's mouth.

"Who in Reorx's name are you?" Dougan demanded in a hoarse whisper. "And what are you doing here?"

Tas replied as best he could, being somewhat hampered in answering due to the hand over his mouth.

"Xrinxmaggle Yurfuuz?" repeated the dwarf. "Never heard of you. Still, you do look kind of familiar."

Tas shook his head violently, squeaked and squirmed and indicated by pointing that they might carry on this conversation more pleasantly if he could talk.

Dougan eyed him a moment, then removed his hand from Tas's mouth. The dwarf sat back on his heels. "Be quiet!" he warned. "They're close. Over there. And though I'm not certain whether or not they can hear, it's best not to take chances."

Tasslehoff nodded, rubbed his head where he'd banged it on a rock, and sat up. "Who's 'they'?" he whispered.

"Who are you?" Dougan whispered testily back.

"Sorry. Forgot to introduce myself." Tas scrambled to his feet. Dougan heaved himself to his feet—which he probably hadn't seen in the past few centuries, or so Tas figured, noting the dwarf's immense girth. The kender extended his hand. "I'm Tasslehoff Burrfoot."

"Oh." Dougan grunted. "So that's where I know you from. I'm—"

"I know. Reorx," Tas said in a loud whisper. "But don't worry. I won't tell anyone," he added hastily, noting the scowl on Dougan's face.

"Nothing to tell," the dwarf snarled, glaring straight into Tas's eyes. "The name's Dougan Redhammer. Understand?"

"No," Tas replied, after a moment's thought. "But then there's lots I don't understand. Death, for one thing. And sheriffs for another. Both seem to take a lot of the fun out of life. And while we're at it, there's the matter of hiccups. Why hiccups, if you take my meaning? And I was also wondering if you could explain—"

Dougan said something about the Abyss becoming an ice-skating pond first, which Tas found rather curious, and he was about to ask the dwarf to explain *that*, but Dougan's hand was over his mouth again.

"Why did you come? What are you doing here?"

He moved his hand slightly, enough for Tas could squeak past an answer. "Raistlin Majere sent me," the kender replied proudly. "I'm to pick up the Graygem."

"*You?*"

The dwarf forgot his own prohibition and spoke this word quite loudly. Cringing, he hunkered down behind the tree, pulled Tas down with him.

"You?" Dougan repeated, apparently quite shocked. "He sent you?"

Tas wasn't sure he liked the nasty way Dougan kept saying *you*. It didn't sound very complimentary to Raistlin.

"I *am* a Hero of the Lance," Tas pointed out. "I've fought dragons before, and I captured a prisoner once, no matter what Flint might have said to the contrary. I rescued Sestun from a red dragon, and I've been to the Abyss and back *twice*, and—"

"Enough!" the dwarf howled quietly—an interesting feat, and one Tas would have said offhand a person couldn't do, if he hadn't just seen Dougan do it.

"You're here, so I guess I'll have to make the best of it," Dougan grumbled, adding something about why hadn't the mage sent along a party of gnomes, too, just to make his—Dougan's—misery complete. "Come here," he finished, hauling Tas over to the tree. "I want to show you something. And keep your mouth shut!"

Tas looked, keeping quiet, as ordered, not because he'd been ordered, but because what he was seeing made him want to keep quiet—very, very quiet for a long time.

Seven dead pine trees stood in a circle. The pines had all been ravaged by fire, but—unlike the other trees that had been reduced to blackened and withered stumps—these pines were still whole. Now they stood, like ghastly skeletons, their peeling limbs twisted and contorted in agonizing death.

A whimper—in sympathy for the once magnificent trees—tried to slip out, but Tas managed to swallow it back. In the middle of the ring of dead pines stood a heap of wood. Marvelously and inexplicably, the wood had not been consumed by the terrible blaze that had burned everything else on the island. Something sparkled near the bottom of the woodpile, sparkled red, reflecting the blaze of the fierce and stubborn sun, which was still refusing to properly set.

Tas put his hand to Dougan's ear, leaned over, and said softly, "Is that the Graygem?"

"Split in twain," the dwarf answered back, his face dark, his expression grim. "Its two halves lie upon what is left of the altar. I hid them from Himself. He could not find them, though he searched long and hard. And that made me stop and think."

"Think what?"

"Never you mind," Dougan said severely, looking very serious. "The first thing we have to do is recover the gem."

"Then let's go get it. What's stopping us?"

"They are." Dougan gave a gloomy nod in the direction of the altar.

Tas looked back. He didn't see a dragon. He didn't see draconians. He didn't see hordes of goblins or ogres or kobolds or death knights or banshees or skeletal warriors or any other of the usual guardians of magical gemstones. There wasn't even a sheriff. There wasn't anything—a fact he pointed out.

"Been hitting the dwarf spirits again, eh?" Tas said with sympathy.

"I'm not drunk!" Dougan returned indignantly. "The guardians! They're there, between the trees."

"There's nothing but dark shadows between the trees," Tas observed.

"That's them," Dougan whispered. "Only they are not shadows. They are shadow-wights, fearful warriors of Chaos."

"They're made out of shadows?" Tas asked, impressed.

"They are made of holes in the fabric of mortal being. You do not look at them, but through them, into their realm, which is the plane of nonexistence. If they touch you, you become as they are: nothing. That is the doom Chaos prepares for this world and every person, every animal, every rock, tree, and plant, every river, stream, and ocean. All, all will be nothing."

Tas experienced a sudden hollow, unhappy feeling in the pit of his stomach. He thought of himself being nothing, of everything around him being nothing, of everyone being nothing . . . all disappearing into the darkness of oblivion, with no one anywhere ever knowing that it had all once been something.

"Are . . . are you sure, Dougan?" Tas asked, gulping and rubbing his hand over his stomach, to try to convince the unhappy feeling to leave.

"Aye, Laddie. I'm sure. It's what Himself promised, and he'll keep that promise. It'll be all he keeps," Dougan added ominously.

"But if we get hold of the Graygem, we can stop him?"

"I'm thinking so, Lad. Mind you, I'm not sure. It's just a bit of an idea I had." He sighed. "It's the only idea anyone's had, so far. And so we thought we'd give it a try."

"Let me see if I've got this straight," Tas said, peering back at the shattered altar beneath which lay the two halves of the Graygem. "We have to get those broken halves away from those shadows?"

"Shadow-wights," said Dougan in a low voice.

"Yes. Well, this shouldn't be too difficult. I have"—Tas plunked himself down on the ground, began to rummage through his pouches—"this very powerful magical artifact. . . ."

"You do?" Dougan squatted on his heels, tried to see into the pouch.

"Yes, I do. It was given me by my Uncle Trapspringer—"

"Of course. Who else?" Dougan muttered sourly. "Would that be it now?"

"No, that's a dried-up lizard. At least, I think it's a dried-up lizard . . ."

"What about that?"

"A handkerchief with the initials 'FB.' Hmm. Who do I know with the initials FB? Oh, well . . . No, that's not it, either. Aha!" Tas cried.

"Shhhh!" Dougan gestured frantically.

"Aha!" Tas whispered. "This is it! The Kender Spoon of Turning."

Dougan eyed the spoon, snorted in disgust. "It might be of some use, if the shadow-wights all turn into shadow soup, which I don't think likely." Getting to his feet, he stomped about in irritation, groaning and tearing at his beard. "Why me? Why is it always me?"

"This," said Tas, drawing himself up with dignity, which put him taller than the dwarf, not counting the hat, "is a very famous kender artifact. You watch. You'll see how it works."

Tasslehoff walked out from behind the tree, headed toward the altar, holding out in front of him Dalamar's silver teaspoon.

22

Tasslehoff in trouble.
Dougan's plan. The thief.

as? Where are you?" Palin called out.

There was no response.

Every traveler on Krynn, either brave or misguided enough to journey in the company of a kender, knows that while it is nerve-racking to be in the same party with a kender, it is ten times more unnerving to discover that the kender has wandered off on his own. Being quite fond of having adventures, kender have the interesting habit of bringing the adventure back to share with their companions, whether they want it or not.

Roundly cursing himself for his mistake—though he'd only turned his back on Tas for about five minutes—Palin searched the area and soon discovered the set of small footprints, leading off down the path.

"Where does this go?" he asked Usha.

She looked around sadly. "It's all so different. It's hard to recognize. I think . . . Yes, that must be the path leading to the altar the Irda built for the Graygem."

"Dear god. That's where he's gone, then." Palin gripped the staff hard, asked a silent prayer, and then, watchful and wary, he and Usha followed Tas.

What remained of the fire-ravaged trees lined the pathway: burned stumps, cremated limbs, ashes. It began to seem to Palin as if there were only three colors in the world: char black, ash gray, and the fire red of the sky.

"Are we close to it?" Palin asked.

"We must be! It wasn't far." Usha said. She was silent a moment, searching, then she pointed. "There! The seven pines . ."

The massive trees, once proud guardians, stood damned and blasted, skeletal warriors forever constrained to watch over the object that had brought about their doom. In the center of the dead grove lay a pile of wood. Palin caught the slightest glint of what might have been light reflecting off the facet of a gemstone. But then a shadow passed between him and the trees.

Palin cringed, froze in fear, the way a rabbit freezes to the ground when the shadow of the hawk's wings flows across its back. The fear passed, almost immediately. The shadow flitted across the woodpile, obliterating it from sight, and disappeared among the dead trees. He could see again that faint sparkle of light.

Despite the heat of the merciless sun, Palin shivered, drew his robes more closely around him. He was puzzling over the strange sensation of fear, was about to ask Usha if she had experienced a similar feeling, but she was staring off in a different direction.

"Look, Palin!" Usha said. "Isn't that Dougan?"

"Yes. Where's Tas, I wonder?"

They spoke softly, but the sound must have carried. The dwarf pivoted, peered around. Catching sight of them, he began to make frantic hand motions.

"Come quickly!" he mouthed, alternately waving his hands and wringing them. "Quiet! Quiet!" he cautioned. "But quickly!"

Having a sick feeling that this urgency had something to do with Tasslehoff, Palin hurried forward, moving as silently as he could through the ashes and fallen logs. He had the distinct and uneasy impression that something was watching him.

"Dougan!" Palin said softly, approaching the distraught dwarf. "Have you seen Tas—"

Dougan answered by directing Palin's attention toward the dead grove.

Palin shifted his gaze, was alarmed to see the kender heading straight into the pines.

"Tas! Tas, come back here!" Palin started to follow him.

Dougan caught hold of the sleeve of Palin's robe, held on with a deathlike grip. "Don't go after him, Lad," the dwarf warned in a deep, grim voice. "There's nothing you can do. I tried to stop him . . ." Dougan's shoulders slumped. He bowed his head, shook it, and groaned.

Palin stared at the kender.

"What in the name of all that is holy is he doing?"

Tasslehoff was slowly advancing toward the pine grove, moving at a funereal pace, walking with measured tread, solemn mien. He held something shining in his hand.

"A spoon?" Palin said, bewildered. "What's he doing with a spoon?"

"The Kender Spoon of Turning or some such thing," Dougan muttered.

"Yes, I remember! From the tower." Palin swore softly in frustration. "Damn it, he didn't realize . . . that was all my uncle's doing. Where's he going?"

"To try to recover the Graygem." Dougan gave another great groan, tore at his beard. "It's there, under what's left of the altar. Don't go after him, I tell you, Laddie! He's walking into terrible danger. Did you see . . . something like a bit of shade . . . gliding from out the trees?"

"Yes," said Palin, shivering again at the recollection. "What—"

"Shadow-wights, Laddie," Dougan said in low, dread tones, "creatures of Chaos. They'll draw you into oblivion, first your soul, then your body. You will vanish as if you had never been."

"I felt their touch," Palin said softly, "though I didn't understand what it was."

"I don't think you understand yet, Lad," Dougan said grimly. "When I say you will vanish as if you had never been, I mean just that! Your memory will vanish from the minds of all who knew you. Your mother will forget she ever bore a son. Your father will not recognize your name. Those who love you will not mourn for you, not pray for you, never think back on you with loving thoughts. It will be as if you had never been!

"This is what Himself plans for all the world. We gods will forget all we created, then we will die, and Creation will forget us. And then the stars themselves will forget."

"Palin, I think they've seen him," Usha said urgently. "He's getting too close!"

"How, Dougan?" Palin rounded on the dwarf. "How can we stop them?"

"The Graygem!" Dougan had worriedly twisted his beard into knots. "We must have the Graygem!"

"But how do we get it if those creatures have it surrounded?"

Tas was drawing closer. The shadows had begun to move.

"Tas!" Palin risked a low call. "Tas, come back!"

But the kender didn't hear because, at that moment, he began to speak.

"Out of my way, you soul-sucking scum! Leave now, lest I unleash the lethal power of my ancestor's tableware! Leave now, lest I use this spoon to scoop out your shadowy innards!"

"Tas!" Usha raised her voice. "Tas, please! Come—"

"Hush!" Dougan clutched at her, nearly knocked her down. "Look! Look! They're coming for him!"

Darkest, deepest, blackest night glided out from beneath the charred pines. All light, all sound, all color, all movement, all hope was sucked into that fathomless darkness, never to find the way out Four of the awful formless shapes converged, began slipping over the ground, moving toward the kender. The shadow-wights blotted out the sun, the trees, the sky, the ground.

"Lad, Lassie! Look!" Dougan whispered in a state of high excitement. "They've left the Graygem unguarded!"

Palin had difficulty seeing the altar, had trouble even remembering where it was. Behind the shadow-wights, nothing existed. When they moved, objects reemerged, looking as if they had just at that moment sprung into existence.

"Fool kender! I'm going after him," Palin said. He ran over his catalog of spells in his mind, wondering which—if any—might destroy the shadow-wights.

"I'm going with you," Usha announced.

"No." Palin shook his head. "You stay here with—"

"You go after the Graygem, Lassie," Dougan interrupted, his black eyes gleaming with cunning. "You could nip in there and swipe it before those creatures ever knew it was gone. You've been trained to the art, Lass. I've seen your work. . . Nine-Fingers says you're one of the best . . . No time for questions now, Lass. Can you lay hold of the gem?"

"Would that stop the shadow-wights?" Usha asked.

"Aye, Lassie. Aye, it might," Dougan said. "At least," he added, "it can't hurt."

"Turn me into nothing, will you?" Tasslehoff's voice rose shrilly, though it quavered a bit, as the shadow-wights drew nearer. "Well you can take your nothingness and put it where the sun don't shine—"

"Now, Lass!" Dougan urged.

Usha dropped her pack on the ground, to leave her hands free. Ignoring Palin's protests, she gave him a swift kiss on the cheek, patted his arm, and—slipping out of his grasp—sped off with silent tread through the trees.

Palin eyed Dougan grimly. "You're a god—supposedly. Why don't *you* do something?"

Dougan appeared no end astonished. "I am, Lad! I am! It was my idea to send the girl after the gem, wasn't it?"

"I mean against those creatures!" Palin waved his hand at the shadow-wights.

"Ah, Lad," Dougan said softly, "they are formed of the same stuff I am. They are god-beings, same as me. And though I am immortal on your plane, I am not on theirs, if you take my meaning. And what would happen to the world if they destroyed me, Lad?"

"I don't know," Palin said coldly. "Perhaps you'd care to place a wager on that?"

Dougan scratched at his beard. "I think you'd better go now, Lad. Your kender friend appears to be in a bit of trouble."

"If anything happens to either him or Usha, by Paladine, I'll make you regret it!" Palin promised.

"*Shirak.*" He commanded the staff to light, hurried forward toward the seven pines, toward Tasslehoff.

The kender was about halfway there. The shadow-wights were lined up in front of him, leaving the Graygem unguarded.

A kender's taunting could unhinge the most easygoing person, drive him to commit murder and mayhem. But had Tas's insults truly provoked the shadow-wights into leaving their post? Palin had the uneasy feeling that this was not the case. He considered it far more likely that the otherworldly creatures had small interest in guarding the Graygem. They had only one objective, and that was destruction.

But if they noticed Usha trying to take the Graygem, they would turn on her fast enough. Palin watched her out the corner of his eye, afraid to look at her directly, lest the shadow-wights follow his line of sight and discover her. She slipped with silent ease through the burned wreckage of the forest.

At least, for the moment, she was safe. The shadow-wights were completely focused on Tasslehoff. And in a short time, they would have another subject—Palin.

He was too preoccupied to be afraid. He had to form a plan that would rescue Tas, at the same time keeping the creatures' attention from Graygem, and—hopefully—end up by getting them all out of this alive.

He considered his catalog of spells. It seemed logical to him that since the shadow-wights were creatures of darkness they might be sensitive to light, could be either destroyed by light or at least intimidated. The Staff of Magius shed its own radiant glow on Palin. He reached into his component pouch, removed a small ball of bat guano, rolled in sulfur, and—concentrating his thoughts—brought the words of the magical fireball to mind.

* * * * *

Keep your mind on the plunder, Lynched Geoffrey would say. *Touch it, hold it, make it yours in your heart before it's yours in the hand.*

Which meant, don't let anything distract you, turn you from your objective. Think about the Graygem, think about how you want it! Don't think about Palin; don't think about Tas. Don't think about those terrible creatures, who will try to destroy you . . . The Graygem, the Graygem . . . That's all and everything.

Usha watched the shadow-wights slowly drawing nearer the kender. Tas sounded far less sure of himself; his voice faltered now and then, his steps slowed, the spoon—which he had formerly presented so boldly—wavered in his hand.

"I'm not afraid!" Tas cried out. "I'm . . . I'm annoyed! You're really starting to get on my nerves. So . . . just back off! I—" His voice changed, sounded strangled. "Stop . . . you stop that! What do you think you're doing? . . . Quit looking like me . . . !"

Tasslehoff was wild-eyed, staring as if he saw something terrible beyond belief before him.

Palin strode out from among the trees. The crystal atop the Staff of Magius shone with a white, vibrant light.

"The gem, girl!" Dougan's voice came to her. "That's the only way you can help them! Get the gem!"

She tore her gaze from Palin and Tas, refocused on her objective, as she had been taught.

Entering the ring of seven dead pines, she slipped through their unseeing guard. The woodpile that had once been the altar stood in the center. Now that she was close, she could see the terrible destruction. Some gigantic hand, working in rage and fury, had pummeled the once-beautiful, hand-polished, rune-covered wood to splinters.

Usha had a sudden poignant memory of the Irda building this altar, of them working long hours with their tools and their magic, carving, smoothing, sanding, planing, weaving their spells into the wood, spells that would hold the Graygem fast.

Prot had not approved. Prot had been opposed to the plan from the beginning. She remembered him watching, remembered his foreboding.

"You were right, dear friend, dear father," Usha whispered, her tears gathering, threatening to blind her.

"The gem, girl! The gem!"

Usha blinked back her grief. The altar was a dead thing now. The Irda were dead. She couldn't bring them back. But she could try to undo the mischief they had done.

The Graygem, which had once shone with its own eerie gray light, lay in two pieces on the ground, partially buried by the splintered wood. The gem was split in two, like a cracked walnut shell. The inside of the gem was hollow, as though some insidious worm had been gnawing away at it for long, long years.

Even broken, the gem enthralled, fascinated. It was so beautiful it was ugly, so large it was small, so shiny it was dull, so hard it was soft. Usha stretched out her hands to it, touched it, lifted it. The gem weighed nothing, yet she was conscious of a great weight. The innumerable facets were sharp, cutting, soft. The gem was cold to the touch, burning cold.

She was about to slip the Graygem triumphantly into her pouch when a fear-rimed cry chilled her soul.

Palin stood in front of Tasslehoff. The staff's light still shone, but it was fading, dimming. The shadow-wights were closing in. Already, she could see very little of Tas—only the very tip of his topknot. She could see Palin's shoulders and his face.

And on his face, the same expression of wild-eyed, staring horror that had overcome even the fear-immune kender.

23

I am not nothing!

P alin was coming up on Tas. The kender had ceased to taunt his foes. It seemed that Tas was attempting to bolster up his own courage—unheard of, for a kender.

"I'm *not* afraid!" Tas cried out. "I'm . . . I'm annoyed! You're really starting to get on my nerves. So . . . just back off! I—" His voice changed, sounded strangled. "Stop . . . you stop that! What do you think you're doing? Quit looking like me!"

Palin had not been watching the creatures. He'd been thinking of his spell, which meant he was visualizing in his mind the words he must speak. The rest of his attention had been divided between Usha, now inside the pine grove, and Tasslehoff.

At Tas's cry, Palin looked for the first time directly at the shadow-wights. He couldn't look away.

He found himself staring at himself. Palin stood before him.

"Who are you?" Palin demanded, his voice shaking. He looked into the wight's eyes, saw nothing, not even his own reflection. "What are you?"

"Who are you? What are you?" The wight mocked him.

"I am myself," Palin said, but even as he spoke, he felt himself start to slip away.

The shadow-wight was pulling his life from his body.

"You are nothing," the shadow-wight told him, speaking with Palin's mouth. "You were born of nothing. You will return to nothing."

Look away! came Raistlin's warning voice, vibrating through the staff. *Look away! Don't look into the eyes!*

Palin tried to wrench his gaze from the image of himself, but he couldn't. He stared, rapt. The words of his spell were blotted out by drops of darkness that fell into his mind, like raindrops onto paper, causing all remembrance, all the knowledge of himself to blur, run, become indistinct and muddled, slowly start to wash away.

He had a vague impression that he heard Usha cry out a name, "Palin!" and he wondered dimly who that person was.

*   *   *   *   *

"Palin!" Usha cried from within the grove of dead pines.

The shadow-wights were drawing nearer Palin, were creeping up on

Tasslehoff. She could see almost nothing of the kender now, nothing except his bright yellow socks and the tip of his topknot.

"Palin! Tas! Get away! Run!"

But neither of them moved or even reacted to her words. Palin stood staring at the wights with that dreadful expression of horror.

"Quickly, Lass, or they're goners," Dougan cried out.

"What . . . what can I do?" Usha asked helplessly. Her pack, with all the magical artifacts the Irda had given her, was lying far away at Dougan's feet. There was no time to try to reach it.

"The Graygem!" Dougan yelled. "Try trapping them with the Graygem! I'll help you, Lass. You can do it!"

Usha was doubtful on that point, but she could think of nothing else. She had to act swiftly. The darkness was stealing up over Palin, had almost engulfed Tasslehoff.

Holding one half of the Graygem in each hand, Usha crept toward the shadow-wights.

"Don't look at 'em, Lass!" Dougan cautioned. "Whatever you do, don't look at 'em!"

Usha didn't want to look at them. Every time her gaze brushed across them, she shuddered in a terror that twisted her up inside. She fixed her gaze on Palin, on his beloved face, now contorted in fear.

And then, suddenly, Usha was standing before her.

Usha blinked, amazed and appalled.

"Don't look into the eyes, Lass!" Dougan howled. "Don't!"

Usha looked at Palin, concentrated on Palin, ignored the wight's voice that was trying to lure her to darkness. Head turned away, she reached out blindly, thrust the Graygem into the image of herself.

A terrible, painful, numbing cold froze her fingers. She almost dropped the Graygem. The agony was unendurable. Shards of ice shot through her veins. She was losing consciousness, spiraling down into darkness.

"Catch it!" Dougan commanded. "Trap it in the jewel!"

Desperately, despairingly, Usha slammed the two halves of the Graygem together.

The chill was warm.

The darkness was light.

The shadow-wights were gone.

Usha stared around, wondered dazedly if they had ever truly been there. She gazed down at the Graygem, pressed tightly together in her hands, and she began to shake.

Dougan came dashing up, panting and puffing, his thick boots clomping, raising clouds of choking ash.

"Well done, Lass! Well done. We've got 'em now." In a muttered aside he said, "Some of them, at least." Then he added hastily, "I'll take that," and plucked the Graygem from Usha's hands.

She had wanted it before. Now she was only too glad to be rid of it.

"Palin?" she said anxiously, grasping hold of the mage's arm. "Palin, are you all right?"

He was staring straight ahead, that dreadful fixed expression on his pallid face. At the sound of her voice, her touch, he looked slowly around.

"Palin. *I* am Palin."

She flung her arms around him.

He embraced her, held her close, his eyes closed, body trembling.

Dougan bent over Tasslehoff.

The kender had fallen to his knees. He clutched the spoon in his hand still, and was sobbing, over and over, "I'm *not* nothing! I'm *not* nothing! I'm *not* nothing!"

"Lad! Lad! They're gone!" Dougan called, pounding Tas on the back in what was a good-natured attempt to bring the kender around, but which had the effect of knocking most of the air out of Tas's small body.

He coughed and wheezed and blinked his eyes. Catching sight of Dougan, Tas smiled vaguely.

"Oh, hullo."

"Do you know me, Lad?" Dougan asked anxiously.

"Well, of course," Tas said. "You're Reorx."

Dougan shook his head. "Never mind about that now. The important thing is, who are *you*, Lad? Do you remember?"

Tas gave a relieved and contented sigh that started at the toes of his yellow socks, surged warmly all through him. He flung his arms wide.

"I'm me! That's who! I'm me!"

*   *   *   *   *

The Graygem rested in the dwarf's hands. He looked very old suddenly. His hands shook; the fingers trembled. His face was worn and aged. He had removed his hat with its jaunty feather, set it aside. His clothes were ash-covered, the buttons undone, laces dangling. He held the gem and regarded it sadly, drew a deep, shivering breath.

"I remember well the day I crafted this," he said. "A bit of Chaos, that's all I wanted. It was all I needed. No more than a lock of hair or a shaving of a fingernail, to put it into mortal terms. Himself was hanging about, snooping, as always. Our world—the world we'd made without him—was ordered then, you see. He couldn't bear that. Disorder, confusion, anarchy—he'd have enjoyed watching our creation sink to that.

"He especially hated my forge. The crafting, the making, the building of things, was anathema to Himself. The breaking—that's what he liked.

"Himself has many children. But these three children: Paladine, Takhisis, Gilean, these were his favorites. He gave them great power, and then he was furious when they used it—used it to thwart him—or so *he* felt. To make a world and then populate it with living beings, to breathe the breath of the gods into those beings, to give them life, so that they could continue the crafting and the building and the ordering. None of his other children had ever dared try such a thing before. Himself couldn't stand it.

"He wanted to wreck it, but we were too powerful. We held him back. Himself had given his children the means to do that, you see, and how he regretted it! Paladine and Takhisis, Himself despised them, the two who always longed for order, plotted and schemed to achieve it. Gilean—he was the favorite child, but he proved a sad disappointment.

"It was mainly on account of Gilean, I believe, that Chaos held back from destroying the new-peopled world at the very beginning. Himself thought Gilean would see to it that Chaos reigned. But Gilean had always been of a studious turn, his nose in a book, refusing to be bothered. And so Paladine and Takhisis had their way. The balance shifting from one to another with Gilean flipping pages in between."

Dougan stared at the two fragments of the jewel, hefted them both, peered intently into the hollow center.

"They say I trapped him inside, that I grabbed for a tiny bit of Chaos to put in here and ended up with it all. The gem was to be an anchor, don't you see? It would do what Gilean, lost in his books, was not doing. The plan sounded good to me at the time. Perhaps, if I'd thought about it . . . But I didn't, so there's an end to it.

"But I don't think I trapped him. No.

"He did it on purpose. Himself saw his chance, and he took it. He popped into that gem, right before I sealed it. It was Himself who took off soaring over the world, changing this and altering that, throwing all that we had done into disorder. A good time he was having with it, too: wars, the Cataclysm, his children battling among themselves. And then, you see, it was the Irda ruined it all for him. They broke the jewel, spoiled his fun. So now he blusters and rants and raves and—since he can no longer influence the world—he'll destroy it. That's the truth of the matter, to my mind."

The dwarf nodded emphatically, and—balancing the gem carefully on his broad knee—wiped his sweating face with his hand.

Palin shifted restlessly. "*You're* not to blame. Paladine's not to blame. Takhisis is not to blame. No one's to blame, it seems. That's all very well, but I don't suppose it will matter much when our world is broken like this wretched gem and we're all dead and forgotten."

"True, Lad, true," the dwarf said morosely.

"But there must be some way we can defeat Chaos," Tasslehoff observed. "We have the Graygem now. I don't suppose I could hold it—for just a second. I'll give it right back . . ."

Dougan clutched the gem to his breast. "Go away!" he ordered fiercely, glowering at Tas. "Go on! Stand over there! No, farther back. Keep going . . ."

"If I go any farther, I'll drop off the end of the island," Tas complained.

"Good riddance," Dougan muttered.

"Stay where you are, Tas," Palin said. "Look, Dougan or Reorx or whoever you are, we've got to do something!"

"The gem destroyed the shadow-wights," Usha began hopefully.

"Not all of them," the dwarf corrected her, "not by a long shot. The wights will spread like darkest night across the land, starting with the High Clerist's Tower. It's there, you see, where Chaos figures he can strike hardest at his two most powerful children, Paladine and Takhisis. Once they are destroyed—and they both will be if the High Clerist's Tower falls—then he will send his fiends in force into the rest of the world."

"We should go to the tower, then," Palin said, frustrated. "We can use the Graygem to help the knights defeat Chaos—"

"The knights have help, Lad, though they may not know it. The other gods are not idle. Their forces are at work throughout Ansalon. But this"—Dougan touched the Graygem with caressing fingers—"this is the key to it all. If my idea works, we can stop Himself, send him and his fiends packing."

"You have a plan, then," Palin said.

Dougan fixed him with a cunning eye. "You want to do something, you say?"

"Of course," Palin answered impatiently. "We want to do whatever we can."

"No matter that it's dangerous, that you likely won't survive? Or, if you do, you'll be changed forever?"

Tasslehoff raised his hand. "I'm going, too! Raistlin said I could!"

"I'll face the danger." Usha glanced back toward the dead pine trees, toward where the shadow-wights had been. "Nothing could be as bad as that."

"Wanna bet?" the dwarf growled.

"From what you say, everyone on Ansalon will be facing danger. We'll take our chances with the rest. What do we have to do?"

Dougan held out the two pieces of the Graygem, one in each hand. "You must capture Chaos, put him back inside."

Palin gasped. "You're mad! That's not possible for us! We're not gods!"

"It *is* possible, Lad. I've thought it all out. I've talked with the others, and they believe it might work. As for we gods, we have our own problems. Paladine has agreed to help us—*if* he survives. Desperate as Takhisis is"—Dougan shook his head—"she still fights to rule the world. She had much better fight for her own survival, but she can't see that. They're doing battle at the High Clerist's Tower."

Dougan sighed heavily. "Takhisis may yet win. If she does, she'll finally be on top. But she may find herself on top of nothing but a heap of ash."

24

The Dark Warrior. Plotting.
The Nature of the Enemy.

he knights fought in the red heat of the sun that would not set. The garish light bloodied their sword blades and gilded their spears with flame. The Knights of Takhisis rallied to defend the High Clerist's Tower against an awful, dread, and deadly foe.

Lightning forked out of a cloudless sky; thunder boomed and roared continuously. Wherever the lightning struck the mountainside, the tinder-dry trees burst into flame. Smoke hung like a pall over the valley. Flowing beneath the smoke, the unnatural darkness surged down from the mountains to the north, heading for the northern wall of the High Clerist's Tower. The knights were prepared to face it—whatever it was—having been warned by the dragons that this unnatural darkness was no friend to those who worshipped Her Dark Majesty.

The dragons—golds, reds, blues, silver, and all colors of dragonkind—reported that a vast rift had opened in the Turbidus Ocean, a rift erupting with fire that caused the sea water to boil. Out of this rift came the darkness.

"It is a vast river of endless night that flows over the mountains. In its wake, devastation worse than the fires," reported an ancient gold dragon, a lord among his kind. "Every living creature the darkness touches disappears, vanishes without a trace, leaving nothing behind—not even a memory."

Ariakan listened, skeptical, particularly of the gold dragons.

"What is this darkness?" he demanded to know.

"We cannot say, Lord," answered a red dragon, young, newly risen to leadership, with the scars of battle fresh on him. "We have never seen its like. You can judge for yourself, though. It is upon you."

Lord Ariakan went to his command post, taking up a position on the battlements of the Knights' Spur. As the dragon had said, the attack had already been launched. Archers, lining the walls, fired arrows into the darkness, which flowed like water up to the base of the structure. The arrows disappeared without leaving a trace, doing no damage that anyone could see. The darkness rose, began to seep over the walls.

A line of brutes, commanded by knights, was drawn up in defense, prepared to attack the darkness with sword and spear. Among their ranks were Knights of the Thorn and Knights of the Skull, ready to fight this new enemy with sorcery and prayer.

"What the—?" Ariakan swore. "What's going on? I can't see!"

The sun shone brightly on the horizon, yet night had fallen on the northern wall of the High Clerist's Tower. Ariakan heard hoarse cries of terror, horrifying screams coming out of the darkness. What he could not hear worried him more. No sounds of battle, no clash of sword on shield, or sword against armor. No officer's commands. He heard the voices of his wizards, the beginnings of magical spells, but he never heard the ends. Prayers of the clerics, rising to Her Dark Majesty, ceased abruptly.

At last, Ariakan could stand it no longer. "I'm going down there," he announced, brushing aside the remonstrations of his commanders.

But before he could take a step, the darkness retreated as suddenly as it had come. It flowed back down the wall, glided in among the trees, mingled with the smoke. The knights on the walls cheered at first, thinking that their forces had beaten back the foe. The cheering ceased when the light of the angry sun rushed in to replace the darkness. It was then apparent that this was not victory. The darkness had retreated for a reason.

"Blessed Majesty!" Ariakan whispered, stunned and appalled.

Of the hundreds of soldiers who had mounted the defense of the tower on the northern wall, not one remained. The only indication that these people had ever existed was the physical objects they'd been wearing or carrying at the time. Breastplates, helms, bracers, shirts, tunics, boots, gray robes and black were strewn upon the battlements. Atop a breastplate lay a sword. Near a feathered headdress was a feathered spear. Upon a gray robe lay a bag of rose petals. Beside a black robe stood a black mace.

No living being remained. They had, each and every one, disappeared. No blood was shed, but—by the sounds of those horrible screams—they had all perished in torment. And, what was worse, those who gazed in shock at the awful scene could not call a single face or name to mind. That living men and women had once stood here, no one doubted. There was the physical evidence left behind to prove it. Almost, people could remember. They held the possessions of friends and comrades in their hands and stared at them in awe and fear. Try as they might, they could not remember the vanished.

"What dreadful force is this?" Ariakan wondered in baffled fury. His face was ashen. He stood amazed. Those who had known him before, calm and cool in battle, saw him now shaken to the core of his being. "And how do we combat it? Find someone who can tell me! Bring my clerics and the Gray Knights—those who are left," he added grimly.

But though each cleric and wizard had ideas, none could provide any information for certain.

"At least," ventured Subcommander Trevalin, "the enemy appears to have retreated. Perhaps those who fought it were victorious, though they gave their lives."

"No," said Ariakan, staring out into the impenetrable darkness that lurked beneath the smoldering trees. "No, the shadows did not retreat because they lost. They were drawn back on purpose, so that we could see what happened to our comrades. Their commander—whoever or whatever it is—wants us demoralized, fearful, panicked. But, by Her Dark Majesty, I will not permit that to happen!

"Return to your forces," he ordered his commanders. "Have that mess cleaned up immediately, removed from sight. Interview your men. Try to find anyone who saw or heard anything that might give us some indication as to this foe and what happened to those who fought it. Report all information to me directly. I will be in the Kingfisher's Nest."

His commanders dispersed to reestablish order and discipline among the nervous troops. The knights returned to their duties with only occasional lapses, when here and there one or another would stop and stare at the southern battlements, which were now being called accursed.

Ariakan, accompanied by his bodyguards, ascended to the lookout point known as the Nest of the Kingfisher. He left his guards at the foot of the stairs, climbed the rest of the way alone.

The highest vantage point in the tower, the Nest of the Kingfisher was a small, circular room with slit windows all the way around, providing a breathtaking view of the Vingaard Mountains, the Solamnic Plains, and surrounding territory. Ariakan looked out over the pall of smoke that hung from the valley to the peaks of the Vingaard Mountains. He saw the strange darkness flow among the crags and crevices, devouring the light.

Alone, Ariakan could give vent to his frustration. He paced about the small room, going from window to window, searching for answers, his soul filled with dread and foreboding. He recalled the young mage's story, about Chaos returning, about the gods themselves being threatened, endangered. He had not believed it . . . until now.

As he stared into the mountains, trying to see anything that might give him some hint, he was aware of the sound of booted footfalls coming up the stairs.

"A messenger," Ariakan muttered to himself, hope rising. "My people have found something."

But the person who entered the chamber was not a breathless runner, coming with important information. The person was a knight, one of Ariakan's own knights, presumably, for the man was clad in shining black armor. The knight's face was hidden; he wore his helm over his head, the visor down.

"Who are you, Sir Knight?" Ariakan demanded. "Why have you left your post?"

The knight did not answer. He was immensely tall. The black plume of his helm brushed the roof. His shoulders were broad, the arms thick and muscular. A heavy sword hung at the knight's side, the scabbard was of dark leather, decorated at the top with five bands of color: red, blue, green, white, black. The hilt of the sword was fashioned in the shape of a five-headed dragon. He was cloaked in black, as if he wore the night itself around his shoulders. The knight's eyes were as pale and hot as stars.

Memory stirred in Ariakan. He knew this knight, had seen him before, somewhere in the distant past . . .

Lord Ariakan fell to his knees, awed and worshipful. "Your Majesty!"

"Rise, Lord," said a woman's voice as deep as the Abyss. "The hour of doom is upon us. Chaos has returned, the Father of All and of Nothing. He has come back in anger, prepared to destroy all creation. We fight for our very existence."

"My knights and I are ready, Your Majesty." Lord Ariakan rose to his feet. "You have only to command us."

The Dark Warrior crossed the floor of the small room, came to stand at one of the windows. She gestured, a peremptory motion of her black-gloved hand. Ariakan moved swiftly to stand at the queen's side.

"Doom is at hand," Takhisis spoke softly, "but also the chance for ultimate victory. Ultimate victory, Ariakan!" she repeated, her black-gloved hand clenching to a fist.

"If you defeat Chaos, Ariakan, the people of Krynn will know that they have *me* to thank for saving them. They will be forever in my debt. My hold on this world will be so tight that no one can break it."

"True, Your Majesty," Ariakan agreed, "but how is that to be accomplished?"

"The people of Ansalon will emerge from this war leaderless, confused. Anarchy will reign. That will be our chance. When the forces of Chaos have been driven back, you—my knights—must be poised and ready to seize control."

"We already control much of Ansalon, Your Majesty," Ariakan protested, thinking that she implied fault with himself and his knights.

"Do you rule Silvanesti?" Takhisis asked. "Has the dwarven kingdom of Thorbardin fallen?"

"Not yet." Ariakan was grim.

"Your forces still fight in Northern Ergoth. Rebellion foments in

Qualinesti. And what of Taladas and the distant regions of this world?"

"Your Majesty must give us time," Ariakan said, pale and frowning.

"You don't need time. We will let the forces of Chaos do our work for us. Do you understand?"

"I understand, Your Majesty," Ariakan said, bowing. "What are your orders?"

"Paladine is throwing everything he has against Chaos. The forces of good will be utterly vanquished, wiped out, decimated. We must take care that this does not happen to us. You will hold a certain number of your knights and their dragons in reserve. Keep one of your wings out of the coming battle. Do this in secret.

"When the fight for the High Clerist's Tower is ended and we have won, these knights will be fresh, ready to ride to take over key strategic points on the continent of Ansalon. Your knights will not be alone. I have alerted others loyal to our cause. Draconians, ogres, minotaur, goblins—right now they fight as allies with the forces of good. But when this ends, they will join your army, complete the takeover."

"As you command, Your Majesty," said Ariakan. He gazed back out the window, out at the unnatural darkness. "But first we have to hold the High Clerist's Tower against the enemy. What can you tell me of this foe, Your Majesty? What is it?"

"Shadow-wights—creatures formed of the essence of Chaos. They are without form and without shape. To look into them is to look into oblivion. When they attack, they take on the appearance of their opponent, exact in every detail. They speak words of darkness and despair, depriving their enemies of the will to fight. If they touch a mortal being, they reduce it to nothingness.

"And in the next wave will come daemon warriors. They are creatures as cold as the vast, empty darkness between the stars. A sword thrust into them will shatter as if it were made of glass. A man's hand that touches them will go numb, lifeless, and will never know warmth again.

"Among these troops are the fire dragons with claws of flame and sulfurous, poisonous breath. These are the foes you will face. These are the foes you must defeat."

Ariakan was grim. "How can such creatures be defeated, Your Majesty?"

"Because they are creatures without form or substance, born of Chaos, they can be destroyed by any forged weapon that has been touched by one of the gods. The swords of your knights have all received my blessing. These blades will kill the shadow-wights. The knight must take care not to look into the wight's eyes; yet he must, at the same time, draw close enough to the wight to deal the blow. As for the daemon warriors, a forged weapon will unravel the magic, but the blow that strikes it will be the last. The weapon will be destroyed, leaving the knight who wielded it defenseless."

"What about my magic-users? Your own clerics?"

"Light spells will prevent the shadow-wights from taking their enemy's form, fire spells will destroy them, but the wizard must be able to shut the deadly voices out of their minds or they themselves will be destroyed. Any holy object that touches the daemon warrior will cast it back into oblivion, but the object itself will be lost, sacrificed."

Ariakan was silent, thoughtful. Then he nodded. "I begin to see why Your Majesty wants troops held in reserve. This battle will considerably weaken us."

"It will weaken everyone, Lord Ariakan," Takhisis returned. "And therein lies our ultimate victory. I shall reign supreme. Farewell, my lord."

The queen extended her gloved hand. Ariakan fell again to his knees, to receive her blessing.

"We will fight to the death, Your Majesty!" he said fervently.

Her Majesty withdrew her hand. She was displeased.

"I have souls enough, Ariakan," she said coldly. "It's the living I want."

Ariakan, rebuked, bowed his head.

When he looked up, the queen was gone.

25

Orders. Hidden away.

hat are you saying?" Steel demanded furiously, forgetting discipline in his bitter disappointment. "Trevalin, you can't mean this?"

The other knights of the talon gathered around their commanding officer, echoed Steel's protest.

"I don't like this any better than you do, but I have my orders," Trevalin said. "We are to conceal ourselves in the dragontraps, keep away from the battle, stay there until we receive new orders. And," he added, fixing his men with a stern gaze, "we're to keep quiet about this. Death to the man who speaks of this to anyone outside this talon."

"We're being punished," said one knight.

"What have we done to displease our lord?" asked another.

"Skulking about in secret, hiding in the dark like stinking gully dwarves!"

"People will make songs of our comrades' valor . . ."

"They'll make songs of our shame!"

"That's enough, Gentlemen. My orders came directly from Lord Ariakan himself," Trevalin said, his voice grim. "He has a plan in mind. It is up to us to obey, not to question. If you have any complaints, I suggest you take them up with His Lordship."

That silenced the protests—at least those spoken aloud. The knights exchanged frowning, unhappy glances, but said nothing.

Because of the need to keep their meeting secret, Trevalin had brought his men together in the talon's barracks, away from the main body of the knights. He glanced out the window. The sun was at last starting to sink; was glaring balefully over the horizon as if loathe to leave and miss the coming battle. The tower was readying for the next attack, presaged by immense pools of darkness, sliding down the mountainside, seeping around the walls. Eyes could be seen in the darkness now, the daemon warriors walking among the shadow-wights. Only eyes, nothing more. The eyes were red, hideous, and they gleamed of death.

The Vision permitted each knight to share in Her Dark Majesty's description of the shadow-wights and daemon warriors and how to defeat them. The Knights of the Lily were readying their dragons for flight; the Knights of the Skull were granting the queen's blessing to armor, shield, and weapon; the Knights of the Thorn were gathering spell components, committing spells to memory. Steel's talon was preparing to go away and hide.

"It is time we were moving," Trevalin said at last, reluctantly. "I won't ask if there are any questions, because I couldn't answer them if there were. We are to report to our post down in the dragontraps within the hour. Because of the need for secrecy, go there by ones and twos, take different routes. Knight Officer Brightblade will assign you."

Glumly, the knights prepared to leave to take up their new position, "in the cellar with the old women and the kids," as one put it, though not in earshot of Trevalin.

Steel was as angry at missing the battle as the rest, but—after his first outburst—he said nothing more. He had regained his rank, was once again second in command of his talon and, as a knight officer, he was expected to give Trevalin loyal and unquestioning support. Steel organized the knights of his talon, gave each group directions on their particular route, listened to their grumblings, did what he could to mollify them by talking of "shock troops" and "secret missions." When the last contingent had moved out, he went to make his report to Trevalin.

"You're not far off the mark, you know," Trevalin said in an undertone, as the two headed for the dragontraps themselves. "From what I can gather, we're being held in reserve to take on some important assignment given to Ariakan by Her Majesty herself. I heard from one of Ariakan's bodyguards that the queen met our lord in the Nest of the Kingfisher, that they spoke. The bodyguard knows because he saw Ariakan go up there alone and, afterward, heard two people talking— one of them a woman, with a voice like the knell of doom. When Ariakan came down, he was pale and shaking, like a man struck by a thunderbolt. It was shortly after that these orders were issued."

Steel smiled, pleased. "Why don't you tell the others? It will make them feel better."

"Because we're to obey orders without feeling one way or the other about them. And what I've told you is scuttlebutt, nothing more," Trevalin replied tersely. Relaxing, he shrugged, smiled. "In other words, I can't say anything official, but you could spread the word, Brightblade."

"Our queen herself chose us!" Steel said to himself in exultation as he went through the bronze doors leading to the dragontraps.

But it was hard to maintain the pride, the elation, in knowing that they were singled out, specially chosen, when the darkness of the dragontraps closed around them, cut them off from the rest of their comrades, enveloped them in its shroud.

They sat or stood in silence broken only by the trumpet call to battle, a call they were forbidden to answer.

Steel disciplined himself to sit calmly, await orders. He looked with disapproval on those knights taking refuge in nervous pacing, ordered them to settle down, conserve their energy. He spent the first hour cleaning and polishing his sword, his father's sword, admiring again the craftsmanship, not to be equaled even by the master swordsmiths hired by His Lordship. Ariakan himself had said it was one of the finest blades he had ever seen.

The sword did not really need cleaning—Steel took excellent care of his weapons—but polishing the fine metal gave him something constructive to do and was, at the same time, reassuring. He found himself thinking of his father and the stories he'd heard about his father's courage. His thoughts traveled back through time beyond his father. Steel wondered about the other knights who had carried this sword to honor and glory. Were they gathered now, all the Brightblades? Were they ranged in line behind their leader, Paladine, preparing to ride to battle? The Brightblade ancestors fought in Paladine's name; their living representative, Steel, fought for Takhisis. But he saw little difference—the flip side of the same coin.

He imagined the battle that must be raging in the Abyss, the gods banding together to fight Chaos, his queen in the forefront of her dread legions, leading them to victory. His heart swelled with pride and reverence; he whispered a prayer to Takhisis as he worked, asking her to grant him a small portion of Her Majesty's vast courage. He could almost envy the dead, who would be privileged enough to fight at Her Dark Majesty's side.

His dreams and imaginings and his work took him fairly quickly through the first hour of waiting. The second he spent sitting on the stone floor, sweating in the heat that had found its way even to the inner portion of the tower, and listening to the sounds of battle coming from above. The other knights listened, too, speculated on what might be happening. The sounds were indistinct, muffled and distorted, drowned out by rumblings of thunder that shook the tower to its foundation, the wild blaring of trumpets, the thumping heart of the war engines. Occasionally they could hear, rising above the rest, a terrible, bellowing cry—the death scream of a dragon. At this horrible sound, the knights would all fall silent and study the stone on the floor at their feet.

Time passed and still no word. No breathless messenger came clattering down the stairs, ordering them to saddle their dragons, take to the skies.

The third hour, all the sounds suddenly ceased. An uncanny silence fell. The games of dicing that had been going on halted. All attempts at conversation ceased. Trevalin went to stand at the closed, barred bronze door, staring at it, his face drawn and grim. Steel could stand the strain no longer. He was on his feet, pacing restlessly, bumping into others doing the same.

He felt something wet hit him on the forehead. He put his hand to his head, drew it back, looked at his fingers, and gave a hoarse shout. "Bring a torch someone! Quick!"

Several torches were brought, and the men huddled nervously around him.

Trevalin shoved his way through the circle of knights. "What? What is it? What's the cause of this commotion? Break it up, you men—"

"You'd better see this, Subcommander," said Steel. "Shine that light down here."

One of the knights lowered the torch. Firelight shone in a fresh pool forming on the stone floor. In the sudden silence, they could hear the slow and incessant drip, drip.

Trevalin knelt, dipped the tips of his fingers in the pool, held them to the light.

"Blood," he said softly, staring up at the ceiling.

Trevalin rose to his feet. "I'm going up there," he announced, and several of the knights raised a cheer.

"Stop that," he ordered angrily. "Take up your weapons; make yourselves ready. Brightblade, walk with me."

The others dispersed rapidly, happy to be doing something, even if it was only buckling on their swords and lacing up their armor.

Steel accompanied Trevalin to the doors.

"You're in command while I'm gone," Trevalin said. He fell silent, but did not leave, glanced at the doors and back again, seemed to be making up his mind whether to speak or not.

"Brightblade," Trevalin said finally, keeping his voice low, "have you noticed something strange? Something about the Vision?"

Steel nodded slowly, once. "I had hoped I was wrong, Subcommander," he said quietly. "I had hoped it was just me."

"Apparently not," Trevalin said, with a sigh. "I can't seem to see it anymore. Can you?"

"No, Subcommander."

Trevalin shook his head, pulled on his gloves. "I'm disobeying direct orders, doing this. But, without the Vision to guide me . . . Something's gone wrong. It may be up to us to fix it, if we can. Wait for me. I won't be long."

Taking a torch, Trevalin lifted the heavy bar across the door, opened it, went out. Steel stood inside the door, followed the light with his eyes as it moved down the corridor, watched it until its glow vanished. He remained standing there, the door opened a crack, straining to hear something from beyond.

The other knights joined him, forming a semicircle around him. They, too, were quiet, except for the clink and rattle of armor and soft, measured breathing.

And then the glow reappeared at the end of the corridor. The light wavered, as if the hand that carried the torch was weak, unsteady. Booted footfalls, hesitant, shuffling. Trevalin came into view, leaning against the wall. He came slowly down the corridor, staring at his feet.

Steel opened the door. When Trevalin reached it, he stopped, looked at his men with a glazed, blank expression, as if he had no idea who they were, what they were doing here.

Trevalin's face was ash-white in the harsh light of the torch, which he suddenly let fall to the floor. The torch burned there, sputtering and smoking. No one moved to pick it up.

"Subcommander," said Steel. "What is it? What's going on?"

"Nothing," said Trevalin thickly. "They're all . . . dead."

No one spoke, though someone sucked in a hissing breath.

Trevalin's eyes closed, as if in pain. Tears squeezed out from beneath the lids. "My lord . . . dead!" He spoke with almost a sob. Opening his red-rimmed eyes, he stared around. "Dead! Can't you understand? All dead! Dead . . . All . . . Dead . . ."

He sagged. His knees giving way, he slid down the wall. Steel caught his commander in his arms.

"Sir, you're wounded! Where? Help me get his armor off."

Trevalin caught hold of Steel's hand, stopped him. "No use," he said. "It . . ." He choked, swallowed. "It hit me . . . from behind." Trevalin frowned, angered, puzzled. "Coward . . . hits you . . . from behind . . . I never saw . . . never had a chance to fight back . . . No honor . . ."

"Sir . . . is the enemy out there? How many?"

Trevalin shook his head. He gasped, tried to speak, but only bubbles of blood and saliva came from his mouth. He sank back against the wall. The hand holding Steel's went flaccid.

Steel held his commander's hand a moment longer, then laid it gently, respectfully over the dead man's chest.

"Walk with Takhisis, sir," Steel said softly.

He could see, then, the massive wound that had ripped through the black armor as if it were parchment paper; the charred and bleeding skin; the great, ugly gash in his side.

"Claws did that," one knight said, grim, awed.

"If so, they are claws of fire," said Steel, rising slowly to his feet. He gazed out the door. "I wonder what our orders were."

"It doesn't matter now," said one of the knights. "What are *your* orders, sir?"

It occurred to Steel then that he was in command. He was in command, not only of his talon, but—if what Trevalin had said was true—in command of the High Clerist's Tower. Steel shoved the terrible thought out of his mind. Trevalin must have been mistaken. He had been hideously wounded. Surely they couldn't all be dead!

Steel made his decision. "Two of you, lay the subcommander to rest down here. Cover his body with his shield. The rest of you draw your weapons and come with me. If the tower has fallen, the enemy probably doesn't know we're down here. We may be able to catch them unawares. No light. Make no noise."

Dipping his fingers in Trevalin's blood, Steel smeared it on the black bracers around his arm, as another might wear the ribbon-token of his lady. He drew his sword—his father's sword—and walked out the doors of the dragontraps.

One by one, saluting their dead, the dark knights followed him.

26

The Vision.

Steel crept stealthily through the corridors of the tower, moving slowly. It was impossible to see anything. He had not expected such dense darkness. He sent several of his men back for torches. They would be in more danger bumbling around in the darkness than they would from any enemy who might by lying in ambush.

The strange, stubborn sun had finally set; night had finally come. But where was the starlight, the light of the three moons that should illuminate their way? While waiting for his men to return, Steel groped along a wall, discovered a window, and stared out. He searched the sky, thinking that maybe the drought had broken, that the stars were clouded over.

Lightning flashed through the sky—a clear, cloudless, empty sky. No stars. No moons.

Steel stared into the dark—endlessly dark—sky until his eyes ached, searching for some glimmer of light. He found none. He drew back from the window, not allowing himself to speculate on what meaning this dread phenomenon might hold. The men were returning with the torches, coming along behind him. He kept them moving, ordered them sharply to keep their eyes ahead, if any seemed inclined to go near the windows. They'd find out the truth soon enough, but hopefully after he determined what they were facing.

As they moved through the corridors, they saw the signs of terrible fighting. The walls were scorched and charred and, in some instances, holes had been blasted through them. Heaps of fallen stone clogged the corridors, made the going difficult. And then they began to find the bodies, some of them horribly burned, metal armor fused to flesh by the searing heat. Worse were the piles of empty armor; pitiful heaps of gray robes alongside scattered spell components; black robes, adorned with emblems of Her Dark Majesty, now lying crumpled on the stone floor.

At intervals along their route, Steel ordered his men to halt. Standing in breathless silence, they listened—listened for the orders, for victorious shouts, for gloating laughter, for the screams of captives, the defiant curses of prisoners.

They heard nothing, nothing except the sigh of the hot wind blowing through the wreckage of what had once been the mightiest fortress on Ansalon.

The knights moved on, well disciplined still, though their grim faces, pale in the torchlight, reflected the horrors they saw around them. They entered the central courtyard.

The body of an enormous red dragon almost filled the area. Torchlight glistened on broken scales, on long gashes in the body, tears in the wings, which were bent and mangled. The enormous creature had died of innumerable wounds; its blood made the stone floor wet and slippery.

"Spread out," Steel ordered quietly. He was beginning to realize, chillingly, that his men had nothing to fear, and, by the same token, no hope. "Search for any survivors, report back here."

The knights separated, moving off in groups of two and three, their weapons in their hands.

Steel placed his torch in a sconce, walked around to the dragon's head. He'd seen a human body from where he had stood in the gateway.

Lord Ariakan lay close to the dragon. The red must have been his mount in that last desperate fight, until the beast crashed to the ground, forcing Ariakan to meet his enemies on foot. His sword was still clutched in his cold hand, the blade broken, yet covered with blood, as if he had fought on even after his weapon had failed him. No bodies of whatever foes he had faced were anywhere around him. Steel found oily, charred patches nearby, had a sudden image of daemonic soldiers, touched by forged steel, bursting into flame.

Steel knelt beside the body of his liege lord, beside the man who had found him, raised him to be a knight. He saw clearly, as if in the flare-up of a flaming log, Ariakan as he had come to the home of a twelve-year-old boy, had taken the measure of that boy with his dark eyes.

I offer you hard work, brutal toil, a harsh life with little ease, no comfort. You will gain no personal wealth. The most you can ever hope to earn will be the respect of your comrades-in-arms. You will forego the love of family and friends. Taking their place will be battle, glory, honor. Do you accept these terms, young Steel?

"I do accept, my lord," Steel said now as he had vowed then.

It was difficult to tell which of the many wounds had been Ariakan's death wound. His face was contorted with a grimace—not of pain, but of determination. He had battled valiantly to the very end. The metal of his blade had snapped; Ariakan's courage had not. Steel guessed now why the Vision had died. It had died with the man who had created it.

"Receive his soul, Majesty," Steel prayed, tears choking his voice. He shut the corpse's staring eyes, composed the twisted limbs into some semblance of easeful rest. He found the shards of the broken blade, laid them across Ariakan's chest.

Slowly, Steel rose to his feet. "Now, my lord, you fight at the side of Her Majesty. You fight with honor. Prepare the way for the rest of us."

Standing in the courtyard, his head bowed, alone, Steel wondered what to do. The enemy had been victorious. The High Clerist's Tower had fallen. But this enemy had no care for occupation, for conquest, had no interest in fortresses, lands, cities, wealth, subjects. This enemy had only one objective: dealing death. The mightiest fortress had been taken, and its defenders—the mightiest force on Krynn—had been utterly wiped out. Their main task accomplished, the enemy had surged on, bringing flame and blood and terror with them.

"We're all that's left," Steel said to himself, dazed by the thought. "What do we do? The Vision is gone, but surely it could be reborn!" He looked up into the empty heavens, spread his arms wide. "Dark Majesty! Tell me what to do! Give me your guidance!"

Footsteps—booted footsteps, light footsteps, rapidly approached. Steel's heart jumped; he lifted his sword.

"Who is there?" he called out.

A woman came into view, a knight clad in blue armor. Her hair was short, curly, dark. She smiled at Steel, a crooked, charming smile.

Steel lowered his sword. He had no doubt that this was his queen's response. Now he would receive his orders.

Kitiara walked up to stand in front of her son. Noticing blood on his armor, she looked grave. "You are not wounded, are you, Steel?"

"The blood is that of my commanding officer, who gave his life defending the tower." Steel felt his face burn with shame. "I took no part in the battle, Mother. My talon was ordered to remain hidden—"

"I know all that," Kitiara said, waving away the irrelevant. "I was the one who gave those orders."

Steel stared at her, aghast. "You! Ordered me hidden away from the battle! My honor—"

"To the Abyss with that crap!" Kitiara snorted. "Prattling of honor, you sound just like that hidebound dunderhead, your father. Listen to me, Steel. We haven't much time."

Kitiara moved closer to him. Cold flowed from her, seeped into his body, freezing the bone marrow, making breathing painful. Her words came not through his ears, but pierced through his heart.

"The battle is lost. The war is lost. The forces of Chaos are too strong. Our queen intends to make good her escape, while she still can. She is preparing to leave, and she will take her most loyal followers with her. Through my intercession, you, my son, are one of the chosen. Come with me now!"

"Come with you?" Steel regarded her in confusion. "Come with you where?"

"To another world, my son!" Kitiara said eagerly. "Another world to rule, to conquer! And you will be part of our triumphant force. We will be together, you and I."

Steel was doubtful, troubled. "The war is lost, you say?"

"Must I repeat myself? Hurry, my son. Come quickly."

"My queen would not run away," Steel said, backing up from his mother. "Her Majesty would not abandon, betray, those who fought in her name, those who died for her. . . ."

"Died for her?" Kitiara laughed. "Of course they died for her! It was their privilege to die for her. She owes them nothing! She owes the world nothing. Let it be destroyed. There will be others. New worlds! You will see such wonders, my son. And we will take these wonders, these riches, and make them ours! First, however, you must take off that silly elf toy you wear around your neck. Get rid of it."

Steel looked past his mother, at the body of Lord Ariakan, at the corpse of the ancient, magnificent red dragon. He thought of Trevalin, returning to his command though he was bleeding to death.

The torchlight blurred in Steel's eyes. He sagged back against the wall, struggling to breathe. And it seemed to him that the wall moved. All that was real and solid was being pulled out from underneath him.

Abandoned, betrayed, he had nothing left. The Vision was gone, not because Ariakan had ceased to see it, but because it had ceased to exist. The stars had fallen from the sky, and they had all tumbled down on him.

"Come, Steel!" Kitiara's voice sharpened. "Why do you hesitate? Remove the jewel."

"No, Mother," Steel said quietly. "I'm not going with you."

"What? Don't be a fool!"

"Why not, Mother?" Steel demanded, bitter. "I've been a fool all these years, it seems. Everything in which I believed was a lie."

Kitiara glared at him. Her eyes were as dark as the empty sky. "I was mistaken, it seems. I thought there were the makings of a true warrior in you. The fight! The victory! The power! That is all. *That* is everything! Act like your father, and you will die like your father—alone, abandoned, throwing your life away for some worthless cause. You can't win this one, Steel!" Kitiara hissed his name. "You can't win!"

"You're right, Mother," Steel said calmly. "I've already lost. I have lost my god, my lord, my dream. I have lost everything"—his hand moved to the jewel he wore around his neck, hidden beneath the black armor—"except what is inside me."

"What is in you comes from me!"

Kitiara's anger was like a mailed fist across his face. He turned away his head, averted his eyes.

Suddenly, her mood changed, her anger subsided; her voice was soft, caressing. "You are battle-weary, Steel, grieving for your loss. It was wrong of me to try to force you to make this decision now. Take your time, my son. Think about what I've offered. A new world. A new life. . . ."

The mailed fist was a gentle hand. A soft warmth, like the touch of black velvet, flowed over him . . . and then was gone.

He closed his eyes, leaned back against the stone wall, now firm and steady, supporting him. He was tired, but his weariness ran deeper than battle-fatigue. After all, he hadn't swung a stroke. Yet he was bruised, felt as if he'd been kicked and pummeled, left alone in some dark alley. Left alone to die.

Why should I?

New worlds. Wonders . . . Conquests . . . Glory . . .

Why not? Why the hell not? My mother is right. This world is finished. It holds nothing for me anymore.

The emptiness inside Steel was like a killing gash from a dragon's claw. His queen's betrayal had torn out his soul, drained him, left him a hollow husk.

Why not fill that void with war, the adrenal rush of battle, the ecstasy of victory, the pleasure of its spoils. I will no longer fight for any god. I will fight for myself first. I will be the one who gains!

His hand closed over the jewel.

"She lies . . ." came a voice, another voice, from inside, from outside. It didn't matter anymore.

Steel kept his eyes shut. "Don't try to stop me, Father. It's finished. The battle is ended, and we have lost."

"Kitiara lied. The battle is not over, not for some. Paladine and the other gods fight on against Chaos. The magical children, Lunitari, Solinari, Nuitari, continue to wage war. Sargonnas has sworn a blood-oath to keep on fighting. Chemosh has raised the dead and leads them to battle. All across Krynn, people fight, with no hope of victory. They do not talk of abandoning the world."

"And what will it gain them, Father?" Steel asked. His thoughts went to the body of Ariakan, lying beside the dead dragon. "Who will reward them? Who will sing hero songs for them?"

"You will, Steel," said his father. "You will honor them every day of your long, long life."

Steel said nothing. He held fast to the jewel in his hand, but whether out of need or out of loathing, he couldn't decide.

"What would you have me do, Father?" he demanded, despairing, disdainful. "Chaos can never be destroyed."

"No, but he can be made to retreat. Chaos has opened a rift in the world. Through that rift he has brought his forces: shadow-wights, fire dragons, daemon warriors. But that rift has made Chaos vulnerable. It is a hole in his armor. He has been forced to descend to our plane of existence. Paladine and Gilean both believe that if we can catch him here, on this plane, and defeat him here, Chaos will be forced to abandon the battle and close the rift, lest it consume him as well."

"And how do I fight Chaos? What weapons do I use?"

"A band of knights, bearing the famed dragonlances, must enter the Abyss, confront Chaos and his legions. They must ride forth knowing they will not return. They must ride knowing that their deaths may well be in vain, that no one will be left to sing hero songs for them."

Steel stood, irresolute, undecided, a battle of his own raging within him, a battle that had been fought every moment from the day of his birth. He stood in the torchlight, beneath the starless sky, his head bowed as the warring armies clashed, both sides wounding him, making a ravaged battlefield of his soul.

"Sir! Brightblade, are you all right?"

Steel raised his arm, lashed out. He was exhausted by the struggle, aching from the wounds. And he was angry, angry to be made to go through this.

"Leave me be!" he cried.

"Yes, sir." The knight, startled, stepped back. "I'm sorry, sir. I only wanted to report—"

"No, wait . . ."

Steel blinked, looked around him. He had no idea, for a moment, where he was, how he came to be here. He saw his lord's body, and memory returned. He sighed. He was, he discovered, clutching the jewel he wore around his neck with a strangling, deathlike grip.

Unclenching his hand, he released the starjewel, tucked it back beneath the breastplate. He wiped the sweat from his face. The night was hotter, more oppressive, than the day. The heat and his own exhaustion had caused him to fall asleep on his feet.

"I'm sorry. I must have dozed off. You startled me." Steel forced himself, by an effort of will, to pay attention. "Make your report."

"No sign of the enemy, sir. No sign of anyone at all—anyone alive, that is. There are no survivors. The wounded . . . " The man swallowed. "The wounded were slaughtered, lying on their cots. . . . They never had a chance."

Steel started to commend their souls to Takhisis. He bit off the words.

"Anything else?" he asked wearily.

"There is some good news, sir. We've found a few of the blue dragons still alive. They had been ordered, as we had, to keep out of the battle. And some silver dragons have joined them. They came late, it seems. They were at Silver Dragon Mountain, guarding the tomb of Huma, when they received orders to come to the High Clerist's Tower."

"Orders? Who gave them these orders?"

The knight gazed at Steel steadily. "They claim it was Huma himself, sir."

Steel shook his head. "What else have you to report?"

"Every weapon we have has been shattered, destroyed, with one exception. We've found a pile of lances. Dragonlances, they look like. They've all been stacked up neatly against the wall, here by the staircase, sir."

"Dragonlances." Steel stared at the man. "Are you sure?"

"Well, no, sir, not really. None of us have seen one before. But they match the descriptions we were given."

"Where are they?" Steel asked, a chill creeping through him despite the heat. "Show me."

"Yes, sir. This way."

The knight led his officer through the corridors to the entrance to the Chamber of Paladine. A bright silver glow welled up from below.

"It was the glow caught our eye, sir. We thought there might be someone down there. But all we found were the lances."

Steel descended the stairs, acutely reminded of the time he'd walked these stairs before, in company with Caramon Majere and Tanis Half-Elven, to pay his respects to his father.

All the knights in his talon had gathered here, amid the tombs and the dust. The chamber seemed strangely empty, though the bodies did not appear to have been disturbed. Perhaps the souls of the dead of ages past had risen and gone to the attack. The lances, shining silver in the torchlight, were stacked neatly against the wall. The dark knights stood well back, kept away from the lances, eyeing them with suspicion and doubt, muttering among themselves.

Were these the famed dragonlances, forged of magical silver by Theros of the Silver Arm? Were these the weapons that had helped defeat the Dark Queen? If so, how had the lances come to be in the tomb and why? No one loyal to Takhisis could touch the weapons, blessed by Paladine, dedicated to his service.

Steel walked over to inspect the lances more closely. He had studied descriptions of these weapons, as he had studied all the battles in which the dragonlances had played a part. If they were the famed dragonlances—and they certainly looked it—they were the type known as the footman's lance, shorter and lighter than the mounted lances that were fixed on the dragon saddles.

Bending down to more closely inspect one, Steel marveled at the craftsmanship. Each lance was about eight feet long, the haft and head both made of silver—presumably the magical silver that came from Silver Dragon Mountain. Legend had it that these lances could be forged only by a man with the Silver Arm of Ergoth and the famed dwarven artifact, the Hammer of Kharas. The head was honed to a razor-sharp edge, and barbs protruded from the sides. The lances appeared to be well balanced. Steel reached to pick one up.

A shock, as if he'd been struck by lightning, jolted through Steel's arm, numbing it from fingers to shoulder and sending currents of sizzling fire through his body. For several seconds, he was paralyzed, unable to move. Clutching his arm, trying to rub some life back into it, he fell backward.

"An amusing joke, Father," Steel muttered. "Your god must have gotten a good laugh out of that one. I renounce you all, every one of you." He tried to lift his hand, to take hold of the necklace and tear it from his neck, but his arm spasmed and his hand would not obey his will. "Take the lances, you say! Ride to defeat Chaos! How, when the damn lances are utterly useless—?"

"Not to us."

Steel halted his ranting.

A small band of Solamnic Knights—lean, clad in rags, their arms and backs marked by the stripes of the lash—stood at the top of the stairs.

"The prisoners!" Several of the knights drew their swords. "They've escaped!"

"Put away your weapons," Steel ordered. "They're not here to fight us. At least, I don't think so."

He recognized the knight who had spoken as the same young man who had been lashed for Steel's mistake when they had both been prisoners.

"Why *are* you here, Sir Knight?" Steel asked. "We didn't know you had escaped your cells. You could be on your way to Palanthas by now."

"We were," the young knight said with a rueful smile. He descended the stairs, came to stand in front of Steel. "We were in the dungeons when the attack began. Our guards left us to join in the fighting. We had no idea what was going on. We couldn't see, but we could hear well enough. The horrible sounds nearly drove us crazy. We thought we were going to be butchered in our cells, but the enemy never came below, never found us. Something struck the tower, shook it to its foundations. The walls cracked. Stones began to tumble down. We thought we were going to be buried beneath. Eventually, the shaking stopped. We were still alive and, what's more, our cell door had shaken loose.

"We slipped out. We were about ready to sneak out through one of the side doors on the Knight's Spur when we overheard you"—the knight indicated Steel—"talking to someone about how the war was not lost, that you were planning to lead a band of heroes into the Abyss."

The young knight reached down, lifted one of the silver-glowing lances in his hand. He hefted it easily. The lance was—as Steel had guessed—very well balanced.

The dark knights murmured in warning, drew nearer the Solamnic, ready to run him through.

The Solamnic Knight ignored them. He lowered the lance before him so that the tip touched the floor. "Rarely have we known a man of such courage and honor. If you will accept our services, Steel Brightblade, we will follow you into battle."

Steel gazed at them in wonder. "You could have escaped, gone back to your homes. Why did you return?"

The young knight nodded gravely. "We heard what you said about singing the hero songs. You were right. Perhaps no one will sing them for us. But at least we won't be forced to go through our lives singing them for someone else."

"If we go, we go without hope of ever coming back alive. We cannot even count on our gods to go with us," Steel added with a bitter smile. "We fight alone."

"We know, sir," said the young Solamnic Knight. "We understand, and we are prepared to go. We ask only that you give us back our armor and our swords."

You're a fool, Son! His mother's voice. *They want their weapons so they can turn on you!*

These are your example, Son. His father's voice. *These men go forth in honor, for the sake of doing what is right.*

Steel reached up, unfastened the clasp that held the starjewel. The chain slid into his hand. He folded his fingers over it, held it fast for a moment, then laid it, with a steady hand, on his father's bier.

The warring voices fell silent. The tomb was silent. The knights stood silent, awaiting Steel's decision. He drew his sword, his father's sword, which would break only if he did.

"We will sing the hero songs ourselves."

27

Preparations.

he Knights of Takhisis did honor to their dead with words and song. There wasn't time to do more, to entomb them properly or burn the corpses. There were too many. Some of the knights were disturbed by this, spoke of carrion birds and jackals or other creatures, more hideous, that might prey on and defile the dead.

The dark paladins stood in a circle around the body of their fallen lord, wondering what in haste they could do to protect their dead, when they were suddenly aware of a woman standing in their midst.

She had come upon them silently, no one knew from where. She was beautiful, her eyes the color of moonlight on blue water. Yet—though she appeared serene on the surface, there was dangerous power beneath. She was clad in armor that glistened with water, had the appearance of fish-scales. Her dark hair was bound up with sea flowers and shells. The knights knew her, then, and bowed before her.

It was Zeboim, goddess of the sea, the mother of Ariakan.

She knelt over the body of her dead son, gazed at him long. Two tears slid down her cheeks, fell, gleaming like pearls, onto her armor. She glanced around the tower, with its flickering torchlight, its flitting shadows, its empty corridors and silent halls. Her gaze at last fell on the knights.

"None will come to bother your dead," the goddess said. "Look. Listen. No birds circle in the sky this night. No beasts prowl. No flies buzz. Every creature, from the lowest insect to the mightiest dragon, knows that its fate hangs in balance this night. All wait for the end—as do we."

Steel gestured silently to his men. They left the goddess alone with her dead.

The Knights of Solamnia donned the armor taken from them when they were captured. They buckled on their swords, placed their helms on their heads. The dragonlances in their hands, the Solamnic Knights mounted the silver dragons who had arrived too late to fight in the battle of the High Clerist's Tower.

The dark paladins mounted the blue dragons who had been held in reserve.

Steel was disappointed to find that Flare was not among them. Her comrades had no idea where she had gone. She had been enraged when the orders came that they were to take no part in the fighting. She had nearly blasted the officer with her lightning breath, had blown a great chunk of rock out of the mountainside. Sulking, she had disappeared. No one knew where, but it was assumed she had disobeyed, gone to do battle on her own.

Steel searched among the bodies of the dragons, hoping to find Flare, that he might do her honor before he departed. His search had been, of necessity, a quick one, and he had not been able to find her corpse among the other blues. He could only conclude that her body lay somewhere in the forests, among the rocks of the Vingaard Mountains.

He was about to climb into the saddle of a strange blue dragon when there came an angry call from above. Wings whipping up clouds of dust, Flare descended from the skies, landed right in front of the strange dragon. Her neck arched in challenge, her wings spread, tail lashing, she advanced on the stranger.

"This is *my* knight!" Flare hissed. "He rides to battle with no one except me!"

Steel hastily intervened before a fight broke out, for the blue he rode had no intention of backing down. Steel asked the strange blue politely to join those dragons who were going along on their own. The blue agreed, stiffly, making it clear he was offended. Flare did not attack the stranger, once Steel had asked the dragon to leave, but she got in a nip on the stranger's tail as he departed.

Dragon and rider greeted each other joyously, each pleased to see the other still alive and, apparently, unharmed.

"The others said you left in anger," Steel said. "Where have you been? Where did you go?"

Flare tossed her head; her blue mane glistened in the torchlight. "I went to see this rift of which everyone talked, to see for myself if it existed or not. I admit," she added, with a sidelong glance at the silver dragons, "I thought it might be a trick." Her voice deepened, and she lowered her head. "It is not a trick, Steel," she said. "A dreadful battle rages within the Abyss. I've been there. I have seen it."

"How does the war go?"

Flare's eyes glinted. "Our queen fled. Did you know that?"

"I knew." Steel's voice was soft, grim.

"Some of the gods left with her: Hiddukel was the first one out. Zivilyn departed, saying he had seen all the endings and feared to influence the outcome if he stayed. Gilean sits, writing in his book, the last book. The other gods fight on, led by Kiri-Jolith and Sargonnas, but they—being on the same immortal plane with Chaos—can do little against him."

"And we can?" Steel asked.

"Yes, that is what I came to tell you. But"—Flare glanced around at the mounted men—"it seems you have already heard."

"I have, but I am glad to have the information confirmed."

Steel climbed onto Flare's back. He raised the standard of the Knights of Takhisis, the flag bearing the death lily, the skull. The Solamnic Knights raised their own standard, decorated with the kingfisher, holding in one claw a rose, the other claw a sword. The flags hung limp and lifeless in the hot, breathless night.

No one cheered. No one spoke. Each man took a long, last look around him at the world he was never going to see again. The Solamnic Knights dipped their standard in salute to the High Clerist's Tower. Steel dipped his standard to the dead.

Their dragons took wing, bearing their riders up into the empty, starless, godless sky.

28

The Gift. Instructions.

"hat are we waiting for?" Usha demanded, nervous and irritable. "Why don't we go somewhere, do something?"

"Soon, soon," Dougan murmured.

"I agree," said Tasslehoff, scuffing about dispiritedly, kicking up clouds of ash with his boots. "Things picked up considerably when those shadow-what-ma-jiggers tried to snatch us. Mind you, I wasn't afraid. Not really. It sort of gave me a turn to see me standing in front of me when I knew I wasn't. Wasn't me, I mean. And then to hear myself saying such really awful things to myself . . . all about how I was nothing. When I'm not, you know."

Palin shuddered. "Don't talk about it anymore. I agree with Usha. We should be doing *something*."

"Soon, soon," Dougan repeated, but he didn't move.

The dwarf sat on a charred stump, fanning himself with the plumed hat. He was solemn and preoccupied and seemed to be somewhere else. He would cock his head, as if he were intently listening; peer straight ahead, as if he were intently watching. Once he groaned and covered his face with his hand, as if what he both heard and saw was too much for him to bear.

The other three watched him anxiously, continuing to ask questions, receiving no response. At last, they gave up. Usha and Palin sat together, holding hands and talking together in quiet tones. Tas, complaining about the ash that made him cough, began to rummage through his pouches.

"That's it, then," said Dougan, jumping to his feet with a suddenness that startled everyone. "They're on their way. We must be there to meet them."

"Not yet," said a voice. "Not yet."

Raistlin materialized inside the center of the grove of seven pines, near the shattered altar.

"Fine!" Dougan muttered, eyeing the mage with no great pleasure. "This is just *all* we need."

He stomped across the ground, kicking irritably at bits of tree. Raistlin watched with a thin-lipped smile of amusement.

"Uncle!" Palin called out gladly. "What news do you bring? Did you see those creatures who attacked us?" He went to meet Raistlin.

Usha followed, reluctantly.

"Wait! Wait for me!" Tas yelled, but at that moment, something upturned all his pouches, spilling the contents. He was forced to scramble around to gather everything back up again.

Palin and Dougan entered the grove. Usha remained diffidently behind, though Palin would have drawn her forward. "You go talk to your uncle," she said, drawing her hand out of his. "This is important. I'd only be in the way."

As Raistlin watched all this, his golden eyes narrowed in impatience and disdain. Palin, uncomfortable, feeling somehow that he had betrayed his uncle's trust, left Usha without another word, hurried into the grove.

Raistlin gazed at his nephew steadily. "You very nearly failed." His gaze shifted to the spot where Palin had been standing when the shadow-wights attacked.

Palin flushed. "I—I am sorry, Uncle. It was . . . so horrible and . . . strange and . . ." His voice trailed off lamely.

Raistlin shifted his cold-eyed gaze to Usha. "Perhaps you were distracted, unable to concentrate."

Palin's flush deepened. "No, Uncle. I don't believe so. It was . . ." He shook his head, straightened, faced Raistlin directly. "I have no excuse, Uncle. If it hadn't been for Usha, I would be what the creature told me I was—nothing. It won't happen again, though. I promise you."

"It is said we learn more from our failures than our successes. I hope this adage holds true for you, Nephew, for all our sakes. You are to be entrusted with an enormous responsibility. Lives—many lives—hang in the balance."

"I will not fail you, Uncle."

"Do not fail yourself."

Raistlin's gaze went again to Usha, who sought refuge in the shadow of a burned tree.

"Enough of this nonsense," Dougan growled. "To my mind, the young one handled himself well enough, Master Mage, considering his age and his inexperience. And if he was a wee bit distracted by his love for the lass, it was her love that saved him in the end. Where would you be now, Raistlin Majere, if you had counted love a strength, not a weakness?"

"Probably sitting in my brother's kitchen, making gold coins come out my nose for the enjoyment of little children," Raistlin retorted. "I gave my all to my magic, and it never disappointed me. It was lover, wife, and child. . . ."

"You even killed your own brother for it," said Dougan.

"I did," Raistlin replied calmly. "As I said, we learn from our failures.

Enough of this. We are running out of time—literally. Dalamar returned to the tower. His adventures were many and dangerous, and I will not waste what moments we have left detailing them. Suffice to say, he and the others have discovered a weakness. Chaos has been forced to manifest himself on this plane of existence. He has taken on physical form. This makes him vulnerable."

"About as vulnerable as a mountain to a gully dwarf with a pickaxe," Dougan muttered.

"I did not say he would be easy to defeat." Raistlin flicked a disparaging glance at the dwarf. "But there is a fault in the rock."

"Aye, I know it." Dougan sighed.

"Then you know what must be done?"

"I know that, too." Dougan shifted his feet uncomfortably. "I'll see to it."

"What are we to do, Uncle?" Palin asked.

"You are to go to the Abyss. There you will join Steel Brightblade and a small band of knights, who have taken on the challenge of fighting Chaos and his minions. The knights need a wizard. That will be you, Nephew."

"The knights don't trust wizards," Palin said. "They won't want me."

"It will be your task to convince them otherwise. I won't lie to you, Nephew. This is the main reason you are being sent, and not some stronger mage. You are the only wizard your cousin Steel would even consider accepting."

"I will go, Uncle, and I will do my best," Palin said, adding ruefully, "but I don't think I can be of much use fighting Chaos with rose petals and bat guano."

Raistlin almost smiled. "You'd be surprised what you can accomplish with those. However, we will arm you better than that. The Conclave sends this to you—a gift."

Raistlin held out his hands. A book appeared, shimmering out of the ash-filled air. The book was old and very worn. The pages were dried and brittle. Its leather binding, red, was cracked; the lettering on the front had been stamped in gold leaf, was almost completely worn off. Only the imprint remained, covered with dust and cobwebs.

Magius.

Raistlin handed the book to Palin.

He took it reverently, trembling. Awed, he stared at it, at the name on the cover.

"The most valued spellbook in the Conclave's collection," Raistlin said. "Only those who have risen to the highest ranks have been permitted to read this book, and then it was never allowed outside the Tower of Wayreth. Few in this world even know it exists. The spellbook of Magius, the greatest war-wizard who ever lived.

"He trained with Huma—though in secret, for the Solamnic Knights would have never permitted otherwise. In defiance of all the rules, he fought openly at Huma's side. His spells are war spells and counterspells. You will need them. But they are complex, difficult. You don't have long to commit them to memory. They will require your utmost concentration."

Raistlin's eyes flicked to Usha, who had moved out a little from behind her tree.

Palin, troubled, followed his uncle's gaze. He was silent a moment, then—stretching out his hand to her—he said quietly, "I know what you mean, Uncle. I don't want to make you angry, but I will not forsake her. I know that if she is your daughter, we can never be more to each other than we are now. Her love is a blessing that will be my armor, my shield—even in the Abyss."

Usha took Palin's hand in hers. She kept her head bowed, clasped Palin's hand tightly.

"I hope you can understand this, Uncle," he said deferentially.

Raistlin's eyes flickered. "Perhaps better than you suppose, Nephew. But come. It is time. You have the spellbook. Stand here, by the altar, and you will be transported to the Abyss. The Portal stands wide open now. Her Majesty has no more need to guard it."

Palin embraced Usha, kissed her on the cheek. She clung to him for a moment, whispered her love, her good-byes, and let him go. He walked over to the shattered altar, the Staff of Magius in one hand, the spellbook of Magius in the other.

"Is Dalamar casting the spell?" Palin asked suddenly, remembering his uncle's ominous words.

"Dalamar may not even be alive at the moment," Raistlin answered coolly. "It is Dunbar Mastersmate who now works the spells. Farewell, Nephew. May the gods—those who are left—go with you "

Dougan waved his hat.

"Wound Chaos!" the dwarf shouted. "That's all you need do, Lad! Just wound him!"

The magic began to work, lifting Palin and carrying him away, floating like a seabird on a gale wind.

*　*　*　*　*

Usha and Raistlin and Dougan stood in the grove of dead trees, near the broken altar.

Usha's eyes filled with tears. "I'll never see him again."

"Oh, I rather think you will, my dear *daughter*," Raistlin said, his lip curling in a sneer.

"You needn't be sarcastic," Usha said quietly. "I'll tell him the truth. I was going to in Palanthas." She shook her head. "I couldn't."

"Probably just as well you didn't," Raistlin said dryly. "Then he *would* have found it difficult to concentrate."

"He'll hate me for lying to him. He won't want to have anything to do with me anymore."

"I doubt that, Child. Palin is like his father. He has a large capacity for loving . . . and forgiving." Raistlin placed his hands inside the sleeves of his black robes. "And now I must return to the tower, to the Pool of Seeing. Farewell, Usha, whose name means 'dawn.' Let us hope that your name is of a prophetic nature."

Lifting his head, he spoke to the ash-filled air. "I am ready, Mastersmate, when you are."

Usha, no longer afraid of him, watched him leave. She would tell Palin the truth. Hopefully, he would love her enough to understand, to forgive her. Usha couldn't quite believe it; that someone would love her that much. Prot had, but no one else among the Irda. She had always been a disappointment to them. Ugly. That ugly human child. It was one reason she had started lying, hadn't been able to stop. She couldn't bear to see the disappointment in her Protector's eyes. . . .

Dougan was tugging on her sleeve. "Lass, I know your heart's gone with your young man, but if the rest of you's not doing anything at the moment, I could surely use your help."

"My help, too!" cried Tasslehoff, dashing up, his pouches—refilled—bouncing around him. "I'm sure you need my help, too!"

"Aye," said Dougan testily. "If I was going to leap headfirst into the mouth of a red dragon, I'd be happy to take you with me. Since I'm not—"

Usha reached out, caught hold of Tas. "We're a team. Where I go, he goes."

"That's right," said Tas gravely. "As you recall, I do have the Kender Spoon of Turning."

"At least until Lord Dalamar gets around to counting his silver. Oh, very well," Dougan growled. "You *have* had your uses in the past, Burrfoot, leastways, according to Flint Fireforge."

"Flint said that? About me!" Tas gasped with pleasure. "I've had my uses in the past!" he repeated, several times.

Bringing out the two halves of the Graygem, Dougan regarded them longingly, covetously. He seemed to be making up his mind. Finally, sighing, he turned his head away, thrust the gem at Usha.

"I can't do it," Dougan said, his voice shaking. "I thought I could, but I can't. Of all the objects I ever forged, that one's caused me the most trouble. And it's the one I love the best. I can't destroy it. You'll have to, Lass. You'll have to."

Usha held the gem, stared at the dwarf with incredulity. "How?"

"A drop of blood, Lass," said Dougan. "You must catch within it a drop of blood."

"Whose blood?"

"Himself's."

29

Into the Abyss.
The book, the staff, the sword.

t was dawn when the knights reached the rift that opened in the Turbidus Ocean. They located it first by the noise, a thundering sound like a thousand waterfalls, made by the seawater cascading into the chasm.

Flying nearer, the knights saw clouds of water vapor rising from it, reflecting the light of the baleful sun, shining with all the colors of the spectrum in a magnificent rainbow. The dragons flew into the cloud, which closed around them in a hot, blinding, suffocating fog. The knights sweated, panted for air, and strained to see through the shifting white mists.

Flare knew the way, however. She had been here once. She could hear the sounds of battle, could see the darkness and the fire through the fog. The rift appeared beneath them.

The dragons spiraled downward amid walls of roaring water. The sound was deafening, the booming of the waterfalls pounding into the head, the vibrations of the thundering cascade threatening to stop the heart.

The knights and their dragons flew deeper and deeper into the rift until darkness swallowed them. With darkness came silence, a silence more awful than the water's tumult. It was a silence that made each man fear, for horrible moments, that he had gone deaf.

When Steel spoke, it was mainly to hear the sound of his own voice. "Where are we?"

"We have flown into a tunnel that leads into the Abyss," Flare replied. "This is the path we dragons take. It is secret, unguarded. It comes out near the Portal."

The dragons sped through the tunnel, and soon the knights could see a glimmer of red light at the end. They emerged from the tunnel into a landscape that was more barren and empty than the darkness from which they had come. Empty except for a lone figure, clad in white robes, who stood near the Portal and seemed to have been awaiting their arrival. When they flew within his range of sight, he raised his hand to stop them.

"Who is that?" Steel demanded, peering down at the figure.

"A White Robe," replied Flare disdainfully, neither slowing nor pausing in her flight.

Steel stared at the figure, thinking it was familiar. His eyes caught the glimmer of white light shining from atop a staff.

"Halt!" Steel ordered. "Take me down. I know him."

"Master, there is no time!" Flare protested.

"This won't take long," Steel promised. "He is in contact with the mages. Perhaps he has some news."

Flare made no more complaint, but spiraled slowly down. She landed near the Portal, claws skidding on the gray, red-tinged rock.

Steel leapt from the saddle, walked swiftly toward Palin, who advanced to meet him.

"What is it, Majere?" Steel demanded. "Why do you stop us? Make haste. We ride to battle."

"I know," Palin replied. "I stopped you for that reason. Take me with you."

Steel frowned, said slowly, "I thank you for the offer, Majere. I honor your courage now, as I have in the past. But I must decline."

The other knights and dragons spiraled overhead, silver dragons flying side by side with blue, dark knights riding with the knights of light.

"Go back to the world above, Majere," Steel said. "Go back to the woman you love. Go back to the parents who love you. Spend what time you can with them. Don't worry about missing the battle. If we fail, the battle will come to you. Farewell."

Palin moved to block Steel's way.

"I can keep you from failing," Palin said, and he held out the spellbook. "Look at the name written on the cover. The book was given to me by the Conclave of Wizards. And I am to tell you this. All you need to do to Chaos is to wound him."

"Wound him?" Steel was doubtful.

"That's all. The god, Reorx, told me this as I was leaving."

"That's *all*?" Flare snaked her head down to take part in the conversation. "That is everything! This is not some ogre chieftain we're talking about! This is the Father of All and of Nothing. Even in his mortal form, he is terrifying beyond belief. He stands taller than the Vingaard Mountains. His arm is the width and breadth of the River Torath. His hair is pure flame, his gaze is doom, his hand is death. He is surrounded by fire dragons and shadow-wights and daemon warriors. Wound him!" Flare snorted.

"We can. You and I," Palin said calmly, his hand upon the spellbook. "We walked through Shoikan Grove together and came out alive. Few other mortals can say that."

"True," Steel said with a half-smile. He pondered, but only a moment. "A warrior never turns down a useful weapon. Very well,

Majere, you ride with us. But understand this—we cannot spare the manpower to defend you. If you get into trouble, you must get yourself out."

"Agreed," said Palin. "I will not let you down. I have learned much since my first battle."

Steel remounted his dragon. Reaching down his hand, he assisted Palin to sit in the saddle behind him.

Flare spread her wings, flew to join the rest of the knights. The red-orange glow in the sky grew brighter, stronger. The air was hot and fetid, difficult to breathe.

"How many spells do you have?" Steel asked, shouting over the rush of wind in their ears. "Are they powerful? What do they do?"

"I may not speak of such matters," Palin answered, clutching the spellbook under one arm. "It is forbidden."

Steel looked back at him, suddenly grinned. "The hell it is. You don't have that many, do you?"

Palin smiled. "They are very complex. And I didn't have much time to study them."

"How many *do* you have?"

"One. But," Palin added gravely, "it's a good one."

30

Chaos. The Father.
All and Nothing.

'll say this for him," Tasslehoff Burrfoot remarked, looking up and up and up. "He certainly is ugly."

"Hush!" Dougan whispered in an agony of terror. "Himself will hear you!"

"Would he be offended?"

"No, he won't be offended!" Dougan snapped furiously. "He'll just squash us all like bugs! Now shut up and let me think."

Tas fully intended to keep quiet, but Usha looked so pale and frightened and unhappy that he couldn't help but whisper, "Don't worry. Palin will be all right. He has the staff and the spellbook."

"How can he possibly win against . . . against that?" Usha said, staring in awe and dread at the fearful giant.

A word from Dougan had transported Usha, Tas, and the dwarf to the Abyss. Or rather, the god's magic seemed to have brought the Abyss to them. The grove of seven dead pines remained around them, but the rest of the island on which the grove stood had vanished. The broken altar of the Irda stood in the middle of the grove, which stood in the middle of nowhere. Dougan, Tas, and Usha crouched behind the altar.

Above them towered Chaos.

The giant was alone. He had apparently not noticed the grove or the altar, which had sprung up behind his back. He gazed straight ahead, into time, into space. He was silent. All was silent around him. Yet it seemed that in the distance could be heard the sounds of battle.

"The people of the world fight Himself and his forces," Dougan said softly. "Each person in his or her own way, wherever they may be, battles him. It has made allies of ancient enemies. Elves fight side by side with ogres. Humans and goblins, dwarves and draconians—all have abandoned their differences. Even the gnomes—may the gods bless them and help them." Dougan sighed. "And the kender are doing their part, a small part, but a valued one."

Tas opened his mouth to make an excited comment, but Dougan frowned at him so fiercely that Tas kept silent.

"And that is why, Lass," Dougan said, patting Usha on the arm, "that we have this chance. If we had to face Chaos and all his legions . . ." The dwarf shook his head, wiped his hand over his sweating face. "It would be hopeless."

"I don't know if I can do this, Dougan," Usha said, trembling. "I don't know if I have the courage."

"I'll be with you," Tas said, squeezing her hand. The kender looked back up at Chaos. "Humpf. He's big—really, really big. *And* ugly. But I've faced big, ugly things before. Lord Soth, for example. And I wasn't the least bit afraid. Well, maybe just the tiniest bit, because he *was* a death knight and awfully powerful. He could kill you with just a single word! Imagine that! Only he didn't kill *me*. He just sort of bowled me over and I got a bump on the head. I—"

Dougan glared at him.

"Shutting up," Tas amended meekly, and clapped his hand over his mouth, which—he had learned—was the only way to keep himself quiet . . . for a short time, at least. Until his hand found something more interesting to do, such as rifling through the preoccupied dwarf's pockets.

Usha clutched the Graygem tightly. She stared up at the giant. "What is it . . ." Her voice cracked, and she had to start again. "What is it I have to do?"

"Only this, Lass." Dougan spoke so softly that Usha had to lean close to hear. "The knights and your lad, Palin, will attack Chaos. He'll summon his legions and fight. It will be a hard battle, but they're strong, Lass. Don't you worry. Now, if any of them manages to wound Chaos— just nick him, mind you, that's all we need—a single drop of blood, caught in the Graygem, will put Himself in our power. We will have captured his physical essence, don't you see? He must either stay here— in this shape and form. Or he must leave."

"And what if he decides to stay?" Usha demanded, dismayed. The entire idea sounded ludicrous.

Dougan stroked his beard. "He won't, Lass." The dwarf tried his best to sound confident. "He won't. We've thought this all out, the magical children and I. Himself hates being confined, you see. That body of his represents order, though you wouldn't think so to look at it. His troops, his legions—all of them demand orders and commands. He has to tend to them, send them here, send them there. He's growing tired of it, Lass. It's not fun anymore."

"Fun . . ." Usha thought of her people, of the ruined houses, the charred bodies. Her eyes filled with tears. She made herself stare at Chaos, stare at him long and hard. Seen through tears, blurred and indistinct, he didn't appear so formidable. It would be an easy task after all. Sneak up behind him when he wasn't looking . . .

Chaos suddenly roared, a bellowing roar that rumbled through the ground, caused the burned branches of the pines to break and topple, shook the broken altar behind which the three hid. The Father did not roar in anger. He roared with laughter.

"Reorx! You puny, sniveling, whimpering, misshapen, undersized, sorry excuse for a god! You're traveling in low company these days."

Dougan put his finger over his lips, pulled Usha down behind the mound of wood. He made a grab for Tas, but missed. The kender remained standing, gazing up at the giant.

"I'm not afraid of you!" Tas said, swallowing an unaccountable and annoying lump that had suddenly jumped into his throat, a lump about the size of his heart. "I'm awfully glad I got to see something as big and as ugly as you, but now that I've seen you, I really do think it would be best if you went away."

"Went away?" Chaos sneered. "Oh, yes. I'll be going. When this ball of dirt you consider a world is scattered like dust in the void. Don't bother to hide yourself, Reorx. I know you're there. I can smell you."

Chaos turned. His lidless eyes, which held nothing in their fathomless depths, focused on the three, seemed to suck their souls out of them. "I see a god, a human, and a thing—I don't even know what it is."

"A thing!" Tas repeated, indignant. "I'm not a *thing*! I'm a kender! And as for being undersized, I'd rather be short than look like something that got belched out of Mount Doom."

"Tas, stop!" Usha cried, terrified.

The kender, feeling considerably better, was just hitting his stride. "Is that your nose or did a volcano erupt in your face?"

Chaos rumbled. His empty eyes began to narrow.

"Dougan, make him stop!" Usha pleaded.

"No, Lass, not just yet," Dougan whispered back. "Look! Look what's coming!"

A flight of dragons, silver and blue, materialized in the red-orange sky. On their backs rode knights—those dedicated to darkness, those sworn to light. As they drew near Chaos, the dragonlances and swords they carried seemed to catch fire, gleamed flame red.

Leading the knights was a blue dragon bearing a knight clad in black armor. A white-robed mage rode behind him.

Chaos did not see them. His attention was focused on the kender.

Desperate to keep Chaos from looking around, Dougan scrambled to his feet. "You big bully!" the dwarf shouted, shaking his fist.

Tas eyed Dougan severely. "That's *not* very original!" the kender said in an undertone.

"It doesn't matter, Lad," Dougan said, mopping the sweat from his face with the sleeve of his coat. "Just keep talking. A few more seconds . . . that's all . . . "

Tas drew in another deep breath, but the breath and the rest of his insults got expelled in a big whoosh, as if he'd been hit in the stomach.

Chaos held in his enormous hand the sun—a huge ball of flaming, molten rock. The three could feel the heat beating down on them, scorching their flesh.

"A drop of my blood? Is that what you want?" Chaos said in a voice as cold and empty as the night sky. "You think that will give you control over me?"

The Father of All and of Nothing roared again with laughter. He juggled the sun, tossing it carelessly into the air, catching it again.

"You will never control me. You never have. You never will. Build your fortresses, your walled cities, your stone houses. Fill them with light and with music and laughter. I am accident. I am plague and pestilence. I am murder. I am intolerance. I am drought and famine, flood and gluttony. And you"—Chaos raised the flaming ball, about to hurl it down on them—"you are nothing!"

"You are wrong!" came a clear, strong voice. "We are everything. We are hope!"

A dragonlance, shining red and silver, arced through the air. It smote the sun and shattered. The sun burst into a thousand pieces of flaming rock, which rained down in fire to the ground, grew cold when they hit.

Chaos turned.

The knights faced him, drawn up in battle formation, their dragonlances leveled and ready, their swords raised, the metal glowing silver and red. In their midst sat a white-robed mage, wearing no armor, carrying no weapon.

"Hope?" Chaos laughed again. "I see no hope! I see only despair!"

The fragments of rock changed to daemon warriors, imps of Chaos that were formed of the terrors of every person who had ever lived. Colorless and shifting like bad dreams, the daemon warriors appeared different to each who fought them, taking on the shape of the thing each person feared the most.

Up from the rift came fire dragons. Made in mockery of real dragons, the fire dragons were formed of magma, their scales obsidian, their wings and manes flame, their eyes blazing embers. They belched noxious gases from the bowels of the world. Sparks flew from their wings, setting ablaze anything over which they flew.

The knights stared at these monsters in despair; their faces blanched in dismay and fear as the horrible creatures surged forward to attack. The standards slid from shaking hands, began to dip toward the ground.

Chaos pointed at the Solamnic Knights.

"Paladine is dead! You fight alone."

Chaos turned to the dark knights.

"Takhisis has fled. *You* fight alone."

Chaos spread his enormous arms, which seemed to encompass the universe.

"There is no hope. You have no gods. What have you left?"

Steel drew his sword and raised it in the air. The metal did not reflect the fire, but shone white, argent, like moonlight on ice.

"Each other," he answered.

31

The light. The thorn.
A knife called Rabbitslayer.

I must set you down, Majere," Steel said to Palin. "I cannot fight with you behind me."

"And I can't fight from dragonback," Palin agreed.

Flare alighted on the ground. Steel gave Palin his arm, swung the young mage off the saddle. Steel started to withdraw his grasp. Palin kept hold of the knight's hand for one brief second.

"You know what to do?" he asked anxiously.

"Cast your spell, Sir Wizard," Steel said coolly. "I stand ready."

Palin nodded, clasped Steel's hand tightly.

"Farewell, Cousin," he said.

Steel smiled. For an instant, the dark eyes were warm.

"Farewell . . ." He paused, then said quietly, "Cousin."

Flare, with a shrieking battle cry, leapt into the air.

Their own courage ignited by Steel's words and example, the knights of darkness and of light lifted their fallen standards and flew to the attack.

Chaos was ready for them with confusion and madness and terror and pain. Fire burned, and nightmare creatures gibbered. Wielding the dragonlances, the Solamnic Knights attacked the fire dragons. The silver dragons risked the deadly flames to carry their riders close. The knights, sweating in the awful heat, squinted against the fiery light and threw the lances. Their faith and their strong arms launched them straight and true. Several of the fire dragons fell, plunging to the ground to explode in a rush of flames. Many of the silver dragons fell, too, their faces burned, eyes blinded, their wings scorched and shriveled.

The dark knights fought the daemon warriors, slashing at them with accursed swords. The blue dragons battled with claw and lightning. But whenever a weapon struck the heart of a daemon warrior, the cold of the dark void that had existed before the beginning of time caused the metal to shatter, froze the hand that held it. The knights bore the pain, switched the blade from the useless hand to the good, and fought on.

Palin stood well behind the front line of knights and, for the moment, he was out of the battle. The fury of the knights' onslaught drove the daemon warriors and the fire dragons back, put them on the defensive. They would not be on the defensive long. Chaos, with a wave of his gigantic hand, was bringing up reinforcements, not from the rear, but creating them from the bodies of the fallen.

Palin had to cast his spell quickly. He opened the spellbook of Magius to the correct page. Holding the spellbook in his left hand, Palin took hold of the Staff of Magius in his right. He ran through the words of the spell one last time. Drawing a breath, he started to speak them, looked up and saw Usha.

He had not noticed her before. She had been hiding behind the broken altar. But now she had risen to her feet, was watching the battle fearfully, holding the Graygem in her hands. What was she doing here?

He longed to cry out to her, but was afraid that doing so might draw the father god's deadly attention to her presence. Palin needed to go to her, to protect her. He needed to stay here, to cast his spell, to protect the knights.

The magic began to writhe and crawl about in his head; the words to the spell started to slip away, to hide in the crevices of his shattered concentration. He could see the words on the page, but he couldn't think how to pronounce them, how to give them the correct enunciation that was all-important. They were fast becoming meaningless gibberish.

Love is my strength!

Once again he was back on that terrible beach, watching panic-stricken, paralyzed with fear for his brothers' lives, wanting to help so desperately that he had been an utter failure. It was useless to say the odds were overwhelming, that he'd been wounded, that they had never had a chance . . .

He knew he had failed. And he was destined to fail again.

We learn from our failures, Nephew, came a soft, whispering voice.

The words to the spell suddenly made perfect sense. He knew how to pronounce them.

He placed the staff in position, spoke the words clearly, strongly. *"Abdis tukng! Kumpul-ah kepudanya kuasahan!"* He waited, tensely, eagerly, for the sparkling tingle in the blood that was the beginning of the magic.

"Burus longang degang birsih sekalilagang!"

The magic wasn't there. He was near the end of the spell. He knew he'd spoken it correctly, knew he had made not one mistake. Only a few more words . . .

"Degang kuashnya, lampar terbong kilat mati yangjahat!"

Chaos towered over him. Fire burned him. Death surrounded him. Steel would die, Usha would die, Tas and Dougan, his parents, his two little sisters, and so many others . . .

Sacrifice. Sacrifice for the magic. What have you ever sacrificed for the magic, Nephew? I gave up my health, my happiness. I gave up love—of my brother, of my friends. I gave up the only woman who might have loved me in return.

I gave this all for the magic.

What will you give, Nephew?

Palin spoke the last two words of the spell. *"Xts vrie."* And then he added, quietly, calmly, "I give myself."

The words on the page of the spellbook began to shine with a silver-white radiance. The radiance seeped through the red leather binding into Palin's hand.

A shivering, tingling sensation swept over him. He was filled with the ecstasy of the magic, sublime pleasure, exquisite pain. He was not afraid of anything, not of failure, not of death. The radiance flowed through Palin, gathered within him, within his heart.

Atop the Staff of Magius, the crystal, clutched in the dragon's claw, began to glow with a silver-white light. The glow grew stronger, brighter, until it shone more brilliantly than the flames of Chaos. The silver armor of the Solamnic Knights reflected the light, brightened it. The black armor of the dark knights absorbed the light, but did not dim it. The scales of the silver dragons glinted like diamonds in the magical light. The scales of the blue dragons were glittering sapphire.

Where the light struck the daemon warriors, they screeched in pain and anger. The shadow-wights wafted away, like smoke sucked up into a chimney. The fire dragons swerved to try to avoid the light, and fell victim to the silver shining dragonlances.

Chaos became aware of the light. Seen out of the corner of his eyes, the flash was annoying, irritating. He determined to get rid of it.

Chaos shifted his attention from leading his legions, searched for the damnable light. He discovered the staff and the small and insignificant being holding it. He looked at the light, looked directly into it . . .

The magic surged through Palin with a jolt that drove him to his knees. Yet he held the staff steady. The light burst out of the crystal, shot a bright, blinding beam of radiant white straight into the giant's eyes.

"Now, Steel!" Palin shouted. "Strike now!"

Steel Brightblade and Flare had been hovering on the edges of the fighting, impatiently awaiting their moment. The waiting had been difficult for them both. They had been forced to watch comrades die and could do nothing to aid them or avenge them. Steel had seen Palin falter, had urged him silently to hold on. His cousin's success brought intense satisfaction and—it must be admitted—a warm and unexpected feeling of brotherly pride.

He did not need Palin's yell to know when to commence his attack. The moment the light from the crystal smote Chaos full in the eyes, Steel raised his sword, dug his spurs into Flare's sides.

Chaos howled in rage and fury, sought to shut out the light that had stabbed into his head, blinding him and hurting him. But his lidless eyes could not close. Whirlpools of darkness, they sucked everything they looked at inside, including the debilitating light.

Flare flew straight for Chaos. The giant wrenched and jerked his head about, trying to break the light's hold. Steel guided the dragon, shouted words of encouragement, urged her through the roaring flames that were the giant's hair and beard.

Almost blinded himself by the fire, Steel shielded his eyes with his hand. He had chosen his target, aimed straight for it. The heat was horrific; it beat on the metal of his armor, made it hot to the touch and unbearable to wear. His helm was suffocating him. He yanked the helm off, flung it to the ground. The fire seared his skin. He couldn't breathe the superheated air that burned his lungs. Still, he rode on.

Chaos wore a breastplate of adamant and glowing hot iron, but the plate covered only his chest. His arms and hands were bare.

"Veer off!" Steel yelled to Flare, tugged the reins to the right, to turn the dragon's head. "Take me near his shoulder!"

The dragon, lowering her head, soared through the fire of the father god's beard, spat her lightning breath. Jolts of electricity struck Chaos, further irritating, further enraging him. He knew an enemy was close, began to lash out blindly, flailing with his arms. Steel ducked, protecting himself by hiding behind Flare's neck.

The dragon lifted her right wing, flipped over, flew so near the glowing breastplate that the heat radiating from it scorched her wings. Steel gasped for air. His eyes watered from the heat, yet he kept them open, kept them fixed on his target.

The dragon flew close to the giant. Steel, leaning perilously out of the saddle, lifted his sword and, with a ringing battle cry, stabbed the blade into the enormous arm.

*　*　*　*　*

"He's done it, Lass! He's done it!" Dougan shrieked, dancing up and down. "Quickly now! Quickly!"

Steel's sword was embedded in the giant's flesh. Chaos bleated and bellowed. Unable to see what had stung him, he jerked his arm back, dragged the sword from Steel's hand.

A drop of blood sprang, glistening, from the wound.

"Now, Lass, now!" Dougan panted.

"I'll come with you!" Tas cried. "Wait a moment, though. Let me find the spoon . . ."

"No time!" Dougan shoved Usha. "Go, Lass. Now!"

"I'll just be a second." Tas was rummaging through his pouches. "Where is that dratted spoon? . . ."

Usha cast an uncertain glance at Dougan and at Tas, searching his pouches. Dougan waved his hand.

Usha crept forward.

Concentrate on the objective. Don't think about Palin, don't think about Tas, don't think about how frightened you are. Think about the Protector and the others. Think of how they died. I never did anything for them, never told them how grateful I was. I left without thanking them. This . . . is for my family, the lost Irda.

Usha kept her eyes fixed on that drop of shining red blood welling out from beneath the sword.

She drew closer, closer to the huge legs, the enormous feet that stamped upon and shook and cracked the ground.

The drop of blood hung, dangled like a jewel far out of reach.

It did not fall.

* * * * *

Steel's sword—his father's sword—stuck like a rose thorn in Chaos's flesh.

In jerking his arm back, Chaos had wrenched the sword from Steel's grasp. The blade hadn't done much damage to the giant. It had drawn only a single drop of blood.

Steel needed to strike again, but first he had to retrieve his sword. His strength was failing, and so was the strength of his dragon. Flare was badly burned, one eye gone, the scales of her head withered and bleeding. Her blue wings were blackened, the fine membrane torn.

Steel couldn't seem to find air enough to fill his lungs. Every ragged breath came with excruciating pain. He was dizzy and light-headed. His skin was burned and blistered.

He gritted his teeth, bent over Flare, patted her on the neck.

"We have to go in again, Girl," he said. "We have to finish this. Then we can rest."

The dragon nodded, too exhausted and hurting to speak. But Flare found it within her to snarl in defiance as she flew forward, forced the tattered wings to carry her and her rider back into battle.

The dragon flew near the wounded arm, dipped her wing at the last possible moment before crashing headlong into the giant. Steel caught hold of the sword's hilt and, with his last strength, yanked it out of the giant's arm.

The drop of blood fell, glittering, from the wound.

* * * * *

Usha saw the blood fall. Hope lent her courage. Heedless of the trampling feet, she ran forward to catch the drop.

But at that moment, Chaos, swearing savagely, swung his arm up and swatted at what was to him a stinging, annoying insect.

The dragon lacked the power in her wings to carry herself and her rider clear of the flailing, crushing hand. Chaos smashed the dragon, as he might have smashed a fly.

The dragon, her neck broken, fell from the sky, carrying her rider with her. There came a flash of silver light, and both crashed to the ground near Palin. The dragon's wing struck the mage a glancing blow, knocked the staff and the spellbook from his hand.

The silver-white light vanished.

The drop of blood, won at such enormous cost, fell to the ground and was immediately soaked up by the gray, parched soil.

Usha cried out in dismay. Going down on her hands and knees, she began scrabbling at the moist, blood-red dirt, trying desperately to recover some of the blood.

A shadow fell over her, chilled her to the bone, froze her hands, numbed her heart.

Chaos could see her now, bending over the spilled blood, the Graygem in her hands.

He understood his peril.

Injured and dazed, Palin searched frantically for his staff, which lay somewhere beneath the dead dragon. The lengthening shadow darkened all around him. He looked up. The giant's black, empty eyes—now able to see clearly—were focused on Usha.

Palin scrambled to his feet.

"Usha, look out! Run!" he cried.

She didn't hear him over the giant's roar. Either that, or she was ignoring him. Desperately keeping her gaze fixed on the bloodstained ground, she tried to salvage a drop to place into the halves of the Graygem.

Palin abandoned the fallen staff, ran to help Usha.

He never made it.

Chaos swept down an enormous hand that seemed to catch hold of the wind as it came, dragged the wind along. A blast of hot air smote

Palin, hurled him backward, slammed him into the body of the dragon. Pain burst in his skull.

"Usha," he murmured, sick and dizzy. He fought to stand, and, in his mind, he was on his feet, but his body lay in the dragon's blood. His own blood trickled warm down his face, and he was a speck of dust in one of the giant's empty eyes, and then he was nothing.

*　*　*　*　*

Tasslehoff tossed objects from his pouch left and right, littering the ground around him. A bit of blue crystal, a piece of petrified vallenwood, a lock from a griffin's mane, a dead lizard on a leather thong, a faded rose, a white ring with two red stones, a white chicken feather . . .

"Where is that dratted spoon?" he cried in frustration.

"Usha! Leave it, Lass! Run!" Dougan screamed.

"What's going on? What's happening?" Tas lifted his head, eager to see. "Am I missing something?"

Usha crouched, piteously digging in the dirt, tears streaming down her face. Palin was a huddled doll, lying in a pool of dragon's blood.

The giant's huge, booted feet shuffled, rolled over the ground with the rumbling, grinding sound of gigantic boulders, crushing the bodies of the dead knights, the dying dragons. Usha and Palin lay directly in the giant's path.

A cold fist—hurtful, like the giant's fist—squeezed the kender's heart.

"He's going to squash them!" Tas cried. "Squash them flat! This . . . this is worse than Lord Soth! My friends can't be squashed flat. There's got to be somebody big around to stop him!"

Tas looked about wildly, searching for a knight or a dragon or even a god to help. The knights and dragons who were left alive were fighting their own desperate battles. As for Dougan, the dwarf was a huddled heap, his head bowed, his hands flaccid in his lap, moaning, "My fault. My fault. . . ."

Tas stood up and, as he did, he realized suddenly that he was the tallest, the biggest person around. (Left standing.) (Aside from the giant.) A feeling of pride swelled the kender's heart, burst the clutch of the chill hand that had been squeezing the life out of it.

Tasslehoff flung his pouches aside. Drawing his knife—the knife that Caramon had once dubbed Rabbitslayer—the kender ran toward his fallen friends, using the speed and agility that is born to the kender race and is one reason they have managed to survive in a world of angry minotaur, infuriated shopkeepers, and enraged sheriffs.

Tasslehoff flung his small body in front of Usha. With a kender cry of defiance, "Take that!" he plunged the knife called Rabbitslayer into Chaos's big toe.

The magical knife pierced the leather of the giant's boot, struck flesh.

Blood spurted. The god jerked his injured foot up, prepared to stomp on the insignificant, infuriating creature who had injured him.

Chaos smashed his foot into the ground.

Clouds of dust rose. Tasslehoff disappeared.

"Tas!" Usha cried out in grief and anger. She started to try to rescue her friend, when she heard Dougan give a tremendous shout.

"You've done it, Lass! Look down! Look at the Graygem!"

Usha, dazed, looked.

A single drop of blood glistened in the center of one half of the Graygem.

"Close the two halves, Lass!" Dougan was on his feet, jumping up and down. "Close them! Quickly!"

Chaos shrieked and thundered around her. His flames scorched her. His winds tried to flatten her. She was going to die, but it didn't matter. Palin was dead. The cheerful kender was dead. The dark and stern knight was dead. Prot was dead. All were dead, and nothing more remained. Hope was dead.

Usha brought her two hands together, brought the two halves of the Graygem together with the blood of Chaos trapped between, then . . .

Silence.

Silence and darkness.

Usha could see nothing, hear nothing, feel nothing, not even ground beneath her. The only solid object she could sense was the Graygem, its cold, sharp, faceted edges.

The jewel began to glow with a soft gray light.

Usha dropped it, but the gem did not fall.

The Graygem rose from her grasp, rose higher and higher into the darkness and then, suddenly, the gem exploded.

Millions of shards of sparkling crystal burst outward, expanding, pitting the darkness with pinpricks of light.

They were stars. New stars, strange stars.

A moon rose, a single moon, a pale moon. Its face was benign, yet uncaring.

By the moon's light, Usha could see.

Chaos was gone. Dougan was gone. All around Usha were the bodies of the dead. She searched among the dead until she found Palin.

Putting her arms around him, Usha lay down beside him. She rested her head on his breast, shut her eyes, shut out the sight of the strange stars, the cold moon, and sought to find Palin in the darkness.

32

Rain. Autumn.
Farewell.

A drop of cool water fell on his forehead.

It was raining, a gentle rain, cool and soft. Palin lay in the wet grass, his eyes closed, thinking that it would be a dreary, gray, and gloomy day for a ride, that his older brother would complain bitterly about the rain, prophesying that it would rust his armor and ruin his sword; that his other brother would laugh and shake the drops from his hair and comment on them all smelling of wet horse.

And I will remind them that we need the rain, that we should be thankful the drought is broken . . .

The drought.

The sun.

The burning, blazing sun.

My brothers are dead.

The sun will not set.

Memory returned, horrifying and pain-filled. The liquid falling on him was not rain, but blood. The clouds were the shadow of the giant, towering over him. Palin opened his eyes fearfully, stared up into the leaves of a vallenwood tree, leaves that were dripping wet with rain, leaves that were just starting to change color, transforming into the warm reds and golds of autumn.

Palin sat up, gazed around in vast confusion. He was lying in a field that must be near his homeland, for the vallenwood grows in only one place on Ansalon, and that is Solace. Yet, what was he doing here? Only moments before, he had been dying in the Abyss.

In the distance he saw the Inn of the Last Home, his home, standing safe and sound. A thin curl of smoke rose from the home fire, drifting—sweet-smelling—up through the falling rain.

He heard a whimper near him, looked down.

Usha lay at his side, curled up like a child, one arm flung protectively over her head. She was dreaming, and her dreams were terrible.

Gently, he touched her shoulder. She stirred and called his name. "Palin! Where are you?"

"Usha, it's me. I'm here," he said softly.

She opened her eyes, saw him. She reached out her arms, clasped him, held him close.

"I thought you were dead. I was alone, all alone, and the stars were all different, and you were dead . . ."

"I'm fine," Palin said, and was astonished to know that he *was* fine, when the last thing he remembered was agonizing pain.

He smoothed back the beautiful silver hair, gazed into the golden eyes that were red-rimmed with tears.

"Are you all right?"

"Yes, I . . . wasn't hurt. The giant . . . Tas . . . Oh, dear gods!" Usha thrust away Palin's hands, staggered to her feet. "Tas! The giant!"

She turned, caught her breath in a sob.

Palin looked past her, and now he saw the dead.

The bodies of the Knights of Solamnia lay next to the bodies of the dark Knights of Takhisis. Of all those who had ridden forth into the Abyss to do battle with Chaos and his dread legions, not one had survived. The warriors lay in state, each man with his hands clasped over his chest, each face smooth and peaceful, all trace of blood, fear, and pain washed away by the gentle rain that fell on them all alike.

Peering through the rain, Palin saw movement, saw something stir. He'd been mistaken. One of the knights still lived. Palin hastened swiftly past the rows of dead. Drawing nearer, he recognized Steel.

The knight's face was covered with blood. He was on his knees, so weak he could barely hold himself upright. He placed the cold hand of a young Solamnic Knight over his chest. Then, his strength failing him, Steel fell into the wet, brown grass.

Palin bent down beside him. A glance took in the scorched, shattered, bloodstained armor, the pallid face, the labored breathing.

"Steel," Palin called softly. "Cousin."

Steel opened his eyes, which were shadowed and dimming. "Majere . . . " He smiled briefly, fleetingly. "You fought well."

Palin took hold of the dark knight's hand. The flesh was chill. "Is there anything I can do for you? To give you ease?"

Steel's head turned, his gaze shifted. "My sword."

Palin found it, lying near the fallen knight. He lifted the weapon, placed the hilt in Steel's hand.

Steel shut his eyes. "Lay me with the others."

"I will, Cousin," said Palin, through his tears, "I will."

Steel's fingers closed over the sword's hilt. He tried, once more, to lift it. "*Est Sularus . . .*" His last breath whispered the Solamnic words, *My honor.* His last sigh carried with it the conclusion, "*oth Mithas*," *is my life.*

"Palin." Usha stood at his side.

Palin raised his head, wiped away the rain and the tears. "What? Have you found Tas?"

"Come see," Usha said softly.

He rose to his feet. His robes were soaked with rain, but the air was warm for the beginning of autumn. He walked past the bodies of the knights, wondered, now that he thought of it, what had become of the dragons.

And then, with a pang of fear, he remembered his staff and the spellbook.

But there they both were, the Staff of Magius lying in the grass, the spellbook nearby. The red leather binding on the spellbook was blackened and charred. Palin touched it gingerly, lifted the cover. No pages remained inside. They had all been consumed, destroyed in the last spell.

Palin sighed, thinking of the great loss. Yet he was certain that Magius would have been pleased to know that his magic had helped defeat Chaos. Palin picked up the staff, was startled and vaguely alarmed to note that the staff had a strange feel about it. The wood, which had always before been warm and inviting to the touch, was cool, rough and uneven. The staff was uncomfortable to hold, felt wrong in his hand. He laid it back down, relieved to let go of it, wondered what was wrong.

He walked over to where Usha was standing, staring down at a pile of scattered pouches. Palin forgot about the staff as he bent over the kender's most prized possessions.

He sorted through the various objects. He didn't recognize any of them; not surprising, with a kender's pack, but he had almost managed to convince himself that these pouches belonged to some other kender, had been abandoned by their owner (probably to enable the kender to flee faster) until he lifted one pouch. A bundle of maps tumbled out.

"These are Tasslehoff's," he said, fear cold in his heart. "But where is he? He never would have left them behind."

"Tas!" Usha called, searching. "Palin, look! Here's his hoopak. It's . . . it's lying in a pile of . . . chicken feathers."

Palin moved aside the chicken feathers. There, beneath the hoopak and the feathers, was a handkerchief with the initials FB, a silver spoon (of elven make and design), and a knife, stained dark with blood.

"He *is* gone!" Usha sobbed. "He never would have left his spoon behind!"

Palin looked up the road, the road that ran eagerly along until it joined another road, and another road after that, coming together, branching apart, but always traveling onward, going everywhere, only to lead, at the very end, back home.

The road was suddenly a blur.

"There's only one reason Tas would have left his most prized possessions behind," Palin said softly. "He's found something more interesting."

* * * * *

The gentle rain ceased its fall. The gray day faded to dark night. The strange stars came out, scattered over the sky like a handful of seeing stones tossed on black cloth. The pale and uncaring moon rose, lit their way.

Palin looked up at the stars, at the single moon. He shivered, lowered his eyes, and met the golden-eyed gaze of Raistlin.

"Uncle!" Palin was pleased, yet ill at ease.

The staff no longer supported him. It was heavy and burdensome. He couldn't figure out what was wrong.

"Have you come to stay with us, now that the war is at an end? The war *is* over, isn't it?" he asked anxiously.

"This war is over," Raistlin added dryly. "There will be others, but they are not my concern. And, no, I have not come to stay. I am tired. I will return to my long sleep. I merely stopped on my way to say good-bye."

Palin gazed at his uncle in disappointment. "Must you go? There's still so much I have to learn."

"That is true, Nephew. That will be true to the day you die, even if you are an old, old man. What's wrong with the staff? You're holding it as if it pains you to touch it."

"There's something the matter with it," Palin said, fear growing in him, fear of things guessed at, suspected, but unknown.

"Give it to me," Raistlin said softly.

Palin handed over the staff with a sudden reluctance.

Raistlin took it, gazed at it admiringly. His thin hand stroked the wood, caressed it. "*Shirak*," he whispered.

The light of the staff glowed, but then the glow began to dim, darken. The light flickered and died.

Palin gazed in dismay at the staff, then looked up at the single moon. His heart constricted in fear.

"What is happening?" he cried in terror.

"Ah, perhaps I can answer that, young man."

An old wizard, dressed in mouse-colored robes, with a disreputable, broken-pointed hat, came tottering along the road from the direction of the Inn of the Last Home. The wizard wiped his mouth with the back of his hand.

"Fine ale," he was heard to remark, "some of Caramon's best. This will be an excellent year." Sighing, he shook his head. "I'm sure gonna miss that."

"Greetings, Old One," Raistlin said, leaning on the staff, smiling.

"What? Eh? Is that some sort of comment on my age?" The wizard glared from beneath bushy brows.

He turned to Palin, caught sight of the kender's handkerchief, which Palin had tucked into his belt. The wizard's beard bristled.

"That's mine!" he shrieked, and made a grab for the handkerchief. Retrieving it, he exhibited the cloth. "There's my initials. FB. It stands for . . . Mmmmm. Foos ball. No, doesn't sound quite right. Flubber. No . . ."

"Fizban," said Palin.

"Where?" The old man whipped around. "Drat him, he's always following me."

"Fizban!" Usha stared at him in wonder. "I know about you! The Protector told me. You're really Paladine!"

"Never heard of him!" the old man stated testily. "People are always mistaking the two of us, but I'm much better looking!"

"You're not dead!" Palin said thankfully. "Chaos said you were dead. That is, he said Paladine was dead."

Fizban was forced to pause a moment, to consider the matter. "Nope, don't think so." He frowned. "You didn't leave me in a pile of chicken feathers again?"

Palin was comforted, cheered, no longer afraid. "Tell us what has happened, sir. We won, didn't we? Chaos was defeated?"

Fizban smiled, sighed. The befuddled expression smoothed away, leaving an old man, benign, sad, grieving, yet triumphant.

"Chaos was defeated, my son. He was *not* destroyed. The Father of All and of Nothing could never be destroyed. You forced him to flee this world. He agreed to do so, but at a high price. He will leave Krynn, but his children must leave as well."

"You're . . . not going, are you?" Usha cried. "You can't!"

"The others have already gone," Fizban said quietly. "I came to give you my thanks and"—he sighed again—"have a last glass of ale with my friends."

"You can't do this!" Palin said, dazed, disbelieving. "How can you leave us?"

"We make this sacrifice to save the creation we love, my son," Fizban answered. He shifted his gaze to the bodies of the knights, to the handkerchief he held in his hand. "Just as they sacrificed to save what they loved."

"I don't understand!" Palin whispered, anguished. "What about the staff? What about my magic?" He pressed his hand over his heart. "I can't feel it inside me anymore."

Raistlin laid his hand on Palin's shoulder. "I said that one day you would become the greatest mage who ever lived. You fulfilled my prophecy, Nephew. Magius himself was never able to cast that spell. I am proud of you."

"But the book is destroyed . . ."

"It doesn't matter," Raistlin said, then shrugged. "Does it, Nephew?"

Palin stared, still not understanding. Then the meaning of what his uncle had told him penetrated, struck him to his very soul.

"There is no more magic in the world. . . ."

"Not as you know it. There may be other magic. It is up to you to find it." Fizban said gently. "Now is begun what will be known on Krynn as the Age of Mortals. It will be the final age, I think. The final, the longest, and, perhaps, the best. Farewell, my son. Farewell, my daughter."

Fizban shook hands. Then he turned to Raistlin. "Well, are you coming? I don't have all day, you know. Got to go build another world. Let's see. How did that go? You take a bit of dirt and mix in some bat guano . . ."

"Good-bye, Palin. Take good care of your parents." Raistlin turned to Usha. "Farewell, Child of the Irda. You not only avenged your people, you redeemed them." He glanced at the dejected Palin. "Have you told him the truth yet? It will cheer him considerably, I think."

"Not yet, but I will," Usha answered. "I promise, Uncle," she added shyly.

Raistlin smiled. "Good-bye," he said again.

Leaning on the staff, he and Fizban turned and walked across the field, where lay the dead.

"Uncle!" Palin called desperately. "The gods are gone! What will we do now that we are alone?"

Raistlin paused, glanced back. His skin gleamed pale gold in the light of the strange stars; his golden eyes burned.

"You are not alone, Nephew. Steel Brightblade said it for you. You have each other."

* * * * *

Palin and Usha stood alone, together, in the field near the town of Solace, a field that would afterward be held sacred.

In this field, the people of Ansalon came together to build a tomb made of stone brought all the way from Thorbardin by an army of dwarves. The tomb was simple, elegant, built of white marble and black obsidian. Around the tomb the humans planted trees, brought from Qualinesti and Silvanesti by the elves, led by their king, Gilthas.

The bodies of the Knights of Solamnia were placed within the tomb, side by side with the bodies of the Knights of Takhisis.

In the center Steel Brightblade rested on a bier made of rare black marble. He was clad in his black armor. He held his father's sword in his hands. On another bier, carved of white marble, lay the body of Tanis Half-Elven. He was clad in green, in leather armor. At his side lay a blue crystal staff, placed there by the children of Riverwind and Goldmoon.

The vault was shut and sealed with double doors made of silver and of gold. The Knights of Solamnia carved on one side of the door a rose, on the other side of the door a lily. They engraved the names of the knights on the blocks of stone.

But over the door they put only one name, in memory of one of Ansalon's most renowned heroes.

Tasslehoff Burrfoot.

Beneath his name, they carved a hoopak.

The Last Heroes tomb, it was called, and it commemorated all those who had died during the battle at the end of that terrible summer.

Far from being a solemn place, the tomb became a rather merry one (much to the discomfiture of the knights). Kender from all over Ansalon made pilgrimages to this site. They brought their children and held picnic lunches on the grounds. While eating, the kender would tell stories of their famous hero.

It was not long—within a generation, at least—that eventually every kender you came across would show you some interesting object—a silver spoon, perhaps—and swear to you on his topknot that it possessed all sorts of wonderful powers.

And that it had been given to him by his "Uncle Tas."

Epilogue

lint Fireforge paced, back and forth, back and forth, beneath the tree. He had to keep moving, for the forge fire had gone out, and the old dwarf was chilled to the bone. He clapped his hands to warm his fingers, stomped his feet to warm his toes, and grumbled and complained to warm his blood.

"Where *is* that dratted kender? Said he'd be here. I've waited and waited. Tanis and Sturm and the rest left eons ago. I can imagine where they are, now, too. Probably sitting in some nice, cozy inn, having a glass or two of hot, mulled wine, talking of the old days, and where am I?"

The dwarf snorted. "Nowhere, that's where. Underneath a dying tree, next to a cold forge, waiting for that doorknob of a kender. And what's he up to? Ah, I'll tell you!" Flint huffed until he was red in the face. "He's likely in jail. Or maybe some minotaur's strung him up by his topknot. Or some irate mage has turned him into a lizard. Or he's tumbled into a well, like he did that one time, trying to grab hold of his own reflection, and it was up to me to haul him out, except that he pulled me in, too. If it hadn't been for Tanis—"

Flint grumbled, paced, clapped, and stomped. So intent was he on grumbling, pacing, clapping, and stomping that he never noticed he'd gained a partner.

A kender, dressed in bright yellow pants with a jaunty red-and-green plaid jacket, hung all over with bulging pouches, had crept up behind Flint and, stifling his giggles, was mimicking the dwarf.

The kender paced, clapped, and stomped on Flint's very heels, until the dwarf—stopping in mid-grumble to light a pipe—reached into his leaf pouch and discovered another hand there already. A quick count bringing the number of hands up to three, the dwarf roared and spun around.

"Gotcha!" Flint grabbed the thief.

The thief grabbed Flint.

Tasslehoff flung his arms around his friend. "Flint! It's me!"

"Well! About time!" Flint humpfed. "You doorknob! See what you did? Made me drop my pipe. There, Lad, there. Don't take on so. I didn't mean to yell at you. You startled me, that's all."

Tas tried laughing and sobbing at the same time, only to discover that the laugh and the sob got all tangled up in the throat, which made breathing a bit difficult. Flint pounded his friend on the back.

Recovering his breath, thanks to Flint beating it back into him, Tas was able to talk.

"I finally made it. I bet you missed me, didn't you?"

Ignoring Flint's resounding "NO!" Tas prattled on. "I missed you. I had the most wonderful adventure. I'll have to tell you."

The kender divested himself of his pouches, spread them around him, settled down to sit beneath the tree. "Where shall I begin? I know. The Kender Spoon of Turning. It was given to me by—"

"What do you think you're doing?" Flint demanded. Hands on his hips, he glared at the kender.

"Resting here underneath your tree," Tas returned. "Why? What do you think I'm doing?" He looked interested. "Is it something different from what *I* think I'm doing? Because if it is—"

"Confound you!" Flint growled. "It's not what you're doing or what you think I think you're doing, it's what you're *not* doing!"

Tas eyed the dwarf severely. "You're not making any sense. If you think I'm not doing what I'm supposed to be doing, and if I think I am doing what I'm not supposed to be doing, then—"

"Shut up!" Flint groaned, clutched at his head.

"Is something the matter, Flint?"

"You're giving me a headache! That's what's the matter. Now, where was I?"

"Well, I wasn't doing—"

"Stop!" The dwarf was breathing heavily. "I didn't mean that. And get back up. We don't have time to laze around. We're due to meet Tanis and the others up there aways." He waved his hand vaguely.

"Maybe in a little while," Tas said, settling himself even more comfortably. "I'm awfully tired. I think I'd like to rest right here, if you don't mind. This is an awfully nice tree. Or it would be if it wasn't all brown and sad-looking. I think the tree's shivering. It *is* chilly here. I'm cold. Aren't you cold, Flint?"

"Cold! Of course I'm cold! I'm nearly frozen stiff. If you had come when you were supposed to—"

Tas wasn't listening. He was assessing the situation.

"You know, Flint, I think the reason that you're cold and I'm cold and the tree's cold (I really do think that's what's wrong with it), is that there's no fire in that forge."

"I know there's no fire in the forge!" Flint howled, so infuriated that he started to splutter. "I . . . But . . . You . . ."

"Well, it's a good thing I came back," Tas said resolutely. "Look where you'd be without me! We'll catch up with Tanis and the others later. By that time, they will have gotten themselves into no end of trouble, and you and I'll have to rescue them. Just like the old days. Now, why don't you light the fire, and I'll sit here under this nice tree and tell you stories. Oh, and by the way, I've got this for us." Tas rummaged through one of his pouches, came up with a silver flask, which he exhibited proudly. "Caramon's finest!"

Flint stared at the tree. He stared at the forge. He stared at the kender. Then Flint stared at the flask.

Especially at the flask.

The dwarf scratched his head.

"By Reorx," he muttered, "it wouldn't hurt to have a nip. Just to warm myself, mind you. I suppose you paid Caramon for it?"

Flint took hold of the flask, popped off the cork, sniffed at it eagerly.

"I will," Tas said, leaning back, his head on his pouch. "The next time I'm there. Now. Where was I? Oh, yes. The famous Kender Spoon of Turning. Well, there was this specter, you see, and . . ."

The kender prattled on. Flint tasted the brandy, found it to his liking, took several swigs, tucked the flask in a hip pocket.

There would be time enough to join Tanis and the others. An eternity, if you wanted to get right down to it.

"I might just build that fire after all," Flint decided. "Anything to keep from listening to the chatter of that rattle-brained kender."

Flint gathered up wood, stoked the forge, lit a spark. He began to pull on the bellows, and their breath fanned the spark into a flame.

The forge fire soon burned bright, warmed the dwarf, the kender, and the tree.

Flint sat down, decided he'd taste the brandy again, to see if it was as good as he'd thought it was the first time.

It was.

He handed the flask to Tas, who tried it and handed the flask back to the dwarf.

The forge fire glowed hotter and brighter.

* * * * *

And in the night sky over Ansalon there burns a new star—a red star—which will remain forever fixed and unchanging, a sign that, even in the Age of Mortals, mankind is not alone.